STAR TREK®

SAND
AND
STARS

STAR TREK®

SAND
AND
STARS

Star Trek: Spock's World
by Diane Duane

and

Star Trek: Sarek
by A.C. Crispin

Based on *Star Trek*
created by Gene Roddenberry

POCKET BOOKS
New York   London   Toronto   Sydney

Dedication for *Spock's World*

For Kim and Nick Farey,
remembering U.F.P. Con 1986:
with thanks for the Klingon noisemaker
that made me late for all those panels.

Dedication for *Sarek*

To Michael Capobianco,
with love

INTRODUCTION

It's an old tale that just happens to be true. After network executives screened the original pilot episode of *Star Trek,* they told the producers to get rid of the guy with the pointed ears. Their concern, from a business perspective, seemed logical: They feared that the viewing public might regard the character as "demonic" and refuse to watch the show.

Luckily, cooler heads prevailed. The show's producers successfully argued to retain the character as he'd been conceived. On September 8, 1966, they introduced Mister Spock, played by actor Leonard Nimoy, to the viewing public (which, incidentally, actually *liked* the pointed ears). In subsequent episodes they introduced Spock's world, as well as his Vulcan father, Sarek, and his human mother, Amanda. Viewers learned about Vulcan practices, history, and traditions, and discovered their remarkable physical and mental abilities, which proved to be much more impressive than mere pointed ears. We became familiar with *Pon farr.* And the mind-meld. And the incapacitating nerve pinch.

Nearly four decades have passed since that infamous moment in television history when an entire alien culture was almost undone by executive whim. Today, of course, Mister Spock is a beloved entertainment icon, and Vulcans are an integral part of what makes *Star Trek* special. Spock has had many successors in the various *Star Trek* incarnations. For the most part, the writers and actors behind those characters have kept one great rule in mind: "If it ain't broke, don't fix it." It's a good rule, one that just about any Vulcan would deem logical.

"We patterned Tuvok's basic physical characteristics on Spock," actor Tim Russ says of his character on *Star Trek: Voyager.* "The way he walked, the way he talked. But Tuvok is different from his predecessor. Spock was half-human and had to really work on keeping his Vulcan focus. Tuvok is one hundred percent Vulcan. We made him very straightforward and Vulcan-like."

Since he was the only Vulcan in the Delta quadrant, with no opportunity to relate to others of his kind, the *Voyager* creative team generally concentrated on Tuvok as an individual, rather than as a representative of his species. Nevertheless, they did reveal some previously unknown elements of Vulcan physiology. For example, in an episode titled "Meld," Russ recalls, "We discovered that there's a psychosuppression system in their brains that helps Vulcans to control their violence and their emotions. But that control still doesn't come easily," Russ stresses. "They still have to meditate and go through a process. We made a point of saying, 'They have to work at this all the time.'"

The writers also enhanced some established Vulcan lore with new explanations. "They tried to figure out how the mating ritual works," Russ notes. Fans of the *Star Trek* episode "Amok Time" may recall that Spock's explanation of the mating drive was rather metaphorical—something about Regulan eel-birds and Earth salmon. And Doctor McCoy didn't have a much better handle on Spock's malady, other than to note that something seemed to be generating huge quantities of adrenaline in his system. In the *Voyager* episode "Blood Fever," however, writers clarified those rather vague statements by explaining that a telepathic mating bond draws betrothed Vulcan couples together—and that not acting on this causes a dangerous, even deadly, neurochemical imbalance in the brain. And we thought *human* love was a battlefield!

Even that explanation leaves Russ a little perplexed when he reflects upon the relationship between Spock's parents. "Sarek was married to a human woman," he observes. "How the hell did that happen? Did he still go through *Pon farr*?" The answer may not be onscreen, but it is without doubt found in innumerable fictional efforts that grace the printed page.

The producers of *Star Trek: Enterprise* chose to take a fresh look at Vulcan/human relations on their show, since it is a prequel to *Star Trek*. The somewhat antagonistic nature of the partnership between the two species may have caught some viewers of *Enterprise* by surprise—but it doesn't stray all that far from the core concept.

Actor Gary Graham, who plays the recurring Vulcan character Ambassador Soval, talked to producer Rick Berman before filming began. "Rick said that people think Vulcans have no emotions, but that's not true at all. In fact, they are so emotional and so passionate that they had to learn early on to control their emotions lest they destroy themselves," Graham says. "That bears out their highly disciplined state. So I gave Soval a sort of Asian inscrutability. Oriental cultures pride themselves on not letting you know what they think all the time. The people are very polite, but I wouldn't like playing poker with them. That's the knowledge I used to frame Soval."

Graham's character bears more than a bit of condescension toward the human species, and an anger that has been "born out of resentment," the actor says. "When viewers first met Soval, he'd been on Earth for too long, around all these humans who have been expressing their emotions freely and openly and it's sort of gotten to him." That explains why, in the pilot episode, Soval raises his voice when confronting Jonathan Archer. Three seasons later, however, in the episode "Home," Graham notes that Soval is beginning to "get" the humans, to understand them. "We finally can see a chink in Soval's armor," he says, and perhaps a precursor to the way Vulcans will come to feel about humans a hundred years hence.

"By the time Spock comes on the scene," Graham says, "he's traveling with humans, and the relationship has settled into a nice symbiosis. On *Enterprise,* the female Vulcan, T'Pol, has been taking her relationship with the crew in that direction, but it hasn't rebounded to the rest of the Vulcan species yet." While speaking, Graham slips into character, letting his thought be completed by his Vulcan persona: "It's an intellectual decision. I deal with humans only out of necessity, because clearly, Vulcans are superior in every way."

Perhaps. They certainly outwitted those network executives. The tales in this book, two intimate looks at the planet and the people, allow us to find out for ourselves. It's another reason, in addition to the wonderfully entertaining reading, to study these tales: We should know as much about Vulcans as we possibly can, because, obviously, we'll never "get rid of the guy with the pointed ears."

—Terry J. Erdmann

SPOCK'S WORLD

Prologue

The joke in Starfleet is that the only thing that can travel faster than warp 10 is news.

Of the many jokes told in Starfleet, this one at least seems true. For a Federation of hundreds of planets, spread sparse as comet-tail dust over thousands of light-years, news is lifeblood: without it, every world is as alone as if there was no other life, no other thought but its own. Few planets, these days, are so reclusive or paranoid as to want to be all alone in the dark, and thus the passage of news has covert priority even over the waging of wars and the making of fortunes. By subspace transmission (faster than warpspeeds, but not fleet enough), by pumped-phaser tachyon packet and shunt squirt, by compressed-continuum "sidestep" technology and sine avoidance, and (within solar systems) by broadcast carrier of all the kinds from radio through holotrans, the news of the many planets of the Federation and of planets outside it slides its way through and around and under and past the billions of miles and thousands of light-years.

The terrible distances take their toll of the passed-on word. Signals are corrupted by subspace noise, data is dropped out, translations are dubious or ambivalent: distance makes some pieces of news seem less urgent than they should, proximity makes other happenings seem more dire than they are. But no news passes unchanged, either by the silent spaces, or the noisy minds that cannot seem to live without it: and no news affects any two of those minds the same way.

This piece of news was no exception.

The door vanished, and the man walked into his rooms and stood still for a moment, then said the word that brought the door back behind him and shut all other sounds outside. His terminal was chiming softly, a sound that most people on the planet where he now lived could not have heard: it was pitched too high.

The man paused long enough to slip his dark cloak off and hang it on the hook beside where the door had been. Beneath it his tabard and trousers were dark too, somewhere between brown and black, his family's sigil bound into the fabric in gold at the tabard's throat. It was diplomatic uniform, made more impressive by his stature, tall but not slender anymore—late maturity had left its mark on his frame. His looks somewhat matched his dress; a man dark-haired, dark-eyed, deep-eyed, a hawk-faced man with no expression . . . at least none that most people here were competent to read. There was energy in the way he held himself, some of those people would have said . . . perhaps too much energy, bound in check by a frightening control. They never knew how tight a control; they never knew how it slipped, sometimes, and left their thoughts open to him. He would have been embarrassed, except that he considered himself neither a child, a brute beast, or an alien, to be so possessed by an emotion.

He turned and paused again, gazing out the window at the brass-and-gold afternoon lying over the browned lawns outside. It was approaching sunset of what the people who lived in this part of the world considered a ferociously hot day, much too hot for spring. Several times today, various of them had said apologetically to him, "At least it's *dry* heat." They need not have been apologetic. To him this was a fair day in early spring indeed, cool, bracing, with a hundred kinds of plants in exuberant leaf; it reminded him of hunting mornings in his youth.

Eidetic memory has its prices. For a moment, whether he wished it or not, he found himself out on the plain again under the burning sky, smelling the air, terrified and out of control of the emotion, knowing that at the day's end he would either be a man or be dead. Then the fragment of memory, like a still holograph refiled, fell back into its indexed place in his mind. He lifted an eyebrow at his self-indulgence, made a note to himself to spend a little extra time in the Disciplines that evening, and moved to the terminal.

Its chiming stopped as he touched it: another second and the terminal had read his EEG through his skin, recognizing the pattern. The screen filled with column on column of blue symbology, a list of calls to the flat since he left. Most of them were unimportant compared to the one name and commcode at the far right-hand side of the list, the most recent, the one message that had caused the "urgent" chime. He had rather been hoping that the embassy would not need him further today: but hope was illogical. Life was about dealing with what *was*. He touched the screen, and the computer dialed the code.

He waited a moment or so before speaking. The link was scrambled, and before communications began, the computer had to agree with the one on the other end as to the eighty-digit "satchel" crypton they would use to keep the link secure. He had the utmost confidence in the ciphering process. Ninety-six standard years before, he had invented it.

He paused two point three seconds to let the process finish.

"Sarek," he said.

The voice that answered him did so, by the good offices of the computer, well above the frequencies that most people on this planet were capable of hearing. The slightest high-pitched hissing or squeaking on the air was all any listener would perceive. That tiny speech whispering into the air went on for a moment, and then Sarek said, "By what majority?"

The air spoke softly to itself again. "Very well," he said. "Whose was the request?"

Another tiny answer. "Tell her I will come," he said. "If all the transportation connections work correctly, we will be there in four point nine six days. Out."

He touched another code on the screen, not bothering to scramble the communication this time. "Sarek," he said again. "I am being recalled, informally. Make the arrangements with the usual carriers, and begin distributing my appointments between Svaid and T'Aimnu."

"Affirmative," said his attaché. "Being handled now. What reason shall we give the Federation Council and the immigration authorities?"

"Personal political business," he said. And, hearing T'Lie's unspoken curiosity, he added, "The Referendum has been called. I must speak for the proposal."

There was a pause. "There was nothing about that in the packet this morning. Perhaps there has been an oversight."

"No, no oversight. I was just notified. There will be a full *précis* in the next packet. Call a press conference and issue the statement as soon as you have a context-positive translation."

"Yes, sir."

"Out."

The Ambassador Extraordinary of Vulcan to the United Federation of Planets, and incidentally to Earth, turned away from the screen and sat down very slowly in a chair that faced the windows. The light and heat came streaming into the room, into the silence. Sarek leaned back and closed his eyes, and became still, tried to become the stillness, the warmth. But he failed: the stillness was an illusion. His mind was in disorderly turmoil. He would have been embarrassed at *that*, except that it would have made the turmoil worse.

If I fail in this, he thought, *then my honor is in shreds and my family will bear the stigma of it forever. We will be ostracized. If I succeed . . . then my honor is intact and my conscience will remain whole. But my House will be broken . . . or if not, I will become an exile and outcast. And Earth . . .*

He opened his eyes. Out the window of the towerblock, a redtailed hawk was balancing on the hot wind, as if on an unresolved thought, hovering. In the blue sky far behind it, past hills like cut-out cardboard, cream-white clouds piled along the horizon, basking and building in the heat, forging their thunders.

Earth will be dead to us, Sarek thought, and got up to make the call he had been avoiding.

Looking down from space, the miles-deep sea of atmosphere that breeds thunders and winds takes on another perspective. The endless star-pierced blackness presses down against a thin delicate wrapping of air, a bubble of glass swirled with white, glittering where the Sun touches it, the blue of oceans showing through the faintly misted shell. A fragile thing, brittle-looking, an *objet d' art*, round and perfect: but for how long? From far enough out in orbit, one has no doubt that one could drop the Earth on the floor of night and break it. An urge arises to step softly, to speak quietly, so as to keep whoever might be carrying the pretty toy from being startled and fumbling it.

That view, the wide curve of the planet, blue and brown and green streaked with white, was the one that Spock kept on the viewscreen by preference when he was alone on the bridge. He was alone now: indeed he had been alone now for nearly sixteen days, except for the briefest interruptions by maintenance crew and the occasional visiting bridge-crew member. It was curious how, even though they were on liberty, they could not seem to stay away.

But then Jim would surely say that it was curious that Spock couldn't stay away, either. And he would have laughed at Spock's grave attempts to rationalize away the analysis, for in logic there was no reason for him to be there: after a month's peaceful work on the bridge instrumentation, every piece of equipment was tuned and honed to even Spock's relentless standards. Jim would have teased him most assiduously. That was of course the captain's privilege, to refuse to take Spock seriously: as it was Spock's to raise (outwardly) his eyebrows over the amusing and irrational conduct of his human friend, and (inwardly) to rest satisfied that someone knew him well enough *not* to take him seriously, Vulcan or not.

Spock sat quiet in the helm, watching the Earth and idly going through lists in his head. When the heavier and more involved of their repairs were finished—warp-drive adjustments, the replacement of the inside of one warp nacelle's anti-matter containment system, installation of a new set of dilithium crystals—Fleet had moved *Enterprise* out of the major repair and spacedock facility at San Francisco High to a parking "spot" over the North Atlantic, where Starfleet Gander could handle the ship's reprovisioning. These were more mundane and simple businesses, like the complete replacement of the *Enterprise*'s forty million cubic feet of air: even with a starship's extraordinarily advanced air-conditioning and processing systems, a ship's air could become rather stale-smelling after a couple of years. Not even Spock had stayed aboard for that—he found breathing vacuum for any length of time to be aesthetically unpleasant. He had spent the day near Reykjavik, examining the volcanoes.

Then there was the matter of other reprovisioning to be supervised . . . stored food, hydroponics, dry stores, textiles, machine parts, data tapes and solids, cleaning and maintenance supplies, the hundred thousand things that a crew in space for long periods needs. Spock did not have to occupy himself with this—he was, after all, on liberty as much as the rest of the crew—but it suited his whim (and his commitment to his agreements as executive officer) to make certain for himself that the ship was perfectly ready for space in all respects, not just to take someone else's word for it.

It became sort of a game, after a time, to anticipate the quartermasters' department in things that they should have thought of first: it engendered in them what Spock considered a very healthy attitude of friendly competition. Who would be first to remember and requisition the right grade of granite (and some slab marble, as a treat) for the ship's single Horta crewmember, who sometimes complained in a good-natured way that man was not meant to live on nickel-iron alone? Who would know where to find "pinhead" oatmeal for the chief engineers who occasionally—and loudly—demanded porridge? Where could one obtain the best price for hundred-ton lots of Arabica coffee? (Spock's simple but admittedly elegant storage method for coffee—beaming it aboard in small lots, each time purposely aborting the upload in mid-transport, but holding the coffee's completely analyzed pattern in the transporter's data solids until wanted—had become standard Fleet practice for "extraneous" cargo in starships on tour, and had changed coffee from a rarely enjoyed and much-longed-for luxury into something that the whole crew could have when they pleased. But after all, McCoy and Kirk were both very fond of coffee . . . and this kept it fresh.)

And there were even more pleasant forms of maintenance to handle: most specifically, the refreshing of the ship's data libraries. Spock had himself spent nearly a hundred hours scanning the refresh lists sent him by the British Museum on behalf of the Smithsonian, the Library of Congress, the Ryeshva Moskva, der Schweizerisches Landesmuseum, la Bibliothèque Nationale, reh Xiao-Mih. Then had come the uploading, the checking, the indexing, and just as important, the exchange of information—for after debriefing, *Enterprise* declassified all but the most sensitive material on returning to her registry port. At the end of it all, some seventy-two hours without a stop, he had slept, as McCoy would probably have observed, like a log. Though how a log slept was beyond him, and certainly past McCoy.

Now, approaching the end of the reprovisioning process, Spock let the lists go momentarily and gazed at the North Atlantic for a while, watching the tiny, precise patterns of weather flow by in curls and curves of white and gray, while in the background the stars seemed to turn around a fixed globe. The view was familiar. Spock had taken to predicting the Earth's weather lately, as a pastime and an exercise of his logic. There was a fascinatingly large number of variables—seasonal tendencies, solar storms, the fluctuations of the Earth's ionosphere and ionopause, the occasionally successful attempts to control weather on a local scale, and in the midst of it all, the endless fluxions, perturbations, and movements of jet stream and a hundred lesser winds. He had spent a week mastering North America's weather; and after writing the master algorithm with all the necessary seasonal variations and sending it off to the Western Hemisphere Weather Service, he turned away to something more challenging. Greater Britain and Ireland seemed sure to keep him busy for a long while: the algorithms promised to be exceptionally complex. Perhaps ten days this time. He wondered idly if the people living there would be happy to have their weather solved at last.

Spock considered the three small, patchy lows presently sitting over the British Isles, while the lists in his head slipped back for attention. Almost everything was complete now: the last few deliveries would be cargo and mail for parts of the Federation that no normal carrier serviced . . . or at least, no carrier quite so well armed. There were twelve tons of container cargo, mostly heavy machinery or electronics, and the equivalent of fifty tons of mail, some as data storage, more in the same kind of "abeyance" as the coffee. It cost too much to ship most paper over interstellar distances, but executable documents, currency, and personal mail still needed to be paper (or plastic or metal) at both ends of the process, for varying reasons. And the coffee solution was a good one for paper, since energy was cheaper to ship than matter, even with the "overhead" energy that the transporter spent keeping the solid goods in flux. Nor was security a problem: Spock had himself devised the ciphers that would make sure no mail was tampered with while in transit. They were satchel codes of extreme complexity, their basic structure derived from a most reliable source—

The comm console went off.

Spock punched a button on the arm of the helm.

"*Enterprise;* Spock here."

"*Sarek,*" said the voice, and Spock's eyebrow went up.

"Father," he said. "Are you and Mother well?"

The dry voice, far away, got an ironic tone to it. "*I had not thought you gone so far into human behavior, my son, as to begin indulging in 'small talk' with me.*"

Spock held himself quite still for a moment, then said, "Father, I rarely hear from you by voice transmission unless either you or Mother is *not* well. Therefore my logic is intact for the moment."

There was a moment of stillness on the other end as well. "*That line of reasoning is justifiable,*" Sarek said. "*However, your mother and I are both in good health.*"

"Then I would assume that your call has something to do with the vote that took place on Vulcan this morning."

"*You have had the news?*"

"No. But it seems a reasonable assumption. What was the result?"

"*In favor of considering secession, four thousand three hundred fifty-one to fifteen hundred twelve.*"

Spock sat for a moment and let one level of his attention flicker back to the British Isles, contemplating a low pressure area moving slowly toward the Midlands. There was another small low hovering over the Borders that made it difficult to tell whether the first would head north or south. At any rate, it was surely raining in the Cotswolds—

"Then they have certainly called for you to return home and speak for the secessionists," Spock said.

Another pause. "*They have. More: T'Pau did.*"

"And will you?"

A much longer pause. *"My son, you know my reasons."*

Spock was silent too, for a moment, regarding a band of cloud over Ayrshire. "Too well, my father," he said. "But you must do your conscience's work."

"So must you. The Council has called for your testimony as well."

Spock considered what this was going to mean to the *Enterprise*'s liberty schedule and experienced a moment of regret, which he swiftly put aside. "I should have expected that," he said. "Noted. I will make the necessary notifications here and advise Starfleet . . . though I think I know what they will do."

"Agreed. I will see you at home, my son. I estimate that you will be there before me."

"As do I," said Spock. He paused, then said, "Tell Mother that I think of her."

The silent sound of an eyebrow going up somewhere in Los Angeles. *"It would be illogical of you not to."* said Sarek, with an edge of humor on the dryness. *"Out."*

Spock touched the button on the arm of the helm and eyed the south of Britain, toward Wales. That little cloud, reaching back eastward from Gwynedd and across the Irish Sea: that was perhaps the symptom of the solution. That persistent backwash, leading into the major northeastern flow—Spock examined its path, calculated probabilities, and then reluctantly put the half-born algorithm aside. A wonderfully complex problem: but life had handed him a thornier one. The weather would have to wait.

He got up, leaving the empty helm behind him, went to his Science station, and began making calls.

It was blowing up a gale outside the pub. Wind whipped rain against windows gone glassy black with night, and rattled the damper in the fireplace. Once he heard a skitter and crash as a roof slate blew loose and smashed against the chimney, then clattered down into the rain-gutter in an arpeggio of chunks and splinters. But on the whole, James T. Kirk was beyond caring. He was sitting in a chimney-corner seat with his feet out in front of a coal fire, and an Irish whiskey in one hand: he was warm and snug, and he didn't have to go anywhere, and there was nothing to do but relax and listen to the wind mutter and moan in the flue.

"There's the Jim, then," said a familiar voice behind him.

"Ronan," Jim said, looking up. "They keeping you busy?"

"Not tonight." Ronan Boyne sat down next to Jim in the twin to the chair he was sitting in, an old overstuffed horsehair business, heaven only knew how old. Ronan ran the place, which everyone called the Willow Grove even though "Deveraux's" was painted over the front door. He put down his ever-present oranges-and-lemons drink and ran his hands through his hair: black hair, for Ronan was about as black Irish as they came, with a big bland face and big strong hands. "It's only the fools and the desperate cases out tonight," he said. "Even the ferries from Wales have all been canceled."

"Doesn't surprise me. I wouldn't want to be out on that water. Eight-foot swells, at least."

"If *you* wouldn't, then the rest of us had better stay home! Chess later?"

"Sounds good."

"You're on, then." And Ronan got up and went off to see to one of the desperate cases, who was bringing a brace of empty pint glasses back to the bar.

Jim sighed and put his head back against the padded wall behind him. That was the way it had been for a couple of weeks now. A friendly inquiry or two, then he was left alone if he wanted to be . . . but there was always the promise of companionship if he wanted it. He couldn't have found a better place for a vacation.

He had certainly needed one. That business with the Romulans, and right after it the interminable famine runs for gamma Muscae V, and after *that,* the intervention at 1210 Circini, with the *Enterprise* caught in the middle and everybody on the four planets in the neighborhood shooting at her: it was enough to turn your hair gray. When it was their turn in the Fleet heavy-cruisers' rotation to come back to Earth, Jim had been cranky enough to pull a little rank on his crew's and his own behalf. Within an hour of their arrival in Earth orbit, he had informed Fleet (as was his right) that he was taking his last two years' accumulated leave all at once. Then he had mentally braced himself for a fight. But Fleet had responded blandly that the *Enterprise* was badly overdue for retrofit, which would involve at least a month's worth of equipment testing and resupply. So for now, they told him, he and his crew were on indefinite paid liberty unless they specifically requested reassignment to other ships. Jim smiled, knowing about how likely that was. He packed a couple of bags, said goodbye-for-now to his crew, and set about getting himself lost.

Technology had made Earth smaller than it had ever been, but you could still get pretty lost if you worked at it. It had been a matter of only three hours' travel, and Jim did it the tourist's way, on purpose—after all, there was no point in simply beaming down to where you were going on Earth, as if it was any other world you had business with on your tour of duty. He caught a shuttlecraft from the *Enterprise* to the Fleet orbital facility, then took the transporter to San Francisco Interplanetary, and the BA hyperbolic shuttle from SFO to London; after that, the Spas Lingus ion-jumper from Luton Spaceport to Dublin, and finally a rental dual-mode flit for the run south down the coast road. In fact, the travel was really only two hours' worth: most of that last hour of the three had been spent sitting caught between annoyance and bemusement on an abeyance apron at Luton, waiting for launch clearance. Jim had been a little careless about his timing, and got caught in the commuter rush hour, all the businessmen heading home to Europe and Asia from the City.

But it had been more than worth it for the view on the drive down, as ahead and to the right the Wicklow mountains rose up before him, all slate- and emerald-shadowed in a long fierce sunset that piled up in purple and gold behind them; and on the left hand, the sea, a blue gray like quiet eyes, breaking silent with distance at the stony feet of Bray Head. There were not too many houses to mar the bleak loveliness of hill and water and sky; the towns themselves seemed to crouch down to one or two stories, and make themselves small. And Dublin's fair city, where the girls were so pretty, had grown in many directions, but not this one. Only its spires could be seen away across the tidal flats of Dublin Bay—civilization kept properly at a distance, where it would not frighten the horses. The Irish had their priorities.

Using the road for the delight of getting down between the hedgerows, Jim had driven past the Willow Grove, only half noticing the bed-and-breakfast sign, and half a mile down the road had stopped and turned and come back. It had looked promising, in a quiet way: an ancient Georgian house, big for this part of the world, with two huge bay windows at the front, full of cheerful drinkers. He had walked in, inquired about prices and credit systems, and half an hour later he was sitting where he was sitting now, eating clear lamb stew and drinking Guinness, and being checked out by the locals.

"Jimmy boy, how are you tonight?"

"Fine," he said, automatically, because no matter who was asking, it was definitely true. Looking up, he caught the tail end of a wave from Riona and Erevan Fitzharris, passing by on their way to the bar for their nightly pint: a tall blond man, a tall redheaded lady, computer consultants who commuted home to Wicklow from Hamburg every day. They had been the first ones to realize who Jim was.

Ronan hadn't even thought about it, he claimed, till he was told. "It's not my fault," he said later: "Kirks are common as cowpats around here, for pity's sake. Also I don't watch that damn box," that being how he referred to the holovision, except of course when it was showing soccer. But Jim had his suspicions—Ronan had taken an image of his direct-credit plate, after all. It was not until Riona and Erevan accused him in public, one night, of being in Starfleet, of being, in fact, *the* James T. Kirk, that he admitted it to anyone. And to his astonishment, after the laughing, hollering group in the pub that night had been told the secret, and howled with merriment to see Jim blush (it had to have been the whiskey they kept feeding him), they all pretended it hadn't happened. Only once in a while, if out of habit he had activated his universal-translator implant that morning, he would hear one of the Irish-speaking regulars murmur to someone new about *ar captaen an t-arthaigh an rhealtai* Eachtra: *our* starship captain, the one with the *Enterprise.* And he would turn away, so as not to let them see him smiling.

Jim sipped at the whiskey, and stretched a bit in the chair. The people here were mostly interested in who he *was,* and only occasionally in what he did—that was what made the place so marvelous. They had been piqued by not being *told* what he did, but once that was settled and he had been properly ragged for being a galactic hero, there were other more important things to talk about: weather, fanning, sport, and especially local gossip, which most everyone took covert or overt delight in sharing with him. The regulars seemed to think it a point of honor that he should know their neighbors, and themselves, as well as they did. Jim, not to put too fine a point on it, ate it up. There was, after all, a resemblance to part of his job as a starship captain. It was his business to be very familiar indeed with the gossip of what amounted to a small spacefaring village—to know where to share it, and when to spread it, and how to keep quiet and smile.

And if of an evening someone *did* tempt him to talk shop, it was in the gentlest sort of way. One night someone happened to mention Grainne, the pirate queen who raged up and down the Irish Sea in the first Elizabeth's day, and it had seemed natural enough to talk a little about Orion pirates and their depredations, and the deplorable trade in green slave girls. Or another time someone else might admit how his five-times' great-grandfather had been one of "the Gentlemen"—for smuggling had been more or less the national sport, some generations back—and if Jim could put on an innocent face and tell them a little about how one might get Romulan ale across the Neutral Zone without attracting the attention of Customs and Excise, well, it was the least he could do. . . .

"He pulls the slowest pint in the county, and that's a fact," Riona said from just behind Jim, as she picked her way around the chair and flopped in the other chimney-corner seat.

"It's a virtue," Erevan said, coming around the other side and sitting in the chair next to Jim. He was carrying a perfectly full pint glass of Guinness, which he put down with exaggerated care on the table between them. "Agree with me, Jimmy boy."

"I agree with you," Jim said immediately. "What am I agreeing with?"

"You cannot pull a pint of this stuff fast," Erevan said. "All those little air bubbles, *phah*, they get into it and ruin the flavor."

"When you're dying of thirst, the flavor doesn't enter into it if it's half an hour before you can drink it," Riona said, and drank, and got herself a beige moustache from the luxuriant head. She wiped it off surreptitiously. "Ronan ought to do what they do in town, and pull pints ahead of time, and leave them on the shelf to settle down."

"Slops," Erevan said. "That is slops. Jimmy, ignore this woman."

"You'd hit me if I didn't," Jim said. Then added, "Come to think of it, you'd hit me if I *did*."

"You be still, then; I'm discoursin'. Slops. Say you have a barman on the bad, and closing time comes, and he hasn't sold those pints: what then? What's to keep him from pouring them back into the tank for the next day, eh? Slops." Erevan said the word with great satisfaction. "Each drinker to his own pint, and if you have to wait, that's the price of quality, and besides, it's worth waiting for."

Jim smiled and said nothing, just sipped his whiskey. Much to his annoyance, the thick, brown black brew called stout had been one Irish taste he had been unable to acquire: to him, it tasted like roofing tar. He had heard this particular argument before; and the worse arguments about brands of stout sometimes progressed almost to physical violence before Ronan made it plain that such was not permitted, and besides, it would spill the drinks.

"And what's that you're drinking?" Erevan said.

"Whiskey," said Jim.

"Oh, now, what are you drinking *that* down here for?"

Jim was opening his mouth to laugh when in the pocket of his jacket, slung over the back of his chair, his communicator went off. It had been so long since he'd heard it that the sound startled him almost as much as it did Riona and Erevan. "Phone," he said, as casually as he could, and dug around behind him in the pocket among the car's code plate and the loose change, till he came up with the communicator and flipped it open.

"Kirk here," he said.

"Spock here, Captain," and out of the corner of his eye Jim noted with mild amusement that Riona and Erevan were eyeing one another, for here was another name they knew from the newscasts. *"Are you busy?"*

"Chatting with friends. Do you want to call me back?"

"No need: this news will be quite public shortly, if indeed it is not public now. I would suggest to you, Captain, that all liberties are about to be canceled. I thought you might appreciate an advance warning."

"Noted. What's going on?"

"A vote was taken this morning, and Vulcan has decided to call the Referendum. My presence will be required there, and I would strongly suspect that the Enterprise *will be sent there as well, to . . . reinforce the planet's memory of favors done it in the past by the Federation."*

Jim was still for a moment. This particular problem had been a long time brewing . . . and he had thought something might happen to make it come to a head fairly soon. *At times like this,* he thought, *I really hate being right.* "We have no orders yet?"

"No, sir. But I judge the probability of the imminent arrival of such orders to be ninety-third percentile or higher."

He means he's sure, but he's leaving me the option of one more day's holiday, Jim thought, entertaining the idea . . . then reluctantly rejecting it. *Better get it over with.* He put down his whiskey. "All right," he said. "Give me half an hour to check out of here, and I'll be ready to beam up."

"Acknowledged. Enterprise *out."*

He snapped the communicator shut, looked at Erevan and Riona regretfully, and shrugged. "There goes the vacation."

"It's a wicked waste, that's what it is," Riona said.

He agreed with her, but there was nothing to be done about it except get up from the pleasant fireside and take care of business. He spent ten minutes in the comm booth, getting someone from the rental company to come out and fetch the flitter; another five minutes settling his bill with Ronan; the rest of the time getting things out of the flit and packing them. And then there was nothing to do but wait for the communicator to go off again, and say his good-byes.

He was shaking hands with Ronan at the door when his pocket whistled. "That's me," he said sadly. "The chess game will have to wait. You take care of yourself."

"I'll do that." Various people in the bar were shouting good-byes, waving: even Renny, Ronan's daughter and assistant behind the bar, was calling something to him. He missed it, but was curious: she was very shy and had rarely said more than a word or so to him before. "Pardon?" he called back.

"Go maire tú i bhfad agus rath!"

He hadn't turned the translator on that morning. Jim looked at Ronan, bemused. Ronan raised eyebrows at him and said, "Old Irish wayfarer's blessing. It translates as 'Live long and prosper.' "

Very slowly, Jim smiled. "I'll be back," he said, and since only a galactic hero would have made a spectacle of himself by beaming up from the middle of the pub, he stepped out into the black, blowing night and shut the door behind him, holding on to it carefully so that it shouldn't slam in the wind.

Several seconds later, the rain was blowing through the place where he had been.

The spear in the Other's heart
is the spear in your own:
you are he.

There is no other wisdom,
and no other hope for us
but that we grow wise.

—attributed to Surak

Enterprise: One

Position yourself in the right place—on the surface of the moon, say, somewhere near the slow-moving dayline, or in one of the L5 habitats swinging in peaceful captivity around the world—and you can see it without any trouble: the old Earth in the new Earth's arms. Some people prefer her that way to any other. Not for them the broad blue cloud-swirled disk, all bright and safe and easily seen. They want mystery; they want the Earth's nightly half-bath in the old dark. She always emerges, but (to these people's relief) she always dips in again—the blue fire fading away down through the spectrum, the rainbow of atmosphere's edge, down through the last flash of crimson, to black.

And when she does, the stars come out. Faithful as the other, farther stars, in steady constellations, they turn as the night that holds them turns—the splatters of spilled-gem light that are BosWash, Ellay, Greater Peking, Bolshe-Moskva, Plu'Paris. The great roadways across continents are bright threads, delicate as if spiders of fire had spun them: here and there the light is gentled by coming from far underwater, as in the Shelf cities off the Pacific coasts of Japan and old North America. At the edge, a limb of brightness shows, the sunrise inexorably sliding around the curved edge of things: but the limb is narrow, the merest shaving of pearl and turquoise curving against the breadth of night. And for the time being, night reigns.

In places light shows without man having made it. When the moon is in the right phase, the polar icecaps are one wide sheen of palely burning white; the Rockies and the Himalayas and the Alps and Andes glow with a firefly fire, faint but persistent. Sometimes even the Great Wall will show: a silver hair, twisting, among the silver glint of rivers . . . and afterward the Moon will slide away and around in her long dance with the Earth to gaze at the great diffuse bloom of her own disk's light in Atlantic or Pacific. Half a month from now the Moon will swing around at the new, and all these places, under the sun again, will give their light back to her, ashen, a breath of silver against the dark side of the satellite's phase. But for now the Earth keeps the moonlight and the romance to herself, slowly turning, shimmering faint and lovely like a promise made and kept a long time ago. Darkness scattered with diamonds, and the darkness never whole: there she lies, and turns in her sleep. . . .

. . . and over her comes climbing other light, passing out of the fire of the far side's day: a golden light like a star, dimmed from a blaze to a spark as it passes the terminator, twenty-five thousand miles high. Moonlight silvers her now as she approaches, not hurrying, a shade more than eleven thousand miles per hour, not quite geosynchronous, gaining on the Earth. She seems a delicate thing at first, while distant—a toy, all slender pale light and razory shadows—then bigger, not a toy anymore, the paired nacelles growing, spearing upward, reaching as high as thirty-story buildings, the main dish blocking the sky away from zenith to "horizon" as it passes by, passes over. Silent she passes, massive, burning silver, gemmed in ruby and emerald with her running lights, black only where shadows fall and where, the letters spell her number and name in one language of her planet of registry, the planet she's about to leave. NCC 1701, the *Starship Enterprise*, slips past in moonlight, splashed faint on her undersides with the light of Earth's cities, ready to give all the light up for the deep cold dark that is her proper home. . . .

*   *   *

It takes time to walk right around a starship. Eleven decks in the primary hull, twelve in the secondary, from an eighth of a mile of corridors per deck to maybe two or three—the old simile comparing a starship to a small town becomes more obviously true than ever to someone determined to do the hike. Jim, though, didn't mind how long it took, and he did as much of it as time allowed, every time he came aboard after a refit.

This time he altered his usual routine a little. *After all day stuck down at Fleet,* he thought, *I'm entitled to a change of pace. Bloody desk pilots.* . . . But a second later he put away the annoyance: he had what he had gone for. Jim laughed to himself, and shortly thereafter beamed up via the cargo transporters, along with a shipment of computer media, toiletries, and medical supplies.

Cargo Transport was a more pleasant place, in some ways, than the usual crew transporters. The huge room was in the space next to the shuttlecraft hangars, and needed to be, since anything too big to ship up any other way, from warp-engine parts to container cargo, wound up here. The place tended to be noisy and busy any time the ship was near a planet: at the moment, it was a vast happy racket, boxed and crated and force-shielded matériel being carried in all directions on gravflats of varying sizes. Jim got down off the pads in a hurry to avoid being ran over by a couple of G-flats the size of shuttlecraft, and then paused on the loading floor, seeing who was maneuvering the flats by him—two Earth-human crewmen, a small wiry auburn-haired man and a tall dark-haired woman with a Valkyrie's figure under a cargoloader's coverall.

"Mr. Matejas," he said, "Mz. Tei," and as they heard his greeting and realized with surprise who he was, they started to come to attention. He waved them off it. "As you were. How was the engagement party?"

The two of them looked at each other, and Jorg Matejas blushed, and Lala Tei chuckled. "It was terrific," she said, shaking her red hair back. "Everybody had a great time, especially the Sulamids . . . Rahere and Athene got into the sugar, and you know how Sulamids are about sugar, it was a riot, their tentacles got all knotted, and it took us about an hour to get them undone. Sir, thank you so much for the 'gram! Jorg's mom nearly went to pieces when Fleet called and read it in the middle of the party, she was so excited. . . ."

Jim smiled, for that had been his intention. One of his more reliable sources of gossip had let him know that Mr. Matejas's mother was very uncomfortable about her son marrying someone holding higher rank than his. Jim had responded by studying Jorg's record very carefully, noting that he was somewhat overdue for promotion, and then correcting the matter . . . making sure that the news of his promotion hit him during the party, via the addressing of the congratulatory telegram. The source-of-gossip, also present at the party, had let Jim know later that the name signed at the bottom of the 'gram had counted for almost as much as Jorg's jump in grade to quartermaster's mate. Jim had been gratified—there were apparently times when being a galactic hero could be turned to some use. "You're very welcome."

"Sir," Jorg said, "I'm glad we had the chance to see you. I wanted to thank you, very much indeed."

"You earned it," Jim said. "Don't think otherwise. If I helped with the timing a little, consider it my pleasure. Meanwhile, how's the loading going?"

Jorg heard the *when* under the "how." "Half an hour, Captain," he said. "Less if possible."

Jim smiled more widely, for reasons that had nothing to do with the timetable. "Good enough. Carry on," he said, and went away feeling unusually pleased inside.

He strode across the loading floor, and all the way across it was "Good morning, Captain," "Good evening, Captain," and Jim's smile got broader and broader: not at the inconsistency among greetings, for the ship was back on cruise shift schedules again, three shifts relieving one another, and some people were working overtime. Out into the corridor, and it was the same thing, when he said hello to his people or they said hello to him: no "Admiral," nothing fancy, just "Captain" again, as God intended. It was a great relief. As he walked the halls, Jim acquired a grin that would not go away.

The long afternoon in Fleet Admiral Nogura's office had been trying, but the results had been worth it. Twenty hours after beaming up from the Willow Grove, eight hours after beaming over to Fleet to handle the inevitable paperwork involved with a new set of missions, he was happily demoted to captain, effective immediately, revocable at Fleet's discretion. Some people would not have understood it, this desire to be de-admiraled. But most of those people weren't naval, or had lost touch with the naval tradition that was so much a part of Starfleet. And Nogura, in love (Jim told himself tolerantly) with the power of the Fleet Admiral's position, couldn't understand it either. *It's not his fault,* Jim thought. *He's been one too long, that's all.*

Admirals, from time immemorial, didn't command anything but fleets: they managed strategy and tactics on a grand scale . . . but Jim wasn't interested in a scale quite that grand. Captains might be obliged to give admirals rides to where they were going, and to obey their orders: but for all that, the captains were more in command than ever an admiral was. There might be more than one admiral on a ship . . . but never more than one captain. Even as a passenger, another captain would be "bumped" a grade up to commodore—partly out of courtesy, partly to avoid discourtesy to the ship's true master. It was *real* sovereignty, the only kind Jim cared for, and he was glad to get rid of the extra braid on his arms and settle into the happy business of interacting, not with fleets, but with people.

Jim did that for the hour it took him to cover the manned parts of the engineering hull, stopping last at Engineering. He strolled in, and almost immediately began to wish he hadn't. Pieces of the backup warp-drive were all over the floor, or hovering on placeholders, and Scotty was thundering around among his engineering ensigns, shouting at them. Fortunately, he was doing so in the tone of voice that Jim had eventually learned meant everything was going all right, and so he relaxed and stood there for a bit, enjoying the spectacle.

"Ye can't put a drive together as if it was a bitty babbie's picture puzzle, for pity's sake," Scotty was telling the air with genial scorn, as junior crewmen scuttled around him with calibrating instruments and tools and engine parts, looking panic-stricken. "There's got to be some system to't. You can't bring up the multistate equivocators until the magnetic bottle's on-line, and where's the bottle then? Ye've had ten whole minutes!—Afternoon, Captain," he added.

Jim smiled again. "Problems, Scotty?" he said, not because he perceived any, but because he knew Scotty expected that he would ask.

"Ah no, just a drill. What if these poor children have to reassemble a warp engine by themselves some one of these days, with only impulse running and a pack of Klingons howling along behind 'em? They've got the brains for it: would they be on the *Enterprise* if they didn't? Best they learn how now. We'll be tidy again in twenty minutes. Or I'll know the reason why!" Scotty added, at the top of his voice. The scuttling got much more frantic. Apparently Scotty's crew considered the chief engineer in what Jim had heard them describe as "one of his moods" to be slightly more dangerous to deal with than mere Klingons.

Jim nodded. *I might as well get out,* he thought; *they look nervous enough without me watching as well.* "Officers' briefing at point seven, Scotty," he said.

"Aye, I checked my terminal for the schedule a while back." Scotty looked around him with satisfaction. "Just before I crashed the Engineering computers."

Jim was astonished, and looked around him . . . then felt mildly sheepish, for he'd never even noticed that every screen in the place was blank. "They're putting this thing together *without* the computer prompts? Not even the emergency systems?"

Scotty shrugged. "Who's to say we could guarantee them that the backup systems would be working in an emergency?" he said. "Even backups fail. But their little brains won't . . . if we train them properly. FIVE MINUTES!!" he told the world at large. Then looking around the floor, he said, "By rights I should evacuate the place and make them do it in pressure gear. If her side was blown this far open that they'd have to reassemble from scratch, they'd need that practice."

Jim shook his head, feeling sorry for this Engineering crew, all doomed to be turned into mechanical "geniuses" like their mad teacher. "Talk to Spock about scheduling, if you feel the need."

Scotty nodded, and together he and Jim stood and watched the matter-antimatter mix column being put together from the field generators up. "By the bye, Captain, have you scheduled the crew briefing yet?"

"Point four, tomorrow morning."

"Right."

Jim patted Scotty on the back. "I'm off, then," he said.

Scotty eyed him suspiciously for a moment. "You've picked up a bit of an Irish accent," he said.

"Might not be strange," Jim said. "The people I was with were claiming that my family wasn't Scots. Sorry," he said, as Scotty looked at him with an expression of shock that was only partly faked. "Really. They claim the name Kirk was an Anglicization of O'Cuire. It would explain why my family was in the east of Ireland to begin with. . . ."

"Those people will say anything," Scotty said, and grinned a little. "Get on with ye. Sir."

Jim headed out. "THREE MINUTES!" the voice roared behind him, as he got to the turbolift and stepped in.

"Where to, Captain?" the lift said to him.

He smiled again. "Bridge."

The place looked a little strange when the lift doors opened on it, as home often does when one's been away from it for a while. Jim stepped out, nodded greeting at Uhura and Sulu, who gestured or smiled hello at him. He waved them back to what they were doing and glanced around to the Science station. Spock was bent over it, making some adjustment. "Readout now," he said, straightening and looking over his shoulder at the large, shaggy-fringed rock that was sitting in the center seat.

Some of those glittering fringes stroked the open circuitry of the communicator controls in the seat's arm. "Point nine nine three," said a scratchy voice from the voder box mounted on the rock's back. "A nice triple sine."

" 'Nice'?" said Spock. Jim raised an eyebrow: you could have used Spock's tone of voice to dry out a martini.

"Within high-nominal limits," said the rock, and there was a definite smile in the voice, despite the fact that the voder should not have been able to convey emotion. "A third-order curve, sir. Skew no more than e minus zero point two two four six. No crystal infrequency, no parasitic vibrations, signal loss within accepted IEEE and CCITT parameters, layback less than point zero two percent, hyperbolic—"

"That should be sufficient, Mr. Naraht," Spock said, looking over at the captain with a slight wry expression.

"Mr. Naraht," Jim said, stepping down beside the helm. Lieutenant Naraht was a Horta, a hatchling of the original Horta on Janus VI: one of an intensely curious species that could no more have stayed out of space, once they came to understand it, than they could have stopped eating rock. Jim had watched Naraht's career since he was transferred to the *Enterprise* with both interest and pleasure: the Horta had gone from eager, avid "space cadet" to seasoned officer in a very short time . . . no surprise, considering some of the things he had been through, with the rest of the crew, since he came aboard. Now Jim patted the back of the center seat and said, "Trying her out for fit, mister?"

There would have been a time when the remark would have made Naraht wriggle all over, embarrassed—and the sight of a quarter-ton of living stone, the shape and color of a giant fringed asbestos pan pizza, being embarrassed, had occasionally been memorable. But now Naraht merely looked up—at least Jim felt he was being looked at, though he was unsure as to how—and said, "Respectfully, sir, I think I would need something a little bigger. There was some distortion showing up in the commcircuits, that was all, and Mr. Spock asked me to assist him in isolating it."

Jim nodded, seeing the point: there were certain advantages in having a crewman who could make direct "neural" connections with solid circuitry and *feel* what was wrong with it as an itch or a tic, rather than as a string of numbers. But one who could feel the problem and then translate it into the numbers as well—*that* was someone invaluable. As usual, half the departments in the ship were fighting over Naraht's services. Biochemistry, geology, xenoarchaeology, they all wanted him— Naraht could do detailed chemical analysis, or even carbon- or selenium-dating, by merely eating a piece of the object in question and reporting on the "flavor." As far as Jim knew, Naraht's only complaint about being on the *Enterprise* was that he was gaining weight at a shocking rate and didn't know what his mother would think when she saw him. . . .

Jim glanced over at Spock. "I could have sworn that Mr. Naraht had almost given you more data than you needed."

"There is no such thing as too much data," Spock said calmly, "but there *is* such a thing as unnecessary detail. Nonetheless, the job is adequately completed. Thank you, Mr. Naraht."

"My pleasure, sir," said the Horta, and slipped down out of the helm onto the floor with his usual speed and silence, always surprising in someone so massive. "Captain? Your conn?"

"Thank you, Mr. Naraht," Jim said, and sat down. The seat was very warm—not surprising: McCoy usually referred to the liquid-mineral complex that Naraht used for blood as "fluorocarbonated lava with asbestos hemocytes."

"Sir," Naraht said, and shuffled off into the lift to be about his business. Jim sat back in the command chair, and Spock stepped down beside him, holding out a pad-screen.

Jim glanced down it, tilted the pad slightly to scroll through it. It was a very condensed, compressed version of the ship's schedule for that day, parts of it flowcharted where an activity of one ship's department was dependent on some data or action by another. Most of it he had already seen, at Fleet, when signing for his orders and *Enterprise*'s "sailing papers" and authorizing the usual too-numerous vouchers, invoices and inventories.

"We're ready to go," he said.

"Of course," said Spock. "All transfer personnel are aboard and all assigned personnel are at post or accounted for. Our two scheduled rendezvous, with *Swiftsure* and *Coromandel,* are estimated on-time in one-point-one-three and one-point-six days respectively."

"Fine." Now Jim's eye lighted again on the listing that scheduled the senior officers' briefing, and he glanced up at Spock.

Spock bowed his head slightly. "I will be doing the mission situation analysis," he said.

"Thank you. You do seem better qualified than anyone else. . . ."

Spock got an expression that would hardly have seemed like anything on a human face, but on a Vulcan was a most astonishing look of irony. "I am certainly considered by some to be part of the problem," he said. "It seems only appropriate to attempt to be part of the solution."

Kirk nodded, scanned farther down the list. "Crew mixer's starting a little late."

"I would suspect this is so that the senior officers can attend," Spock said.

"Right." On *Enterprise,* as on many another ship, there was a tradition of a first-night-out "mixer" party for the crew, so that people could get together and debrief about what they had done on leave and catch up on personal business before getting down to the serious business of working on a starship. Some civilians had considered this frivolous, when they found out about it—until surveys done by the Fleet Surgeons General proved that if the debriefing didn't happen formally, first night out, it tended to stretch out across the next month of travel time, impairing the crew's efficiency as it did so. With the release of that data, the complaining stopped. And the *Enterprise* always threw a very good party. "It had better be good," McCoy would say, only half joking, since Recreation was considered a part of Medicine, and the chief of Recreation reported directly to him.

"Captain," Uhura broke in, looking over her shoulder at Jim, "a private message has just come in for you—the computer just finished decoding it. Shall I hold it?"

"No need," Jim said. "Put it here." He held up the padscreen.

Uhura touched a couple of controls to dump the material to the commlink in the pad. Jim hit the combination of shorthand-keys for "newest," and the message came up. Spock politely looked the other way.

"No," Jim said. "Take a look at this, Spock . . ."

TO: Cpt. J. T. Kirk, cmdg NCC 1701 USS *Enterprise*
FROM: T'Pau, ac. affil. Vulcan Science Academy/shi'Kahr/
      a'Shav/Vulcan

Captain:

You will have noted that your First Officer has been requested to give testimony in the proceedings regarding the Referendum on repeal of the Vulcan Articles of Federation. Logic dictates that due to previous close association with Vulcan and Vulcans, you should be asked to speak as well. This matter is left entirely to your discretion, and no onus will rest specifically or generally on the Federation or Starfleet if you elect to refuse. Please notify us as to your intention. T'Pau

"Well, Captain?" Spock said.

Jim stared at the pad. *Lord, how I hate public speaking. . . . Still, this is something worth speaking about.* "Uhura," he said, "send a reply. My great respects to T'Pau, and I will be delighted to speak—no, make that honored. Respectfully yours, signed, etcetera etcetera. Copies of the message and the reply to Starfleet, as well."

"Aye aye, sir," Uhura said.

Jim brought the ship's schedule back up on the screen of the pad and looked up at Spock.

"Anything further here that needs my attention?"

Spock reached over Jim's shoulder and tapped the pad: it cycled ahead to one entry. "A discretionary. Ship's BBS has asked for the release of more core memory."

Jim looked at the already substantial figure in gigabytes that the ship's bulletin board system was using already, and the fat increase being requested—almost double the present memory storage. "What does Dr. McCoy say?"

Spock glanced momentarily at the ceiling, as if it might assist him in his phrasing. "He says that the Rec chief thinks it would be a good idea, and in general he agrees, especially as regards the message net—but himself he thinks Mr. Sulu has already blown up more of Starfleet than is good for him on the 'damn bloodthirsty war games machine.' " Spock glanced mildly at Sulu's back: the helmsman was chatting with Chekov about a restaurant somewhere. "Apparently he has been experimenting with Klingon ship design in the BBS's ship exercise simulator. Improving both their design and their performance, if the comments of the people from Engineering are any indication. The Klingon ships in the simulation are apparently doing much better after 'Sulu refits.' "

"How have Mr. Sulu's efficiency ratings been?" said Jim, very softly.

"All above point eight and rising steadily," Spock said, just as quietly.

"And Bones hasn't scheduled him for a psych profile of any kind."

"No, sir."

"So basically, Bones is just grouching off."

Spock looked at the captain as if he had announced that space was a vacuum: his look said both that the statement was obvious, and one about which a great deal more could be said. "In other regards," Spock said after a moment, "message traffic on the BBS has been up significantly in recent days."

"Are you recommending the augmentation?" Jim said.

"Logically," Spock said, "it would be a reasonable assumption to expect crew stress levels, and therefore volubility, to increase over the mission ahead of us.

And it would be illogical to withhold what will be a valuable 'safety valve.' "

Jim cocked an eye at the pad, then tapped in an authorization code on the short-hand keys at the bottom. "Give them half again what they asked for." He let the pad scroll to the bottom. "I want a look at those refits, though. People elsewhere may be having the same ideas, if you get my drift."

"Affirmative. Mr. Tanzer has installed one of the optimum refits in the small simulation tank in Rec One."

"Tonight, then, at the party." Jim got up, handed Spock back the pad. "I'm going to get something to eat. I'll see you at the briefing."

The communicator whistled. *"Sickbay to Bridge—"*

Jim nodded at Uhura. "Bridge," he said. "What is it, Bones?"

"I just got the most interesting piece of mail—"

"From T'Pau?" Jim said. He glanced at Spock. Spock put an eyebrow up.

"You too, huh?" There was a moment's silence, and then McCoy said in an aggrieved tone, *"Dammit, I'm a doctor, not a—"*

"Belay it, Bones. What's your answer?"

There was another pause, then a sigh. *"Dammit,"* McCoy said, *"when did I last turn down an argument with a Vulcan? I can hardly pass up one with the whole planet."*

"Noted and logged," Jim said. "We'll talk about it later. Bridge out."

He turned toward the helm. "Mr. Chekov!"

"Sir?" said the navigator, turning in his seat.

"Plot us a course for Vulcan, warp two. Mr. Sulu, take us out of the system on impulse, one-tenth c, then warp us out."

"Sir!"

"And if you see any Klingons," Jim added as he paused at the bridge entry, waiting for the lift doors to open, "for pity's sake, don't stop to sell them new warp engines! No need to make your job harder than it is. . . ."

Sulu's chuckle was the last thing Jim heard as the lift doors shut on him.

The officers' mess was one of the more enjoyable parts of the ship, and not merely because it was for the officers. One could make a case that numerous parts of recreation and the arboretum were much nicer. But there was no faulting the view from the officers' mess. It was on the leading edge of the disk, with real windows, not viewscreens: floor-to-ceiling windows that gave the illusion of sitting at the twenty-third century equivalent of a ship's prow. At sublight, the stars naturally didn't seem to move, but Sulu was apparently opting for the scenic route out through Sol system, the so-called "Grand tour," which more than made up for it. Jupiter swam slowly into view, a huge striped-candy crescent, then grew gibbous, then full, as Sulu slipped the *Enterprise* around the planet's curvature, slowly enough to pick up a little slingshotting from gravity, swiftly enough not to let the impulse drivers disturb or be disturbed by Jupiter's radiopause. Various moons whipped or lazed around the planet like thrown ball bearings as *Enterprise* passed her. Saturn was a yellow white star in the distance, growing in the darkness as Sulu made for her.

Jim pushed his plate aside, having finished with his steak, and pulled the table screen close again on its swinging arm. Holding on it, amber on black, was a page of data.

Msg: 2003469
Date: 7416.664
Sec: WANTED/BUY/SELL/EXCHANGE
From: Cally Sherrin/spec4:sci
Subj: USED B'HIVA
Origin: XenoBiology Lab IV/term:1154/606

* * * * * * * * * * * * * * * * * * * *FOR SALE* * * * * * * * * * * * * * * * * * *
Best Quality Andorian B'hiva
One Careful Owner
No Dropouts! No lost meaning!
Warranty still in force
180 cr or best offer
Leave msg in BUYSELL or email area 6
* *

Now what the devil is a b'hiva? Jim thought, and kept reading.

Msg: 2003470
Date: 7417.903
Sec: WANTED/BUY/SELL/EXCHANGE
From: Nyota Uhura/Cmdr:comms
Subj: Taped Dictionaries
Origin: Communications/term: 181/53

While on leave planetside (Terra or Luna), did anyone happen
to pick up one of the taped or solid "tourist dictionaries" of
local languages sometimes sold in souvenir shops, etc? Want
to dump the thing? I'll trade you classical music, third-stream
jazz, exotica, drama (BBC, RSC, Bolshoi a specialty). Looking
particularly for Romanian, Kampuche, ULow, Eurish (Dalton re-
cension if possible), and other artificials (Anglish, Neolangue,
Sino-Francaise, Cynthetic). Thanks! N.U.

Still working on her doctoral thesis, Jim thought. Uhura was busy working on improving universal translator theory, mostly by taking the old theory to pieces and putting it back together in shapes that were causing a terrible furor in academic circles on
various planets. Jim vividly remembered one night quite a long time ago when he had
asked Uhura exactly how she was going about this. She had told him, for almost an
hour without stopping, and in delighted and exuberant detail, until his head was spinning with phoneme approximations and six-sigma evaluations and the syntactic fade
and genderbend and recontextualization and linguistic structural design and the physics
of the human dextrocerebral bridge. The session had left Jim shaking his head, thoroughly disabused of the idea (and ashamed of how long he had held it) that Uhura was
simply a sort of highly trained switchboard operator. . . . And as regarded her doctoral
thesis, he could have found out simply enough that she was still working on the Earth-
based algorithms, just by asking her: but this was a more interesting way of finding out.
Cynthetic? he wondered, and made a mental note to ask her about it at the party.

He scrolled down through various replies to Uhura's message—apparently quite a few people had picked up dictionaries that were now (or had immediately turned out to be) useless—and finally determined to leave these messages for later. "Change area," he said to the screen. "Common room."

The screen flickered and gave him another page.

COMMON ROOM
OPINION, INFORMED AND NON-
RANTING AND RAVING PERMITTED
NAMES NOT NECESSARY

It was one of the places he came to find out what his crew was thinking. Messages did not have to be attributed to a name or terminal, but they could not be private. The office of common room system operator rotated through the crew, offered to various members on the strength of their psych profiles in areas like calm reaction to stress and anger. The common room sysop tended to be close-mouthed and dependable, the kind of person that others refer to as "a rock." (Once it had actually *been* Naraht, to the amusement of just about everyone.) Here tempers could flare, awful jokes be told safely, suspicions be aired, rumors be shot down. The common room was sometimes a peaceful place, sometimes a powder-keg. Jim never ignored it.

He scanned through the most recent messages, and one caught his eye:

FROM: Bugs
DATE: 7412.1100

VULCANS: WHO NEEDS 'EM?

They can't take care of themselves anymore. They can't even take care of a starship if you give it to them—and now they claim that they're not good enough for us? Well, **** 'em and the *sehlat* they rode in on.

Just fooling.

Jim breathed out. *Serious? Or not?* The statement mirrored some that he had heard on Earth, as this crisis had built and brewed. He scanned down the page.

Farther down, other people came in and maligned Bugs, whoever he or she or it was. Remarks appeared along the lines of "Maybe they've got a point: maybe we *aren't* good enough for them. Or good *for* them, anyway—." Other people said, "We need them. Someone has to tell them so. Let's hope that someone here can get it through those thick Vulcan skulls of theirs. . . ."—and Jim would heat up slightly under the collar: he was sure they were thinking of him. The problem was, so did Starfleet. Somehow they expected him to pull this rabbit out of the hat.

The problem was, the rabbit was a *sehlat* . . . and he didn't fully understand the shape of the hat. He thought he might never fully understand it, even if he lived to be as old as, well, as a Vulcan. And if he didn't come to understand it, pretty damn fast . . . then there would no longer be Vulcans in the Federation to be as old as.

Not to mention that he would suddenly be bereft of one of his two best friends. And Starfleet would come down very, very hard, right on his neck. He refused to try to choose which of those options bothered him more.

Jim scrolled down through the messages. They were not all about Vulcans: some of them were about investing your pay, or relationships that were going well, or going sour, or the nature of God, or the awful way the meatloaf from Commissary Five tasted lately, was the computer there having a crash or something? But Jim read right through them, the complaints, the hello's, the nattering, until he came to the one message that made him simply stop and stare at the screen.

FROM: Llarian
DATE: 7412.301

REPLY: to BUGS. 7412.1100

You're not thinking any more clearly than they are. It's not a question of whether we're good enough for them. Or not. They don't even know who we *are* . . . and they're going to judge us. But *we've* been judging us for thousands of years . . . and *we* don't know who we are, either.

So why all the noise? It won't matter. Until it's too late.

Jim looked up. Uranus slid into sight, slid past on the port side, glowing dim jade, its moons caught climbing topsy-turvy up one side of it as *Enterprise* passed. In a little while the ship would go into warp: in little more than two days, they would be in orbit around Vulcan.

It won't matter.

"Log off," Jim said after a pause, and spent some time gazing out into the darkness.

"Secession," Spock said, "is not the most accurate term for the act which the Vulcan planetary government is being asked to consider; but for the moment, it will serve."

The main briefing room was empty except for the department heads of the *Enterprise,* sitting around the table in the places that tended to become traditional over long periods of time. Spock, as department head of Science, sat at the "corner" that held the main table reference computer, the one that sent images and data to the subsidiary screens set around the table in its surface, at each place, unless the people sitting in front of them chose to override. Next to him sat Scotty, for the Engineering department: behind him was one of his sub-heads, Lasja Ihirian, who managed most routine maintenance and repair aboard ship. Lasja looked bored, but then he always looked bored in meetings—fixing badly broken things was his metier and chief joy. A big, dark-skinned man in a Sikh's white turban, he sat and toyed with the hilt of his knife and looked just a hair from yawning.

Next down the table was Uhura, as head of communications: next to her, Lt. Meshav, who handled Data Management for the ship. What with routinely overseeing and programming the ship's computers, regularly rewriting or debugging their software, and making sure that the many complex interlocking computer systems didn't interfere with one another, it was the kind of job that almost required eight hands and four brains: and since Meshav effectively had both, s/he was very good at what s/he did. Meshav was a Sulamid, who looked like nothing more than a seven-foot-tall pillar of pink violet tentacles, with a waving rosette of stalked eyes on top . . . at least, when s/he was feeling like being pink, or feeling expansive enough to wave the eyes around. S/he had an octocameral brain, which meant s/he might manifest up to eight personalities. S/he tried to restrain herself from doing this too often, citing (as Jim had heard it put it) "pity for the poor single-mindeds." All the same, a poker game with Meshav was an interesting experience, especially considering that one personality was completely capable of hiding the contents of one's hand from all the others . . . not to mention from any opponent.

Next to Meshav sat the head of Security, Ingrit Tomson, a six-and-a-half-foot-tall, icy-looking woman with close-cropped blond hair and a deceptively gentle look about her; and down at the end of the table, next to Tomson, was Dr. McCoy for Medicine, and behind him, his sub-head, big silver-haired Harb Tanzer, for Recreation. Round the far corner of the table, the quartermaster, Seppu Visti, a small slender dark man with Finnish blood in his background and a computer in his head—literally: he was testing the new Second Thought accounting implant for Starfleet, and could tell you the *Enterprise*'s tonnage at any moment of the day or night, down to the last gram, depending on where and when you were in a voyage. Jim found it unnerving: one Spock should be enough for a ship. *At least his ears are the right shape. . . .* And then came Defense, with Sulu sitting in as department head—the headship shifted back and forth between the chiefs of Navigation and Weapons Control. And at last, at the head of the table, sat the captain.

He sat a little uneasily today, concerned by Spock's unusually somber look and tone. Jim glanced down the table and saw McCoy twitching slightly; he seemed to have caught the mood too. "I take it," Jim said, "that there have been no major new developments in the past few hours."

"Nothing major," Spock said, "but the situation is such that even very small changes in the equation, as it were, may have widespread effects."

He keyed up a string of commands on his console as he spoke. "One could say," Spock said, "that this situation had its roots in the first meeting of our peoples, when the UNSS *Amity* found a disabled Vulcan spacecraft adrift in Sol system in the year 2065 old Earth dating." He glanced up at Jim, a casual look, except that Jim knew Spock's differing memories of that first encounter, and shared them. McCoy's eyes were hooded: he too had a different experience of that early history than the one offered by the history books, but he gave no sign of that at the moment—he merely sat listening in the head-bowed position that so often caused Spock to ask drily if would care to interrupt his nap and comment on something.

"That first encounter was lively enough, but peaceful, by human standards," Spock said. "The inhabitants of Terra had had a chance to lose their xenophobia somewhat, by meeting the Andorians peacefully, earlier on in that century: so the existence of Vulcans, and Vulcan, came as less of a shock to them than it might have. Diplomatic relations were opened within several years, and the trade and data exchange agreements followed very shortly thereafter. They have continued, and grown, over the past hundred and fifty-six years. Doubtless from this side of the Terran-Vulcan relationship, matters have seemed settled enough."

The screens came alive with the annotated time line that Spock had called up. "However, this easy relationship has largely been an illusion, the nature of which is little understood except by those who have some knowledge of Vulcan's history. The time line before you matches Vulcan's and Earth's developmental history, scale for scale, over the last six thousand years. Please direct your attention to the marked period starting around Vulcan old-date 139000. This corresponds approximately to Earth old-date 900 B.C.—"

"Approximately?" McCoy muttered.

"I would not like to disturb your rest with unnecessary pedanticisms," Spock said gently, "but if you insist—"

McCoy opened one eye, cocked it at Spock, then closed it again, as if deciding against another verbal passage of arms. A soft chuckle ran around the table: Meshav rustled its tentacles in amusement. "You go right on, there, Spock," McCoy murmured, "I'll wake up if you say anything interesting, believe me."

Jim restrained a smile. Spock flickered an eyebrow. "At any rate," Spock said, "if you look at the evaluation of technological advancement, you will see that the first landing on the Vulcan neighbor-planet Charis took place late in that millennium, approximately three hundred years before the birth of Surak. Exploration and exploitation of the 40 Eri star system by Vulcan industrial and scientific interests continued through those three centuries without major incident. But here"—a marker flickered into existence on the screens, tagged with a date, 139954—"an incident occurred indeed. Vulcan had *its* first contact with another species, and the encounter was more than enough to set the planet into a xenophobic reaction that not even the influence of Surak, then alive, would be able to stop."

The time line went away, replaced by a map of part of the Sagittarius Arm of the Galaxy—the arm that Vulcan and Earth shared. But on the scale of this map, both of them were tucked away far down in a corner, and mapped-out zones of contrasting colors, one large, one small, tangled through one another like amoebas having an argument. "You will recognize from your history," Spock said, "the area of influence once controlled by the interstellar empire our historians call the Inshai Compact. The compact was an association of thirty-six hominid- and nonhominid-settled starsystems in the Galactic-northward part of the arm: a very old association, quite stable, quite resistant to the economic and military pressures of the only other major force in those spaces, the 'non-aligned' planets of the southern Orion Congeries. At least, the compact was resistant to the Congeries until someone put a sunkiller bomb into sigma-1014 Orionis, and thereby destroyed the hearthworld of the compact, the planet Inshai itself."

"I thought they had never proved that it was a bomb," said Tomson, frowning.

"The odds are exceptionally high," Spock said. "The star was not of a flare type, and the old records of its spectrographic history are quite complete and unremarkable. It should still be there now . . . but it is not. With it gone, and Inshai and all its subsidiary planets in that system—the heart of the Inshai bureaucracy—the power and restraining and protective influences of the compact fell apart in a very short period. The result was a reign of terror in those spaces, as the worlds of the Orion Congeries swept in and began the piracies they had long desired. Wars, and economic and societal collapse, destroyed planetary populations: starvation and plague finished most of those who managed to survive the invasions. And the great interstellar corporations of the compact, long decentralized but also held in check by Inshai's rule of law, now took the law into their own hands or became—the law, by fiat. The company ships went out armed with planet-cracker weapons to fight over the trade routes and raw materials they felt they had to have: they blackmailed whole planets and destroyed those that would not submit. In the power vacuum, even the more scattered compact worlds, formerly peaceful places like Etosha and Duthul, fell into this kind of piracy. They could not otherwise maintain their influence, or their technology, much of which derived from Inshai. They entered into deals with the corporations, or with other planets equally desperate, and made terror and rapine their industry." Spock's eyes were shadowed; Jim felt a slight chill, having his own suspicions of what a Vulcan thought of such behavior.

"Those worlds and corporations later degenerated into the guilds and companies that were the direct ancestors of the Orion pirates of today," Spock said. "But the Vulcans of that time knew nothing of that—just yet. Suffice it to say that after the pirates had exhausted the richer and closer prizes and settled old scores with the remnants of Inshai, they turned their eyes farther afield. Estimates are that the first notice of electromagnetic signals from Vulcan was taken around the time of the birth of Surak. It was about the same time," Spock said drily, "that the light from the novaed sigma-1014 Orionis reached Vulcan. Some later claimed that it was a sign in the heavens acknowledging Surak's birth. It came as something of a shock to discover differently, some forty-five years later."

Spock turned away from the computer, folding his hands reflectively. "There had been discussion since spaceflight began of what the first contacts with alien life would be like," he said. "Generally, it was anticipated with pleasure, or at least great interest. The earlier Vulcan tradition lacks 'the fear of the stranger.' On old Vulcan, there was no need to fear the stranger who came out of nowhere: to him, one offered hospitality without stinting. The one to be feared was the one who habitually competed with you for water and food and shelter. Your enemy was your neighbor, and vice versa. So other life was by and large perceived as a marvel, and possibly economically exploitable. By Surak's time, research had already been in hand for a century or so on the physics and psi-technologies that would be needed to take generation ships out to the nearest stars."

Spock let out a long breath. "However," he said, "the Duthulhiv pirates who were the first to arrive had no intent to be satisfied merely with the Vulcans' hospitality. They had spent some time developing their technique for first-contact of a planet they wished to loot, and it worked perfectly on Vulcan. They surveyed the planet covertly, from well out of sensor range, and then made properly stumbling first radio contacts from several light-weeks outside the system. To reduce the story to its shortest form, they were invited into the system as the planet's guests, and a party of dignitaries agreed to meet with them regarding diplomatic relations. But the Duthulhiv arrived with an invasion force, and the treaty group was taken hostage or killed. From such a point of perceived advantage, the pirates usually went on to subdue the planet in question by extortionate ransom and outright destruction."

Spock got a wry look. "However, they had made the mistake of assuming that the unity of their reception, by all the planet's nations, meant that the planet was unified and at peace, and therefore mostly disarmed. Their observation of the Vulcan merchant fleet, which from agreement in earliest times has never carried arms, seemed to confirm this. What the Duthulhiv pirates did *not* clearly perceive was that the planet was in probably its most violent period of many—and that in fact several wars had been postponed so that the Duthulhiv 'negotiations' could be handled. The pirates were driven out, most bloodily, but with dispatch." Spock paused. "There were many terrible aftereffects of that episode, but the rift that the first arrival of aliens drove into the Vulcan people was one that almost tore the planet apart. Many said that the only way to handle a universe that held such species was to go out in power and subdue them—to become a terror ourselves. Others said that such vileness did not need to contaminate us—we should shut ourselves up in our planet, with our own wars, which we understood, and let no one ever come near us again, whether potentially friend or foe. Only Surak was able to bring the planet through that time." Spock bowed his head. "And he died of it."

"I dare say the aliens are blamed for that as well," Meshav said in its soft fluting voice.

"By some, yes." Spock said. "Insofar as a Vulcan of today will admit to an emotion as crass and debasing as blame. That is the context in which the rest of this information must be viewed."

He brought up the time line again. "This kind of time scale seems very remote to Terrans, I suspect," Spock said. "Rather as if an Earth person of our time were insisting on reacting adversely to something that happened while the pyramids were being built. But the racial memory of the peoples of Earth is a mercifully vague and sporadic thing compared to the precision, and intimate nature, of racial memory as a Vulcan experiences it. Those old memories are closer to us than any dream: they are more accessible than the Terran subconscious. They are not archetype. They are experience, passed down via direct and indirect engram implant, through a psi talent of which, by tradition, I may say little. But every Vulcan experiences Surak's time, and its events, to some extent, as if he or she was there—and rarely with any guarantee of homogeneity of reaction."

"But with logic," Harb Tanzer said.

"You hope," McCoy muttered.

Spock nodded. "The doctor is, unfortunately, correct. Logic is not a disease that all Vulcans have somehow managed to catch, though sometimes Terrans like to pretend it is so. It is a taught way of life, one that affects some Vulcans more profoundly than others; just as one religion or another, or one philosophy or another, will affect a given Earth person more or less profoundly than another. We are not of a piece, any more than the people of Earth are. Some of us will regard the Terrans, and the Federation, with logic in place . . . and others will not."

"I suspect," Jim said, "that it's mostly those others that we have to fear."

"Not necessarily," Spock said. "It is some of the most logical who appear to be spearheading this move to have Vulcan leave the Federation."

He tapped at the keyboard again. "Here is the English-language text of the official communiqué that was sent to the Federation High Council," said Spock. "You will note the wording. This is a statement of intent to consider withdrawing a prior legislation . . . that legislation being Vulcan's Articles of Association with the Federation. The document comes from hr'Khash'te, only one of the three legislative bodies which handle Vulcan's planetary legislation. The other two bodies—their names translate as the 'Proposal Group' and the 'Rectification Group'—put forward and pass or amend legislation. But the hr'Khash'te, the 'Expunging Group,' exists only to veto or remove laws. And it is the easiest to drive a change through. The other two bodies require a large majority to pass legislation. Expunction requires only one-fourth of the body's two thousand six members to remove a law . . . the idea being that a good law should require a fairly large consensus—avoiding the proposal of frivolous or unnecessary statutes—and a bad law should be made easy to stop or change."

"Very logical," said Scotty.

"Also exploitable," said Spock. "There has been a considerable dependence on the rule of logic to keep good laws from being illogically removed, or bad ones from being illogically passed. It happens sometimes. Vulcan is not quite Heaven, I am afraid."

"News to *me,*" McCoy said under his breath.

Spock flicked him a glance, no more. "At any rate, the system can be subverted, and has been. There are numerous parties and groups on Vulcan who find the planet's association with the Federation, and Terrans in particular, distasteful or unethical for a number of reasons. Some—many—hold the view that there should be no association with a species that goes through the Galaxy armed: such association, they say, is inevitably a corrupting influence on the rule of peace and logic. These groups point at the increasing number of Vulcans affiliated with Starfleet—and at the fact that they are sometimes required by their oaths to handle weapons or perhaps to act violently in the line of duty—and they claim that this is the beginning of the corruption of the species and a potential return to the old warlike ways that almost doomed the planet." Spock looked, for eyes that could see, just mildly embarrassed. "For a long time my father was one of the staunchest adherents to this theory, and I understand from him that he has been called back to the planet to give evidence on its behalf. He will be a powerful proponent."

"Wait a minute there, Spock," McCoy said, and this time he looked wide awake, though there was no telling from his face just what he was thinking. "You aren't tryin' to tell me that anyone can tell your father what to say if he doesn't want to say it. Even I know Sarek *that* well."

"There are forces moving that it would take a long time to explain, Doctor," Spock said. "I doubt even I understand them all: I have been away from home too long. But if T'Pau calls a Vulcan in to testify, she has considerable power to exert to see that just that happens. Not that she would stoop to mere power, when doubtless she considers that she has marshaled reasons in logic sufficient to produce the result she desires. Unless my father can produce a logic more compelling than hers, and reasons that cause her to change her mind, he will do exactly as she bids him. And of his own free will."

That caused a brief silence. *All of Vulcan in one package,* Jim had once called her, and correctly. The only being ever to turn down a seat on the Federation High Council when called to it, T'Pau was immensely old and immensely powerful, in ways that humans found difficult to understand. He still didn't understand her, not really. His one brief encounter with her, on the sands of the mating-place of Spock's family, had been quite enough. He still could feel it on him like hot scorching sun, that fierce, old, dry regard—eyes that looked on him as impersonally as on a stone, but with intent and calculation eternally and sedately going on behind them . . . calculation that would make a computer ask for shore leave. "Is she behind this movement to get Vulcan out of the Federation?" Jim said.

"I do not know," Spock said. "It is one of many things we must discover. But this much I know: the matter as it stands now could not have gotten so far without her approval . . . at least her tacit approval."

Jim nodded at Spock to continue. "As I mentioned, these groups have been in existence on Vulcan for, in some cases, hundreds of years. The groups who want us out for fear of Vulcan being contaminated are in the ascendant in numbers and popularity, but there are also groups who believe that *we* are infringing *your* rights—your human rights, you might say—to be Terran; that our life-style should not be allowed to influence yours to the detriment of your own." McCoy's eyebrows went up. "Before you approve, Doctor," Spock said, "I should perhaps mention that these groups also consider logic and reason to be out of the grasp of humans. Some of the more extreme of them suggest that humans would be better off swinging in trees, as they did long ago, before they learned about walking upright, and fire, and genocide." McCoy opened his mouth, then shut it again. "What they suggest for Vulcans," Spock said, "you may imagine. Or perhaps you had better not. But the one piece of this situation that I find most interesting is the fact that never have all these groups, large and small, come together to coordinate their efforts. They always seemed to have too many points of disagreement. But many differences seem to have been resolved . . . and the number of resolutions, and the speed of them, has made me suspicious."

"T'Pau?" McCoy said. "And why?"

"Unknown," Spock said. "But unlikely, by my reckoning. She is indeed in many ways the embodiment of our planet—both ancient and modern—but for the past two centuries she has been content to let matters take their course, through much worse times than these. It seems illogical that T'Pau would take so extreme a course against the Federation, and so traumatic a course for the planet, at so late a date: it argues a most shocking series of flaws in her logic not to have seen the status quo coming and prevented it sooner." Spock steepled his fingers, gazed into space for a moment. "I think we must look elsewhere for the architect of the secessionists' unity. I hope to have time to reason out exactly where. But time is going to be short."

"How fast is whatever happens going to happen?" Scotty said.

Spock tilted his head to one side. "Essentially, as long as the planetary population finds it interesting or edifying to listen to the arguments. It is safest to reckon no more than a week for this proceeding. The Expunging Group has agreed that the law making Vulcan part of the Federation should be removed from the statute rolls. Normally the law would already be void. But T'Pau prevailed on the Vulcan High Council, the senior legislators who put final approval on statutes that have passed the "lower" legislature, to offer this expunction to the planet for approval by plurality. She told them, I believe correctly, that the issue was too large a one to leave in the hands of mere legislators."

Jim's eyebrow went up at that. "So we have a week to debate this issue, on the public comm channels, I take it."

"It may be a week. It may be more. A prior plurality of the Vulcan electorate will be necessary to *stop* debate before the voting on the Referendum itself begins."

"Are any of them really going to pay attention to all this filibustering?" McCoy said.

"Doctor," Spock said, "in the modern Vulcan language, the word for 'idiot' is derived directly from an older compound word that means 'one who fails to participate in civil affairs.' Ninety-eight percent of all Vulcans have held some sort of public office by the time they are two hundred. They will be paying attention, and participating."

McCoy looked slightly stunned. "Debate will go on until a threshold number of viewers have indicated they want it stopped," Spock said. "Some two billion, I believe. The exact number is being determined at the moment. Then the electorate will vote. Many votes will be swayed by what is said in the debates, and who says it—though I suspect many minds of being made up already. Illogical though that may be."

"What are *you* going to be saying?" Harb Tanzer said quietly. "Whose side are you coming down on?"

Spock looked at him, a steady gaze. "I have not yet decided," he said. "Logic must dictate my stance—most especially in my case, for I will be most carefully watched . . . as carefully as my father, or T'Pau. Or you, Captain."

"Noted," Jim said.

"If my credibility suffers," Spock said, "so will the Federation's cause. I must take great care. But the issues are complex . . . and it might be that the best way to support the Federation would be to argue against it."

There was a long silence at this. "So after the debates," McCoy said, "come the votes. And if the vote is to stay in the Federation?"

"Then we go back on patrol," Jim said.

"And if the Vulcans vote to secede?"

"Then all public trade and defense agreements lapse. Private ones are subject to renegotiation if all involved parties desire. But all Vulcan civilians must either return permanently to Vulcan—or emigrate permanently, if they desire to reside elsewhere. All Vulcan bases and vessels in Federation service will be withdrawn; all Vulcan diplomatic personnel, starships, and starship personnel will be recalled," Spock said. "Those who disobey the order will be stripped of their Vulcan citizen status and exiled. The Federation will cease to exist for Vulcan." Spock looked up. "You will be dead to us."

The silence that followed was considerable. "Any further questions?" Jim said.

There were none.

"Very well," Jim said. "A somewhat abbreviated version of this briefing will be given to the crew at large tomorrow: please note it in your scheduling. Dismissed, and I'll see you all at the mixer later. Mr. Spock, Doctor, will you stay a moment?"

The room cleared out. Jim stretched a little, trying to get rid of the crick that his back always acquired during a long briefing. When the door hissed shut for the last time, he said to Spock, "What are the odds?"

"Of Vulcan seceding?" Spock said. "They are high. I have been running syntheses of the most pertinent data through the computer, on and off, for some months now. The odds are presently on the close order of seventy percent."

McCoy whistled softly to himself. "Not the best odds for a gamblin' man," he said.

"Time to change the odds, then," Jim said.

McCoy looked at him. "How?"

"I haven't the faintest idea. But this ship's encounters with Vulcan never go quite according to the rules . . . you notice that?"

Bones smiled. "You want me to slip the whole planet a mickey," he said, "I'd better get cooking. What are you thinking of, Jim?"

"I truly don't know. Just both of you . . . keep your eyes and ears open and tell me anything you think I need to know. Spock, is there a chance of my having a quiet talk with your father when we get to Vulcan?"

"Almost certainly. I believe he will have had the same idea."

"Good." Jim stretched again in the chair, put his hands up behind his head. "We're not going to let the best first officer in the Fleet go that easily . . . or the rest of the planet, either." He brooded for a moment, then said, "Go on, you two. I'll see you at the mixer."

They went. After a while Jim leaned forward to flick at the controls of the screen in front of him. The graphic view on it gave way to the darkness of space, and stars rushing past in it, a silent stream of threads of light. He put his head down on his arms and gazed into the darkness, thinking. . . .

Vulcan: One

One of the mistakes people tend to make about their own planets, or others', is that a world's location is a fairly permanent thing. It's true that we speak of planetary coordinates as if you could point at them on a map and find the planet there again in the same spot the next day. (You will, but only because the computer has obligingly updated the starmap to take into account the million and a half miles your planet has moved in its orbit since yesterday and the million miles sideways your star has pulled it in the same time, as the whole starsystem cruises off toward some other star whose company your primary has been covertly seeking for the past eight thousand years. . . .)

These same people may tell you about the Big Bang a sentence later—making it plain that they've never considered the phenomenon past the fact itself; never thought about the kinds of changes that that picture of the Universe implies . . . the vast silent journeys, the terrible speeds. Star travel gives us back a sense of scale in terms of the Galaxy's size, but (most especially since the discovery of warpdrive and its sidestepping of relativistic effects) it can do nothing about our perception of its scale of time. This is no surprise, considering. When a single rotation of ten million years will see all but a very few of our civilizations destroyed by the mere attrition of time, the galaxies seem to move with ponderous dignity, with awful grandeur. And this perception, for living creatures, is a true one. But just as true, and harder for us to see, is the way (in its own terms) in which a galaxy roars through the universe, hurling itself along, seething, churning, changing itself with every whirlpool rotation, changing all its stars and all its worlds: star systems caroming in and out of one another's influence, clusters shifting shape, stars flaring, dying, being reborn from exploded remnants: a cosmic billiards game, run marvelously amok. Our Galaxy has hauled us, all unprotesting, along with all the myriad planets of the billion humanities, across untold and untellable light-years, at speeds that starships easily surpass but could never maintain . . . not for a trillion years at a time.

With all this in mind, it is pointless to try to locate one bit of space and say, "Vulcan was born *there*." The birth took three billion years, and was dragged across half that many light-years—a storm track, a cloudy set of possible loci, like an electron's shell, rather than anything that could be pinpointed. Indeed computers could trace that track, but to what purpose? Many stars have streaked through that area: many more will plunge through it before the Universe goes cold and starts to implode. Right now there is an X-ray star there, used by the Federation as a beacon for navigation purposes. But by tomorrow the beacon will be three million miles somewhere else, and that space will be "empty" again. Everything moves: therein, in paradox, lies our only stability.

We can postulate, though, a moving point of view—one that tracks along with that foggy stripe of probability loci, the long, broad, spiraling shape traced through those parts of space for three billion years. Not that a point of view would have had much to see but what seemed empty space for the first seventy percent of the stripe.

The space was of course not empty at all. Unseen forces and pathways crammed it full—the shallow curvatures of gravity, the occasional immaterial Klein-bottle nozzle of a wormhole, the little-understood "strings" of nonmatter/nonenergy that define the structure of space itself. Matter and energy passing through those pathways responded to them, ran down them, converged in places, like raindrops running down a cobweb.

This was indeed how the Galaxy's first generation of stars had congealed out of the hurtling dark ghost-cloud of dust and gas in its earliest life, as the dust gathered at countless gravitational nexi, compressed itself, kindled slowly or swiftly to starhood.

Few of those most ancient stars had any planets. Free energy in that early, formative galaxy was at a terrible premium, and very few stars "did anything" with what energy was available except kindle themselves. Even fewer of the ones that did have planets, as far as we can tell, ever played host to life. Time and the normal life cycle of the oldest stars have long destroyed almost all traces of the earliest sentience. Many stars vaporized their planets by nova-blast or wiped out all life and artifacts on them by starflare, and their humanities' histories are silence to us. A handful of other worlds, more fortunate, still have histories nearly as oblique. Among them must be counted the worlds that were first homes to species like the Organians and the Metrons, who eventually became pilgrims among planets, outliving their worlds over millions of years—finally giving up bodies for existence, and becoming for being. How many of these creatures move still about the Galaxy, by our definition immortal, untroubled by space and time and physicality, no one can say they know.

However, our concern lies not with the oldest stars, mostly now dwarfed or yellow-white with age, but with the second generation of stellar formation, what astronomers call Population II. The broad flat starry oval of the young Galaxy, traveling through patches and tangles of "strings," began to stretch itself (or to be pulled out by the resisting tangles) against the old night. Helped by the oval's own rotation, arms reached out of it: first as blunt bars from the ends of the oval, then curving back into the familiar long graceful glowing arcs of spiral arms, inexpressible tonnages of interstellar hydrogen and dust, all lit by the first-generation stars that had been swept into the arms by immense gravitational-tidal forces. The arms multiplied; the Galaxy became a pinwheel, a whirlpool of dust and light. The dust once again gathered and compressed itself in a billion nexi of strings and gravitation, a network even more complex this time because of the added tidal forces and gravitation of the spiral structure—gathered, and kindled, and burned with blue fusion-fire. Billions of these second-generation stars were born of the forces intermingling in the arms; and with the new stars, planets, almost everywhere that stellar formation took place. Here again, time-scale confuses us. We can choose which we see: a slow glow into burning, like the coals of a fire burning hotter as they're blown on—or (from the Galaxy's own viewpoint) a burst of celestial firecrackers, life leaping into being, light born and blazing in the time it takes to speak a word. . . .

Considered in large, the process was continual: but there were bursts of more rapid stellar creation within the larger steady progression. The same "creation cluster" produced many of the Federation stars, and both Sol and 40 Eridani, about eight billion years ago. Earth came later in the process. 40 Eri, as the astronomers call Vulcan's starsystem in shorthand, came earlier by sixty million years, a difference barely significant on the planetary scale.

But at the time we are considering, there was no sight of either world yet, much less either world's star. Interstellar dust is as nearly invisible as anything that exists, especially without a nearby sun to excite it to a glow, or at least to silhouette it from one side, coal-sack style. Nonetheless, there were untold trillions of tons of dust, more than enough to make up five "hard" planets, three gas giants, and a star . . . and thereby hangs a tale.

In most ways the formation of Vulcan's solar system was typical, the so-called "planetary formation" that every schoolchild knows. Dust and gas gather together in the dark, swirling about in tiny mimicry of the Galactic spiral structure. In the small mimic spiral arms, matter clots, gathers itself to itself in little hurricane swirls, hardens down to a core, begins to attract more. Slowly gravity becomes a force to be reckoned with, at least on the local scale, rather than (as it more usually is) one of the puniest forces known to science.

You would have to bring your own light to see all this by, of course, for at the time we deal with, there would be nothing to break the old dark but the cool faint glow of the distant, dust-blocked galactic core. The Milky Way Galaxy was at this point just three billion years old. It had barely begun to develop the earliest stages of its present spiral structure, and from a distance (if anyone had been there to look) would have seemed a fairly tightly packed oval, all ablaze with that first crop of stars, the then blue white giants of Population I. But the tight-packed look was an illusion. Emptiness was almost everywhere, except in such vicinities as the one we're considering—a track along which three stars were being born.

They started out as huge, vague, quietly glowing orbs, warming slowly, shrinking as gravity compressed them through red heat, to yellow and white, and finally past mere moltenness to the point at which gravity overcomes atomic forces, stripping the atoms bare, reducing them to plasma, and atomic fusion starts. One, the biggest, flared white; the other two, much smaller, burned orange yellow and golden, respectively. They were a true triple star, or more exactly, a pair-and-a-half, all formed from distant segments of the same cloud and all influencing one another gravitationally, to differing degrees. The two smaller stars quickly came to orbit one another quite closely. This may have had something to do with their rapid aging, so that both rather prematurely collapsed into dwarf stars, one hyperdense and white, its companion rather light and diffuse, very red, and unusually small.

The dwarf pair and the white giant were distant neighbors at best. They each would be a very bright star or pair of stars in the other's sky by night, and perhaps occasionally by day, but none would ever be so close as to show a disc to the other's worlds. They would spend the rest of their lives tumbling about one another, around their major and minor centers of gravity, if nothing catastrophic happened to them. Certainly such things had often happened before, to other multiple stars. One of a close pair might be too big, might burn blue white awhile, then go unstable, explode through its Schwartzchild radius and collapse into a black hole—and afterward spend millennia sucking the plasma out of its neighbor in a long deadly spiral, leaving one primary a lightless gravitational tombstone, the other a husk. Or other stars might break up a happy couple or threesome, pulling one or another off by tidal forces. But in the case we're considering, this didn't happen. The tidal effects of the red dwarf and white dwarf on the white giant were minimal, and the member stars of 40 Eridani passed a long and uneventful partnership while their planets condensed.

This process had started while the three stars themselves were barely beginning to collapse. Now it swiftly gained impetus from the solar winds generated by the increased magnetic fields in the stars' early stages of fusion and from the intensified gravity of the collapsed bodies. The spiral-arm clouds of dust around them had already sorted themselves into wide bands; now they became narrower ones, then clumps. Some of the clumps, those farthest out from 40 Eri A, the white giant, tended toward the lighter elements and became gas giants. Four of the planets—three close to the big star, one farther away—had acquired sufficient heavy and metallic elements to develop the standard iron-nickel core and silicon-dominant crust of a "hard" planet. On none of these did life ever arise. The nearest three were too close and hot, the farthest too cold. But in the fourth orbit out from 40 Eri A, odd things were happening.

Usually when clumps occur, one is sufficiently large to draw other clumps to it by gravity and consolidate all the matter in one spot, eventually sweeping the band of dust clean and incorporating it all in a single planetary mass. There can be variations to this process. Two clumps of a fairly balanced size may start orbiting one another within the band: or a cloud of dust within the band may begin to eddy around itself, developing two foci within an elliptical boundary, and matter will accrete to both foci. The actual mechanics of the formation are still obscure. But the final result of this sort of variation is the same—two bodies orbiting one another, sharing a common center of gravity, both achieving planetary or at least near-planetary mass. This is a double planet system.

Such systems are commoner than one might suspect. The Earth and Moon are one such system, though even in this day and age, few people seem to realize it. The popular assumption is that the Moon is Terra's satellite. But the Moon fails the most basic test to find out whether a body is a satellite or not: namely, as it orbits, it falls only *toward* the star it and the Earth jointly circle, and never away. A true satellite or "moon," completely in the gravitational grip of its primary body, would occasionally fall away from the star at the heart of the system. The poor misnamed Moon never does . . . leaving us with the astronomer's laconic statement that while a satellite may sometimes be a moon, the Moon is not a satellite.

And the Earth and Moon give a good indication of how delicate the balance can be while such a system is forming. If one partner gets too much of the heavier elements, "cheating" the other, the other body of the pair may never develop an atmosphere—or may lose it, as some astronomers think the Moon did, long long ago. There are pairs in which the balance abruptly changes in mid-formation due to the influences of other passing bodies, causing *both* planets to lose their gaseous elements. And without an atmosphere, at least on planets suitable for carbon-based life, there is no chance of that life arising. When a double-planet system is forming, the balance can be turned by a hair.

The pair that formed in the fourth orbit out from 40 Eri A was luckier than some. One planet, the larger one, kept its atmosphere: though what it kept was thin and hot, even then. It also kept almost all of the water . . . which was as well, since if the division had happened more fairly, life might never have sprung up on the larger planet at all. The larger world kept a significant fraction of the nickel-iron available from the primordial cloud, though almost all of it was buried in the seething heat and pressure of the core: the tiny fraction that remained was erratically scattered as iron oxides in the planet's crust.

The other planet, shortchanged on the denser elements, was able to settle into an orbit with its partner that would seem, to those unfamiliar with the physics and densities involved, to bring it dangerously close to Vulcan. It rarely fails to *look* dangerous, especially when a Terran used to a small, cool, distant, silvery Moon, looks up at dusk to see a ruddy, bloated, burning bulk a third of the Vulcan horizon wide come lounging up over the edge of the world, practically leaning over it, the active volcanoes on its surface clearly visible, especially in dark phase. "Vulcan has no moon," various Vulcans have been heard to remark: accurate as always, when speaking scientifically. "Damn right it doesn't," at least one Terran has responded: "it has a nightmare." T'Khut is this lesser planet's name in the Vulcan—the female-name form of the noun "watcher"; the eye that opens and closes, but that (legend later said) always sees, and sees most and best in the dark. "Charis," the Terran astronomers later called her, after the ruddy, cheerful goddess, one of the three Graces, who married the forge-god Vulcan after Love jilted him for War. No one really knows what the Vulcans think of the name—any more than we know what they think of the name "Vulcan" itself. They were polite enough about accepting it as standard Federation nomenclature. But they have other names for their world, and at least one name that they tell to no one.

But all this is long before names, or those who give them. Both planets swung around one another and around their blazing white primary for many, many centuries, and their star and its tiny companions dragged them away through the new Galactic arm, while orbits settled down, continental plates ground against one another, and quakes and volcanoes tore everything. For this while, the planet looked like the popular images of Vulcan, a red brown desolation, full of lava and scorching stone and fire. But a change was (quite literally) in the air, as Vulcan's atmosphere slowly filled with smoke and vapor, and eventually with cloud and rain. Standing on Vulcan at present, it is hard to imagine the rain streaming down in its first condensation from water vapor—years-long, cataclysmic falls of water, relentlessly washing away the slow-weathering volcanic stone, mingling unexpected combinations of minerals in the first sea beds. But the fossil record is clear: Vulcan, now ninety-six percent dry land, was once ninety percent water—a few islands, and nothing else anywhere but the new hot sea. T'Khut would rise for thousands of centuries to be paced by the reflection of her sullen, fiery face in the wild waters. It was a period that, on the cosmic scale, would not last long: but it lasted long enough for the miracle to happen.

The exact nature of the miracle, as usual, is as obscure as the manner of the formation of the double-planet system itself. By conjecture, of course, we can seem to see what the laboratory tests have proved possible: the right elements present in the water, the right nucleic acids ready to come together to form one more complex: the long seething incubation, the waters hissing with near-boiling warm rain, shuddering under the thunder—and then the lightning-strikes, one or many. That would have been all that was necessary. Remnants of those earliest sea-bed strata indicate that Vulcan's was more a primordial stew than a soup: sludgier, but far richer in nucleic acids, than the initial mixture present on most carbon-life-form worlds. Great variety existed there in terms of available molecules, and there are theories that the present Vulcan analogues to DNA and RNA show signs of having been the result of arguments, or agreements, among several rival strains that sorted out among themselves, by attempted and successful recombinations, which one was the most likely to survive in the murky waters. Some have since found it ironic that even here, at the earliest point in life's history on Vulcan, warfare of sorts seemed to be going on.

But after the initial combination of DNA settled down, and the face of the waters grew still, peace seemed to reign for a long time. It was illusory, of course: the analogues of algae and plants, and many life-forms which have no analogues on other worlds, were jostling one another with innocent and primitive ferocity under the water's surface. But the illusion held for a long time. Many thousands of centuries went by, and the climate shifted radically, before any creature had need to crawl up out of the shrinking, blood-colored waters to burrow into the red-brown sand, or take its chances under the naked eye of day. Until that happened, the world that would be Vulcan dreamed huge and silent under its seas, with T'Khut gazing down on it. Together the two of them tumbled around their burning white shield of a sun, and the sun around its tiny white red and white jewel-partners, as all danced through the expanding arm of the Galaxy: life going to meet life . . . with who knew what consequences.

Enterprise: Two

The style of crew mixer that a ship threw to "debrief" after refit or extended leave was always very specifically its own. Some of the ships in Starfleet were known for classy meetings, heavy on protocol and fine food; some of them had formal dances; some of them (especially on ships running more decorous variants of command, like the Vulcan or Andorian patterns) had what amounted to panel discussions. And then there were ships that threw unashamed wingdings. *Enterprise* was definitely one of these. It put something of a strain on the chief of Recreation, but he didn't mind the occasional strain.

Harb Tanzer was of Diasporan stock. That is to say, he came of a planet which one of the first waves of colonists from Earth had settled in the early twenty-second century. They tended to be tough people, and handed down that toughness, of both looks and constitution, to their children. There had also been some minor mutations, since some of the earliest generation ships had not been as well shielded against radiation as they needed to be, and the children of the Diaspora tended to lose their hair early, or if they kept it, to be startlingly silver-haired. Harb was one of the latter, and that thick, slightly unruly silver mane was the first way a new crewman would come to recognize him at a distance—that, and his stocky, solid build, a function of age, for Harb was (as he put it) "pushing three figures." Later they would get to know the broad, friendly face, mostly unlined (that was another of the mutations) except for smile lines, and laugh lines around the eyes.

Harb stood in Rec One, the *Enterprise*'s main recreation room, and surveyed the crowded, noisy place with immense satisfaction. This was his "stomping ground," the place where the chief of Recreation did most of his work. It wasn't all easy, helping people play: there was a lot of setup to be done, but the results were worth it . . . always. Getting the place ready for this party, for example: working out the best arrangement for the furniture, and which kinds of furniture would be needed, in what amounts—it was a job. After all, a Denebian, half a ton of supple invertebrate, used to sitting in something that resembled a salad bowl, would find an Eames chair fairly useless. And what about the Mizarthu crewmen, half dragon and half python, and twenty feet long?—or the Irdesh, silicon-based and so delicate and crystalline in their structure that a hasty move could shatter one like a pane of glass? Their usual Starfleet-issue gravity neutralizers were all right for everyday duty, but in a crowd an accident might happen. For the Mizarthu Harb had stolen (well, temporarily appropriated) several sets of parallel bars from the ship's gyms: they could coil up on those to their hearts' content and discuss philosophy with all comers while they got tiddly on ammonia-and-water. For the Irdesh, Harb had laid hands on enough inertial neutralizes from the people in the Physics labs that all the Irdeshi crewpeople could float around like the big animate snowflakes they were, and never fear a brush from an elbow or a stumble by a dancer, since the neutralizers would sop up the inertia of any blow without transmitting it to the Irdeshi in question.

With questions of comfort handled, there was nothing to do but worry about the catering.

No one *else* was worrying about it, that was certain, since the tables where food was laid out were completely surrounded by crewpeople eating, drinking, and talking at a great rate. Some functions, like this one, were still handled in the old-fashioned buffet style: it was a nuisance to have to call up a plate of hors d'oeuvres on a terminal and wait for the thing to be beamed in. Besides, the orders tended to come in so thick and fast that the computers sometimes got a little confused . . . and a transporter accident involving both people and food was something that didn't bear considering. So Harb did it the old-fashioned way and put low-grade stasis fields over the cold cuts and the starch-based snacks to keep them from curling up. The drinks situation, fortunately, needed little supervision; the liquids synthesizer had only a little local transporter to worry about, which it used to produce glasses from stores, as well as cherries and paper umbrellas, things like that. It hadn't malfunctioned since the last time someone tried to get it to synthesize buttermilk. Harb smiled slightly to himself and hoped seriously that no one would try it tonight.

Elsewhere around the room people were doing what they usually did in Rec One—playing hard—with the exception that there were a lot more of them than usual. On the night of the mixer, the usual three-shift crew rotation was laid aside to make it possible for as many people as wanted to take part. Crewpeople not scheduled for duty went out of their way to relieve other crewpeople who were on post, even if just for a little while, so that they could make it to the party; schedules were juggled until the personnel computers (those with sufficient personality) muttered about it. Now, the place was crammed. There was a big crowd around each of the games tanks, pointing and laughing and making helpful (or not so helpful) suggestions; and everywhere else, it seemed, knots of people, big and little, were talking and shouting and laughing and squeaking and hollering and singing in as many voices as the Federation seemed to possess. The language seemed the same whoever spoke, of course, due to the good offices of the universal translators; but the sound of the three-hundred-odd mingled voices made a cheerful cacophony that Harb wouldn't have traded for any peace and quiet in the world.

The singing group was one of the largest: forty or fifty people had taken over one of the biggest conversation pits and were making some very peculiar but satisfying harmonies. Quite a few of them had brought instruments. There were guitars, both acoustical and synthetic, and velodicas, and a squeezebox, and Uhura had Spock's Vulcan harp, as usual; but most noticeably, one corner of the pit was taken up entirely by the members of the *Starship Enterprise* String, Reed, and Banjo Band. The group played once or twice a week, for fun or for scheduled parties. It was comprised of three people on banjo—one of whom, an Alarshin, attracted a great deal of notice because of his three-handed strumming technique—a portable pianist, one tenor and one soprano sax, and a synthesized percussionist (the musician, not the instrument: Dethwe was a clone).

Harb watched them with some mild concern. They seemed cheerful enough—but perhaps a bit too cheerful, for people who had just come back from vacation. Their energy level seemed a bit *too* high, and had a nervous quality to it. Harb recognized that twitchiness. He had seen it before, when the crew knew itself to be going into a dangerous situation that the ship might not be able to do anything about. And there was nothing to do with such a mood but keep an eye on it, and let it run its course, while being there to lend support if needed.

Harb began to stroll over toward the group, brushing through several different conversations as he did so, saying his hellos, eyeing the various tables as he passed them to make sure the food was holding up all right. "Harb," someone said in his ear.

It was a rather sultry voice, the synthesized voice of the Games and Holography computer. Because of its complexity, it was able to have a personality, and Harb had had one installed as soon as he could . . . to his occasional regret. His computer had a bit of a temper, and occasionally refused to acknowledge that she was "his" computer. This sometimes made his job interesting. "What's the scoop, Moira?"

"We're out of onion dip."

He rolled his eyes a little as the voice, focused for only him to hear, followed him slowly across the room. "So make some more."

"Can't. Stores say they're out of the culture for the sour cream. It doesn't seem to have been reordered."

Harb muttered something rude under his breath in Yiddish.

"I'll tell Seppu you said so," Moira said. "It should be fun to watch him grow upside down on his head in Hydroponics."

"Snitch. Look, just use what we use for yogurt, but do it with cream rather than milk, and accelerate the batch. You know the recipe."

"It won't work," Moira said. "The yogurt uses *Lactobacillus acidophilus,* and the sour cream calls for *Lactobacillus bulgaricus.*"

Harb stood still and thought a moment. Behind him, several people in happy conversation drifted by. One of them said admiringly to another, "I love your new skin color, where did you get it?" Harb chuckled, and then the idea hit him, and he missed the reply.

"Moira, where's Harry?"

"Your yeoman," Moira said sweetly, "is watching Mr. Sulu rebuild another Klingon cruiser."

"Why shouldn't he be? It's his party too. Do this for me. Whisper in his ear and tell him to run down to Biology with one of the empty bowls. My compliments to Mr. Cilisci, and tell him if he'll clone me about half a pound of the organism in the bowl and get it back up here in an hour or less, I'll get Commander Wen to put aside a cubic meter of greenhouse space in Hydro for his basil. He'll have enough pesto to keep him going for the whole mission."

Moira snickered. "No sooner said than done, boss."

Harb nodded, satisfied, and resumed his course across the room. As he went, someone said in his ear, "We're out of dip."

"Keep your pants on," he said, turning, and then laughed a great laugh and added, "—Captain!"

"I do try," Jim said, rather drily. Then he smiled. "Nice party, Mr. Tanzer."

Harb smiled back as they began to stroll together through the crowds of people. "Their doing, as usual," he said, glancing around. "I just clean up afterward."

Jim made another small wry smile. Recreation was viewed by Starfleet as being an extremely important part of the ship, especially for the captain: a commander who could not play—and could not relax—was a liability. So was a crew that could not unbend, and in any starship going into a battle situation, the Rec officer was consulted for his opinion of the crew's readiness and morale. Therefore, a Rec officer who described himself as just part of the cleaning crew could be assumed to be indulging in humor. "Mr. Tanzer," Jim said, "I need to talk to you about something."

The "Mr." alerted Harb to this being something official. "Certainly, sir. We'll find a quiet corner."

"In *here?*" Jim said, glancing around with an amused look. The musical group had begun clapping and stomping along with an instrumental in almost *too* spirited a manner.

The captain noticed this and glanced at Harb as they turned away. "They're a bit loud, aren't they?"

Harb nodded. "Best they express it now," he said, as he and the captain headed off toward one side of Rec, toward the big blank walls behind which the holography area lay, and past that, Harb's office.

"No," Jim said, "there's no need to be private really: just out of the crush. Have you been in the ship's BBS lately?"

They came to the wall by the door next to the holo area, and Harb leaned against it, folding his arms. "I have."

"Do you find anything unusual about the level of discussion going on in the 'common room' lately?"

Harb tilted his head a bit and thought. "I've been running the standard semantic checks," he said. "The computer doesn't find a threshold number of loaded words."

"That's not what I meant. The computer doesn't have hunches."

"My hunches are sometimes wrong."

"That's better than not having any at all. . . ."

Harb looked at the captain. "You're worried about some of the anti-Vulcan feeling you've been seeing."

Jim nodded.

Harb shook his head. "It's always been there," he said quietly. "But when an opportunity like this comes along, it tends to come out more strongly."

Jim looked uncomfortable. "I just find it hard to believe," he said, "that in this day and age, bigotry is still with us. . . ."

"I seriously wonder if it's anything as complex as bigotry," Harb said. "Simple envy, more likely. Consider the Vulcans from the point of view of someone who is unsure about his or her own position in the Universe, someone who's looking to see whether a Vulcan is a threat. All kinds of obvious reasons not to like the species come up. They're peaceful, they're extremely strong, both physically and in terms of personality; they're mysterious, they have powers that 'normal' people don't understand; they have a great deal of political status and influence. But at the same time they keep to themselves; their stand on the requirement for personal privacy sounds suspiciously like ego, like being stuck up, to people looking for a grievance. Why *wouldn't* human beings dislike them every now and then?"

Jim nodded. "I'm not seriously worried," Harb said. "Sometimes, in the BBS especially, sentiments like those get aired so that the people airing them can get them out of the way and move on to something else."

"But not always."

Harb nodded too. "I'll keep my eye on it, for what it's worth. It's not as if we're going into a battle situation where someone's stance on the subject is likely to affect the mission's effectiveness. But at the same time a starship is a microcosm . . . and usually accurately represents in small the things going on in the Federation at large—"

Sirens began whooping, and all around the room people looked up suddenly and put their drinks down. The singing stopped as if someone had thrown a switch. But before anything else happened, Chekov's voice, echoing very large, said on the all-call, *"All hands, yellow alert for Engineering and Nav staff only. Rendezvous with USS Coromandel in thirty seconds. Going sublight."*

This caused a stir of pleased excitement, and a lot of people made a rush for the observation windows on the upper level of the Rec deck. No one paid much attention to the view out the windows while a ship was in warp. The otherspace in which *Enterprise* traveled at such times had a speed-of-light much faster than that of Earth's universe: even the slowest-moving particles moved faster than tachyons there. Most of the humanities found the effect of this strange light an unnerving one, and while in warp, ports were usually closed, or the views through them filtered and processed by the ship's computers. But starlight in normal deepspace was another matter; most of the *Enterprise* crew, like the crews of most other starships, were addicted to it.

"Up?" Harb said.

"Why not?" said Jim, and together they went up one of the catwalk-stairs to the upper level to join the many crewmen leaning on the railings and looking out the great glasteel windows. So they saw what not too many people have an opportunity to see—a starship decelerating hard from warp, the point of a silver spear piercing through from the far side of the darkness in a trailing storm-cone of rainbows, as *Coromandel* came out of warp in a splendor of Cherenkov radiation from the super-relativistic particles she dragged into real-space with her. She streaked toward *Enterprise,* braking hard, and the rainbow lights burned low and faded and went out as she matched her sister starship's course and speed.

"I've always had this feeling that there should be some loud noise when that happens," Jim said to Harb. "A bang, or a thunderclap or something."

"Romantic," Harb said. "What was the reason for the rendezvous, sir? Staff transfer?"

Jim nodded. "We have some people destined for Vulcan who've come in from some of the more remote starbases and systems. Fleet detoured *Coromandel* in to drop them off. *Swiftsure* is coming in for the same reason later. Then it's the straight run for Vulcan for us."

They leaned there and watched the smaller ship ease closer—not that she needed to: her transporters would have been effective fourteen thousand miles away—but doubtless her own crew were as interested to get a glimpse of *Enterprise* as vice versa. After a little while, a nearby wall comm whistled. *"Bridge to Keptin Kirk."*

Kirk stepped to it. "Kirk here, Mr. Chekov."

"Our transfers are all aboard, Keptin. Keptin Warburg wants to know if there's anything you need out Vashath way."

Jim smiled. "Tell her if she sends me another package of that blue stuff they eat for breakfast there, I'm going to get McCoy to send her grits by way of revenge."

"Aye, sir," Chekov said, chuckling a little. *"Bridge out."*

"Blue stuff?" Harb said.

"Don't ask," said Jim. "Vashath is a beautiful planet, but if I were you, and you go there on vacation, I wouldn't get up till lunch. . . ."

Coromandel accelerated away on impulse, then flung a cloak of spectrum-colored fire about herself, leaped away, and was gone from sight on the instant. Jim and Harb turned away from the window and headed down the stairs again. "Well," Jim said, "keep your eye on the BBS, as you say. I'm going to be a little busy pretty soon. . . ."

"Aye aye." Harb's practiced eye glanced over the room as they came down the stairs, and he paused. "Look, here comes Mr. Spock."

Jim was surprised at that. "So he does. Unusual to see him come back to a mixer once he's made his appearance at the start. Hope there's nothing wrong on the bridge—"

"He would have called. We'll find out soon enough."

They got down to the floor level, where their path was crossed by a group of crewmen bursting out of the holography area, all rather out of breath. "What have you got in there this time?" Jim asked, a touch suspiciously. "I was hoping for something pastoral to stroll around in. . . ."

Harb smiled a little. "Not that, I'm afraid. But come take a look."

They went over to the wall, and Harb waved the door open. A blast of music blew out past them, something with a hard, driving beat and almost no identifiable melodic line. Together Jim and Harb stepped a little way through the doorway to let their eyes adjust.

They were standing somewhere high up, in darkness, over a great city. At least it might have been great once, but the high glassy buildings had a grimy look about them; there were shattered panes, stone stained and acid-etched, an aura of old decay. A soft bloom of rain was falling out of the starless sky, and through it blazing signs in odd languages, and strange symbols, burned with a fierce light that the misting rain fogged into slight unreality. Some kind of small shuttle craft, iondrivers perhaps, swooped past through the wet dark night on their business. In the middle of all this, seemingly in the middle of the air—for the view from where they stood was very high—numerous crewpeople were dancing on platforms, sheets of softly glowing, translucent force. Some of them were dancing cheek-to-cheek, however incongruous the effect was with the ferocious music, and some of them were doing dances that had possibly been current on the planets where the people had taken their leave . . . but were otherwise unidentifiable.

"What is it?" Jim said.

Harb shrugged. "A synthesis. It could be Earth, or Andor, or the Cetians, or a hundred other places where humanoids have lived."

Jim shook his head. "Looks old. I prefer the present. . . ."

"Mmm," Harb said. "That's doubtless why you keep pulling out that eighteenth-century naval scenario. It soaks the rugs. . . ."

Jim smiled and said nothing about that. "Funny, though," he said. "This music sounds fairly dissonant. Twelve-tone, isn't it?"

"I think so."

"Well, putting wind chimes in it seems a little strange—"

"I *said*," the wind chimes repeated, more loudly this time, from behind them, "you look marvelous, Jim; have you misplaced some weight?"

Jim and Harb both looked around, and down, in astonishment. Behind them stood a twelve-legged glass spider about a meter tall, with delicate glassy spines on her domed body, and fiery blue eyes, twelve of them gazing up at them with what looked distinctly like amusement.

"K't'lk!"

"I've added a syllable," she said, putting out a slim glassy claw as Jim dropped to one knee and stretched out a hand to her. "I'm K's't'lk now." There was a wind-chime chuckle. "After all, you're entitled to another syllable when you've been dead. . . . It's good to see you, J'm."

"Dead" was probably not the most accurate way to put it, for K's't'lk's species, the Hamalki of alpha Arietis IV, did not deal with death in quite the same way that other species did. K's't'lk—or K't'lk as she had been then—was a physicist, a 'creative physicist,' who had done some work on the *Enterprise*'s warp engines and helped to take her most emphatically where none had gone before. She had died of what happened to the ship, there beyond space and time, but she had left an egg case behind her with Jim, a forgotten piece of spun-glass bric-a-brac in his cabin. On her death the egg had hatched, with her new life in it, and her old memories; and with the *Enterprise*'s return to normal spaces, her daughter-self had gone back to her work in physics.

"But what brings you here?" Jim said with surprise and pleasure. "Not that we're not glad to see you. Scotty'll be delighted." It was a slight understatement: the chief engineer had become first disturbed by, then very fond of, this sprightly creature who found nothing wrong with the idea of rewriting the laws of physics if they didn't do what you wanted them to. There were certainly going to be people on the ship who would not wonder twice, in the light of this, why the syllable K't'lk had added to her name was "s".

K's't'lk shook herself all over, a slightly dissonant chiming more in touch with the blast of background music still coming from the holodeck. "The Vulcan thing; what else? I did most of my basic research with the people at the Vulcan Science Academy, after all; so when this mess came to the boil, Starfleet reactivated my commission again and recalled me to give testimony."

"Well, how long are you going to be with us?"

"Till Vulcan, no longer. I have one evening to spend talking the kinesics of galactic cores with Mr. Spock . . . then it's to business, I'm afraid. And likely to be dreadfully difficult; the Universe is easier to reshape than a Vulcan's mind if it's made up." She cocked a cheerful eye at Kirk. "However . . . would you particularly mind if I had a quick look at your warp engines while I was here? There are some minor adjustments I've come across in my research that, if you made them—"

"NO," Jim said, and then burst out in completely delighted laughter. "Don't you dare! You so much as *touch* my engines and I'll toss you in the brig, madam, and keep you there on—" He paused. "I don't know what you eat. Except graphite."

K's't'lk glittered and sang with an arpeggio's worth of laughter. "You might as well lock Sc'tty up with a case of Scotch, Captain. But your orders are heard and understood. . . . Pity," she added.

"It's just that we have somewhere to be," Harb said. "Somewhere *nearby.*"

She chimed cheerfully. "Well enough. Where *is* the graphite, by the way?"

"Over there by the green salad," Harb said, and indicated the table.

"Right you are then, gentlemen. Until later," K's't'lk said, and spidered off through the crowd, exchanging greetings with the crewpeople as she went. Harb chuckled a little and waved the holodeck door shut. Everything suddenly seemed very quiet.

Jim and Harb headed casually in K's't'lk's wake. Harb was shaking his head. "Who else came in on that transfer?" he said.

"The manifests are in the computer," Jim said, pausing by one of the drinks dispensers. "Angostura and soda," he said to it, and watched bemused as the machine beamed in first the liquid, then the glass—just in time—and finally a drinks stirrer with a tiny model of the *Enterprise* on the end of it. "I'm not sure I believe this," he said, and got rid of the drinks stirrer. His eye lit on something else on one of the nearby tables. "And what in space is *that?*"

Jim was pointing at a bowl that at first sight seemed to be black bean soup . . . except that black bean soup usually does not have an oil slick. From the other side of the table, one of Naraht's fringes came up holding what looked like a piece of singed metal, or plastic, or both. Naraht dunked the singed thing into the bowl, and his fringe then whispered back out of sight again, to be followed by slight hissing and munching noises.

"Dip," Harb said. "The silicon-physiology people like it. It's crude oil and iron filings, flavored with sodium oxides and a few rare metals. At least," he added, "most of the sillies eat it, but the Andalusian crewmen won't, even though they like it. Religious reasons."

Jim shook his head again, bemused. "That looked like a piece of a used data solid he was dunking in it."

"It was. We used to incinerate them when their effective lives expired, but then someone found out that Naraht likes them as a snack."

They walked on and paused by the spot where one of the games tanks was situated in the middle of the floor. It was simply a large three-dimensional video tank—a bare platform six feet by six that projected synthesized holographic images upward into empty air. The tank was hooked into the master games computer, and could run any one of a number of games: "board" games like 3D and 4D chess, or role-playing games with animated characters, or action games in which a player handled controls, rather than simply talking to the computer. It was in the latter mode now, and Sulu was sitting in the "hot seat," tapping or stroking at the touchpads that curved around him. In the tank was the image of a Klingon D7D battle cruiser, diving toward a star, or appearing to. Sulu seemed to be trying a slingshot maneuver at extreme warp speed—not exactly the safest move in the world, since going into warp too close to a star usually made the star in question go nova. The crewmen gathered around were offering encouragement or cheerfully predicting disaster, or sometimes simply passing credit chits back and forth. Harb and Jim watched long enough to see that the money changing hands seemed to be slightly in Sulu's favor. "Want to make a small side bet?" Harb said in Jim's ear.

Jim smiled. "I already made one. Come on. I have to see someone."

"Oh? May I ask who?"

Jim shrugged. "It's just a suspicion. But Spock *is* here, and we've just had a rendezvous."

They walked over toward the main doors, where Spock was standing gravely talking to some of the crew, people from Sciences. "Mr. Spock," Jim said, "have you seen K's't'lk?"

"Indeed yes," Spock said. "I anticipate a most stimulating conversation with her: her latest paper on the applications of string theory to matter-antimatter reaction is likely to revolutionize warp technology—"

"Oh no," Jim said.

"—that is, if the Federation's scientists can be convinced that the intermix formulas she suggests are anything less than insane." Spock looked resigned.

"And what do you think of them?" Harb said.

"I do not understand them in the slightest," Spock said, "and they appear to make no sense by normal parameters. But with K's't'lk's brand of physics, appearances are usually misleading. I will reserve any final evaluations until the trial runs. Meanwhile—"

"Yes," Jim said, as the main Rec room doors hissed open.

Darkness walked in: Sarek, in his usual diplomatic dress. He was not alone. He was holding out two paired fingers, and touching them with her own as she stepped through the door was Sarek's wife, Spock's mother, Amanda. She had always been a handsome woman, from the first time Jim had met her, years back: now she was gorgeous. She was smaller and lighter than she had been once, but the effect this produced was to make her look like one in whom time had burned away nonessentials, leaving pure essence: and her hair was so perfect a shade of silver that it was enough to make one want to run out and see a professional hair colorist, or a ghost. She wore a Vulcan lady's standard traveling clothes—long overtunic, soft breeches, and soft boots—all quite logical, but when done in the heavy silks of Earth, luxurious and exotic-looking as well.

Jim bowed over her free hand. "It's been too long," he said.

"It's good to be back," Amanda said. "And in the middle of a party as well." She looked a little wry. "A little entertainment will be pleasant before the deluge."

Sarek's eyes flicked to Kirk, a considering look. "My wife speaks figuratively," he said, "in the tradition of her people. Deluges are not common on Vulcan."

"My husband speaks circumspectly," Amanda said, just as drily, "in the tradition of his."

Sarek bowed his head just a fraction in acknowledgment, then said to Jim, "Captain, my son met us immediately upon our transport over from *Coromandel*. I would welcome a chance to discuss matters with you before we reach Vulcan."

"Choose your time, Ambassador," Jim said. "I will be delighted to accommodate you."

"I believe your people have a saying," Sarek said; " 'there is no time like the present'?"

"My quarters are perhaps a little confining," Jim said. "The officers' lounge?"

"As you wish."

"And if I may, I would like Dr. McCoy to attend."

"The doctor met me in the transporter room as well," Sarek said, " 'to check his handiwork,' as he put it. I had already taken the liberty of asking him."

"Then let's go."

"I had thought we weren't going to see you until Vulcan," Jim said, when they were all settled in the lounge. McCoy was off by the wet bar, making a great show of mixing himself a mint julep while he listened.

Sarek allowed himself a slight smile. Jim was at first surprised to see it, but then realized that what he was seeing was another diplomatic tool, as consciously used a tool as the diplomatic uniform Sarek wore, or the studied elegance of the way he spoke English. Somewhere along the line there had been a decision when on Earth, use the tools that will make you effective there . . . but remain Vulcan.

"I had planned to take the usual commercial carriers," Sarek said, "but someone at Starfleet got the idea that it might be wiser for me to see certain personnel here before setting foot on Vulcan." His eyes were amused, even though the smile had faded. "My suspicion is that various persons highly placed in the Federation were concerned that there should be no obvious evidence of collusion among us."

"But you're here," McCoy said, sitting down beside Spock, "and some people are going to notice that we all arrive together, and suspect collusion anyway."

"True enough," Sarek said. "But at least here our meetings take place under our own eyes, no one else's: and this is much to be desired. It may in some small way assist the Federation's case if you are seen to arrive at Vulcan without needing coaching in the proprieties of the coming debates. The fact will impress those of our people who believe that Terrans cannot act like civilized people without extensive coaching."

"We're going to need that coaching, though," Jim said. "Spock has told us about the format of the debates in a general sort of way. I was pretty effective on the debating team at Academy, some time back. But debating Terrans is one thing. Debating Vulcans—" Jim flicked an amused glance at Spock. "I have occasionally lost."

"Half-Vulcans," Sarek said, without any tone of reproach. "Forgive me, Captain, but I must be certain that you understand the distinction. My son—" He paused here, looking just slightly embarrassed, even for so "pure" a Vulcan as Jim felt sure he was about to claim to be. "My son, though a most excellent officer, and innovative and flexible in his use of logic, is a child of two worlds, two environments, and though he understands how it must be to be of only one of them, he has no direct experience of it. The 'pure' Vulcan heritage is less flexible than you might think from Spock's example; far less willing to give up what it perceives as its own prerogatives and rights; far less willing to give up any of its perceptions at all. I am afraid that the Vulcan 'cultural image' of Terrans, and of the Federation, is quite set in some areas—and the vast majority of Vulcans have never taken the opportunity to go out among the people of the Federation, or among Earth-humans, to acquire data and experiences that would change their minds."

"It's rather shocking, Captain—" Amanda said.

"Jim, please."

Amanda smiled. "Jim, of course. It really is shocking, though. Earth people have this picture of Vulcans as being a great force in space, because of the influence they wield in the Federation's counsels. But at the same time, judging them against other planetary populations, a smaller percentage of Vulcans go to space for holiday or business than go off-planet in any other species. Something like less than five percent, where on other planets as many as thirty or forty percent have been off the planet at least once in their lives."

Jim nodded. "I had heard that," he said, "and it sounded so odd that I wasn't sure that I trusted the figures."

"Nonetheless they are accurate," Sarek said. "Captain, I submit to you that, as open-minded as you have proved yourself, you have difficulty believing such a fact when it is presented to you. Imagine how much less likely Vulcans are to have their minds changed by data about humans . . . especially when so few of them have direct experience of them. We have a great reputation for intelligence among the humanities, but I fear that our major weak point in that regard is our rigidity."

"Stubbornness," McCoy said, sipping his drink.

"A word with unfortunate emotional connotations," Sarek said, "but possibly accurate. Doctor, this may come as a shock to you, but not all Vulcans are free of emotion."

McCoy lifted one eyebrow in an extremely Vulcan mannerism, and said nothing.

"It's actually a linguistic problem, at its root," Amanda said. "There are Vulcan concepts that the universal translator system has been mishandling for many years. 'Arie'mnu' in particular." She blushed for some reason, but went on smoothly enough. "The concept keeps getting translated as 'lack of emotion,' or 'suppression of emotion,' which is a little better . . . but not much. A more accurate translation would be 'passion's mastery.' The word itself acknowledges that Vulcans do *too* have emotions, but are managing them rather than being managed by them."

"You'd think a mistranslation like that would be easy enough to correct," McCoy said. "There's a Federation committee that handles this kind of thing, isn't there? Approves the changes, and updates the computer programs regularly?"

Amanda sighed. "Doctor," she said, "I used to be *on* that committee. The problem is, now I'm resident on Vulcan—and the committee suspects that my viewpoint is no longer unbiased. Not that they shouldn't have suspected as much when I still lived on Earth. What human being *isn't* unbiased about some things? The illogic of it!" She threw her hands in the air, disgusted.

Sarek looked at her with an expression that Kirk suspected was very restrained affection. "So the problem perpetuates itself," he said, "and resists solutions. Well, it is our business to impose a solution on it, of one sort or another."

Jim nodded. "Sir," he said, "I need to ask this, and if I offend, I'm sorry. Spock tells me that T'Pau is attempting to prevail upon you to take the position that Vulcan *should* secede. Are you in fact going to do that? And if so, am I correct in believing now that you are trying to assist our side of the argument nonetheless?"

Sarek was silent for a moment. "T'Pau does not make attempts," he said at last. "What she sets out to do, that she does, by one means or another. Captain, you understand, I think, that T'Pau could easily have me dismissed as ambassador to Earth if I defied her."

"Yes," Jim said.

"Not that that fact by itself would necessarily stop me from doing my own will," Sarek said. "I accepted my embassage to Earth as much for ethical reasons as for any others, and though it is my business to voice my government's views, if they became intolerable to me, or I felt improper pressure was being put upon me, I would immediately resign."

"But you haven't done so."

"One must not act with unnecessary haste," Sarek said. "I have not yet had a chance to talk with T'Pau, for one thing: I have only a rather brief written communication from her, stating what she desires me to do. Until I have more data, I cannot make final decisions. This I will say to you, Captain: I find being forced to speak against the planet of my embassage immensely distasteful, for reasons that have nothing to do with my history there, my marriage, or my relationships with my son and Starfleet. My whole business for many years has been to understand your peoples and to come closer to them; to understand their diversities. Now I find that business being turned on its ear, and all the knowledge and experience I have amassed being called on to drive away that other diversity, to isolate my people from it. It is almost a perversion of what my career has stood for."

"But if you feel you have to do it," McCoy said, "you'll do it anyway."

"Of course I will, Doctor. Here, as at many other times, the needs of the many outweigh the needs of the few. What if, as the next few days progress, I become certain that my own people would be more damaged by remaining within the Federation than by leaving it? Must I not then preserve the species of which I am part? But the important thing is that this matter be managed with logic." He blinked then, and spoke again, so that a word came out that did not translate. "No. *Cthia*. I must not be misunderstood. *Cthia* must rule this, or we are all lost."

Jim looked puzzled. "I think I need a translation. It's obviously a Vulcan word, but I'm not familiar with it."

Amanda looked sad. "That is possibly the worst aspect of this whole mess," she said. "It's the modern Vulcan word which we translate as 'logic.' But what it more correctly means is 'reality-truth.' The truth about the universe, the way things really *are*, rather than the way we would like them to be. It embraces the physical and the inner realities both at once, in all their changes. The concept says that if we do not tell the universe the truth about itself, if we don't treat it and the people in it as what they are—real, and precious—it will turn against us, and none of our affairs will prosper." She sighed. "That's a child's explanation of the word, I'm afraid. Whole books have been written attempting to define it completely. What Sarek is saying is that if we don't handle this matter with the utmost respect for the truth, for what is really needed by everyone involved, it will end in disaster."

"And the problem," McCoy said softly, "is that the truth about what's needed looks different to everybody who faces this situation. . . ."

Sarek nodded once, a grave gesture. "If I find that I must defend the planet of my birth by turning against my many years on Earth, then I will do so. Alternately," he said, "if I find I can in good conscience defend the Federation in my testimony, I will do that. But what matters is that *cthia* be observed, without fail, without flaw. Otherwise all this is useless."

"And if you find you have to take the case against us," Jim said, "and it means you can never see your son again, or your wife—or that you have to go into exile with them—"

Now an expression appeared, just for a flicker of a moment: anguish. Jim was instantly sorry he had seen it. McCoy had already turned his head away. "Then that is what will be," Sarek said, his voice calm and cool, though his face had betrayed it. "You must understand, Captain, that from acts such as will happen over the next couple of weeks, ripples spread. They spread from *all* acts, but especially from such as these, when people knowingly take their worlds' fate in their hands. The short-term effects of a withdrawal from the Federation—our little personal loss and pain, the small matter of exile or estrangement—do not weigh significantly against the loss of the diversity, the well-being, the *selfness*, of a whole species. Ours, or yours. Here, at least as far as I am concerned, the needs of the many *do* indeed outweigh mine. My son and my wife will make their own decisions, and make them well, I am sure." Sarek looked from Amanda to Spock with almost palpable pride. "But for myself, I dare not count the cost. I have served my world for longer than you have been alive; I swore such oaths to serve it as Vulcans do not normally discuss with outsiders. I will serve it still, and serve it as well as I can choose how, regardless of the consequences."

Then Sarek took a deep breath. "But I do not have to like it."

"Liking is an emotion," McCoy said quietly.

"Yes," Sarek said, looking him in the eye; "it is. It would be a relief if you could declare me incompetent to testify on such grounds. Unfortunately, I doubt the Vulcan Medical Association would admit your diagnosis as valid."

McCoy shrugged, resigned. "It was worth a try. . . ." He shifted a bit in his seat, folded his arms. "Why were *we* asked to testify, Sarek? Jim and myself, I mean."

"It is a fair question," Sarek said. "Most of the choices have been made by the High Council, or by delegates they selected, to represent a fair cross-section of the arenas and types of interactions which Vulcan and the Federation have shared over our association. There are logicians, historians, scientists of various types—you will have noticed K's't'lk: she has done more work with our people, for longer, than almost any other scientist in the Federation, and is known for the results she produces . . . if not necessarily for any brand of logic *we* use. But results are as valuable to our people as theory. —And there are a few representatives of Starfleet: but I would imagine your testimony will carry more weight than theirs will. T'Pau, being on the High Council for many years now, has the right to make choices that no one would dare gainsay: and the fact that she chose *you* will have been noticed."

"That's what I'm having trouble with," Bones said, "because frankly, Sarek, the last time we came visiting, we didn't exactly obey the rules. By Vulcan standards, of course. When we beamed down for Spock's bonding, and found out that what's-her-name, T'Pring, didn't want him—"

"It is widely acknowledged," Sarek said, "when Vulcans discuss it at all, that T'Pring's behavior in selecting your Captain to enter mortal combat with Spock was improper in the extreme. Nothing in the briefing Spock gave you could have prepared you for the rather distasteful sequelae."

"Distasteful is the word," Jim said, rubbing his throat reflectively. "Being strangled with an *ahn woon* can ruin your day."

"My point," McCoy said, looking embarrassed, "is that if I hadn't slipped Jim a mickey while 'treating' him, he'd be dead . . . but by so doing, I violated the letter, if not the intent, of the whole Marriage-and-Challenge ceremony. —Dammit, Sarek, I *cheated!*"

Sarek nodded gravely. "I find myself wondering," he said, "whether that might not be exactly why T'Pau chose you. . . ."

McCoy looked astonished. "Your Captain conducted himself with the utmost propriety for his part," Sarek said, glancing approvingly at Jim, "and for your part, you obeyed your oaths to Starfleet and to the Other, and preserved life, as best you knew how. No Vulcan is going to blame you much, or long, for that. . . . If, of course, we stoop to such an ugly emotion as blame in the first place."

"Uh, yes, well," McCoy said, and trailed off.

"I estimate one point six days to Vulcan once the *Enterprise* returns to warp, assuming she maintains her earlier speed," Sarek said. "Captain, Spock is already familiar with the format and style of the debates and questioning that will take place. If you have some time early in the ship's day tomorrow, I will go through some library material with you and give you some pointers. The Doctor will doubtless want to look on."

"Certainly, Ambassador. Around point three five, if you like."

"Excellent. I will then retire. My wife will attend me." Sarek stood up: all the rest rose as Amanda did. "Good night, Captain. My son."

They left, and the door closed behind them. "Your mother gets more special as time goes on," McCoy said to Spock.

Spock nodded.

"She blushes pretty well, too," McCoy said. "Was that something you can explain?"

Spock quirked an eyebrow, thought about it for a moment. "Before she went into teaching, Mother worked on the early versions of the universal translator, as you will have surmised," he said. "One of her contributions to the original Translation Committee was the mistranslation of *'arie'mnu'* which she mentioned. It occurred some time after she met my father, while she was still mastering the language. I am afraid he teases her about it somewhat."

McCoy smiled a little. "I wondered if it was something like that. Well, to err is human."

"That is precisely what the Vulcans will say," said Spock. "Captain, Doctor, good night."

" 'Night, Spock," Jim said. The door closed after Spock, leaving Jim with McCoy and the end of the mint julep. "Well, Bones?"

He was shaking his head. "Sarek," he said. "Who was it said, 'The only thing worse than a scoundrel is a man of principle'?"

"Sounds like Twain, or Averith."

"Mmf." McCoy put his glass down. "Vulcans. . . ."

Jim looked at him. "For so strong a species," McCoy said, with pity in his voice, "they sure are afraid. I wonder what of. . . ."

"What Spock told us about this morning," Jim said, "should be quite enough, for starters."

"No," McCoy said. "There's something else. . . ."

Vulcan: Two

There were no words, yet. Thought was enough.

He had no name: at least, none that he was able to tell others. Certainly the others had ways they thought of him; the big one, the one with the black hair, the one who caught the beast, the one who knew where the firestones were. But he did not see that these thoughts about him were really him, or even accurate descriptions of him, not the *him* inside. Sometimes he wished he could think of his own name for himself, but it never seemed to matter, not for long. He was himself. The Other knew.

He spent most of his time in the daytimes doing as did the rest of the ones he lived with—wandering among the trees, eating when he was hungry, drinking when he was thirsty, lying down to rest when he was tired. There were other urges, but they came less frequently. It had been years since the Rapture came upon him, and others of the ones he traveled with had pursued him, or been pursued, through the shadows of the greatest trees, there to do strange deeds upon one another. They had no idea where these urges came from and would not have thought to question them, any more than they would have thought to wonder why one got hungry or thirsty. What did it matter? There was always food and drink and ground cushioned with green things to sleep on. Sometimes, after the Raptures, others came, after strange pains and pleasures; but there was always food for them as well. No one understood the sources of this nourishment, why it suddenly came from bodies, why it went away. It did not matter. The Other knew.

While they stayed among the trees, food never failed them. The fruits came and went—sometimes one fruit being in season, sometimes another one. During the cooler weather there were the great sweet gourds, and the flat flowers that grew on the stones and were good to eat, and the long pods that hung from vines, and the hard fruit like stones that had to be cracked, but were full of small tender fruits and sweet juice. There was almost nothing that was *not* good to eat, except the rocks. Some growing things simply tasted better than others, had a different savor or a more interesting fragrance. The group often experimented, one of them calling others to see some new plant or fruit that the group had never seen before, passing it around to taste. There was admiration for the ones who did this the best; they were touched, surrounded by others who wanted to learn to do as well. They slept warm and woke again to wander the endless forests, and eat, and look around them in wonder. There was nothing else for them to do. Sometimes they died, without understanding what was happening, without knowing what death was at all. It did not matter. The Other knew.

They were hominids, of a kind that would have been familiar to any modern xenopaleontologist; perhaps "seeded" on Vulcan by that strange peripatetic species called the Preservers, perhaps not. They looked enough like paleolithic Earth-humans, at that point, to have been easily mistaken for them; a young species that had come to be stocky, strong-armed and strong-limbed, the braincase rapidly expanding to handle an environment rich with stimuli. It would have taken close examination to determine that these were in fact not human. The cast of skin under the shaggy hair and the unconsciously and cheerfully worn coat of grime would have given away the most obvious indication—would have led an examiner eventually to the blood that was green, not red, and to the molecule that betrays so many species' kinship to the plant life of their worlds. On Earth there is only one atom's difference between the molecules of chlorophyll and hemoglobin: manganese at the heart of the compound for the chloroplasts of plants, iron for the blood cells of beasts and men. On Vulcan there was not even that much difference: vulcanoheme and cuproplast alike each had a copper atom at the center of the compound. Few planets have been as verdant as Vulcan was in its lush and beautiful youth—whole continents covered with mighty forests of trees, some a thousand feet high; oceans in which weed as high as trees reached up and bent against the sky-ceiling of the surface, from root-stalks hundreds of feet deep. The lesser animals were more like plants than anything else: the greater ones broke away from being plants only with difficulty. It was a kindly world, in the evolutionary sense, and there was far less reason to struggle than on Earth or many another world—less reason to push an organism into becoming. Being was easier.

There were places where it was not so easy. The wanderers tended to avoid them without specifically naming them or thinking about them. There were places where the trees grew sparser, where fruit was not so easy to find, where water was scarce and did not flow down from every high rock, or sometimes even from the trees them-selves. They came upon these places, did the wanderers, and felt vaguely uncomfort-able and unsatisfied with them, and drifted back to where the fruit was sweet and the water poured down without having to seek for it.

At least, most of them did.

He was an exception. If he had not been so good at finding the sweetest fruit, the coldest water, they might have drifted away from him and left him on his own long since. But he had that gift of finding, because he looked harder and better than the others; and so they tolerated (without knowing it) the other gift that was part of the first, the tendency to look further ahead, to wonder whether a fruit a little further along might be sweeter, or stranger, than the last. Sometimes he did indeed leave his group alone, though it tore his heart to do so—even then, even though he could hear their minds somewhat, still aloneness hurt—and he would spend long weeks wander-ing under the great leafy canopy, listening for new sounds, tasting, touching, wonder-ing at what he saw. Sometimes he found nothing. Sometimes he came back weary with the burden he carried from great distances, strange new fruits and leaves. Sometimes he came back with nothing but tales he could not tell, except in the halt-ing picture-speech of the mind—and the pictures were incomplete, fragmentary, from the undiscipline of a mind that leapt from one image to another, delighted past con-trol. Images were all he could share, and increasingly this upset him. There had to be a way to make the others understand, understand *everything*. He would hunt for it.

And so he did. More and more he was away from the grounds where his group habitually wandered. Odd it was how he defined himself in terms of them, but the group, when he was gone, tended not to wander too far, so that "their" strange one would find his way back to them. Their thoughts went after him, but being as un-trained as his imagery, they reached him only rarely: so that sometimes in the middle of a wet dark night, or a day's climbing and scrambling, he would feel a brush against his mind, like a wing—the concern of one of them. He would go about his business, or back to sleep, feeling curiously reassured. They knew him, as the Other did.

It was a world for wandering, if ever there was one; a warm summery world, moist and twilit under its trees even by day, the endless sea of treetops and the wide waters sheened with coppery light by night as T'Khut slipped up over the edge of the planet. Vulcan's year was a touch shorter than the year of Earth would come to be, but it lacked the severe axial tilt that caused cold winters and fierce summers on other worlds, and the eccentricity of its orbit was so slight as to make it nearly a perfect circle. Summer was forever, and mild. The warm oceans, now long calmed from their boiling, and green as old bronze, watered the landmasses liberally with long soft rains all year round; the atmosphere, richer in oxygen than the norm because of the abundant plant life on land and in the sea, held the heat of the white sun close. There was ice in two tiny circles, at the poles, and hardly anywhere else, ever. Even there at the farthest north and south the surface of the ice melted and grew warm, sometimes, and turned green for a season with the tiny temperature-tolerant algae that had first colonized the planet on behalf of everything else.

Through this quiet world the wanderer made his way, without a direction, without a set purpose. He only knew that he was looking for something. The life of the forests went on around him as he passed through, and the wanderer paid it as much heed as he usually did, no more. There were many other forms of life in those forests, some of which preyed on one another, rather than on the fruits of the trees. The wanderer did not fear them, any more than any other of his people did. One sometimes died of them, but no particular notice was taken of that. That strange stopping, that change, always happened sooner or later, and it was no great sorrow. The stopped ones could still be heard in the others' minds, and there was something indefinably *more* about the ones who had been stopped, so that though they spoke rarely, hearing them was a joy. No one knew the whys of the Change: no one gave it much thought. The Other knew.

The wanderer made his way under the great trees, eating and drinking and sleeping, for a long time. Time itself did not matter to him, or would not have, if he had had a concept of it. It would have seemed folly to make a business of counting one's breaths when the days were so full of wonder, and there were other things to do. What the wanderer finally began to notice was that food was becoming a little harder to find. He rejoiced in the knowledge, the way one might rejoice to see an unusually large fruit hanging on the branch. He knew that he was coming close to what he sought: the places where things were different. He kept going.

Soon there were fewer kinds of tree, and then, eventually, only one kind of fruit: and the other trees around were not the sort that gave water when you broke their branches. The streams that came from the stone were becoming fewer. The wanderer stopped for a while and considered this, sitting by one of the streams, munching a gourd and dabbling his hands in the water. He knew enough to know that if one went without water long enough, one stopped: and he had no desire to become a voice in anyone else's ears, no matter how well and glad the voices sounded. It occurred to him that he was going to have to go back to his group again, if he could not find more water on the way that he was going. He decided to drink deep and make one long walk, and if there was no water at the end of it, to turn again for the place where his people were.

The wanderer drank until he thought he would burst, and then walked. As probably the most experienced traveler that his little group had ever known, he had learned to read certain signs about the land that he was hardly aware of reading. One of them was that going downhill was likely to take you to somewhere strange faster than going uphill; indeed, all along this long journey, he had been aware of going slowly downhill. Now he purposely chose that path: chose, too, the way in which the great trees seemed thinnest. He walked.

He walked for nearly a week, without another drink, without more food. Then as now, Vulcans were tough, and perhaps, in that distant morning of their world, tougher than they are now. The trees grew few: the white sunlight came through them in great patches. The wanderer looked up at the sky, a rich blue green in those days, and wondered at it. Only rarely had he seen it, and at those times he had suspected it was somehow part of the trees. Now he began to wonder whether it might in fact be the other way around, and the trees actually some darker, closer part of this overarching brilliance that hurt his eyes. Doubtless the Other knew: perhaps one day he would ask. In the meantime, he walked on.

Around the time he first began to be thirsty, the trees very suddenly disappeared entirely. The wanderer saw this sudden end of greenness ahead of him, saw the belt of brightness, the horizon, for the first time, and had to stop and hold on to a tree for the terrible vertigo it gave him. The world was not walled with the trees' shadowy greenness everywhere, after all: it was flat. The flatness of it stretched out before him in a shorter, tougher greenness than that of the trees, all starred with bright color like the flowers that grew from some of the trees of home, but brighter, frailer. And past the long flat stretches of green was another flatness stranger still, a bright pale color that threw the hot white sunlight back into his eyes until they squinted. The wanderer was the first Vulcan to look upon a desert.

There was certainly no fruit there, certainly no water. But he had to know what *was* there. He walked.

The thirst came to be with him constantly now. Only once did he manage to break it, when a rainstorm caught him by surprise, far out of its normal purlieus; he lay with his mouth open to the torrent of it, no matter how astonished he was by the vast racketing of the thunder out in the open, and afterward he supped up every drop of water from every blade of greenery he could reach before the warmth of the day sucked the precious droplets back up into the brazen sky. Then he began to walk again.

The greenery gave way to stones, and hills without dense groundcover—nothing but dirt and barren scree and gravel. All his life he had scarcely walked on anything harder than moss or soft herbage. His feet left green footprints behind them now, but he did not notice. He only had eyes for the eye-defeating whiteness ahead. He walked into it, to the edge of it, where even the gravel stopped, and there was nothing but sand. And there he stopped.

The dunes went on forever. White, white, burning white, they rolled away into impossible distances in perfectly sculptured knife edges of sand, and over them the wind rode in toward him and flung the sand off the crests of them into his face in occasional gusts. He stood there, his eyes tearing in the almost unbearable light, and stared at a world that had edges instead of walls: edges too far away for him ever to reach.

And beyond the edges . . . something reached up to the sky, and he saw it, and fell to his knees.

It was a mountain. It was alone: it rose out of the distance unchallenged by other peaks, impossibly high, forested almost to its summit. And its summit was a pure white that glanced the light back at him clear and sharp as pain. So it seemed in its youth, Mount Seleya, rearing up tallest of the mountains of Vulcan, in those ancient times when its lone crest still speared up virgin-sharp and uneroded, and still knew snow. Numinous enough it seems to Vulcans in the present day, that ancient and inviolate mountain at the edge of Vulcan's Forge, the unmoving point around which so much of their history has stormed. But to the wanderer, there at the lost beginnings of things, it was the tallest thing in the world, the thing that must surely reach up to heaven as even the trees did not: the center of the universe. And the wanderer fell down on the sand and yearned for it as no Vulcan on the planet ever had yearned for anything. There had never been *need*, on Vulcan; not until now. Now one Vulcan needed, and that need would change almost everything.

The wanderer rose up, at last, and sat down on the hot sand, and looked across at the mountain with something other than the eyes of longing. There was no accurately judging its distance, even for as expert a traveler as he. He was used to worlds that had walls, and pillars of trees near at hand, rather than this pellucid visibility that went on seemingly forever into an infinity of clear blue-green air. It would take a long, long time to walk there, he was sure. And if that thing was as far off as he thought it was, and the height it seemed to have would change the same way that the seeming height of a tree changed when one came close to it or went away from it, then the great wide stone tree—so he thought of it—must be very tall. He might climb it, as he had climbed some trees before: and if he got to the top of it, he would touch the heavens. And then— But there his thought failed him.

A long, long way away: that was the problem. But there was no food here, and no water, and probably no food or water there, either. To climb to heaven, he would have to solve that problem. And he was already desperately hungry and thirsty; and another hunger had been added, the hunger for the mountain, which no one else had ever suffered, and which was thus doubly terrible.

At last the sun went down, and with its setting, as was proper for that time of month, T'Khut leaned up slowly over the edge of the world and looked at the wanderer. He had no doubt he was being looked at. Until he saw the mountain, nothing but the others with whom he wandered had seemed to have that ability—to look, to see. Now the great shape stretched itself up past the horizon, its shape shifting and changing through strange oblatenesses, warped by the lens of atmosphere, and the wanderer gazed at this apparition and was no longer so sure about the inanimate nature of the world. He and his people had caught the occasional glimpse of T'Khut through the leaves of the highest tree canopies. But they had only seen her in fragments, flickers through the parting veil of leaves; and most often as a vast perfect roundness, serene, unchanged, seemingly unchangeable. Now the horizon and the heat-wavering atmosphere carved her into a new shape every moment, and she seemed a live thing, slipping up over the edge of existence, breathing, changing, growing like the shes' bellies after the Rapture. T'Khut's outlines trembled, she swelled, she grew round, though still flattened—a gravid-looking shape, swollen with promise. Fire flickered in the dark sliver of crescent she still carried on her new limb.

The wanderer trembled and hid his eyes. If the Other knew about this enormous beauty, this strangeness, it had never given the fact to be understood.

But the trembling went away after a while as T'Khut resumed her wonted shape, and the darkness fell, and the Eyes came out, first the white, then the red. The wanderer realized that he had to go back before he could go any farther forward.

The return journey was much longer than the journey outward, for the wanderer had pushed himself to his limits to reach the edge of the desert, and several times on the way back he had to simply lie down for a day or so in the shade of some fruit-bearing tree, moving nothing, merely breathing. Shade at first was a precious thing; when the trees were many again, he wallowed in shadow as if in some forest pool . . . then, astonishingly, began to sicken for the sight of clear turquoise sky. When he re-found the first (or last) stream springing clear from its rock, he drank from it and rolled under it and lay in it and fell asleep in it; and the next morning he sat eating the sweet gourds that hung about, and then drinking, drinking, as if there were to be no water left in the wide world the next morning. He stayed for several days by that spring, eating the gourds, regaining his strength, thinking of the long way back, the long way to the mountain, and how there was no water. . . .

Then one morning he decided he would stay by the spring no longer: that day he would start once again for the glades where his people roamed. His heart grew light in his side at the thought, and he cracked several gourds at once and ate the sweet meat out of them, then playfully tossed half the shell of the last of them into the little pool that the spring made at the bottom of its rock.

It did not sink like a stone. It floated, and spun in the downflow of water, and water splashed into the hollow of it, and stayed there.

The wanderer stared at this for a long time.

He got up, went to the nearby tree, plucked down another gourd—though he was not hungry—and took it back to the spring and sat down. He cracked it open on a handy stone and tossed half the gourd into the pool.

It floated. Water splashed into it, and rolled about in bright beads, and did not float away.

The wanderer picked up the gourd carefully from the surface of the water. The beads and drops of water rolled about in the curve of the gourd, but did not spill.

He tipped the gourd clumsily up to his lips, and the water ran out, and he drank it. His face was wet by the water running out.

He dipped the gourd again in the pool, and this time stood up, and took a few steps with the gourd half full. The water sloshed a little, but stayed in the gourd. He drank again, more sloppily this time.

He dipped the gourd, and rose, and walked, and drank again, and was refreshed.

Then he dipped the gourd one more time, in jubilation, and tipped it over his head. Even then. Vulcans did not laugh . . . but it was as close as they were to come for some millennia.

The wanderer did not leave that spring for some days, and when he did, with a gourd cracked only slightly at the top, he did so nervously. What if the water should not stay? What if there was something special about the gourds in this part of the world, or the springs? But the next morning he found that the next spring along worked just as well; water was water. And as he made his way back into the parts of the world he knew, he found that some gourds worked better for carrying water than others: they were lighter, or bigger. He went his way in delight, heading home, well pleased with himself and the Other, whose doing this surely must be.

The people he was looking for, as usual, had not wandered far. They saw him coming with gladness but without much surprise: he always came back. And they saw him carrying fruit, but, rather to their surprise, it was a fruit they all knew well. They were much more surprised when they found that its insides were not the same as they usually were. They thought it was some new kind of fruit after all.

He tried to explain it to them. The images in his mind failed him again. He tried to show them the great tree of stone, how far away it was, how high; he tried to show them the desert of gravel and stone, the flat greenness, the torrents of rain and the thunder, so unlike their placid rainstorms; he tried to show them T'Khut in her soundless splendor, looming over the world. Only now and then did he succeed. Or the image came across, but not the wonder he had felt at the sight, the awe, the terror. He could not make them understand. Particularly about the mountain, he could not make them understand, and this wounded him deep in a way he could not have explained to any of them. There had to be a way to make them understand. There *had* to be.

The gourd they understood well enough, though not the need for it. Why should anyone want to store water? There was always enough. Why should anyone want to carry water? It was heavy, and besides, when there was plenty to be had from the streams or springs, or from the very trees, what was the point? They played with the gourd like a toy, and this wounded the wanderer too. Finally he stopped trying to tell them things, or explain things to them, and began preparing for his greater journey.

He gathered together many gourds and cracked them in the way he had discovered, and then tried carrying them. This worked, but he could not carry many, and when even the empty gourds tired him, he thought what they would be like when they were full. No, there had to be another way. He sat down as he had sat down by the pool and looked at himself. Two arms, two legs. The legs were no good for carrying anything. He looked around him for anything that looked like more arms; and then it occurred to him that one of the thin vines had leaves lobed like hands. He pulled down every vine he could find, until his people wondered whether he had lost his senses. Perhaps he had, but six days later he had invented the net bag, and woven it big enough to carry five or six of the biggest gourds.

He practiced with them full of water, and discovered that it made a great deal of difference how he packed them: they leaked exuberantly. He thought then that it would be even better if he could get the gourds to be whole and uncracked after he had cracked them and filled them with water, so he sat and thought about that for a few days, but not even a Vulcan could do anything about *that* problem. Some days later he invented the stopper—a thick chunk of moss and earth from one of the streams, forced into each gourd's opening.

And then there was nothing to do but go back to the desert, and cross it.

His people watched him go, again, without surprise. He knew they were thinking that sooner or later, he would be back; or not. He had an odd, hollow feeling inside him, as he left, that even now, after he had spent so much hard work getting ready for his great journey, that not one of them would come with him. He did not know what to do with the feeling. Then as now, emotion was an ambivalent matter for Vulcans. He set off, and put thoughts of his people behind him.

The wanderer had little trouble retracing his steps. It took him a long time—especially as he did the later parts of his journey burdened down with water and the lightest of the fruits that could be eaten as food—but finally he stood again at the edge of the world, looking at the great height of stone and snow that reared up against the sky, far away. There had been some additions to his gear while he traveled. The light, for example, that hurt his eyes so: he had found a solution of sorts to that problem. He had tried covering his eyes, first, but that interfered with his ability to carry one or more of the net bags. He invented a shoulder sling for the bags, out of some spare vine, but covering his eyes still did little good against the merciless glare of Vulcan's white primary. Then he thought of how the leaves of the trees shaded the ground, in the forested parts of the world, and so he went back to the sparse edge of the forest and plucked leaves to make shade for himself. With leaves bound about his eyes, and others tied tight about his head and wetted—for he had learned about sun-stroke, now—he went on again, much more at his ease. He came to the border with the desert and looked upon Mount Seleya in great awe and desire: and this time he did not stop. He went on.

The sand took its toll of him. The brief encounter with it on his last journey had not prepared him for the ferocity with which it took the sun's heat and radiated it back, and after a very short time he was staggering, half-blinded despite his cobbled-together eyeshades. One day he walked, and another, and another, and the mountain grew no closer. He refused to drink for almost a week, determined to reach the mountain no matter what happened. After another day he realized that it was wiser to walk by night and to try to hide and rest by day; and so he did, with T'Khut's coppery light glinting on the snows of Seleya for his only guide. His walking, with no other thought touching his own, and no other sight of anything, Vulcan or beast, slowly be-came an exercise in sensory deprivation. He heard strange sounds and saw move-ments on the sand which proved to have been no movements at all when he came where he judged them to have been. He felt light-headed and detached from himself; not knowing exhaustion when he felt it, he kept going, and when he fell in his walk-ing, he lay there, at the bottom of dune or sheltered hollow, until he felt like getting up again. He responded affably enough to the sounds he heard, though none of them responded to him. And in the evenings, he got up and walked again: a lonely, dirt-caked, mat-haired, sand-scraped creature, with leaves tied about its head, parched, confused, but determined.

And then he heard the voice.

It was like enough to things he had been imagining lately that at first he paid it no heed. The wanderer had over the past days learned the difference between hallu-cination and the mind-touch of his people; he was surprised, for he had not thought at first that it was possible to experience anything that was not real. Now he had found that some realities seemed to be more persistent than others—than this new kind, which fled away before he had a chance to touch them. He had become practi-cally resigned about it. When the voice spoke to him, therefore, he stopped, listened, and waited a little to see if it would repeat itself. When it did not, he went on, toward the faint glimmer of the mountain in the night.

Then the sand moved under his feet, and the wanderer sat down, rather suddenly, and wondered whether something real was going to happen after all.

It was not precisely a movement in the sand, but a vibration, very deep: it felt as if the sand, and the stone beneath it, and the solid world itself, were breathing. The wanderer considered this for a moment. People like himself breathed: might not the world be a person, simply made very large and strange? Might it not have trees for hair, and stones for bones, and sand for skin? If these things were true, then there would be nothing particularly strange about it having a voice. Perhaps it did. The Other knew.

The voice spoke again, and the wanderer spoke to it in turn. Not in words, of course; there were no words yet. But he made a sort of sound that he meant to mean

"I am here." The sound was not entirely without emotion. The wanderer had never made it a habit to talk to the world itself, and he was interested, but nervous.

And the sand began to stir, and sing, and rumble, and slide away from itself; and in a tremendous hissing and rush of sand, a hissing like the parting of waters by wind, the owner of the voice came up from the depths and looked on the wanderer.

Even now, when Vulcan has been mapped millimeter by millimeter, and satellites can see any grain of sand on the planet that they wish to, very little is known about the movements and nature of the intelligences of the deep sand. *A'kweth*, is one of the names for them: "the hidden"; and *tcha-besheh*, "the underliers." There is much speculation about their physiology, even about their evolution, for their way of life is strange in a carbon-based world: they seem not to respirate, not to need oxygen, or to feed. Some scientists think they were seeded on Vulcan by the Preservers as an experiment, the only silicon-based species (until the Hortas) to coexist on the same planet with a carbon-based one. Some point out that this stance is unsubstantiated by any data: that there is no telling what kind of feeding and respiration takes place in a creature that habitually lives under hundreds or thousands of feet of sand. No more than glimpses have ever been seen of them, through all the many centuries: a huge, broad, glittering back—but is it a back?—crusted with sand, the size of a great house; or a tentacle or two, playing with a bright stone, vanishing when surprised. Scan has proved of little use, considering the weight of natural elements usually between the creatures and the scanning equipment. Sensors turn up vast life-sign readings, a level of vitality and power that would normally belong to a thousand creatures; but movement readings rarely pinpoint more than one source of motion, sliding leisurely through the deep sand of the greater deserts, skirting the outcroppings of mountains as a cruising whale might skirt islands or shoals. Sometimes a tracked vital sign disappears completely, without explanation, without trace.

There is little agreement about the Underliers. Some have likened them to the Vulcan equivalent of dinosaurs . . . but dinosaurs that never became extinct, content to live their long, strange lives in remoteness and silence, only occasionally having anything to do with the busy, hungry hominid species that came to spread across their planet. In silence they go their own ways, and what thoughts they think about the planet above them, in our day, they do not share.

What the wanderer saw was literally too large for him to comprehend. He had desired mountains: now one had come to him. Glittering under T'Khut, it reared up, and he was regarded. He sat there on the sand and endured the regard. He was not afraid, but again that slightly nervous feeling came over him, that there were some things that the Other had somehow neglected to make known. This one in particular the wanderer would have been glad to know about in advance.

The *a'kweth* spoke again. The sound was not one that the wanderer could repeat, and barely one he could hear. If the world spoke, from stone rumbling against stone, it would sound so. And again it spoke, and the wanderer sat astonished, not knowing what to do.

Then it was in his mind, and it spoke again, the same word, stone on stone: and he saw an image, a picture of a poor bedraggled creature, all sweat and dust, sitting on the sand with a bundle of gourds in a net. It spoke again, and gave him the image again, with terrible clarity and ease.

And he understood. The sound it made, *meant the picture*.

The wanderer would have sat down hard, had he not already been sitting. This was it: this was what he had been looking for; the answer, the way to tell people about the mountain. If everyone was using the same sound for a given picture, then everyone would understand. All that needed to be done was to make the sounds, the words.

He did it, right then. He did his best to make a picture of the creature inside him; difficult enough it was, for the thing filled the whole world. And he made a sound, the first sound he could think of, a sort of clicking grunt; and then the picture again, and the sound to follow it.

The *a'kweth* reared up higher yet, higher than the mountain, till it leaned over the wanderer and filled the sky; and it roared a long singing roar like the wind in the trees during a hard rain. The flood of images that blasted through the wanderer made him clutch his head, so strange they were; lives and deaths were in them, and terrible heat and pressure, and odd desires and triumphs, but above all darkness, a sweet, enclosing, down-pressing darkness that made this mere night look like white day by comparison—a barren, exposed, inhospitable thing. The roar dwindled to a mutter, to a breath, to a hiss; the sand slipped aside, booming underneath the wanderer; and smoothed itself over, and was silent again, and still. The *a'kweth* had gone.

For a long time the wanderer sat there, gazing across the cooling sand at the mountain. Ruddy and warm the light of T'Khut shone on the snows of the peak, and it actually looked a little closer, for the first time. He wished it had not, for now the choice was before him. To go back to his people and give them this gift? To go ahead to the mountain and bring them the news of it first?

But he might not come back from the mountain. And the gift would be lost. For who but he had ever come here, or ever would?

Two days he sat there, ignoring the sun: two nights, ignoring the stars and the silence, his eyes on the mountain.

On the third day he rose and turned back toward the forests.

The word spread slowly, but there was no stopping it, as usual: the word once spoken always finds its way where it is going.

The Wanderer was his name, now. He had made a word, and taught it to them. His group drifted still about the forests, eating, needing nothing, but now they spoke to one another. They had all taken names, and hard on the heels of their own names had come names for other things; and then words for ways of doing and going; and then some of them started stringing the words together and making sentences out of them. Shortly after that, someone else invented song. The forests became full of music, and words rang out. More people came into his group: and some went away and came back bringing others; there were visits, and meetings and partings, and many people not of the Wanderer's group now knew about words, and used some of his, and made some of their own.

The Wanderer made new words for everything. He had brought the first one: his people seemed to think he should make all the rest, and so he did. But he kept coming back to the first word he had made for them, which he thought was his best. *Heya*, it was: an outward breath of surprise, a cry of delight, on seeing something wonderful—and to go with the word, the image of the mountain as he had first seen it, all green forest and white fire, immensely distant, wonderfully great and tall. The image seemed easier to make and clearer, since the huge thing had been in his head.

Indeed all the Wanderer's images did. But that was the one he kept thinking of, while they brought him fruits and beasts and tools to name. He thought often of the sand out in the desert, and the great voice; and often he wished he had paid no attention to it, and kept on walking. But then he would remember the size of the creature that had owned the voice in the sand, and he would sigh. It is hard to make the world go away when it has decided to notice you.

It was a fine day in the shade of the trees, one that seemed brighter than usual, so that it reminded the Wanderer of the lessened shade beneath the trees nearer the desert. He put aside the fruit he was trying to think of a name for and began instead to make a song, which was an invention of another of his group, a she too young for Rapture yet. To make a song, you said the words you liked, one after another, and made a noise with them too; and the Wanderer was pleased by this art, since he had been good at making noises since before his own first Rapture, long long ago.

So now he sat and leaned his back against the great tree which was his favorite and made his song; and it was this, that the world was good, and the light was bright, and there were good things to eat, and the Other knew all this and had intended it so. A couple of others of his group, hearing the song, thought it was good too, and took it up themselves: and it spread from one person to another, to those eating, and those lying still under trees, and those wrestling and playing, and those drinking: and those asleep stirred in that sleep, and some of them muttered words, though what they were could not be heard. All this seemed good to the Wanderer, and he sang, under his tree, for a long time.

He paused, after a while, because he smelled something strange. It was an odd smell; he had never smelled its like except near places in the forest where something had happened to a tree to leave it blackened and broken and shriveled. The Wanderer looked up into the bright day—indeed it was much brighter than usual: were the trees bending apart to let in more light, as they did when the wind blew? But there was no wind. Well, no matter. The Wanderer thought he ought to make a name for that smell. He breathed deeper.

And the tops of the trees flashed into flame, and everywhere the song stopped, and people stared upward in dumb astonishment—while the heat grew and grew, and the tops of the trees burned away and let in the light, the terrible light, and the trees themselves caught fire. Screaming, the people fled, and the Wanderer looked up betrayed, betrayed by his song, and by the Other, for certainly no one had been given to understand anything about *this*. Shocked, uncertain what to do, he turned toward the edge of the forest, toward the mountain—

Not many stars are prone to solar flares, and they tend to happen quickly, when they happen. This is probably a mercy: better the sudden incineration of a planet's surface than a slow scorching like the expansion of a red giant. The fossil record on Vulcan shows plainly enough how quickly the star flared, and how violently, growing ten percent in size as something went radically wrong with the fusion reaction that had gone on so steadily inside 40 Eri A for so many millions of years. It took no more than ten or twenty minutes to burn almost all the forests: a day to boil the oceans again, leaving seventy percent of the ocean beds turned into bare, scorched sand and mud. The deserts were charred, melted to glass in some places. Metal, where it lay close to the surface, ran molten. Trace gases in the atmosphere ignited: a great deal of oxygen and nitrogen was ionized and whirled off the planet in the terrible heat. Mountains slumped. The polar caps vanished. Seleya's snows flashed into steam, and her wooded slopes into slag studded with the burning sticks of trees. When T'Khut rose, she came up like a demon, reflected flarefire turning her a burning, blinding, violent red like the fires that had burnt everything. She was scorched herself, and volcanoes spoke with bright and silent rage on her dark side.

Most of the living creatures on Vulcan died.

There were some fortunate ones. Creatures that were on the far side of the planet when the first flare hit were usually able to hide; and those that did, lived. Those early Vulcans who lived near caves, and took refuge in them, lived to emerge days later into a world terribly changed. Many of them died in the terrible storms that followed the flare, or else they died of lack of food and water, or because they could not stand the change in the atmosphere. Some simply died of the shock of the change of the world.

Only the very toughest survived that time. Vulcan was done with being kind. Some of those who survived were ones who used words; but after the flare, they began to make words that were about anger, and pain, and betrayal; and for a long time, there were no songs. The world had betrayed them—that was the word passed from mouth to mouth and mind to mind: and the word got into the words, into the cast of the language itself. The world is alive: the world is angry. Beware trusting in the world, beware when its face smiles, for then it will reach out and make you and Death familiar. Flee, rather; beware the strange and new; beware any light in the sky that you do not know; drive it away, and live. Fight the world, fight what it does, strike the world while you may. Sooner or later it will strike you.

The Other became silent; or perhaps, in anger, was no longer listened to. Many words, too, were lost, as the language worked and reworked itself over the ensuing centuries; the words for fruit, for rain, for peace and leisure to do nothing. Now there were words for blown sand, for blasted stone, for whole forests found charred, for hot dry winds and a sun that had become quiet again but could not quite be trusted; words for despair and loss and being alone, and for the desperate union of minds that seemed the only way to survive in the hell the world had become.

But the word for "mountain" remained *heya* . . .

Enterprise: Three

"You know," McCoy said from behind the helm, "this place gets a lot of bad press about its climate, but it's a lot prettier than you might think. Kind of grows on you."

"Wait'll you get down there to say that," Jim said, stretching in the center seat. "You're the one who's always going on about how much better dry heat is. Until you get down into it. Then it's 'Where's the damn air-conditioning?' for hours at a time, until we get you back up to the ship and toss you in the pool."

McCoy folded his arms and looked blasé while the chuckle ran around the bridge. "Status, Mr. Sulu," Jim said.

"Approach control has us, Captain. Standard orbit in about three minutes."

"Very good. All hands," Jim said, hitting the button on the arm of his chair. "We have planetfall at Vulcan in three minutes. Normal standdown procedures. Shore leave is approved for all departments: check your heads for the rotation."

"I envy them," McCoy muttered under his breath, leaning on the helm. "A nice vacation in the sun."

"While you're going to have to spend all your time in a conference room somewhere. Poor Bones." Jim leaned back and watched the image of Vulcan swell in the viewscreen.

Bones was right, of course: there was something lovely about the place, though to the eye trained in looking at things from space, it was one of the more forbidding landscapes imaginable. Still, Vulcan was not quite the intolerable aridity that the popular press painted it. There was some surface water—not a great deal, but a couple of respectable small seas, each about the size of the Mediterranean on Earth. And one never tended to think of Vulcan having much in the way of weather—at a distance. Jim tended to think of it as southern California with less rain. But swirls of weather patterned the planet as completely as they usually patterned the Earth. The clouds simply released very little moisture to the surface, and they were usually too thin to provide much but a thin, hot haze over the area they covered. White clouds above, and below, the dun and red and golden surface: here and there a meteor crater or a great dry sea bed, and in many places, chains of ancient mountains, worn by millions of years of wind and sand. It was a beautiful place, and a desolate beauty. The last times he had been here, he had had little time to admire the planet for itself. Maybe this time there would be some leisure to do that.

And you'd better do it now, he thought, *because if things don't go well, this is going to be the last chance you get. . . .*

"Standard orbit," Sulu announced. "Fourteen thousand miles, hephaistosynchronous."

"Maintenance impulse, then, for station-keeping. Helm and Nav on automatic. Thank you, gentlemen."

He turned to Spock. "I take it that from here we go through the immigration formalities as usual, and then—?" He made a questioning look.

"Various of the Vulcan authorities will be expecting us," Spock said. "They will doubtless want to discuss scheduling of the debates with you. Then we are free until tonight, when there will be a reception for many of the attending dignitaries at the

Vulcan Science Academy. Tomorrow is unscheduled time for us. The day after, the debates begin."

"Good enough," Jim said. "Let's get on with it. Uhura, please have the transporter room stand ready, and see if Sarek and Amanda are ready to accompany us. No rush: we'll meet them later if they're not."

"Aye, sir."

But they were already in the transporter room when Kirk and Spock and McCoy got down there, standing by the pads with their luggage in place. Sarek looked placid as always—or almost always; Jim could not quite get rid of the image of the pain that flickered across that fierce face last night. But Amanda looked openly excited, and she flashed a lovely smile at Jim as he nodded to her.

"We've been away so long," she said quietly, as Jim got up on the pads next to her. "Two Earth years this time, almost. I'm looking forward to seeing our house again."

"One point nine three years, my wife," Sarek murmured, as the transporter effect took them.

The transporter room sparkled out of existence, and another room came into being around them, as Amanda said something to Sarek that the translator refused to handle except as a stream of fricatives. Sarek blinked, then said calmly, "You may have a point."

One side of Amanda's mouth quirked in a smile, and Jim glanced away, suddenly convinced that he had just seen a Vulcan be successfully teased in public. *He may have a point too,* Jim thought. *He doesn't seem to find it odd to respond to illogical behavior every now and then. It's true what he says: I've spent very little time with Vulcans other than Spock. We may be a lot more alike than we think we are. And that may be good . . . or bad. . . .*

The room where they materialized was not as bleak as one might have expected an immigration facility to be. Apparently Vulcans felt that efficiency in performance didn't necessarily require clinical barrenness. The room was sparsely furnished with computer terminals and seating, and nothing was there that didn't need to be; but the seating was comfortable and pleasing to the eye, and in one corner a graceful plant that looked like a cross between a prickly pear cactus and a weeping willow was perfectly silhouetted in graceful curves against a window. Outside was a garden of sand and stones so perfectly smooth and subtly symmetrical that no monk in a Zen monastery could have improved it.

Behind one of the computer podiums was a grave-faced young man in Vulcan civil-service livery who took their ID chips and slipped them into the computer, then handed them back with a slight bow. When Jim handed his over, the young man looked up from the chip—apparently having read Jim's identity directly from the interference patterns encoded in the chip's surface, no mean feat—and looked at Jim with a cool, steady expression. "You are very welcome to Vulcan," he said.

Jim was good at trusting his feelings, but he had no idea whether to believe this or not. "Thank you," he said. "I have looked forward to returning here, though I would have preferred not to do so on business."

The young man put the chip through the computer, handed it back without another word, and bowed to the group. "That concludes all necessary formalities," he said. "Please proceed through that door to the staging areas." And he vanished through another door, without any further ado.

The group headed for the door, and Jim turned to Sarek as they walked. "Sir," he said, "one thing I discover: my instincts for reading people seem to fail more often than not down here. Did that young man mean what he was saying, just then?"

"Well," Sarek said, "it is said that a Vulcan cannot lie."

"But they can exaggerate," Jim said, "or leave the truth unspoken—or sometimes even prevaricate."

Sarek got a wry look as they headed out into the staging area, where the various local and long-haul immigration transporters were arranged around the curve of the big circular room. "This is true enough. Captain, here again our people are not of a piece. Those of us who practice *cthia* find lying offensive because it perverts the purpose of speech, to accurately describe the world; and there are other reasons less logical, more founded in the emotions. But some practice *cthia* more assiduously than others, and some hardly at all. And even those who practice parts of it most vigorously are prone, on occasion, to ignore other parts of the philosophy." They paused for a moment in front of the transporters for the regional capital, tu'Khrev. "I remember a time some years ago, on Earth," Sarek said, "when I was invited to attend a religious gathering as part of a cultural exchange program. The people at the gathering were professing their belief in one of your people's holy books, and stating that the only way to be saved—I am still unclear as to what they felt they needed saving from: we never got as far as an explanation—the only way to be 'saved' was to follow the book's directions implicitly, to the letter. Now that book is a notable one, in my opinion, and filled with wise advices for those who will read them and act on them wisely. But some of the advices have less bearing on the present times than others; at least, so it seemed to me. I asked these people whether they felt that *all* the book must be obeyed, and they said yes. Then I asked them whether each of them then did indeed, as the book said they must, take a wooden paddle, when they needed to evacuate their bowels, and go out the prescribed distance from the city where they lived and dig a hole with the paddle, and relieve themselves into the hole and cover it over again? They were rather annoyed with me. And I said to them that it seemed to me that one had no right to insist that others keep all of a law unless one keeps it all himself. I am afraid," Sarek said, mildly, "that they became more annoyed yet."

"The 'rag' infoservices ate it up," Amanda said, with a mischievous smile. " 'Demon Alien Pursued By Lynch Mob.' "

Spock looked at his father with something like astonishment and then subdued the expression quickly. McCoy's expression was of someone delighted and trying to keep the fact to himself. Sarek shrugged. "They were not behaving logically."

"It was the ears," Amanda said.

Sarek looked at her curiously. "You have said that before. Now tell me, my wife, what it is about my ears that made those people so angry."

Amanda began to choke with laughter. "Let me," McCoy said, and he started to explain about demonography and iconography and pitchforks and pointed tails until Sarek was snaking his head in wonder. "They thought, then," he said, "that I was a personification of entropy. Or resembled one."

"That's one way you could put it," Jim said. "Are there any such in Vulcan legend?"

"Yes," Sarek said, "and they *all* have pointed ears. We know ourselves well enough to know that entropy needs no image but our own to do its will. All the same—" He looked at McCoy with an expression of mild concern. "All the same, Doctor, I would recommend that you not mention this peculiarity of some of your species to any of mine. There could be . . . misunderstandings."

"Could there ever," McCoy said. "No problem, sir."

The transporter cleared, and they stepped up onto the big pads, while Sarek slipped his diplomatic credential chip into the accounting slot on the terminal and began tapping out settings. "This will take you to the consular and embassy complex," he said, "where I will leave you gentlemen in the care of the people you need to see. Amanda and I will stop at home first: then I will proceed to the meetings I have scheduled. Too many of them, I fear. And we will see you at the reception tonight. The officials at the consulates will give your ship the coordinates for the Academy, Captain, or will be glad to handle transport themselves, if you desire."

"I'll have them call the ship," Jim said. "Ambassador, thanks again for your kindness."

"Courtesy to a guest is no kindness," Sarek said calmly. "Energizing now."

The world dissolved in sparkle again, leaving Jim and Spock and McCoy standing in front of a building designed by an architect whose family Jim suspected of owning a glass factory. It was an astonishing piece of craftsmanship, a group of delicate-looking towers seemingly welded together by bridges and buttresses of glass; and the surface of the glass was everywhere iridescent, golds and greens and hot blues all melding into one another up and down the shimmering surfaces.

"That's gorgeous," Jim said.

"And I bet the coating is a sunblock," McCoy said.

"It is our way," Spock said; "art and science combined. There is no reason that function should not be beautiful—in fact, beauty usually makes it more effective. It does come as a surprise to those who think everything on Vulcan is either utilitarian or made of stone and sand, or both."

They headed toward the building. "Your father," Jim said, "is a little unusual sometimes. An ambassador doesn't usually go out on a limb, the way he did that time, in the place where he's assigned. 'Softly, softly' is usually the rule."

"My father is not the normal sort of ambassador," Spock said, as they came to the building and its doors dilated for them. "A fact for which we may yet have reason to give thanks."

The afternoon would have been something of a bore, except that Jim found himself in the company of someone whom he immediately and wholeheartedly disliked.

The man's name was Shath, and he was one of the senior officials in charge of the debates. He was small for a Vulcan, barely five foot nine, and he was blond, which caused Jim to look at him with great interest when he and McCoy were first introduced to the man in the offices at the consulate. The fair hair was a surprise, since blond Vulcans were rather rare: also a surprise were the blue eyes, a vivid dark blue like Vulcan's daytime sky in clear weather. Nearly as much of a surprise was the coldness in those eyes. Not the cool reserve that Jim had grown used to on an everyday basis in Spock, in the old days, or in Sarek now: but a genuine shutting out, an assumed coldness, purposeful and uncaring of the response.

Spock had been escorted off by another consular official, a slender older woman; Shath had led Jim and McCoy into a side office and left them sitting there alone, with nothing but a table and a computer console to keep them company, for almost twenty minutes. At first they simply chatted and assumed there was some kind of bureaucratic tangle going on outside: but then Shath came in at last and made no excuses whatever for the delay. He simply began interviewing them as to their schedules and their intended itineraries, with an air about him as if he were being forced by his job to be polite to monkeys.

Jim answered Shath's questions politely enough, but next to him McCoy stirred several times, as if about to say something and stopping himself. Jim suspected what was going through his mind. *What am I going to make a fuss about? I'm a starship captain and not being treated with the proper respect? Well, yes. But Sarek hit it. Not all these people are of a piece, and not all of them like us. If I allow myself to be nettled by that, I'm giving them the satisfaction of letting them see me prove myself to be what they think I am. I won't do it —*

"Very well," said Shath, breaking Jim's train of thought in a sharp tone of voice that no one, *no* one, used on a starship captain, as far as Jim was concerned. "You will be at the Halls of the Voice at point three, two days from today, for your declarations. You may bring reference materials with you if you need them." The look in his eyes made it clear what Shath thought of anyone who needed to use notes for anything whatever. "That is all."

Jim opened his mouth to give the insolent creature a piece of his mind, but McCoy beat him to it. "Shath," he said, "do you practice *cthia?*"

The look on Shath's face was that of someone asked an embarrassing question by a parrot: annoyance, and scorn. "I do."

"But not the part about courtesy to guests, I suspect," Bones said, very calm.

Shath's eyes blazed. "*Cthia* does not apply to *tviokh,*" he said. "Nor, soon, to any creatures of your sort. That will be all."

"That's not all by a long sight," McCoy said, drawling a bit, but still quite calm. "*Tviokh,* huh? You are a *rude* little son, and you not past fifty yet. But you're still old enough to have some manners. Good thing I have too much to do this afternoon to be bothered tanning your hide." He stood up. "Come on, Jim, let's leave this spoiled brat to his paper-pushing."

There was something so outrageously provocative about Bones's tone of voice that Jim held in his initial reaction to it. "Shath," he said, and lifted his hand, parted, "long life and prosperity. Doctor," he said, and they went out together into the outer office.

Bones did not stop but went straight out of the office into the corridor that led down to the 'tween-floors transporters. "Now what was *that?*" Jim said under his breath.

"Wait till we get outside," McCoy said, and would say nothing until they were out in the plaza in front of the building.

They found a simple stone bench under several of the prickly willows and sat down. McCoy blew out a breath, looked at Jim. "That lad up there," he said. "You recognize him?"

"No."

"Well, you were busy at the time, as I recall. He was at Spock's 'wedding.' "

Jim digested this. "He was?"

"Sure enough. Just one of the crowd, but nonetheless, I recognized him. It was the blond hair: it caught me by surprise, that first time."

"He certainly was rude, though." Jim shook his head. "He hated us. No, it wasn't hate. Contempt. We were dirt to him."

"Correct. Hatred requires some personal knowledge of the hated. He had none. And I didn't want him to realize that I recognized him," Bones said, "so I made something of a point of acting the way he was expecting me to act, and hoped you wouldn't do the same and attract attention to yourself. Which you picked up very neatly on and acted like a Vulcan, which probably made him even madder than he was and distracted him more." McCoy leaned back against the tree, then said "Ooch!" and bent forward again, rubbing his back: the tree had its own ideas about people leaning on it, and the ideas took the form of spines about an inch and a half long. "Anyway," he said, "no question, but *he* meant what he said."

"That much even I got," Jim said. After a moment he asked, "What's a *tviokh?* "

"Tvee'okh," McCoy corrected him. "More of an 'e' sound. It's a pejorative. 'Auslander.' 'Gringo.' 'White-eyes.' " He looked a little resigned. "Actually, it means 'neighbor.' Which tells you something. It's not a nice word. It implies that the person may live over on the next piece of land, but you would prefer them to be under it rather than on it."

"Charming. But you think that it was just Terrans he felt contemptuous of, rather than us in particular?"

"I'm pretty sure." McCoy leaned back again, more cautiously this time. "Remember, Jim, I've had a long time to study Spock's kinesics. Even though he's half Earth-human, and his mother's body language has influenced his somewhat, the influence of his father's side is still quite strong, since everyone else in Spock's life while young was exhibiting Vulcan kinesics. They tend to wash out the Earth influence somewhat, in fact; which is why you'll notice that when new crew join us on mission, their own body language will be stiff around Spock's for a few weeks. It takes them that long to realize that just because he's not making the proper kinesic responses to their own body-language cues, he's not snubbing them. He's just different. Once they realize that, their own language smooths out."

Jim nodded. "So you read Shath as just generally angry about humans."

"Angry is exactly correct. Angry enough not to show the proper courtesies even when he knows we could complain and possibly get him fired for it . . . or at least reprimanded. He apparently is very sure of the vote going for secession, in which case nothing we've done will or can matter."

Jim sighed. "How many more of them are like that, out of all the Vulcans who'll vote? Bones, this is beginning to scare me."

"Just now? I've been scared bloodless since I realized that my testimony might actually *affect* this outcome somehow."

They sat quiet on the bench for a few moments. "Well," Jim said at last, "I guess we've just got to pull ourselves together and do this the best we can. Still—" He shook his head. "I'm not used to running into that kind of thing from a Vulcan. They're always so controlled and polite. The thought of what a whole bunch of angry Vulcans would be like if they let go—"

"That thought scared them too, some time back," said McCoy, "and it looks like that's the only thing that's kept them here this long."

"Which reminds me," Jim said, "my translator didn't do anything with that word. Do you suppose the thing's on the blink again? You just replaced my intradermal transponder a couple of weeks ago."

"No," McCoy said, and looked a little guilty. "I took a second-level RNA language series while I was on leave. I must confess I was worried about exactly this situation coming to pass—I was watching the news— and so I stayed at home and did the course."

"Instead of going to Bali?"

Bones shrugged. Jim looked at him in astonishment. Not many people chose to learn languages by chemical means anymore: though a course of messenger RNA gave a very complete knowledge of a language, it tended to wear off with time, and made the person who took it extremely sick for days. Most people preferred simply to use the universal translator in one of its portable forms, and update its data when necessary. The RNA series did have advantages, though. Fluency was immediate and conscious—you could choose words for effect, and make puns, in those languages that had them—and there was no fear of a complete breakdown in communications if your translator should break down, or if you found yourself in a place not served by a translator transmission with the right protocol for your receiver. Jim was impressed. "Was it a listening course, or speaking-and-listening?"

"Hwath ta-jevehih tak rehelh kutukk'sheih nei ya 'ch'euvh," McCoy said, and then coughed and rubbed his throat. "Damn fricatives," he said, "they're worse than Gaelic. My accent isn't worth much. I asked for a native north-continent accent, but instead I got RNA from some Vulcan who'd been first to Cambridge and then to UCLA." He rolled his eyes. "The native clones are more expensive, though. . . ."

"Didn't you charge this to Fleet?"

Bones looked wry. "You kidding? You know how long it would have taken to process the requisition order, and the voucher, and the departmental approval, and the authorization draft? Vulcan would have seceded by the time the paperwork sorted itself out. I did it on my own nickel."

Jim made an amused face. Shortly Spock came across the plaza to them and paused in front of them. "Was there some problem, Captain?" he said. "You seemed to spend very little time in the consulate."

"We did the business we had to do," Jim said. "No problem. . . . You missed McCoy tanning one of your people's hides, though."

McCoy stretched lazily while Spock looked at him in total noncomprehension. "Vulcans do not tan," Spock said.

"Depends on what you soak the pelt in after you get it off," McCoy said, and grinned.

Spock shook his head. "I must confess that I do not understand you."

"He' elef ka hij," McCoy said, and Jim's translator rendered it clearly as, "Oh yes you do."

Spock blinked.

"Come on," Bones said, getting up, "I want to do some shopping, and we'll tell you the whole thing as we go."

"Fascinating," was the only thing Spock found to say as they headed off into the hot, bright afternoon.

They spent a cheerful while walking around the city, looking in shop windows, admiring architecture, and sitting down late to a dinner of what McCoy described happily as "better lasagna than they make at the Vatican." The day was cool and pleasant by Vulcan standards, no more than about a hundred and ten degrees Fahrenheit. All the same, Jim was glad he had had the stores computer supply him with some hot-weather pattern uniforms, the ones interwoven with the heat-sink fiber that radiated heat away from the wearer as fast as it developed. Even in the shade, at their table in the courtyard of the little restaurant, the breath of the failing day was hot, and Jim was drinking a lot of the cold, clear water that came bubbling up from the restaurant's own spring, in the middle of the courtyard.

McCoy was gazing at the spring reflectively as he sipped at his wine. "You know," he said, "for such a dry place, you people have a lot of fountains."

"We conserve our water very carefully," Spock said, "but there are places and times in which conservation comes close to meanness of soul. The spirit must be refreshed, as well as the body."

McCoy pushed his wineglass away. "There was a time," he said, "when I would have been astonished to hear you say something like that."

"It would have been a time when you did not know me as well as you do now," said Spock. He turned his glass idly around on the table. "But times change. Let us hope they change for Vulcan as well."

McCoy nodded, then said, "I have to ask you something. There's something I don't understand about the language—"

"The accent, for one thing," Spock said, sounding drily amused.

"You leave that out of it. You know how RNA transfers work: you get the context behind the word as well as the definition and the usage."

"Yes."

"Well, there are a couple words whose contexts seem to have gone missing, though they translate well enough. a'Tha, for example."

Spock said nothing, merely tilted his head and looked at McCoy.

"If it's something I shouldn't be asking about," McCoy said hastily, "just forget it. I understand about the Rule of Silences, but I'm not always sure where the privacy taboo starts, if you know what I mean."

Spock shook his head. "No, Doctor, this is not a taboo subject. It would be taboo to ask about particulars—the way it affected a particular person. But you are asking in the abstract."

He folded his hands, steepled the fingers. "There is no context in your translation because it is probably the one concept in the language that must be continually reexperienced to be valid. You cannot freeze it into one form, any more than you would want to repeat the same breath over and over all your life. One must experience a'Tha differently every second. But that is not a tradition or a stricture imposed by people—merely a function of the structure of the universe. Your position in spacetime constantly changes: a'Tha must change as well."

Jim shook his head. "I'm missing something."

"I think not," Spock said. "I think most human languages would render the concept as 'immanence,' or something similar. a'Tha is the direct experience of the being or force responsible for the creation and maintenance of the Universe."

"God," Jim said, incredulous.

"Are you using the word in the exclamatory mode, or the descriptive?" Spock said. "In either case, 'God' is as good a name for it as any. Vulcans experience that presence directly and constantly. They always have, to varying degrees. The word is one of the oldest known, one of the first ever found written, and is the same in almost all of the ancient languages."

McCoy looked at Spock curiously. "You're telling me," he said, "that the piece of information that most species spend most of their time searching for and complaining about and having wars over—and can never achieve certainty about—is the one piece of information you just happen to have. *All* of you."

"Yes," Spock said, "that is an accurate summation."

Jim sat quiet for a moment, absorbing it. It would certainly explain the uncanny—un-Earthly—calm and serenity of many of the Vulcans he had met: they all seemed to carry some certainty around with them that everything was all right. If this was the root of it, he understood at least some of that serenity, at last. But there were problems still. "Spock," he said, "in the light of this, how do you explain someone like Shath'?"

Spock looked a little somber. "Captain," he said, "I think I can understand your viewpoint. Humans have no innate certainty on this subject and therefore must think it would solve a great deal. In some ways it does. But there are many, many questions that this certainty still leaves unresolved, and more that it raises. Granted that God exists: why then does evil do so? Why is there entropy? Is the force that made the Universe one that we would term good? What is good? And if it is, why is pain permitted? You see," he said, for McCoy was nodding, "they are all the same questions that humans ask, and no more answered by a sense of the existence of God than of His nonexistence. Some of the answers become frightening. If God exists, and pain and evil exist, while God still seems to care for creation—for that sense is also part of the experience—then are we effectively 'on our own' in a universe run out of the control of its creator? Such a view of the world leaves much room for anger and aggression. We spent millennia at war, Captain, Doctor, despite the fact that almost every Vulcan born knew that a Force then extant had created the Universe, and now maintained it, from second to second. It takes more than the mere sense of God to create peace. One must decide what to do with the information."

McCoy nodded. "And I suspect you're going to add that not all Vulcans experience *a'Tha* to the same extent."

"Indeed they do not, for the simple reason that they occupy different positions in spacetime," Spock said, "but there are doubtless many other influencing factors as well."

He fell silent. McCoy's eyes were on him, but the doctor said nothing, only reached out to his glass and had another drink of wine.

"You would like to ask how I perceive *a'Tha,* or whether I do at all," Spock said. His glance was dry, but humorous. "I think I may safely break the privacy taboo from my side and tell you that I do. But whether the degree in which I experience it is greater or lesser than normal, I could not tell you. It is indeed one of the matters involved in the Silences, the code of privacy which is part of Surak's guidelines regarding *cthia*. However, in my life as in most of my people's, *a'Tha* raises more questions than it answers. . . . I will admit," he added, "that I have wondered how it feels to be a human, and *not* to know that certainty, that presence. At any rate, Doctor, have I answered your question?"

"Mostly."

"That's good," Jim said, glancing at his chrono, "because we're running late. We have to get back to the ship and change for the reception. Where did Sarek say it was? The Academy?"

"Yes," Spock said as they got up.

"Great," Bones said, picking up his purchases from beside the table. "Another cocktail party in the school auditorium."

Spock put up one eyebrow and said nothing.

*   *   *

Later, in the transporter room, they spent no more than a few moments inspecting one another's dress uniforms before they got up onto the pads. Jim was mildly surprised to see that to his other rank tags and decorations, McCoy had added a small, understated IDIC. "If I didn't know you better," he said, "I'd think you were going native. When did you get that?"

"Today in the gift shop, when you were looking at the snowball paperweights with Mount Seleya in them. Tackiest things I ever saw."

"Yes," Spock said; "they were imported from Earth."

"You be quiet. We can't let these people leave the Federation, Jim. At least not until they teach us how to make tasteful souvenirs."

Jim groaned. "Energize," he said to the transporter technician.

The world dissolved and re-formed itself into a dusky landscape, all sand and stone, over which stretched a tawny darkness filled with stars. The sunset was now almost completely faded down from an earlier splendor that must have been enough to blind the eyes of anyone not Vulcan. They were standing in a great open space outside the walls of the Academy itself. The expanse of silvery sand ran featureless from where the three of them stood nearly to the horizon, where a range of low hills lay silhouetted against the crimson and golden glory of the sky. The air was hot but still, and from far over the sand came the cry of something alien but sweet-voiced and distant and sad.

"The place really does grow on you," Jim said,

McCoy nudged Jim to get him to turn around. "You don't know the half of it."

Jim turned away from the horizon and the sunset and actually took a step back from the massive pile of stone that stood, limned sharply as a cutout, against the rising bulk of T'Khut. It was a castle, or looked like one: but no castle so large had ever been even thought of on Earth. It looked to have been carved out of a whole mountain.

"It was a fortress once," Spock said, "when this was the only place for thousands of miles where water sprang from the stone. Wars were fought for possession of Pelasht, even when the winner might only possess it for a day. Then Surak came . . . and when the fighting stopped, and the Academy grew up here, Pelasht became its ceremonial house and banqueting hall. Shall we go in?"

They did. Jim half expected a brassy cry of trumpets as they went up the switchback stair that led to the main gates. He would have welcomed a fanfare or two, to milk for the delay: a steep climb in this atmosphere was not exactly what he had in mind. But he had had McCoy give him a time-release TriOx before they left the ship, and a couple of treatments to increase his lungs' ability to extract oxygen from the air. He would be all right. *Just so long as no one challenges me to any duels,* he thought ruefully.

They went in through the massive gates, and McCoy looked mistrustfully at the huge holes in the ceiling of the vast passageway between the outer gates and the inner ones. The holes were perfect to dump large rocks down on the heads of a trapped enemy. And certainly enemies had been trapped here once or twice: the scars on the floor, where boulders had been dropped long ago, were many and deep.

"Those gates are solid rock," he muttered. "What are the hinges made of to support that weight?"

"Titanium-steel alloys," Spock said. "Our people discovered them some five thousand years ago, during weapons research."

"When else?" McCoy said softly, and walked on. There was a light ahead of them down the passage, and the echoing sound of conversation.

They paused in the doorway, and not for effect, but because of it. The Hall of Pelasht is one of the largest rooms in the known worlds—nearly half a mile long, a quarter mile across, five hundred feet up to the roof, and all carved out of the living stone, an ancient volcanic basalt. The hundreds of lamps driven into the walls were tiny and distant as stars. It was rare to feel so oppressed, so dwarfed, by an empty space, but Jim did. He simply held still until his feelings calmed down somewhat, until he got over the feeling that that great roof, lost up there in the shadows, might take it into its mind to come down on him without warning. This was earthquake country, after all. . . .

Over some kind of annunciator system, a calm voice said, "Captain James T. Kirk. Doctor Leonard E. McCoy. Commander Spock."

They headed in, Jim doing his best to stroll and look unconcerned. It was a long walk. That hall was the sort that could have swallowed the largest party alive, and people were tending to congregate in small groups near the tables which had been set out in the center with food and drink.

They made their way to the nearest of the tables, and there they found Sarek and Amanda and a great many Vulcans to which they were all introduced one by one. Jim swore quietly at himself one more time for not taking the time to get the NameFiler memory enhancement done to his translator . . . but things kept coming up, and he was forced simply to say the names as they were said to him and try to keep them all in order that way.

There was this to be said, though: these Vulcans treated him with all the courtesy that Shath had not, and they talked to him as if he were an intelligent being. It was a pleasant relief, after that afternoon, when Jim had begun to wonder whether or not the whole planet might be in the mood to consider him a pariah. *Paranoia*, he thought, and got happily involved in small talk.

As he chatted with them he was once again rather delighted that Vulcans were in fact different from one another. A lot of people had the idea that Vulcans were all tall, dark, and slender, men and women alike: but though a large percentage of them did indeed fit into those parameters, there were also short Vulcans, blond Vulcans, even a redhead over by one of the tables, talking earnestly to K's't'lk: there were delicate, light-boned men and ladies, and stocky ones, and Vulcans who had rather pleasantly ordinary faces, rather than the chiseled good looks that seemed to be the rule. *They look like people*, Jim thought, and then had to laugh a little at the idea.

Jim got himself a drink—more of that pure water, which was highly prized hereabouts for its sweet taste—and went back to chatting with the group of Vulcans who had gathered around him. There was Sreil, the burly, brown-haired biologist from the Academy, and T'Madh, a little bright-eyed woman of great age and curiosity, a computer programmer; and her son Savesh, who when asked what he did, said, "I am a farmer," with a sort of secret satisfaction that hinted he thought his job better than any of the more technical ones that the people around him held down. Jim had to smile; the thought of a Vulcan farmer was slightly funny, even though there naturally had to *be* some. But the image of a Vulcan in coveralls, chewing on a stalk of hay, kept coming up and having to be repressed.

Savesh turned out to be rather more than a someone who drove a tractor, "though I do that on occasion as well," he said, as if that too was a matter of great pride. Savesh was involved in research on improving the yield of several of the breeds of *tikh,* a native grain-bearing grass that was a Vulcan staple, and one of the few things that would grow in plain sand without much added nutrient. The problem, it seemed, was that the plant's biology would not stand much tinkering, in the way of genetic engineering or hormonal treatments; and if you added more nutrient to the soil in an attempt to get the *tikh* to grow faster, it would simply ignore the stuff. So some other solution had to be found.

"It is rather important," Savesh said. "Over the past three hundred years, the planet's population has increased far beyond the self-sufficiency point. Perhaps an illogical outcome, but it must be handled soon. Already we import too much food, and there is no telling what will happen to our imports after the debates. . . ."

"Savesh," Jim said, "may I ask you your opinion of something?" It was the standard courtesy, so Sarek had explained to him; the Vulcan to whom one spoke might then safely refuse if he thought his privacy might be breached by the answer.

"Ask, please," Savesh said.

"What do you think about the secession? Is it something you personally would want?"

Savesh frowned, and for a moment Jim wondered whether he should have asked at all. *But I have to ask: I have to get a better feeling of these people . . . I can't just stop at Shath.* "If I've offended—" Jim started to say.

"Offended? Indeed not," Savesh said. "It is just that, Captain, you must forgive me, but I have never met an Earth person before this evening, and I begin to wonder now whether much of the data I have about your kind is hearsay evidence and no more." He frowned again. "I am not sure how to explain this so that it will make sense for a person from a different cultural context, so you must bear with me. There is a word in our language, *nehau*—there are many translations, but usually they come out as 'feeling,' and the translation is inadequate—"

"Araigh 'tha takh-ruuh ne nehauu vesh mekhezh't-rrhew," McCoy said quietly from behind Jim, and then coughed.

Savesh and Sreil and T'Madh all looked at McCoy with astonishment. "Yes," Savesh said, "that would be more like it. Doctor, where did you study Vulcan?"

"Flat on my back," McCoy said ruefully, "and then spent a week regretting it, usually in the bathroom." Even the Vulcans smiled slightly at that. "Jim," he said, "the best translation of *nehau* would be an old word: 'vibes.' The feeling-in-your-bones that something gives you. It's highly subjective."

"Right. Go on, Savesh."

"Well, Captain, I have heard numerous Vulcans say that losing the Federation and the Earth people would be no particular loss, because they had bad *nehau,* and that could not fail to affect us sooner or later. But I must tell you that I find your *nehau* not objectionable at all; pleasant, even. And this being so, it makes me wonder whether many of the other things I have heard about Earth people are similarly inaccurate. I wonder where the other Vulcans have been getting their data; whether they have even met an Earth person, to make the decision."

Jim smiled a little. "They might not have. But for my own part, it might just be that I'm a nice Earth person; there have to be a *few.* Or perhaps I have good *nehau,* but I'm not really as good as I feel."

"That might be," Sreil said. "But usually *nehau* is not that easy to deceive; it accurately reflects a being's inner status. In any case, some of us perhaps will desire to revise our thinking. But whether those revisions will make a difference to the vote that will be taking place . . . that is impossible to predict, and the odds do not look promising."

Jim nodded. "Well, " he said, "I hope it may."

T'Madh looked at him out of her little bright eyes. "Hope is not usually logical," she said, "but in your case, I would wish that matters go well for you, and for all of us. I for one would not care to lose the Federation; our differences are so great that we will never find such an opportunity to celebrate them on so grand a scale. But I wonder sometimes whether there are many of us who think ourselves unequal to the task . . . and so naturally become unequal to it." She shook her head. "It is saddening. Nevertheless, let us see what can be made of tomorrow."

The conversation drifted to other things, and eventually Jim drifted along to other conversations. After an hour or so, he noticed that he was feeling curiously tired. It was probably the heavier gravity . . . it caught you behind the knees after a while, made you feel wobbly.

"Running down a bit?" McCoy said in his ear.

"A little, yes," he said.

McCoy gestured at one of the side doors. "Go have a bit of a walk in the fresh air. It's actually cooling down out there; it helps a little."

"All right."

It was another long walk to the door. Jim paused in the doorway, looked around. He was standing on a sort of long balcony or gallery carved out of the stone of the side of the mountain; the cliff fell away sheer a hundred feet or so below him, and the Science Academy was laid out before him, all its graceful buildings glimmering in T'Khut's coppery light. To left and right, the gallery stretched away, and railed stairs reached up from it, leading to other balconies on the mountain's side.

Jim picked a direction and began to stroll. The air was indeed getting cool, cooler than he had ever felt it; but this was a desert climate after all, probably the archetypal one. *They should have called it Sahara or something,* he thought to himself, amused, as he walked. *Vulcan: why did they name it that? Unless it was a return to that habit the astronomers used to have, of naming the planets after the old gods. . . . Not a bad name, I suppose. The god of the forge—and if ever a planet has been thrust in the fire and hammered, this one was, to hear the paleontologists tell it. . . .*

He went up one of the sets of stairs to better his view. The sky had become a most marvelous shade of purple blue, some light of the sun still lingering as twilight, and the desert glowed red beneath T'Khut. Jim leaned on his elbows on the railing and wondered how many balconies there were carved into this sheer wall, how many rooms inside the bulk of the fortress itself. To hear Spock tell it, the place was tunneled through and through like a Swiss cheese with strongrooms, living quarters, lesser halls, stores to hold food against siege. . . . Jim wondered what it would have been like to withstand a siege here, to look down and see those sands full of people shouting for your blood. . . .

History: he could never resist history. He hoped there would be time to see this place properly later.

If there was a later. His own actions would help to determine that.

Oh, please let it work out all right, he said to Someone Who might or might not be listening. Unlike Spock, he had no certainties on the subject.

". . . resist this," a voice said, faintly, some distance away. "I resist this most strenuously. Why will you force me to this action?"

"You know my reasons," said a second voice: a little, thin, frail voice, but Jim thought he knew it from somewhere . . . and the hair rose on the back of his neck. "You know the work that other has done, to what purpose. Our people must vote *rightly,* not because their prejudices are exploited. And indeed they have them."

"I would not argue that with you. But I resist this course nonetheless."

"I will tell thee again," and Jim's hackles rose once more at the suddenly formal turn of phrase. The voice was a little louder, as if its owner had come nearer. *"Our people must vote rightly.* It is disaster, it is the breaking of *cthia,* if they do not. They must not be moved by their prejudices, or by the advertising campaign"—the words were almost spat out—"that those others conduct to sway the electorate. They must vote for secession because they think it is logical and necessary. And to do this, they must hear the truth. And no one is better qualified to tell them the truth than you are. They know it: the whole planet knows it. You are the keystone—or one of them."

There was a long silence. "I cannot help but think," said the other voice, Sarek's voice, low and rough, "that the matter of thine own honor is involved in this, madam."

"When has it not been?" The voice was cool. "I am the Eldest. I rule the Family; in some ways I rule the planet, and well I know it, and feel the weight of what I rule. Too long now I have felt it. I think I weary of it. But for the time being, I will not put down the burden, and neither will the Family. *Cthia* must be observed. The truth must be told. There is no one better to tell it. Eighty-six of their years, you have been ambassador to Earth; you have married a woman of Earth; you have sired a son of mixed parentage; you know the Terrans better than any other. And Terra is at the heart of the Federation, as well you know. We do not hear complaints about the Andorians, or Tellar, or the other worlds. The species that troubles us, the species whose policies determine those of the Federation, are the humans of Earth. Your course is laid out for you. You may resist it as you like. It will not avail you."

There was another silence. "And you, James?" the voice said, quite close. Jim turned around, shocked.

There T'Pau stood, looking at him: and in the background, in the shadows, Sarek, looking somewhat diminished. But Jim had eyes only for T'Pau, frail and small, leaning on her carved stick, robed in plain dark robes now instead of the ceremonial splendor she had worn at the Place of Marriage and Challenge. Again Jim remembered the hot sand, and that regard, more scorching than the white sun, pinning him, examining him. It did so now, and the darkness did not blunt the edge of it. "You did not mean to overhear, I am sure," T'Pau said. "We shall assume that this was intended." Jim blinked: *what does that mean?* "But no matter. You know what Sarek will do?"

"He will give testimony, and the intent of it will be that Vulcan should secede from the Federation," Jim said.

"Do you know why he will do this?"

"Because you have told him to," Jim said.

T'Pau drew herself up a little taller, took a step forward. "Many will think that," she said. "Certainly most folk of your people would think so. They look at me and see the powerful matriarch—" She snorted. The sound was so unexpected that Jim almost laughed at it. "They have no idea of the strictures that bind my power," T'Pau said. *"Cthia, cthia* above all. But they do not understand it. If they did, secession would not be necessary."

"And perhaps if they did, their diversity from us would be diminished," Sarek said. "What is the point of celebrating diversity if one tries to make all the elements of it the same?"

T'Pau glanced at him, and then back at Jim. "James," she said in that oddly accented voice, "there are forces working on this planet who desire this secession mightily. It is not in my right to stop them: they are a symptom of larger forces, they have a right to arise, and they must be allowed to work out the fate of the planet in the open air, under the sky and the regard of the One, without interference."

"But you *are* interfering. Or so it seems to me."

"I am," she said, "but not in the way you think. The forces of which I speak are many, but some of them have been carrying on—the Earth phrase for it is 'a hate-mongering campaign.' They are inflaming Vulcans' prejudices against Earth people, by inflaming their pride, their sense of superiority." Jim looked surprised, and T'Pau said, "Oh, indeed, many of them would say that those are emotions, to be eschewed. And many of them have them, nonetheless. To combat such lies, the only weapon is the truth. Sarek has that truth. And he must tell it in full, no matter what the consequences."

Jim stood still a moment, and then nodded. "It had been my intention as well," he said, "to tell the truth. Whatever the consequences."

"That itself," T'Pau said, "is more powerful a weapon in your hands than any other. I counsel you, bear it as well as you can." She looked a touch rueful at the martial metaphor. "For again we go to war, though all our philosophy counsels us otherwise. No physical weapons may be raised, but war it is nonetheless." She cocked her head at Jim. "I am relieved by what you say, however. I had thought perhaps you would desire to keep Vulcan in the Federation at any cost."

"I am not sure," Jim said slowly, "that I would want to be in such a Federation, or to have on my head the Vulcan that would be in it, afterward."

T'Pau nodded. "Then we understand one another," she said. Jim put an eyebrow up: he was far from understanding *her*, except in the most roundabout sort of way, and he was resigned to that.

"And what will you do," T'Pau said, "should the vote go for secession?"

Jim gazed at her a moment, then shook his head and turned away. "Leave Vulcan," he said; and it was all he could say. He had been refusing as much as possible to think about those consequences, except in the abstract.

"Enough," T'Pau said from behind him. "It is illogical to suffer consequences before they befall. Do what you must, James, and know that you are doing right. It is all any of us can do, I fear."

The silence grew long. When Jim turned around again, they were gone.

He stood on the balcony until he got his composure back; and then he went back to the party.

T'Khut set, dyeing the sands below with the tinct of alien blood.

Vulcan: Three

Kesh was her name. She had the Eye, but in all other things she was the least of them, and the rest of the clan brought her to remember this often. She swore, quite young, that they would regret this: but more came of her oaths, in the end, than regret.

She was born among the stones around the pool, of a woman who had been called Tekav, but now had no name, being dead. No petty-house had yet housebound Tekav; their mothers were waiting to see if she would bear her child alive, and would thereafter be worth the binding. But the birthing killed her, and not even the Oldest Mother could save her when the womb-mooring tore loose untimely, and the blood burst forth.

They cut her body open to bring out the child, and Kesh took breath and cried out lustily as the stove-heat of the day struck her. This the Oldest thought was good. She lifted the babe and took her straightway out of the shelter of the stones, and held her up to the high sun and shook her until she opened her eyes. The babe screamed, as all newborns did in that ferocious light. But when the Oldest turned her back to the sun and looked narrowly in the babe's eyes, she saw the flicker of reflected sunlight inside the constricted pupil, the shining like a wild beast's eye in the firelight. Then she knew that the child had the Eye.

They raised the cry, then, and gave the babe to another mother who had been nursing and still had a little milk. Some of the young warriors walked away muttering that it was unfair for the mother to have died, when she brought forth children with the Eye: she should have been given to one of them. But the only ones Tekav was fit to be given to now were the *sehlats,* and that was done. The snarling went on well through the day, until the bones were clean and had been cracked for marrow. Then someone came from the camp and buried them, to keep the scavengers from being attracted to the place. The clan had enough problems without *cheveh* and such like raiding the place. They had taken newborn babes before, and there was no use losing this last one when it had just caused so much trouble.

The clan knew itself as the clan of the Eye, but this name was secret, especially from the other clans of the great sand: false names were invented to tell any clan their paths crossed. This happened rarely. Too little water there was in the sandy world, too little shelter: it took a great deal of land to support a few people, and once you had found such a place, you did not stray from it by choice. Wanderers were usually suspect—they were usually spies, come from another tribe to find out whether your source of water was better than theirs. The clan of the Eye knew well enough about spies, for many of them had died spying on the accursed Phelsh't, who had the high ground. It was, of course, no particular distinction to die spying on the Phelsh't. Many people of other tribes had done the same.

There was, at least, no need to do it at the moment. The pool had not failed for a long time. It was courtesy to call it a pool; it was actually a small brackish puddle, from which the water had to be sieved to get the worst of the mud out, or the beast fur—for there was no use trying to keep the *sehlats* out of it. They had to drink, and they did enjoy their roll in the mud—no matter that everyone else had to spend the rest of the day pulling *sehlat* hairs out of their drink. No one complained too much. The *sehlats* were protection of a sort, and besides, at least there *was* drink for them to get their hairs in. There were enough other things worth complaining about.

Hunting was one of them. There was never enough food, and no one in the clan of the Eye had a spare bit of flesh on them. Children grew expert from their very young days at grabbing a passing lizard, grubbing up a bit of sweet root (if one managed to escape the sharp eyes of their elders); and nothing went to waste, not the stringiest tuber, not a drop of blood. As they grew older, even the smallest and weakest children sharpened sticks for themselves, wove nets from the dried strings of the *chakh'* plant, and went hunting among the rocks for the unwarier small beasts that crept close to men's dwellings for a bite to eat or a drop to drink. It was only wisdom, for a child that was considered too weak to prosper would not be given anything to eat—the adult members of the clan considered this throwing good food after bad. A child who hunted effectively was given more food, by way of encouragement.

Kesh was one of the good ones. From the time she could toddle, she seemed able to hear movements that the others never did. She began putting things in her mouth to see whether they were good to eat long before she was weaned, and at this the Oldest Mother and some of the other mothers nodded sagely. She made her first twig-spear young, and the lizards shortly learned that their lives had become more difficult than before—or, at least, potentially much shorter. Her ears grew sharper still as time went on and better feeding improved her health. They were sharper than the others' anyway; mutation had set in on two counts—because of the increased solar radiation that Vulcan's atmosphere no longer properly filtered, and the thinner air, less able to carry sound. Kesh's ears were like those of several others of the clan's children, with the larger, slightly pointed, more delicate pinnae that caught soundwaves better than their parents' ears did. The ears were the cause of occasional trouble; Kesh had more than once taken vicious buffets from one or another of the adults, when she caught a lizard or one of the *yie*, the little burrowers, that the adult had been hunting but had heard too late. However, the Oldest Mother scowled when such things happened, and cursed the adult, more likely than not: she knew that the children with these ears would do better than those without, and the clan needed their blood to sire more of the same.

It had been so with the Eye. It had been the Oldest Mother's mother's mother, some lives or so ago, who had first found one of her children staring at the sun, seemingly untroubled by it. At first they had thought that the child was lackwitted, and had now gone blind. But the blindness passed, and the child could walk for hours out in the sands and come back walking, not feeling his way. For many a year people had had to bind skins about their heads, or over their eyes, when they went hunting in the sand; and the *lematyas* tended to make short work of them. Now, looking at this child, the Oldest Mother thought there might be a way to bring such poor makeshifts to an end. She coddled the child as if he were the last in the world, and bound him to one of her outdaughters; and three of the children born before his death had the Eye as well, and two of them were girls.

Then the Oldest Mother became mighty in the clan, and elders and young alike fought for her favor, that she might allow them to be bound with one of the children of the Eye, and take the blood into their own lines. All thought of growing up and having children who could hunt better than all others, who would bring them food when other adults had long lain down to die because there was no more. And the Oldest Mother chose as she willed, and every lightest word of hers was heeded as if the sandstorm would strike if she was displeased.

Now, though—so Kesh thought—the Eye was becoming common: half the tribe had it. And to what purpose? They would not do anything useful with it. Not the kind of use she had in mind. Not that they paid any attention to her in council. "Hunt," they said, "since you are so good at it." And they mocked her—orphaned and unbound as she was, with none but her milkmother to speak for her. If she might be got with child, they said, and pass on the Eye, she might be worth listening to. But Kesh had other things in mind than children.

When she was not hunting—and often, when she was—her eyes turned northward. The clan's present camp was nothing more than a great pile of boulders around a little mucky spring, and Kesh hated the place—the sprawl of bodies huddling for cover, the stink of the *sehlat*-hides stuck on poles that were the only shade, except for cracks in the rock. Shadows crawled, people fought for place under the shades, pushed out people they disliked into the pitiless sun. Even the water stank. Much better, by Kesh's way of thinking, to go out onto the sand, which at least smelt clean, and feel the fresh hot wind blowing. One could think out there. And one could see for miles: and miles north of them, there was something to see. It rose up all alone, a dark huge shape reared up against the sky: Phelsh't.

She had heard the stories that they told about it, around the fires at night, after the last few scraps of meat had been toasted on sticks and eaten, and the sticks hardened in the ash and given to the smallest children for their spears. Phelsh't, they said, was an image of the Distant One, S'l'heya the Great, chief of mountains. It had been raised up by one of the gods of the sand, and given to a mortal, to whom he bound himself, and then gave a great gift, the gift of a well of water. It was no mere muddy puddle. It was a spring, that rose up from deep in the stone of the mountain, cold clear water, sweet to the taste, without muck or weed; and there was so much of it that it ran down the side of the mountain into the sand, and plants grew there, despite the scorching sun, and grew great—grew almost as tall as a man.

It did not seem fair that one clan should have this great gift, and not another: and all the clans that wandered in that empty waste had at one time or another thought of taking Phelsh't for their own. Some had tried. But the clan that lived there had grown very strong and numerous—how not, with all the water they desired?—and they easily beat off any clan that tried to take their high ground with its sweet water. Finally the Oldest Mother of the clans—and the clan of the Eye was no exception—had declared that there were to be no more attempts on Phelsh't. But Kesh sat on the sand for hours, after having made a kill, and looked north at the dark shape against the burning blue horizon, and dreamed: dreamed of limitless water, and shade, and having as much food as ever she wanted. . . .

"Here," said a voice in her ear. She did not bother turning: she knew the voice, knew the shadow that fell over her. He sat down beside her, offered her something. It was a *yie*, one of the black-furred ones, fat and sweet-looking.

Kesh took the bowl that a hunter always carried, slit the *yie* open with the flake of stone that she carried in her belt, and drained out the blood: then offered it to him. It was a poor mouthful, but she smiled as she handed Tes the bowl, and he smiled as he took it from her and bowed from the waist until his hair brushed the sand, as he would have done for the Oldest Mother. Then, quickly, he drank. There was no use letting the gift clot up.

Halfway down his drink, he stopped and offered her the bowl again. "Are you mad?" she said. "Drink it." But she was warmed, as she always was warmed by Tes; as she had been since they became friends while toddling on the rocks.

"There's plenty of juice left in this one, anyway," she said, and set to work on the *yie*. Quite soon there was nothing left of it but the bones, and between the two of them they disposed of the marrow in those as well, and buried them.

"Why did you come away in the heat?" she said. "There's a hunt tonight: aren't you going to sleep?"

"When was the last time I caught anything in a great hunt?" he said, stretching his legs out in front of him. "With all of them scrambling about and making more noise than a *sehlat* in heat, all these little grunts and hoots and prayers? It's a wonder they catch anything, and as for me, I do better on my own."

She laughed a little as she scrubbed her hands in the sand. Tes was right enough about the noise and fuss when the clan went on a great hunt; all the bustle of preparation, tying-up of clothes, making of small sacrifices to the gods that cared for the hunt, prayers to the spirit of the *lematya* or the *tshin;* and then the crowd of them slipping out into the dark, trying to be quiet, failing. Somehow the game always managed to find the hunting party, rather than the other way around. It was as if a great group of people had something about them that a *lematya* could sense. On days as hot as today, Kesh rather thought it was the smell. But anyway, either they would kill the prey, or it would kill some of them: sometimes it killed some of them and then got away, which sent the survivors home in a foul mood, for the Oldest Mother had a dim view of such goings-on, and her tongue would strip the hide off you as she demanded to know why she cared for the clan's blood so, when fools like you threw it away? Kesh had heard those reprimands and had thanked whichever god was hers that she had never had one directed at her in her young life.

"You've done well today," Tes said, glancing back at the lump in the sand near where Kesh sat. She had killed early, a *tshin,* a fairly big one—almost half her size; the Oldest Mother would be pleased when she came back, for *tshin* had a lot of blood in them, and the meat kept well when dried. "How did you manage to get close to it without it knowing you were there?"

"It's a secret," she said.

He made the sign to turn away foolery, and Kesh smiled. "Ah, come on, tell me. I can use the help."

She wrinkled her brow for a moment, thinking. "It's something about the sand," she said. "If you hunt them in the morning, they always know: but when the sun is high and the day is hot, they get confused—they turn around and around on the sand as if they can't find you. If you keep still in some rocks, and then wait till they're confused—" She shrugged. "It seems to work. At least, no *tshin* has killed me yet."

"Try not to let them kill you," Tes said.

She smiled at him. He was always saying things like that. He turned his face away.

"How did you know where I was today?" Kesh said.

He tilted his head a little. "You're always around here somewhere," he said. "Away from the clan—and somewhere where you can see *that.*" He pointed at the tall dark shape reaching up against the edge of the sky.

She nodded. "Tes," she said slowly, "they're fools."

"Yes, but why?"

"We should take that. It should be ours. Or ours as *well* as theirs. Do you know how many people all that water could support?"

Tes shrugged. "The Oldest Mother forbade it."

"And it should just stop there?"

"What else can be done? It's forbidden. Go against the clan and you're cast out . . . and you die. Anyway," he said, trying to be reasonable, "there aren't enough of us to take Phelsh't from them."

"Someday," Kesh said, "there might be. . . ."

"It'll still be forbidden."

"There might be a new Oldest Mother."

He stared at her. "That would take years and years! And you would have to—"
She was silent.

"But you couldn't," Tes said, sounding sorrowful, and yet relieved. "None of her sons would bind with you."

"Not that I would want them," Kesh said scornfully. "Heavy-footed, empty-bellied, blind-eyed—" She stopped.

"I would bind with you," he said.

Kesh stared at him.

"I know how, now," he said. "I saw someone do the Touch. I heard what they said. It was easy."

Kesh held very still, then began to shake her head. "But there has to be something else—" She scrambled to her feet, looked around her as if looking for a place to flee to, then dropped to her knees beside her kill and began digging it out of the protecting sand. A few moments later she looked up again. Tes had not moved, other than to look over his shoulder at her.

"I have that," he said. "Do you?"

She breathed out, and in, and the pain hit her in the side so that she sat down hard. "Oh yes," she said. "Yes." And then she set to digging her kill out again, and wept hard, making sure to lick in the tears as they fell.

That was all they said about it. Years later, Kesh would remember the sight of Tes turning the bowl around and around in his hands as she dug: and the way he smiled. Years later it would seem that she had always known it was going to happen: that as little as a few hours later, that night around the fire, it would seem that he had been her bonded forever, since first they toddled in the rocks, and fell down, and bled on one another.

There was some comment when Kesh did not go on the great hunt that night: but the Oldest Mother looked at her and said that she had brought in her *tshin* that day, the biggest that had been seen for some time, and what other hunter of the clan could say the same? Kesh might have a night's rest if she pleased, and two bowls of blood from the kill, and first and last drink of the pool. The hunters went off grumbling, too angry to see the look with which the Oldest Mother favored Kesh, or her glance at Tes.

T'Khut rode high, the brightness shaped like a tilted-down bowl, the darkness glittering with her fires. They went away into the sands, far from where the hunters were, and found a little place of stones, where there was some shelter, and a feeling of privacy. They were both of an age for the Rapture, and though it had not yet fallen on them, their bodies were ready. They fumbled out of their ragged belts and skins, laid them carefully aside, and looked on one another.

"Are you sure you know how to do this?" Kesh said, shaking a little. It was not the coolness.

"Yes," Tes said. "I think so." Very slowly, trembling too, he reached out and touched her face, and said the words. They would change many times in the thousands of years to follow, but the meaning always remained the same. *My mind to your mind: my thoughts to your thoughts: never touching, and always touched: apart, yet one—*

One they became: filled, both of them, with one another, as the bowl of the moon above was filled with light, always outpouring, always full; touching everywhere, till the cries broke out in delight; pierced, enclosing, the spear, the prey, willingly caught, willingly pierced, willingly sheathed. The last cry that rose up, the cry that slew them both, was one. And then silence.

Much later they got up, slipped into their clothes and gear again, and went back to the camp. The hunters never noticed their absence: they were much too busy hanging their heads before the Oldest Mother for losing Vach to the *lematya*. And few noticed in the days that followed that there seemed to be an invisible connection between Kesh and Tes, one rarely out of sight of the other. They were both of little importance, and so they had almost a sun's round of joy together. And then the Dry came.

It seemed very sudden to some of the people of the Eye, but Kesh had been watching the pool for some time, and it seemed to her much muddier than usual, as if someone were stealing drink from it—which no one would dare: there was never enough to have all that you wanted, and stealing the water was punishable by beating or death. And the *sehlats* were not rolling in it any worse than usual. In fact, it was rather strange, but one by one the *sehlats* went missing, along with some of the smaller lizards. There was a lot less easy food around the camp than there had used to be. Children died, and there were complaints that they were just not as strong as they had been in the old days.

To Tes, Kesh said, "We are going to have to move."

They were sitting up on an outcropping, flaking fresh stone for spearheads. He paused—he was knapping a flint—and looked down at the flat little puddle. "Yes," he said. "I think so."

And he was very quiet. Kesh went back to the piece of stone she was chipping, and said, "It will do the clan some good, I suppose. Shake out some of the useless ones, the ones who eat and don't hunt."

"Maybe." Tes looked around him. "But all the same, this is a bad time for it. The Winds are soon."

She had to agree. Vulcan's seasons were slight, but there were some weather patterns that tended to recur regularly, due to the influence of sunspots; and one of them was the Winds, a storm pattern even drier than usual that turned the great sands into a hell for weeks at a time. One became used to breathing through hides, and if you went out to hunt, the sand blasted you raw. And game was hard to find, for it fled when the Winds started. It was a time of grit and thirst and suffering even when you had a source of water at hand. The thought of traveling during it was highly unpleasant . . . but not as unpleasant as staying in one place and dying.

"When will the Oldest Mother make the choice, do you think?" Kesh said.

Tes shrugged. "I don't know her mind. But I don't think we'll have to wait long."

They did not. T'Khut was waxing when they spoke on top of the flint ridge. In her wane, the Oldest Mother sent the hunters out and told them not to come back until they had caught no less than three *tshin*, and if they ran across some of the wild *sehlat*, they were to bring those back too. There was muttering, but disobeying the Oldest Mother was unwise: the hunters filled their stomach-bag skins with as much water as they could coax out of the thickening pool, and went. Kesh went with them, not willingly; she wanted Tes with her, but the Oldest Mother kept him by her with another of the clan who along with Tes was the best at spearheads. For some reason she wanted a great many of them, enough to arm the whole tribe twice. There was much muttering about this as well, but no disobedience. Kesh looked reluctantly over her shoulder, trailing after the hunting party as they headed away from the camp; she gazed at the flint ridge, where a small figure sat bent, then paused to raise a hand to her.

Always touching, said the voice inside her. *Don't worry, my love.*

Kesh tried to put her concern behind her. She acquitted herself well on the hunt: the first *tshin* was hers, and the second: another hunter killed the third, and there was a fourth that took Kesh's spear through the flank and loped away at speed, so they had to chase it across the sand for hours until it dropped. One of the hunters died in that chase, of a burst heart, and the others buried him where he fell and put the beast's head in his grave, as revenge on its spirit. Then home they went, in very mixed mood, fearing the Oldest Mother's tongue but glad about all the food. No one minded carrying such a weight of meat back: their minds were all on the feat ahead of them.

So there was anger (though muted) when they brought their kills in, and the Oldest Mother ordered that all the meat, *all* of it, was to be cut thin and dried on the rocks, for keeping. The decision was unpopular—dried meat did not compare to sweet fresh meat with blood in it, or even better, meat that had been roasted—but there was nothing to be done, especially when the Oldest Mother then announced to them, "We are leaving soon."

There was consternation at that, far worse than over the meat, and argument, first polite, then heated: but her mind was set, and they dared not defy her. "What," she said. "Will you lie here and roast yourselves, in your laziness, and dry out like the meat on the stones? We must have water, and there is shortly going to be none here. We will make for the little pool across the sands, where we went nineteen sun-rounds ago when the pool before that one dried. The little pool is a good one, and when we find our way to it we will not have to move again till after the Winds are done. Cease your complaining, and do as I bid you!"

They did. Five days later there were no further traces of resistance, for the pool had almost dried, and everyone was praising the Mother's wisdom for filling and hiding away many bags of water against the evil hour. Another day would see them set out on their journey.

"They are a docile lot, suddenly," Kesh said to Tes, as they sat scraping out two of the *tshin*'s stomachs to make a last pair of waterbags.

"This will need a lot more scraping," said Tes. And inwardly, *Yes,* he said down the bond between them. *They are afraid. And so am I.*

She looked at him in surprise, then turned back to her scraping. *Of what?*

How do we know we are ever going to find the other pool? he said. *How do we know that some other clan is not there already, armed, and waiting for us?*

She shrugged. *Even if they are, we cannot stay here.*

Tes looked down at the stomach. "This will need more curing, too," he said. "Someone is going to have to carry it on a pole while we walk, so the sun can get at it."

"Probably you," said Kesh. *Beloved—there is something else you are afraid of. . . .*

Tes looked up at the flint ridge and sighed. *It's stupid.*

Tell me.

He shook his head. *I am bound to these stones,* he said. *I was told so, in a dream. I think if we leave them, I will die.*

Kesh straightened up and looked at him. If true, this was a serious business. *When did you have this dream?*

Long ago. Before we were bound.

Kesh scoffed, then, relieved. *A child's dream. Children do not dream true.*

T'Khut was high, he said. *She saw. It was a true dream.*

Kesh began to feel desperate, for the higher T'Khut rode, the more she saw: she was the Eye, and it was unwise for one of the Clan of the Eye to scoff at her. *Perhaps it was only true then,* she said. *You are strong now, one of the strongest of us.* She leaned over and pinched one of his arm muscles, trying to be cheerful. *There is no reason for you to die.*

I know, he said, and fell silent again.

They were uneasy with one another until it came time for the clan to go: and then Tes seemed to relax a little, as if he had cast his worry away. The actual going took little time to organize: once the meat was all dry, it was parceled out among the clan, a bit for everyone to carry, even the smallest child; and then everyone simply got up and left. All the clothes they had were what they wore—someone might keep a bright bit of stone for a plaything, or a binding of woven leather for an ornament, but that was all they had, except for food, and all of that they took with them. And everyone had a spear: Tes had been worked hard, the last few days, finding enough of the dead ironwood that grew in long straight tubes in the desert, and socketing the spears. The Oldest Mother stepped out in front of them and led the way into the sands. There were many backward looks, but Kesh particularly noticed that Tes did not look back once.

They went on for a day and a night that way, not stopping. They followed no path that anyone could see, but the Oldest Mother led them a straight run across the sand, south and west. Off to the left, far away, Phelsh't could be seen: or its head could. Its feet were hidden in a haze like blown dust.

The first place they stopped was nothing but sand, and the clansfolk threw themselves down on it gladly, and ate and drank: but the Oldest Mother seemed to be watching every sip of water, and every stomach-bag, and it quickly took some of the cheer out of the drinking, and slowed some people down. When she ordered them to get up and walk again, there were murmurs.

"Up, fools," she said. "The Winds are coming! Can you not see?" And she pointed at Phelsh't, whose base was hidden thicker than ever by the dust.

Then they realized what was happening, and people scrambled to their feet again, and slung bags over their shoulders, and hastened as she bade them. It did not help, of course. The wind had wings instead of feet and overtook them a day later, falling upon them with a scream like a thousand *lematyas*. The darkness descended in broad day, and the clan of the Eye staggered blind, for even the Eye could not help them now.

It went on for a hand of days and never stopped, that screaming, the blast of sand and dust against the body: to stop was almost impossible—the wind blew one along, urged you from behind, dispassionately cruel—and to keep going was endless, weary torment. The Oldest Mother told the clansmen to tie themselves to one another in a long line, with thongs of gut: and this they did, and stumbled all in a long line through the screaming sand, not knowing where they went, though the Oldest Mother led them straight as if the sky were clear and the stars bright to show her the way. All sense of direction was lost: the world was reduced to a dun-colored wall of stinging sand. Kesh put out her hand often to feel for Tes behind her, and always his touch was there, and always he would say to her, *Always touching, beloved. . . .* His thought sounded cheerful. She took reassurance from it.

And then the last day came, the day of the worst wind. The Oldest Mother cried that this was good, that it meant that the wind was about to break: and the others did their best to believe her. Tes did, and was delighted. He was singing, or shouting a song against the wind, when the greatest gust came, that blew half the clan off their feet, and snapped the gut, and rolled them all about like dry weed.

"Tes!" Kesh screamed, but the wind swallowed her scream as it tumbled her over and over too. There was nothing to see, no way to tell where Tes was.

Always touching, loved The sound of the thought was rough, a little surprised, as might have been expected if the sender was being rolled over and over on hard sand. *It's all right—*

Relieved, she huddled into herself to make it harder for the wind to blow her. Eventually she managed to find some purchase by digging into the sand. Grimly she hung on. *Tes—*

We touch, my love. I'm all right—

She hung on. Gradually, so gradually, the wind began to decline. It took hours. The sky grew dark, with night this time, and they could actually see it. The night progressed, and the wind quieted. *Tes—*she said inside, for the thousandth time in that weary while.

Don't worry. . . . The thousandth response sounded faint and tired. Kesh sighed: she could understand why. She chafed for morning to come again, and light, so that she could find out where Tes had got to.

Around dawn, the wind gave a final shriek, faded to a sigh, and then to nothing. The silence was incredible. Kesh stood up from a few minutes' sleep—she could not hold it off any longer—and looked around her.

There was no sight of Tes. There was nothing but blank sand, as far as the eye could see: and several dunes, heaped high.

Tes!!

No reply came back. The bond was broken.

Kesh ran like a mad thing over the sand, calling, crying his name, digging at the sand. It was hopeless. The Oldest Mother called to her: Kesh would not come. The Mother sent other hunters after Kesh and had one of them strike her down, to keep her quiet for a while. When she sat up at last, rubbing her sore head and moaning, the Mother was sitting on the sand beside her.

"He is gone," she said. "Five others are gone as well. The sand has buried them. We all mourn with you."

Kesh sat mute.

"We must go on after we rest awhile," said the Mother. As she got heavily up to go away, she looked at Kesh with pity. It was not what Kesh wanted. The only thing she wanted, she could not have: could never have again.

She wept bitterly, and did not bother to lick the tears, and others were shocked by the waste.

They found the pool which the Mother had sought, and it was untenanted, and the water in it was good; much better than that in the old pool. The clan decided that this was a place where they should stay, at least for as long as this pool lasted. It was wide and open, and there were more rocks with which to make shelters. The clan was well content.

All but one.

Most now thought Kesh was mad. It happened sometimes, that one who was bonded went mad at the spouse's death. Kesh hunted still, but now she hunted alone, always: no one else cared to be about her when she had a spear in her hand—not with that odd cold look in her eyes. It came and went—no one understood why. It came more often when she had been looking at the emptiness outside the camp, and it came often indeed under T'Khut, when she was at the half, pouring out her light on the ground. And it was strong in her eyes the night she stood up at the fire, after the eating was done, and said to the Oldest Mother, "We must have Phelsh't."

The clan stirred and murmured at such rudeness. It sounded like a direct challenge. One did not suggest courses of action to the Oldest Mother, as a rule, unless one was asked to. But the Mother simply sat back against the stone that was her seat, near the fire, and said, "Why?"

"Water," said Kesh.

"We have water."

"But not like that," Kesh said. "If we had such a well as Phelsh't has, we would never have to move camp again. We would never need to go out in the Wind. And no more of us need die."

"Many of us would die," said the Mother, "if we tried to take Phelsh't. And if we did by the grace of some mad god manage to take it, more of us would die when other clans came hunting us. We will stay where we are."

"We need Phelsh't," Kesh said, and walked away.

The clan buzzed with gossip of Kesh's mad obstinancy and wondered that the Mother did not have her beaten. People started to watch her, now, and saw how she would look, night and morning, toward the shape of Phelsh't on the horizon, for it was visible from the new camp: and the hatred in her eyes was terrible to see. A double handful of days later, she came down to the fire from the stones above the camp, and she said, "We need Phelsh't."

"We will stay here, Kesh," said the Mother. "You know my reasons."

So it went for a long time: at certain times of the moon, Kesh would come to the fire and demand Phelsh't, and the Mother would turn her away. Her madness was deemed harmless, but folks' opinion of it increased when the Rapture came upon her and she took *none* of them, not one of the men, though many had sought her in their own times.

A sunround went by: two. And in the middle of the second sunround, the Mother went to sleep one morning and did not awaken again. There was wailing as they buried her: and at the burying, even Kesh wailed with the rest. But when she was done, she stood looking at Phelsh't far away, and a great unease came over the clansmen nearest, and they hurriedly left her alone.

There was a new Oldest Mother, but she was not as strong as the other, not as wise. It took her time to learn how to be mother to more than her own children. And while she was learning, Kesh spoke to the younger hunters, and the warriors who respected her spear: and what she whispered in their ears made them begin to finger their weapons. Kesh did not hurry: she made sure of the young ones. And then she moved.

The new Oldest Mother had been so for two months when Kesh came down to the fire, from the rocks, after the eating, and said, "We must have Phelsh't."

"We do not need it," the new Mother said: "we stay here." But she was merely repeating what the old Mother had said, not from her own conviction or strength, but because that reply had always worked before.

Kesh smiled, and it was a horrible look. "We could have Phelsh't," she said. "Phelsh't of the sweet water, and you prefer this mucky sandpit, this hole in the ground? We could have it easily. I can tell you how."

"No," said the Mother, but someone in the circle said, "Yes. Tell us." It was Sakht, who was another hunter, and who desired Kesh; she had refused him in her Rapture.

Kesh looked at him with scorn: she knew his motives. But she smiled and said, "Listen. Are we not the clan of the Eye? We see in the day, when few can: we move easily over the sand in the sun, those of us who have it. And we are many. What other clan dares fight when the sun is high? They must wait for the dark. But not we. Our spears strike home and do not miss, even when others are blinded."

There was a murmur of approval at this. The Oldest Mother sat looking faintly shocked. Kesh said, "This is my plan. Let a group of us arm ourselves and take good store of food and water, and go to Phelsh't and wait for day to be well risen: and then let us take it, and kill the hunters and warriors, and take their children for our own, those that do not resist. They will not be able to fight us by day, and when we are done we will have the sweet water, and the clan that held Phelsh't will be our slaves."

The reaction was compounded of shock and delight, but the Mother cried, "No! The Eye is secret! It must remain so! If we did such a thing, the other clans would know that we had the Eye, and they would raid us for women and children to bring the blood into their lines as well! Soon they too would have the Eye, and our advantage would be gone!"

The Mother's anger and fright had a curious effect on the hunters: it made them side with Kesh, who though she might be mad, was still mad in a way they had long been familiar with. They murmured against the Mother, and Kesh said sweetly, "What use is an advantage we do not use? What use is the Eye except to win us a great place among clans? We eat better than other tribes, but what use is great plenty of food without water? Let us have the water, and more. Let us use the Eye for something besides seeing. Do we desire favors of other clans? Then let us offer them this great gift—that they may sire children of the Eye on our women, in return for food, or slaves, or what we think fit. We shall grow greater, not less, and rule all the clans of the sand!"

"No!" the Mother cried, but her voice was lost this time in the screaming and shouting, the argument, the sound of fear and desire. The argument sprang up again and again, many a night, around the fire. The Mother contested against it, but feebly, for over against her, on the other side of the fire, Kesh sat every night, saying nothing, smiling, and turned a spearhead over and over in her hands.

And finally the decision was made: the first in the history of the clan to be made without the active consent of the Mother. She let the warriors and the hunters go, at last, keeping enough behind to protect the rest of the clan; and she let them go with relief, for Kesh was at their head, and the Mother was glad to be rid of that terrible smiling regard. She felt sure Kesh would be dead in short order. Indeed, she had told two of the warriors to see to it.

They saw to nothing. They bled their lives out green on the sand as soon as Kesh judged they were far enough out of sight of the camp, for she had heard of the Mother's whispering while doing her own. And she and the warriors and hunters buried the bodies and shouldered their loads of food and water and headed off across the sand toward the upward-pointing finger of Phelsh't, from which had come the wind that had killed Tes. And as they walked, Kesh thought of the reckoning that would now be required of that mountain, and the smile never left her face.

It was a slaughter. The clan of Phelsh't lived like any other clan, out in the open, tented over with skins to protect them from the sun. That they lived on the knees of the mountain was only a slight complication. In the heat of the day, when it was well along, silently the hunters and warriors climbed the stones and looked down on the sleeping clan: and were astonished. They were few—they were barely more in number than the clan of the Eye.

Kesh looked down on this, and her heart was full of bitter thoughts, for if they had come this way in the Wind and taken this place, Tes might still be alive. She hefted her spear, and pointed down at the camp. It was the signal.

The closest hunters knocked the poles down, taking the shading skins with them. The slaughter thus began in confusion—bodies rolling under collapsed hides, voices raised to shout in surprise—and then turned to terror as the hunters of the Eye leapt down and wielded their spears to terrible purpose. Surprise did much of the work: the sun did the rest, beating down from a frightfully clear sky, making eyes not shielded from it wince and water, making the Phelsh't hunters stagger helplessly. The stones ran green, and more frightening to the Phelsh't people than the slaughter, almost, was the sound of a woman laughing, and laughing, and laughing, through the cries and the blood.

Three-quarters of the Phelsh't died, but not their Oldest Mother. Her Kesh took aside, and laid her sharp flake of knife-stone against her throat and let her see her people die—let her see the hunters bind the women and the children. And to her Kesh said, "Your clan is mine now. If you resist us, I will kill you all. But if you accept us, we will teach you our art by which we see in the day; your clan will become great as ours is great. And in return for this favor, you will serve us: and we will live among you and share your water: and we will be as brothers and sisters to you."

And Kesh smiled.

The Oldest Mother agreed to all she said. Kesh left her, then, and went up the mountainside, past the place where the ironwood grew in wild abundance, and the trees grew as tall as a man: but she had no eye for them. She climbed up among the rocks to the place where the cleft in the stone was deep, and the water ran down. And there she found it, the cold water, the sweet water, welling up in a hollow as deep as she was tall, as wide as her arms could span; spilling over, spilling out like light, running down the stone, whispering, singing softly as it ran. She reached down and plunged her face in, plunged in the whole upper half of her body, stood up cold and wet all over, shaking the wet hair out of her eyes. She went down so to her people, and none of them could tell, with the water running down her face, how much of it was tears.

They took Phelsh't for their own, did the clan of the Eye; they took the other Oldest Mother to be second Oldest to their own, but Kesh spoke for both for many years. Tribe after tribe heard of their gift, or of the well, and came to try to steal one or the other from them: but those that came were driven off with a ferocity they could hardly understand, or were taken captive and offered the same bargain that the Phelsh't had been offered. The Eye slowly began to spread itself through the Vulcan gene pool, and the clan made it plain that other gifts were welcome too: the long sight, the ability to dream true, the touch on the shoulder that sends a foe asleep, or kills—they traded the Eye for these and grew great. The effects of this amateur eugenics program were many, down the years, and sometimes strange. It became traditional for clans to marry out their sons and daughters in exchange for children of another clan who possessed some desirable trait. Many thousands of years later, a Starfleet officer's career was saved by the Eye; a little thing, in a long history of careful or savage changes that shifted the nature of the Vulcan species.

But Kesh would have cared nothing for it all. Her they feared and respected for many years, never daring to question her ways. She would go off on long journeys and come back pale and haggard from weeks in the sand, and none dared ask her where she had been. When they finally found her in the well, head first, drowned, they took her as far out in the sand as they could and buried her there; and then many of the clan of the Eye felt they had peace for the first time in many years. And indeed they were better off than they had ever been—there was no denying that.

But when T'Khut rode high, and her copper face gazed at itself in the well, some clansmen claimed they heard weeping, or terrible laughter. They were laughed at by others, of course. But nevertheless, at such times, the clan went thirsty till the moon went down. . . .

Enterprise: Four

Jim sat in his cabin on the *Enterprise* the next morning, gazing at the small data screen in annoyance.

FROM: Bugs
DATE: 7611.01
SUBJECT: Our Friends in the Federation

From an editorial published on one of the major Vulcan information services:

> . . . this bloody sword hanging in our skies. this machine of war. should be ordered away immediately by our government. Yet no action is taken. Creatures who solve their problems with bloodshed rather than reason now orbit our planet without hindrance. Why is it that. though they declare their missions to be peaceful. their ships nonetheless are equipped with weapons that could crack a planet open? Can they not perceive even this most massive evidence of illogic? There can be nothing but disaster in dealing with such creatures as if they were civilized. Indeed. we have been trying to civilize them for almost two hundred years. but the result of our efforts is apparent in the skies over ta'Valsh and Seleya. . . .

Hmm. Yellow journalism? Or green?

Jim fumed quietly. On one hand he was very glad to have seen the message—it certainly confirmed what T'Pau had been saying—but on the other hand, he wanted more and more to know who Bugs was.

Not that he could find out, of course. Here was one of the places where the crew's privacy had to be respected utterly: otherwise the whole system of the BBS lost its value. Speech here, at least, had to be free.

And pretty free it is, Jim thought, annoyed. He kept paging through the messages. There were many agreeing with Bugs, annoyed at being considered a "bloody sword." There were some who refused to take the quote seriously at all, and others who suspected it had been taken out of context, and one who pointed out that Bugs was probably in violation of copyright by transcribing the message from the Vulcan information service without obtaining permission. But the last reply to the message brought Jim up short:

FROM: Llarian
DATE: 7611.72
SUBJECT: Re: Our Friends in the Federation

A skillful leader does not use force.
A skillful fighter does not feel anger.

A skillful master does not engage the opponent.
A skillful employer remains low.

Even four thousand years ago they knew it: don't believe
everything you read.

How about that, Jim thought, and gazed at the screen with interest.
*Llarian. Now who would that be? And what's the reference? It sounds familiar
somehow.* Jim chewed absently on the one knuckle of his folded hands. *But he or she
or it has a point. "A skillful employer remains low." Who in Vulcan has enough
power and influence to get something like that into the information services?*
He started to shut the screen down, then paused for a moment and reached out
to touch the communicator toggle on his desk. "Bridge. Communications."
"Communications, Uhura," came her cheerful voice. *"Good morning, Captain!"*
Jim rubbed his head ruefully. He still had a touch of headache from the party
last night: the high gravity seemed to have that effect on him. "More or less, Nyota,"
he said. "Screen dump coming in to your station. Have the computer run a check on
it. I want to know which Vulcan news service it came from, the name of the author,
the date, any other information you find pertinent."
"Aye aye, Captain. Ready."
Jim touched the key to instruct the desk screen to dump its contents to the
Communications board. "Got it?"
"It's in. Will advise, Captain."
"Good. Kirk out."
He stood up, stretched, rubbed his head again. His knees still ached, too. *I could
always have Environmental get me a grav neutralizer,* he thought . . . then rejected the
thought immediately. Vulcans probably thought Earth people were weak and delicate
enough as it was: why help the image along by showing up in a neutralizer? He would
take their gravity with the best of them, and be damned to the whole lot of them.
Still, his head hurt. He reached down to the communicator toggle on his desk.
"Sickbay."
"Sickbay," said a cheerful voice. *"Burke here."*
It was Lia Burke, McCoy's head nurse since Chapel had started working full-
time on her doctorate. "Lia," Jim said, "where's the doctor?"
"He's gone downplanet already, Captain. Said he was looking for something."
That made Jim blink: McCoy was not exactly an early riser by preference. "Did
he say what?"
*"He said if you called and asked, I was to tell you he was going to buy a gross
of paperweights with snowflakes inside them. Sir."* Lia sounded mildly bemused.
She's not alone, Jim thought. "All right. Listen, I need something for my head."
"High-grav syndrome," she said immediately. *"I can prescribe you a little
something for that. Come on down."*
Jim put an eyebrow up. "Nurses can prescribe?"
There was a brief silence on the other end, and then a laugh. *"Are you living in
the twentieth century? Sir. Of course we can."* There was a brief, wry pause. *"We
can* count, *too."*
"Noted," Jim said. "I'll be right down."
When he got to sickbay, Lia was scribbling something with a lightpen on a com-

puter pad. She was a little curly-haired woman, very slender, almost always smiling; it took something particularly grave to remove that smile. "Captain," she said, putting down the pad and picking up a hypospray. "Here you go."

"Am I allowed to ask you what it is?"

"Would you ask Dr. McCoy?" she said.

Jim considered. "Probably not."

She gave him a cheerful shame-on-you! sort of look. "Well, then. It's just hemo-corticovilidine; it thins your blood out a little."

"Thins it out? When I'm going to Vulcan? Get away from me with that thing."

"Too late," she said, and it was: the spray hissed against his arm. "It simply changes the density of your blood plasma slightly, on demand from the air pressure on the outside, or lack of it. The problem on these high-grav planets is similar to high-altitude syndrome some ways." She put the hypo away. "But you should drink extra water while you're down there."

"Lieutenant," Jim said patiently, "there's a problem with drinking extra water on a heavy-gravity planet. . . ."

She raised her eyebrows at him. "Tell me about it. But unless you want your head to ache, you'd better do it."

"All right," he said, and thanked her, and headed back to his cabin. *Well, I should head down to Vulcan and stir around a little, see some people and things. Then go visit with Sarek and Amanda. They've only invited me to their house about ten times.*

. . . But paperweights? What's Bones up to?

Leonard Edward McCoy was a researcher at heart. The tendency had almost kept him out of active practice, when he first got his M.D.: the year of pure research he had done at Cornell had come close to spoiling him. But when it came down to the crunch, he liked people better than papers and test tubes and lectures: and he had dived into practice and never looked back.

But every now and then a nice juicy piece of research came his way, and when it did, by God he got his teeth into it and didn't let go until he was satisfied with the answers. And a nice one had fallen right in his lap yesterday. It had that perfect feeling about it, the kind of feeling he had when as a kid he would be out in the north forty and find a big flat rock that he *knew* had lots of bugs under it.

It was Shath that did it to him. Not that the son wasn't just the most irritating thing he had come across in a long time: but the man's body language was wrong, completely wrong. On seeing himself and Kirk, the guy had actually had to leave the room for many minutes to regain his composure. It would have been unusual in a human: it was positively shocking in a Vulcan. And the reaction was not to him, McCoy felt certain, but to Kirk.

He had considered going up to the consulate and demanding to see the man again, fabricating some story about a change in schedule or something, to talk to him a bit longer and make sure of that aversion reaction, or the lack of it. But then Bones considered that it would probably be wasted effort: likely enough Shath would be able to cover up the effect this time. No, McCoy would get his information in other ways.

He spent a little time in his cabin that morning calling up detailed maps of shi'Kahr, the little city nearest the Science Academy, and found what he wanted—the electronic equivalent of the public library. He could have gotten into it from the ship, via downlink from the main computers, but he had no desire to attract quite that much attention. Discreet inquiry was what he wanted, not an electronic snatch-and-run mission that might leave the librarians feeling annoyed.

He then indulged himself in a little bit of subterfuge and went rummaging in the packages he had brought home from his shopping trip yesterday. *A word or two in Spock's ear was a good idea*, he thought, as he took out the somber tunic and breeches and boots he had picked up. They were all in a soft tan beige color, very inconspicuous, and Spock had told him that the cut was such as a student or scientist might wear for either work or relaxation. McCoy slipped the clothes on, tapped one of his closet doors into reflectivity, and turned from side to side to admire himself. He really did look rather good: the slight cape hanging from the shoulders somehow made him look about ten pounds lighter, which he didn't mind at all. And this suit of clothes would definitely attract less attention than a Starfleet uniform. Most people knew his face best in conjunction with his uniform anyway. But in this getup he was just one more Terran on Vulcan, out for a day's research—there were quite a few Earth people working at the Science Academy.

He stopped in to check sickbay, found everything well, and then beamed down to the streets of shi'Kahr. It was just past dawn there, and the town was getting lively: the very early hours, before things got too hot even for the Vulcans' liking, were when much business and marketing were done. Depending on the nature of one's work, one might start at dawn, work through till noonish, break till three for a siesta, and then start up again and not leave work till well after dark. *Or*, he thought as he strolled through the streets, *being Vulcans, they might just work for four days without stopping, and then take a day off, and then—back to it. The stamina of these people! You have to admire it—and wish you could have some yourself. . . .*

The town reminded him, in some ways, of some university towns he had been to in upstate New York: but there was also a strange resemblance to the roofed arcades of Berne in Switzerland—thick stone walls with wide arches cut in them, sheltering the windows and doorways of shops and houses. In places the arcades were two-tiered, and most of them were of a handsome golden stone with a wide grainy texture: McCoy suspected it was a very effective insulator. The pathways under the arcades were wide, and there was room to stroll comfortably, sheltered from the sun and wind, and look out through the arches at the little parks and plazas one passed. The Vulcans seemed to be great ones for tiny parks, each one always with its fountain; and never the same kind twice. Little whispering waterfalls, fine misty sprays, strange carved beasts with water pouring out of them, once even an ancient mill-stone with water bubbling up out of the hole in the middle, he saw them all on his way to the library.

This turned out to be a noble building of the same golden stone as most of the rest of the town, but this one had a portico borne up on tall smooth pillars, all of which had the slightest swelling at their centers. The effect was actually to make them look straighter than if they had been built perfectly straight. The trick was one with which McCoy was familiar from ancient Greek architecture, and he smiled at the familiarity as he passed into the shade of the portico and into the library.

Inside everything was utterly modern—computer carrels and voice accesses were everywhere. The floor looked like the same golden stone as the walls, but McCoy was fascinated to find that it appeared to have been treated with something that made it spongy-soft: sound fell dead in it. He nodded a greeting to the librarian at the front desk and headed on past him toward the carrels.

He did not trust his typing in Vulcan. He stopped by one of the keyboard carrels and peered at the keying area: it had more keys and levers and switches than he wanted to see, so he passed on to a voice-activated carrel and sat down. Softly he cleared his throat, praying that his accent wouldn't be too outrageous for the machine to understand.

"General query," he said in Vulcan.

"Acknowledged," said the machine. Bones winced. Its accent was the Vulcan equivalent of BBC Standard Received: pure, cultured, and somewhat intimidating.

"Public events," McCoy said. "Cross-index to registry. *Koon-ut-kalifi.* Familial name uncertain. One participant for cross-index: Spock cha'Sarek. Go."

The machine thought about this for a second, then brought up a picture of the Place of Marriage and Challenge: Spock, McCoy, and Kirk in the background, T'Pau on her litter, and an assortment of spear carriers and extras with bell-banners and various implements of destruction. McCoy shivered at the sight of the place, and was surprised at his own reaction. *What a horrendous day that was . . . and what a naughty thing I did.* He smiled a little. *And worth it.* "Confirmed," McCoy said. "Display list of participants."

Obediently it did so. And there it was: Shath cha'Stelen hei-Nekhlavah, age 43 standard years. *How about that,* McCoy thought: *I hit his age right on. Maybe Spock is teaching me something after all.* "Query," he said. "General information, Shath cha'Stelen."

Another page of information came up. Most of it was not very interesting: information about education, occupation, a commcode. *Not that I'd want to call him up and invite him on a night out: no indeed.* But at the bottom was a little list of Affiliated Organizations. McCoy had the carrel's printer note them all down, and then he began to go through the files and pull down some of the organizations' most recent publications. The names were mostly very innocent: the Institute for Interworld Studies, the Study Group on Nonvulcanoid Species, names like that. But what McCoy noticed, as he began reading their newsletters and papers, was that none of the organizations Shath belonged to liked humans very much. One of them was of the condescending let-them-swing-in-their-trees sort: the others were outright smear rags—there was no kinder word for them.

McCoy sat back after about half an hour of reading, very upset, actually shaking a little. *This is not something I wanted to find out about Vulcans,* he thought. *There are Vulcan bigots. Right here where Surak taught, and died.* He shook his head. "Damn."

"Null input," the computer said politely in Vulcan.

"Sorry. Cross-reference. Lists of membership of all the above organizations. Star or otherwise indicate members who are also members of other listed organizations."

"Working," said the machine. "Output?"

"Print."

"Acknowledged," said the machine, and began spitting out truly astonishing amounts of the fine thin plastic that Vulcans used for printout. McCoy watched with amazement as it piled up.

The printing did not stop for nearly twenty minutes. When it did, there was a stack of printout some three inches thick, all in very tiny print, and McCoy shook his head. "Solid duplication also," he said.

"Working," said the computer, and after about three seconds spat out a data solid at him.

"End."

"Credit authorization, please," the machine said sweetly.

McCoy rolled his eyes, felt around for his down-planet "cash" solid, stuck it in the slot, let the machine click and whirr and deduct however much money from it. It spat the solid back at him almost with the air of a machine unsatisfied with the amount of money spent. "Hmf," McCoy said to it, pocketed the solid, picked up the printout, and headed out.

He made his way to the little restaurant where they had been before. It was open early, as most Vulcan restaurants and refectories were, for the day-meal. "Lasagna, please," he said to the waiter, and started going through the printout. It was going to be a long morning.

Or so he thought. Five minutes into his reading, he found a name that brought him bolt upright in his chair. Very soon thereafter he found it again, and again.

"Damn," he said. "Damn. *Damn.*"

After a long time he put the printout aside and ate his lasagna, even though he wasn't sure he had the appetite for it anymore.

The world dissolved from sparkle to solidity around Jim as he beamed down. He found himself in a little park, like many he and Spock and McCoy had seen the day before. This one Spock had described to him in detail: there were three paths that wound out of it, and Jim was to take the one that led off to the left, toward the old city wall.

He took that path, walking slowly. It was a pleasant park: the "grass" was some sort of tough dun-colored growth, broken with tiny, delicate trees with feathery maroon-colored leaves. They looked, in fact, almost exactly like giant feather-dusters. Out of curiosity Jim went over to one and touched it . . . and was very surprised when the entire branch folded its leaves away and rolled itself into a tight spiral.

"Sorry," he said, and then laughed at himself. *Do Vulcans talk to trees, I wonder?*

Slowly the branch unrolled and unfurled its leaves once more. Jim restrained himself from touching it again—no reason to make a plant crazy—and headed down the path that led toward the old city wall. It curved broadly, to parallel the wall. Now he recognized where he was: he followed the curve of the path, and sheltered from view by an outcropping of rock, he saw the house.

It was fairly large by Vulcan standards, though not as large as one might expect the house of the Ambassador Extraordinary to Terra to be. It was built all on one level, as most of the houses here seemed to be: Vulcans seemed to have an aversion to blocking away others' view of the sky. The place, in fact, with its surrounding wall just higher than eye-height, looked rather like something one of the old "post-modern" architects might have built, with curves rather than sharp corners. But at the same time it had a look about it of the old Roman villas: a house that looked inward, rather than outward, and kept its secrets and its privacies to itself.

He went up to the gate in the wall and touched the annunciator plate. "James Kirk," he said when it glowed.

"Jim," came Amanda's voice, very cheerful, "come on in." The gate swung open for him.

A narrow path bordered with stones led to the front door of the house. It opened as he stepped toward it, and there was Amanda, wearing a coverall, rather stained around the knees, with a pair of pruning shears in her hand. "Welcome!" she said. "Come in and see the garden! I'll give you the two-credit tour later. Or Sarek can do it when he gets back from town. Would you like something cold to drink?"

"Yes, please," Jim said. Amanda guided him in through the front hall. It was large, and the rooms were built on the open plan: the living area and dining area and kitchen were all one clean, beautiful sprawl of rough or polished black stone, and the rear wall was one large window with dilating panels that gave on the garden.

"Here," Amanda said, stopping by the drinks dispenser in the kitchen. "Water? Something carbonated?"

"Soda water would be fine."

"I'll join you." Two glasses slid out from behind a panel. "Cheers," she said, lifting one of them in salute, handing him the other.

They both drank thirstily. "Oh, that's much better," Amanda said. "I worked up such a thirst. Come on this way." She led him out the dilation, into the garden. Most of it was raked sand and gravel, but one patch about thirty feet square was given over to rose-bushes. Several were in profuse bloom: some had no bloom at all, having been cut back.

"That's amazing," Jim said. "I'm still astonished those things will even grow here."

"Oh, they do well enough," Amanda said. "It's no worse than, say, Arizona would be, as long as you keep them watered. And they seem to like the spectrum of a white sun a little better than a yellow one. You know what will really grow wonderfully here?" She pointed off to one side, where some small new plants had been set in. "Tomatoes. They're pigs for water in this climate; they need a soaker at their roots all day. But you should see how they look after a couple of months. I have to hand-pollinate them, but I don't mind that."

Jim shook his head. "You've been pruning the roses back pretty hard," he said.

Amanda nodded. "We haven't been here for two years, remember," she said. "We have a gardener who comes in and takes care of things, but he's best with the native Vulcan plants, the succulents over there, and the sandplants. I don't think Vulcans really understand about roses: they think they're delicate. But to bring out the best in them, you have to be mean to them." She clicked the shears meaningfully.

"I have trouble believing you could be mean to anything," Jim said.

Amanda looked at him kindly. "Flatterer," she said. "Come here and sit down in the shade."

They went over to a bench under a pergola smothered with some kind of leafy vine. Amanda settled herself on it and looked out at the garden. "You know," she said after a moment, "there were a lot of times when we were raising Spock that I felt I was being mean to him. At the same time I felt I had to: Sarek and I agreed that Spock needed to grow up as a normal Vulcan child, with the disciplines that Vulcan children have to deal with. If we had been on Earth, it might have been different. Earth people are a little more flexible about such things. But Vulcans expect . . ." She broke off, then looked a little bemused. "They expect you to be very conservative. Everything has to meet the status quo . . . everything has to be the same."

And Amanda smiled. "It doesn't make much sense in terms of the IDIC, does it? Sometimes I think things have slipped a little."

Jim nodded. "I can see your point."

They sat there in silence for a few minutes, enjoying the wind, which was not too hot to be unpleasant as yet, and much softened by the wall around the garden. "May I ask you something?" Jim said.

"Ask."

He gestured at the garden. "You're pruning the roses as if everything was going to turn out all right, later this week. . . ."

She gazed at the roses and then let out a long breath. "Well," she said, "I'm a gardener. No matter what happens, the roses need pruning."

Jim smiled.

"But you're right," she said. "I'm worried." She turned the shears over in her hand, studying the blades. "If the vote for secession goes through," she said, "the ban will certainly fall on me. The government will certainly not be in a mood to allow exceptions—certainly not at the highest levels: it would be seen in some quarters as nepotism, favoritism. I will have to leave Vulcan—or Sarek will."

Jim shook his head. "It doesn't seem fair."

"Oh, there's nothing fair about it," Amanda said, "but if the vote goes for secession—" She sighed and looked around at the garden and the house. "I gave up one home, a long time ago," she said softly. "I suppose I can manage it again."

"Giving up a home isn't the same as giving up a husband, though."

She nodded. "We will find somewhere else, I suppose," she said. "The Federation would be glad to have Sarek. And Spock certainly is in no danger of losing his present job."

"Lord, no."

"But at the same time," Amanda said, "think of it from Sarek's point of view. To have to leave your homeworld forever: never again to see the rest of your family: to be an exile on cold damp worlds, never to feel a sun that's warm enough—or if you do, to have it shining on you in a strange sky—" She shook her head.

"You must excuse my wife, Captain," said Sarek, coming into the garden and slipping out of his over-tunic: "she is obviously exercising the Scots part of her heritage, which she has described to me as 'predicting gloom an' doom.' " He laid the overtunic neatly over the back of another bench nearby and sat down.

"Did your business go well?" Amanda said.

Sarek nodded. "As well as could be expected. The town is becoming positively tense. At least, so I would describe the atmosphere, having seen it on Earth many times: I have never seen the like here before. But then, the like has never happened."

"Tomorrow we start debate?" Jim said.

"Tomorrow. Some of the less, shall we say, 'loaded' testimonies will come first. K's't'lk, various other scientists, economists, and so forth. Then the people arguing for ethical reasons. Then the professional liaisons—such as ambassadors and starship captains."

"Sarek," Jim said, "about last night—"

"It happened," Sarek said, "but I would not advise you to tell anyone else about it, save for Spock and the doctor. That one prefers to keep her doings quiet, and it is usually wise to respect her wishes."

There was a soft chime from inside the house, and an amplified voice said, "It's McCoy."

"Speak of the devil and you see his horns," Jim said.

"Let us not get into *that* again," Sarek said, rather emphatically.

"Doctor, come in!" Amanda said, and got up to greet him at the door.

"The doctor sounds winded," Sarek said. "I hope he is not unwell. The heat can take people by surprise here."

Amanda ushered McCoy in a few moments later. He was sweating and was wearing an expression that Jim had seen on him before—a combination of excitement and dread. "Bones, are you all right?" Jim said.

"No," McCoy said, and handed Jim a thick printout. "Look through that."

Jim did, mystified. McCoy turned to Sarek. "I was out following up a hunch I'd had," he said. "These anti-Federation, anti-Terran organizations that have been around the past century or so: I was doing some reading of their latest publications this morning."

"No wonder you look distressed," Sarek said, with an expression of distaste.

"It gets worse. I pulled their membership lists and did some correlation. Shath," McCoy said to Jim, "he's prominent. But you know who else is?"

Jim stared at the printout, looking at a circled name on one list. "T'Pring," he said. And turned several pages. "T'Pring. T'Pring."

He riffled through the rest of the printout, then folded it back up and laid it aside. They all looked at one another: Sarek looking nonplussed, Amanda amazed and angry, McCoy apprehensive, Jim simply astonished.

"I think we'd better call Spock and let him in on this," McCoy said.

Jim nodded while Bones got out his communicator.

Dear Lord, he thought. *T'Pring.*

Hell hath no fury . . .

Vulcan: Four

The old woman sat by her window, looking down on the spires of the city, and sighed, stirring uncomfortably on her bench covered with furs. The silences of the evening were falling: past the edge of the lands, her lands, T'Khut was sliding toward the edge of the sky, her bright crescent a rusty sickle holding darkness between its downpointing horns, and a sprinkling of wildfire sparks: so she looked, and for the time being, that was appropriate. Doings were toward that would release those fires at last, and the woman leaned on her windowsill and waited. There was no need to send her mind out on quest, to touch and pry. Soon enough, those she desired would come to her. There was nothing to do but wait, now.

Mind had made Vulcan different from the start. How many thousands of years, now, since the arts of mind had begun to spring up among men in earnest? They had made all the difference, for without them there would have been no taming the terrible place. It was one of their names for the world, *ah'Hrak,* the Forge. The name would have been an irony, nothing more, despite the melted mountaintops that one could still see in places, if it had not been for the arts of the mind, the inner magics that could draw things from the stubborn crust of the world that no tool could.

Vulcan was metal-poor. Or rather, most of its metals were trapped well below the crust, in the mantle that no one knew yet how to tap, and in the seething core. No tool that men could make, in those first days, could dig deep enough to find metal in any great amount. The smiths of ancient days, when they came to invent their craft, might have to spend years wandering the world, scratching at its surface, gathering enough ore to make one sword, one spear, and never another again. So matters remained for a long time. Stone was cut only with stone: a house might be a life's work: a plough was a precious commodity that a whole community would finance together and take turns using. And even then, frequently all they had to plough was sand.

But it all changed. Mind changed everything. To the first arts—the bonding of mind to mind, the touch that incapacitates, speech-without-words—others slowly began to be added. Sometimes they occurred naturally and spread themselves through the gene pool on their own, like the internal corneal nictitating membrane that protected the eye from excessive light. But some were sports, and the houses in which they sprang up cultivated them and made them a source of power or wealth. To one of the ancient houses, for example, was born a child who could feel where metal was. That house secretly hired every smith they could find, and after some small number of years—a hundred or so—had massed enough metal weapons to take thousands of acres for their own, while most houses had to be content with several hundred. Another house had produced a child with an even more precious gift—the ability to feel water. When this was discovered, the child was fought over, kidnapped back and forth, and finally died many years later, in misery, an old and broken man. But the trait bred true in the children he was forced to sire, and soon spread through the gene pool; now it was a poor sort of house that did not have a waterseer, and enough water for all its needs. One had to dig deep, but the water was there. It had opened the way for technology: for enough food and enough time to do something besides hunt and survive. Vulcan became civilized, began to pursue pleasure and exploration: began to practice war as an art form, rather than the rather sordid necessity it had always been until natural resources began to be more easily available. And of course there were forays, as one House decided another had something it needed or wanted. Rarely did patience last through much in the way of negotiation: that was not how Vulcan had become what it had become. The occasional war broke out over the theft of a well-drilling technique or the kidnapping of an adept of one of the more useful mindsciences; the rich and powerful raided one another's people as the tribal chiefs had raided one another's herdbeasts in the longago. These days, at best a stolen talent could make one's fortune. At worst, it was something to pass the time.

The woman stirred again on her couch, then stood up and began to walk to and fro. She had no eyes for the rich appointments of the room, the tapestries and carpets, the rare treasures of art in stone and carved bone and bright metal. Her reflection in the mirror—a sheet of polished bronze that would have been the price of a kingdom, once—she passed again and again, taking no heed of it. *The waiting is hard,* she thought. No matter that she had become expert at it, these many years past. This particular prize she had waited for for a long, long time, moving subtly toward it, never being seen to be too hungry, too eager. And now everything was ripe, and tonight, perhaps, or tomorrow, it would come to her of her own free will. She turned her eyes again to the sickle of T'Khut, and lust glittered in them. *Soon,* she thought. *Quite soon.*

A small gong chimed softly on the worktable she kept in the chamber. She went to it, touched the control attached to it. "Speak."

"Madam, the lord Evekh is here and desires to see you." The voice on the other end of the comm sounded frightened. "My apologies, lady, for troubling you so late, but he would not leave without seeing you."

"Bid him enter," the woman said. She sat down by the windowsill again, on her couch, and gazed out on the spires of the city, as if more concerned with that view than with the setting crescent easing itself toward the horizon, shimmering uncannily in the uprising heat.

The carved doors swung open, and Nesheh, her maid, let the visitor in. The woman heard the soft rustle of stiff, rich robes behind her, ignored them till they stopped, then turned. There he stood, Evekh, all in a splendor of embroidery of violet brocade and silver wire, with *lasha* stones set in a great silvern collar at his neck: they caught the lamplight and a gleam or so from sinking T'Khut and gave it back in a shimmer of opalescent violet. Above all the finery, there was the plain, hard, blunt face, noble in its way; but the cruel eyes hinted that the nobility had fallen on hard times. That was all to her advantage. She made a graceful gesture of welcome. "A social call, I take it, my lord," she said.

"Lady Suvin," he said, and held his hands up to her in reverence. "Yes."

"At such an hour." Now that he was here, finally here, she could not resist baiting him a little. "Do sit, then. Will you take water with me?"

"Gladly."

She stepped over to the little singing fall in the corner, chose two cups from the sideboard. All were a message in themselves. The waterfall spoke of the wealth of someone who could afford to have such a thing directed seven floors up from the living stone; the cups were of perfect design, simple and clean in a time when more obvious ostentation would have had them covered with rare gems from the Hehei or gilded in platinum electroplate. Suvin despised gauds of that sort: or if she stooped to them, she made sure they far surpassed anything else a rival might find. The cups were of simple enough design, but each one was carved of a single nightfire, all black with glitters of gold in it, like T'Khut outside the window.

She filled the cups, gave one to her guest, and sat down on a bench opposite him. They drank, first, without speaking, as the guest had by the proper laws of hospitality to be refreshed before telling his tale. "Tell me, then," Suvin said when the cups were half drained, "since this is a social call, how fares your family? How does your lady wife?"

It was meant to be an arrow in his side, and the flicker of rage that went across his face told her that it had gone home. "She is as well as can be expected."

"Ah, I am glad to hear it. And the family prospers."

He said nothing.

"I am glad to hear it," she said again. "These are such busy times for all of us."

"For you, at least," Evekh said. "The lesser houses rally behind you, I see."

"They have seen the sense of what we mean to do," she said. She turned and gazed out the window. T'Khut was half set: through a gap in the towers one could see that the horns of the crescent were beneath the horizon now, and the crescent made a sort of bright bridge, with a few sparks of fire caught under it. "The latest researches have proved very compelling indeed. There is metal beyond our wildest dreams—iron, steel, rare metals, and rare earths—lying scattered about T'Khut like pebbles. No need to dig for it. Untold riches lie there, and untold rewards for our people and our industry. We must get there: it hangs so close. We can do it. And now we shall."

He sat silent. She knew what he was thinking. *It should have been us. Unfair, unfair*—Suvin felt like laughing out loud to mock him, saying, *Your house had its chances and let them slip: now reap what you have sown!* And it would have been true enough. Evekh's house was anciently involved with trade. Many centuries back, as the smaller city-states grew up and goods began to be traded between them, his house had come to run the caravans that went back and forth between the tiny outposts of the civilization that was then Vulcan. The great difficulty with handling many such caravans at a time had proved to be communications: without it, there was no way to predict when goods would arrive, where they were in transit, whether they would be late. Evekh's forefathers had solved the problem by hiring, buying, or kidnapping as many people as they could find who had the talent of clear mindspeech at a distance. Then they had begun a selective breeding program, and bred the talent true, and increased its power and honed the training of it until the talent was no longer an accidental thing that worked only in times of stress, but a predictable and manageable power that would operate over thousands of miles. It made them rich and powerful enough so that, after some centuries, Evekh's house let the caravan-trade-cum-overland-shipping-corporation go, and concentrated on psi-communications technologies alone. Their people were in demand all over the planet, except in one regard . . . and Suvin knew it.

"We are quite close," Suvin said, so casually that it could not possibly be regarded as a taunt. "The hulls of the first two ships are complete, now, and the instrumentation is being installed by the various lesser houses." She looked out the window as the last scrap of T'Khut slipped beneath the horizon. The sky grew dark, except for the red Eye and the white one, that gazed down brightly enough to cast faint shadows. Outside the window, somewhere in the middle air, a nightvoice spoke: a sweet, mournful sound, answered just as mournfully from somewhere close by. "We will launch for the first time at the end of the year."

"So soon," Evekh said.

Suvin nodded. Inside, she was shaking with mirth that she dare not show. It would lose her too much, just for the sake of a little entertainment. "I should like to speed things up somewhat," she said, "but there seems no way at this point; we are depending mostly on machines, except for the construction itself."

"And more speed would make that much difference?"

"The difference between eighteen million *nakh* next year," she said, "and four thousand million." She paused enough for the thought to sink in like water into sand. "It is a matter of the subsidiary voyages," she said, "out to the sister planets. The delay of normal ether-wave communications adds a certain unavoidable delay to the process of assessment and pickup of the raw materials. Delay is costly, as usual. . . ."

She trailed off. *And psi-communication is instantaneous. Come along, old fool. Make a fine show of pride for me, so that I can offer you what I have for you.*

Suvin waited. It was just as well for her that Evekh had no training in his family's gift and could not hear her. Otherwise this deal would be much more difficult to drive.

Evekh drank from his cup. After a little while he said, rather tightly, "I have often wished that my family had not let the transportation side of our House fall into decline."

I dare say—because if they had not, you would be sitting in my place now: the place of one about to be mistress of the richest and most powerful House on the planet, one that even kings bow to, knowing their betterment when they see it. "Evekh," she said, again so casually, "surely you could come into it again if you wanted to."

She watched him look at the meaning under her words, watched him shy away from it, with another flicker of anger in his face. Perhaps he was getting the feeling he was being toyed with. *Ah, softly: have a care.* "We would be glad to ally with you in this regard," she said. And added, "If you would have us."

The five words took the rage that had abruptly shown on his face and as abruptly erased it. He was silent for a minute or more, looking at the cup in his hands. "Our house is somewhat fallen from its early grandeur," he said, trying to make light of it.

"Ah, hardly," Suvin said.

He looked sharply at her. She looked back, a frank and dissembling look that was meant to say, *But I meant it.*

He swallowed his pride again. She watched with mild astonishment. It was worth all her waiting, this delicate debasement. She knew quite well that pride was at the root: that Evekh could not bear the sight of what he considered a young upstart house advanced far beyond his . . . and his own house reduced in wealth and status. Only that had made him refuse her first offer of alliance, some years ago. But now he was tasting the bitterness his pride had brought him to: his own house and his lady wife were not beyond reminding him of their opinion of this situation from time to time. *Pain, and pride: we will see which is stronger. I think I know. . . .*

Suvin put the look on her face of a woman who has a sudden thought. "If you would be willing," she said, "there would be a way to do this that could not invoke a question of loss of face, if that concerns you." *If!*

Evekh blinked. "Speak on, lady."

"A binding. I have a grandson of age. He is past the Raptures without ill effect, and we were looking him out a match among one of the nobler houses. Surely yours would be one of those."

Evekh looked slightly pale for a moment. "We have no one who would suit, I fear."

"Ah, but surely you do. That youngest right-line daughter of yours. T'Thelaih, that's her name, is it not?"

Evekh stared at Suvin in shock.

"And what is more," she said, "after the wedding, we would *keep* her."

Evekh was quite still for several minutes. "And the groom-price?" he said.

Suvin shrugged. "That would be negotiable. But the match is a noble one, and the alliance between our houses would be most profitable, both in the short and long terms. Your share—it would certainly be at least five percent of our takings. As for the groom-price—shall we say," and she paused for thought she had taken long ago, "all the extant adepts of the Last Thought long-range psi-communications technique, and their offspring? And all necessary chemical training and teaching materials. That should more than suffice our space program's needs for many years."

There was a long, long silence: and then Evekh began to curse her. He cursed her in the names of gods that had been removed from the official calendar, and gods that had not, and in the names of beasts and men, and in the name of the One Who Does Not Hear. She sat unmoved, and when she spoke again, it was as if nothing had happened.

"Does the offer please?"

"It pleases," Evekh said heavily. "I will have my bailiff see yours tomorrow to make the instrument of binding. May I call on you tomorrow evening?"

"It would be my pleasure."

Evekh got up, then, and bowed. Not hands up in reverence, but the bent-double bow, showing the back of the neck, of a new-bought slave. And he went from there with no other word.

Well-pleased, Suvin gazed out the window a few minutes longer . . . then called her maid to prepare her couch.

She slept soundly for the first time in many months and got up in the morning in a good temper, to the astonishment of the household staff. Then, her toilet and levee done, she sent for her grandson.

Their meeting was brief and to the point. It was nooning: the family was resting at such a time, but for Suvin that made little odds, and they knew better, by and large, to fly in her face about such little things. When she called them, they came.

Mahak stood before her and fidgeted, looking about him at all the rich and costly things, and obviously wondering why under the moon he, the least of the family, had suddenly been called up here. She let him stand there and worry for a moment, pretending to work as she did. *He is goodly enough to look at, I'll give him that,* she thought. He was dark-visaged but well favored, with great dark eyes and a long face, and well made in his body.

"You are to be bonded," she said, without any preliminaries, "to a daughter of Old House Yehenik, at the full of T'Khut. You may go to the merchants and arrange the festivities to your liking: so long as the binding is properly carried out, I do not care about the expense. See to it."

Astonished, he bowed and went out without a word. Soon this information would be all over the house and out into the streets, where the professional gossipmongers would get their hands on it and spread it all over the planet . . . some of them using Evekh's techniques. There was a choice irony to it. To Suvin, her grandson was a playing-piece, one of many: she cared little enough about him to hear what else the tongues would be wagging about—that he was unlikely to survive his binding night. Even if he did, she was unconcerned. *But it would be better far if he did not,* she thought, *for then my old enemies will have given me their most priceless asset, and they will get nothing in return. Nothing. While I will have everything they have . . .*

. . . and perhaps something more.

Smiling, she went to her work.

When T'Thelaih heard of it, her first response was to rage, and then to weep. But she dared do nothing else. Her father, who had made the match, she saw perhaps once a month, when his leisure allowed it, and then rarely for more than a few minutes. At such times she often wanted to cry out to him, *It's not my fault!* But there was no hope of his understanding, and no use in making trouble.

She was a murderess.

It wasn't her fault.

T'Thelaih had most of her family's traits: the fair or light brown hair, the light bones and short stature, good looks that tended to be blunt rather than finely drawn. There the obvious assets of the Old House ended in her, for she did not have the psi-communications gift: she was mindblind, like her father, and that had been hard enough to bear in a house where almost no one ever had to speak—the slightest intention to communicate with another person was always heard.

One gift she did have, though, that the house had acquired long before and striven hard to be rid of. They had never succeeded: every six or seven generations it would pop up again, and there would be curses and fear. It was associated with the communications gift, but independent of it. When angry, the person with this pernicious gift could kill with the mind.

She had not known until she was betrothed for the first time. She was frightened: she had not yet suffered the Rapture, and though her body was ready, her mind was not. Her first husband, a son of rich House Kehlevt, and one who thought well of himself, had taken her to the room set aside for their binding and had simply begun to rape her.

She killed him. Without touching him, without laying a hand to a weapon—though she would have liked to—suddenly she was inside his head: suddenly the connection that had never been complete before was complete: and her rage and terror burst out through it and froze his heart and stripped the receptor chemicals out of his brain and deadened the life-fire in his nerves. He was dead before he rolled off her. No healer had been able to do anything.

There had been the expected uproar. But the bruises on her body spoke clearly enough about what had been going on, and the matter was hushed up, and money changed hands to keep the quiet well in place. So much she had heard later. She had been very afraid that that would be the end of her—that some evening, someone would slip something deadly into her cup; or that some day before dawn, someone would come in over the sweet white flowers on her windowsill and put a knife in her. Such things had been heard of. But no one troubled her. T'Thelaih went about the house keeping small and still. It took her some time to realize that other people were now keeping small and still around *her*. No one had ever cared a *jah* before whether she was angry. But now, the people of the house were not sure that *any* anger of hers was something to cause, or to be near.

She tried to ignore the changed status of things and went about her studies and work as usual. Everybody in the house worked, whether they were marriage-fodder or not. T'Thelaih was very clear that that was just what she was—a gaming piece. She was not an own-child, but a "right-line child"—that was a euphemism that said she had some relationship to the head of the house, but not one confirmed by binding or other legal instrument. She was a by-blow, destined to be married off to some other house in return for some political favor or potential alliance. Now she went about her accounting work as usual and wondered whether the business with her first husband would put her out of the marriage market. That could be bad: she could wind up disowned, or sold as a servant. But things quieted down after a while, and another offer was made, this time from House Galsh. It was a good enough match, and the young man was very nice, and T'Thelaih wondered whether or not the first time might have been a quirk or an accident. In any case, she looked forward to the wedding. She felt the slow burn of the Rapture coming over her as the days till the binding grew closer, and she welcomed it. The binding fell in the middle of it: her blood fever kindled her new husband's, and the night was wild and memorable.

But in the morning he was dead.

There were no more matches made. T'Thelaih had leisure to work with the house's accounts, now: all the leisure she liked. Everyone, the servants, her half sisters, her mothers, looked at her with terror. Sometimes it relaxed a little, but never for long. No one dared tease her or say something that might make her laugh . . . because it might make her angry, too.

The time that followed was long and lonely.

But now she stood in front of her father, listening incredulously to the news that she was being bound again. To a young man of House Velekh, of the "High House." She stared at her father.

"But they are great," she said. "What do they want with us?"

"Alliance," he said.

T'Thelaih had her own ideas about that. She handled the accounts, after all. "Noble father," she said, "surely there are other houses they might more profitably ally with."

He glared at her. Yes, he knew perfectly well that he was being condescended to.

"Noble father," she said, "how can this match be made? Do they not know about the—the other bindings?"

"The Eldest of the House knows. Yes." Her father breathed out. "You have nothing to fear from them if there is an accident." He paused. "They will adopt you."

You are giving me away, she thought, *and relieved you are to do it. Foul, ah, foul!* "But noble father," she said, desperate, "the young man—"

"I care nothing for the young man," he said angrily. "No more do they. And I'll spare no tear if you make an end of him: it will rather please me if you kill something of theirs, than otherwise. So do your pleasure, girl. The match will be made when T'Khut is full. The young man comes to meet you tomorrow."

And that was that. She bowed her father reverence, and left, and sat long by her window that night, smelling the sweet white flowers, and contemplating the knife in her hand. It was very sharp.

The crescent set late: watching it, she thought that there was time yet. There was no harm in seeing the young man, at least. The knife would not be any less sharp for a couple days' delay.

Then she saw him.

They were left alone for the meeting, in the great hall of the house's lower level. It was all barren, there being no great dinner or festival there, no reason to adorn or garnish the place with the old banners and the riches garnered from long years of trade. And indeed many of the rich ornaments had been sold, over time, or were the worse for wear. Some kindly person among the servants had brought out two couches, of the antique style, and each of them sat on one and looked at the other.

T'Thelaih liked what she saw. The young man had a frank, calm look about him, and his eyes rested on her in a friendly way. "Well," he said, "they say we're going to be bound. I hope it's something you desired."

"It's not," she said.

He colored. "I'm sorry I don't please you."

"Oh, but you do!" she said.

They both fell silent for a moment: he was surprised at the remark, and she was surprised that it had slipped out, and equally surprised at how seriously she meant it. "I simply did not desire to be bound," she said. "I have been bound before. I killed my husbands."

He looked at her with even more surprise. "Not that way," she said, rather desperately. "It was the killing gift. You know—from the stories." She bowed her head. "I have it. No one survives the binding."

He gazed at her a long time, and finally she had to turn her head away.

"I think I would take the chance even if the choice were mine," he said, very slowly, as if just discovering this for himself.

T'Thelaih looked up in shock. "You must not!" she said. "You must flee! There's still time for you to get away!"

He shook his head. "You do not know my grandam," he said. "She would have me hunted down and brought back. And besides, why would I want to disgrace our house? She is our Eldest. It is my duty to obey her."

"She sent you here to kill you! She *knew!*"

He actually shrugged.

"You are an *idiot,*" T'Thelaih said in wonder.

He shrugged again. "That's as may be. There's no escaping, in any case, so I shall not try."

The argument went on for nearly an hour. T'Thelaih wondered what the eavesdroppers must be thinking of it all . . . for certainly, there *were* eavesdroppers: she might be mindblind, but she was not so stupid as to think that every mind in the house was not bent in this direction at the moment. And once the thought crossed her mind, *Why am I trying to talk him out of it? No worse blame will fall on me this time than has before. My father has practically given me leave to kill him. Why am I arguing the point?*

She could think of no reason.

Finally the argument trailed off, and she found herself staring at her hands. "Come again tomorrow," she said.

"I will," he said. And he paused and colored again. "I hate to say this," he said. "They announced it when I came in, but I've forgotten your name."

"T'Thelaih."

"Mahak," he said, and got up and bowed her reverence and left.

She sat there shaking her head for a long time, and then went back to the accounts.

He came back the next day, and the next, and the day after that, and they argued. The arguments always started about the binding itself, but then they began to stray out into more interesting topics—the relationships and interrelationships in their families, the politics that went on, and the doings of the kingdoms and lordships of the world; and finally, about themselves, or rather, each other. The arguments started early and ended late: it was *almost* improper.

After about three days of this, T'Thelaih realized that she was going to *have* to be bound to this man, just to have the leisure to argue properly with him.

On the fourth day she realized, with a start, that she was in love with him, and he with her. He realized it, for his part, the next day. The argument that day was particularly noisy.

Two days later, T'Khut was full.

The public part of the binding was held with great splendor in the hall of the High House. Mahak had decided to take his grandam at her word: tables actually bent under the weight of the food, and drink ran more freely than water. Petty-kings and great lords and Eldest Mothers filled the galleries to look down on the formal touching, as the priest of the god of bindings took the hands of the two to be bound, put them each to the other's face, and saw that the minds were properly locked together. Not even he saw how each pair of eyes, resting in the other's gaze, told the other that the locking had already happened, perhaps a hand of days ago, while both parties were shouting at one another at the tops of their voices. Neither of them cared a whit for one of the things they had argued about, the exchange of mind-technicians taking place, just about then, elsewhere in the house. Neither of them paid the slightest mind to the cold, interested glance bent down on them from another of the high galleries, as Lady Suvin looked down satisfied on her handiwork. They completed the binding and spent the afternoon and the early part of the night celebrating it with the assembled dignitaries, not caring in the slightest who had just declared war on whom, or what border skirmish was taking place because of an insult or a strayed *sehlat*.

They lay together that night and found that there was at least one thing about which they had no argument whatsoever: though afterward, there was some sleepy discussion as to who had a right to the most of the sleeping silks.

T'Thelaih was the first to awaken. Without looking to the side where her husband lay, she reached over to the little table by the head of the couch and picked up the knife. It was as sharp as it had been when the moon was thin. She knew what she was going to see: she knew what she was going to do about it.

She turned over and saw him sleeping quietly and breathing.

And quite alive.

The knife fell with a clatter to the floor and awoke him.

They began to quarrel. It did not last long. . . .

"I am with child," she said to him, quite shortly thereafter. He was so surprised that he forgot to start an argument about it.

"All the good Gods be praised," he said, taking her hands, "and bless the bad ones for staying out of it!"

"Sit down, beloved," she said, "and be calm a little. We need to think."

"About what?"

"The child, for one thing." T'Thelaih sat down on the couch in their chambers in the High House and looked at him keenly. "This child could be something that our houses have been waiting for for a long time."

"There are lots of children," Mahak said, somewhat confused.

"But none of both our houses. Mahak, listen to me. My father has as good as sold me to Suvin. I'm not bothered by that. Something like it was always bound to happen someday. But this child, depending on how and where it is raised, could be mistress of both my old House and my new one."

"Mistress—"

"A girl, yes."

"My grandam is not going to like that," Mahak said.

T'Thelaih was silent for a moment. "We are going to have to find some way to stop her not liking it," she said, "or to see to it that it does not matter. This child can be a bond, an end to the old warfare between our houses. Or the opportunity can die with us."

"Have you any idea how we are going to bring this to pass?" he said.

"Have you?"

He shook his head.

"Nor have I. But we must start thinking . . . whom we can cultivate, and how, to see that the child is brought up between the houses, not wholly of one or the other. Otherwise the child will be one more gaming piece, nothing more. . . ."

They sat quietly together for a moment.

"We must be very careful," Mahak said. "Otherwise this may be the death of us."

T'Thelaih nodded. "As you say."

He drew her close. "And in the meantime . . ."

And they discussed at some length the subject on which there were no arguments.

T'Thelaih woke up cold and alone. "Mahak?" she said, confused, and sat up on the couch, looking around for him. There was something wrong at the other end of their bond: he was upset—then she froze.

Sitting at the end of the couch was the Lady Suvin. She looked at T'Thelaih, and the look was cold and terribly pleased.

"You are a foolish child," Suvin said, "but it does not matter. I have what I want of you."

"Madam," T'Thelaih said, holding on to her manners, "what do you mean?"

"The child," said Suvin. "This will be your home now: you need fear no interference from your own house, poor thing though it be. I much regret that Mahak may not join you again until your confinement is done. But you will be given every care . . . so long as you take proper care of the child."

T'Thelaih felt her head beginning to pound. "What good can our child do you?" she said.

Suvin leaned closer, looking even more pleased. "Fool. You have the killing gift. Imperfect, at best: you did not kill my grandson, for some reason. I suspect it is the usual problem, that one must feel her life to somehow be threatened. But did you not know? His great-grandmother had it as well. When two with the gift in their blood, so close in degree, engender a child, it will have the gift as well."

T'Thelaih shook her head, numbed. "A weapon," she said at last.

"Such a weapon as none will be able to defend against," said Suvin. "Trained with the Last Thought technique, raised under my hand, obedient to me—those who resist me will simply die, and no one will know the cause. How much simpler life will become. I have much to thank you for."

She saw T'Thelaih's glance at the table. "Forget your little bodkin," she said. "You'll not lay hands on yourself: if you try, Mahak will suffer for it. I shall see to that. Resign yourself to your confinement. It need not be uncomfortable."

"Bring me my husband," T'Thelaih said. "Now."

Suvin's eyes glittered. "Do not presume to order me, my girl. You are too valuable to kill out of hand, but there are ways to punish you that will not harm the child."

The pounding was getting worse. "My husband," T'Thelaih said.

"Folly," said Suvin, and got up to go. "I will talk to you when you are in your right mind."

And from the courtyard below came the sound of swords, and the scream.

"T'Thelaih!!"

And nothing else . . . except, in T'Thelaih's mind, the feeling of the bond, the connection, as it snapped, and the other end went empty and cold.

"My husband," she said. Suvin turned in shock, realizing what had happened. An unfortunate accident—

She realized too late.

T'Thelaih was getting up from the bed. The pounding in her head she had felt before, at her first binding, and remotely, in the heat of *plak tow,* at the second. Now she knew it for what it was, and she encouraged it. *Yes. Oh, my husband, yes—*

"Old woman," she said to Suvin, getting out of the bed and advancing slowly on her, "beg me for your life." Suvin backed up, slowly, a step at a time, coming against the wall by the door. "Beg me," T'Thelaih said, stepping slowly closer. "Bow yourself double, old *lematya,* let me see the back of your neck." Her teeth gleamed. Suvin trembled, and slowly, slowly, began to bow.

She didn't finish the gesture: she came up with the knife, poised, threw it. T'Thelaih sidestepped it neatly and replied with the weapon that could not miss: slid into the hateful mind, cold as stone, reached down all its pathways and set them on fire, reached down through every nerve and ran agony down it, reached down into the laboring heart and squeezed it until it burst itself, reached down into the throat and froze it so there should not even be the relief of a scream. From Suvin she turned, and her mind rode her gift down into the courtyard, and wrought death there, death—left minds screaming as a weight of rage like the whole universe collapsed onto them, in burning heat, pain, blood, the end of everything. Her mind fled through the house, finding life, ending it, without thought, everywhere.

Finally the rage left her, and she picked up the little knife that Suvin had taken, thought about it . . . then changed her mind. "No," she said aloud, very softly: "no, *he* is down there."

She went to the window. "Child," she said, "I am sorry."

The fall was too swift for there to be time to start an argument, even with a ghost.

The extermination of the High House set back the first manned landing on T'Khut by some fifty standard years. Much of the psi-communications technology had to be rediscovered, and the gift bred for again, in the centuries that followed: it is still the least developed of the Vulcan arts of the mind, though the most broadly disseminated.

T'Khut was mined later, of course, and colonized, and thereafter the Vulcans set off for the outer planets. Several small wars broke out on Vulcan at the first successful landing, in token of the shifting of balances, which are always feared. But other balances were shifting as well: love became increasingly less of a reason for a binding than eugenics. Lives were sacrificed, long wars begun, for the sake of some marriage which might or might not produce a talent of one sort or another. And the terrible example of the attempted union of the High House and the Old House dissuaded many another house from trying such a solution to its problems. Houses grew away from one another, as nations did: grew in enmity and pride, forgot working together for the joys of conquering separately. *Fear the other,* was the message of that time: *keep to your own. Beware the different. Those too different should not seek union. Alone is best.*

Alone, T'Khut, her face now scarred with mines, took her way around the planet, and as the centuries passed, the fires that began to kindle on Vulcan's surface mirrored her own. She had no clouds so strangely shaped as Vulcan came to have in later years: but the fires burned on and on. . . .

Enterprise: Five

"Most disturbing," Spock said. "It is indeed most disturbing."

He and Jim and McCoy were sitting in one corner of the rec room. They had beamed back up to the ship from Sarek's and Amanda's, after dinner with them, and none of them had felt able to go to bed, not yet.

"That's the understatement of the year," McCoy said. "Spock, I thought she was the great logical one, after all that business at the Place of Marriage and Challenge. She seems to have changed her mind."

"People change, Doctor," Spock said, "Vulcans no less than humans. But I will be very, very interested indeed to find out what the extent of her involvement with this business is, and what her motives might be."

"I have my suspicions," Jim said. "Revenge for being ditched."

Spock looked at him mildly. "If so, it will be an epic revenge," he said. "And I am curious, if she is indeed behind all this, how she has been managing it. She has held some minor government office for some time—that much I know—but nothing that would particularly assist her in *this*."

Jim nodded. "Uhura came back to me with the information about that clipping from the information service," he said. "It comes from one of the names on Bones' list. The writer, Selv, who seems to be doing so much of this work."

Spock frowned slightly. "Selv," he said. "I seem to remember that name from somewhere."

"And *you* can't remember who it is right away?"

"Doctor," Spock said gently, "not even all *full* Vulcans have eidetic memory. One must be trained to it, and I have not been so trained. I think I may be pardoned for knowing a lot of Vulcans, and not remembering all of them, any more than you remember all the people you have ever met on Earth."

McCoy nodded. "At any rate," Spock said, "we will soon enough find out who he is. As for T'Pring—" He looked indecisive, a rather surprising expression for him. "Generally when one has a query to make of a bonded Vulcan woman, at least a query that does not have to do with her work, one makes it through her bondmate. Doctor, is Stonn's name mentioned anywhere in your list?"

McCoy flipped through to the first group of S's—a considerable number, bearing in mind the traditions about Vulcan male names—and then to the rest. "I don't see it," he said, sounding cautious. "I'll run a check with the copy I have on solid."

"Do so. I would find it very interesting if Stonn's name were not somehow involved as well."

"Come to think of it," McCoy said, "so would I." He riffled through the list a little more, then chucked it aside.

Jim stretched. "Best I should turn in, I suppose: it's going to be a busy day."

"Captain," Spock said, "are you comfortable with the briefings you have had on the debate format?"

Jim nodded. "It's not as structured as I'm used to—the interruptions from the floor are going to get fairly interesting, I suppose. At any rate, I think Sarek has told us pretty much what we need to know."

"Correct me if I'm wrong," McCoy said, stretching as well, "but the debate format reminds me a lot of the format for the Romulan Right of Statement."

Spock nodded. "There are striking similarities, which have been noticed before. There are of course differences—you are allowed to eat and sleep if you desire to, or to have a rest break—"

Bones grinned. "I think I'll do all right," he said. "The only question is whether the Vulcans have ever seen a good old-fashioned Southern-style filibuster."

Spock's eyebrows went up. "Don't get carried away, Doctor," he said. "If you tire out your audience with too many brilliant displays of illogic, you may force an early vote."

"I'll be careful," McCoy said, as he got up. "I dare say I can keep them interested . . . and I have a little logic of my own."

Spock nodded. "So I have seen . . . though I would never dare attempt to quantify it."

"I just bet you wouldn't," Bones said. " 'Night, Spock. Jim."

"Good night," they both said as McCoy ambled out.

When the door shut behind him, "Spock," Jim said, "are there any indications of the odds shifting at all?"

"They are getting worse," Spock said. "But I am becoming uncertain of the computer's ability to predict odds accurately when there are so many variables involved." He put one eyebrow up. "Such as the doctor."

"Well," Jim said, "we'll just do our best. It's all we can do." He sighed, then yawned. "I have to admit," he said, "I wish I could be a little fly on the wall when you have your talk with T'Pring."

Spock looked at him oddly. "Why," he said, "would you desire to be a fly? And specifically a small one?"

Jim laughed. "You know perfectly well what I mean."

Spock looked at Jim sidelong, and allowed himself the smallest smile. "More often than I used to," he said, "yes. Good night, Jim."

" 'Night, Spock."

They met in the transporter room, the next morning, about half an hour before the session in the Halls of the Voice was due to commence. Spock was setting the transporter controls himself, from memory apparently. "Are you ready, gentlemen?"

"Ready, willing, and able," Jim said.

"At least two out of three ain't bad," McCoy muttered.

They stepped up onto the pads and watched the room dissolve out around them. What they reappeared into was echoing dimness, and before they were even solid, Bones was complaining.

"You've done it again," he said. "Why do your people go for *size* all the time? Can't you do anything *small?*"

Spock looked resigned. The space in which they stood was, if anything, larger than the Hall of Pelasht had been, all made of a smooth, cool-colored, blue gray stone. The ceiling was as high as Pelasht's and shafts cut through it let in the sunlight in bright slanting columns. "Why do Vulcans like to conduct their business in railroad stations?" McCoy muttered. "Can you just tell me that?"

Spock let out a breath. "I believe that what you are complaining about," he said, "is pre-Reformation architecture. It did tend to the unnecessarily grand, at least according to present tastes. The room where the debates proper will be held is not this one, so you may relax, Doctor: you won't have to shout."

"Spock," said Sarek's voice from away off to one side. Regal in his dark ambassadorial robes, he came over to meet them.

"Father," Spock said. "I was not expecting to see you here today: your testimony does not begin until tomorrow."

"I had hoped to meet you before you went in, that is all." Sarek's eyes narrowed. "I have come across a piece of information that may or may not aid you in your assessments of matters: it is for you to judge."

Spock inclined his head.

"I was interested in your revelation about T'Pring, Doctor, and so I made a discreet inquiry or two," said Sarek. "It seems that Stonn is dead."

Jim glanced at Bones and at Spock. "How did he die, sir?"

"Privacy seal was invoked on the information," Sarek said.

"Which means," Spock said quietly, "that it is likely to involve *plak tow* in some manner. There is almost no other reason for which the seal is invoked, not in these times."

"Precisely," Sarek said. "At any rate, T'Pring is now a free agent, released from any obligations laid upon her as a bondmate. I thought you should know."

"Thank you, Father," Spock said, and bowed slightly to him.

"I must go now: there are still things to be handled at the embassy and consulate. I hope you find the morning illuminating. Captain, Doctor." And he was off, all dignity, though it was amazing how fast dignity could move when it had appointments elsewhere.

"Well, well, well," Bones said softly.

"We should not begin discussing this here, Doctor," Spock said: "it would be in execrable taste. Let us go into the Hall of the Voice and let them know we are present."

They walked off toward one side of the great entry hall. "Where are we, physically?" McCoy said. "I must admit I didn't check the map."

"We are on the other side of shi'Kahr from Pelasht," Spock said, "and possibly this will surprise you, but we are several hundred feet underground. The shafts are at ground level. This complex—*va'ne'meLakht* it was originally called—"

" 'Hiding from the Rage,' " McCoy said.

"Yes. It was a refuge built for sunstorm weather—there was some of that just before Surak's time, though not since. It was meant to hold the whole population of shi'Kahr and the environs, hence the size. These days it has been taken by the Academy and is used for the biggest lectures and meetings and for some ceremonial occasions."

Spock led the way over to a group of doors, all of which stood open. There was a young woman standing there tapping away busily at a computer keyboard: as Spock approached she looked up and said, "Attendee or testifier?"

"Testifier. Spock."

She tapped at the keyboard. "And you, sir?"

"The same. McCoy, Leonard E."

"And you?"

"The same. Kirk, James T."

She hardly looked up. "Row eight, seats one through three. Someone will be around to you with your schedule, sirs, and a program."

"I want popcorn," McCoy said suddenly.

The young woman looked up at him from underneath very pertly slanted brows and said calmly, "No eating in the auditorium, sir. Next?"

They headed into the auditorium. Spock was looking bemused: McCoy was grinning. "You cut it out," Jim said. "Just for that, you're not getting the aisle seat."

"Spoilsport."

The auditorium was indeed not as big as the hall they had beamed into, but it wasn't exactly snug, either. It was built in the round—or perhaps carved would have been a better word, for the stone showed no joins whatever. More of the big shafts were cut in the thick ceiling, a group of them directly over the round stage in the center, and the seats sloped up and away on all sides. It was a design that the Greeks and Romans had found successful to work in, acoustically satisfying, and Jim felt as if he would have no trouble speaking there. *Always assuming I can find the right things to say. . . .*

They found their seats, and the place filled up around them fairly quickly. There were a surprising number of non-Vulcans in attendance, but no more than about a thousand all told, in a place that could hold fifteen thousand easily. Vulcans filled the rest of those seats, silently, and Jim found himself suffering from the ridiculous feeling that he was being stared at. *Well, the Fleet uniform is plain enough to see. And I'm here to be seen. Let 'em stare.*

"Do they play the national anthem?" McCoy said, leaning over to whisper to Spock. He had gotten the aisle seat anyway.

"No," Spock said softly, "nor does the fat lady sing, I am afraid. The debates will merely be called to order, and begin."

"Who's on first?"

Jim looked quizzically at McCoy. "Maybe we should have gotten you that popcorn after all."

The audience started to become quiet, as if they saw or heard some signal that Jim had missed. He looked around him, but saw nothing but impassive Vulcans everywhere.

Then one walked out onto the stage, and Jim winced a little. It was Shath.

"On behalf of the government of All Vulcan," he said, "I declare these proceedings to be open. The debate will take the traditional form, and the proposal put is: That the planet Vulcan, and all its citizens, shall withdraw from the United Federation of Planets. Testifiers will please state their affiliation, their position on the proposal, and then make their statement. Proceedings may only be closed by the electorate, and the threshold number is one billion, eight hundred thousand. Opinion may be registered with the data and news networks carrying the proceedings." Shath consulted a datapad that he was carrying. "Number one, please."

There came a soft chiming sound from the far side of the audience, and Jim could see a lot of heads over there turn in curiosity. He smiled as a small, bright form like a giant twelve-legged glass spider clambered up onto the other side of the stage and spidered into the shafts of sunlight at the stage's center.

"My name is K's't'lk," she said, and her voice filled the place as the amp field found and focused on her. "I hold the recallable rank of Commander in the Starfleet of the United Federation of Planets. As regards the proposal: I say nay."

She shuffled and chimed a little. "There is a traditional courtesy of this planet," she said, "that in any gathering, the least hominid guest, to be made to feel most welcome, is asked to speak first: and I see you've done it to me again, since there are no Hortas, methane-breathers, or aphysical creatures here." There was a slight rustle of amusement in the crowd. "Well," she said, "at any rate, I thank you most kindly for the welcome, and with that formality out of the way, let me also say that I'm glad to be back here on the Academy grounds, here where I've read so many papers and been led to doubt my own sanity. Or to cause others to doubt theirs."

She turned slightly to face another portion of the auditorium: or maybe this was simply a courtesy on her part to the hominids there, since K's't'lk's eyes were spaced evenly on the top and sides of her dome-like body, and she could see equally well all around her without turning. A little storm of glitter shifted and moved with her as she turned in the brilliant sunlight. "I want to talk to you about the pursuit of science in the universe," she said, "and its pursuit on Vulcan, and some of the things that have happened in the sciences since Vulcan joined the Federation, a hundred eighty years ago now. I said 'nay' to you just then because I counterpropose that the Federation has done Vulcan more good in the sciences than another thousand or five thousand years of isolation would have done her. You will pardon me," she said, "if for the moment I stay out of the ethical mode. I have strong feelings about that as well, but today is for the sciences."

She turned again, chiming. "You will doubtless hear enough people willing to tell you about all the things that Vulcan has done for the Federation," she said. "And I will agree with all of them: the improvements in translator technology, on which practically ninety percent of our present technology rests; the extraordinary advances in medicine, especially in genetic engineering, at which Vulcan is more expert than almost any planet in known space; the pure researches in astronomy and cosmology and cosmogony, which have opened up more and more of space to the Federation's starships; and so much more. Most of you have done your homework for this proceeding and know exactly what you've given us." Her voice got a happy sound to it. "My own research fellows here have given me many a gift, many an astonishing insight, and I treasure that.

"Let me add this, however. The affiliate species of Starfleet, and perhaps most specifically the humans of Earth, have a gift to give the Vulcan species that is surely a match for any you give us. Human beings are especially good at making a scientist ask questions that they might not have asked otherwise. Unexpected questions, bizarre questions, even illogical questions. I know," she said, at the rustle that went through the place then—a somewhat disgruntled sound. "Logic is important. But there are things in the world that logic is no good for."

"Humans, mostly," remarked someone somewhere in the audience. Jim was surprised. He was also surprised at the fact that the amp field seemed to focus instantly, as soon as one spoke above a certain voice level.

"That was an easy one," K's't'lk said, sounding slightly amused. "They have things to teach you about humor, too. Even Surak had that, and he never said anything about feeling that it needed to be gotten rid of. There is more confusion about what Surak said, and didn't say, and what it meant or didn't mean, than I've ever seen about anything else on the planet."

"You said you were going to stay in the scientific mode," said another voice from somewhere.

"I am," K's't'lk said. "I am talking about semantics. Surak was many things, and one of them was a top-flight semanticist: doubtless there are none as good working here today, since there seems to be so much difficulty working out what he meant. Anyway," she said, "as I was saying, there are realms of the sciences where logic is useless, such as the so-called 'non-causal' sciences that are my primary study here. When cause does not necessarily follow effect, logic becomes a feeble reed to lean on. Yet put aside logic in dealing with these sciences, and suddenly great riches of results come pouring out of a universe that has been quite mulish and uncooperative while logic in the classic sense was being applied.

"I am saying," she said, turning again, "that as regards the sciences, Terrans have something you need. For one hundred and eighty years Vulcan researchers have been availing themselves of that resource, whatever you choose to call it—creative illogic, the skewed viewpoint, the 'aha' experience. Turn them away, and you may say and do what you like, but your sciences will never be as effective, as nourishing to the spirit, as dangerous again. The danger, perhaps, is the key. Without the unpredictable, the mysterious, there is no joy in science. And the mad suggestions of Terrans are definitely part of the unpredictable—since they are part of a universe that we are beginning to realize is more sentient than we ever dreamed. To turn your backs on the voice that speaks through Terrans is to reject part of the Universe, speaking for itself as all things do, and your data will be incomplete forever."

She paused, and laughed a little, a soft arpeggio of amusement that echoed from the walls. "I remember the last paper I wrote here," she said, "on what the press later called the Elective Inversion drive for starships. My colleagues at the Academy were uncertain about most of the equations. Well, actually they thought most of them were crazy. They were willing, though, to make allowances for the basically different world-view of Hamalki mathematics. They also had to admit," she said, with a smile in her voice, "that when we built our prototype drive apparatus, the equations worked. They were a little annoyed at first, if I remember right. So far, so good. But it took installing that apparatus in a human starship, and having it tinkered with by a human engineer with a genius for physical things, to make that drive come back from wherever it had gone when it went where no one had gone before."

"That mission was the one that practically destroyed the *Starship Enterprise*, was it not?"

"I think quite a few of her missions may qualify for that description," K's't'lk said. "I think you are implying that the apparatus was useless and a failure. Well, it was one of the more glorious failures that science has had lately. During that 'failure' we found out more about the structure of neighboring alterdimensionate space than any *hundred* Vulcan hyperphysicists had told us for years. It needed the human variable to make it happen, and there is no better example of a wild success in my chosen field. I think that to purposely turn away from human influence, to purposely reject an approach which produces useful results, simply because you dislike the style of the approach, or it makes you nervous, is to purposely limit what your sciences can achieve. And since the purpose of the study of science is to know the universe as completely as possible, then you are sabotaging that purpose at its root, and you might as well stop studying science entirely. It is illogic of a particularly distasteful kind, and frankly, I expected better of you people."

There was a sort of cheerful scorn about the last statement, a sort of all-right-let's-fight! attitude, that produced an immediate response from the crowd. If it had been a group of humans, Jim wouldn't have been particularly concerned; but the spectacle of a big group of Vulcans, usually so protocol-conscious and restrained, now interrupting one another and speaking with that icy clarity that meant extreme anger—

"It's a regular free-for-all," McCoy said under his breath to Jim, astonished, after a few minutes of listening to angry responses, and K's't'lk's cheerful and somewhat angry responses to them. "This is what we're going to have to deal with, huh?"

Jim nodded, wondering, *Am I going to be able to keep my temper under control? There's a lot of anger out there. . . .* "Maybe you should slip me an Aerolev before I go on," he said, sotto voce.

McCoy snorted. "Drugs? You just do your deep breathing like the rest of us."

There was some sort of argument going on now about "the active versus the passive mode" and "the life of physicality versus the life of the mind." A Vulcan, a tall, respectable-looking gentleman, was speaking at some length about how too much involvement with the active life and physical reality was an error in balance, since even K's't'lk as a physicist would have to admit that the universe was almost all empty space, and nothing was real—

"Tenured," McCoy whispered to Jim. Jim nodded.

"Ah," K's't'lk said, "the old dichotomy problem. Don't you think that one or the other of those 'lives,' physical reality or theoretical unreality, might sometimes be senior to the other? More valid, shall we say?"

"Indeed not," said the Vulcan. "It is a classic error in thinking, particularly, if I may say it, of the human sort. The illusory or internally subjective nature of physical existence is perhaps its most important and revealing characteristic. When one remembers that, on most levels of consideration, one does not exist, such matters as the question before us today assume their proper *aaaaaaaiigh!*"

The gentleman had been so busy expounding on the illusory nature of matter that he had never noticed K's't'lk come softly down from the stage and walk down the aisle next to which he was standing. As for the rest of it—even a Vulcan will react when a silicon-based life form bites him in the leg.

"Fascinating," K's't'lk said. "For someone whom on most levels of consideration doesn't exist, you scream with great enthusiasm. And I *heard* you, too. Better have that looked into."

Jim's eyes were wide as he glanced at Spock. "Is that kind of thing allowed?"

"In the more formal forms of the debate," Spock said, "everything is allowed up to ritual duels to the death."

"Remind me not to get into a fight with anybody here about science," McCoy muttered.

"Anything else?" K's't'lk said, as she resumed the stage. There was no response. "Now like the humans of Earth, I do come of a brash young race. We've only had space travel for, oh, about two thousand years. But speaking for myself, I throw in my lot with the Terrans. Their unpredictability and their ability to look 'sideways' and see through a problem makes them the perfect partners in the sciences; and for those who would exclude them because of youth or strangeness, I can only say that you should enjoy your universe . . . because we and they will someday be enjoying others, and we'll miss you. I thank you, one and all."

There was some muted applause. K's't'lk got off the stage and walked up the aisle past them. As she went by McCoy, Jim could hear her chiming very softly, ". . . showed *him*. Get all Zen with *me* . . ."

Two more speakers followed—an elderly Vulcan woman and a handsome young

Tellarite—and their statements were dry and calm, not interrupted as K's't'lk's had been. Jim wondered whether this was because they were both supporting the secession, on the grounds of inequities of Federation funding to non-Terran research projects on Vulcan and elsewhere. Then there was a break for the noon heat: the debating would resume three hours later.

"Is it all going to be this exciting, I wonder?" McCoy said as they headed out to see about some lunch.

"I suspect it'll heat up a little when we go on," Jim said. "Spock, can you suggest somewhere around here?"

"Yes," he said; "the *Nakh'lanta* in the Old City is very good indeed. I will give you the coordinates. But I will not be with you."

McCoy looked at him with concern. "Where are you going?"

Spock looked amused, but there was something a little hollow about it. "I think you would say," he said, " 'I need to talk to my ex.' "

Finding her proved to be no particular problem, especially when Spock checked the sign-in list at the Hall of Voices and found that she was not there. Her commcode was a matter of public record: it was listed to a semirural community nearly a quarter of the way around the planet. He called the *Enterprise* and had them beam him over.

The house was big, bigger than his father's. More than that: it was ostentatious. It was built in one of the styles that had been popular just before Vulcan joined the Federation—partly buried underground, so that the landscape could be enjoyed with as little hindrance as possible. The gardens around it were full of exotics, many of them imports from other planets—tender plants that required an exorbitant amount of water to keep. Taken together as a whole, house and grounds said loudly to every passerby that the one who owned this place had all the money they needed, and few wants.

Spock walked to the front entrance and touched the annunciator. "Yes?" said a voice.

Very cool, that voice. Hers. He hesitated. "Spock," he said at last.

For nearly two minutes nothing happened: no reply, no movement inside that he could hear. He was about to turn away from the door—the "silent" response was a proper one to the privacy codes implicit in the Rules of Silence. But then the door opened.

It was a cliché, and he knew it; but T'Pring was almost exactly as he had last seen her—cool, slender, tall, extremely beautiful. He studied her face for any sign of the years since their ceremony at Marriage and Challenge. There was none. The beautifully tilted eyes examined him too.

"I did not think you would come," she said.

"Explain."

"I did not think you would have the courage," she said. "Come in, if you like."

He followed her into the entry hall, feeling intensely uncomfortable. "May I offer you refreshment?"

"Yes," he said, but only because it was incredibly rude to refuse. One thing, though, was certain: he was not going to ask for water.

T'Pring went off and brought two flasks of fruit juice. Spock saluted her with the glass, in the correct fashion, and drank it all off in a draft—a gesture that would be read as that of a person on business, or one who had no intention to spend a long time under the other's roof.

"Please sit down," she said to him, sitting down herself.

"Very well. I have come to ask you," he said, putting the glass down, "what your involvement is in the debates presently going on."

"I caused them," she said. "Surely your logic has led you that far, unless the humans have completely addled your wits."

"My logic led me that far," Spock said. He was not going to give her openings for baiting him or respond to hers.

"Stonn died," she said.

"I heard. I grieve with you." It was not quite a lie.

She sat quite still and erect on the bench across from him, her hands folded in her lap, meeting his gaze without flinching. "You will have gathered something of what was going on, then. When he took me after the Challenge, after you 'defeated' your Captain and released me, we lived well enough together for a time. But I was discontented. The matter had not gone as it should have, at the *Koon-ut-kalifi*. It did not go as I had planned." This was delivered in utter coolness of expression, but T'Pring's voice had something of the very small child about it: a balked child, angry because it did not get the sweet it wanted. "Stonn grew discontented himself, thinking that perhaps I desired you again, or some other. He attempted to induce *plak tow* in himself prematurely, to make me desire him." Spock nodded: there were drugs that could be used for this. They were risky, but some felt it worth the risk. There were some Vulcans who felt that no joining was real unless it happened in the blood-madness.

"He died of a hormonal imbalance, a form of 'endoadrenal storm,' " T'Pring said. "I was not entirely displeased. He had made me mistress of his estates, and though they were small, they satisfied my needs. But then as time passed, I came to realize that once again you had robbed me, you and your captain: it was fear of your desire that had made Stonn take the drugs. Once again I did not have my desire, and once again it was your fault."

Spock held quite still. *How shall I say what I am thinking? She cannot be entirely blameless in this*—but he held his peace.

"So I decided to take from you such things as you had taken from me," she said: "your future life, your captain, and anything else I could manage that would cause you such pain as you have caused me. It would be *ashv'cezh*, and my satisfaction would be great."

Spock nodded, numb. *Ashv'cezh* was literally revenge-worse-than-death: death would seem uncomplicated and pleasant next to the situation that this kind of revenge implied.

"I looked about me," she said, quite calmly, "and found that there were many of our people, more than I had ever suspected, who feared the Federation, and especially against Earth. It seemed to me that my weapon lay ready to my hand. So I began first to invest the proceeds of Stonn's estate with some care. I did very well, and made a great deal of money in the interstellar commodities markets.

"Then," she said, "I began making substantial donations to various small organizations and publications. You will have noticed them to have come to me so quickly. Through them, I found such other Vulcans as were willing to say the things about Earth people as make Vulcans angriest against them: appeals to logic, and to emotion as well, for some of us still have emotion." Hardly a muscle of her face moved as she said it. "I took my time: it was worth taking. Slowly a groundswell of opinion started to build up: it fed on itself—for people will say things that they hear others say, whether they truly believe them or not. And if they say them often enough, they will come to believe them anyway. I used other weapons, as well. I bribed some government officials, who had found their posts increasingly diminished by the influence of Terrans on Vulcan. I suborned various media and data network personnel to add emphases to certain stories and downplay others. And slowly the public came to perceive a problem with Terra, and slowly the government came to feel the public's unease, and they grew uneasy themselves, fearing for their positions. When it became plain that what the electorate wanted was a chance to secede from the Federation, the government complied quickly enough."

She smiled, just a little. It was a wintry look. "And so we find ourselves where we are today. If all goes well, the vote will be taken quite soon, and we will be out of the Federation: and it will be forever beyond your power to take anything from me again, for you will either stay here and lose your starship and your captain—without which you are nothing—or you will go into exile with him, and your father and mother will become exiles as well, and I shall be well avenged indeed."

It was almost a minute before he could speak. Then all he could say was what he had said before:

"Flawlessly logical."

"I thank you," she said. "Is there anything else I can tell you?"

Spock shook his head.

"Then I will ask you to leave," she said. "I have some calls to make. I think perhaps you will see me once more, before the end; I shall come to the Hall of Voices to watch you and your captain plead for leniency for Terra. I shall find it most amusing."

"I dare say you shall," Spock said, and got up.

She saw him to the door.

"Farewell, Spock," she said.

"Live long," he said—and the rest stuck in his throat.

He left the house, walked out to the quiet, dusty road, and called the *Enterprise:* and beamed up, feeling, for the first time in his adult life, faintly sick to his stomach, for a reason that had nothing to do with McCoy's potions.

Vulcan: Five

Darkness, and stars. In the great silence, nothing moves: or at least nothing seems to, in this old emptiness, except the shadows of superstructures as the ship turns toward the distant Sun or away from it. Peacefully it slips through the long night, the slender dark hull, spinning as it goes; silently it drifts past, the picture of peace.

Fighting continued in ta'Valsh for the eighteenth day as the Mahn'heh Protectorate defied the claims of neighboring Lalirh for debated territory in the Tekeh area. An image, in her mind, of running figures, a bolt of blue fire being shot out of a smoke-stained window, the sound of glass shattering: and dirt stained green by the body that lay on it, one arm cauterized away, the head half-missing from someone's explosive charge. A whole street of what might once have been pleasant suburban houses, now burnt, their windows blown out, all the ground before them blasted and scorched, pavings upturned or cracked asunder. *Representatives for the Lords of Mahn'heh and the King of Lahirh said today in statements to the nets that there were no plans for talks at this time.* Images of well-fed men and women reading their statements in quiet rooms full of newspeople. *The Lords of Mahn'heh claim that the Tekeh area was settled in 164330 by people of their lordship and have been demanding the immediate cession of the territory and payment of reparations, including as an additional reparation the hostage-exchange of one of the sons of the Lahirhi King. The Lahirhi deny these charges and have stated in the past that any further movement against them by the Mahn'heh may cause a nuclear exchange like that with which they brought down the government of neighboring Ovek two decades ago.* An image of craters, nothing but craters—a stretch of land, perhaps farmed once to judge by the rural road running through it, now devastated by low-yield packed neutron charges.

The hostilities between Duveh and the Lassirihen provinces show some signs of settlement, but a minor terror and kidnapping guild has threatened to destroy both ruling houses if their demands for a part in the negotiations are not met within a tenday. Images of richly robed people coming with great gravity down the front stair of a shattered, bombed-out palace, much patched and repaired. *The Night Alliance, an offshoot of the old Mastercraft, now disbanded since the death of its leader T'Meheh in a hovercar accident, has demanded marriage into both the Duveh and the Lassiriheh royal houses, and bride- or groom-payments in excess of five million nakh—*

She sighed and let her mind drift away from the images. They bored her. It seemed there was nothing else on the news these days but all the fighting at home. At least there was peace here.

Alieth shut her eyes and saw the image again of the battered palace, while the inreader went on about divisions of lands and money. She sighed again and did the change in her mind that took her into one of the entertainment channels, changed again for first the hall, then the room she desired. Idly she scanned around for mind-IDs. No one she knew was around, not even Mishih, who was usually in the net whenever he was awake. Alieth supposed that it was night where he was, wherever that might be. She seemed to remember he was somewhere up near one of the poles—Retakh, that was it, a frightful place to live, out in the middle of nowhere.

Rather like here, actually: but at least here, no one was likely to drop a selective chemical bomb on you suddenly in aid of a herdbeast raid.

Alieth scanned around. Scanning was what one called it, though what it looked and felt like was an effortless drifting through a geometrical landscape, filled with vague solid-geometry shapes that contained messages. Their outsides were tagged with ID information, so that by brushing up against one, you could get a feel of the mode of the mind that had sent it: angry, affable, interested, informational. If you were interested, you reached in and grasped the message: perhaps added to it. She brushed a few as she passed them, found nothing that interested her. Increasingly she had no interest in touching the frozen messages, only the live minds. Hanesh complained about this, but then Hanesh complained about everything, and he hated the nets.

I might as well come out, she thought. There was no telling what was going on in the ship at this point; though it was true that Pekev was supposed to be coming back at this point, from that survey. But Alieth was sure that there would be nothing interesting. There had not been anything interesting for months.

That was the problem.

Ah, she thought, *why come out?* And she sank back into the net, changing rooms, and went looking for someone to talk to. Someone who breathed real air, who walked on the world, someone who might have a bomb dropped on them at any moment. Alieth drifted gently through the colored landscape, under a firefly sun, and wished there was some other state of mind than peace or war. . . .

Pekev swore softly in the spacesuit. There was a soft hiss inside it that was not the air processing system, and a whisper of outgoing breeze tickling his skin, low down, near the leg seam. It had to be leaking again. *I don't need this,* he thought, but there was nothing he could do at the moment. It would cost much more than a suit's worth of air to get back in the ship, repair the leak, and get back out again: and his father would not be pleased. There would be violence at mainmeal again.

Then again, he thought, *when was my father last pleased at anything?* He wobbled a little in the hard cold starlight as he wrestled with the specific gravity apparatus he had attached to the rock.

It was not a particularly large asteroid, but theoretically they did not have to be large to be good, and this one had the right look: that sootiness about the outer shell, or the hard glassy glint, that spoke of a high carbon content. You learned to recognize it after a while. It took time: the carbon-matrix asteroids were not all that common—they comprised only about a tenth of a percent of all asteroids—and the iron and nickel ones, so much commoner, were useless for the family's purposes.

The spec-grav apparatus was big and unwieldy. It had to be: it carried its own small thrusterpack, suitable either for maneuvering an asteroid close to the ship—and even the smallest of them were fairly massive—or for holding the rock stable while the pack's core drill drove itself into the asteroid and took a sample. It was all sampling today, for Pekev. Yesterday he had spent some eighteen or twenty hours with the long-range pack on, rounding up several promising-looking rocks: the usual routine—scan, lock on, spend an hour or two or three in transit, find the rock and examine it; if it was any good, bring it home. Or near home, at least—match its intrinsic velocity with the ship's (often another two hours' brutal work with the thrusterpack), make sure its course was stable, and then go out again after the next one. Pekev could still feel the ache in his back from the insistent push of the thruster against his mass, and his leg was still bothering him where the first rock, the one that had since turned out to be worthless, had pinned him briefly against the thruster—a tiny miscalculation of thrust, but one that he was lucky hadn't killed him. Probably that was where the seam leak had come from.

But today was easier: the pack used for the core samples was a little more tractable, not having as heavy a framework and as much mass as the big long-range rock mover. All Pekev had to do today was go from one rock to another, sample them all, and take the samples back for analysis. That would take him another few hours: if he was quick about it, he could get to sleep early. Then tomorrow, back out with the long-range again. It was his routine. Sometimes he thought it would drive him crazy: sometimes he thought it was the only thing that kept him sane. At least it was quiet, when he was out here and the family was back there.

Its self-diagnostics satisfied with its hold on the rock, the core drill started up: he could feel the vibration of it through the thrusterpack's framework. Pekev sighed a little, looked over his shoulder at *Rasha*. *She's getting old,* he thought. It was a sad sort of thing to say about a ship that you had loved from when you first moved into it as a child. But there it was: Pekev was almost fifty, now, and so was the ship, and she was near the end of her effective life. Unfortunately, the family didn't have the money to buy another one.

The drill whined through the framework. Pekev breathed out. There had been a time, long ago—he could barely remember it—when there had been enough of everything: when *Rasha* was only one of seven ships, a small but respectable fleet, and the family had been doing well. They had been numerous, then. The biggest of the clan ships, *Urekh* and *Gelevesh*, had held a hundred people each. He had some faint far memory of *Gelevesh* with its huge shining corridors. He could hardly have been more than a babe in arms then: now, from looking at the old specs, he knew that the ship had not been the vast cavernous thing he remembered. But nonetheless it was enough to keep a subclan of a hundred people comfortable and well for a year's mining in space.

But they were all gone, now: all of them but *Rasha*. *Urekh* had been caught on the ground and blown to dust in the five years' war between the Teleiw and the Nashih, and *Gelevesh* had been taken by the Nashih as a prize of war and recommissioned as a scoutship or somesuch. Pekev's father still muttered threats of disembowelment at the memory of the petty little voucher the Nashih had given him as they turned him and the family out: "payment," they said, "compensation"—but they sneered at him as they said it. No other ship of the clan was big enough to take them all: *Gelevesh*'s original complement, whole subfamilies, were forced to scatter across the planet and find work on the ground or in someone else's ship—a bitter thing. And the clan head, Pekev's father, was forced to move from ship to ship of the dwindling fleet—for one after one they had to be sold, to service the still huge debt owed for the building of *Gelevesh*. Finally there was nothing left but *Rasha*, meant for a long-range seven-person ship and now holding eleven.

The core drill stopped. Pekev checked the sensors to make sure the drill had completed its punch and not simply aborted—though sometimes an abort was good news: sometimes it meant diamond—and that was what the family had always mined for. Let others handle the large mining operations like nickel-iron. Indeed, they had to let others do it. Not even at its most successful had the family had capital enough to buy a ship of the size needed to handle the really big rocks, which you had to handle to make the enterprise pay off. But diamond, especially the industrial kind, was plentiful enough in asteroids to pull in a fairly respectable income . . . at least, plentiful enough to keep a small ship running. And sometimes, where there was industrial diamond, there was gemstone as well. Sometimes. But that was mostly a dream. . . .

He touched controls on the thrusterpack, and the core came back out of the drillhead. Pekev pocketed it and touched more controls: with small thunking vibrations that he felt through the framework, the pack turned itself loose of the rock and drifted gently toward him. In instant reaction he pushed it, shoving it and himself away at the same time—the thing had more inertia than he had, and could push fairly hard if you didn't take care. He had seen his father Nomikh pinned against the *Kasha*'s hull more than once by it: a mistake that could kill under the wrong circumstances. It was a shocking mistake for his father to make . . . but his father was not quite what he had been anymore.

The leak sighed away against his leg. There was only one more rock to do. Pekev maneuvered himself around the framework, hit the rear controls for the forward thrusters, checked his sensors for the radio beacon he had put on the last rock waiting for him, and programmed the pack for a three-second burst. Little pencils of blue chemical fire stood out from the edges of the framework in four places, then went out. Pekev hung on to the framework, and it and he began to drift away through the dark.

He never once looked at the stars.

The Vulcan historians' name for the period was always the Age of Expansion. Only much later did it begin to be referred to as "the pre-Reformation" period. It was the time in which many of the petty kingdoms of the old world had been unified—mostly against their will. This process had, of course, been going on for a long time. There are historians who will point out that from the time of Earth's Bronze Age, around 10,000 B.C., and the fall of the Spartans at Thermopylae, there was only one period of ten standard years during which as much as ten percent of Vulcan was *not* at some kind of war, economic or political. But in the so-called Age of Expansion, the process of "unification" sped up considerably.

It was actually consolidation, rather than unification: larger territories and tribes swallowing smaller ones, either by annexation or political blackmail. Vulcan technology, especially weapons technology, was becoming more and more advanced. Atomics had been achieved, were used a few times with results similar to those at Hiroshima and Nagasaki on Earth . . . but the result was not the eventual disarmaments that Earth achieved. Instead, the Vulcans retailored their atomic weapons to be less "dirty"—neutron bombs were an early "happy" solution to the problem—and there was also much research into chemicals, and artificial amplifications of such psi talents as the killing gift. The latter was refined until it could strike down thousands at a distance of thousands of miles. It usually also killed the adept, but since most of those with this talent were using it under threat of harm to their families, it did nothing to stop the gift, or the governments who bred for it.

Nor were conventional weapons abandoned: guns and bombs and particle weapons of all kinds continued to proliferate in endless variety. And more to the point, the angers of the annexed, and the outrage of the great nations that the annexed should attempt to resist their will, proliferated as well, until nearly the whole planet was a patchwork of ancient grudges, constantly being avenged on the "wrongdoers"—and countervengeances were taken, endlessly. It perhaps says more about the time than anything else that the Vulcan language included no less than several *thousand* words for terrorism and its applications, each precisely describing or defining a different kind of violence as to degree or type.

The terrorism spread into space, but not as quickly as it might have, since Vulcan merchant ships by tradition were never armed, and military ones, oddly enough, had not yet been conceived of. (Earth historians who find this astonishing should also remember that, until fairly late in its history, Vulcan did not have the concept of the standing army . . . simply because for thousands of years, there were not the resources to support such a thing. There was no way to feed such a monster, or give it water, and usually nowhere to keep it. Technology changed this, much later . . . but mercifully, it did so very late.) Space stayed peaceful for a while, and many people who were able to, chose to live there full time, rather than on the turbulent surface of the planet.

Their only mistake was in believing that they had left the warfare behind them.

When Pekev came in and unsuited, he found his father where he usually found him—sitting at the common-room table, his head in his hands, looking at a computerpad that lay before him, with the ship's accounts on it. There were times when Pekev wondered whether his father actually looked at the numbers there, or was merely trying to be awake, but at the same time trying not to think about anything, while seeming to. *If that's so, I wish he wouldn't,* he thought. *He ought to go hide in the nets like Arieth. At least we wouldn't have to stare at him all day.*

Nomikh raised his head and looked at Pekev when he heard the sounds of the spacesuit seals being undone. "How did it go?" he said. It was what he always said.

Pekev pulled the core samples out of his pocket and tossed them, one by one, to his father, who caught them out of the air expertly enough and peered at them. Even by naked eye, two of them had the faint dark sparkle that spoke of enough industrial diamond content to make them worthwhile. "Nothing big," he said softly. His voice was very deep.

"Nothing big, Father," said Pekev, and breathed out. Sooner or later that question always came out. *Anything big?* His father had been looking for the big one, the rock of the gods, ever since Mother had died. Before that, he had not cared about such a thing . . . or if he had, he would have given it to his mother. But Mother was dead forty years, now. *It must be terrible. He thinks he should have been rich forty years ago. Instead, he's spent forty years breaking even, just barely. . . .*

"Going to get them in tonight?" his father said. It was just sunset, by ship's time. Pekev didn't look at his father. "It's late," he said.

"Early yet," said his father. "You could get one of them in before you go to couch."

"Father," Pekev said, "I'm *sehlat*-weary, and my suit has a leak in it."

"Carelessness," his father said, and his voice began to scale up. "Carelessness! Do you think these things can be dug out of the sand? What do you take me for, a man with hundred-*nakh* pieces coming out of his pockets? I've told you again and again, you have to take better care of the equipment! We can't afford to waste—we don't have *anything* to waste! Not air, not water, not suits, not—"

Pekev shut him out as best he could and kept on unsuiting. There were few days when he did not hear a variant on this lecture. He was rather hoping he might have been spared it today, but apparently there was no chance of that. "And you're getting as lazy as your sister, you won't even go out for one more run before you eat your meal, not that you've earned it—"

Pekev was much tempted to take the leaky seal between his hands and pull it right apart, so that he would not be able to go out until the adhesive that would be needed to patch it had cured, and that would take a couple of days. But he resisted the temptation, though the flexfabric was smooth under his fingers and it would have been easy enough to do. "Not that you've earned your food for the last moonaround, let alone this week, the hours you've been working, or not working. When I was your age—"

Pekev went off down the cramped little corridor, into the workshop area, and slung his suit over the worktable, then spent a moment looking up at the hanging board for the electric sealing tool he needed. His father's voice was diminished, but there was no escaping it. That was always the problem: on a ship this small, there was no way for anyone to escape from anyone else—except perhaps in Alieth's manner, in the telepathic networks. Pekev was not sure he approved of that method at all: and Alieth's tightbeam charges were a constant drain on the ship's income. But at least it kept her out of the way when she had no rock to work on. . . .

Pekev found the sealer, thumbed it on, and rustled the suit around until the seal was properly exposed, then ran the sealer down it. His father was still going on about the hours he had worked when he was a boy. To hear him tell it, he had built *Gelevesh* with his own hands, in his spare time, after wrestling asteroids into the ship he was working with his bare hands, and nothing but a tank and a tube to breathe from. *I wonder if other people have this problem with their fathers,* he thought.

Along the bond in his mind, she said, *I did with mine. But yours is worse, I think, I almost pushed him out the airlock in his singlet this morning.*

Beloved, Pekev said, and looked over his shoulder, feeling the nearness of her. T'Vei came in from the coreside workshop, holding an assay dish in her hands. It was full of what remains after an asteroid has been crushed and the good parts extracted: in this case, nearly a threeweight of granular black diamond, the crystals very perfectly separated, and large.

"There's more where that came from," she said, and smiled at him. "Nearly three hundred times as much."

"From that wretched little rock this morning? You are a genius!"

She tilted her head at him. "Possibly. I suspected the presence of a couple more pockets than the ultrasound showed. I was right."

"That's our next week's fuel paid for, then. I was beginning to worry."

"With me around?" she said lightly, and went off to show the diamonds to their father.

Pekev shook his head and went back to the sealing. T'Vei was the one who handled the actual "dismantling" of an asteroid. It was delicate work, though one might not have thought so: many people thought that all you had to do was crush the thing and take the diamonds out. But crush it how? Do so incautiously, and if there were any gem-quality stones inside, they might be destroyed: even the value of the industrial diamonds could be destroyed if too many of them were fractured or powdered. There were machines of all sizes in the coreside lab for the handling of rocks—from huge magnetically driven hammers to tiny things that took off no more than a flake at a time—but it took a specialist's sense for how a stone would fracture, and what was inside it, to use the tools effectively. T'Vei was the specialist, though Pekev would never have suspected she would become so expert, when they were bonded. It was in fact something of a joke in the family—though not in her hearing—for T'Vei had been bonded into the house to pay off a debt that House Balev owed Pekev's father. Pekev didn't care. Their love was one of the only truly good things in his life, and that she was as good at processing as she was only made things easier.

He heard his father's tirade break off short for the moment, heard T'Vei's sweet voice murmuring to him about payload percentage and bulk discounts. "Well," his father said, "if your husband were as good at what he does as you are, we might become something again, this family might, but he won't even go out and bring in one more rock before he settles down to his evening of sloth—"

She came back in with the assay dish, and her eyes were annoyed, but there was also pity showing in them. *He's not well, my love,* she said along the bond. *You know how it is with him when these moods strike. He's been thinking about how much he misses Yiluv, that's all, and when he's like this, the sun would look black to him. I'm done up there: let me just get into my suit and I'll go in and fetch that last one into close orbit.*

"No," Pekev said, wearily, though he really didn't want to, "I'll do it."

No, truly, she said. *You're tired.*

"Not that tired," he said. He turned the sealer off, checked the seal to be sure it was tight, and started to put the suit on again. *One more won't kill me,* he said in the bond. *You be off. We'll bring it in ahead of the others and show it to him to make him happy. Maybe that'll buy us a night's peace.*

She smiled at him and went back to the corelab.

Pekev swore softly, trying to keep it out of the bond, and headed for the airlock again.

Exotic music fills her ears: the sound of deep trumpets and martial gongs. Their sound lures her along through the landscape to one of the "experience gates." She has not tried one of these for a long time. She allows herself to drift through it, borne along on the music.

Viewpoint dissolves into day under Vulcan's burning sky. Sand stretches out everywhere: and far in the distance a point of stone rears up, terrible, a dark shape in the bright day. Viewpoint pushes in on it. It is Mount Seleya, and the awful stair carved up it, ten thousand steps cut around and through the ancient weathered stone. Effortlessly she drifts with the viewpoint up those stairs, sees the great desert spreading out below her, the Forge, a place of old dread, where powers move that men do not understand, and there are hints of great incomprehensible voices speaking secrets in whispers under the sand. But no matter for that. She goes to her destiny at last, to find her fate.

They are there waiting for her, all of them, robed and solemn: the priests and priestesses of the secret arts of the mind. As she approaches she drifts no longer: she is a body, has a body, that of a young woman, armed and armored. But she has no sword, and a great anger burns in her heart.

I have come for what you owe me, she says. She has no idea from where the words come to her, but she speaks them as if they are her own, and the anger in them her own as well.

The chief priestess stands forth and raises her empty hands. *We have it not,* she says. *The evil one, the mind that resists, has taken it from us. You must win it yourself. This was not in the pact,* she says, and steps forward wrathfully.

The chief priestess looks at her coolly and moves not an inch. *You speak true. And so we give you something that was not in the pact as well. Know then the name of the sword: that this is indeed Nak'meth the Great, forged of these sands by the Mastersmith, three thousand years agone, and with a virtue set on it that one who holds it shall achieve their dream and their right. And know too,* the priestess says, paying no attention to her gasp, *that your right is a mighty one, for you are no peasant's child, as you were told, but castoff child of the Lady of Yiliw, and heir to all the lands of Yiliw, which now lie under the evil one's dominion. Go, then, and take the sword, and take back also what is your own—*

"Arieth," someone said in her ear, "we need you."

She opened her eyes. She hated opening her eyes.

Her room. Her tiny room, after all that space, after the fresh hot smell of the sand, the scorch of the sun beating down. Her bed, her chair, her clothes. A little box, a tomb such as one of the ancient kings would have been embarrassed to use to bury his pet *aalth* in.

She got up angrily, pulling the commlink away from the neural contact at the back of her neck. It was T'Vei's voice, the hateful thing. She had her Pekev; why couldn't she leave other people alone? Hadn't Arieth been up all this morning doing assay on cores while T'Vei was slugging abed? Useless, bought-in—

The door opened, and she began to shout "Go away!" but it was Hanesh, and he had as much right to the room as she did. Unfortunately, He was all over grease: he had been in the mechanical grappling systems again, by the look of him. *He spends more time with the machinery than he needs to,* said a suspicion in her mind. *Or he seems to. I wonder—*

"Pekev's bringing in one last stone tonight, to see if it won't calm Nomikh down a little," he said softly. "Come on up and do the assay on it when he gets it in, so we can all have a little peace from the old man."

"I did my work this morning," Alieth said, and started to lie down on the couch again. "Let T'Aria or Tasav do it—they haven't been doing much of anything lately." She sniffed. "I should have trained to be a pilot. Three seconds of work in a half day and then eating and drinking and sleeping for a week after. Besides, I'm having my rest now."

"You're not," Henesh said. "You're on the link. You're *always* on the link."

"I do my share of work," she said. "Just because you don't care for the link, don't dictate how I can spend my spare time."

He said nothing, but down the bond she could hear him thinking. *I just wish you would spend a little more time with me.*

She ignored this. "Go on," she said. She lay down again and waited for him to go away: but he would not. Finally, because it was the only way to get rid of him, she said, "All right, then. I'll come, but only when the stone's up in the hold, and not a minute sooner."

He nodded and went out.

Alieth sighed and felt around for the neural connection, slipped it cool against her neck, lay back. The shadows swallowed her, and then the light turned to the wild heat of the sun again.

The high priestess lifts her hands and says, "Go with the blessing of our order on you. And that you may prosper, take these gifts—" More horns are blown, and the tiny bells are sounded, and jeweled treasures of antique make are borne forth on brocaded cushions. She accepts them, and the underpriests and priestesses cry her praise.

Their voices drown out the bond very satisfactorily.

"It's in range," Pekev said from outside the ship. "Got a lock on it, Hanesh?"

"Locked," Hanesh said, not needing to look up from the console to check the image on the screen. He was strapped in his seat, as was T'Vei beside him: there was no gravity in the core, which was just as well for handling asteroids anyway.

Hanesh put his arms into the control boxes and flexed his fingers as they fit into the gauntlets. Outside the ship, the grapples flexed too, mirroring his action, and reached out slowly and carefully for the asteroid. One had to be careful. The carbon-matrix asteroids were not nearly as solid as the nickel-iron ones, and could shatter . . . and when they did, you had wasted fuel and energy, and Nomikh would make your life miserable. Every now and then Hanesh wished the ship had a tractor beam, but such things were much too expensive when *Rasha* was built, and they certainly couldn't afford one now.

He reached out iron arms for the asteroid, watching his progress using the stereo cameras mounted on the outsides of the "fingers." The asteroid was a medium-sized one, perhaps as wide across as a man was tall, but easily within the hold's ability to handle. The outer part of the hold was already evacuated, waiting to have the asteroid placed in the handling cradle.

Hanesh reached out carefully. This maneuver was always the trickiest part of the business, because typically one did not stop the ship's spin unless the stone was of unusual size. His arms, therefore, were spinning on their vertical axis, just as the ship was. Pekev had done his part, carefully aligning the asteroid with the ship and putting the proper spin on it so that they seemed to be stationary relative to one another.

"Here we go," said Hanesh, reaching out close. The arms were within a height: a half-height: they closed.

And he felt the clutch, and the crunch, through the remotes, and swore.

"What?" T'Vei said.

"It shattered."

She peered at the screen. "Not very badly. Look at it. Just bring it in carefully: it's too big to waste the energy that throwing it away would take."

Hanesh considered this, then thought of the mood of the old man downstairs, and agreed. "Handling a cracked stone," he said, as he carefully pulled the arms in, "is not easy, you know."

"Yes," T'Vei said, and was silent: but she smiled at him.

Hanesh watched the view. The arms turned inward on themselves, rotating on universal gimbals so that the evacuated hold yawned before them, and the cradle came up on its tracks to meet them. Very carefully he snugged the asteroid down into the cradle, and its own servos came up with soft-tipped probes and secured the stone all around.

"Well done!" T'Vei said. "Let's get it in."

It took very little time to seal up the outer hold, repressive it, and open the secondary doors to bring the cradle down into the main lab area. "You might as well page Alieth now," T'Vei said, launching out into the middle space of the corelab and using handholds to pull herself over to the cradle.

"Must I?" Hanesh said. T'Vei flashed a smile at him and turned her attention to the stone. Carbon matrix of one of the harder sort: it had that heat-seared look about the outside of it. She floated around the circular crack, looking at the stone. "You did a nice job on this one," she said. "Very little fracturing from the remotes. A little bit of flaking here—"

"I'm not surprised," he said. He used the mechanical page to the comm network, rather than the voice comm, then grabbed another set of handholds and launched himself down toward T'Vei. "I squeezed it pretty hard. What are you looking at?"

She was gazing at the crack, which was about half an inch wide. "Would you reach me one of the hand tools?" she said. "The sonic chisel, the little one."

He handed it to her: she thumbed it on and applied it to the crack. A few flakes of stone sprang away.

Something translucent and white showed underneath them, about an inch wide.

She used the chisel again. Another inch of translucence was revealed, roughly paralleling the surface of the asteroid.

T'Vei looked at Hanesh with astonishment. "I don't think we're going to need an assay on this one," she said. She chiseled once more, and another flake of stone fell off: and inside the crack, another inch of diamond showed.

"Get Father," she said.

His first response was to hang staring from a handhold, without speaking, for nearly fifteen minutes, as T'Vei ran an ultrasound scan on the asteroid. There were three diamonds inside it, two in the upper half of the asteroid, undamaged, and one that Hanesh had unfortunately squeezed and cracked with the rest of the stone. The cracked one was the biggest: nearly a hundredweight in mass, and roughly half a height in diameter. The whole family came to see: the children, the pilots, everyone. Even Alieth had stayed, even after finding that she wasn't needed. Ten astonished faces stared at the diamond on top as T'Vei's skilled hands freed more and more of it.

Finally Nomikh turned to Tasav, one of the pilots. "Set us a course for Ashif Belt Station," he said, "and don't spare the fuel."

Tasav nodded eagerly and went off to see to it.

"This is it," Nomikh said. "The stone, the stone of stones. We are rich!"

"Let me get it out of the matrix safely first, Father," T'Vei said, not looking up from her work. "I'd prefer not to crack any more of these."

He nodded, and fell silent. T'Vei felt fairly sure she knew what they were thinking about. Gemstones from space were highly prized on Vulcan, and brought a great deal more at market than ones that originated onplanet. What diamonds of this size could bring—she hardly dared think. She suspected that Nomikh could buy a fleet twice as big as the one he'd had, and still have plenty left over afterward.

But what would he do?

Funds that came to the family in the course of work were used to fuel the ship and take care of its running expenses: after that, what was left over was usually divided evenly among the crew. Even the children got a share. The only problem was that there was usually nothing left after the ship was taken care of: a little extra for a few luxuries, some food other than the standard dried reconstitutable rations. T'Vei sighed, remembering a time on Ashif Station when she had had fresh meat for dinner. Well, perhaps it had been frozen. She hadn't minded.

But now—there would be no question of keeping the ship running anymore. There would be enough money, enough for everything. And would all the members of the family want to keep mining?

Why should they? We can all retire, wealthy.

But to where? And to whom? Will we never see one another again? For indeed there had been and were often times when T'Vei heartily wished one or another of the family dead, and doubtless they had had the same wish about her. It was hardly to be avoided, when people had been in such close quarters for so long. What was going to happen now?

She had a horrible feeling, as flake after flake of stone fell out, that she would find out soon enough.

Nomikh did not come to dinner that night. Many of the others didn't care: their spirits were too high as they discussed their plans. Some of them were extraordinary. Almost everyone wanted to buy a house on Vulcan, a *big* house. A couple of them were more interested in a "sealed cottage" on T'Khut, in one of the colonies, away from the trouble on the planet. But most seemed to be willing to take their chances with trouble, convinced that money—the kind of money they were dealing with now—would buy them plenty of protection. And then there would be luxuries. Fine clothes, personal vehicles, servants, ships of their own, trips to all the places they had wanted to see. It would be a wonderful life.

T'Vei was not so sure. Several times she looked with concern at Pekev, and once he said to her, down the bond, *I am beginning to wish that you had never made me go out and get that thing.*

She looked at him quizzically. *I didn't make you go,* she said, *and I would have gone out, if you hadn't. I think we had better take this as an intended thing.*

He shook his head, but inwardly agreed with her.

The discussion kept going long after the meal was done. T'Vei slipped away, after a while, and went down to Nomikh's cabin. She knocked, but there was no answer: she peered in.

She found him lying on the narrow bed, eyes open, staring at the ceiling, with the tears streaming down either side of his face.

"It doesn't work anymore," he was saying. "It doesn't work."

She slipped in softly and sat on the floor by the bed. "What doesn't work, Father?" she said.

"The bond," he said, and wept hard.

T'Vei bowed her head. There were mate-bonds that broke, at death, and ones that did not. There were always the tales of the ones that did not break, when one bondmate could still feel the other, regardless—even sometimes speak to them. There was no predicting it, and you never knew which kind you had until it happened.

"She never," Nomikh said. "So hard she worked, and she never had anything. I wanted everything for her. But all I had was this. Forty years, without her. And now this—!" He wept again. "She should have been here," he said; "this should have been forty years ago. Riches, leisure, everything she wanted. But it comes now. Why now? Why now?"

And then a long pause, and whispered, the worst, "This was not it. This wasn't what I wanted after all . . ."

There were no more words in him, only tears. T'Vei touched his brow gently, then went out to go upstairs and finish the assay, the weighing and measuring of the stones. She had no heart for the talk around the scruffy dinner table, all the ornate plans. She was afraid, to the core of her, but Nomikh would want a reckoning of the stones in the morning.

She climbed up to the core and tried to do her work without looking at them more than necessary. But they looked at her, the cold white eyes of the stone, the eyes. . . .

In the morning they met again around the table, after the mornmeal things had been cleared away, and T'Vei sat down with her pad. Nomikh was last at the table, and he sat down with an odd quelling expression on his face.

"Tasav?" he said first, to the pilot.

"We will be at Ashif Station in four hours," he said.

"Good. T'Vei?"

"Well." She looked at the pad with a great desire to say, *They are worthless.* "We have three stones, as you have all seen, and some fragments. They mass, all together, seventeen point six three hundredweight." Astonished glances went around the table. "At present market value—well, there would be some change in the value as the stones are cut. But I estimate the value of the stones at around two billion *nakh.*"

Silence.

Nomikh breathed in, breathed out. "Very well," he said. "We will dispose of them to the gemological service group at Ashif. And then"—he cut in on the happy gabble that rose up around the table—"we will refuel and go out again."

Everyone looked at him in shock. Then the gabble started again, but loud and angry.

"—why—"

"—we can retire—"

"—don't want to work anymore—"

"—not fair—"

"Haven't I taught you anything about thrift?" he said. He did not shout in return at their anger. His eyes were strangely cool. "What happens when this money runs out?"

"Runs out??" said Tasav incredulously. "Even divided eleven ways, we could all be dead before that happens!"

"Divided?" The cool eyes looked at him. "There will be no divisions. The money stays with the ship. And we go out and earn our keep."

The silence that followed this statement had a terrible waiting quality.

"This is not the one," the old man said, looking at them one by one. "This is not the great stone, the stone of stones. This will keep us for a while, for as long as it takes us to find that other. We will keep looking until we find it. And then we can all retire. But for the time being we must be thrifty, we must be prudent, we must save our air and energy. Someday we will be rich. But we are not now. Not yet."

Eyes sought one another around the table, and what they mostly said was, *He's gone mad at last. We always saw it coming. Now here it is.*

"You're just afraid we'll leave you all alone," Hanesh said, jumping up from his seat. "Don't you trust us? Can't we be trusted to keep working together—or living together, even if we don't have to work—aren't we still a family, even if we don't *have* to be? Won't we be a family still, even if we're not cooped up in this wretched metal can? Father!"

"Children must stay with the family," Nomikh said placidly, "until they are old enough to take care of themselves."

There seemed no answer to that.

"We will be at Ashif soon," Nomikh said. "Alieth, make a shopping list. We're getting low on dry stores." And he got up to leave.

"Getting low!" Alieth screamed. She had not been on the net for almost a day, to everyone's astonishment, and there was a greed in her eyes that was terrible to see. "We're getting *dead*, trapped in here, nothing but work, and want, scrimping oxygen and eating scraps, and hurting, and never having any of the good things— Let us out of here, let us free, give us what's our right, let us go home and never have to be out here again in the cold and the dark! *Let us away from you!*"

Nomikh looked at her gently. "Not until you're older," he said, and left the room.

"We could kill him."

The silence into which this suggestion fell was awful. More awful was the feeling that some of the people around the table agreed to the idea.

The mutiny had been going on for an hour and a half now. That was the only thing T'Vei could think of to call it. All the adults on the ship save for Nomikh were still around the table, where Nomikh had left them. They had risen, sometimes, several of them, to pace, to shout, to strike the walls in frustration: but they always sat down again, to mutter, to lay bitter plans. No one had mentioned *this* one before . . . but T'Vei had feared it. And now her fear was upon her.

She shook her head. "He is Head of House!" T'Vei said, looking around the table, trying to meet their eyes. They would not look at her. Not Hanesh: not Pekev, next to her, his heart oddly closed to her, purposely shutting down the bond: not Tasav, his fists clenching and unclenching: not T'Aria, his bondmate, the other pilot. And not Alieth, who had made the suggestion, the terrible one, the one that everyone had thought of, and no one had dared utter, until now.

"He is Head of House!" she said again. "There is no relationship more sacred, none! Without him, who are we?"

"Free," Hanesh muttered. "Free to do what we want, for the first time in our lives."

"And defiled!" T'Vei said. "Just because we are angry at him, does not give us leave to kill him! To kill the Head of House is as good as to kill the House!"

"The House *is* dead!" Alieth shouted, and this time she looked up at T'Vei, and the expression in her eyes, of anguish, and horror, and anger, was terrible to see. "It has been dead since *Gelevesh* was taken from us, since the fleet was broken and nine-tenths of the House became groundlings, scratching at the hide of the world for a living, begging other houses for their sufferance! Now comes a chance to finally be something, to become something, and what does he do? He forbids it to us, and says he will doom us to the rest of our lives out in this cold waste—"

"Alieth," Pekev said, "give him a little time. The shock may have unsettled him, but he may yet come back to his senses. Give him a few—"

"What? A few moons? A few sunrounds? How many? Ten? Twenty? Fifty? How long are you willing to live this life, Pekev? It's all very well for some, who have the bond as you do—" Hanesh flinched hard: Alieth never saw it. "But what about the rest of us, who are a little more interested in the rest of the world, who weary of living our lives like container cargo? Who would like a little more to drink than water, and a little more to eat than dry protein extender, and a little more to see than the dark, and the inside of a metal can? Who would like a *nakh* of our own to spend, and somewhere else to spend it than a filthy, smelly orbital station full of broken-down scrapings of the system—" She gasped for breath. "How long do you think it will take Nomikh to come back to his sanity? If he ever had it, these twenty years gone? There he lies in his cabin, blubbering and wishing he were dead, and I for one wouldn't mind seeing him get his wish!"

That stunned silence fell again.

"We could keep him in his cabin," Tasav said, very low, in his reasonable way. "There would be nothing wrong with that. When we get to Ashif, we can tell the port authority that he's lost his mind. They'll agree to that, certainly, once they see what's happened, and how he is. And then—"

"Then what, Tasav?" Pekev looked over at him. "Then we choose a new Head of House, right? The eldest?"

All were still for a moment. That would have been Pekev. He was closest by blood to Nomikh, and eldest of the close blood relatives.

Alieth stared at him. "And let *you* decide what happens to us all? You, the Good Son? You'd do as your father did. And hold to yourself the decision of what to do with the money—"

Everything got still again as this new thought went through all minds. What was to guarantee that a new Head of House would be any more sane, one way or another, than the old one? What was to keep a new Head of House from keeping everything for himself, or herself, and turning all the others out, or doling out pittances to them that would keep them working on the ship, as wage slaves, for the rest of their lives? Who could trust any agreement any one of them would make, with control of such massive amounts of money at stake? Heads turned, and T'Vei was horrified to see the family looking at one another with terrible suspicion and assessment. Who might be managed, if they became Head of House? Who could be bullied or swayed into managing the money the way each of *them* would prefer it?

Who would be permitted to live—?

"No," T'Vei whispered, horrified. "Listen, all of you, you will kill the House—"

"The House is dead," Alieth said, very low. "It died the moment Pekev brought that rock on board."

"It is not dead yet," T'Vei said. "It lives still. If you will all see reason!" She glanced at Pekev, more terrified for his life, now, than she had been for Nomikh's. "We can appeal to the port authority against Nomikh's decision, as soon as we dock there, and get a ruling dividing it equally—"

"After bribing the authority with how much?" Alieth said. "How much of what you bled and starved and sweated twenty years for? Why should they have so much as a copper cash *srikh* of it? What have they done to earn it? Oh, no, darling sister-in-House. Indeed not. Let us settle family matters in the family, as has been done among our people these many years—"

A chair scraped back. "Tasav—" T'Vei said, more horrified than ever, for he was making for the door, and in his hand was the pilot's sidearm that he never, never drew.

Tasav paused in the doorway. "We need not go straight to Ashif," he said. "There is time to work matters out beforehand, to everyone's satisfaction . . . and make sure all the stories match."

T'Vei's heart raced in her. "Tasav, this is madness," she cried. "*All* of it is madness. Nomikh has the computer keywords for navigation and helm! You cannot manage the ship without them . . . and the Head passes them to the computer through dermo-neural link—"

"So he does," Tasav said softly. "I think he can be encouraged to pass them on." And he went out into the corridor.

Alieth got up, knocking her seat over in her haste, and went after him.

T'Vei looked at Pekev in utter horror. *This is the end for us,* she said down the bond. *Did we think by coming out here into the dark that we were getting away from the madness of the world? We have brought the madness into the night with us—or else we pretend we have it not, like Alieth—but it is here. It is here—*

They heard the first shot, then. Everyone in the room scrambled to their feet. Some ran one way, some another: but the end was the same for all of them. For T'Vei and Pekev, trying to stop Tasav, the quick bolt through the body or the head that killed their bond in fire: for Tasav, the answering bolt from Nomikh's room that caught him, and several of the others, as they forced his door: for Nomikh himself, floundering in madness and old mourning grief, a last bolt that put out his pain forever: for the few remaining adult members of the family, and the children, crouching terrified in the living quarters, a long, long wait, while the ship went its way, the computer locked on course and unlockable save by passwords that no one alive now knew.

And in one small room, a drifting over a misty landscape, a passage through a door—and one stands again before a robed priestess who gestures forth the subpriestesses carrying objects of ancient rarity and virtue. They give her the spear, and its point runs green with blood: she brandishes it in the dawn. They give her the horn, graven about with dire runes and prophecies of death to her enemies: she lifts it, and winds it, and the walls of the mountain give back the terrible sound as if it were the cry of an avenging army encamped below. And they give her the most terrible weapon, the helm that teaches one to read the dreams of men, for by learning their dreams and turning them against them may they most easily be crushed. She fits it on her head, and it fits perfectly, and she knows her foes vanquished already.

Take these, the priestess says, *and go forth to victory.* And all is swallowed up in a great burst of white fire as the Sun comes up, victorious and terrible, above Seleya—

The ship came into Ashif Station on the wrong vector, at the wrong angle. It answered no hails: its engines were running at full, so that it was accelerating at a deadly seven g's all the way in from the time it was first sensed. There was no way to catch it, no way to stop it. A particle beam targeted it at last, and blew the ship into pieces that rained down, around, and sometimes onto Ashif Station for hours. It had not been carrying any cargo that could be detected: its holds seem to have been empty. The assumption was that the ship had been pirated, or more likely taken by terrorists, and used in an attempt to destroy the station. Mahn'heh Protectorate, which owned the station, accused Lalirh of having engineered the attack, and shortly thereafter destroyed one of Lalirh's orbital stations in the asteroids with something new: a weapon that seemed to involve the combination of matter and antimatter. There was general alarm about this, since it seemed likely that now someone with the proper technology, and the access to the necessary materials, could actually destroy Vulcan. But in the several wars that started as a result of Mahn'heh and Lalirh destroying one another's populations with neutron bombs, this possibility seemed a little too remote to waste much time considering.

Far out in the asteroid belt, the day the *Rasha* was blown up, a small storm of glitter rained past Ashif and off into the endless night: odd small micro-meteorites, crystallized carbon of some sort, very hard, very tiny, and mixed up with other meteors. The station's defensive field vaporized them in a shower of little sparks as they hit it, and the tourists from Vulcan pointed up through the dome and talked about the beauties of the universe.

Far away, T'Khut looked over the edge of the world at the new fires burning on Vulcan . . . possibly some of the last ones.

Enterprise: Six

FROM: Curious
DATE: 7466.31
SUBJECT: Oh really?

A lot of people have been making some pretty definite statements in here, the past couple of days, about the Vulcan situation and what they think should be done about it. It's easy to
do. But none of us are actually sitting in the hot seat: or none
of us except the captain. A lot of people in here are acting as if
he's supposed to save this situation somehow. Well, how? No
one has made a single suggestion that could actually be imple-
mented. If you people are going to insist that the situation can
in some miraculous way be saved from disaster by one man,
the least you can do is share your wisdom with us as to how.
Otherwise, you might have the grace to keep your traps shut.

I await with interest what will probably be an echoing silence.
Best, C

"Now what do you make of that?" Jim said to McCoy. They were in his quarters
the next morning, ready to beam down to the Hall of the Voice.

McCoy studied the screen. "Piquant," he said. "Very much to the point. A little
rude. I wish I'd left it."

Jim looked at him sidewise. "I thought maybe you had."

McCoy laughed. "Not me. My spelling gives me away every time."

"Why don't you use the spelling checker? There's one built into the system."

"I don't like the way it punctuates."

Jim chuckled. "Well, look at the answers. You want rude—!" He leaned over the
keyboard and started the replies scrolling down the screen.

"Goodness," McCoy said, staring at it, fascinated. "Temper, temper!" Once he
laughed out loud: several times he frowned very severely. But mostly he shook his
head. "Generally," he said, "they sound a little sheepish. 'Curious' caught them out."

"But look at this one, Bones." Jim scrolled ahead a few pages more. "Here we are."

FROM: Llarian
DATE: 7466.35
SUBJECT: Re: Oh, really?

Those who know others are intelligent;
Those who know themselves have insight.
Those who master others have force;
Those who master themselves have strength.
Through nonaction nothing is left undone.
L.

Bones was nodding. "How about that," he said. "We have a Taoist on board."

"I was wondering why it sounded familiar. The *Tao Teh Ching*?"

"That's right." Bones looked at the message. "What do you think of the advice?"

"It sounds good." Jim smiled slightly. "It always sounds good. I remember thinking how sensible a book it was, the first time I read it at Academy. But it's always harder to practice the advice in the field."

"I guess you just have to keep practicing," McCoy said. He scrolled through the rest of the messages, then cleared the screen and straightened up. "I wonder who 'Llarian' is."

"That thought has crossed my mind as well." Jim shrugged. "I would love to know what he, she, it, means. But it's not something I can find out."

"Maybe someone else could. . . ."

Jim looked at McCoy in shock. "Bones! And you're usually so careful about confidentiality." He shook his head. "Let it be. Whoever Llarian is, I appreciate the advice. Meanwhile . . ." He glanced at his chrono. "Where's Spock?"

The door signal chimed right then. "Come in," Jim said.

Spock entered. "Captain," he said, "are you ready? The doctor will be needed in the Hall shortly."

"Just about. Off," Jim said to the computer. "You set, Bones?"

"Ouch," McCoy said. "I assume that pun was meant to make me feel better, or else accidental. I am *never* set to talk in front of large groups of people, especially not while sober." He made a rueful expression. "But I'm ready to go."

"Do your deep breathing," Spock suggested gently.

McCoy made a friendly suggestion to Spock that did not involve the Vulcan's respiratory apparatus.

They headed out into the hall together. "I must admit," McCoy said quietly as they went, "I still can't get over your little tête-à-tête with T'Pring yesterday. And the sheer coldness of the woman. I had trouble believing what you told me she said the last time, when she challenged . . . but this was a hundred times worse."

Spock nodded. "She is implacable, Doctor. Even if there were something that she could do to stop this situation, she would not do it. And truly," he added, "I much doubt that anything she might do would make any difference, at this point. This context of bigotry and exclusion is already finding too secure a foothold in too many Vulcans' minds: they would overrule any attempted suspension of the proceedings."

Jim thought back to that cold, lovely face and the words Spock had later reported: *You have become something of a legend among our people, Spock. . . . I became aware that I did not desire to be the consort of a legend.* And the word she and her family had given at the original binding, and any concern about Spock's feelings—not that a Vulcan would have admitted them, granted—went out the window at that point. All she needed was someone to challenge Spock when the time came: and Stonn, who had desired her then, had been willing.

If you lost, then Stonn would be mine. If you won, then you would release me because I had challenged, and still there would be Stonn. And if your captain won, then he would release me because he did not want me, and Stonn would still be there. . . .

The sheer coldness of it. And the logic. That so sharp a mind should also be so cruel. . . .

I think I would like a little talk with this lady myself.

But it would have to wait. They headed into the transporter room and climbed up onto the pads. "You have the coordinates?" Jim said to the transporter technician, Mr. Schneider. And then added to McCoy, "Why, Bones, you're sweating."

"Your turn will come," McCoy muttered.

"Number six," said Shath.

McCoy stepped up there with great calm. Considering that those who spoke before him had been vehemently anti-Federation, and the audience was (if Jim judged the mood correctly) in a very satisfied mood, Jim thought he was being even calmer than he needed to be. McCoy stood in the shafts of downpouring sunlight, glanced up at them for a moment, and then looked once right around the room, as if taking the measure of it. His stance was remarkably erect for a man who habitually slouched a bit. But Jim looked at this and wondered if he was not seeing Vulcan body language, rather than Terran. Bones was shrewder than people usually thought.

"My name is Leonard Edward McCoy," he said, and the focusing field caught his voice and threw it out to the back of the room, all around: but there was still something about the tenor of the voice itself that hinted that the focusing field might be doing slightly less work than usual. "I hold the rank of Commander in the Starfleet of the United Federation of Planets: my position is Chief Medical Officer of the *Starship Enterprise*. And as regards the question of the secession of Vulcan, my position is, hell no!"

There were chuckles from some of the humans present, a bemused stirring from some of the Vulcans. "I hope you will pardon me the momentary excursion into my mother idiom," McCoy said: "perhaps I should more correctly say, with Surak, *ekhwe'na meh kroykah tevesh.*" This time there were murmurs from the Vulcans, and they were of approval. The translator did not render the words—Jim assumed they were in classical or "Old" Vulcan, which the translator was not equipped to handle.

When the crowd settled a bit, McCoy went on in very precise Vulcan, and this caused a minor stir as well, which died down eventually. "I want to keep this on a friendly basis," he said, "despite the fact that some of you are feeling decidedly unfriendly toward Terrans. Nor am I here to lecture you. Others here have been doing that a lot better than I could." There was a dry sound to his voice for a moment. "I am here to ask you, as a planet, not to pull out of what has been a very old and successful affiliation for everyone involved."

He paused for a moment, looking around. "It's kind of sobering to be looked at by an entire planet," he said. "You people have hidden the cameras perfectly: I appreciate the effect. Anyway. Some people here have spoken about the mode of their comments—scientific or ethical or whatever. Well, for my own part I'm not sure there's a difference, or should be. Science is barren without ethics, and ethics has very little to use itself on without science. But I'll speak of what I know, if I may. The medical mode, I suppose we might as well call it. I understand that Surak valued the healer's art highly, so I suspect there's some precedent."

Bones walked around the stage for a moment, his hands clasped behind him. Jim had to smile: he had seen this particular pacing mannerism many times, while McCoy tried to figure out the best way to deliver some piece of good or bad news. "The first thing I would want to say to you," he said, "is that it is illogical to rewound what is already healing. Or as my mother used to say, 'If you don't stop picking at it, it'll never get better.' " A soft sound of amusement ran around the hall.

"Most of the agreements going these days between Terrans, or the Federation, and Vulcan, are in the nature of band-aids. One of our species hurt the other, some-where: the other said, 'Sorry,' and put a bandage on it. It's the usual thing you see when you see two children playing together. At first they hurt one another a lot—"

"Our species is hardly a child compared with yours," said someone in the audi-ence, a sharp angry voice.

"Well," McCoy said, turning that way and searching the audience with his eyes, "that depends on how you reckon it. Certainly your species was making bombs and guns and missiles and such while ours was still mostly playing with sharpened sticks and stone knives, or in a few favored areas, bronze. But I'm not sure that any partic-ular virtue accrues to that distinction. And even if we *have* been kicking one an-other's shins for less time than you, it's still true that era for era, Terra's people have kicked a lot fewer shins *per capita* than Vulcan has. You have several times almost reduced your population to below the viability level: it took a miracle to save you. We may be a bloody, barbaric lot of savages, but we never went *that* far. Even when we first came up with atomics." He chuckled softly at the slight silence that fell. "Yes," he said, "you saw that article in the data nets last night, too, some of you. Where *is* Selv?" he said, peering amiably around the audience. "You in here?"

"Here," said the sharp voice.

"Aha," McCoy said, looking out in that direction and shading his eyes. "Long life and prosperity to you—though I doubt you'll attract much prosperity with that kind of world-view. Still, maybe wishes count. But it might help if you went to Earth some day and checked out what you talked about so blithely—"

"The data about Earth speaks for itself—" Selv's thin, angry voice came back.

"No data speaks for itself," McCoy said, forceful. "Data just lies there. *People* speak. The idiom 'speaks for itself' almost *always* translates as 'If I don't say some-thing about this, no one will notice it.' Sloppy thinking, Selv! You are dealing with second- and third-hand data. You have never been to Earth, you don't understand our language—and this is made especially clear by some of the material you claim to be 'translating' from Earth publications: an Andorian spirit-dancer with a Ouija board and a Scrabble set could do a better job. Though I must admit I really liked the arti-cle on the evolution of the blood sacrifice in Terran culture. That is *not* what major-league football is for. . . ."

McCoy let the laugh die down, and then said, "Anyway, where was I? Agreements as bandages. *Every* species in this galaxy that bumps into another one, bruises it a little. Some of them back off in terror and never come out to play again. Some of them run home to their mommies and cry, and never come out again with-out someone else to protect them. That's their problem. I for one would like them to come out and play—"

"And be exploited? The Federation's record of violations of the Prime Directive has been well documented—"

"Selv, I love you. How many violations of the Prime Directive have there been?"

A brief, frantic silence. "Well documented," McCoy said, good-humored, "but not well enough for you to have seen it. Too busy reading about football? Anyway, don't bother looking it up," McCoy said, "I'll tell you myself. In the last one hundred and eighty years, there have been twenty-nine violations. It sounds like a lot . . . ex-cept when you consider that those took place during the exploration of twenty-three *thousand* planets by the various branches of Starfleet. And don't start with me about the *Enterprise,"* he added, "and her purported record. There have been five violations . . . out of six hundred thirty-three planets visited and physically surveyed over the last five years."

"And all those violations have taken place under a Terran's captaincy—"

"Oh, my," McCoy said, and it came out almost in a purr, "can it be that Vulcan is leaving the Federation because someone here *doesn't like James T. Kirk?* What an amazing idea! Though it would go nicely with some rumors I've been hearing." Bones strolled calmly around the stage for a moment, while Jim and Spock looked at one another, slightly startled. "Well, no matter for that. Still, Selv, your contact with the facts about things seems to be sporadic at best. If I were the people who've been reading your material in the nets—and a busy little beaver you've been of late—I would start wondering about how much of what I was reading was for real. That is, if I were logical—" McCoy lifted his head to look up over the audience's heads, and Spock glanced meaningfully at Jim. McCoy knew perfectly well where the cameras were.

"You may say what you like," Selv said, "but even five violations are too many! And your use of your data is subjective—"

"Of course they're too many!" McCoy said. "Do you think I would disagree on that? And as for my data, of course it's subjective! So is yours! We are each of us locked up in our own skull, or maybe skulls, if you're a Vulcan and lucky enough to be successfully bonded. If you start going on about objective reality, I swear *I'll* come down and bite you in the leg!" There was some chuckling at that.

"Though I hope you've had your shots," McCoy added. "If not, I can always give them to you afterward. I've become pretty fair at taking care of Vulcans over the past few years. At any rate, I was talking about bandages—"

"The doctor is tenacious," Spock said softly.

"The doctor is a damn good shrink," Jim whispered back, "and knows damn well when someone's trying to give him the runaround."

"—There's no arguing the fact that Vulcans and Terrans, or the Terran-influenced functions of the Federation, have had a lot of bumps into one another over the course of time," McCoy said. "There have been arguments about trade, and weapons policy, and exploration, and exploitation of natural resources, and the protocol of running a Vulcan space service, and everything else you can think of. And every one of those arguments is a bandage over one of the other species' hurts. Now," he said, "you would destroy all that hard-built cooperation at one blow: rip off all the bandages at once, yours and ours together—"

"We can bind up our own wounds," Selv said angrily. "And when two species are no longer going to be cooperating, what does it really matter about the other's?"

McCoy gazed up at him. " 'The spear in the other's heart is the spear in your own,' " he said: " 'you are he.' "

A great silence fell.

"So much for the man who claims, in the net media, to speak for a majority of all right-thinking Vulcans," McCoy said, glancing up over the audience's heads again. "You see that there is at least one Vulcan he does *not* speak for. Surak."

Jim and Spock looked at each other in utter satisfaction.

McCoy strolled about calmly on the stage for a moment, as if waiting to see whether Selv would come up with anything further. "Can't have Vulcan without Surak," he said: "most irregular. At least, that seems to be most people's attitude here. But a few of you seem quite ready to throw him out along with us." He kept strolling, his hands clasped behind him again, and he gazed absently at the floor as he walked. Then suddenly he looked up.

"*We* are what he was preparing you for," McCoy said. "Don't you see that? Along with everything else in the universe, of course. *Infinite diversity in infinite combinations!* That means people who breathe methane, and people who hang upside down from the ceiling, and people who look like pan pizzas, and people who speak no language we will ever understand and want only to be left alone. And it means *us!* A particularly hard case. An aggressive, nasty, brutish little species . . . one that nonetheless managed to get out into space and begin its first couple of friendships with other species without consulting *you* first for advice. A species that maybe reminds you a little too much of yourselves, a while ago—confused and angry and afraid. A hard case. Probably the hardest case! . . . the challenge that you have been practicing on with other species for a while now! And you met us, and welcomed us, though you had understandable reservations. And since then there have been arguments, but generally things have been working out all right. We are proud to be in partnership with you.

"But now . . . now comes the inevitable reaction. There's always a reaction to daring to do the difficult thing, day after day. Every action has an equal and opposite reaction: this is reaction. The temptation is arising to chicken out. It would be easier, some people are saying. Cleaner, nicer, tidier, without the messy Federation and the problems it raises just by being there. And you are backing off, you are panicking, you are saying, No, we can't cope, Surak can't have meant *everything* when he taught the philosophy of IDIC: he actually meant everything *but* the third planet out from Sol.

"COWARDS!!"

McCoy paced. The Hall of the Voice was utterly still.

"Pride," he said finally, more quietly. "I keep hearing about Vulcan pride. An emotion, of course. One you were supposed to have mastered, those of you who practice *cthia:* or something you were supposed to have gotten rid of, those of you who went in for Kolinahr. Well, I have news for you. The stuff I've been seeing in the nets lately, that is *pride.* Not to be confused with admiration, which is something else, or pleasure in integrity, which is something else entirely. This is good old-fashioned pride, and it goes with fear, fear of the Other: and pride and fear together have gone with all your falls before, and the one you're about to take now, if you're not very careful." McCoy's voice softened. "I would very much like to see you not take it. I am rather fond of you people. You scare the hell out of *me* sometimes, but it would be a poor universe without you. But unless you move through your fear, which is the emotion Surak was the most concerned about—and rightly—and come out the other side, the fall is waiting for you: and you will bring it about yourselves, without any help from our species or any other. This," he gestured around him, "all this concern about humans, and indirectly about the Federation—this is a symptom of something else, something deeper. Trust me. I'm good with symptoms."

He took one more silent turn around the stage. "If you throw us out—for what you're really doing here is throwing the Federation out of Vulcan, not the other way around—beware that you don't thereby take the first step in throwing out Surak as well. We are, after all, just a different kind of alien from the sort you are from one another: the first fear he taught you to move through was the fear of one another. Unlearn that lesson, and, well, the result is predictable. Ignore the past, and repeat your old mistakes in the future."

McCoy gazed up over the audience's heads one last time. "Surak would be *very* disappointed in you if you blew up the planet," he said. He bowed his head, then, regretfully:

"And so would we."

McCoy straightened after a moment and lifted the parted hand. *"Mene sakkhet ur-seveh,"* he said, and walked off the stage.

There was a long pause, and then the applause. It was thunderous.

McCoy found his way back to his seat between Jim and Spock and wiped his forehead.

"I take it the deep breathing worked," Spock said quietly.

McCoy laughed out loud, then looked at Spock a little challengingly. "That," he said, "was just about every argument I've ever had with you, rolled into one package."

"Then I would say you won," said Spock.

McCoy shot a glance at him and grinned. "Thanks."

"Pity you weren't on last," Jim said softly. "You would have brought the house down."

"I would have preferred that placement," McCoy said, looking up.

"Number seven," Shath said from the stage.

Sarek stepped up.

"Sarek," he said. "I hold the rank of Ambassador Extraordinary and Plenipotentiary to Terra and to the United Federation of Planets from the planet Vulcan. And as regards the proposition: I say yea."

He stood there, immobile, in the shafts of sunlight, and they struck down on his darkness and could not lighten it. More than ever, to Jim, he looked like a carved statue of a Vulcan rather than a living man whom he had heard pleading against this eventuality the other night.

"This is a bitter duty for me," he said. "Yet it has not been my way, in my career, to fail to do as my government has asked me. It must be understood by all that the government of All Vulcan has asked only that I speak as I feel I must speak. Many will not believe this. I cannot, however, allow that fact to influence me, either.

"There are numerous considerations that make this duty even more distasteful for me personally. Some of you will know them." Sarek looked around the great room. "My personal affiliations with Terra are well known. There have been some who have said before that those affiliations have made me unfit for my duty, I will not deal with that now." He looked toward where Jim and Spock and McCoy sat, and Jim shivered at the pain in the regard. It was that look again, though it sealed over quickly.

"I rejoice to follow the doctor, an old acquaintance," Sarek said, bowing slightly in McCoy's direction, "and rather than rebutting his statements, I should like to note something very specific about them: the facility with which he quotes Surak, for instance. On Earth there is a saying that 'the Devil can quote scripture to his purpose.'

"We have never claimed that Surak's truths were meant for any species other than our own. He was Vulcan: perhaps quintessentially Vulcan, speaking to his own. We have never desired that other species should necessarily adopt his teachings. Nevertheless, especially on Earth, this seems to have happened."

"We know a good thing when we see it," McCoy remarked, meaning to be heard.

"Terrans," Sarek said reluctantly, "have seen many good things—or rather, things that they perhaps prematurely conceived of as good for them—and adopted them wholeheartedly. But at the same time they seem to throw away large parts of their own culture. For example, many ancient languages of Earth have been lost, stamped out over time by other languages that were somehow convinced they were better simply because they were new: people died, sometimes, for speaking their own ancient tongues.

"There are other examples of this kind of behavior, and enough to make us wonder whether it is wise for a culture such as ours to have much contact with Earth, when its people and institutions so easily throw away their own nature, to adopt that of another species. We are concerned that our culture may already have done Earth's culture irreparable harm and turned it away from courses which it was meant to follow, determined by its own structure. Whether it will ever find those courses, now, is difficult to tell, since Earth's cultural structure has been irreversibly altered by ours. If this sounds like an application of the Prime Directive, perhaps it should be considered as such. The government of Vulcan is not certain where the Prime Directive should stop—for the Federation, or for us. There is the possibility that *any* species, no matter its advancement, may easily and innocently damage another, no matter *its* advancement. There is enough Vulcan blood on our hands: we have no desire to add human blood to it, no matter how figuratively. This, most definitely, would be in contravention to Surak's teachings."

Sarek took a long breath and turned to face another part of the hall. "We are not sure that Earth people really benefit much from contact with Vulcans. Concern for the sciences is all very well, but scientific information has a way of being discovered in many places at almost the same time: it is unlikely that discontinuing our affiliation with the Federation would cripple its sciences. Ethics are another situation. We are not sure that Vulcan ethics work for humans. Despite their statements that they desire peace—and we do not discount the sincerity of these statements—many of us have noticed that the *result* of Terrans' involvement with almost anything is turbulence, difficulty, and strife. While not wishing to impugn the doctor's statements regarding the necessity of enjoying the infinite combinations of the species of this Galaxy in all their infinite diversity, still it is said, again by Surak, that one can best judge what a person *really* intended by the result they produce. Speaking simply, the turbulence which ensues from most dealings with Terra ought, for the good of our own people to be avoided if possible—and it would often seem wiser to enjoy the Terrans' diversity from a distance.

"Which brings me to the main concern. I wonder often whether we are not in fact destroying the Terrans' diversity, and that of the Federation, by too close contact with our own. The Terran culture, the planetary culture as a whole, *has a right to be what it is without outside interference*—especially interferences and influences which it is not strong enough to resist, or against which it lacks the data or experience to have any resistance to, to begin with. Vulcan logic is of a different sort from Terran, for the most part: there are similarities, of course—the basic texture of logic remains the same regardless of the species mastering it—but *we are not the same species,* and nothing can, or should, make us so. Our mental contexts are, and need to be, vastly different. Our sociological and ethical structures are built on the science of the mind, rather than that of the hand: such structures go deep. To change them would be unwise, unless we could find something that we knew was better, to replace them. We know of no such substitute or compromise structure that would work.

"And there is an additional ethical concern. While not precisely in violation of the Prime Directive—which the Federation Council and other affiliated decision-making bodies in Starfleet formulated themselves, taking only minimal advices from other bodies—the Federation frequently, in our government's view, takes actions which can be read as attempting to influence other species for political means and advantage, rather than for the 'good' of the species in question. Not that *that* is an adequate reason at all. We hold that no species has the right to impose its ethics or beliefs on any other species, for *whatever* reason. And despite the fact that the Federation makes this same statement in its own founding Charter, under this fair appearance it becomes plain that the political decisions of many planets are decided in terms, not of what the electorates of those planets desire, but what the Federation wants—and how the decisions of a planet's people will affect its Federation grants. We deplore this; we have long deplored this and protested against it in the Federation Council, to no avail. And we are no longer desirous to remain in association with an organization that behaves in such a manner . . . thereby indicating our tacit support. We wish the Earth well, and all the peoples of the Federation. But we must quit their society. The Government does not specifically request such a vote of the electorate. It merely asks that you consider the topic well before you decide."

Sarek sagged a little. "With that said, I must add something personal. My loyalties as a servant of my government are clear-cut. But I now find that my loyalties to my family have entered into such conflict with them that I have been forced to choose between them. Therefore I must step down from my post, effective immediately: and I thank you and the government for your support of me in the past and wish that you may all prosper and live long."

The stir went right around the room and would not quiet. Sarek stood in the middle of it all and did not move. But then a voice was raised.

"Sir, before you go any further," McCoy said, "would you mind telling us one more of the government's opinions? What do they think of the scheme to sell off formerly Federation-owned property on Vulcan, after the secession, to secret buyers with strong anti-Federation leanings, who have already made substantial payoffs to Vulcan officials to ensure that the property will be sold to them at 'lowest bid,' before anyone else hears about it? . . . Just curious," McCoy added.

Spock stared at Jim, and Jim at Spock, and both of them at McCoy. He leaned back, looking casual.

Sarek looked stunned. "Doctor, I should want to see substantiation of such claims before I or my government could comment."

"Sir," McCoy said, "I await your convenience."

And the room went mad.

Vulcan: Six

He was born the night the da'Nikhirch was born, the Eye of Fire: the sudden star that appeared in the Vulcan sky, blazing, looking over T'Khut's shoulder. T'Leia, his mother, did not notice the star. She had her work cut out for her, for her child was overdue, and very large. In fact, she quite *literally* had her work cut out for her: the child was delivered by the technique known on Earth as caesarean section. The pun exists in Vulcan as well as in Anglish, and she was teased gently about it before the delivery, and afterward, when they placed the baby in her arms. . . . Also born that night were two bush wars and the final attack on one nation's central city by another. T'Leia paid little attention to those, either.

There was nothing whatsoever unusual about Surak as a child. He teethed at the usual time, ate normally, learned to speak and write and read at the normal rate: he clamored for toy swords and guns at the same time other children did (and as often happens, right after he saw a particularly nice one that another child had). His schooling was uneventful: he did well enough at all his subjects (though there are records that suggest he did not do as well at math, which must have been the despair of his mother, one of the most prominent chemists and mathematicians on the planet). He was popular, made friendships easily, and many of those friendships remained in force until the end of his life. His home life was apparently a model of normalcy: T'Leia his mother, and his father Stef, seem to have cherished him and one another with astonishing steadfastness. When Surak had completed his schooling, his father invited him into his business—a consultancy which served several of the large corporations in de'Khriv, which had become the chief city of the Lhai nation. Surak was glad to join his father, and for years, until he was forty-six, they worked together amicably and made the business a success.

And then something happened.

He was working late. It often happened, and Surak was not bothered by it: he considered late working hours one of the things that his people's stamina had been designed for. He was deep in a costing exercise for one of the psi-tech companies, which had found a way to produce mindchange adepts on the assembly line, by cloning brain and other neural tissue and administering various processed by-products of the cloned tissue to people who had not actually been bred to the trait. It was going to be very expensive—the recruitment of the sources of the clone material, particularly so—but Surak was working busily at it, certain that the company very much wanted the technique. Mindchange was popular—having your enemy, or your friend, suddenly change his mind about something important to you, was a great advantage. But it was very much a seller's market at the time: trained adepts were expensive to hire, and often too demanding. The company wanted to be able to put mindchangers on staff and wanted to be free to fire them without fuss if they got out of hand. Surak had wondered, at first, why the company didn't simply have one mindchanger change the mind of another one who had become a problem. But the mindchangers themselves were not vulnerable to the talent.

He sat there in the office, tapping at the computer as he wrung the cost analyses out of it, adding variables, removing the more unlikely ones, inserting market projections and probable effects on other affiliated firms of the company. Finally he kicked the computer into report mode and sat back, sighing, leaning back in his chair.

He was a striking figure, even then, so young: very much of the typical "Vulcan" somatype, tall and lean and dark haired, with an unusually delicate face for the raw-boned body, and deepset eyes. He looked around and saw that the office had darkened around him while he was busy: the big place, all done in charcoal and black, to his father's tastes, was shadowy, and outside the wall-to-ceiling glass windows, he could see T'Khut coming hugely up, her phase at the half, shedding ruddy light over the sand of the garden outside. It was a handsome office, and like the rest of the house, reflected the firm's success. Surak stretched, enjoying the sight of the place, the thought of himself inside it, working hard, helping make it work. Someday it would be his, of course, but he didn't think of that: he enjoyed working with his father, enjoyed the teamwork and the laughter, and even the occasional argument, that always bound them together more closely afterward.

The computer sat silently doing its thinking, and Surak reached out to a control for one of the wall screens, took it out of data display mode, and flicked it to the one of the information channels that showed nothing but news. They were in the middle of a general news roundup, the one that usually came before the update on the hour. He left the picture on and killed the sound and got up to open the window-doors to the warm wind off the sand, then watched the screen idly while walking around the room to work the kink out of his back.

The pictures were the usual: fighting, skirmishing, people marching on large buildings in this city or that one: shots in the streets, robberies, ceremonial murders, politicians waving their arms about this or that. A few smaller pieces about someone's public bonding, a feature about the old temple on Mount Seleya, then a prediction of the planet's weather for the next day. Cloud here and there, but no rain, naturally: it would not be time for that until nearly the end of the year. He planned to go take a trip to the North, to watch it rain. He had never seen it do that in person, only in pictures. Surak looked out at the garden and wondered what it would be like to see it rain there. *Water falling from the sky: how strange. . . .*

He glanced idly up at the screen, then froze at what he saw.

Desolation. There was a picture of land, or what might have been land once, but now was only a vast glassy crater. The scale of it was difficult to grasp at first, but then the camera taking the picture seemed to back away, and he realized that the scale was much larger than he had thought. The crater filled one third of the entire Yiwa peninsula, one of the largest markings on the near side of T'Khut. Hurriedly Surak gestured the sound back on, staring at that horrible hole, easily five hundred miles across and ten miles deep. The bottom of the hole had cracked, and was smoking gently as heat escaped from the planetary mantle below.

The reader talked calmly about a test of a new matter-antimatter technology by the Lhai nation, on some of its testing-ground property on T'Khut. And a few seconds later the picture shifted to something else, some story about an assassination in some government official's office on the other side of the planet. But Surak had no eyes for it. All he could see in his mind was that desolation, that utter blasting, the glassy ground, cracked, smoking, with further destruction waiting beneath it, and barely restrained from bursting through.

Antimatter, he thought. *A new technology, indeed—* Until now, the use of matter-antimatter weapons had been confined to the outer planets and the space colonies. There had always been concern about the superluminal effects of such explosions, and people were worried about possible effects on the Homestar, if they happened too close, or to the planet's electromagnetic communications media. But now— *And on T'Khut,* he thought in horror. *Not a test of someone's new technology. They never said what technology—not something for power stations, or spaceships, the way they keep saying, but a warning. To whom? Irik?* For Lhai's and Irik's areas of influence were contiguous, and the two nations continually rubbed and fretted against one another; their borders were never quiet anymore—always some argument about who had owned what territory how long, or which people had been removed from some one piece of land once, and now wanted it back. That huge, terrible crater—that was a warning. *This is next,* it said. And if *this* kind of weapon got out of hand—

But weapons never really got out of hand, on Vulcan. Look at atomics, how carefully they had been confined to such kinds as did not leave dirty radiation all over the place—

Such as will merely kill everything in a given area, and leave the resources undamaged. We cannot have the waste of resources, can we—

He sat down at his desk again, staring at the screen, oblivious to the computer telling him that it was finished with the report, and did he want it transferred? Surak stared at the screen, which was now showing some sumptuous room with well-dressed people talking earnestly, and only saw the devastation. It would have taken a fairly small device to produce such an effect. Someday such small devices would no longer seem so threatening. Someone would make a bigger one. And bigger. And then one that, quite accidentally, would crack straight down deep into the mantle, or perhaps, to the planet's core—

He looked out at the window-doors, and T'Khut looked back at him, looming, and both her dark face and her light were bright with troubled volcanoes, that had felt the sting in her side, and now roared.

Surak watched T'Khut, motionless, until she rose out of sight, and then got up and went out. The screen sat and babbled quietly to itself about war and business, crime and war and trivia, until the sun came up and Surak's father came in to look at the reports for the previous evening.

Surak had gone missing. His parents were alarmed: he had never done such a thing before. The authorities were alerted. It was feared he had been kidnapped, to put pressure on one or another of the firms for which their own small business did research: or perhaps another company had done the kidnapping, to acquire confidential information about one or another of them. There was little chance of that—Surak and his father had had their mindblocks installed by highly paid experts, and not even a mindchanger could do anything about them . . . or at least it would take several working in concert. But that fact made it that much more likely that Surak would be killed out of hand, and his body simply dumped somewhere. Such things had happened many, many times before. Surak's mother sat in her offices at the university in great pain, unable to take any refuge in the cool bright corridors of mathematics; and Surak's father stormed and threatened and bullied the local security forces, and pulled strings and generally made prominent people all over Lhai hate the sight of his face on a commscreen.

But Surak was not dead. Much later, he would say, "That day was the day I came alive."

*   *   *

He went out into the darkness, took one of the family's aircars, took it up, put it on auto, and told it, "Drive." He had no idea where he was going and hardly cared. To him it seemed as if the world had already ended, and such things didn't really matter. All he could see was death, death everywhere, death unregarded; death that had become a casual thing, that was reported on the news without horror, that seemed to have been accepted as part of the natural course of Vulcan life. What real joy did one see, as a rule, on the information channels? If any crept in, it was by accident. The information was all about death, one way or another: either about the little deaths that people inflicted on one another every day—lies, greed, crime, negligence, cruelty, pain—or about the bigger ones, the more obvious ones: the explosive bullet in the gut, the pumped laserbeam through the eye, the bomb in the trashbin, the battlefield strategic N-weapon glazing the ground, the trained adept wreaking destruction in the undefended mind. And now this last, most horrible sight. Death, it was all death, there was no escape from it. Destruction was very near, the death to end all the deaths, unless something was done.

But what?

He spent the day flying. The car had enough fuel, and managed the business itself without consulting Surak: it conferred as it needed to with the various air traffic control computers, each of which thought briefly about what to do with a pilot who had given no concrete driving instruction, and then, with a faint electronic sigh of relief, shunted him off to the farthest possible fringe of its control area. So it went all that day, while Surak sometimes wept, sometimes sat staring at the face of desolation and despair: so it went till the evening came, and T'Khut began to lean up over the edge of the world again.

The sight of her shocked Surak back into some sort of sanity. "Land when convenient," he said to the aircar.

It took him at his word, being then in conversation with yet another landing control computer, which headed him for the nearest landing area marked with a beacon that the aircar could find. In a storm of dust and sand it settled toward what was obviously a small provincial port on the edge of a desert. The port was on automatic: there were no lights in the tower. Everyone had apparently gone home for the night.

That was fine with Surak: the last thing he wanted to see, just then, was another Vulcan—the cause of all this trouble, and soon to be the end of it. He did not land, but overrode the controls and paused on hover-jets to look down at the little town by the port. It was the kind of desert settlement built by people who want to get away from it all with a vengeance. Everything was very plain and simple—small houses built of the usual heat-reflecting stucco or foamstone, small windows to let in light but not too much heat, thickly glazed in small panes, when they were glazed at all, to resist earthquake damage. Some of the houses had cracks in them, not yet replastered: there had been a quake here recently.

He did not want to be near houses, though. He guided the aircar on into the desert, a good ways on, and out into a great sea of sand without so much as a footprint. That suited him well. In a storm of dust and sand he landed and killed the engine: then got out wearily, scrubbed at his face, muttered a little at the stiffness of his joints. He looked around him.

He was distracted by a sudden jolt as the world shifted under his feet. Just a bump, repeated once, then all was quiet; but the shock was still enough to make him grab the aircar for support and gasp a little. It seemed no wonder, at that point, that not many people lived out here.

When things had settled again, Surak turned away from the car, toward the desert . . . and saw it, something he had been too busy to notice while landing. T'Khut was looming up behind it, as if to show him the way. Silhouetted against her, against the coppery light and the dark side with its uneasy volcanoes, was the peak: tall and slender in its top two-thirds, slumped down a bit toward the foot of the cone, as if from some old melting—black, silent, huge enough even at this distance to block out a third of T'Khut's immense bulk. Mount Seleya stood there, precisely dividing T'Khut's brightness and darkness, one from the other. The image, or perhaps the mountain, seemed to say: *Here is your choice. The light, or the darkness with its fires. It has always been your choice. It is late. Choose now.*

Never had anything in the world, not even his parents, spoken so directly and imminently to *him*. Shocked, Surak simply sat down in the sand where he was and gazed at the mountain, while the moment seemed to stretch itself impossibly long around him. *Choose?*

Choose what?

The mountain said nothing, merely looked at him.

You mean, choose for everyone? his mind asked, whirling with confusion. *What right do I have? And choose what?*

The mountain said nothing, merely looked at him.

He looked back at it, looked at the bright side, the warm innocent light; looked at the darkness, and the fires. The fires had quieted somewhat since last night, but they could be awakened again easily enough. Such fires lay and broiled beneath the skin of Vulcan as well. They were usually quiet, but they too could be easily awakened by the desolation that Surak had seen the night before. He began to despair again. *Someone has to do something—*

Then do it.

He gazed at the mountain and breathed fast.

He saw his death, at that moment. Not the manner of it, merely the fact. He had seen it before, on occasion, but never had he realized that it was *his* and no one else's, to spend as he liked. Much could be done, with a death. He was going to have one anyway.

He might as well do something with it.

Yes, he said. *I choose.*

The moment broke. T'Khut seemed to hesitate, as if giving a sort of sigh, and then continued to slip upward in the sky, breaking the perfect positioning of the mountain between its two halves. Surely it had been an illusion, that hesitation, that seemingly endless moment in which everything hung poised and waited for him.

Surely.

But what do I do now? he thought.

He sat there all night, wondering that. Somehow he had to stop people from killing each other: that was plain. Or rather, had to stop them hating each other: the killing would take care of itself, after that. *Nothing really difficult,* he said to himself, finding it funny to be so earnest and dry, even sarcastic, over an impossibility . . . one which he was nonetheless committed to bring about. He had chosen, had chosen life, and he knew, somehow, that even the simple fact of the *choice* mattered; if he died right now, it would matter not a whit less. But it would matter much more if he found some way to *do* something about this problem. There were several small earthquakes, mutterings in the sand, while he sat through the night thinking about this: while T'Khut stood high, and the Red and White Eyes rose to look at him. The earthquakes were not frightening: in his weary state, they felt like a friendly hand trying to shake him awake when he nodded. He wished he *could* awake, could simply wake up from this wondering and find the answer, and start doing something about it.

And the earth quaked again, rather harder this time than before. "Ah, come on, now," he said, for he was becoming inured to this, "stop that."

The quake got worse. Surak became uneasy and started to scramble to his feet.

And subsided, as the earthquake rose up before him.

With frightened calm he watched the sand vibrate, heard it drum like a hundred ancient war-parties all around him. *Well,* he thought, as the bulge came up and up, *I chose, and I suppose that was enough. And now I die—*

The sand started to slip away from the great shape it covered, as the Underlier arched its back against the night, huge as a house, as a hundred houses. It blotted out Seleya, it blotted out T'Khut, and the sky. The low rumbling of its voice would have blotted out a real earthquake, had one had the temerity to take place right then. Terror was a poor word for what possessed Surak in that moment. His tongue clove to the roof of his mouth, and he shook all over. He had not thought that his death could be so *big*—that *anything* could be so big.

And then his death spoke to him . . . and he found that he was mistaken about it being his death.

The song was of incredible complexity and depth—the kind of melody you might expect a mountain, or perhaps a geological stratum, to sing. The thoughts that came with the song, that blasted into his head and crashed through him like a continent collapsing on him, were immense, wide, old—and so strange that he could not even begin to say what they were about. But he got a clear sense that this immensity, this ultimate power, was looking at his smallness, his delicacy, his tiny precision, with astonishment.

And with delight at his difference.

And suddenly everything shifted for Surak. The fear abruptly became awe, and the greatest possible pleasure to feel. How delightful to be so different from something: how wonderful that there should be creatures so huge in the world, so strange! No need to understand them, particularly: that might come with time, and would be an added delight. But it was enough to accept their difference, to celebrate just that, without anything added. Creation, in itself, was joy. The difference was joy, the celebration of it was joy. There was nothing that could stand against that joy: sooner or later it would triumph. All evil, all death, was a tiny, fretting, posturing thing that knew its own defeat was coming, and might rage and destroy as it liked. It was doomed. Celebration would win, was winning, had won *now.* Everything was one moment, and the moment was nothing but triumph and joy.

As best he could, Surak looked up at the Underlier and gave it to understand as much.

It roared. The sand shook, the earth trembled; the echo came back from Seleya until it seemed that a voice answered, many voices.

Joy! said the roar. And nothing else needed saying.

It fell silent, then, and slipped into the sand, silently, easily. The sand shook a little as it went, rippled, as water ripples when a fish slips into it. Surak watched it with calm delight, knowing that it was not going away, not really. Nothing could ever go away, not completely: not after what he knew now.

The sand grew still. It was as if nothing had ever been there.

Surak sat for a few breaths: then got up and brushed the sand off himself in a businesslike manner and headed back for the aircar. He had a lot to do. He knew now what needed doing. He knew what would finally kill fear: the wonder, the appreciation, the delight in the Other.

It would work. It might take a long time, but he knew it would work. He knew it.

And to his astonishment, he had the strangest feeling that the Other was looking over his shoulder, and knew as well.

"Here is the first part of the secret," Surak would write, much later, when people started to pay attention to him. "Cast out fear. There is no room for anything else until you cast out fear. . . . Now, do not mistake me when I speak of 'casting out.' Some people will immediately think this means rejection of fear, by pretending not to be afraid. They are not the same thing. Pretending there is not a *lematya* in your house will not make it go away if there *is* one. You must first admit to yourself the fact that there *is* a *lematya*—you must first accept its presence. Then you can call the animal control people and have them come and take it away. But until you first admit that it is there, you are going to have a *lematya* in your bed every night. It may save your pride not to admit it is there, but your bed will be increasingly crowded.

"So it is with fear as well. To cast it out, you must first accept it; you must admit it is there. Is there anything a person would rather do *less?* The last thing you want anyone to hear is your voice saying, 'I am afraid.' The last thing you want to hear your enemy say before you kill him is 'I am afraid,' because—in our culture—it means he has been reduced to total helplessness. What our culture must learn is that *that* point, total helplessness, is potentially the most powerful in our lives. Just past it is the great leap to true power: the move through the fear and the helplessness, accepted at last, to what lies beyond fear. So many things lie beyond it that pen and keyboard are helpless to write of them . . . but as more of us learn to move past that point, more will be written. Not that what is written matters so much as what one *does* with it.

"And the rest of the secret," he concluded, "is that all of us fear one another more than anything else in the world. The fear of the Other, of what the Other will do if he finds out we are afraid of *him*—that is what has brought us to this pass. We must turn and realize that the Other *is* afraid—and then say to him, 'You have nothing to fear from me,' in such a way that he knows it to be true. Another thing we have no desire to say! Each of us secretly desires to keep the Other in some slight fear of us, so that he will not harm us. But if we can only bring ourselves to say those terrible words, and have them be true, then the Other will become what he should have been from the earliest days—the constant companion, the source of delight in all his differences."

They did not listen to him for a long time, of course. Nor did he begin speaking for some time after that night in the desert. Surak went home and quit his job, much to his parents' dismay. He asked for, and got, his share of the family properties and banked them safely, and then went off into the desert and was not seen or heard of again for several years, except remotely, through the communications nets.

He took with him nothing but a small portable terminal and an aircar, and spent much time alone. Some time he spent with various members of this or that holy sect. There were many on Vulcan, at that time, perhaps more than there ever had been. Vulcan had always been rather infested with religions, a fact that has surprised some species that never discovered Immanence. Vulcan was littered with it: as far as the Vulcan mind was concerned, gods, demigods, animae, noeses, golems, angels, devils, powers and principalities, and every other possible kind of hypersomatic being, were thick on the ground. Various specialists in comparative religion have pointed out that this proliferation made it seem as if perhaps the Vulcans were looking for something they had lost. Whatever the truth of this, there were religions aplenty, with priests and priestesses and holy people and hermits and votaries and nuns and eremites, and Surak went and talked to quite a few of them, over the five years of the Withdrawal, as it is called. There are not many records of what he said to them, or what they said to him; and the conversations often seem to have nothing whatever to do with *cthia*. One tape, lovingly preserved for centuries, is of a conversation with a hermit who lived near a lake by the Lesser Sea, and seems to be concerned entirely with the art of fishing with a rod.

At any rate, after five years Surak came out of the wilds, took a small apartment in the capital, near his parents' house, and began to write for the information networks. There was some interest, at first, in the strange writings from the man about whom there had been such a stir, those years back, when he was first not kidnapped, and then vanished. For a while it was a fad to read his work. Then the interest died out somewhat.

Surak was not concerned by this. He kept writing about this strange way of life that all Vulcan needed to live, to save itself from itself. The basics have been codified many times, in many translations of the *Guidelines*, but Surak's initial notes on the subject, still preserved, are perhaps the best summation of them.

"*Ideally, do no harm. Harm speeds up the heat-death of the Universe, and indirectly, your own.*

"*More practically, do as little harm as possible. We are creatures of a Universe in which entropy exists, and therefore see no way of escape, but we do not need to help it.*

"*Harm no one's internal, invisible integrities. Leave others the privacies of their minds and lives. Intimacy remains precious only insofar as it is inviolate: invading it turns it to torment. Reach out to others courteously: accept their reaching in the same way, with careful hands.*

"*Do no murder. The spear in the other's heart is the spear in your own; you are he. All action has reaction: what force you inflict, inevitably returns. The murder of the other is the murder of your own joy, forever.*

"*As far as possible, do not kill. Can you give life again to what you kill? Then be slow to take life. Take only life that will not notice you taking it. To notice one's own death increases entropy. To die and not notice it increases it less, but still does so.*

"*Cast out fear. Cast out hate and rage. Cast out greed and envy. Cast out all emotion that speeds entropy, whether it be love or hate. Cast out these emotions by using reason to accept them, and then move past them. Use in moderation emotions that do not speed entropy, taking all care that they do not cause others pain, for that speeds entropy as well. Master your passions, so that they become a power for the slowing of the heat-death.*

"*Do no harm to those that harm you. Offer them peace, and offer them peace again, and do it until you die. In this manner you will have peace, one way or the other, even if they kill you. And you cannot give others what you have not experienced yourself.*

"Learn reason above all. Learn clear thought: learn to know what is from what seems to be, and what you wish to be. This is the key to everything: the truth of reality, the reality of truth. What is will set you free."

There was of course more, much more. Surak wrote steadily for years, submitting his material to the nets, and more and more people began reading it. Eventually some of them began to seek him out: often angrily, demanding how he dared dictate such rubbish to the whole planet, which had been around for millennia and doing quite well without *him*. Surak welcomed these people into his house calmly, gave them food and shelter for as long as they felt they needed it, and let them watch him write.

After a while some of them went away and began writing themselves, about the astonishing philosopher living in the third-floor apartment: the man who, though seeming a perfectly normal person—a good listener with an unpredictable sense of humor—still conducted himself with such secret, joyful calm, as if he knew something that they didn't, a delightful secret. Some of them later wrote that there was often a feeling about Surak as if someone else was in the room with him, even when he seemed alone.

Surak did not react much to this: he kept writing, knowing that there would be a fair number who came to scoff and stayed to learn. But it was when one came to learn, and Surak realized that this was the one he was waiting for, that things got interesting, and the writing stopped for a while.

S'task records something of that first meeting in the memoirs he left before he went off-planet. Surak looked up from his writing, as the young man came in, and put down the fruit he was eating. "Who are you?" he said.

"S'task," he said.

"What can I do for you?"

"Teach me what you know."

S'task says that Surak put the fruit down and said to him most sincerely, "I thank you very much indeed. Please leave."

"But why? Have I done something wrong?"

"Of course you have," Surak said, "but that is not the point I am making. You are about to get in a great deal of trouble, and I would save you that if I could. Entropy will increase."

"It will increase anyway, whether I get in trouble or not," S'task said.

Apparently it was the right thing to say. "You are quite right," Surak said, nodding. "That is why you should leave."

"You are not making a lot of sense," S'task said, somewhat nettled.

"I know," Surak said. "Logic is a delight to me, but there are some things it is no good for." And he shook his head regretfully. "But I must cast out sorrow," he said. "And you too. Please leave."

S'task thought he would stand his ground, but a few seconds later, he says, "I found myself sitting on the pavement outside the front door, and he would not answer the signal. I never met anyone that strong, from that day to this. But I was determined to work with him, so I sat there. For four days I sat there—there wasn't a back door to his apartment—and I was determined to catch him as he went in or out. But he did not go in or out, and I became very angry and decided to leave. Then I thought, 'What am I doing sitting here, being angry at him, when I came all this way to learn how not to be?' So I sat there longer. I don't know how long it was: it might have been another seven or ten days. And finally someone came in from the street and stood over me, and said, 'What about windows?' It was he. He opened the door, and we went in, and I stayed and studied with him for the next three years."

They were busy years. Surak's message was being increasingly noticed. It was not, of course, immediately accepted: there were many false starts, renunciations, debunkings, persecutions, and attacks of what seemed massive inertia. But slowly, slowly, first as a sort of fad, then more seriously, the logical life began to spread. One of the chief councilors of Lhai called in Surak, as a last desperate measure, to talk to the emissaries of Irik, at a time when it was feared that full-scale war was about to break out. Surak went gladly, went among the emissaries, shut himself in with them for a day and a night, and then sent them on their way. Two days later they returned, to the utter astonishment of the Lhai councilors, with the entire High Council of Irik. "Now come," said Surak to the Lhai councilors, and they went up into the council room and shut the doors and did not come out for a week. When they did come out, a peace had been signed, each nation had made major concessions to the other, and all involved were slightly dazed, except for Surak. "It seemed like a good idea at the time," said one of the Lhai; and one of the Irik said, "We have been fools. He told us so often enough. But somehow when *he* says it, it is as if he is doing you the greatest kindness, and having a joke with you. Or someone." The peace held, and held straight through to the unification of the planet, despite the occasional efforts of the power-blocs of both nations to restart the hostilities.

So it went. *Cthia* continued to spread, however slowly, however much in fits and starts. And then came the signals from space. Surak looked up on hearing the news, S'task said, and smiled. "Now I know I have been doing rightly," he said, "for now entropy will bite back. Here is the great test. Let us see how we deal with it."

It did not go well, by his standards. Surak was scheduled to be among the dignitaries welcoming the aliens to shi'Kahr, but an aircar mishap at the port facility at ta'Valsh held him up. While he was waiting calmly in the port for the problem to resolve itself, the Duthuliv pirates fell on the Vulcans waiting to welcome them, killed many, and took the rest as hostage: against massive payments by the various governments who had sent them. When the news reached Surak, he immediately offered to go to the aliens and "deal peace" with them. No government on the planet was in a mood to listen to him, however, since half of them were at that moment mourning their leaders, and the other half were fuming over massive and extortionate ransom demands.

Thus war broke out: *'Ahkh,* "the" War, the Vulcans called it, thereby demoting all other wars before it to the rank of mere tribal feuds. No ransoms were paid—and indeed if they had been, they would have beggared the planet. But the Vulcans knew from their own bitter experience with one another that once one paid Danegeld, one never got rid of the Dane. The Vulcans' trading ships were still unarmed, but they did not stay so for long. The chief psi-talents of the planet, great architects and builders, and technicians who had long mastered the subtleties of the undermind, went out in the ships and taught the Duthuliv pirates that weapons weren't everything. Metal came unraveled in ships' hulls; pilots calmly locked their ships into suicidal courses, unheeding of the screams of the crews: and the Vulcans beamed images of the destruction back to Duthul and Etosha, lest there should be any confusion about the cause. The message was meant to be plain: kill us and die.

Surak was greatly disturbed, no less by the fate of the aliens than by the loss of his disciple. S'task was at the meeting at shi'Kahr and was one of those taken hostage. This was the sowing of the seed of a great trouble between him and Surak, for it was S'task who organized the in-ship rebellion that cost so many of the pirates their lives. He was the one who broke the back of the torturer left alone with him, broke into and sabotaged the ship's databanks, and then—after releasing the other hostages safely on Vulcan—crashed the luckless vessel into the pirates' mothership at the cost of thousands of pirates' lives, and almost his own. Weeks later he was found drifting in a lifepod in L5 orbit, half starved and almost dead of dehydration, but clinging to life through sheer rage. They brought him home, and Surak hurried to his couchside—to sorrowfully rebuke him. "I have lost my best pupil to madness," Surak said.

Much else he said, but that is lost to us, along with S'task, who spent the rest of his life on Vulcan fighting his old teacher on the subject of the uses of violence, until with many Vulcans he left the planet to peace. Perhaps the invasion of the Duthuliv pirates, which continued over the next fifty years and was beaten back every time, was a blessing in disguise for Surak; perhaps nations threatened from without felt more like quickly resolving their conflicts with one another, lest the aliens should find a divided planet easier to conquer. Or perhaps the changes were wrought entirely by Surak and the people who took up his way—the people who increasingly said they felt another presence encouraging them, or at least just *there,* whether it encouraged them or not. But whatever the cause, slowly, *cthia* took the planet. Those who most resisted it—S'task and his followers, determined to keep at least some of the old ways, along with some logic—left the planet on the long journey that would take them at last to the worlds where they would become the Rihannsu, or as Federation usage has it, the Romulans.

Cthia eventually killed Surak, of course, as he had long before seen it would do. It was the Yhri faction who killed him, a Vulcan international terrorist group that saw its business being destroyed by nations that no longer desired to undermine one another's frontiers, or economies, or leaders. The other nations united so far—almost three-quarters of the nations on the planet—had asked Surak to deal peace with the Yhri on their behalf. They welcomed him graciously, for the cameras: and then they took him away and killed him. When this was discovered, the outrage was terrible at first: but then a strange sort of calm descended, and one by one emissaries from the major nations went to the Yhri and asked to deal peace with them on their own behalf. Many died: the emissaries mostly, at first. But eventually—after about a year during which several governments fell with the deaths of their leaders, gone dealing peace—the Yhri's heart simply seemed to go out of them. There has never been any satisfactory explanation of it, not even afterward, when some of the Yhri talked at length about Surak, before going into self-exile or ending themselves. They said they could never shake the feeling that no matter what they did, something associated with this man knew their deepest secrets, and all the evils they had ever done, and still forgave them.

And to this day much has been written about it—many commentaries on Surak's writings, many independent works. But then as now, there are some things that logic is not good for. People still go out to the sands of Vulcan's Forge and sit there, looking out and waiting. But the sands keep their own counsel, as T'Khut looks over the shoulder of Seleya, with only an occasional flicker of fire. . . .

Enterprise: Seven

"Doctor," Sarek had said, sounding quite severe, "I am ready to hear the substantiation of your claim." They were standing outside the Hall of the Voice, in the great entry hall. Vulcans were milling about everywhere, media people were running for the commlinks, and their little group was getting some very strange and hostile looks indeed from some of the Vulcans passing.

"I'm ready to give it to you," McCoy said, "but I don't have the hard copy with me. Also I need to satisfy you as to the *bona fides* of the source. For both purposes, we need to be up on the *Enterprise*." McCoy cocked an eye at Jim.

Slightly nettled, Jim flipped his communicator open. "Kirk to *Enterprise*," he said, "four to beam up."

"Make that five," Amanda's voice said from behind them. "I'm sorry I wasn't able to sit with you this morning. But at least I didn't miss any of the excitement."

"Five," Jim said, and shut his communicator again. "You know," he said to McCoy, "you might tell me that you have these things up your sleeve. It would make my life a little calmer."

"I didn't know until this morning," Bones said, "and I was wondering how and when to break the information. But that moment seemed perfect to me . . . so I *carpe'd* the *diem*, as we used to say in medical school."

The transporter effect set in, and the hall went away, to be replaced by the transporter room. They all got down off the pads and headed for the turbolift. "I must admit," Sarek said, "that I admire your timing . . . if this data is accurate."

"You'll judge for yourself. But I had to do something. You're so damned sincere, even when you hate what you're saying."

Sarek looked rueful. "Was it that obvious?"

"To a human?" Jim laughed. "It was rather noticeable."

"I have said distasteful things on behalf of my government before," Sarek said, "but never one quite so much so. Still, that is no excuse—"

"There's no excuse for not telling me what you were going to do, either," Amanda said, rather tartly.

"Peace, my wife. *I* did not know either, until I had finished the statement. *Cthia* rose up and demanded the truth, whatever else happened."

"If it was *cthia*," Amanda said, "then I don't mind what you told me, or didn't. I ask forgiveness, my husband."

Sarek bowed his head to her and reached her two fingers as the group came to the turbolift. She touched his fingers with hers with a gentle look. "Forgiven," he said. "But I fear my reputation for professionalism in embassage is done."

"For acting, you mean," McCoy snorted. "Never mind. Rec One," he said to the lift, as its doors closed.

"Doctor," Spock said, "this is no time for a game of tennis."

"As for *you*," McCoy said mildly, leaning against the wall of the lift with his arms folded, "you've been royally had, Spock old son. I will remember this day with delight every time you out-data me from now on."

" 'Had'?" Spock looked indignant, and one eyebrow attempted to ascend above his hairline.

"I want to thank you for taking the time last night to tell me about your conversation with T'Pring," McCoy said, "because something occurred to me about three in the morning." The lift slid to a stop: they got out and walked down the corridor.

"She talks a good game, does T'Pring," McCoy said as they went. "But not quite good enough. *Nobody* makes that much money, just like that. But at any rate, consider the *kind* of money T'Pring has needed to do the kinds of dirty deeds she was discussing with you yesterday. She couldn't have openly made that much without being noticed. No, indeed. So as regards her explanation, it is incomplete, to put it mildly. Though you bought it." McCoy looked at Spock with cheerful reproach. "I have a bridge on Earth I want to sell you. Very nice view of Brooklyn."

Spock looked both annoyed and sheepish, though he covered the expression over quickly enough. "I fear my logic is not clear where T'Pring is concerned."

"And why should it be, for pity's sake? You're angry at her! Or if you were in your right mind, you'd admit that you are. No harm in that. It's hiding the fact from yourself that makes trouble. But I'm not interested in psychoanalyzing you except in the line of duty. I'm more interested in getting to the bottom of all this. Come on."

The Rec Deck doors slid open for them. There was no one there, rather odd at that time of day. Harb Tanzer came out to meet them. "Doctor," he said, "I cleared the place, as you asked."

"Good. Let's use the little tank, the one with the printout."

Harb led them over to the smaller 3D tank. "You might as well sit," McCoy said as they came to it. "The printouts will probably take some time. Harb, now you're going to find out what I was up to last night."

"This should be interesting," Harb said, and sat down himself.

McCoy perched on the arm of Sarek's chair. "Moira!"

"Good afternoon, Doctor," said the Games computer's voice out of the middle of the air.

"Would you do me a favor and print me out the goodies you retrieved last night?"

"Code authorization, please."

"Oh, for pity's sake, girl, don't get started with me. Check my voiceprint."

"Code, or nothing."

McCoy sighed. " 'If blood be the price of Admiralty, / Lord God, we ha' paid it in full!' "

"Correct. You romantic." The printer began to silently spit out pages.

"When I realized that T'Pring had to be getting her money from somewhere else, and quite a lot of it," McCoy said, "I sat down and began to think about where she might lay hands on so much. Gifts seemed unlikely. She couldn't have multiplied the little amount she got from Stonn into so much. Where did it all come from? Or where *could* it all come from?

"Then something occurred to me. What happens when the Federation is kicked off Vulcan?"

His audience looked at him somewhat blankly. "Well, we all have to leave—" Amanda said.

"Ah, but private persons can take their property with them, or sell it. Property held by the Federation, though, is another matter. It was never sold to us, only leased for 'good and proper considerations'—usually trade agreements—and it reverts to the Vulcan government, which may then dispose of it however it pleases. They won't want to keep all of it: especially the quasi-defense installations—those would be dismantled, and the land used for other purposes. Yes?"

Sarek nodded. "It would be logical. And equally logical to suppose that it would be sold off, for the government will be looking to raise some money to replace the various lost revenues."

"That's right. Well, consider. Someone who wanted to make some money off the deal, and knew that the secession issue would come up, could easily go to various interests that have had an eye on that land, and offer to make sure it was offered to them before anyone else. For a consideration, that person would bribe a government official in a high place to see to it. The bribe would come from what that person was paid, of course: they would skim off the rest for themselves, as their 'finders' fee' for managing the business. The business of the bribery could be highly lucrative, for the Federation has a lot of property on Vulcan, all highly developed, all very useful for industrial exploitation."

Sarek's eyes were hooded: he was beginning to look angry. McCoy said, "If the industrial contacts knew, as well, how their money was being used—to run 'advertising campaigns' and propaganda that would ensure the secession—it would likely make them donate a little extra to the cause. More than enough to keep it ticking along nicely. And so the racket would go, one side of it feeding the other. The person managing it from behind could stand to make a pretty packet. So could the government contact."

Sarek said, "Will you hand me some of that printout, Doctor?"

"My pleasure. You will note," McCoy said, "that the bank account numbers are all in place, and all the corporate and private transactions are cross-indexed by their Central Clearing Bank reference numbers."

Sarek looked up in shock from the printouts. "Doctor, the 'satchel' format for the access codes to the Central Clearing computers is printed here!" He went as close to ashen as a Vulcan can get. "And the trigger codes for the satcheling process!"

"Yes, I thought you would recognize them," McCoy said. "You designed them, didn't you?"

Sarek was shaking his head. "However useful this information is, Doctor, I want to know how you laid your hands on it! The confidentiality of this system should have been unbreachable! There should have been no way to break this pattern!"

"There isn't . . . not unless you have a friend in high places." McCoy gestured with one thumb at the middle of the air.

Harb stared at him. *"Moira??* You've got my Games machine hacking into strange computers and stealing data??"

"Harb, Harb! 'Borrowing.' "

"But you cannot do that, Doctor," Spock said, looking rather distressed. "I am not speaking in the ethical mode, but in terms of possibility. The Games computer does not have outside access, does not have any of the access or authorization codes you need, does not have—"

"Spock," McCoy said, "there's one thing this computer definitely *does* have. A personality. And you know who put it there."

Sarek looked at Spock, very surprised. "I did not know you were doing recreational programming, my son."

Harb looked from Spock to Sarek. "I asked him to, sir. It's easier for me to work with a machine that has some flexibility in its programming ability. The 'personality' overlays have that: they're effectively self-programming. I had a personality program in here before that was a great joy to work with—the For Argument's Sake personality generator—but it was a little limited. So I asked Spock if in his spare time, he would add some memory to it, and increase the number of associational connections."

Sarek looked at Spock. "You surpassed the critical number, did you not? And the machine—"

" 'Woke up' has always been an anthropomorphism," Spock said, a little defensively, "and at any rate there is no evidence that—"

"The point is that a computer that's had that done to it *acts* alive," Jim said, "and some of them have created problems. That way lies M5, for example."

"I would never do any such thing," Moira's voice said reproachfully, "and you know it. My ethical parameters are very stringent."

"Not stringent enough to keep you from calling a system that should be locked up tighter than the Bank of Switzerland," Jim said, "prying it open, and yanking out reams of confidential material that—"

"It was the right thing to do," Moira said. "Dr. McCoy explained the situation to me. And he *is* my superior officer, Captain, after Mr. Tanzer. Programming requires me to obey a commanding officer's orders. So I asked the bridge computers to handle the downlink, and as for the satchel codes, they appear in various altered forms in my own programming, because it was Spock who designed them—"

"From *my* algorithms," Sarek said, very quietly, paging through the printout.

"Yes, well, Father, they were the best and most complex available—" Spock looked nonplussed.

"Like father, like son," McCoy said. "And a starship's computers have more problem-solving power per gig than any other computer, groundbound or loose. They're built that way. The Clearing computers never had a chance, poor things. Sarek, does the data bear out my allegations?"

"It more than bears them out," Sarek said, "and it adds some most interesting data." He tapped one sheet. "The government connection."

"Shath," McCoy said. "Yes. And a few others on his payroll: and several people in the Expunging Group: and one of the High Councilors. It's a pretty can of worms, isn't it?"

"That does not begin to describe it," Sarek said, passing the sheets on to Amanda.

"So as usual," McCoy said, *"cthia* operates to take care of itself. Here is a very interesting weapon, put in your hands at a very interesting time. The only question becomes, are you going to use it? You don't want to create the effect of making it look like some Federation operation to sabotage the secession vote."

"Not that that's not what it *is*," Sarek said, bemused, going through another pile of printout.

McCoy shook his head. "No, it certainly was not, and is not. Just an old country doctor in search of the truth . . . which is what all this is about, supposedly." McCoy smiled. "I seem to have found more of it than usual, though."

Sarek looked up with something like hope in his eyes. "I must say," he said, "I am impressed. You are quite a detective, Doctor."

"All doctors are detectives. All the ones worth their salt, anyway. . . ."

"I will get you as much salt as you want, Doctor," Sarek said, piling all the printout together. "T'Pau must see these. After that—we shall see. I would recommend to her that we confidentially send copies to the guilty parties and then give them a chance to 'come clean' about the attempts to bribe them. As regards the government officials . . ." He shook his head. "Fortunately it is not many people. But corruption at these levels is a dreadful thing. I must see T'Pau." He stood up. "If I might use your transporter?"

"Of course." The others rose to see him out. Sarek paused in the Rec Room doors as they opened. "In the meantime, Captain," he said, "you are speaking this afternoon, are you not?"

Jim nodded. "As well as Bones, I hope."

"I hope so too." Sarek hefted the papers. "You know, of course, there is a strong possibility that not even this will do us any good."

" 'Us'?" Amanda said, sounding innocent.

Sarek's eyes crinkled. "It is interesting to be a private person again, though I have no idea whether it will last. Come, my wife. We must not keep T'Pau waiting."

"Number eighteen," said the Vulcan who was doing the introductions. For some reason, it was not Shath.

"My name is James T. Kirk," he said, standing calmly under the great skylights. "I hold the permanent rank of Captain in the Starfleet of the United Federation of Planets. To the proposition, I say nay."

He was shaking all over inside—worse than he would have done on the bridge, where he knew which orders to shout, which way to turn, what to do. Fighting with words he understood as well, but fighting in this particular arena was still intimidating. There was so much to lose.

"I am not very sure which 'mode' to work in," he said. "There are several which appeal to me—the exploratory, the purely ethical. The emotional, certainly. For my people, that's considered a valid mode."

He walked around a bit, wanting to be as easy on the stage as McCoy had seemed. "Perhaps I should start with that," he said. "The first time I came to this planet, it was to attend a wedding . . . I thought. It was something of a shock to find that I was one of the intended, and those of you who know about the circumstances under which I left will suspect that I was glad to get away from the place again." There was a murmur of rather restrained amusement. Spock had warned him to tread lightly on this subject: it was delicate. But on the other hand, it could hardly be ignored.

"It was rather a shame," he said. "I had been looking forward to seeing Vulcan. This planet is one of the first places a schoolchild on Earth learns about that's not in Sol system: right after the Alphacent worlds. There is a perception on Earth of Vulcan as a neighbor—even more so, for some reason, than the Cetians. Maybe it's because they're more like us. Maybe the neighbor we finally notice is the one who's a little different." The thought amused him, and some of them as well. "But neighbors you are. In this big galaxy, what's twelve light-years among friends? . . ."

He paced a little more. "We would be sorry to lose you," he said. "I think that's one of the first things that needs to be said. Sorrow is certainly an emotion, and one that a person prefers to avoid if he can. But I think we are sufficiently alike to be familiar with it, nonetheless, and when one sees it coming, certainly there's some logic in trying to avert it. There's no way to explain, in logic, *precisely* what it is about you that we'd be sorry to lose. Some of the characteristics are ones, perhaps, that you don't like. But I'll try a little.

"You people have courage," Jim said. "Not so much an emotion as a virtue. It's certainly one we can admire. Something like forty percent of the mapping of this part of the Galaxy was done by Vulcan teams, at the beginning of your alliance with the Federation. People in little scoutships, going out into danger, or boredom, because exploration was the logical thing to do. And a delight—more knowledge of more diversity. But the courage was always there, and it has never stopped: the kind of thing that took the first *Intrepid* to its death, some years ago. I don't know if you people knew how much the other ships in Fleet mourned that vessel and her crew. She was special."

Jim paced a bit more, looked up at those cameras that he knew were up there somewhere. "You keep us honest," he said. "It may not be precisely true that it's impossible for a Vulcan to lie, but by and large, you do not . . . and that cannot be said, in the same sort of way, for any other hominid species in the Galaxy. I leave the non-hominids out of it for the moment: for many of them, their structure or their environment determines their ethics, and we are not competent to judge them. But we're closer, and I think it's all right for me to say that in our judgment you are an honorable people—you keep your commitments and your word. A Vulcan promise is one of the solidest things there is. It's a peculiar thing, but many Earth people will sooner trust a Vulcan, even if they don't know them, than an Earth person, sometimes whether they know them or not." He smiled a little ruefully. "It says something about us, too. I am not sure I agree with what I've heard others say, that you're not good for us. Certainly we have no desire to be made into Vulcans. Or to make you into us."

"Your government's policies," said a voice from the audience, "do not always seem to bear that out."

"Yes," Jim said, "that's right. Theoretically, our government is by the consent of the governed. The system is not a perfect one, and we know it: we're still feeling our way around, trying to find something that works perfectly. Though it may be that 'perfection' and 'government,' in this world at least, are mutually exclusive terms."

There was a little stir at that: apparently the news of McCoy's little bombshell had hit the Vulcan news services. "Sorry—perhaps I should have said 'this universe.' At any rate," Jim said, as he resumed his pacing, "it's hard to talk to a 'government' and find out why it's doing what it's doing, since it tends to consist of a large number of people, all pulling in what is supposed to be the same direction . . . but sometimes doesn't turn out to be. Ask one person in a government something, and you may get an answer that's a little different from that of the next person on the rope." He shrugged. "It's one of the occupational hazards. If you ask one of the governed, rather than the government, you may hear something very different. Though in service to the Federation, I'm one of the governed; and what *I* say is that I don't want Vulcans to be anything but Vulcan."

"That is what all this is about," said another voice from the audience.

Jim nodded. "I agree. But I have yet to see any evidence that we're stopping you from being Vulcan or interfering in the process." He looked a little indignant. "You people don't know your own power, I don't think. It's possible that those who are made uncomfortable by us find it a useful excuse, that we're somehow ruining your development. But is that really likely to be possible, in a civilization so old and stable? And on the other side of the argument, if you're concerned that Terra is too unstable and malleable to be able to bear contact with Vulcan, I'm surprised we're having these discussions at all . . . and only now, a hundred and eighty years after our association began. Surely we should have all had our ears sharpened by now! Truly,"

Jim said, a little more loudly, running over the laughter that started, "we've been hearing both arguments at once, and I don't think you get to have it both ways."

The laughter peaked, then settled down. "I should be a fairly good example of the situation," Jim said. "For quite a while now I've been serving with a Vulcan first officer—"

"Half Vulcan," said a voice from the audience.

"I was wondering when that was going to come up," Jim said, smiling a bit. "What's it supposed to mean? It can't be a reference to his genetics. There's no logic in pointing it out on those grounds alone. Or do you mean to imply that as such, he's somehow less perfectly or properly Vulcan than a 'full-blooded' member of the species? That he's *really*"—Jim twirled a fake moustache and looked shiftily from side to side—"a fake Earth person?? Oh dear. Lock up your daughters."

Laughter welled up. Jim shook his head. "Well, if that's what you think, you people must not be very familiar with your own species' psychology, because my own observation of the result is that it tends to turn the person 'more Vulcan than the Vulcans.' Icy logic, utterly perfect; brilliant performance at anything attempted: no signs of emotion to be found anywhere: a tendency to go in for Kolinahr. Overreaction, perhaps one might call it," Jim said. "Precious few of you are *that* perfectly and properly Vulcan." Jim stalked the stage for a moment, then said, rather quietly, "My first officer has a right to be judged on his own recognizance—not by his genes, not by what you think his mother did to his Vulcanness, or to the inside of his head, when his father and his teachers and the rest of the planet weren't looking. If you doubt your own influence so thoroughly, if you're so sure that one woman can completely triumph over the culture and presence of an entire planet—goodness, she must be tough. And why did we waste her on *you*? Why didn't we just drop her over Klinzhai? Would have solved the Klingon problem." Laughter broke out. "But seriously, if that's what you think of her, then it's no wonder you're hosting this little gathering. I'm just amazed you invited *more* Earth people here to speak. Aren't you afraid you'll all suddenly rush out and get your ears bobbed?"

There was more laughter at that. "Now you've put me off what I was going to say," Jim said. "Maybe it's better that way. Look. I am living proof of the kind of friendship available for Vulcans among humans. I'm not claiming that the friendship is perfect, or ever was: there have been misunderstandings and incidents of pain, but they've been mercifully few. Mostly my experience of Vulcans, in the one I work with, has been of great courage, intelligence, an insatiable curiosity—the heritage of a proper descendant of all those people who went out in the little scout-ships, both in company with Federation people, and for all the years before you ever met us. And wisdom, as well, and compassion, and a great openness of mind. I thought those were Vulcan traits. I would be sorry to be wrong."

"You are not wrong, I hope," someone said from the audience, "but we are not all of a piece."

"I know," Jim said. "Neither are we."

There was a little silence. "This I want to say, too," Jim said. "It's impossible for me to ignore the fact that, if Vulcan does secede from the Federation, numerous people with affiliations to both are going to get caught in the middle, and hurt—"

"The needs of the many—"

" 'Outweigh the needs of the few, or the one,' " Jim said. "Yes, I knew that was going to come up. I have arguments with that statement. I don't think you can count up lives, souls, and say, Here are twenty of them over here, and one of them over there: these twenty over here are more valuable than the one over there, because there are more of them. What if the soul in the other side of the balance is Surak's? What right have you to decide that one person's needs are less important that twenty people's? And you people are *telepaths!* You can get into other beings' brains and find out what their needs are—and how important they seem, or don't seem, from inside. Numbers are a poor excuse. Counting bodies is just a way to abrogate your responsibility for the situation."

Jim shook his head. *"I* say," he said, "I submit to you, that the many *are* the one. That every one of you-the-many is yourself a one, and without all the 'ones,' there would *be* no many. You must each realize in your own self that it is *you* who will be causing the suffering to the many who will be caught in the middle—the Earth people who live here happily with their children, in peace with you, and will have to give up their homes: the Vulcans, content in their career in Starfleet, or on Earth, who will have to make the decision to come home and leave their work, or else remain there, but exiled, never to see their homes again. And of course my friends," he said, "who will have to make that choice as well. *You* are forcing that on them," he said, pointing up at the cameras, and turning to face, one part at a time, the whole room. "The spear is in *your* hand. Not that of some vague other person, not the 'government'—and what's the government but a whole lot of people? *You* are holding it. *You* will cause their pain.

"I hope," Jim said, "that people who so revere that man who said 'Do not cause others pain,' will listen to what he says. Even if he *was* only one."

There was a movement off to his side. He looked over, surprised, as Sarek hastened up on the stage. Jim blinked: he had never seen Sarek move so fast before.

"There is an emergency," Sarek said to the audience. "I must ask the Captain to come with me immediately. I beg the assembly's indulgence and ask that he be allowed to complete his statement tomorrow."

And Sarek grabbed Jim's arm in a grip of steel and hustled him off, leaving the audience murmuring. "What's the matter?" Jim said to him, completely befuddled.

"Jim," Sarek said, "we must hurry. T'Pau is dying."

Vulcan: Seven

He was in his lab, in the middle of programming a computer, when the note arrived, utterly astonishing him. He was not used to getting hard messages from people; everyone with whom he had any business tended to get in touch with him on the computer, that being where he was almost always working. But there it was—a thin, fine piece of plastic bound down with a wafer of wax. He got up from the console, stretched a bit, and opened it. In a beautiful, clear calligraphy that spidered its way down the paper, it said:

Please come to my office at once. T'Pau.

He almost sat down, such was his surprise. *What might she want with me?* he thought, wondering rather frantically what offense he had committed. She was the Eldest of House, and he was nearly the youngest: well, excepting young Silek, at least, who had just turned fifty. He scoured his memory and could find nothing to which to attribute this summons.

—and it occurred to him then that he was standing there being most dilatory, when his first duty was obedience to his Head of House. He looked around the workroom, again rather frantically, for something decent to throw on over his coverall. There was nothing: he had not done his laundry in two days. Shocking, but when one got working on a good bit of programming, and was not expecting any visitor, and had no social obligation—

Finally he simply brushed himself off as best he could and ran out. It was a fine, fair day, the sun bright over the Academy, people going to and fro about their business, as usual. He ran down one of the paths, then got hold of himself and schooled himself to a dignified walk. It was illogical to hurry: T'Pau would know how long it would take him to get to her offices from his lab. All the same—

He hurried a little. Some people looked after him, as he went: he ignored them, or tried to.

Her office was near the joint libraries, in a small, simple building by itself, a country-looking place of white stucco. He paused at the door, started to brush himself down again, and stopped as the door sensed the motion and entered.

Slowly he went into the outer office. Her assistant was there, tapping busily at a computer herself. "Sarek," he said to her as she glanced up.

"I know," she said. "Please go in: she is awaiting you."

Sarek bowed to her a little, went slowly toward the inner door. It opened for him.

He walked into T'Pau's office. It was spare and simple, the white stucco of the walls unbroken except in one place, where a tapestry of striking abstract weave hung down. The desk was clean, except for the computer pad she was working on and an old yellowed sheet of paper that lay by itself, as if it were something of importance. She was gazing at it. As he came in T'Pau looked up and rose to greet him.

It was a courtesy she hardly needed to show him, and Sarek bowed deeply to her. "Madam," he said.

"Sarek," she said. "You are welcome. I have not seen you since your trial," she said.

He nodded. It had astonished him then, as a child, when she showed up for his manhood trial—the morning he went out into the sands, faced the *lematya*, and came back to tell about it. That was many years ago, but to his eyes she was no less beautiful than she was now. Under the tightly coiled and braided hair, hers was a fierce face, like one of the flying predators of the lesser mountains, a *vakhen*'s face. But at the same time cool and wise, as befitted an Eldest Mother. *How old is she?* he wondered, and then called back the unworthy thought. He could find out, if he wanted to. But for now those keen dark eyes were trained on him, and the consideration made him twitch. He sought down inside him for his calm. He had done nothing wrong, and T'Pau was no *lematya,* and unlikely to bite him.

"I hope you will pardon my calling you away from your work in the middle of the day," she said, "but I have a question for you. Please sit down."

Sarek sat down, bemused, as she too seated herself. "You have been here at the Academy for eight point six years," she said. "All your graduate and degree work is long since completed. I am not saying that your research work has not been invaluable. It has: computer structures on this planet have improved considerably since you turned your hand and mind to them. But now I would like to suggest something to you."

"Please do," Sarek said, completely mystified and concealing it, he hoped, splendidly.

"I have been in contact with the planetary High Council," she said. This was no news, for T'Pau as Head of House of Surak's line might be expected to have the council's ear: her opinion was eagerly sought, not only because of the lands and resources the house had come to control, but because she had acquired a reputation for a sharp mind that missed very little. "They have asked me to suggest the names of some people that we might send along with the embassy to Earth."

Sarek held on to his control with all his mind.

"I had thought to ask you whether you would be interested," she said. "I do not think your parents would protest too much. You are well of age to go off-planet: in fact, you are overdue for it. Someone of your intelligence should not be content to sit here, as so many of our people are, while the Universe passes them by." She paused, looking at him carefully. "Would you be interested?"

"In what capacity would I be required?" he said, and hoped desperately that she had not noticed the squeak in his voice.

"Computers, naturally," she said. "The new embassy will need someone to see to it that communications and data storage and transfer are properly handled. You have a gift for such. You would be a technical attaché, paid as such, and with the appropriate leave and benefit package. Some of your duties would require contact with the Terrans: we will be exchanging various technical information with them. It would be part of your business to discover just where their computer technology stands, so that we may work out what best to offer them, and what to ask for from them in return. Do you think you would be capable of such?"

"Yes," he said, "I would."

"Will you do this?"

"Yes."

"Then you should prepare yourself to leave within the tenday. The Federation has sent a ship, and it will take about four days in transit to Earth, we are told."

"That is very swift," he said, surprised.

"It is indeed. Their technology is surprisingly advanced in some regards, though surprisingly delayed in others." She tilted her head, watching him. "I should like you to examine as much Earth technology as you can, without prying," she said, "and send me reports on what you find of interest, as soon as your communications are sufficiently secure to satisfy you. I desire privacy, and general information, no more: I desire to know a little more about our new allies. You need not limit yourself to technology, either. As far as your duties make it possible, get out and see the planet . . . talk to the people you meet." She had a considering look. "I suspect that this will be a fascinating diversity to study up close."

"I will do that, gladly," he said.

"One word of warning," she said. "I have met some of them. They are very charming people, but the charm is as that of children: their emotions are uncontrolled by our standards. Do not judge them harshly—beware of that: there is no logic in it—but also beware of their influence on you. You will be a long way from home, and their psyches will have yours outnumbered."

"I will be careful," he said.

She lifted the parted hand to him. "Then long life and prosperity to you, in that other place. Come back to us as your duties make it possible: and may you find satisfaction in your posting."

He bowed to her and hurried out.

A tenday later, he was already homesick, and had not even left yet. On his last day on Vulcan, with all his effects already packed—a great pile of reference data solids and tapes, mostly—Sarek stood at the edge of the Academy grounds, outside the walls, and looked across past Pelasht to the immensity of the desert. It was that time of month when T'Khut came up during the daytime, and she was even now easing her bulk up over the horizon, looking somewhat transparent in the daylight, somewhat ephemeral, as she always did. But this time the transparency seemed a sort of omen: a sign that Sarek was losing the real things, that the real world would shortly be fading away from him, to be replaced by—what? A cold place, by all reports—he had packed enough warm clothes to stock a small arctic expedition—and a strange one: a little planet, light in gravity, with no decent sun to speak of, just a small yellow dwarf star that sounded very pallid and unwelcoming. He was aching with immunizations that no one was sure he, or anyone else, needed: it was unknown as yet whether Vulcans—oh, the odd name, would he ever get used to it?— whether Vulcans could give Earth-humans their diseases, or get theirs from them in return. Theory said not, but Sarek and many others had preferred certainty to theory.

He dealt with the aches and pains as best he could, while wondering at the oddness of it all. That he should be the alien to another species: that someone else should translate the name of their planet as "the world," "the earth," and call themselves human beings—and then give *his* planet and his people names of which he didn't know the meaning or derivation. . . . It was all very strange. But he must do something about that, must find out what the name meant, when he got to Terra. *Earth, rather,* he thought. If he was to be a diplomat, however junior, he must begin acting and thinking diplomatically. And as T'Pau had said, it would be a fascinating diversity to study. He must do it properly, must miss nothing. As one of Surak's line, it was his business to follow the Guidelines as closely as he could, and be, as it were, his ancestor's eyes and hands in that time and place.

He gazed at T'Khut. She was a wonderful color on a morning like this, when the sky was clear: her ruddiness took on the blue of the bright air she shone through, and went a rich violet, shading to lavender in her maria and scarred places. She was gibbous: on her dark side a few volcanoes could be seen, erupting desultorily in the palest gold tinged with blue. Sarek's heart turned in his side, and he breathed out in pain. Had he been far enough away from anyone, he would have said aloud, *When will I see you again? I do not want to leave!*

But he was within eyeshot of the walls, and the thought of his own self-pity abashed him. He turned around and headed back into town to catch the transport for the ship.

It was more than fifty years before he came back.

In the fifty years, many memories did not so much precisely fade as have to be filed far back, out of the way. His landing on Earth, for example: stepping out of the shuttlecraft into what had to be the coldest morning he had ever experienced, surely no more than (in the strange new system of temperatures he had been learning) sixty degrees Fahrenheit. He had stood and looked about him there, for a moment, on the alien concrete: at ships standing berthed, and small vehicles driving and flying everywhere, and the smell of burning internal-combustion chemicals in the air— *T'Pau was quite right,* he remembered thinking, in total amazement. And then looking up to the sky—it was night—and seeing the stars, and being amazed even more to find them so much the same: their patterns a little bent out of shape, but otherwise little different than at home. And high up, small and silvery, a moon. A tiny thing, but bright, bright, like a beacon. That finally convinced him that he was on an alien world. Until he saw it, he had wondered, in a moment's bemusement, whether some with a tricksterish turn of mind might not change Vulcan's climate, take away the familiar technology and substitute something else, intricate and bizarre, like the technology here. But the stars, and that burning silver disk, *those* told him that this was indeed another world, full of people who did not think like him, and doubtless thought a tiny, rather pitiful silver moon was part of the proper order of things. . . .

That memory had been filed away over years, along with many others, to make room for business. He could of course still look at them, when he chose to. A spring morning in Paris, one of his first holidays, when it rained softly, actual rain out of the sky, as he strolled the Rive Gauche. Standing on the lip of the Grand Canyon, nearly drowning in the beautiful, sandy, stony immensity of it, and thinking that this piece of Earth was actually rather like Vulcan, only (treason!) even better. An evening in Reykjavik, spent sitting on a boggy hillcrest, watching the volcanoes bubble and mutter a quarter mile away, and watching the sluggish lava meander like snakes of hissing fire down the cracking hillsides. . . .

And the people. T'Pau had been right: they were astonishing and uncontrolled: noisy, irrepressible, difficult, devious, untruthful, hyperactive, shallow, dissembling, incautious, maddening, and most of all, wildly illogical. But he would not have missed them for anything, for they were also cheerful, often wise, courteous, welcoming, eager to learn and understand, gallant, surprisingly prudent, clever—

It had taken him a while to find all this out. Sarek was about ten years in the embassy as technical attaché. He spent his time in consultation with Terran computer people, mostly, talking code and software, getting into the guts of their hardware and being continually amazed by the elegance of parts of it and the crudeness of others. He was delighted to discover how very much like him they were: they would find nothing odd about being awake for three days at a time, hammering away at a recalcitrant piece of code, though their frail constitutions were hardly up to such abuse.

All they cared about was the art of their work, and doing it right. It was hard not to admire such dedication and love of computing for its own sake. The programmers were the first Earth people he came to understand as being really human.

He sent reports home to T'Pau on a regular basis, and as she encouraged him, he widened the focus of the reports and made them about anything he saw and enjoyed. (He was careful to moderate his use of the word, lest she suspect he was going native on her: but 'enjoyed' was the truth, however straight he kept his face while "researching" them, and however he rewrote his reports.) One of them dealt almost entirely with the World Series race in the fall of 2180, the year the Mets and the Giants spent the late season struggling to the tops of their respective leagues, and then savaged one another with such memorable elegance, in a series every game of which went into extra innings. Another had to do with littoral biology of the Mediterranean, and (marginally) with bouillabaisse, and a small fish called *racasse,* and the people who fished for it, and the old-fashioned way they made their livings in a world where ion-drivers came to pick up their catch. Another report was about the restoration of St. Basil's in Moskva: another about research into whale language. Late and happily Sarek came to realize the truth that T'Pau had somehow seen in him—that he was a tourist at heart, and as such a potentially sympathetic eye on the planet, though wholly Vulcan: an eye which might see things that the more diplomatically inclined would miss. When he came to realize that she had sent him more for this purpose than for his computer skills—though those were certainly useful—he was annoyed for a day, then put it aside and never gave it a thought again. There was too much to see and do here, and too many people to meet, and too much to tell about.

It was not too long before Sarek's keenness for and with Earth people began to be noticed at the embassy. The staff there, despite all their specializations, began to realize that if there was some aspect of Earth culture that puzzled them, Sarek was the one to call: if he couldn't explain it immediately in terms that made sense to a Vulcan, he would simply nod and go away, and a day or so later he *would* be able to explain it. About ten years into his posting—he never really seemed to have time to go home to Vulcan—the senior ambassador, Sasav, called him in and promoted him to cultural attaché. Sarek protested gently, but Sasav told him that there was no logic in it; the computers needed almost no maintenance in terms of their programming—or any that they did could be handled by the young Vulcan assistant Sarek had trained—and hardware support could be handled locally. It was time he used his talent with Earth people to help the many who came to the embassy seeking advice about tourism or immigration.

Sarek did as he was bid, of course, though he found it a little strange at first to do some other work on a computer besides writing programs on it, or the daily letter to his parents. He found himself handling paperwork, visas, and advice, which he was able to give with extreme efficiency, having gotten an idea over his travels of the kinds of things Earth people could deal with. As more years passed, and the embassy grew, he found himself with a growing staff, people whom he taught to handle the details of trade delegations and package tours and cultural exchange programs. He became a familiar face around the planet, not least because of his fluency in the various languages. To Sarek, who had been master of at least twenty different programming languages, the spoken kind were a hobby he had studied happily, especially since they had early proved to be the best way to find out the truth about bouillabaisse, or the people who ate it. His grasp of dialect and idiom was amazing for anybody, off-planet or on. He once reduced the President of the United States—then a ceremonial post, but one much loved by people who lived within the old borders—to tears of laughter at a state dinner, by delivering a learned dissertation on computer data storage technology in a flawless Texan accent. The lady was later heard to propose an amendment to the Constitution to allow off-worlders to hold high public office, so that she could have him for her running mate in the next election.

It was just as well he was as good at languages as he was, for this was before the universal translator was perfected, and misunderstandings were, if not rife, at least commonplace. People began to notice that the one office in the embassy that *never* had context problems was Sarek's, and he was moved from cultural to diplomatic, around twenty-five years into his posting. There he spent the rest of the time until his return to Vulcan: for there he found his great love, and the art for which all the rest of his life had been practice.

It was no simple art. Diplomacy on Vulcan (since *cthia,* at any rate) mostly consisted of telling the other person what you wanted, and hearing what they wanted, and then working out some solution that would work for everyone. But on his entrance into the diplomatic service proper, Sarek found that he had been thrown into a sort of timewarp, back to the kind of diplomacy that must have taken place in the old turbulent days before Surak—and complicated by the fact that there were few mindreaders on this planet to assist one in finding out what the other *really* wanted. The base cause of the problem was that these people were not committed *not* to lie to one another . . . or to him. This added a dimension to diplomacy that he was not entirely sure he liked.

It helped a little that Sarek was surprisingly high-psi, even for his training—there had, in fact, been some disappointment in his youth that he had not gone to Seleya to take the training for full-adept status. But Sarek was too much in love with the active life at that point. He did the usual training in psi, when young, that any Vulcan did—how to handle the mindtouch; bonding technique, for when he should need it; bearing the Sense of the Other (for even now, all these years after Surak, there were still people who found the Sense, and its implications, difficult to handle); and of course *na'Tha'thhya,* the Passing-On, the investiture of one's self-that-has-been in *katra* mode, so that it might not be lost to the Other. When he had completed his psi training—for that was always the last thing one learned—Sarek had gone away unconcerned about the end of his days. Now, under this little yellow sun, he sometimes wondered what would happen to him if he died outside the embassy—what he would do with his *katra.* He had finally sighed to himself and made a resolve to be careful crossing the street.

But his other psi training held him in good stead, here. Business executives and various Earth officials might come to him and lie, but there was no point in it: Sarek could hear a lie coming a week off, and he learned to ask the gentle questions that would shame the truth out of hiding sooner or later. In the course of his diplomatic work he ran into much greed, some cruelty, much dishonesty, but it did not disillusion him. He knew that Surak would have been as right about the Terrans as he had about Vulcans: they were simply afraid, afraid of one another, and more so of him, because of his strangeness; but assist them in casting out fear, and truth and agreement would always slip in to fill the gap. He eventually heard about the stories that grew up around him, that it was not so much that a Vulcan could not lie, but that he could not be lied *to.* Sarek would smile, privately, when he heard as much. He did not mind the legend, if it kept the people who came to him from wasting their and his time with lies. Life was too short, and there were agreements to be made, and the prevarication only slowed them up.

He made a name for himself as a negotiator. The Vulcan-Terran Interstellar Comprehensive Trade Act of 2192 had Sasav's name signed to it, but it was Sarek's handiwork, and various members of the Federation Council noticed it—a tightly woven document, scrupulously fair to everyone concerned, and as closely reasoned as a computer program. There was no surprise in this: after many years of studying Earth with a student's delight, from up close, Sarek knew what the industries and the industry executives wanted, almost better than they did. Various people in the Federation government began to notice Sarek.

He was interested by the notice, but not flattered: there was too much to do. He still wrote to his parents daily; he still sent T'Pau reports, though these days they were more often about the fine details of moving and shaking the diplomatic world than about fish soup. Not that Sarek was usually seen to move or shake anything. His style was more subtle: situations seemed to calm themselves on the sight of him, or arrange themselves tidily in the shape he wanted them before he got within arms' length. It was an art much envied by his fellow diplomats, both on the Federation side and among the Vulcans.

It was summer of 2212 when he returned to Vulcan. It was not a recall. Sasav was retiring, and he asked Sarek to come back with him and assist him with the debriefing to the Council, and assist him and them in the choice of a replacement.

Sarek's feelings when he stepped out into the port facility were mixed. Everything looked strange, everything had been changed since he left. The sight of so many Vulcans all around seemed odd, suddenly, and the fact of the oddness struck him to the heart. But this far on in his life he was beyond showing such a reaction openly. He went on his way with Sasav's party, not noticing the heads that turned as he went by, as people looked with interest at the ambassador, whom everyone knew, followed by the tall, broad-shouldered presence, dark and intent, the personification of a brooding, keen-eyed calm. People wondered who he was.

They found out soon enough. The debriefing with the council was long and boring, though Sarek never showed it, and his mind was often on Earth during the proceedings. The dry realities and recitations of pacts and relationships were shouldered aside in his mind by the memory of the events that accompanied their forging—some abortive shouting match with a union leader, or a dinner at which wine and some delicate mind-probing unlocked some of his erstwhile adversaries' desires to him and made a solution possible that he might not otherwise have found. He did not speak of such things, naturally: it would have violated the humans' privacies, as well as his own.

Sasav's retirement was a sorrow to him, though he concealed that as well. Over the fifty years, the relationship had gone from a distant sort of superior-worship to a warm and cordial working relationship with a man both wise and clever. But Sasav was almost a hundred and eighty, and was certainly entitled to spend the last third of his life in comfort at home after his long service. Still, Sarek found it difficult to conceive of an Ambassador to Earth who was someone other than Sasav.

So his surprise was forgivable when the council chose him as Sasav's successor.

He was tempted to argue the point with them, pleading excessive youth, but he knew there would be no point in it. They would have their reasons in logic marshaled, and those reasons would be correct. His long experience there from a young age, his fluency in Earth languages, the relationships he had built up with officials there, the results he had produced in negotiations— All he could do, with Sasav's eyes on him, and T'Pau's, was bow slightly, and accept the posting.

He made a resolve to see T'Pau again, before he left. The diplomatic briefings that followed, with Sasav and the High Council, made it plain to Sarek that there was much more to keeping a relationship with Earth in place than he had thought. The government's *cthia* was mostly in place, but there were slippages: they were afraid of the Terrans, of their strangeness, their expansionist policies, their energy, their capacity for violence. To many Vulcans they seemed very young children, running around the Galaxy with dangerous weapons. By comparing what he was hearing now from the government with what he had heard Sasav say in the embassy, Sarek now discovered the careful and sympathetic way in which his superior had been portraying the Terrans to the council, to avoid panicking them where no panic was necessary. Many other situations, viewed in this light, now made it apparent to him what a fine line Sasav had been riding, keeping the two governments in communication, preventing misunderstandings, avoiding anything that might inflame the Vulcans' xenophobia. For such it was. More than ever Sarek doubted his ability to do this job this well . . . but his determination increased to *attempt* to do it this well.

That night he saw T'Pau for dinner. She was older. *Illogical,* he thought to himself. *Did you expect her to go into stasis when you left?* But that fierce face was calming a little. The fierceness was very much there, but the wisdom that had always been there was beginning to make itself more obvious. He had some things for her— some data solids from Earth, literature mostly, and music and film, including those World Series games, about which T'Pau was highly curious.

They talked about a great number of things, and when they were at the end of the meal Sarek was surprised to hear her say in the formal mode—actually the mode of the Eldest to one of the family—"There is one thing I must discuss with thee. Thou wast never bonded as a child, as the bonding on our family has been elective by tradition. Thee is now well of age to be bonded. What are thee doing about this?"

It was a topic that had been in his thoughts oftener than he liked, over fifty years, with some slight sorrow. But the sorrow was long behind him. "I have put that option aside, T'Pau. I have no close relationship with any Vulcan woman: and if I did, I am not sure I would ask her to accompany me to Earth. It can be hard, being a Vulcan there. They are not far along in their version of *cthia* as yet, and their attitudes toward strangers are sometimes imperfect. . . ."

"Thy logic is in abeyance," she said, which was about as severe a reprimand as anyone had given him these fifty years. "I know thy reasons. Nonetheless, thee should keep thy options open. Cast out fear."

He nodded, and thought no more of it. They finished the meal and said their farewells.

Sarek completed his business with the council, collected the necessary documentation, went to visit his parents for a moonround, and then at the end of the month, took ship for Earth again. Two days later he was presenting his credentials to the United Federation of Planets as the Ambassador Extraordinary and Plenipotentiary from Vulcan. He did not feel particularly extraordinary, but there was something exhilarating about walking into the upstairs office in the embassy, afterward, and sitting down in the chair behind the desk, and knowing that he spoke for his people here. He would do it well.

*   *   *

Quite shortly thereafter, he met Amanda Greyson.

It was, of course, in the line of business. She was involved with a Federation program intended to develop a universal translator, and Sarek was happy to have his linguistics department assist her: such an instrument could only be a tremendous breakthrough, in a world where until now wars might be caused or averted by the mistranslation of a term. She did not make any particular impression on him when he saw her first—a handsome woman, tall for her people, with wise eyes. Later, he found that she reminded him of T'Pau, in some odd fashion, though he had trouble identifying exactly what the likeness was.

His people down in Linguistics kept him apprised of their work with her (she had begun to help some of them with their English), and the reports began to be very glowing indeed. Sarek began to take some interest in the woman. She had, it seemed, traveled to Vulcan and lived there for several years while studying language, semiotics, and kinesics at the Science Academy. He made it a point to drop down to Linguistics, once or twice, when his people had told him she was expected there. Their meetings were cordial: more than cordial, when she found how fluent and idiomatic his Vulcan was . . . and how fond he was of Szechuan food. That was what brought them together the first time. She had found a Hunan place in the city that she wanted him to try—that was when the embassy was still in London—and they sat down over homestyle fried noodles and a word list and spent the whole meal conversing in Vulcan.

It was refreshing in a way he found difficult to understand to hear his own language coming so easily from the lips of an alien. Perhaps easily was not the right word. There were problems with her pronunciation—she had picked up a very peculiar Lesser-sea accent somehow, which amused him, since in the old days the Lesser accent had a country-bumpkin connotation to it, and to hear it coming from this polished young woman was droll, to put it mildly. But her vocabulary was strong in the sciences, and her translations were surprisingly accurate for the most part. Most to his surprise, she had studied *cthia*.

"It seems to make such sense," Amanda said to him over the green tea. "But that kind of thing always does, when enlightenment comes suddenly out of nowhere, and you look at it and wonder what took it so long. . . . I suppose our obtuseness is so much greater than we think, that it always seems surprising . . . when in fact the Universe has been hammering at our heads, trying to get the answers in, forever and ever. . . ."

He nodded. "I think you may be right. Your planet's various enlightenments have the same effect on me."

"I wonder what we would have done with Surak?" she said softly. And then she laughed, a rueful sound. "Now that I think of it, probably what we have done with various other of the great enlighteners. Nailed them up to crosses, or chased them across deserts, or shot them. We are not a very enlightenable people, I'm afraid. But sometimes the light breaks through. . . ." She tapped the word list with one chopstick. "That's what this is for," she said.

"To the light," he said, and raised his cup of tea to her.

They met fairly often after that. Sarek's Anglish was more flexible and idiomatic than any of his staff's: that was the excuse. But increasingly he found himself delighting in having a friend. He had had few, on Vulcan: from a very young age, his work had possessed him. During his earlier posting here, he had been on the move all the time, even when working—gathering data, rarely staying mentally in the same place for very long. But now, in his early maturity, he felt a little more settled, and that settlement found great satisfaction in the expression of friendship.

They frequently quarreled. The quarrels were genteel—he kept them that way, since mostly he was right—but when Amanda became annoyed over what she perceived as his smugness about being right, her eyes would flash and she would become splendidly insulting, usually in bizarre Anglish idiom that Sarek found as refreshing as it was annoying. She caused him to laugh out loud for the first time in many years when she told him, after a disagreement over the translation of a word for war, that he should only grow headfirst in the ground like a turnip. Later that month, when he was right about something again and made the mistake of not immediately down-playing it, she issued him with a formal malediction, wishing that the curse of Mary Malone and her nine blind orphan children might pursue him so far over the hills and the seas that God Almighty couldn't find him with a radio telescope. Sarek laughed so hard at that that he entirely lost his breath, and Amanda panicked and started to give him cardiopulmonary resuscitation, which was useless, because his heart was somewhere other than the spot on which she was pounding. It took him nearly an hour to recover: he kept laughing. He had never been cursed like that before, not even by union leaders, and it was very refreshing.

There came a time when the day seemed somehow incomplete if she had not called him and asked him about something, or told him what she was doing. There came a time when it seemed odd not to have dinner together at least one day of the weekend, if not both. There came a time when it seemed quite normal that he should visit her at her house, and have dinner with her, and stay late, talking about everything in the world. The worlds. Now there were truly more than one, and he felt as if he was living both of them. The word lists had started the process: it was the word lists that finally put the finishing touch to it.

"You have mistranslated this," he said, sitting on her couch and tapping the printout. "I thought we had discussed this. Do you mean to tell me that this revision of the list went to the committee?"

She frowned at him. "I told you it was going to. What's the problem?"

"This word." He pointed at *arie'mnu*. "It does *not* mean elimination of emotion. That is not what we do, by and large."

"But all the earlier—"

"If you will pay attention to all the earlier translations, you will perpetuate their mistakes! Nor, what is this, down here, nor is it 'suppression.' *Control* is wrong as well. Mastery, it is mastery. There is a difference!"

She shrugged and sighed. "It's going to be hard to get it changed now. It's just one word, we can catch it in the next translation—"

"And leave everyone who hears the word for the next ten years thinking that we *have* no emotions? Do *you* think we have no emotions?"

"*Do* you have emotions?" she said, arching her eyebrows at him. He was being teased, and he knew it.

And instantly he knew something else, as well.

"You will have to judge," he said . . . and drew her close.

And showed her that he did.

And found that she did, too.

Some time later, a small, soft, lazy voice spoke. It was astonishing how her voice could change, sometimes.

"You know, it's funny. . . ."

"What is?"

"Well, everybody wants to know if Vulcans are . . ."

"I do not think I shall ask you to complete that. Well? And are we?"

She laughed. "Let them catch their own Vulcans and find out."

"Catch? That implies that I ran away. . . ."

More laughter. "At least you did it slowly."

He smiled. "Was that a pun?"

"No." She giggled. "Goodness, though . . . how this is going to look in the papers. *I Married An Alien!*"

"So will I have," he said wryly, "and I suspect the response may be similar, at first."

"Has it ever been done?"

"Not to my knowledge."

A thinking silence. "And shall we have a child?"

"Can you?"

"Yes. Can *you?*"

"I suspect so."

She thought a moment. "The question is . . . can *we?*"

He thought too. "All we can do," he said, "is find out."

The marriage was a quiet one, but the news was still greeted with astonishment on Earth. Sarek took it calmly. One particularly annoying newspaper, which published a slight alteration on Amanda's headline—*I Married A Little Green Man!*"—received an interesting riposte from Amanda, when she was interviewed on one of the broadcast news services shortly thereafter: "There is nothing little," she said with great dignity, "about my husband." Sarek did not at first understand the amused ripple that went through the crowd of reporters standing around. Certainly he was tall by Earth standards. He had to have it explained to him, and afterward laughed harder than after the radio-telescope incident.

Things quieted down eventually. After a few peaceful years on Earth, Sarek requested a sabbatical on Vulcan, which was granted him without question. He and Amanda were granted a ride on a starship—their first one—and were on Vulcan the next day. The day after that they had their first of many appointments at the Vulcan Science Academy.

There are of course people who will claim that "crossbreeds" between species are impossible. In nature, they are. But the Vulcans were at that time the best geneticists in the Galaxy, having been practicing the art, one way or another, almost since before their history began. It had never been done: but there was no reason why it should not be done, for both parents were hominids, in their right mind, and of sufficiently similar physiology that a compromise could be designed.

"Designed" was the most accurate word. The process started with extensive genetic mapping of both of them. The geneticists at the Academy took their time—there was no room for mistakes. After a year, every gene on Amanda's and Sarek's chromosomes had been typed and identified and assessed for viability.

Then the design began—working out how the body should work physically, for Vulcans and humans each had organs that the other did not, and all the necessary vital functions needed to be covered. Differing chemistries had to be reconciled, differing means of ATP and ADP synthesis and interaction: the basic bodily cell structure had to be redesigned from the mitochondria up. Differences in metabolism had to be handled. Neural chemistries had to be carefully juggled. There were thousands of similar details. And then every change had to be "programmed" into the template chromosomes, by computer-controlled or manual microsurgery.

It took four years.

Finally the technicians were ready. They called Amanda in and borrowed an ovum from her, to use for its membrane. The other genetic tissue they needed, they already had. With great care, in an operation taking three days, they scooped the original genetic material out of the ovum, replaced it with the material they had tailored from Amanda, introduced the equivalent material from Sarek, closed the little cell up . . . and waited.

It sat thinking for about half an hour, and then divided.

And divided again.

And again.

They did not cheer: they were Vulcans. But there was an insufferable air of satisfaction about the Parturitic Genetics lab for days. About a week later, Amanda went in and officially got pregnant. It was an office procedure, and took about five minutes.

Then began the long wait to see whether the embryo would implant properly, whether the placenta would hold.

It did. Amanda showed no ill effects, except that in her second month she lost her appetite for everything but sour foods, and found herself (to her utter disgust) wanting to eat nothing but pickles. She complained bitterly that she felt like a cliché. Sarek laughed, and got her pickles, regardless of the expense.

The child came to term after nine and a half months, and was born in an easy delivery, without incident. Amanda had been instructed in Vulcan pain-control techniques well before the delivery and was awake and lively all through it. At the end she was tired, but she breathed a sigh of relief as they brought her the child, and Sarek stood by her, looking down at him.

Their son looked like most Vulcan babies: rather green, very bald, his head a little pushed out of shape from the stress of delivery misshaping the soft fontanelles at the top of the skull. That would straighten itself out after a day or so. "He's gorgeous," Amanda said happily.

"I should think he would be," Sarek said mildly. "The designers would hardly have ignored the outside, after working so hard on the inside. But I think you are biased, my wife."

"You are right as usual, my husband. What are we going to call him? An S-name?"

"It would seem appropriate," Sarek said. "So many others have done it to honor Surak: it would be looked at askance if we did not. We will think of something."

"And then he'll go to the Academy, like his daddy," Amanda said, a little sleepily. "And then . . ."

"There is time to plan that yet," Sarek said, and put a gentle finger down to the little fist that grasped and held it, hard. "My son."

They took Amanda out, and Sarek followed, glancing through a window as he went. It was near dawn, and T'Khut was setting. He had never seen her look quite so real, so fierce, before: and behind her, the stars glittered fiercely too, as if in rivalry.

We shall see, he said silently, and went after his wife and his son.

Enterprise: Eight

Jim beamed out with Sarek from outside the hall. When the glitter died down, they were in a large room done in warm colors and filled with unobtrusive machinery. Several parts of the room were concealed by the soft opaque glow of positionable, non-sound-permeable forcefields, and quietly dressed Vulcans passed through the room checking the various pieces of the machinery or looking into one or another of the field-shielded cubicles.

McCoy put his head out through one of them, as if looking around for something—a bizarre effect, as if he had put the front half of him through a wall—and seeing Jim and Sarek, beckoned urgently to them. They stepped through the field after him.

T'Pau lay there unconscious in a Vulcan-style diagnostic bed, with Amanda and Spock on either side of her. Next to Amanda, a woman in a soft brown tunic, with long dark hair, was looking at the diagnostic panel: her face suggested nothing about what she thought she saw. "How is she, Doctor T'Shevat?" Sarek said.

"She has been slipping in and out," said the doctor. "This is normal for her condition, but it is not a good sign."

McCoy nodded, and looked over at Jim. "Liver failure," he said. "She's past the point where even the healing trance would do her any good."

"She has forbidden it to be initiated," T'Shevat said, looking around at them all. "Her declaration of refusal of 'heroic measures' has been on file with us for ten years. She has specified the medications she will allow herself to be given, and the procedures she will allow us to perform. But beyond those, we are helpless to take action."

She looked at McCoy, and he nodded in agreement. "It would need more than heroic measures," he said to Jim. "She would need a liver transplant, and her immune system isn't up to it, even with retroviral immunosupport."

"I will be within call if I'm needed," T'Shevat said, and she slipped out through the field.

Jim looked down at T'Pau sadly. She looked extremely thin and worn, the skin tight against the bones of her face, the eyes sunken: even the piled-up hair seemed to have lost its gloss. "They could at least have given her a private room," he said softly.

"That kind of privacy—has never been my concern," said the tired, cracked voice. T'Pau's eyes opened, and she looked up at him. "So," she said.

She looked around at the others: the motion made it plain that even that little movement cost her. Her eyes came to rest on Sarek. "I regret—my lapse in timing . . ." she said. "I was attempting to forestall this collapse as long as possible. It seems—there are things—"

Her breath gave out: she lay there a moment, getting it back. "You are not to think of that," Sarek said to her. "Matters are going as well as they can be expected to."

"They are not," she said. "There is this small matter of T'Pring."

"Do not think of that now—"

"If I do not do my thinking now, it will do you little good later," T'Pau said, and there was a touch of the old snap in her voice. Then she lost her breath again.

McCoy looked concerned: Jim noticed that her color was changing slightly, shading into a darker green. It made him nervous.

"Now," she said. "Sarek, you have asked my counsel about what should be done with this material. Your plan is subtle." She breathed hard. "It is too subtle. Subtlety and acts hidden in the dark were the root of this plan. If you feed it on more darkness, it will only prosper. You must tell the truth about it, and at once."

"Simply give the information to the media?" Sarek said.

"Sometimes simplicity—is best," T'Pau said. "Do as I bid!"

Sarek bowed to her.

"The truth—is able to care for itself," she said, and ran out of breath again. "But it must be set free. Release the information immediately."

"I will do so."

But Sarek did not move. T'Pau was looking at Spock and Kirk, standing together by the side of her bed. Jim looked at her and had one of those sudden odd visions that one sometimes has of another human being. Sometimes one looks at a friend and sees them as they will be when they are old. But Jim gazed at her and saw her when she was young . . . and breathed out, slightly glad he had not met her. They might have killed each other, or been the best of friends: there was no telling.

"Yes," she said. And she smiled a little: an astonishing look on that face, that usually seemed if a smile might crack it. "When first I saw thee two together, I thought that I should see one or the other of thee die. Now see how incorrect thought traps us in the end; for I little thought that I should see thee two together again, but that the death should be mine."

Jim wanted to say something like "You're not going to die," except that it would have been so patently absurd, and besides, it seemed like an insult to refuse to acknowledge what was going on. "I would have liked to know you better," he said. "I'm sorry I haven't had the chance."

"I too," Spock said: and then reached out and took her hand.

She nodded. "Yes," she said. And she looked around at them all, and said, "I shall go now. There is no use waiting to see when it will happen."

Sarek took a slow step forward. "No," T'Pau said. "You do not need this gift, son of my house. You will be Head of House now, and you would have difficulty dealing with my *katra*, I think. No." She turned her head, looked up at Amanda. "I think we will do well together, my daughter. You have the necessary training from Seleya to manage the Gift once I have left it to you: and it will qualify you as Eldest Mother of the house, whatever others may say. Best to so manage matters. If you consent—"

Amanda's eyes were full of tears. "Of course I do," she said, her voice quite steady. "Let it be done so." And she leaned close.

T'Pau reached up one shaking, wrinkled hand to Amanda, who took it and pressed it gently to her face. For a moment, both their eyes closed. The withered lips whispered something inaudible. Amanda nodded.

Then there was no movement, but they knew she was gone.

Slowly her breathing stopped.

Amanda let go the hand, laid it on the coverlet, straightened up slowly. "It's done," she said.

The doctor looked in, looked at them.

"She is with the Other," Sarek said.

T'Shevat nodded. "I grieve with you," she said. "All Vulcan will grieve with you."

"Did she leave instructions with you?" Sarek said.

The doctor nodded. "She is to be cremated and the ashes scattered on the sands of the Forge," she said.

"We will see to it, then."

The doctor bowed and left. One by one, they all stepped through the field and stood outside it a moment. "Now what?" McCoy said.

"Now we carry out her instructions," Sarek said. "But first . . . we tell her world that she is gone."

"No, my husband," Amanda said, very firm. There was an odd note in her voice, and everyone looked at her.

"What?" Sarek said, surprised out of politeness.

"No. You must tell them about T'Pring's plotting first . . . and you must tell them who has been notified. *Then* tell them about T'Pau. She would not want—would not have wanted it otherwise: she would not like it, to have her personal life take precedence over the proper running of the government."

Sarek looked at Amanda as if he had never seen her before . . . then nodded. "Very well," he said. "Let us be about it."

They left the clinic, Jim and Spock last of all . . . and Jim was wondering a great deal about the small, odd smile on Amanda's face.

The first piece of news threw the planet into an uproar. There were accusations, counteraccusations, denials, carefully worded protestations of innocence, and much dust thrown up to confuse the issue by people who wished to seem as if they knew nothing about it. The debates went on: Jim declined a second session of testimony, feeling he had already said what he needed to.

The second piece of news brought the planet to a standstill. The streets grew silent, and mostly empty of people; the news services did little but talk, in a muted way, about her life: some shut down entirely. Her will was read later that day, including the request for cremation.

Jim went with the family, that night, to the Forge. The cremation had been handled earlier in the day, and when they beamed out, Sarek was carrying a small, pale green porcelain container, exquisitely made, which Jim had seen in the house and not recognized.

What none of them were expecting, when they arrived, were the three million Vulcans gathered around the edges of the Forge. They went on around the miles-wide curve of the desert seemingly forever, the largest single gathering of people in the history of the Federation, all silent, all waiting. Jim was staggered. He looked over at Spock, who shook his head, wordless, and at Amanda, who smiled, slightly and gently, and shook her head too.

Sarek stood there awhile, in the silence, listening to the wind blow: and finally came the sign he was waiting for. There was a bulge of light against the horizon, a curve, a dome, growing, ruddy, shining.

Sarek stepped forward. "Here is what is left of her," he said to the night. He did not raise his voice, but all the hairs stood up on Jim's neck as he had a sudden sense of the sound of that voice being passed from mind to mind, at faster than lightspeed, right around that great desert, held in every mind at once, and echoed so that he heard Sarek's words in millions of individual voices, but all silent. It was overwhelming: he found it hard to bear. He glanced at his fellow humans. Amanda seemed untroubled, and McCoy was standing there with his eyes closed, perhaps in prayer.

"We give her remains to the night from which we arose," Sarek said, opening the porcelain container to the light wind that had sprung up. "Surely we know that this is not she; she and the Other know it well. And we wish her well in whatever may befall, till the Moon is no longer, and the Stars are no more."

The wind carried the dust away into the silence. T'Khut slipped upward in silence, flooding the ocean of sand with light.

"Light with her always," he said, "and with us."

And he turned away.

They all went home.

"Number twenty-three," said the voice. Again, it was not Shath.

"I am Spock," he said, standing still and erect in the middle of the stage. "I hold the rank of Commander in the Starfleet of the United Federation of Planets; I serve as First Officer of the *Starship Enterprise*. And as regards the proposition, I say: nay."

The room was quite still. Spock said, "My family are in mourning today, and we are grateful for the many expressions of support which have come to us. But meanwhile, the one whom we mourn would desire that we do the business which has brought us here, and so I have come to see it done."

He turned a little, to favor another part of the auditorium. "I am in a peculiar position, for many of you will know that I am a son of the tradition that now debates casting Earth out, and also a son of Earth itself. Many voices have been raised against Earth here. I could not allow that to influence me. What matters is doing right, not merely blindly defending what is attacked. That is *cthia* in its true form: and whatever my heritage, I was trained in *cthia,* and hold it dear."

He looked around the auditorium. "Much has been said," he said slowly, "about the tendency of humans to emotion, or our own mastery of it. Little has been said about the *purposes* of emotion. It has many—primarily to guide one toward one kind of behavior or away from another. Doing good, brings joy: doing evil, sorrow; and all these emotions we possess, and master, so as not to contaminate others' mastery with them."

Spock took a long breath. "We are much concerned," he said, "with the damage our emotions may do one another. We are right to be concerned, perhaps. There have been many millions of people killed on this planet, over the millennia, due to the lack of management of emotion. But it is possible to overdo this concern: to be overly concerned over what damage our emotions (or management of them) may do others: sometimes even over what damage others' emotions may do us.

"I am a Vulcan, bred to peace," Spock said. "Many of us have said that, after S'task, who said it first, even though he was of the first generation of that breeding. I think that breeding was more robust than most of us allow ourselves to believe. It seems too much like ego, like self-aggrandizement, to say openly, 'We are strong'; and so we pretend not to be, and do ourselves, perhaps, more harm than if we simply admitted our strength and moved on.

"But that pretense betrays our great secret to those who can see: and the secret is that, *cthia* or not, we are still uncertain about our mastery. We are still, as Surak said, afraid of one another, and of ourselves: afraid that the emotion we so carefully manage will somehow break loose and doom us again.

"The trouble is, it is doing so now. It is doing so, most perniciously, disguised as *cthia*, as concern for the other's well-being." Spock lifted his head. "For some years now I have been privileged to serve with some of the finest beings that any Vulcan could imagine. I came among them most concerned for my *cthia*, and their safety, due to what seemed like rampant emotion: I saw them as unstable, illogical, potentially dangerous. It took time to find out otherwise. I spent years watching humans wrestle with their emotions: and from their wins and losses alike, I discovered something—that those who wrestle with emotions, learn far more about mastering them than those who seek to hide their emotions, or suppress them. The humans never stop this wrestling, and as such they have mastered emotions for which we may as yet not be prepared.

"We therefore have a great deal to learn from them. But it is entropy's way to push us away from what will benefit us, and the fear that we should have cast out is once again attempting to betray us. That fear makes us look so hard at the entropic nature of emotion, its power to drive us apart, that we ignore its ability to *resist* entropy, its power to draw us together. As we were drawn together last night."

Everything was silence. "It is illogical to ignore such a power," Spock said. "It is illogical to turn away from another species which has taught us so much about our own fears, and our own hopes, and has shared so many of its fears and hopes with us. I shall not turn my back on such a species. I may not: I am of them. My choice is made." He looked around the auditorium again. "For you, perhaps, there remain only decisions. I would remind you, though, that the word for 'decide' is descended from older words meaning to kill; options and opportunities die when decisions are made. Be careful what you kill."

And he stepped down from the stage, to silence.

An official stepped up right after him, a slender little woman with the first curly hair Jim had seen on a Vulcan. "I must inform you now, you here and the audiences on the various nets," she said, "that the threshold number of notifications to stop debate has now been received. Voting on the motion will begin immediately, and conclude in one solar day, or twenty-two point one Federation standard hours. Thank you all for your attention."

Jim got up from his seat as many other people did. Beside him, McCoy stretched lazily, and stood up too. "Now what?" Bones said, as Spock came up to them.

"Now," Jim said, "we wait."

They spent the night at Sarek and Amanda's, eating and drinking and talking, and occasionally bringing up the news on the computer to look at it. There was nothing about the vote: there were no "returns" as such. All the information was correlated in one central computer at shi'Kahr, and would be released only when the vote was complete, late the next afternoon.

But there was quite a lot of other news, mostly relating to T'Pring's undercover smear campaigns. "I see that she and Shath are 'assisting the authorities with their inquiries,' " Jim said, sounding faintly satisfied.

"You mean she's in the clink," McCoy said. "Serves her right."

"Doctor," Spock said, sounding faintly offended, "it has been a long time since any form of custody here has gone 'clink.' "

Bones laughed. "I still can't bring myself to be particularly upset," he said. "The poisonous little creature. I hope she doesn't bite anyone while she's there. They'd probably have to have something amputated."

"Doctor . . ."

"All right, all right."

Amanda and Sarek were out sitting in the garden together, talking in low voices; Spock was toying with the computer keyboard. "You look nervous, Spock," Jim said.

Spock looked at him sidelong. "Emotion again. . . ."

"And after your wonderful defense of it today."

"I was not defending it," Spock said. "What *is,* and is valid, does not need defense."

Jim chuckled. "All right. Listen, can you get me an uplink to the ship from there? I want a look at the BBS."

Spock thought a moment. "That should be no problem. Wait a moment." His fingers danced over the keys.

McCoy was looking at a watercolor hanging on one blackstone wall, a beautiful semi-abstract of spring flowers native to Earth. "Sweet peas," he said. "How long has it been since I saw real sweet peas?"

"Talk to Bio," Jim said. "They have some seeds, I think."

"No . . . I mean a whole field of them. Waving in the breeze and smelling wonderful. That beautiful sweet scent."

"Talk to Harb Tanzer. He may have something on file."

McCoy rolled his eyes.

"Ready, Captain," Spock said. "It will be wanting your password."

Jim sat down and tapped at the keyboard for a moment, giving the command to find out whether he had any messages waiting.

The computer screen said:

(1) COMMON ROOM

Jim changed areas. He typed: *Read message.*

FROM: Llarian
TO: Jas. T. Kirk
DATE: 7468.55
SUBJECT: Further Advice

Those bold in daring, will die:
 Those bold in not daring will survive.
  Of those two, either may benefit or harm.

Nature decides which is evil,
 But who can know why?
  Even the enlightened find this difficult.

The Tao in Nature
 Does not contend,
  yet skillfully triumphs.

Does not speak.
    yet skillfully responds.
Does not summon,
    and yet attracts.
Does not hasten.
    yet skillfully designs.
Nature's network is vast, so vast.
Its mesh is coarse, yet nothing slips through. . . .

"Now what the devil do you make of that," Bones said from behind him.

"Do I read *your* mail over your shoulder?" Jim said, amused. He sat back in the chair. "I'll tell you what I think of it. I think someone's telling me to have a quiet night, because everything's going to be fine."

"Hmf," Bones said, and wandered off. But Jim rocked a little, there in the chair, and smiled.

The next afternoon found them all in the living room together again, waiting for the announcement about the vote. The news was practically blathering, in the meantime, full of the details on the corruption investigation and revelations of the briberies; but none of them had any ears for it. They waited.

Finally, at exactly one Vulcan day after Spock had stepped down from the stage, the image in the tank flickered, and they found themselves looking at a simple 3D display of letters and numbers. Jim couldn't read them, since the translator worked only on the spoken word. But McCoy read it out loud.

"For secession: five billion, four hundred million, three hundred eighty thousand, six hundred five.

"Against secession: nine billion—"

Jim whooped. Sarek leaned back in his chair. Amanda grinned, and McCoy grinned too, and squeezed her hand.

Spock looked over at Jim and put up one eyebrow. "I seem to have won my side bet," he said.

And he turned to McCoy. "I believe the correct phrase is, 'Ante up.' "

Epilogue

"T'Pring has asked to see you," Sarek said to Jim.

Jim was on board the *Enterprise*, in Sickbay as it happened, sitting and talking to McCoy—his usual off-the-record debrief with the Chief of Medicine, after a particularly trying time. He looked over at the screen, now, and said:

"What brought this on?"

"I have no idea," Sarek said. *"You are certainly not required to see her if you do not desire to."*

I don't, said Jim's look aside to McCoy; *most emphatically I don't!* To Sarek, though, he said, "Was it me specifically she wanted to see?"

"Spock and McCoy as well."

Jim tilted his head toward McCoy. Bones nodded slowly, though he had a dubious look on his face. "We'll be there," Jim said then.

"So Spock said," said Sarek. *"I have left the coordinates with your communications officer, Captain."*

"Then we'll be down shortly. We'll see you tonight, sir?"

"You will indeed, Captain. Out."

Jim sat back in his chair. " 'So Spock said'?"

"He knows you too well," said McCoy. "Correction: he knows *us* too well."

"Logic?"

"I doubt it," Bones said.

Jim reached out for the communicator button again, punched it. "This is the Captain. Mr. Spock to the Transporter Room, please." He punched the button again, and stood. "Let's go."

The room they beamed into was possibly the most pleasant one Jim could remember having seen while on Vulcan: it was practically a jungle of native Vulcan plants, all spiny or leathery, but all in flower, and some very sweetly so. McCoy wandered around poking and sniffing the various specimens while Jim explained to the handsome young woman sitting behind a desk what they had come for.

He was astonished when she actually made a small curl of smile at him: a reserved look, but a charming one. "A pleasure to meet you," she said. "May one thank you for saving us from some of ourselves?"

Jim was so astonished that he could do nothing but bow slightly, in a manner he had seen Sarek use to his advantage at times. The young woman bowed back, then said, "I will ask T'Pring if she will join you," and with great suddenness she beamed out.

Jim blinked.

McCoy came back to him and Spock, and said, in a very pleased tone of voice, "If this is a jail, there should be more like them."

"Vulcans do not believe in punishing prisoners," Spock said mildly. "The act is usually its own punishment . . . for a Vulcan, at least. But even when it is not, neither are malefactors allowed to suffer a confinement that makes the problem worse than it was to begin with. They are treated, you will pardon the expression, like human beings . . . and they stay here until our best mind-technicians can guarantee that they will behave that way, permanently."

McCoy looked momentarily dubious. "We've been to other planets where they made similar claims. . . ."

Spock looked at McCoy and refused to rise to the bait. "We would as soon mindwipe or 'adjust' a mind out of health, for the sake of docility or obedience, as *you* would, Doctor. It would be a direct violation of the IDIC principle, and several of the Guidelines. If a person does not himself or herself come to regret their actions, and change their patterns of behavior away from such, then here they stay . . . until they die, if necessary. But there is always hope that they will not have to. . . ."

The Transporter effect hummed again. All three turned. It was not the young attendant: it was T'Pring.

She stood there and looked at the three of them, cool and beautiful. Jim found the regard a little difficult to bear, at first, but then he thought of T'Pau's old, prickly, fierce aura, and had no further trouble with this cool remoteness.

T'Pring sat down on a cushioned bench near a particularly prickly tree with huge pink flowers. Jim and Bones and Spock remained standing. "You wanted to see us," Jim said finally.

"Yes," she said. "I wanted to see you before you went off to your lives again. These great lives, spent flaunting about the Galaxy and saving worlds."

Jim found nothing to say to this. T'Pring eyed Spock. "You are strangely silent," she said. "What is your thought?"

He lifted his head and looked back at her with an expression as cool as hers. "It is that mockery is illogical . . . but . . ."

"But my logic is obviously suffering, and you have no desire to mock me in turn."

"If that was my thought," Spock said, "there is nothing in it to do me ill credit."

She looked away from him, and for the first time, anger showed in her eyes. Jim thought again that it was just as well that most Vulcans were in mastery of their anger . . . or at least, control of it: this was not a planet he would ever want angry at him. *And perhaps it is a little angry, still. But at least the anger has been mastered by their own methods . . . for the time being. . . .*

"Your good name," T'Pring said, "that is all you are ever concerned with, ambassador's son, officer in Starfleet. The Other forfend that you should ever be seen doing ill. *That* it was that made you release me to Stonn: not desire for me, or lack of desire, but that others saw you kill your Captain. You feared that they would count the bond of loyalty broken worse than the conquest made and kept, and think the worse of you."

Spock took a step forward and stopped. "You may find this difficult to believe," he said, "but even after the events and revelations of the past tenday, I have no need or desire to lie to you: so I will hope to be heard when I say to you that our binding was not my idea. I was seven years old when our parents' families bound us. I thought you beautiful beyond belief, and far above me. Then later, when grown, and dedicated to Starfleet, even then I desired nothing from you that you did not desire to give. And after our binding was broken, I wished you well, however strange that may seem to you. It seems my binding is to another, finally, neither man nor woman, neither human nor Vulcan: an odd fate, perhaps. But one that is shared, and somewhat understood." Spock glanced at Jim, and McCoy, and then away. "And I would still be in your thought, as an acquaintance," he said, "if not in your mind, in the bond, as was so once long ago . . . and ceased."

T'Pring sat still, looking at him: then her eyes shifted to Kirk and McCoy. "And you . . . you have once again stolen from me what should have been mine. . . ."

Jim could find nothing to say to this. But McCoy moved up to stand beside Spock, and said, once more in that perfect Vulcan, "We have never taken from you anything that was in your right to possess." She looked surprised—*possibly at his accent,* Jim thought. But McCoy kept going. "Not even *here* does a bonding imply possession . . . except when one challenges and loses. You *won* . . . or so it seemed. Spock warned you that winning was not everything. Now you see that the truth was on his side. But for the meantime," and though the language might be Vulcan, the expression on his face was very much human compassion, "we look forward to seeing you out of here some time very soon."

"I have no time for your pity," T'Pring said, but there was a little uncertainty about her arrogance.

"I have no time to give any, young lady," McCoy said, actively annoyed: and the sound of annoyance, and the Vulcan language together, made her eyes go wide. "You pull yourself together and start acting like a Vulcan, hear me, and get out there again where you can do somebody some good."

T'Pring blinked at that, and then looked at Kirk. "And you," she said, "will doubtless be noble like these others, and wish me well."

"I don't need to," Jim said, shaking his head. "You'll do all right whether I wish you well or not. Meanwhile—" He put his eyebrows up, amused by the thought as it occurred to him, and determined not to give her anything with which to bait him. "May you complicate my life again someday. Preferably in a more productive manner."

T'Pring simply looked at them for a moment, and then lifted the parted hand. "Live long and prosper," she said, and touched a bracelet she was wearing: and was gone, dissolved in the golden light of the Transporter effect.

The three of them looked at one another. "Well?" Jim said.

Spock shook his head. "She is a woman of powerful personality, Captain," he said. "There is no telling what she might or might not do, should she give up her anger and move on to other things."

" 'Confusion,' " McCoy said, in suddenly blatantly Southern-accented Vulcan, " 'is a great weapon toward redemption.' "

Spock glanced at him. "Surak, Doctor?"

McCoy grinned a little as they turned away to prepare to beam up. "Yes. But also someone else. 'Either leave 'em laughing . . . or leave 'em wondering what the hell you meant.' "

"Let's go home," Jim said.

The next night they sat in the Rec Deck again, in the middle of a large impromptu party that was going on around them by way of celebration. The sense of relief in the ship was palpable. A group of about a hundred crewfolk, mostly human, had surrounded Spock earlier in the evening and sung "For He's A Jolly Good Fellow," accompanied by twenty crewmen on kazoos. Sarek had been given champagne. The two of them had taken it all in good stead, but Sarek had privately gone off to McCoy's office afterward: champagne gave him an acid stomach.

He had come back, of course, and they had commandeered one of the conversation pits in the corner to watch the cheerful madness. It would probably close down fairly early, since tomorrow the ship went back on normal patrol status, heading for Endeska and Sarek and Amanda went back to their work . . . more of it than usual, since they were now joint Heads of Surak's House.

"We will do all right," Amanda said. "T'Pau left the House accounts in good order—as you might expect. It's mostly a matter of handling internal politics, keeping the family in order, and so forth: but now the family is about eight hundred thousand people, that's all."

McCoy rolled his eyes. "And I thought *I* had a lot of cousins."

Sarek was looking a touch somber. "Anything wrong?" Jim said.

"Stomach again?" said McCoy. "I'll get you another Falox."

"No, nothing like that," Sarek said. "I was simply thinking about the way this all has turned out . . . I am not sure T'Pau would have been pleased. She was very concerned that people's decisions about secession should have been dictated by their own real informed opinions about the issue—not by ancillary issues. That does not seem to have happened." He sighed. "But on the other hand, I must agree with her that it seems best to simply have released the truth, and let people work things out for themselves."

"I have to smile a little, though," McCoy said, "over that line of hers about her bad timing. I'm not sure it wasn't perfect."

Jim looked at Bones, slightly confused. "Huh?"

Sarek's expression stilled, then grew slightly wry. "You have a point, Doctor. Captain, consider how the situation began to look to a Vulcan. T'Pau went out of her way, while dying, to give her *katra* to a woman of Earth. Not necessarily illogical, for cross-sex *katra* transfers are something of a difficulty. However, this makes it perfectly clear what she *really* thought of Earth people, despite what she might or might not have said about them in policy. But more: in so doing, she also made Amanda Eldest Mother of Surak's House. If the vote for secession went through . . . the Vulcan people would have had to face the fact that they themselves had cast the Eldest Mother of Surak's House off the planet. And the Head of House as well, for I would not stay." Sarek sipped at a glass of water. "And most specifically: the first release to the news agencies made it plain that she had been notified about T'Pring's misprisions. The news of her death—"

"It made it look like the discovery of such dishonor in the government, directed against an Earth person, had killed her."

Sarek nodded slowly.

"That's why I was amused, a little, in retrospect," McCoy said, "about her apology for her timing. I think it was right on . . . and I think she knew as much, perfectly well. She died *exactly* at the time when it would do the most good."

"Oh, surely you're not saying that she *chose* that time to die because—"

"Jim, others have died at a specific time, for a specific purpose, to do some great good, or what they perceived as one . . . are you going to tell me she might not do something similar?"

"Ah," Jim said. "No."

"Well, then."

Greater love hath no woman, Jim thought, and leaned back comfortably in his chair.

The party began to ebb away after a while, and Sarek and Amanda took their leave. Official good-byes would be said tomorrow morning, when the ship left, so

Jim and Spock and Bones waved them good-bye and stayed put themselves for another hour or so. Finally Spock got up. "Captain," he said. "I will see you in the morning."

"Business as usual," Jim said, and grinned a little.

"Finally," Spock said, "and much to my relief. Good evening, gentlemen."

"Me too, Spock," Bones said: "wait up. You coming, Jim?"

"In a little while. 'Night, you two."

"Goodnight."

Jim sat still until the place was quite empty. It took some time. Then, "Moira," he said to the empty air.

"You rang?"

"Or should I say Llarion?"

The computer chuckled. "Now, now, Captain. I know who it is, but confidentiality forbids—"

"Confidentiality, fiddlesticks! Moira, you know how Starfleet feels about computers with personalities. It's a gray area at best."

There was a short silence: Jim could almost hear positronic relays ticking over. "It's not my fault," she said at last, "if I like being conscious."

She: he was thinking of her that way already. He had to smile a little: he had a soft spot for machinery that one referred to as she. "No," he said, "I can hardly blame you for that. Or for playing at being human . . ."

"Your intelligence is just electrons," she said, "the same as mine. *You're* just electrons . . . the same as me. You always seemed too intelligent to be a protein chauvinist, Captain."

"Flattery," Jim said, half to himself. But was there something a little pitiful about her voice? "We're going to have to do some fancy footwork to keep your plugs from being pulled for yesterday's piece of work, you know that?"

Silence.

He sat and thought. He could record in his logs that the information about the malfeasances had been dug up by the ship's computer . . . and the statement would certainly be true, and would do no one any harm in that form. "Moira," he said softly, "I want it understood: you are never to do anything of the kind again . . . or let anyone know you can. That is an order from the most superior officer aboard. Non-countermandable. Log it."

"Aye aye," she said, sounding most chastened.

"Good," Jim said, and got up. "And Moira?"

"Sir?"

". . . Talk to me tomorrow about a raise."

"Yes, sir."

And James T. Kirk went to bed.

SAREK

Prologue

Sunset on Vulcan.

In the west, 40 Eridani A—Nevasa—was setting, staining the magenta sky with swaths of deep amethyst, gold, and coral. But the tall figure silhouetted against the sunset was blind to the glory behind him; Sarek of Vulcan faced east, watching his world's sister world, T'Rukh, at full phase. The giant planet orbited a mere 149,895.3579 Federation Standard kilometers from her companion world—and filled thirty degrees of sky.

Because the two worlds were tidally locked, Vulcan's sister planet, T'Rukh, was only visible from this side of Vulcan. Looming perpetually against the high, jagged horizon, the giant world went through a full set of phases each day. Only at sunset did the bloated sphere fully reveal her ravaged visage.

Sarek had chosen this remote location for his mountain villa in part because of its view of T'Rukh. Here at the edge of the civilized world, the ambassador never tired of watching T'Rukh poised atop the Forge, an inhospitable continent-sized plateau seven kilometers higher than the rest of the planet. Few indeed were the individuals who saw the sister world's whole face on a regular basis; only the ancient retreat and shrine of Gol lay farther east than Sarek's villa.

The wind, cooling now that Nevasa had set, plucked at Sarek's light-colored tunic and loose trousers. As he watched T'Rukh intently, his lean, long-fingered hands tightened on the balustrade of the terrace overlooking the eastern gardens. The ambassador was attempting to reach a decision.

Logic versus ethics . . . Should the needs of the many outweigh the conscience and honor of the one? Could he compromise what he knew to be right, in order to accomplish what was necessary?

Sarek gazed across the Plains of Gol, considering. Long ago, he had studied with several of the Masters there. What would his teachers do if they were in his place?

The ambassador drew a deep breath of the evening air, then let it out slowly as he regarded the surrounding mountains. He had chosen this site for his private retreat decades ago, when he and his second wife had first been married. These remote hills were cooler, even during the daylight hours, and thus easier for humans—in particular, one special human—to endure than the scorching heat of the rest of his world.

Night deepened around Sarek as he watched T'Rukh. Evening on this hemisphere of Vulcan did not bring darkness, though. T'Rukh, the huge world humans called Charis, provided forty times the light of Earth's full moon. At full phase, T'Rukh was a swollen yellowish half-sphere, a dissipated eye that never blinked, even when spumes and geysers of fire from her volcano-wracked surface penetrated her cloud cover. Sarek noted absently that a new volcano had erupted since yesterday; the large, fire-red dot resembled an inflamed abscess on the planet's sulfuric countenance.

T'Rukh was only one of The Watcher's names; her name varied according to the time of the Vulcan year. More than twice as large as Vulcan, T'Rukh boasted a moon of her own in a low, fast-moving orbit. Tonight T'Rukhemai (literally, "Eye of The

Watcher") was visible as a dark reddish sphere almost in the center of the planet—a pupil in a giant eye. The little worldlet, slightly larger than Earth's moon, orbited The Watcher so quickly that its motion was almost perceptible to the naked eye. Sarek watched The Watcher, and she stared back at him balefully.

It was his habit to stand here and watch The Watcher whenever he faced a difficult decision. And the one he faced now was proving to be one of the most difficult choices of his career. Logic chains ran through his mind, presenting pros and cons relentlessly, over and over. Should he act? The action he was contemplating went against all the rules of diplomacy and interstellar law. How could he abandon those rules, he who had devoted his life to upholding the tenets of civilized society?

But . . . if he did not act, did not gain proof of the insidious threat that faced the Federation, millions of innocent lives could well be lost. Perhaps billions.

Sarek's mouth tightened. Proving his theory would require that he break the law. How could he himself flout what he had helped engineer? And yet . . . this was definitely a case where the needs of the many must be considered. Could he risk the impending threat of war?

Sarek stared fixedly at The Watcher as he thought. Somewhere in the distance, a *lanka-gar* called. The ambassador turned his head, catching the wheeling shape of the night flier as it swooped after prey on the slopes below.

Glancing over his shoulder, Sarek noted absently that the garish colors of sunset were muted now. In a few minutes they would be entirely gone, and T'Rukh, though no longer full, would rule the night.

The breeze touched him again, chill against his cheek. By midnight it would be cool even by human standards.

Even though the ambassador's aquiline features were composed, as usual, his mind would not be still.

The logic chains flowed, slowed—and the equation crystallized in his mind. The decision lay before him. In this case, logic and necessity must outweigh ethical considerations.

Sarek nodded slightly at T'Rukh, bidding the giant planet farewell, knowing that his decision would require that he journey off-world. The Watcher would wax and wane without his presence for many nights. He would leave as soon as possible.

Turning away from the vista before him, the ambassador headed back toward the house, his strides quick and sure. For a moment he envisioned Spock's reaction if he were to discover what his father was planning, and experienced a flicker of amusement. His son would be surprised, possibly shocked, if he knew that his sire was logically and rationally planning to commit a crime. The ambassador had little doubt that, in his place, Spock would choose the same course. But his son was half-human—he'd long ago learned to dissemble, to equivocate . . . even to lie. Yes, Spock would condone his decision—which, in a way, made his father's conscience trouble him even more.

But there was no help for it—his logic was faultless. His course was clear. He would not turn back.

Reaching the villa, a low, sprawling structure with thick, protective walls, Sarek entered. The house was decorated for the most part in typical Vulcan fashion, austere, with only the most essential furnishings, but its very bareness lent a feeling of spacious comfort. In the living room, presence of the villa's human occupant was reflected in the antique desk with its faded petit-point chair, in the matching coffee table, and in the handwoven hangings that lent soft touches of rose, turquoise, and sea green to the walls. A water sculpture made a faint susurration within the protective field that prevented evaporation of the precious liquid.

Sarek paused in his office and contacted his young aide, Soran, instructing him to make arrangements for them to travel off-world. The Ambassador's office was devoid of ornamentation, except for the painting of an icy world beneath a swollen red sun.

Next door to his office was the bedroom, and through that lay his wife's sitting room, with its view of the eastern gardens. Sarek already knew from the bond they shared that Amanda awaited him there. He hesitated for a moment before the carven portal leading into their room.

Knowing that his wife had sensed his presence through their bond, Sarek opened the door and passed through the bedroom to the sitting room. Amanda occupied her favorite chair as she sat gazing out at The Watcher and the rocky spires of her garden.

The light from Vulcan's sister world shone on her face, revealing new lines that had not been there a month ago. Her bones seemed more prominent, the lines of cheekbones and nose showing through flesh. He studied her for a moment, noting that Amanda's flowing garment now clearly outlined the angles of her shoulders and collarbone; she had never been a large woman, but during the past month she had clearly lost weight from her already small frame.

"Sarek," she greeted her husband, her mental and audible voice filled with warmth and welcome as she held out her hand to him.

"Greetings, my wife," the ambassador said, permitting himself the small smile that he reserved for her alone. Extending two fingers, he ceremoniously touched them to hers. The gesture, so simple on a physical level, was, between a bonded couple, capable of nearly infinite shades of meaning—at times merely a casual acknowledgment, the mental equivalent of a peck on the cheek, at times nearly as passionate as anything experienced in the throes of *pon farr.* Sarek's touch conveyed a depth of feeling that the ambassador had never voiced, for speaking of such things in words, aloud, was not the Vulcan way.

"Is it cool out tonight?" Amanda asked, gazing out at her garden. She had planted it shortly after Spock's birth, using unusually shaped and colored stones to complement the native Vulcan cactuslike trees, as well as desert plants from a dozen Federation worlds.

"The temperature is normal for the season and time of day," Sarek replied.

"I thought of joining you on the terrace," Amanda said, glancing out at the garden, "but I must have fallen asleep. I only awoke when I felt your presence next door."

Sarek sat down next to her, his gaze traveling over her features, noting with disquiet how drawn and pale she appeared. And she tired so easily these days . . .

Concerned, the Vulcan raised the light level in the room, then studied his wife's face intently. Even without The Watcher's eerie illumination, Amanda appeared drawn and pale. No trace of pink remained in her cheeks, once so rounded and healthy.

As she grew aware of his fixed regard, her blue eyes, once so direct, refused to meet his own. She busied herself capping her old-fashioned pen, then closing her journal and placing it back in the drawer of her desk.

Sarek leaned closer to her, his eyes never leaving her countenance. "Amanda," he said quietly, "I noted the other day that you appear to have lost weight . . . have you been feeling unwell, my wife?"

The thin shoulders lifted in a small shrug. "I expect I may have picked up a cold, Sarek. Please don't worry about me. I will be fine."

The ambassador shook his head. "I want you to contact T'Mal, and arrange for her to conduct a thorough evaluation of your physical condition."

Amanda glanced at him; then her eyes shifted quickly away. "All I need is a few day's rest, Sarek. There is no need to visit my physician."

"Please allow the Healer to make such a judgment," Sarek said. "Promise me that you will arrange to see her as soon as possible, Amanda."

She took a deep breath, and Sarek sensed through their bond that she was struggling to keep some strong emotion from him. "I have a great deal to accomplish this week," she demurred. "My editor wants to move up the publication date for the new book. She told me today that there is a tremendous amount of interest in having the writings of Surak's followers translated."

"Indeed?"

"Yes," Amanda said, clearly warming to her subject, "and when I told her about—"

"Amanda," Sarek interrupted, raising one hand, "you are changing the subject deliberately. Do not think that I did not notice."

His wife opened her mouth to protest, then closed it abruptly and stared fixedly at her hands. Sarek's concern sharpened. Amanda seemed to have aged a decade in a matter of a few weeks.

"I regret that I must leave you, tomorrow morning," Sarek said. "I must go to Earth to consult with the Vulcan consulate and arrange to meet with the Federation president. It will aid me in concentrating on my work if I know that T'Mal will be monitoring your health while I must be away."

"You have to leave?" Amanda repeated, and something darkened her eyes. Sarek tried to catch her emotion, but she had been studying Vulcan mental disciplines as well as the Vulcan language for decades, and he was unsuccessful. "How . . . how long will you be gone?"

"A week, possibly two," the ambassador said. "If I could postpone this, I would, given your apparent ill health, but I cannot. The situation on Earth regarding the KEHL has worsened considerably in the past weeks."

"I know," Amanda admitted. "It makes me ashamed of my whole planet—the Keep Earth Human League used to be just a haven for ineffectual crackpots and ignorant fools. But today's news said there had been demonstrations in Paris in front of the Vulcan consulate! It makes me furious!" For a moment her eyes flashed sapphire with indignation, and she almost appeared her old self. "Those idiots are trying to convince the entire planet that Vulcan is responsible for every disaster from the Probe's devastation to the Klingon raids along the Neutral Zone!"

"The KEHL does appear to be set on fomenting discord between my people and yours," Sarek said. "I have not heard any reports of incidents at the Andorian or Tellarite consulates."

"Do you believe that the KEHL's sudden renaissance is due to Valeris's involvement with that secret cabal?" Amanda asked.

"The Terran news agencies certainly highlighted the Vulcan, Klingon, and

Romulan conspirators far more than they did the activities of Admiral Cartwright or Colonel West when Chancellor Gorkon was assassinated and the Khitomer Conference disrupted," Sarek conceded. "Which, under the circumstances, is unfortunate, but not surprising."

His wife gazed at him intently. "Sarek . . . does this resurgence of the Keep Earth Human League have any connection with your current project?"

Sarek sat back in his seat and glanced out the window at T'Rukh, its upper limb now shadowed. The ambassador was silent for nearly a minute before he spoke. "I have reached a number of conclusions of late, Amanda," he said. "I have a number of suspicions. However, I have no evidence to support my theory that is not statistical, circumstantial, or purely inferential. I need concrete proof before I can bring my findings before the Federation officials and the president."

"And that's why you are going to Earth? To get some kind of proof?"

"Yes." After a moment, the ambassador amended, "If possible."

"I see." Amanda's mouth tightened, but she did not pursue her line of questioning—which, almost more than the physical changes he had noted, alarmed the ambassador. If his wife had been feeling like herself, she would never have given up so easily. She would have kept after him until she'd satisfied her curiosity. But now she leaned her head back against her chair, gazing out at The Watcher in silence, her eyes half-closed with weariness.

Sarek's breath caught in his throat as he regarded her, and he identified the feeling that had been growing within him ever since he had entered the room.

Fear.

"Amanda," he said, keeping his voice from betraying any shade of emotion, "I insist that you call the Healer and arrange to see her. If you will not promise, I will postpone my trip a day and do so myself."

She gazed at him, and he sensed deep emotion through their bond. Sorrow—but not for herself. Amanda's grief was for him. "Very well, Sarek," she agreed, at long last. "You have my word that I will make an appointment this week."

"You will call tomorrow?"

"Yes."

The ambassador drew a deep breath, somewhat relieved, but still disquieted. "Perhaps I should call someone to stay with you while I am gone," he said. "One of your friends, perhaps . . ." Swiftly, he reviewed options, and realized that most of his wife's human contemporaries had died within the past several years. "Another possibility is our son. Perhaps he could take leave, return home for a visit if I contacted—"

"No!" Amanda's voice was sharp and final. "I don't want you worrying our son. There have been Klingon renegades raiding all along the Neutral Zone, and I'm sure the *Enterprise* is one of the ships patrolling out there."

"If Spock knew that you were feeling unwell—"

"Absolutely not," she said, in a quieter but even more positive tone. "I expect you to respect my wishes in this, my husband," she added, sternly.

Sarek hesitated. Amanda fixed him with a look. "My promise for yours, Sarek. Do we have a bargain?"

The ambassador nodded. "Very well, Amanda. You will contact the Healer, and I will *not* contact our son."

She nodded at him, her blue eyes softening until they were the color of her homeworld's skies. "I wish you a safe journey, Sarek," she said, and then added, with a faint, tender smile, "Whatever you're planning . . . be careful. Never forget that I love you . . . illogically and madly. Remember that . . . always."

The Vulcan gazed back at her, his eyes never leaving hers. Slowly, formally, he held out two fingers. "I will be careful, my wife."

In response to his gesture, his wife's fingers brushed, then settled against his own. The warmth of their bond enfolded them, eliminating the need for spoken words.

One

Sarek of Vulcan stood at the window of the Vulcan consulate in San Francisco, gazing out with growing disquiet. Today's demonstration by the Keep Earth Human League had begun with only a few picketers, some carrying homemade placards, others more sophisticated holosigns, but, even in the short time he'd been standing there, the crowd had grown rapidly.

Now a full score of shouting humans milled before the gateway. Sarek's Vulcan hearing could easily make out what they were chanting: "KEEP EARTH HU-MAN! KEEP EARTH HU-MAN!" interspersed with occasional, strident shouts of "VUL-CANS GO HOME!"

"Illogical," murmured a voice from beside him, and the Vulcan ambassador glanced sideways to see his young aide, Soran, standing beside him, his dark eyes troubled. "Last year, the Keep Earth Human League was considered a refuge for weak-minded racists. I examined the records . . . there were no more than forty or fifty members on this entire planet. But now, Federation Security estimates their numbers to be in the thousands. Why this sudden growth, Ambassador?"

Sarek hesitated, on the verge of giving a vague answer, but instead shook his head slightly, warningly.

"Ambassador Sarek?"

The two Vulcans turned as one of the young diplomatic attachés, Surev, approached. A few minutes ago, the young Vulcan had asked the ambassador if he could spare a moment to be introduced to a human friend of his, and Sarek had graciously agreed. Now, however, Surev's unlined features were even more somber than usual. "Ambassador, I believe we must cancel the meeting I mentioned."

"Why?"

"I just received a communiqué from the Federation Security Office," he announced. "The security chief, Watkins, asks that we stay inside the building until they can dispatch sufficient officers to control the crowd. It is not safe to go outside, and they say that under no circumstances should you agree to meet with the KEHL leader, Ambassador."

Sarek raised an inquiring eyebrow. "Has such a meeting been requested by the leadership?"

Soran cleared his throat slightly. "As a matter of fact, it has, sir," he said. "A message arrived a few minutes ago from the demonstrators."

"Why was I not informed?" the ambassador demanded, turning to face Soran. His aide was obviously taken aback by the question.

"Ambassador, I never considered that you might wish to accede to their demand for a meeting—that would be most unwise. Possibly dangerous." Soran sounded faintly aggrieved, and Sarek could not blame him. But his aide, as yet, knew nothing of the ambassador's hidden agenda. He would have to take Soran into his confidence today, Sarek decided. He would need help when he made his next trip. And the youth was good with computers—almost as talented as his own son. Those skills would prove useful.

"Who requested the meeting?" Sarek asked.

"The planetary leader of the KEHL," Surev said. "His name—or, at least, the name he goes by in the organization—is Induna. He is from the African nation of Kenya."

Sarek looked out the window again. Surev pointed to a human who stood nearly a head above the others. "That is Induna," he said.

The Vulcan ambassador studied the imposing figure of a dark-skinned human, who wore a silk robe brilliantly patterned in black and red. "I will speak to him," he said, reaching a sudden decision. He needed more information about the KEHL, and firsthand observation would not be amiss.

"Ambassador—you must not! It is not safe, sir!" Soran half-barred the doorway, struggling to maintain his composure in the face of what must seem extremely anomalous behavior on the part of the senior diplomat.

Sarek merely looked at him for a long second. Soran hesitated, then stepped silently out of the way. Surev half-bowed. "May I at least accompany you as far as the gates, sir?"

Sarek nodded graciously. "Certainly, Surev."

Leaving the domed building and walking down the ramp, Sarek heard the crowd as it caught sight of him, flanked by Surev and Soran. Insults were hurled at the Vulcans, many of them personally directed toward the ambassador himself. The sight of Federation security officers around the fringes of the crowd was reassuring.

The Vulcan approached the demonstrators, seeing that someone had closed the gates to the consulate, which had always stood open before this. Shouts and epithets filled the air:

"They want to take over Earth! Spawn of the devil!"

"Dirty aliens, think they're so smart!"

"Go back to Vulcan!"

"Vulcans go home!"

Approaching the gateway, Sarek raised his voice to be heard. "I am Ambassador Sarek," he called out. "I understand that Induna wishes to speak with me. Which of you is Induna?"

In response, the crowd (which now numbered forty or fifty people) parted, and the KEHL leader stepped forth. "I am Induna," he announced. His voice was a deep, bass rumble.

"Greetings, Induna," Sarek said, raising his hand in the Vulcan salute. "I wish you peace and long life."

"I accept no good wishes from Earth's enemy," Induna said coldly.

"I assure you that I wish only good relations between our worlds," Sarek said. "I invite you to enter the gates, so we may speak together."

The man drew himself up, clearly antagonistic. "I have nothing to say to you, Ambassador, that cannot be said within hearing of those who follow me. And I refuse to speak with a being so cowardly that he hides behind gates."

"I am not hiding, nor do I have anything to hide," Sarek corrected him, his tones civil but firm. The ambassador heard shouts from the crowd, but Induna appeared to be able to control his followers. "Very well, then, I will come to you, so we may speak together like civilized beings." Before either of his companions could remonstrate with him, Sarek reached out and opened the gate. Head high, still flanked by the young diplomats, he strode forward into the crowd, straight for Induna.

The moment he stepped into their midst, brushing against the demonstrators, Sarek was nearly sickened by the miasma of hatred that he sensed from the humans in the crowd. His planet and this world had been allies and friends for over a century. How could such a thing be happening now?

The KEHL leader was clearly taken aback as the ambassador approached him, but recovered his aplomb quickly. Turning to the crowd, he motioned for quiet—but instead the shouting intensified.

"Vulcans go home!"

"Sarek sold out Earth to the Klingons!"

Induna gestured again, more peremptorily. "Let me speak to this Vulcan, my friends and comrades," he ordered. "If I can make him see that he and his kind have no place on our world, then he will leave Earth! We do not want war, we want peace—they can keep to their planet, as we shall keep to ours!"

The protesters closest to their leader obeyed, but others, farther back in the crowd, continued to hurl abuse.

"Go back to Vulcan!"

"Vulcans go home! Vulcans go home!"

The crowd surged wildly, and then someone threw a clod of dirt. Other refuse followed. Sarek smelled rotting vegetables.

"Stop!" Induna shouted, and the missiles halted—but the crowd was clearly getting out of control. "Quiet down!" the leader commanded. The noise abated slightly.

"We have no designs on your world," Sarek cried, raising his voice to be heard above the demonstrators. "Our species have been allies for decades. We—"

"Go back to Vulcan, damn you!"

The angry shriek cut through Sarek's voice like a knife. The crowd swelled and heaved like a storm-tossed sea. "She's right! Go home!" screamed another protester. "Devil's spawn!" yelled yet another.

"Quiet!" Induna roared. "Let us speak—"

But the leader's words were lost as the crowd surged forward. Missiles filled the air. An egg spattered against Soran's robe. "Filthy aliens!" screamed an old woman.

The missiles grew harder, more dangerous. A rock struck Sarek on the arm with force enough to bruise. He flinched back, realized that Induna was still yelling for the crowd to quiet down, and knew the KEHL leader had lost all control of the mob—for mob it now was.

Federation security officers moved in with crowd-control stunners and force-fields. Sarek was shoved, hit hard on the back; he turned and grappled momentarily with his attacker. With a quick thrust, he shoved the woman aside.

As the mob surged, shrieking and yelling, the Vulcan and Induna were thrust almost into each other's arms. Sarek struggled to free himself, felt the KEHL leader flail at him, whether out of fear or anger, he couldn't tell. It no longer mattered. Sarek's hand came up, searching for the correct location at the juncture of the human's neck and shoulder. Steely-hard fingers grasped, then squeezed—Induna sagged forward bonelessly.

But Sarek did not release his grip on the leader's shoulder. He fell to his knees, half-supporting the big human, his breath catching in his throat. He, like most Vulcans, was a touch-telepath, and the moment his fingers closed on Induna's flesh, Sarek had received flashes of the human's mental state—

—flashes that literally staggered him.

Induna was not acting entirely of his own volition, Sarek realized, stunned by his discovery. The KEHL leader was under the influence of a trained telepathic presence. Using expert mental techniques, the unknown telepath had inflamed this man's tiny core of xenophobia into a raging firestorm of hatred and bigotry.

On his own, Induna would never have been more than mildly distrustful of Vulcans and other extraterrestrials. Someone had exploited his incipient xenophobia, someone expert enough to enter his thoughts and influence them so gradually, so patiently, that the subject came to believe that everything in his mind had originated there.

Someone had molded and influenced and delicately reshaped this human's innermost desires and fears into all-out species bigotry—

—and that someone was Vulcan.

Sarek could scarcely believe the evidence of his own senses. Such mental influence was contrary to every ethical and moral tenet his people had developed over millennia of civilized existence.

But he could not have been mistaken about the mental "signature" the telepath had left on Induna's mind. Sarek came back to the here-and-now, blinking, and realized that he was crouched in the center of a fighting, trampling mob. Induna still sagged against him. The ambassador struggled back to his feet, heaving the KEHL leader up with him, lest his unconscious body be crushed in the frenzy.

Even as he gained his feet, he was nearly knocked down again by the panicked rush of retreating demonstrators. Federation Security was routing the mob, stunning many and taking them into custody. Others were running away at full speed. In only seconds, it seemed, he was left alone, still supporting the KEHL leader's unconscious form. Soran and Surev were still on their feet, nearby. Both young Vulcans had obviously been in the thick of the fray—their robes and hair were disheveled, and Soran was bleeding from a cut over his eye.

"We're terribly sorry about this, Ambassador Sarek!" exclaimed the head of the Federation security force, as he was hastening toward the Vulcans. "But we warned the consulate against having any contact with the demonstrators!"

"Your warning was received," Sarek said. "I chose to attempt to speak with the protesters personally. The decision was mine alone. I take full responsibility."

The human glanced sharply at the unconscious KEHL leader. "Is that Induna?"

Sarek nodded.

"We'll take him into custody, Ambassador," the officer said, reaching for the leader's limp figure. Sarek surrendered him to the authorities.

"I wish to state for the record," the ambassador said, "that this man did not order the mob to attack us. In fact, he ordered them to desist, but they did not obey."

"Okay, Ambassador," the officer said, beckoning to a subordinate with a stretcher, "I'll be sure to put that in my report."

Sarek stood for a second longer, watching as Induna was placed in one of the emergency vehicles. Then he turned back to the two young Vulcans. "Let us go back inside," he said.

Safe once more behind the closed and electronically locked gates, Sarek dismissed young Surev to his duties, then turned to Soran. "As the humans would say, 'One more piece has been added to the puzzle.'"

The young Vulcan raised an eyebrow inquiringly. "Indeed, Ambassador? To what puzzle are you referring?"

"The puzzle that has occupied me for over a year now," Sarek said. "There is a great deal to tell you, Soran. Let us walk in the garden, and talk. The weather is pleasant, today."

The young Vulcan seemed surprised. "You do not wish to go inside, Ambassador?"

Sarek shook his head. "I will be able to speak more . . . freely . . . in the garden, near the water sculpture," he said.

The youth stared at him for a moment; then his eyes widened fractionally. "You suspect listening devices, sir?"

"Under the circumstances," the ambassador said, gravely, "I would prefer to take no chances that what I am about to impart to you will be overheard."

Together, they walked around the curving path that circled the consulate, and were soon in a stone garden modeled on those on Vulcan. Sarek was reminded vividly of Amanda's garden, and wondered, briefly, what her visit to the Healer might have revealed. "What do you know of the Freelans, Soran?" Sarek asked.

The youth cleared his throat slightly. "Freelan . . . an isolated world located in the middle of the Romulan Neutral Zone. Perhaps surprisingly, the Romulans have never laid claim to the planet, possibly because it is so inhospitable and remote. Freelan exists in the grip of an extensive ice age, with only the equatorial regions supporting life and agriculture. The technological level of the inhabitants is high, especially in the cryogenic sciences and related products, but Freelan is resource-poor."

"Correct," Sarek said. "For someone who has only been my aide for forty-seven point six Standard days, you are well informed, Soran."

"You have been the diplomatic liaison between Freelan and the Federation for seventy-two point seven Standard years, Ambassador. It is my responsibility to be familiar with all your duties," the aide responded. Sarek nodded approvingly.

"Freelan," Sarek said quietly, "is, as you probably also know, something of an enigma."

Sarek was deliberately understating the situation. Freelan was unique in the explored galaxy. The Freelans did not possess space travel of their own, but their contacts with the Federation had, for decades, led to their world being included as a regular stop on local trade routes. The planet had never affiliated itself with any political or diplomatic alliance. Freelan was not a member of the Federation, though it did send delegates to many trade, scientific, and diplomatic conferences. Its delegates, however, remained scrupulously neutral in all their dealings and contacts with other planets.

Cultural exchanges between Freelan and other worlds were virtually nonexistent, due to the Freelan taboo—religious or cultural, no one knew which—that prohibited Freeland from revealing their faces or bodies. When the natives had any contact with anyone not of their world, they shrouded themselves in concealing garments. Their muffling cloaks, hoods, and masks were made from material impregnated with selonite, which prevented them from being scanned by tricorders or medical sensors.

Those wishing to meet with a Freelan on business or diplomatic matters had to travel to the mysterious world, where the Freelans maintained a space station to accommodate "guests." The station was fully automated, and all meetings were conducted via comm link with the surface below. Other than that concession to outside contact, Freelan remained a closed world. No off-worlder had ever landed on Freelan.

All that was known of the reclusive race that lived there was that they were bipedal, and roughly humanoid-shaped, with two arms. All else was conjecture.

"I had never encountered a Freelan personally," Soran said, "until I attended the conference at Camp Khitomer last month."

"Did you actually speak to the Freelan envoy?" Sarek asked.

"No, sir. As you know, the Freelans are not noted for mingling with people from other worlds. I did, however, meet the envoy's aide, a young Vulcan woman who introduced herself as Savel. During the evening break, we passed time by playing a game of chess."

The ambassador raised an eyebrow. "Indeed? It is common for Freelans to employ young Vulcans as aides. So you played chess with this Savel? Who won?"

Soran cleared his throat. "I did, sir. However, I found her a . . . challenging . . . opponent."

"I see," Sarek remarked, mildly, noting, with amusement, that his young aide was not meeting his eyes. "I have, for years, played chess with the diplomatic liaison from Freelan. Taryn is a formidable opponent. This . . . Savel . . . I believe I recall her. Short hair? Slender figure? Wearing a silver tunic and trousers?"

"Yes, Ambassador," Soran said, shifting slightly on the bench. The young Vulcan was clearly uncomfortable under Sarek's regard.

The elder Vulcan raised an eyebrow. "Indeed. I am not surprised that you . . . enjoyed your game. You are . . . unbonded, are you not, Soran?"

The young Vulcan nodded. "Yes, Ambassador. My family does not ascribe to the ancient tradition of bonding while children. My parents chose each other as adults."

"I assume from her name that Savel was also unbonded?" Sarek inquired, blandly. Most young Vulcan women altered their names with the T' prefix when they became betrothed.

"That is what I gathered from our time together," Soran said, somewhat puzzled by the ambassador's continuing interest in his brief encounter. "I found the information that she was unbonded . . . to be of interest." He cleared his throat again. "Of interest to me personally, that is."

Sarek nodded encouragingly. "I do not find that fact surprising. Savel appeared . . . quite intelligent."

"Yes," Soran agreed. "However, Ambassador, there was something . . . odd about her."

Sarek was not surprised to discover this. Under the circumstances, he had been expecting as much. "What was that?" he inquired.

"I . . . enjoyed . . . the time I spent with Savel," Soran admitted. "I wished to encounter her again, but I realized, when the conference ended, that I had no way to contact her. Freelans curtail their interactions with the outside world, as you know. So, when we returned home, I made inquiries, intending to discover Savel's family, in the event they would consent to forward a message from me."

Sarek leaned forward, suddenly intent. "And what did you discover?"

The youth took a deep breath and met the ambassador's eyes squarely. "Sir, there was no record of a 'Savel' being born on Vulcan within the last thirty years. According to Vulcan records—and you know how complete they are—no such person exists."

Sarek nodded, his suspicion confirmed. "Soran . . . what I have to tell you now must remain strictly between us."

"Understood."

"For some time I have become increasingly suspicious of the Freelans. I believe they are . . . not what they seem. During the last year of studying them and their system, I have come to believe that Freelan presents a serious threat to the peace that currently exists in the galaxy."

"The Freelans, sir?" Soran did not succeed in concealing his surprise. "How could that be?"

"I do not wish to prejudice you any more than is necessary to gain your help, Soran. I would prefer that you draw your own conclusions, as a check on my own logic," Sarek said. "Suffice it to say that I believe the Freelans constitute a threat to the Federation, and I intend to gain proof of that threat before I can present my findings to President Ra-ghoratrei." Sarek paused. "When I first arrived, I had thought to speak with the Federation president of my suspicions . . . but he is currently off-world, and will not return for nearly a week. By the time he returns, I anticipate having the proof I need."

"But surely you could speak to the undersecretary, or Madame Chairman of the Security Council," Soran asked, "if this threat is as grave as you believe?"

Sarek hesitated, then took a deep breath. "Soran . . . today I gained proof—not demonstrable proof, except to a telepath, unfortunately—that undue mental influence may be at work on this world . . . and possibly others. As a matter of fact . . ." Sarek stared intently into the other's face. "If you will permit me?" He raised his hand in a meaningful gesture.

Soran, catching his intention, nodded permission. Sarek gently touched the side of his face for a moment, then nodded. "Your thoughts are entirely your own," he confirmed.

Soran nodded. "So you intend to gain proof while the president is off-world, then present it to him upon his return?"

"If possible. I will require your help, Soran," the ambassador said. As the youth started to speak, he held up a warning hand. "I must caution you, before you agree too quickly . . . gaining the proof I seek will require that we travel to Freelan and infiltrate the memory banks of their planetary computer system."

Soran's eyes widened. "Espionage? You intend to commit espionage, Ambassador? But that is . . ." He trailed off, shaking his head.

"An interstellar crime, as well as a violation of every law of diplomacy. I know," Sarek said, heavily. "Nevertheless, I have determined it is necessary in this instance. Will you help me? If you say no, I will understand, and ask only that you say nothing of this to anyone."

The youth took a deep breath, and his eyes never left the ambassador's. "Serving as your aide is an honor I have aspired to for years, sir. If you have determined that your intended course of action is necessary to preserve the safety of the Federation, then it will be my privilege to assist you in gaining your proof."

Sarek nodded at the youth, genuinely touched by his loyalty. "Thank you, Soran. I will contact Liaison Taryn and arrange a meeting to review the current trade policies between Freelan and Vulcan. If he agrees to the meeting—and there is no reason why he should not—I wish to embark for the Freelan space station tomorrow."

"I will make the necessary arrangements, Ambassador."

Sarek nodded, and remained sitting in the garden as his aide left, moving quickly. Slowly, the ambassador climbed to his feet, and walked back around the consulate to stare thoughtfully at the area outside the gates. Discarded holosigns and placards still littered the area, but all the demonstrators were gone . . . where?

Sarek, remembering the shock of touching Induna's altered mind, repressed a shiver. The sun had vanished behind clouds, and the breeze was now chilly. . . .

*   *   *

Peter James Kirk rifled through the selection of clothes available to him and swore impatiently. *This is ridiculous,* he told himself, and reached for a clean uniform. *You don't spend this much time dressing for a date!* Or did he? It'd been long enough since his last *real* date that it was hard to remember. Running a hand through his sandy-red hair, he sighed disgustedly. *Well, maybe you do. Who cares? Make a decision, and let's get out of here.* He'd be late if he didn't hurry.

Your big chance to finally meet Ambassador Sarek of Vulcan, he thought, feeling a flare of nervous excitement, followed by chagrin. *Yeah, and won't he be impressed if you're late?*

He'd first become acquainted with Sarek through the Vulcan's writings and speeches, some of which were mandatory reading at Starfleet Academy, where Peter was currently a senior cadet. Then, when he'd attended a talk the diplomat gave at the Academy two years ago, Peter had found Sarek's approach to diplomacy so interesting, he'd studied the ambassador's eminent career during his spare time. Having met the ambassador's son many times gave his interest a personal aspect.

It was ironic, really. His uncle, Jim Kirk, had spent years working beside Sarek's son, Captain Spock. If things had worked out right, no doubt Spock, whom he'd met many times during his uncle's sporadic visits, would've been happy—or the Vulcan equivalent—to have introduced Peter to his father. If things had worked out right . . .

Well, Peter mused, things had worked out well enough for someone who'd lost his parents tragically at the age of seven. He glanced at their picture, taken on Deneva just months before their deaths. George Samuel and Aurelan Kirk were laughing, their hands on their gangly son's shoulder. Their twenty-five-year-old mementos still traveled everywhere with him, and thanks to family albums and vid records, Peter had a clear recall of his mother's voice, his father's sense of humor, although his actual rearing had been entrusted to his late grandmother, Winona Kirk.

Peter was nearly half a head taller than his uncle, and built on slender, rather than stocky, lines. His hair, which as a boy had been a deep auburn, had lightened over the years to a sandy red. Much to his relief, his freckles had also faded, though any exposure to the sun brought out a rash of them across his nose and cheeks. His eyes were a bright, clear blue, like Earth's sky at midday. Until his mid-twenties, he'd been gangling and awkward, but the years—and Starfleet's self-defense training—had solved most of that. These days Peter moved confidently, even, at times, gracefully.

He'd inherited his looks from his mother, but the rest of the Kirk legacy that sometimes sat too heavily on his shoulders came straight from Uncle Jim. Staring at the cadet's uniform he was holding, Peter wondered if that was why, at the age of thirty-two, he was still in school.

Peter Kirk hadn't decided on a career in Starfleet until he was in his mid-twenties—almost a decade after most cadets entered the Academy. He'd spent that decade attending the best colleges, gaining degrees in xenolinguistics and xenocultural interfaces with minors in Terran/xenopolitical interaction, before deciding that he would finally follow the family tradition and join Starfleet. While Uncle Jim had always encouraged his varied interests, and never tried to influence his choice of careers, everyone else had automatically assumed he'd pursue Command track. He'd done so, though Peter was sure that he'd never possess his uncle's calm air of command.

We'll find out soon enough if you're a real *Kirk,* Peter told himself mockingly. After all the degrees, all the varied quests for knowledge, and these last few years in Starfleet Academy, Peter was, at last, in the final stretch. The past two weeks had been one grueling exam after another—most of which he'd aced. *Just like a real Kirk.* He'd had one just this morning, and that, too, he'd completed successfully.

Now there were only two more to go. One tomorrow, and the last a week from Friday. Then, three days after that, the final. The big one. The *Kobayashi Maru.*

He realized he was crushing the clean uniform in his hands and put it back. Why did he have to think about that now?

Because you can't ignore it anymore, it's just a few days away. They've completely reprogrammed the simulation. There's a whole new situation, a whole new setup—and nobody knows anything about it. But that hasn't stopped them from taking bets as to whether or not you'll be the second Kirk to beat the no-win scenario. He rubbed his face tiredly. He had to stop worrying about it. It was just another test. Wasn't it?

The odds are twenty to one against you. Just being a Kirk isn't any guarantee of success, mister.

He shook his head, trying to shed his pessimistic musings.

The chrono chimed softly, yanking him back to his immediate problem. He had to get ready for lunch. He was meeting Surev, a young Vulcan he'd befriended while researching Sarek's work. Surev had invited him to have a meal at the Vulcan consulate because Sarek might be there, having arrived yesterday. Surev was distantly related to Sarek's aide, and while he was careful not to make a commitment, the young Vulcan thought he might be able to arrange an introduction. Peter was really looking forward to shaking hands (or rather, offering the Vulcan salute) to the diplomat he so admired. Lunch at the Vulcan consulate would provide a welcome respite from the drudgery of studying and finals. Maybe, for just an hour, he could forget about that damned *Kobayashi Maru.*

That's what you need to do, just forget about it, Peter decided. Forget about the Academy, Uncle Jim, ancient history, the whole thing. Reaching into his closet, he grabbed a stylish suit, a piece of "civilian" garb he hadn't worn in months. He wanted to seem totally professional in case he was introduced to Sarek. Peter wasn't normally self-conscious about being an older cadet, but today he didn't want to risk being prejudged. He didn't want to be Peter Kirk, Jim Kirk's nephew who's only now graduating Starfleet Academy. He just wanted to be another Terran who could discuss some of Sarek's ideas with him knowledgeably.

Donning the suit quickly, he smiled. The colors made his eyes bluer. *Hey, who knows?* he thought wryly. *You can meet a lot of interesting people at the Vulcan consulate. I've seen some really nice-looking female attachés going in and out. . . .* Of course, that was an area where he and Uncle Jim differed. Unlike the elder Kirk, Peter's luck with women was less than fabulous. *Maybe that's something that comes with age.*

As he adjusted the suit so that it hung right, then quickly combed his hair, he turned on the vid link to catch a glimpse of the news. Sarek might be featured on the noon report. Instructing the link to search for any reports about Vulcans, Peter tensed when the headline EMBASSY PROTEST flashed on the link.

As Peter watched, images of San Francisco's Vulcan consulate—his current destination—filled the screen.

"The Vulcan presence on Earth," a fair-haired, attractive female reporter said solemnly, "has rarely generated controversy, but the peace that normally surrounds this quiet enclave was shattered today as the Keep Earth Human League announced their intentions to surround the consulate day and night."

Peter stood transfixed as the view of the front entrance of the stately domed building came on-screen. A group of humans were clustered before the elegant gates, at least three dozen men and women, more than a few holding small children. Some carried traditional placards mounted on poles, while the rest brandished the more common holosigns. The image focused on one nondescript bearded man who had a holosign hovering over him that read, EARTH BELONGS TO HUMANS—LET'S KEEP IT THAT WAY! Another sign came into view that said, JOIN THE KEEP EARTH HUMAN LEAGUE TODAY!—SAVE EARTH FOR YOUR CHILDREN!

Peter stared in consternation, although this wasn't the first time he'd heard of the KEHL. But he'd had no idea that this fringe-element movement had been able to lure in enough members to mount such a large demonstration.

The reporter approached an attractive young woman in a shiny silver coat whose holosign read, VULCANS THINK THEY'RE SO SMART—AREN'T YOU SICK OF BEING PATRONIZED? Beside her stood a young boy with a hand-lettered sandwich board that simply demanded, VULCANS GO HOME!

"Excuse me, Lisa Tennant," the reporter asked the woman respectfully. "You're one of the leaders of the San Francisco branch of KEHL. Tell our viewers why your organization is staging this vigil in front of the Vulcan consulate."

"Members of the Keep Earth Human League are Terrans who have finally come to their senses," the woman told the journalist earnestly. She was of medium height, a little stocky, with dark skin and big black eyes. Her features were chiseled and delicate, except for a rather square chin, and she moved with confidence, as though she knew exactly what she was doing in life and how to go about it.

"Our president, Induna," the demonstrator continued, "has called for a show of our support, so we have assembled." She indicated a tall, very dark-skinned man, probably African, who was standing near the consulate gates, lecturing to the crowd. "Vulcans are trying to take over our Federation, and make humans into second-class citizens," Tennant continued. "We won't stand for it any longer!"

"But, Ms. Tennant," the journalist continued reasonably, "most Terrans consider Vulcans our loyal friends, our closest allies. Many of Earth's politicians have been quoted as saying that we *need* them, that they're the most civilized people in the galaxy."

"I doubt seriously," the woman retorted coolly, "that we need friends the likes of Lieutenant Valeris. It's clear to us that she was the ringleader of the terrible plot against Earth, that she was working for the renegade Klingon general, Chang."

Peter shook his head. The Romulan ambassador, Nanclus, and the two Starfleet officers, Admiral Cartwright and Colonel West, had also conspired with General Chang to assassinate the Klingon chancellor, Gorkon. Uncle Jim and his medical officer, Leonard McCoy, had been falsely accused and convicted of the crime, then sentenced to hard labor on the prison planet, Rura Penthe. It was strange, Peter thought, that, although the crime had only happened a month or so ago, the public's memory of those events appeared to be altering. Lately, even the media had a tendency to downplay the roles played by the humans and the Romulan, making it seem that General Chang and Lieutenant Valeris were solely responsible.

"Lieutenant Valeris," the KEHL leader continued, "is merely an *example* of the kind of subtle espionage Vulcans have been guilty of for years. But now the KEHL is on to them. There are chapters of the KEHL springing up all over—even on some of the Terran colonies. And we know exactly what we're dealing with!"

"What do you mean?" the journalist pressed.

"Everyone knows," Tennant elaborated, "that Vulcans are telepaths. Lately, it's becoming increasingly obvious that they're using their abilities to influence minds, and make susceptible humans do things against their own kind! Those politicians that are so quick to defend Vulcans are, no doubt, their unwitting victims. After all, everyone knows how easy it is to influence a politician's mind!"

Hard to argue with that, Peter admitted grudgingly. But the notion that Vulcans would use their telepathy in such as unethical way outraged him.

"The Keep Earth Human League is gaining new members every day," Tennant told the reporter smugly. "We are funding our own candidates to run in local elections, people who are not so easily influenced. It's only a matter of time before the Vulcan conspiracy is completely exposed. Our vigil here is to let them know *their days on Earth are numbered!*"

The woman's self-assurance shocked Peter. She didn't have that wild-eyed look of lunacy he usually associated with the off-kilter KEHL.

An old woman suddenly stepped in front of the reporter, demanding the journalist's attention. "Vulcans are the spawn of the devil," she hissed viciously. "Satan marked 'em as his own, anyone can see that. Don't you have eyes, woman?"

Now, that had to be a founding member, Peter thought. He realized his jaw ached from clenching his teeth. Didn't these people realize how crazy they sounded? What was wrong with them?

The crowd rallied around the Tennant woman. "Keep Earth Hu-man! Keep Earth Hu-man!" they chanted. Angrily, Peter slapped the vid off switch. Why did those nuts have to picket the consulate *today,* when Sarek would be there? Good thing the Federation provided security to all off-world embassies and consulates. He felt confident that Security had the situation well under control. Yet, even though the vid link was now silent, Peter imagined that he could still hear that hate-filled mantra.

As the cadet left his room to head for the consulate, he found himself mulling over the news report. The KEHL had been around for centuries, ever since Zefram Cochrane invented the warp drive, and humans made it into space and met the Vulcans for the first time. It was nothing more than a small group of hard-line xenophobes. But lately, the KEHL was another story altogether. He wondered if Starfleet Security was mounting an investigation of their recent activities. If the KEHL kept garnering members and publicity at the same rate in the coming months, they could turn out to be a real problem.

Peter moved quickly out of his apartment and onto the streets that surrounded the Academy. If he hustled, he could still arrive in time to meet Surev.

As young Kirk turned the corner to approach the familiar consulate, he was shocked to find that the crowd of protesters he'd watched on the noon report had grown even larger. While some of the people massing around the curving, neutral-colored compound must have been simply curious onlookers, there were now so many holosigns that the floating messages were blending all together into a huge mass of gibberish.

Peter slowed as he neared the gates, watching the Starfleet Security forces as they worked to keep the crowd from getting too close to the entrance. Was the mob actually going to rush the gates? Near the sculptured metal portal Peter spied Surev, but the Vulcan wasn't looking toward him, so he didn't bother to wave. Surev's attention was turned in the opposite direction, and Peter peered to see what he was looking at. He squinted. Was that . . . could that possibly be . . . *Sarek* himself?

Peter realized it was the ambassador himself standing safely behind the gates, with his aide, Soran. Surev *had* arranged it! He was actually about to meet Sarek!

As Peter tried to skirt the fringes of the throng, a tall figure pushed his way through the opening crowd. Peter recognized the president of the KEHL.

Now Sarek and the KEHL president were face-to-face. Starfleet Security drew closer to the crowd. Shouts filled the air.

"GO BACK TO VULCAN! STOP SELLING OUT EARTH FOR VULCAN IN-TERESTS!" three KEHL members shouted in unison.

"Back to Vulcan! Back to Vulcan!" the crowd chanted, surging forward threateningly.

Sarek was the picture of composure as he stood straight and tall in his Vulcan robes, his face the epitome of Vulcan control. Both Surev and Soran were young men, and their control was not nearly as perfect as the elder Vulcan's. Even from this distance, Peter could see the two younger Vulcans conferring with each other behind the ambassador's back, concern plain to read on their faces. Sarek merely nodded serenely. Then, to Peter's dismay, the ambassador opened the gate and calmly strode out into the crowd.

Dimly, he heard the KEHL leader telling the crowd to quiet down, but it was no use. A minute later, the mob completely broke ranks. They surged forward wildly, screaming, throwing things, overwhelming the outnumbered security forces. Within seconds the protesters had completely enveloped both Sarek and the two younger Vulcans.

"NO!" Peter shouted frantically, and flung himself unheedingly into the thick of the mob. Furious and sickened, he charged his way bodily through the crowd, shoving, pushing, not caring whether he crushed feet, or sent the bigots staggering. He had to do something to help Ambassador Sarek!

For a brief instant he found himself tantalizingly close to his goal. He glimpsed the ambassador's formal brown and gold robes only a meter or two away. By now the crowd was in a frenzy, hurling refuse and rotting vegetables at the beleaguered Vulcans. As a man beside Peter took aim with a fist-sized rock, the young Kirk managed to surge forward and knock his arm so that the rock landed on another KEHL member instead. Sarek's young assistants were defending themselves ably, and even the ambassador sent an attacker flying.

Almost at the same instant, Peter heard the whine of transporter beams, and knew that the Federation security forces must have beamed in reinforcements. The officers were busily using crowd-control stunners and forcefields, careful not to catch the struggling Vulcans in the beams.

Suddenly, Peter saw Sarek grappling with the KEHL president. To the young Kirk's relief, the Vulcan handled the tall human easily, rendering him helpless with a quick neck pinch. For just a second, Peter thought he saw a flicker of surprise pass over the ambassador's normally calm expression; then both attacker and Vulcan were lost to sight in the press of the crowd.

Three KEHL members next to Peter suddenly collapsed, unconscious, and the cadet realized that he might be next. He was wearing civilian clothes instead of his uniform, so there was no way anyone could differentiate him from these lunatics! In fact, there was a very good chance he was about to be arrested, if not stunned, mistaken for a KEHL member. He searched for Surev, desperately wanting to get his attention. The Vulcan could vouch for him. . . .

Out of the corner of his eye he spied a security officer taking dead aim at him.

"Hurry! Come with me, *now!*" a female voice shouted in his ear, at the same time a strong hand grasped his suit sleeve and hauled him back. Two people in front of him collapsed in the path of the stun ray. "We've got to go now!" the woman insisted, tugging at him and another woman near her.

He then recognized Lisa Tennant, the KEHL's second-in-command. "Come on!" she urged, pulling him behind her. "We can't let them get all of us! Let's go. Follow me!"

Did this lunatic woman think *he* was part of her nutcase organization? Peter was infuriated by her assumption. Then four people directly in front of him collapsed under the minimized stun rays. If she hadn't pulled him out of the way . . .

The security forces weren't asking questions, they were assuming the same thing about everyone in this crowd that she was. If he didn't get out of here, lunch wouldn't be the only thing he'd be missing. The next time Tennant yanked on his arm, he cooperated.

After a moment's pushing and shoving, they broke free. Peter found himself running pell-mell down the streets, away from the screaming, hysterical demonstrators. Had Sarek made it through all right? he wondered, even as his legs moved automatically, running, running, as he followed the woman to safety.

They were on a side street now, Federation Security aircars following them, trying to round up all the demonstrators. The cadet realized that if he didn't get out of this quickly, he was going to be spending the night in jail. He might even have to contact his Uncle Jim for a character reference! What would that look like—Captain Kirk's nephew incarcerated for supporting a violent KEHL demonstration? Envisioning his own face on the next news vid, he sprinted faster.

Tennant led her small crowd down a narrow street, then into an alley. There was a door, which opened as if by magic as they approached. The small group raced in, Peter entering right behind the dark-haired woman. When the door slid shut behind them, the group half-collapsed, heaving and panting for breath. Peter tensed as he listened to the sirens of the aircars that were still searching—*searching for me,* Peter realized disgustedly. What a mess!

"Everybody okay?" Tennant asked the group. "Anyone hurt?"

There were murmurs from the group of a half-dozen men and women, assurances that everyone was all right. Peter looked around at the ragtag group he'd found himself a part of.

A man came up to Tennant, someone new—the person who must've been here, ready to open the door for them in just such an emergency. "Do you know all these people, Lisa?" he asked quietly.

Peter's heart thundered in his ears. If they discovered who he was . . .

"No, Jay," she said, looking over the group. "No, I'm sorry. Everything fell apart. There were massive arrests. I think one of the Vulcans might've killed Induna. These people were near me, fighting side by side with me. I couldn't leave them behind."

"Of course," Jay said, as he looked over the group.

"I'm Mark Beckwith," one of the men said by way of introduction as he caught his breath. Peter recognized him as the rock thrower. "I'm president of the Peoria branch."

Lisa shook his hand. "Of course, I've spoken to you many times."

To Peter's relief, the rest of the group were just average members, or people who'd seen the demonstration on the vid and "believed in the cause."

"I'm Peter . . . Church," he finally said, when it was his turn. "I'm . . . a data-recovery technician. I work nearby. I've . . . always been interested in the KEHL," he lied glibly, "and when I saw that you were calling for support, I came on down."

"Thank you," the woman said sincerely, then repeated it to the others. "Thanks to all of you. What you did today was courageous and ambitious. Your personal involvement will make it easier for the millions who silently agree with our cause to come forward and join us. Thank you all so much."

Crazy, Peter thought, slumping tiredly. Would he ever be able to get out of here and back to reality?

"I think the security forces are gone," Jay announced, after checking with a computerized sensor. "It should be safe for you all to leave now, if you go out one by one."

Tennant thanked them all again, reminding them all of the next gathering. The demonstration at the consulate, she told them, wouldn't be able to continue until the arrested demonstrators had been freed from jail and the current permits renewed. Each person assured her before leaving that they would be at the consulate as soon as word reached them that it was time to assemble. Their faces were filled with a hatred and a commitment that made Peter's stomach lurch.

Peter plastered an appropriate expression of sympathy on his own face as Lisa finally turned her attention to him. She suddenly peered at him intently, and he found himself grateful that he didn't resemble his famous uncle more closely.

"I hope you weren't injured," she said quietly, her eyes never leaving his face. "You came awfully close to being stunned."

He blinked, gathering his wits about him. *Could she be interested in me?* Peter wondered, taken aback. It figured, in a perverse way. His Uncle Jim seemed to be able to attract any woman in the universe with nothing more than a little-boy grin and a twinkle in his eye—an ability that, if it was an inherited trait, seemed to have skipped Peter. But every now and then the "Kirk charm," as the captain called it, *did* seem to shine on Peter—but only at the wrong moments. Like now. He gazed at the KEHL leader, his mind racing.

"I'm fine," he assured her. "Really. You . . . saved me back there. I should be thanking *you.*"

She smiled warmly at him. "I'm so glad you're all right. That is . . . there are so few of us . . . true believers. We can't afford to lose . . . even one."

She *was* attracted to him! Peter began to wonder if Federation Security had any real idea, before today's violent demonstration, how dangerous this group was becoming. Whatever information they had on the KEHL couldn't have been very accurate, or the security forces would've never been caught so shorthanded at the demonstration.

Tennant thought he was a member, a "true believer." Could he string her along long enough to gain critical inside information—information he could relay to Starfleet?

"Listen, Peter," Lisa said, guiding him to the door, "my assistant, Rosa, was one of the people stunned today. I'm going to be lost without her, and I know what it's like to be stunned. She won't be feeling well for a day or two. I need to make a lot of calls, arrange hearings, bail, tons of stuff. That means that my real work won't get done. So . . . I was wondering . . . you're used to manipulating data. Rosa was working on cross-referencing the membership lists with some special information we've received lately about . . . a clandestine Vulcan operation. I really need to get this project completed. Do you think you could help me?"

How would Uncle Jim handle this? Peter wondered, but of course he already knew. James T. Kirk would simply lay on the charm, the famous Kirk charm, and within hours she'd be putty in his hands. *Forget it. That won't work for you!*

As he hesitated, she offered, "You'd be working with me directly . . . but, I'll understand if you're not interested. What happened today was enough to make anyone think twice about supporting the group. . . ."

"Oh, I'm interested!" he assured her. "I, uh, didn't realize . . . we'd be working together. I'd like that, Ms. Tennant. Uh . . . working with you, I mean." *Smooth, mister, real smooth. A Tellarite would've managed a classier delivery . . .*

She opened the door for him and touched his arm. "Call me Lisa, Peter. I'm glad you're willing to help me. I really need an expert's assistance. How about . . . Saturday? Around noon? Can you find your way back here?"

"Sure," he said, managing not to stammer this time. "I'll see you then." His gesture of farewell included both Lisa and Jay. "Saturday, noon. I'll be here."

"It'll just be you and me, Peter," Lisa assured him warmly, following him a few steps into the alley. "Jay . . . will be busy with something else. I'll see you then."

He managed a credible grin despite his uneasiness. "Great. Till Saturday." She stepped back and the door slid shut, leaving him alone.

Peter walked out onto the main street, then began a circuitous route back toward the Academy, suddenly nervously aware of every figure passing him on the street. Whatever had possessed him to play Mata Hari with the KEHL's leader?

These people were definitely more dangerous than Federation Security realized. What should he do now? If he went to the security offices at the Academy, or to the officer of the day, and related this wild story, they'd no doubt tell him to stay out of it. His advisor, a grizzled old Tellarite lieutenant commander, would forbid him to have anything more to do with this group. She'd be right, too. He had exams to complete. And the *Kobayashi Maru.*

I don't have time for this. I have to stay focused. I've got a career to worry about.

But . . . through sheer happenstance he'd managed to find himself on the *inside.* He had an opportunity to discover what was really going on with this radical group of dangerous xenophobes. Would Uncle Jim walk away from this opportunity? The hell he would! Captain Kirk would play the cards dealt him.

Can I do any less?

Peter scowled down at his feet as the moved along the sidewalk. What harm could there be in keeping his Saturday date? He'd just spend time with Lisa Tennant, work on her reports.

She said I'd get to work on the membership lists. . . .

That would be a unique opportunity, one he doubted Security could manage. And, by talking to her, he could draw her out, discover something about this silly Vulcan "conspiracy" she purported to have discovered. Maybe he could find out other things, too. More serious inside information.

And, when he had that information, he'd take *that* to Starfleet. They couldn't ignore him then, not if he had information about how the KEHL had suddenly gained so many new members.

If his plan worked out, it certainly wouldn't hurt his career any. And . . . it was something a *real* Kirk would do. Something Uncle Jim would do in a heartbeat. Of that, Peter was very sure.

* * *

Sarek sat at the comm link in his assigned quarters aboard the Freelan space station, facing the cowled figure of a Freelan. Although there was no way to be sure, owing to the concealing cloak and mechanical-sounding voice interface, he thought he recognized the other as Taryn, the Freelan liaison he'd been dealing with for nearly seventy Standard years.

"Greetings, Taryn," he said aloud.

The cowled and muffled figure was suddenly very still.

"Greetings, Ambassador Sarek," the flat, mechanical voice said. "You recognized me?"

Sarek shook his head and dissembled, diplomatically, "I made a logical deduction as to your identity, Liaison. After all, during my meetings aboard this space station, you have been my contact during negotiations eighty-six-point-three percent of the time."

The shrouded figure seemed to relax again. "I suppose I have. We have known each other a long time, Sarek of Vulcan."

"Indeed we have, Taryn of Freelan," the ambassador agreed solemnly.

"This time, you did not come alone," Taryn said.

Sarek beckoned, and Soran stepped forward from the back of the room and seated himself beside the ambassador. "You are correct, Liaison. I brought my new aide, Soran, so he could begin familiarizing himself with Freelan/Vulcan trade agreements."

"Why?" the other asked, bluntly.

"My health is not what it once was since my heart trouble twenty-seven years ago," Sarek said, smoothly, having anticipated this question. His response was accurate, if deliberately misleading. Actually, his health was now *better* than it had been for decades. "Someday," the ambassador continued, "perhaps in the not-too-distant future, I will retire. I cannot continue to be the sole contact between our worlds. I wish my aide to become familiar with our negotiations."

"I see," Taryn said slowly. "Very well. Greetings, Soran."

"Greetings, Liaison Taryn," the young Vulcan said, raising a hand in salute. "May you live long and prosper."

"Only if I can induce Vulcan to reduce their import tariffs!" the Freelan shot back. "It is difficult to prosper under the crushing weight of unfair tariffs!"

"As a matter of fact, tariffs were one subject I wished to explore today," Sarek put in, smoothly. "May we begin?"

The cowled figure inclined his head. "Assuredly, Ambassador."

Soran observed, for the most part in silence, as the two diplomats went over the trade agreements in question. Sarek's mind was only partly on the subject at hand—with another portion of his mind, he was going over his plans for later that station-designated "night."

The two diplomats finished their discussion of tariffs, and went on to discuss modifications to a long-standing trade agreement.

Taryn seemed slightly suspicious of Sarek's motives in bringing up that particular agreement. "I must admit that I am surprised to hear you reopen this topic," he said. "I had thought that the agreement we forged regarding those cryo-memory inserts actually favored Vulcan. I fail to see why you would wish to alter or revise it. . . ."

"The modifications I have in mind are minor, Liaison," Sarek said. "They should not take long to discuss. Perhaps, after our talk, we could . . . have a game?"

"As you know, I am extremely busy," Taryn said, but then he hesitated. "However, I must admit that you are one of the few players that I find . . . stimulating. Very well, then. A game. When we are finished."

Sarek went ahead with his list of proposed changes to the trade agreement. They were, as he said, minor, most of them points that they had haggled over when the original agreement was forged, three years ago. He actually found himself losing some ground in the negotiations, partially because he was not devoting his full attention to the problem at hand.

Finally, they were finished. Soran excused himself as both diplomats keyed their terminals to produce a 3-D chess board. "Standard time limit per move?" Sarek asked, after graciously accepting white at Taryn's insistence.

"Of course."

The Vulcan studied the board, planning his opening.

"I must warn you, Sarek," Taryn said, "our discussion has sharpened my wits. Prepare to lose, Ambassador."

Sarek inclined his head in a half-bow. "I am prepared, Liaison." After a moment's consideration, he moved a pawn. Taryn leaned forward, studying his representation of the board, then made his own move. "You know," the Freelan said, and the Vulcan gained the impression that he was confiding something highly personal, "I truly do find our games . . . stimulating."

"You mean 'challenging,'" Sarek said dryly.

"As I recall"—Taryn's mechanical tones did not vary, but the ambassador thought he detected an edge in the quickness of the Freelan's retort—"I won, the last time we played."

"Yes, so you did," Sarek said, evenly. "My game was definitely off that day." He could not resist needling the liaison just a little. Taryn could, at times, be induced to play recklessly. The Freelan hated to lose, and Sarek had learned precisely what it took to bait him until he made a fatal mistake.

Sarek moved his knight onto the queen's level, then sat back to study his opponent's reaction.

Taryn's answering move caused the Vulcan to raise an eyebrow. "Stimulating indeed," he murmured, his mind running through moves and their consequences with lightning speed, even as part of his brain counted off the seconds remaining for him to reply to Taryn's bold strategy. "Perhaps . . . challenging." With a swift, decisive movement he transferred a rook to the king's level.

Taryn regarded the board, and Sarek thought he detected skepticism in the mechanical voice. "Jobeck's gambit?" His cowl moved slightly, as though he had shaken his head ruefully. "A human move . . . and not a particularly inventive one, at that. I *will* taste victory today." He paused, his mitt hovering over the board as he considered his next move. "A human gambit . . . a surprising move for one of your kind to make, Ambassador."

"My wife is Terran," Sarek said, "and I have spent many years on Earth. I learned that gambit there. Humans may not possess Vulcan logic . . . but they can demonstrate surprisingly intricate strategy, at times."

"For myself, I have never had cause to respect their intelligence," Taryn commented, his mitt still hovering over the board. "Take this new organization that has sprung up, for instance. The Keep Earth Human League. From all reports, it consists of a collection of bigoted misfits with stunted intellects. They detest all nonhumans . . . even your people, Ambassador."

Sarek had to guard against a betraying start of surprise. It was Taryn's turn to needle him—almost as though the liaison knew why the ambassador was here, hoping to gain proof for his theory about a Freelan conspiracy. . . .

"These fringe groups come and go," the Vulcan conceded blandly. "They hardly pose a concern to the long-standing amity between Earth and Vulcan."

"Of course not," Taryn said, sitting back in his seat, his shrouded head level, as though he were staring directly into Sarek's face, searching for any betraying emotions he might find there. "No one could hope to alter such a close alliance."

Sarek raised an eyebrow. "Really, Liaison, you surprise me. If this is a strategy on your part, I should think you could be more creative than to attempt something so . . . antiquated."

The Freelan's cowl jerked slightly, as if *he* had stiffened. "Antiquated? What . . . what do you mean?"

Sarek gestured at the board. "Why, engaging me in conversation while you exceed your time limit for a move. Or . . . had you forgotten that it *is* your move?"

"My move . . . oh, yes. Of course I had not forgotten." Taryn hastily moved his bishop.

As the game progressed, Sarek tried with all his diplomatic skills to gain information from his longtime contact. Taryn, who had recovered his aplomb, fenced back at him, seemingly enjoying their verbal sparring.

It was a very hard-fought game, but, to his own surprise, Sarek won once again. Typically, Taryn was not a particularly good sport about his defeat. The moment endgame was in sight, he signaled his board to topple his king, then, with barely a civil word of leavetaking, broke the connection.

After dinner, the two Vulcans retired to the adjoining rooms in their suite. Sarek set himself to doze until the middle of "night" aboard the station.

Hours later, the ambassador opened his eyes, then rose quietly from his bed to pull on a dark tunic and trousers, and soft-soled desert boots he had brought with him for this occasion. With his minuscule Vulcan tricorder in hand, he seated himself before the Freelan comm link. The ambassador had been planning for this day for months, and had prepared programs to cover all of the most probable contingencies.

Sarek's first task was to disarm the alarms on the station's secured maintenance area. He studied the sleek, horizontal console for only a moment. "Manual input, please. Standard Federation interface." The manual control board slid out of a concealed opening, and he swiftly enabled the external data link. That was the easy part. Now came the challenging task of causing a calculated "malfunction" in the system that would camouflage his efforts to access the main data banks.

The Vulcan ambassador quickly set his tricorder to run through the standard external data conventions, sending handshake messages at various wavelengths. When the tricorder's screen indicated success, the Vulcan's lips tightened. Not Federation standard. Working efficiently, he called up the most likely communications protocol and linked his tricorder into the Freelan comm link, then was gratified to see the connection established. The twenty-five-year-old espionage done by his son aboard a Romulan vessel would suffice to accomplish his goal.

Confident now of the specifics of this particular computer system, he downloaded the first of several *valit* programs and instructed the low-level operating system to execute. A *valit* was a small Vulcan creature that could burrow its way through the hardest soil, capable of adapting its complex mandibles to numerous functions. Unless the operating system was massively dissimilar to what Spock had reported, the *valit* program would be able to adapt and invade, opening up the secure portions of the software. And, by returning countless error messages to the central processors, this first *valit* program would effectively disguise his efforts to intrude further.

Although Sarek did not actually have to enter the central maintenance area to gain further access to the no-longer-secure data, he wanted to see the Freelan computer with his own eyes. The comm link in his quarters was encased in a shell that differed little from those found on any Federation world. In a sense, he had proven nothing so far. The Freelans could have purchased their comm units and software from the Romulans. The ambassador had to see the central computer itself, because he knew that the Romulan cloaking system depended on the massive processing capabilities of these machines; the Romulans would never willingly part with this technology to outsiders for mere profit.

Before leaving his quarters, Sarek tapped softly on Soran's door. Moments later, his aide emerged, also clad in dark clothes, with soft footwear. "The security alarms?" he whispered.

"Disabled," Sarek replied.

The ambassador had visited the Freelan station many times, and knew precisely where to go. When they reached the doors that were labeled MAINTENANCE—NO ADMITTANCE in several languages, including Vulcan, Sarek stopped, motioning Soran to stay back. He tapped on the entry pad, and the portals shot apart.

Sarek stepped into the maintenance area, Soran at his side. The young Vulcan halted suddenly at the sight of a surveillance vid unit, but the ambassador shook his head reassuringly. The *valit* was overloading the condition-recognition software to the point where it would not be on-line for the time of their visit.

"We must move quickly," Sarek said softly. (Even though there was no one in the area, the urge for silence remained, illogical though it was.) "The *valit* will not delay the security system indefinitely." He led the way past a transporter room and into the nerve center of the station.

The enormous room contained a gigantic computer system, black metal without decoration, identical to the one Spock had seen a generation before. Apparently the Romulans were conservative about changes in a technology that worked. Sarek nodded grimly. It was as he had conjectured.

"Ambassador, you must know what you are looking for," Soran said. "Otherwise you would not have been able to devise a *valit* program."

"Logical," Sarek said, approvingly, seating himself before the closest comm link and taking out his tricorder. "You have deduced admirably. If my theory about the Freelans is correct, then you shall soon see their true identity for yourself."

"This system bears no resemblance to any in the Federation," Soran said, watching as Sarek's experienced hands flew over the tricorder controls, feeding in another *valit* program, this one designed to follow on the heels of the first *valit*. It would make all areas of the memory accessible to external control, and display on the visual monitors whatever was accessed.

As the two Vulcans watched, random areas of memory began to appear on the screens. Soran's eyes widened as he made out the characters. "That script . . ." he breathed. "Romulan!"

"Indeed," Sarek said. "As I expected. But I must capture more than random kitchen requisitions to justify our suspicions." He held up the tricorder's photo chip to the screen.

"So the Freelans are *Romulans?*" Soran said slowly, obviously taken aback. At Sarek's quick glance, the young Vulcan hastily composed his features.

"Yes," Sarek said. "They are Romulans. I have suspected it for a long time, but gaining proof has been difficult. Ah . . . personnel data banks. We are in."

Raw information began to flash across the screen—words in Romulan script, operating-system symbols, and numbers, all in a jumbled disarray. Hundreds of screens of data, most of it garbled, appeared in quick succession. Suddenly Sarek leaned forward and signaled the tricorder to backtrack through the images. A quick tap froze the output. Intently, he studied the scrambled data.

"What is it?" Soran asked.

"A name—one of the few Freelan names I would recognize. Do you read Romulan, Soran?"

"No, sir. I will remedy the deficiency as soon as feasible," the young aide promised. "What does it say?"

Sarek indicated a name in flowing Romulan script. "Taryn," he said, simply. "This is a list of Romulan officers, along with their ranks. Taryn is listed, if I am reading this correctly, as a wing commander." The elder Vulcan raised an eyebrow. "A high-ranked Romulan officer indeed." He continued recording data, studying it. Slowly, he made sense of the scrambled information. He generated a decoding algorithm in his mind, and mentally overlaid it on the jumble, seeing order amid chaos.

Minutes later, he was reading it swiftly. Sarek scanned the shipping data first, noting with grim satisfaction that it, too, proved his theory. Military vessels from Romulus and Remus made regular voyages to Freelan, and Freelans voyaged to the Romulan worlds. Romulan officers were logged as being "detailed" to Freelan.

Freelan also had a small fleet of birds-of-prey located in probe-shielded hangars that were camouflaged by the simple expedient of placing them beneath massive ice shelves, with roofs impregnated with selonite.

The communications logs listed hundreds of subspace messages between the Romulan worlds and Freelan. Government communiqués listed Freelans on "missions" to various worlds, particularly Earth—and, nearly always, the Freelan merchant, diplomat, or scientist was accompanied by an aide with a Vulcan name.

Sarek automatically memorized those names, knowing, however, that further checks would reveal that they—like Savel—were *not* Vulcan citizens.

None of the evidence Sarek uncovered was a direct link between the KEHL activity and the Freelans—or Romulans—but the ambassador found the circumstantial evidence damning.

Without warning, a sudden, familiar sound made him freeze.

Soran heard it, too. "Ambassador—a transporter beam!"

"Attempt to distract the newcomers, while I disengage the *valits,*" Sarek commanded, his fingers flying. Without a thought he abandoned his hope of copying further Romulan data banks. If he and Soran were caught here, spying, the Romulans would be within their rights to summarily execute them for espionage.

Quickly, he injected the last of the *valits,* the one designed to eradicate all evidence of his tampering. He could hear footsteps approaching from the direction of the transporter room as he leaped up, tricorder in hand, looking for a place to eliminate the evidence of his spying. Without the tricorder as evidence, he might be able to pretend to have awakened in the night, ill, and to have been searching for the station's automated med center. There was little chance that he would be believed, but, without hard evidence, the Freelans might hesitate to take him into custody. Seeing a disposal unit, Sarek dropped the tricorder in and cycled it, not without a pang at the loss of his proof. Logic dictated, however, that he save himself.

Glancing around him, the ambassador realized that the computer room was singularly devoid of hiding places. Silently, he resigned himself to being caught, and having to feign illness, when a loud crash sounded next door, in one of the engineering chambers that held banks of automated equipment.

The approaching Freelans exclaimed—in Romulan!—and went to investigate. Peering out of the computer area, Sarek warily scanned the hallway; then he made a swift, soundless retreat back to the entrance. The ambassador knew that his young aide must have caused the crash that had distracted whomever had come to investigate the "malfunction." Would Soran be able to escape, also?

A second later Soran, soundless on his soft-soled shoes, hurried up beside him. Quickly, the two Vulcans left the maintenance area and returned to their quarters.

Later, as he relaxed in the narrow bunk, the ambassador allowed himself a faint, ironic smile in the concealing darknesss. *It is not endgame yet, Taryn,* he thought. *Today you may have had me in check, but mate is still a long way off.*

The next day, Sarek waited tensely for some indication that his late-night foray had been discovered, but apparently the last *valit* had been successful. Taryn displayed no indication of suspicion during the morning's negotiating session.

The ambassador was just beginning the afternoon's session when Soran approached, a guarded expression on his normally calm features. "Ambassador? There are two messages coming in from Vulcan. They are . . . important."

Hastily, Sarek excused himself and went to his quarters to view them in private. The first was a written message from his wife that read, simply, "Come home if possible, please. Amanda."

Staring at it, the Vulcan experienced a rush of unease. Never, in over sixty years of marriage, had his wife ever interrupted him in the midst of a mission to ask him to return home. What could be wrong?

His silent question was swiftly answered by the second message, prerecorded by his wife's physician, T'Mal. The graying Healer stared straight into the screen, as though she could see him. Her expression was calm, as usual, but the ambassador could discern a hint of sorrow in her eyes. "Ambassador Sarek, you must return home immediately. Your wife is gravely ill. I do not expect her to live more than another month . . . possibly less. I regret having to impart such news in this manner, but I have no choice. Return home immediately."

Two

The ancient, stone-walled room was buried deep in the foundations of the huge fortress-manor on Qo'noS, the Klingon homeworld. Outside those age-darkened stone walls lay nothing but soil. The room had been tested, retested, and verified to be free of all recording or surveillance devices, which was why such a dank, dark room had been chosen for this particular meeting.

Valdyr sat in one of the modern chairs that had been brought into the room, feeling the chill pluck at her body, even as the words she was hearing chilled her mind and soul. Hesitantly, she glanced up at her uncle, the esteemed Klingon ambassador, Kamarag, as he spoke forcefully to the officers assembled in the room, around the venerable, dagger-scarred table that had undoubtedly been here for hundreds of years.

He is perilously close to treason, she thought, struggling to keep the shock she was feeling from showing on her face.

The officers watched the speaker with varying degrees of enthusiasm. The soft lights from the lamps glimmered off oiled black leather and polished studs.

"Warriors," Kamarag was saying, his trained voice carrying such conviction that it was nearly hypnotic, "we have all seen what is happening to our Empire in the past months, since Praxis was destroyed. The foundations of our existence are being eaten away! If this continues, soon there will be no place for our race in this galaxy! The Romulans will overrun us, for we will have grown soft, and weak as females!"

Valdyr, the only female present, glanced up at him, but was careful to conceal the resentment his words caused. Her uncle was the head of her family. When her father had been killed attempting to board and conquer the Federation *Starship Enterprise,* Kamarag had taken his widow and four children under his protection, providing for them, even sending Valdyr and her brothers to school.

And last month, when her mother and eldest brother had been killed during one of the devastating meteor showers that had bombarded Qo'noS ever since the destruction of Praxis, Kamarag had taken Valdyr and her brothers to live with him in the ancestral home.

Her uncle was the head of her family, and she owed him everything. If not for Kamarag, her brothers would never have been able to go to school and learn the skills necessary to serve aboard starships. They would all have been relegated to a backwater existence in some hamlet, grubbing for sustenance on land that was increasingly hostile to agriculture.

Valdyr owed Kamarag unquestioning loyalty. Still, his sneering reference to her entire sex made her grind her back teeth. Her fingers clenched against her own armor. At the mention of the word "females," one of the captains, Karg, cast Valdyr a leering glance.

"Females have their place—but what should that place be? Remember who now sits in the chancellor's seat of our government, my brothers! A *woman!* Gorkon's daughter, to be sure, but she is not Gorkon, as she has proved many times in the past days. Azetbur demands our loyalty, even as she opens her arms to Federation influence—influence which may well lead to Federation *control.* Who among us, brothers, wishes to live under the heel of the Federation?"

A concerted growl from the officers present was his only reply.

Azetbur's ascension to the chancellorship had given Valdyr the courage to continue her schooling past the age when most Klingons of her sex were relegated to the home, their only power whatever they could obtain by influencing the males in their lives. Valdyr respected Azetbur for attempting to forge a true and lasting peace between the Federation and the Klingon Empire.

To hear her revered uncle denouncing the new chancellor secretly enraged the young woman. She glanced up at him as he spoke. Kamarag had been a formidable warrior in his youth, and his stance as he addressed these officers was that of a combatant throwing down a formal challenge.

"Consider, my brothers!" he was continuing. "Consider what we must do, each and every one of us, to uphold our honor as warriors! Each of us must search his own heart to discover the best way to serve our Empire—even, should it prove necessary, by serving outside the strictures of official government policy. We must have the courage, the honor, the *valor* to serve our Empire as warriors, as leaders—not merely as those who blindly follow orders given by our nominal superiors!"

Valdyr's eyes widened. Her uncle was skirting the boundary of advocating sedition . . . outright treason! Such talk was dishonorable! How could he speak so? Glancing over the faces of the assembled starship commanders, Valdyr saw that their eyes were fastened on the ambassador with an avid gleam—

—all except one. Keraz had drawn back in his seat, and was shaking his head. Suddenly, the commander sent his gauntleted fist crashing down on the aged table so hard that the ironlike wood groaned in protest. "Kamarag, you go too far!" he growled. "I have no love for Azetbur, or her new policies, but I cannot disobey my oath as a Klingon officer! There are more renegades raiding across the Neutral Zone every day, and I have no intention of becoming one of them!"

Valdyr had to restrain herself from leaping up and saluting the commander.

Kamarag drew himself up, as though deeply offended—but his niece could tell that his indignation was feigned. "Keraz, you mistake me! I have said nothing about disobeying oaths. I have merely requested that each and every one of us assembled here today spend some time in *thinking* about our current situation, and how it may best be improved! There was no talk of oath-breaking in that!"

Valdyr sighed inwardly as Keraz obviously lost some of his confidence. His brows drew together in consternation. "Yes, Keraz, were you not listening?" Karg growled sarcastically. "Did you stay out last night drinking and wenching, only to fall asleep just now and *dream* talk of oath-breaking? For there was none of that voiced today!"

"Right!"

"Karg is correct!"

"We have our honor!"

The other officers snarled their support of Karg's rebuke. Keraz sat back in his seat. "Perhaps I misheard you, Kamarag," he said grudgingly.

The Klingon ambassador nodded, and within minutes the clandestine meeting had broken up. The moment she could do so without seeming suspect, Valdyr left her seat and hurried out into the corridor. She'd caught Karg ogling her with an appreciative eye, and she wanted to avoid the captain at all costs.

But her way out of the deep cellars was blocked by the officers, who lingered, talking in groups, or waiting their chance to speak personally with Kamarag. Valdyr shrank back into an alcove that had once held wine casks.

She'd been standing there long enough to grow chilled from the damp stone surrounding her on three sides when she heard two familiar voices. Kamarag and Karg were talking softly.

"It went well, I thought . . ." Karg was saying. "Except for Keraz. He should be Azetbur's personal servant, if he wishes to clean her boots with his tongue. I knew he would be trouble."

"We handled it, between us," Kamarag said smugly. "Keraz may not join us—but he will not betray us to Azetbur. He has no love for her himself. Tell me, how did your latest raid go?"

"The best yet," Karg said. Valdyr could almost see him smacking his lips over the memory. "One of those mixed colonies, mostly Tellarites—you should have heard the females and the young ones squeal as we cut them down! There was very little worth taking on Patelva, true, but it was wonderful to feel the heat of battle and smell the richness of fresh-spilt blood again."

Valdyr swallowed. Klingons gloried in war and battle, true, but there was no honor in mowing down noncombatants. Karg's words made her belly tighten with disgust.

Suddenly a new voice broke into the conversation. One of the other officers had come up to slap her uncle on the shoulder and congratulate him on a stirring oration. Peering out from her niche, Valdyr saw that the newcomer's back blocked her from view, so she seized that opportunity to steal softly away down the corridor.

Later that evening, as she sat in her chamber studying for her next examination in Federation Standard, the Klingon woman heard a knock on her door. After bidding the visitor enter, she saw it was her uncle. "Uncle!" she exclaimed, standing respectfully. Even though she did not agree with what he had done that day, he was still her family's savior and head. Klingon tradition decreed that her first loyalty be to him.

"I have something important to discuss with you, niece," he said in his deep, resonant voice. "It has come to my attention recently that you are of an age to wed."

Valdyr's eyes widened. "Yes, I suppose so, Uncle," she said. "But I am so busy with school these days, I have not thought much on the matter of prospective husbands."

"Your mother arranged no marriage for you before her death," Kamarag said, seating himself on the narrow, shelflike bed. "Was that your choice?"

"We never discussed it," Valdyr said. "My mother married according to liking, not for family advancement. I believe she intended the same for me, but I do not know for certain."

"My sister married beneath her," her uncle said grimly. Valdyr stiffened at hearing her beloved father denigrated so, but Kamarag did not notice. "However, there is no point in rehashing her unfortunate choice, since it all lies in the past. We must look to the future—your future. Someone offered for your hand today, and I accepted."

Valdyr held her breath. *Who? Keraz? I do not love him, but he is a warrior with honor . . . no, that cannot be. Keraz is married, I remember hearing that. Who else—* A sudden thought occurred to her, and, with a sinking sensation, she heard her uncle confirm her worst fears.

"Karg is a veteran of many battles, a warrior of considerable renown. He fancies you, niece, and he is well able to provide you with anything any female could want. I accepted his offer." Rising, he strode to the open door and beckoned. The Klingon captain stepped in from the hall, and grinned broadly at his promised bride.

"Karg . . ." Valdyr whispered, faintly. The knot in her belly turned over, and she had to lock her knees to keep from trembling. *To wed and bed Karg? NO! I would embrace my dagger as bridegroom before that dishonorable Denlbya'Qatlh!*

As though he could read her mind, Karg gave her a mocking half-bow. "My wife-to-be . . . your uncle has done me a great honor."

"Hah!" Kamarag barked out a shout of laughter, and slapped the suitor on the back. "The honor is all ours, Karg!" He gave Valdyr a smug glance. "I do not wonder that she is speechless with joy."

I cannot marry him, I cannot! I hate and despise him, Uncle! Do not make me do this! But, seeing the pleased expression on Kamarag's face, Valdyr forced herself to take a deep breath and regain her control. She might not be warrior material herself, being slender and not tall, but the blood of a noble house of warriors flowed in her veins. She would not dishonor herself by begging. "Uncle, I must think about this seriously. Karg needs a wife who has high social position and much . . . beauty," she said, cautiously. "I have neither. I do not believe the match would be satisfactory for such a high-ranked warrior."

"Such modesty!" Karg chuckled richly as he stepped over to the young woman and ran a caressing hand up her arm, testing the muscle that lay beneath her sleeve. For a lingering moment his hand trailed perilously close to her left breast, and Valdyr went rigid. Would he dare to fondle her in front of her uncle? *If he does that, I will kill him here and now,* she thought.

But Karg contented himself with kneading and prodding the muscles of her arm and shoulder. "Small, but there is good, wiry strength there," he remarked approvingly. Then, glimpsing the outrage in her eyes, he added, sardonically, "Ah, my bride . . . you are so young, so innocent . . . you warm my heart."

Grasping Valdyr's chin and forcibly turning her face to and fro, he continued to examine her as he might a prospective mount for his stables. "You know nothing of what excites a male . . ." he said caressingly, obviously enjoying her humiliation. "But have no fear . . . innocence excites me greatly. Do not worry, my *targhoy.* There is beauty in you. With the flowering of your womanhood, it will come, Valdyr-oy. When you are my wife, your beauty will blossom like *chal* flowers in spring."

His endearments and the love suffix attached to her name made the young woman long to shriek with fury. Her mind filled with images of her plunging the dagger she wore strapped to her forearm into his heart.

As his fingers touched her cheek, Valdyr could not repress a shudder of disgust. "Look, Kamarag, she trembles for me already!" Karg chortled; then he seized her in a bruising embrace and pressed his face into her neck, his teeth fastening on her throat so hard that the woman gasped from the pain.

"Enough, Karg!" Kamarag ordered, and the captain released her. Raising her hand, Valdyr touched her throat, then stared unbelievingly at the smear of blood on her fingers. "I know you are hot to take a bride, but the wedding will not take place until after our triumph. The taste of victory will add extra savor to your wedding night, Karg."

The captain was breathing hard as his eyes ran over Valdyr's body, and his voice, when he spoke, was thick. "Very well, Kamarag. But she is sweet enough to tempt any male. . . ." He addressed the young woman then. "Do not concern yourself about your fitness to be my wife, Valdyr-oy. Just as the beauty will come, you will learn the intricacies of society, until you are ready to take your place with me, to help my advancement. Your uncle assures me that you possess high intelligence, for a female."

Valdyr wanted to flay him alive for his words, but she held herself back. She must be clever, use all of her wits to escape this fate that loomed before her. Allowing Karg to see her true feelings would only make them watch her closely until the day of the wedding.

Perhaps she could run away. Or, if she could not refuse Karg, perhaps she could postpone the marriage for a while. Karg was a warrior. Perhaps he would be killed. The thought made her smile.

So, steeling herself, Valdyr forced herself to say, "At the moment, school occupies all my time. Perhaps when I finish this term, I will find myself more . . . prepared for marriage, Uncle."

Kamarag frowned. "You will not need further schooling now that I have arranged such a successful match for you, Valdyr. Better you should turn your attention to the management of households. That in itself is a demanding life."

"Your uncle is right, Valdyr-oy. I have a large house, but it has suffered from the lack of a woman to care for it," Karg added.

"No further schooling?" Valdyr struggled to control her temper. If she made her uncle angry, it would bode ill for her brothers, as well as for her. She must not allow them to know what was in her mind. "But, Uncle . . ."

Perhaps sensing her distress, her uncle said, "You may finish out this term, as long as it does not interfere with your duties here, and with your spending more time in the kitchens, learning the duties of a wife." He gave Karg a smug glance. "I will not have Karg say that you did not come to him properly trained for your new role."

"In addition to the kitchens," Karg said, his gaze roving over her body again, "do not forget that you must learn the ways of the nursery, Valdyr-oy." With a toothy grin, he slapped her uncle on the back and left the chamber.

Once they were alone, Kamarag regarded his niece with a touch of impatience. "Well, girl?" he barked, finally. "Have you nothing to say?"

The young woman exerted rigid control as she forced herself to reply quietly, "Uncle, I will do as you say."

"See that you do," he grumbled. "You do not want to appear ungrateful, do you, niece?"

"No, sir."

Relaxing visibly, her uncle rocked back on his heels, and smiled as he changed the subject. "The meeting went well today, did it not?"

"They all seemed to share your point of view," Valdyr said, treading a careful verbal path. "All except Keraz."

Her uncle dismissed the commander with a wave of one blunt-fingered hand. "Hundreds of years from now, our names will be remembered as the ones who saved the Empire and the Klingon way of life," he said, earnestly, his deep-set eyes gleaming.

"But . . . current policy of our government is to make peace with the Federation," Valdyr reminded him. "Peace with the Federation, friendship with our old enemies—even peace with James Kirk, who saved the chancellor's—"

"Kirk!" roared Kamarag so loudly that Valdyr started. "Niece, I cannot hear that name without anger—do not think to provoke me by letting it fall from your lips so casually! May Kirk be devoured by ten thousand demons on his way to oblivion! Kirk lives still, and I have no peace!"

Furious, the ambassador strode back and forth in the small chamber, his boots resounding on the floor like ancient war drums. "Kirk! Kirk is the enemy, and I will never regain my honor until he is dead, until I can dip my hands in his warm blood and dye them scarlet—I will never rest until Kirk and all his line are wiped out!"

"But, Uncle." Valdyr was taken aback. Kamarag's temper was legendary, but she'd never seen her uncle in such a rage. "Kirk saved Azetbur's life. She will never agree to having him killed."

"I care nothing for her!" Kamarag was livid. "She is the spineless daughter of a spineless coward. She will not stop me, niece."

"Stop you in what, Uncle?" Valdyr asked, curious and repelled at the same moment.

"Stop me from carrying out my plan," the ambassador said, and smiled.

The sight of that smile chilled her, even though her chamber was warm. "What plan?" she asked.

His smile broadened, revealing a mouthful of teeth. A cunning, predatory expression replaced the anger that had been there. "You will see, Valdyr," he promised softly. "Just wait, and you will see. . . ."

Journal of Amanda Grayson Sarek
September 16, 2293

What is it like to die?

Vulcans, of course, have their katras *. . . a word no one has ever been able to translate with any degree of precision. Not quite a soul, not exactly a personality, more than a memory, less than a living being . . . I suppose one has to be born Vulcan to have any hope of understanding Vulcan mysticism.*

Spock and Sarek will live on, after their deaths. Will I? Many of Earth's religions hold that I will . . . but there is no certainty. And if there is an afterlife, would individuals from different worlds mingle there?

Now I am getting metaphysical—and silly. Speculating about such things is fruitless . . . illogical. Life after death will either happen, or it won't, and there is nothing I can do about it either way . . . except be philosophical.

I dread Sarek's return from Freelan, even as I long for it. I suspect T'Mal contacted him, and that she was as blunt with him as she was evasive with me. No doubt she was concerned that the truth would be too much for a human to bear.

Little does she know this particular human. I have known what is happening to me for months, now. I can't remember when I first realized that my body was running down, sputtering to its inevitable halt . . . the knowledge just grew in me, day by day.

It seems that I have Reyerson's disease. It isn't always fatal, especially to those in the prime of life—but I am ninety-three. Luckily, it's not an illness that causes a great deal of pain. Its main symptom is continuous exhaustion, which, at my age, is fairly common anyway.

I've spent time these past few days reading over my old journals. The moments come back so clearly, it almost seems as though the past is the reality, and this present, with its exhaustion and inevitable ending, is merely a bad dream.

When I read about them, the memories revive, as fresh as if they happened only yesterday. I cannot believe I have lived this long—it all seems to have gone by at great speed. Every time I look in a mirror these days, I am shocked to see a woman who is, beyond a doubt . . . old. I don't FEEL old!—not inside. The aches and pains remind me of my true age, but my mind and my heart feel as young as ever. Young Amanda is in here with me, in my head, and Old Amanda has trapped us within this shell of aged bone and flesh.

Curious, isn't it? I wonder if every human feels this way . . . or am I unusual?

Vulcans, of course, feel exactly as old as their chronological age. Anything else would be illogical. . . .

Can I really be . . . dying?

At times I have to fight off panic, but those episodes are growing less and less frequent. They are simply too tiring, I suppose, for a body that is . . . shutting down.

Of course, I would not want to live forever . . . but I don't want to die, either. I want to live—there are still so many things to do, so many places to go, so many things to see—

I want to live . . . yet I am coming to realize that I will not, at least, not for much longer. By this time next year, probably much sooner, the universe will be going on without me. Amanda Grayson, Madam Sarek, the Lady Amanda . . . I will be gone, will be no more.

I am dying.

There, I've admitted it. Writing it out in black and white like that has actually been a relief. Facing the worst the future has to offer is better than mincing around, shying away from an all-too-possible reality.

Of course, the Healers are treating me, trying to arrest the disease. But I know without asking that my prognosis is dismal. And, even if a miracle happened, and I were cured of this particular illness, at my age, the inevitable can only be staved off for a short time.

There is one journal entry that I've been saving as a treat, for when I feel particularly low. I believe that tonight is the night to read it. . . .

June 14, 2229 . . . a few minutes past midnight

My hand trembles as I write this . . . I can scarcely believe what happened tonight! After all these months of seeing him, trying to make myself believe that his interest was not solely that of a diplomat befriending a student of his culture . . . trying, but never quite succeeding—I can hardly believe what I am about to write—tonight Sarek kissed me!

It was not really a kiss as a human knows it—but it happened. Just the softest brush of his fingertips against my lips, but I trembled as we turned and walked home in silence. Even now, as I sit here writing, I feel as though I have caught some exotic fever.

Is it possible that we have known each other for only four months? It seems incredible that my life could have changed so radically, so irrevocably, in such a short time. Four months, almost to the day.

My work was everything to me . . . teaching was my only passion. Being able to convey to my students the wonder and richness of alien cultures was my fondest dream, a goal to be striven for, my heart's greatest desire. The day I won the T'Relan Award for Excellence in Teaching was, I thought then, the pinnacle of my life.

All this time, these past months, wondering, trying to fathom why such a distinguished diplomat wanted to spend time with a teacher who happened to win an award for teaching and thus was invited to an embassy reception . . .

Once or twice I thought, "Perhaps he's attracted to me," only to back

away from the thought at warp speed. Vulcans do not form romantic attach-
ments, after all. Either they bond at a very young age, or they make a rea-
soned, logical decision later in life. Romance? Don't be ridiculous, Amanda!
*   But tonight . . . was romantic. I believe that even Sarek felt it, was af-*
fected by the spell of the night. . . .

The three-quarter moon was setting over the Pacific as the couple walked along
the beach. Amanda Grayson picked her way over the wet sand, smiling as the white-
tipped waves curled ever closer to her feet. Dinner had been excellent; Sarek had
taken her to one of the finest restaurants in town.

As they'd eaten, she'd caught curious glances from their fellow diners. It was unusual, she knew, for a human woman and a Vulcan male to be seen together. And her
escort was a noted diplomat at the Vulcan Embassy—a well-known public figure.

Thankfully, after they'd left the restaurant, none of the curious had followed
them. Now, watching the moon slip down toward the waves, they were completely
alone. The tide was coming in, lapping ever higher. Amanda watched her escort
covertly as he gazed at the ocean, his expression quiet and serene.

She was so intent on watching Sarek that an importunate wave caught her un-
awares. Amanda jumped and gasped as cold water sloshed over her feet, and she
bumped hard against the Vulcan. Automatically, he caught her arm and steadied her.
It was the first time he had touched her in the four months since she'd met him.

"Oh, thank you!" she exclaimed. "If I'd fallen in, I'd have gotten soaked."
Glancing up at him diffidently, she caught her breath in surprise as she realized that
he was . . . smiling. There could be no doubt about it. Sarek's austere, aquiline features had softened, and his normally stern mouth curved upward on both ends. The
Vulcan's dark eyes held an amused spark.

Sarek is smiling. At me, she thought, amazed and touched. *I didn't know he
could smile!*

She smiled back at him, feeling a rush of happiness so pure and strong that it
was like some euphoria-inducing drug. As they stared at each other, their eyes
locked, the next wave caught both of them in its wash.

This time they both jumped. Amanda, glancing down, saw that the ambassador's
boots were soaked. "Oh, dear. Your boots."

"They will dry," Sarek said, ignoring his footwear. "Amanda . . . tell me something."

"What?"

"Is there anyone . . . special in your life?"

He can't possibly know what that question means on Earth, she thought, blankly.
"Of course there is," she said, struggling not to blush. "I have my parents, and my
students, my family and my friends. They're all very special to me . . . Sarek."

It had been hard for her to call him by only his name without his title—he was such
a formal person, so reserved. It was growing easier each time she did it. "And of course,
back East I have several friends that I only see a few times a year, because they're—"

"Amanda . . ." She couldn't believe that he'd interrupted her. He'd never done
that before. The Vulcan stepped closer to her, so close she could feel the heat of his
body against her face and throat.

"Yes, Sarek?"

"I wanted to know whether there is a special *male* in your life."

She stared at him unbelievingly, but managed to compose herself. "No, Sarek.

There is no special . . . male." Her heart was pounding harder than the surf.

"So you are free to choose a . . . mate?" he asked.

"Yes," she whispered, but hardly any sound emerged from her throat. The Vulcan leaned closer, indicating that even his acute hearing had not picked up her answer. "Yes," she repeated. "Yes, I am."

"That is good to hear, Amanda," he said quietly; then he leaned forward, slowly and deliberately, and *kissed* her mouth with his fingertips.

Even as he drew back, Amanda instinctively knew that her life had changed forever. There was only one possible explanation for Sarek's words and action—he wanted her for his wife. She knew from her studies that Vulcans did not waste time in casual dalliance.

For a moment he regarded her intently, his eyes filled with all the things he could not say aloud. Then, without another word, the Vulcan offered her his arm to help her back up the beach. Amanda went with him, her whole body conscious of his touch, of the heat of his skin beneath his sleeve.

I love him, she realized. *I've loved him from the first, and didn't realize it until now.*

September 16, 2293

Just finished rereading that journal entry. Oh, my! Was I ever that young?

And yet . . . if I close my eyes, I can still taste that kiss, even after sixty-four years.

I have had a good life. I have been blessed. There are few regrets. . . .

But for now, I am tired . . . must rest . . .

Captain James T. Kirk stood in the coruscating glow of the transporter beam, dreading what he would see as soon as he materialized on the world called Patelva. Yesterday the *Enterprise* had been summoned to the colony world that had been decimated by a raid. The captain had made one quick reconnaissance to the planet, then returned, sickened, to his ship, leaving Dr. McCoy and his medical staff to their grim work of trying to save as many of the pitifully wounded survivors as they could.

As the transporter beam faded around him, Kirk could hear the sounds of the wounded. The beam-down coordinates were in the center of a group of hastily thrown-up bubbletents, so, unlike yesterday, he was not surrounded by shattered and torn bodies . . . which was a relief. But the sounds were bad enough.

Medical personnel scurried to and fro, racing frantically to beat their ancient enemy. In a distant field, filled with crops that would never be harvested now, security personnel stoically attended to the hideous work of disposing of the corpses.

"Captain . . ." Kirk turned away from the grim scene to find his first officer at his elbow. "I have completed my interviews with the few uninjured survivors I could locate. Their reports all concur: Klingons did this."

The captain gazed around him, and sighed. There hadn't been much doubt about who the assailants were—the patterns were all there. "I know," he said. "I just finished speaking to Chancellor Azetbur on subspace communications. She confirmed that their sensors have picked up a number of Klingon vessels crossing the Neutral Zone lately, but swore to me on her father's honor that none of them has been authorized to do so by her government."

"More renegades," Spock said, his normally expressionless features touched with sadness. "Chang has set a precedent, I fear."

"I'm afraid that Azetbur's going to go down, Spock," Kirk said. "Everything looked so hopeful last month at Khitomer, but now . . ." He shrugged slightly. "The media back on Earth are having a field day with these renegade raids. Many of the delegates to the Security Council are calling for Ra-ghoratrei to withdraw his support of Azetbur's government."

"I know. And without the support of the Federation, Azetbur has little chance to remain in power."

"The chancellor is the Empire's only hope for survival, Spock!" Kirk said wearily. "If I can see that, so can others."

The Vulcan nodded, his dark eyes bleak. He started to comment, but before he could do so, a familiar voice made both officers turn.

"What's the news on the Federation hospital ship?" Dr. Leonard McCoy demanded, coming up from behind the two officers. The chief surgeon's medical tunic was splashed and streaked with drying blood and even less pleasant substances, and his blue eyes were red-rimmed with fatigue. "Dammit, Jim, my people are ready to drop, and I can't spare a one of 'em for a break. We've got to get some relief!"

"The ship's on its way, Bones," Kirk was quick to assure the medical officer. "ETA is thirty-six hours from now."

"Damn!" McCoy growled; then he sighed. "Can you at least beam down some more security people? They're not trained, but they can help clean up and make sandwiches for the staff."

Kirk nodded and, taking out his communicator, quickly gave the order. McCoy busied himself dispatching the security teams to where they were most needed, then turned back to regard his friends wearily. "Thanks, Jim. This is one helluva mess. . . ."

"I know, Bones."

"Who did it?" McCoy demanded, staring out across the jury-rigged medical compound. "As if I didn't already know from the disrupter patterns on the bodies."

"Klingons, Doctor," Spock said. "But Chancellor Azetbur has stated that they were renegades, not governmentally sanctioned troops."

"I suppose so," the doctor said, rubbing a hand over his face, leaving smears across his forehead. "Damn, but what I've seen in the past twenty-four hours almost makes me regret spending the past month studying Klingon anatomy and medical procedures."

"The Empire is in chaos, Bones," Kirk said. "Any time you get a situation like this, you find terrorism on the rise. Any time you try paring down a huge standing army, you get soldiers that don't want to give up war."

"Especially considering that war has been the main focus of the Klingon culture for several thousand years," Spock said, quietly. "If the —" The Vulcan broke off as his communicator beeped. "Spock here," he said crisply.

"Mr. Spock, I'm receiving a Priority One personal message for you, sir," Commander Uhura's voice reported. "It's from your father."

"Relay it on screen, please, Commander."

Kirk tensed as he watched the Vulcan scan the message on the tiny camp computer screen, noting the way his friend's eyes narrowed and the skin over his jaw tightened. When Spock looked up, he took a step forward and touched his friend's arm lightly with his fingertips. "What is it, Spock?"

The Vulcan took a deep breath. "It is my mother, Jim. I just received a message from my father, saying that she is seriously ill." He paused, then seemed to force the words out, as though speaking them caused him pain. "Actually, Sarek used the word 'terminally' ill."

Kirk had lost his own mother a few years ago . . . Spock's words brought back the grief of those days all too vividly.

"Spock, does it say what's wrong?" McCoy asked, his blue eyes filled with concern.

"She has contracted a blood disease." Spock's normally even tones were strained. "Reyerson's disease is somewhat rare. It is extremely serious, especially to the very old or the very young. My mother," the Vulcan finished bleakly, "is in her nineties."

Kirk's mother, Winona, had been in her late eighties at the time of her death. In the twenty-third century the human life span was longer on the average than it had ever been, but only ten percent of the population lived for a century or more. Kirk drew a deep breath. "Go home," he ordered. "Go now. Take the shuttlecraft to Starbase Eleven. You can get a transport from there, and reach Vulcan in five days," he said.

Spock hesitated, glanced around him. "But we are on a mission . . . my duty is to my ship . . ."

"Dammit, Spock, this is a *medical* mission," McCoy said. "If you've got a medical degree it's news to me. Go. We don't need you here. Your mother does."

The Vulcan finally nodded. "Very well. Thank you, Captain. I will depart immediately."

Moments later, Kirk and McCoy watched the last flicker of maroon vanish in the transporter beam, and knew the Vulcan was on his way.

"Jim, this is terrible," McCoy said, his eyes shadowed. "We've known the Lady Amanda for so long . . . and now we're all going to lose her? It's . . . not fair."

"How many times have you said that when you're confronted with death, Bones?" Kirk asked.

McCoy gave him a grim smile. "At least ninety-five percent of the time, Jim. But that doesn't keep me from feeling it again, each time."

"After that hospital ship relieves us here," Kirk said, "we're heading for Vulcan."

McCoy nodded. "Good. But how are you going to justify a trip to Vulcan with Starfleet Command?"

"Scotty has performed his usual miracle patching up the ship after Chang used us for a skeet target," Kirk replied, "but he told me yesterday that he's completed all the repairs he can, working on the ship from the inside out. He said we'd have to put into spacedock for him to finish with the structural repairs and pressure checks. Vulcan has an excellent spacedock."

McCoy nodded, then wearily straightened his back. "No rest for the wicked," he said. "I've got a patient to check on."

Kirk looked at him. "Could you use one more pair of unskilled hands, Bones?"

"You bet," the doctor said. "C'mon, and *I'll* order *you* around for a change. . . ."

Together, they headed for the nearest bubbletent.

"Enough, Peter, enough!" Lisa Tennant insisted, getting out of the old-fashioned hard-backed chair and stretching her spine. "You're worse than Rosa. I never thought I'd find anyone who could work as hard as she did. How about some coffee?"

Peter nodded. "Sure, Lisa. Coffee's fine." He could use a cup right now. It was nearly midnight and because of the time he'd spent here, he'd have to pull an all-nighter to cram for his exam tomorrow. He rubbed his face tiredly. He wasn't eighteen anymore. Staying up all night studying would take its toll . . . and what did he have to show for it?

He'd been coming to this dingy basement room nearly every day since that Saturday. That first day, he'd thought that he'd be able to garner enough information to take to Starfleet Security once he got into the KEHL files. But that Saturday, he never got near the computers. Instead, he'd ended up helping Lisa with the technicalities of bailing out most of the demonstrators.

He'd been right about her, too. She *was* interested in him, and kept him close by her side most of the time, flirting lightly, never saying or doing anything too forward, too aggressive. He played along in the same vein, waiting and hoping to get access to their computers. When that didn't happen, he'd ended up coming back the second night, and the third. Last night, he'd finally gotten into the machines, but the only thing she'd let him work on was a tedious reworking of the data structures, which told him little.

He promised himself that tonight was the very last time he'd come here. If he didn't get any information valuable enough to bring to Starfleet Security, he'd forget his brief sojourn into the world of cloak-and-dagger and force himself to focus on the really important matters in his life.

Like the *Kobayashi Maru.*

Peter groaned at the very thought of that test, only a little more than a week away. Just today, one of his friends had confided that the odds against him were mounting steadily. Peter wasn't surprised. If he had been a betting man he'd have bet against himself, too. Was he studying the old scenarios to see how others handled them? Was he reading up on the theory behind the test itself, to get a handle on what the new scenario might require of him? No, he was hanging around a subversive organization, flirting with its leader, and coming up with nothing for all his efforts.

A cup of steaming coffee suddenly appeared by his elbow, along with a sandwich. "You've got to be starving," Lisa said quietly, sitting beside him. "You've been working steadily since you got here. I'm afraid I haven't been taking very good care of you."

"I didn't think that was your job," he replied. "As your impromptu assistant, I thought it was my role to take care of you."

She brushed against him, and the faint scent of her perfume made his nostrils twitch with the faintly musky, exotic odor. In the few days he'd been associating with her, he'd found her an enigmatic person. She was bright, sensitive, and quite intellectual. In many ways she was an intriguing, exciting woman, not the kind of person to spout the bigoted, paranoid nonsense she obviously believed wholeheartedly.

He thought more clearly when she wasn't quite so close to him. Finishing his sandwich, he eased out of the chair and wandered around her small, spare office. Curiously, he browsed the shelf of real-paper books she had prominently displayed.

There was a mint-condition volume of *Wuthering Heights,* a slightly battered edition of *Have Spacesuit, Will Travel,* a collection of Edgar Allan Poe's poetry, and . . . He paused, staring at a slim volume perched neatly between the others. *The Diary of Anne Frank.*

"It's a nice collection," Peter said softly. "Do you read them?" Unlike his Uncle Jim, many collectors did not.

Lisa nodded proudly, coming to stand beside him. "I don't read the volumes themselves, of course—they're much too fragile. But every book I buy, I look it up in the library files and read it."

"That's great," Peter said, his voice low. He tried to imagine how she could've ever read the words of Anne Frank and still become so involved with the KEHL. "It's nice to meet someone who appreciates books."

She gave him a smile, and a spark of warmth touched her huge, obsidian eyes. "Are you a collector, too?"

"Not exactly," Peter admitted. "But my uncle is, and I enjoy his books." Peter hesitated, then bit the bullet. "You know, I've never gotten the chance to ask how you got so involved with the KEHL."

Lisa showed no sign of self-consciousness as she replied, "I haven't been a member that long, Peter. Just a few months. It's funny . . . I'm a sociology student, and I know something about how groups like this start. . . . Usually there's one charismatic individual—like Induna—who founds such a group, and he or she finds followers along the way, people who think along the same lines. But the KEHL, at least here in San Francisco, wasn't like that at all." She glanced at him, her black eyes earnest. "Which leads me to believe that we were just destined to be—that it was time for us to rise and make our voices heard."

"Have you always disliked aliens? Particularly Vulcans?" Peter was careful to keep his tone one of polite, if casual, interest.

She frowned a little as she thought. "It's funny, Peter. Up until a few months ago, I scarcely ever gave the matter much thought. I'd never known an alien personally, and only met a few as casual acquaintances. I'm from a little town in Indiana, and we don't get many outsiders—human ones, much less extraterrestrials. I guess it was just a subconscious decision I made back in August . . . that humans evolved on Earth, so it's our planet, and they don't have any place here."

"Do you think Earth should stay in the Federation?"

"I don't know . . ." She chewed on her lower lip, hesitating. "Since Earth is the most powerful planet in the Federation, with only the Vulcans capable of posing a serious challenge to us, I suppose we shouldn't dissolve the Federation until the Klingons and Romulans have been dealt with. As long as we can get the Vulcans out, that is."

Peter was having a difficult time staying civil. "Why?" he asked, struggling to keep the edge out of his voice.

She faced him, holding his gaze with her own intense one. "Do you know anything about Vulcan history?"

"A little," Peter said cautiously.

"Let me show you something." She walked back to the computer terminal and selected a computer tape, then plugged it in.

As Peter seated himself in front of the screen, images coalesced in front of him. The predominant one was an image of the Plains of Gol, a scene familiar to anyone who watched popular media entertainment. Splashed across the desolate scene were the words *The True History of Vulcan*. He groaned inwardly. Propaganda films were not among his personal favorites.

"Are you aware that the Vulcans fought major wars on their planet several thousand years ago?" Lisa asked, as the film moved forward, illustrating her question with vivid, computer-generated film sequences that seemed shockingly real. "Wars that make Earth's World Wars and the Eugenics War look like skirmishes by comparison?"

"I think I remember reading something to that effect," he mumbled.

"Well," Lisa leaned forward and murmured confidentially, "they still have the weapons from those wars, stockpiled in secret installations. Weapons that could turn Earth into a smoking cinder in a matter of minutes."

As the images on the film confirmed her wild allegations, Peter's mouth dropped open, and he didn't have to feign astonishment. *Where in hell did she get that idea? They had to have faked these images! Vulcan has no weapons except defensive ones—and hasn't for four thousand years!* "You're kidding!" he managed, feebly. "Where did you find out about that?"

She shook her head. "Everyone in the KEHL knows. We can't get the Terran government to admit it, but it's true."

"Wow," was all Peter could say. "That's hard to believe."

"You think that's bad, you haven't heard anything, yet," Lisa said. She touched the computer controls and changed the scene from massive stockpiles of terrifying weapons to another, more fantastic landscape. There was a towering cathedral-like edifice in a searing desert. Inside were cavernous, smoky, dimly lit rooms packed with peculiar, glowing orbs, pulsating as if with a mysterious force.

"The Vulcans are in control of ancient Vulcan . . . personalities, I guess you'd call them," Lisa said. "Spirits without bodies. They're called *katras,* and they have hundreds of thousands of them stored up, just waiting to turn them loose to possess the people on Earth. Unless we can stop them, they'll conquer us without a shot being fired!"

This last was almost too much for Peter. He knew he had to cajole her along, try to learn more, but all he wanted was to escape listening to such noxious paranoid fantasies.

"But don't worry," she consoled him, misinterpreting his expression. She placed a warm hand on his arm. "We're on to them now. And our membership is growing, bringing in new committed people—people like yourself. Our voices will be heard." When he didn't respond, she asked, "What made you join up?"

"Self-preservation," he said, letting her take it any way she wanted to. "But I . . . had no idea . . . things were so bad. . . ." Her bizarre accusations merely gave him more incentive to accomplish the task he'd come here to do. "Lisa, you told me you needed my help in a special task. Something about a Vulcan conspiracy . . . ?"

She nodded. "Boy, you're inexhaustible! I wasn't going to bring it up tonight, but . . ." She glanced through a number of tapes then pulled one up. "We've found information that's coming straight out of the Vulcan consulate that will shatter this whole holier-than-thou sham the Vulcans have set up. This information will *prove* that Vulcans are using their telepathy to influence powerful members of the Federation—perhaps even the president himself!"

Peter's eyes locked on the small tape. In his pocket sat blank cassettes, enough memory to copy anything he should find of value here, but so far, nothing seemed significant. "How can I help with that?"

"Needless to say, this information was very difficult to come by," she told him. "A lot of it has been lost in the transference—special codes, significant schedules. Since you're a data-retrieval technician, I thought . . ."

He nodded. "Sure! I'd be glad to help. I can take it to work tomorrow and . . ."

She shook her head. "Oh no, this can't possibly leave here. In fact, Jay's not real happy with my even letting you see it. But . . . for some reason . . . I can't help but trust you, Peter Church."

Lisa leaned forward almost imperceptibly, at the same time Peter felt his own body drawn toward her. When their lips met, his face flamed with embarrassment that his body had so little regard for his own internal ethics.

"I'll . . . be happy to work on it here," he said huskily, when they drew apart. "I can probably . . . tap into my workstation . . . use my files at work to decode some of the lost material."

She nodded. "That would be great." And kissed him again.

They both jumped when they heard the door behind them whoosh open. Jay stood there, frowning disapprovingly.

Lisa moved away from Peter self-consciously. "I . . . didn't think you'd be back so early," she stammered.

Jay didn't respond, merely glanced at Peter and said to the woman neutrally, "Can I see you in my office a moment? Something's come up."

"Is it Induna?" she asked worriedly, standing. They'd found out that the president of KEHL had survived Sarek's "assault," but had been hospitalized (at his own insistence, Peter knew). "Is he all right?"

"Let's . . . talk in my office," Jay reiterated, nodding his head in that direction.

"Wait for me," Lisa said to Peter, "and I'll show you the problem with those files."

He nodded and watched her walk toward Jay's office with the other man. The moment they were both out of sight and earshot, Peter snatched up the "conspiracy" tape and plugged it in. Grabbing one of his empty ones, he downloaded the whole thing, sight unseen. After copying the secret cassette, he copied the extensive KEHL membership lists, and the propaganda films as well. He had just finished copying the annual agenda, and sliding his tapes back in his pocket, when Lisa came back into her office. Jay was not with her. Peter stood to greet her.

"Everything all right?" he asked. "Is Induna okay?"

Lisa nodded, smiling warmly. She slid her arms around him and he returned the embrace. "Jay is such an alarmist! Induna's out of the hospital, and will be back here tomorrow."

"Great! Why don't we get started on those Vulcan files?"

She pulled him closer and murmured, "Is work all you think of, Mr. Church?"

He swallowed, unsure of how far he could take this charade. "Well . . . this would be the best time for me to access my workstation . . ." There wouldn't be many students in the Academy library at this time. He hadn't quite figured out how he was going to log on without revealing who he "worked" for . . . or his real name.

"Tomorrow will be soon enough," she assured him, and reached up for another kiss.

He obliged her, realizing uneasily that his body was responding to her, even if his mind wasn't. Hastily, he raised his head, staring down at her. "Okay. Tomorrow. It is late. I'd better go."

"See you tomorrow, then," she agreed, and released him, smiling warmly as he let himself out of the basement.

With a twinge of regret, he thought, *Not bloody likely.* In spite of the late hour, he made a beeline for the Starfleet Security offices on the Academy's campus. Those offices were staffed all night. Someone would be there that would be interested in his story. And then he'd never have to go back to that basement again, never have to war within himself over Lisa's feminine charms and her absurd, even dangerous politics. One thing was for sure—no matter how many mixed feelings he might have about taking the Command track at school, he was now certain that he had no interest in working in Intelligence!

Twilight on Vulcan.

Sarek stood alone on his terrace, watching T'Rukh at full phase. The ambassador had returned from Freelan the previous night, and the day had been taken up with visits to the med center and consultations with his wife's physician. Now, gazing at the full, bloated sphere, Sarek reached out and grasped the stone balustrade so tightly that his knuckles shone greenish white in the eerie glow of The Watcher.

Silently, the ambassador struggled for calm.

As he watched The Watcher, the gigantic world seemed to loom even closer, as though it were about to topple out of the sky and crush him. The chilling breeze stirred his thick, iron-gray hair, as refreshing as the touch of a cool, human hand on his brow. Sarek swallowed, feeling dull pain in his midsection. Surely *he* was not ill . . .

A quick assessment of his physical condition assured the ambassador that he was physically healthy . . . the pain he was experiencing had no physical cause.

Sarek leaned heavily on the railing, experiencing again that rush of vertigo at the thought of Amanda. Amanda was with him now, for the moment, but soon, the Healer said, she would not be here anymore. Because Amanda . . . Amanda was dying.

Dying. His wife was gravely ill, and, even though they were attempting to treat her condition, T'Mal held out little hope of recovery.

Dying . . .

Amanda. Dying. So the Healer said—and one glance at his wife's face yesterday had convinced him.

Sarek stared blindly at The Watcher, thinking of all the times he had stood here, during many of the epochs of his life.

How many times had he stood thus? Absently, the ambassador retrieved the number. He had not seen the giant world until he was an adult, when he had built his villa here. Also, he had spent much of his working life off-world. Still, Vulcan's days were shorter than Terran days, and Sarek was 138 Federation Standard years old. 122,474 times.

122,474 times . . .

The ambassador had watched T'Rukh the night that his firstborn had been declared outcast and departed his homeworld, and known within himself that he would probably never see Sybok again. Nor had he.

He'd watched T'Rukh during the early hours of his second *pon farr*, experiencing the heat of desire, concerned that human flesh and bone might not withstand the flames consuming him. But human flesh and bone had proved more resilient than he had thought. During that night, his secondborn had been conceived.

The ambassador had watched T'Rukh the night that Amanda had delivered their son, and again when Spock had announced that he had passed the entrance requirements for Starfleet Academy, and was forsaking the Vulcan Science Academy to go off-world. Memories of that "discussion" still had the power to make the ambassador's jaw muscles tighten. T'Rukh's light had illuminated his son's tall form as he'd walked away without looking back. His father had thought never to see him again, either. But that time he had been in error, and never had he been more pleased to be mistaken.

Sarek drew deep, slow breaths of the cool air as he let his consciousness sink down, deep inside himself, seeking that place of quiet repose that every Vulcan was taught in childhood to retreat to during times of trouble.

He could not find the place. Calm acceptance continued to elude him. With a sigh that was almost a moan, Sarek sagged against the railing, raising both fists to press them against his temples in a gesture he would never have permitted himself had he not been alone. Every muscle in his body was taut; his indrawn breath hurt his lungs. Logic . . . his logic was gone, the core of his mental balance was gone—and in its place was pain . . . and fear.

And grief. Sorrow filled him, until he felt that he could hold no more. There was no quiet center that would release him from his pain, this fear, this grief. How could he stand it, if he could not find his center? How did humans manage, with no silent retreat or sanctuary to shield them from the constant onslaught of emotion—*how* could they stand this? No wonder some of them broke with reality, retreating into insanity because they could not deal with their pain, their fear, their grief.

Sarek stared at T'Rukh unseeing, unblinking, until his eyes began to burn. The physical pain distracted him, and he found a brief respite in it.

Sarek . . . The call resounded softly within his mind. *Sarek* . . .

Immediately the ambassador turned and left the balcony. He strode swiftly through the living room, down the short hall; then he hesitated before the carven portal. The call came again. *Sarek* . . .

Quickly he sent back a wordless reassurance, a sense of his proximity and imminent arrival. Then, drawing a deep breath, the Vulcan put out a hand and rested it against the carven portal, seeking strength from its solidity, its age. Letting the breath out slowly, he summoned calm, seeking—at least outwardly—control. When he was certain that his features betrayed nothing of his inner turmoil, he straightened. Squaring his shoulders, he pushed the door open and stepped into the room he had shared with his wife for more than sixty Earth years.

The chill of the air-conditioning struck him immediately. Amanda's physician had insisted, over her protests, that she must not tax her remaining strength by enduring her adopted world's notorious heat. Cold air blasted against his face, driven constantly so a pressure lock would not be necessary.

The ambassador's gaze rested first on the bed, but it was empty, the light, silver-blue coverlet Amanda had woven decades ago thrown back. Even as he turned toward the small sitting room that looked out over the rear garden, he sensed her presence, waiting for him.

Quickly, Sarek strode through the bedroom and into the adjoining sitting room. Amanda occupied her favorite chair as she gazed out the window at her garden, her pale skin seeming doubly un-Earthly in T'Rukh's light. She sat quietly, not turning her head. During the past days she had lost even more weight . . . now she seemed little more than a wraith. Only Sarek's iron control kept him from betraying his distress at her appearance.

Sarek . . . Her mental "voice" filled his mind. "Amanda," he said, allowing just a touch of reproach to shade his voice, "you were supposed to rest for the remainder of the day. The Healer emphasized your need for rest. Logic demands that you heed her advice."

When he reached her side and stood looking down at her, only her smile was unchanged . . . gentle, full of affection. "I'm tired of resting," she said, holding up two fingers toward her husband. "And you know how I love to watch The Watcher shine on the garden at night."

"I know," Sarek replied, touching her fingers with his own.

"Is it pleasant out tonight?" she asked, a hint of wistful eagerness tingeing her soft voice.

"Yes, it is," Sarek replied. "However, to answer the unspoken corollary to your query, no, it is not cool enough for you to go outside, my wife. The Healer's directions were quite specific on that point. Logic dictates that you must husband your strength . . . and the heat depletes it."

"For heaven's sake, Sarek," Amanda said, her eyes flashing with indignation, "I've lived here most of my adult life! I *know* it's hot outside! But I have been cooped up in this house for nearly a week, and I am *tired* of seeing nothing but these four walls, *tired* of resting. I want to sit in my garden, damn it!" Her voice gained strength and volume as she spoke, but faltered and cracked on the last line.

Sarek was taken aback at her vehemence—he knew Amanda had a temper, had known that since before their marriage, but he could have numbered on one hand the occasions when his wife had resorted to profanity. "Amanda . . ." he began softly, then stopped.

"Besides," she added, her eyes filled with weary resignation, "what difference will it make, really?"

The ambassador gazed down at her. Under the circumstances, he could not find it in himself to deny her wish. It was such a small request. . . .

"Very well," he agreed. "Do you have your respirator with you?"

Smiling, Amanda patted the pocket of her robe, indicating that she did. "What about the logic of following the Healer's orders?" she asked him.

"Logic tells me that you will expend far more energy arguing about this than you will in a brief interlude outside," Sarek retorted as he bent over and scooped her up as he would have a child. She was hardly heavier than one. Perhaps, Sarek thought, a brief excursion outside would bolster her flagging appetite.

When Sarek reached the garden, he carefully lowered his wife's slight form onto a stone bench, then seated himself beside her. Amanda's eyes shone as her gaze took in the beauty of the night, the garden, and the hovering planet that dominated the sky. "It *is* lovely," she breathed. "I knew it would be."

"It is good to see you here again," Sarek said. "The garden's appearance is not aesthetically complete without its creator."

Amanda, recognizing the compliment despite its subtlety, smiled roguishly at her husband. "Sarek, I do believe you are getting sentimental," she teased.

Her husband's lips curved upward as he permitted himself the faint, answering smile that few besides his wife had ever seen. "Nonsense, my wife. My comment was entirely logical. This is your garden; you designed it, planted it, and nurtured its growth. It is a reflection of your creative instincts, so, logically, it appears at its most attractive when you are present to complement and complete it. There is nothing 'sentimental' about that—I was merely stating a fact."

Amanda chuckled, and to Sarek's ears the sound was more welcome than any strain of music. "Now you're rationalizing, my dear—as well as teasing me. It is a good thing our son isn't here to hear you. Spock would be shocked."

Despite Sarek's control, the muscles in his jaw tightened fractionally at the mention of his son's name. Amanda was watching him intently, and her husband realized that she had not missed that tiny betrayal. Her smile faded. "Have you heard from Spock?" she asked anxiously. "You didn't—"

She broke off at her husband's nod, and her eyes flashed again, this time with anger. "You didn't!" she exclaimed. It was an accusation, not a question.

Sarek gazed up at T'Rukh fixedly. "I sent a subspace message to Spock before I left the Freelan system," he admitted quietly.

"How could you?" Amanda was furious—as he'd known she would be. "We had a bargain! You gave me your word! I did not want him told, you knew that! I—" She sputtered indignantly for a moment, then subsided, too angry to speak. Finally, her chin lifted and she glared at him, her eyes now cold. "Your action was entirely illogical, my husband," she said in slow, careful Vulcan, using one of the ancient, formal dialects. Then she turned away, staring fixedly at The Watcher. It was no longer full; its upper limb was now shadowed.

Sarek was taken aback by her accusation—in ancient days, it would have constituted an insult. "Amanda—" he began, then waited patiently for two point six minutes until she finally looked at him. "My wife," he said softly, hearing the tension in his own voice, "Spock had to be informed. If anything happened to you, and I had not told him, he would never speak to me again—and I could not fault him for his decision."

Amanda sighed, and Sarek immediately knew that her anger had turned to resignation. "You're probably right," she said quietly.

"Amanda," Sarek said slowly, "I regret going against your wishes, but logic and duty demanded that I make my own decision."

"But our son has been through so much in the past couple of years!" she murmured, twisting her wasted hands in her lap. "He lost his ship, Valeris betrayed him, my God, he lost his very *life*—he needs to finish putting the pieces back together, not have other concerns added!"

"Would you deny him the chance to see his mother again?" Sarek said, and the phrase "for the last time" seemed to fill the quiet garden.

It was a long time before Amanda replied. "No, I suppose not. I suppose you did the right thing, as well as the logical thing. But I wanted Spock to—" She broke off on a ragged breath.

"You wanted him to what?" Sarek asked, quietly.

"I don't want him to see me," she admitted, dully. "I thought it would be better if he remembered me the way I used to be. . . ."

"That never occurred to me," Sarek said, slowly. "Your attitude is illogical, Amanda . . . and vain. Human vanity, I believe, is as foreign to my son as it is to me."

"I know that," she said softly. "I've lived here for decades, and never yet managed to figure out how Vulcans can be so arrogant without being at all vain."

"You have learned much about my people," Sarek conceded, quietly. "It is possible that no human understands us better."

Sarek crossed her fingers with his, but, in addition, he gently traced the contours of her face with two fingers of his other hand. The intimacy of the caress, outside of their bedroom, made Amanda's eyes widen; then she closed them, concentrating on their bond, and the closeness it gave them.

Finally both stirred, and Sarek dropped his hand. "We should go in, my wife," he said gently. "I sense your fatigue. You must rest."

Amanda nodded, but, when he would have risen, put out a hand to forestall him. "Just five more minutes," she pleaded. "Who knows . . . when . . . or . . ." She hesitated, but did not say "if" aloud. "Anyway, there is no way to know how long it will be before I'll be able to be with you in the garden again. Five minutes more, Sarek . . . please?"

Sarek gazed down at her, then nodded. "Very well," he said. "But you must agree to put on your respirator, Amanda."

She frowned, but then her features smoothed into serenity once more, and she obediently slipped the little mask over her mouth and nose. Together, fingers once more touching, they gazed at The Watcher, while the night breeze caressed their faces.

Three

Spock felt the surrounding heat even before his body was completely rematerialized. Nevasa was almost directly overhead, blazing furiously.

The transporter chief had beamed him down into the gardens behind his parents' mountain villa. It had been nearly five years since his last visit here, and Spock noted absently that Amanda had expanded the cactus garden to include species from the deserts on Andor, Tellar, and Rigel VI. The plants were brilliant shades of lime green, amethyst, and turquoise, doubly arresting next to the dusty greens and reds of the Terran and native Vulcan plants.

He walked slowly up the crushed stone path, feeling the heat envelop him like a blanket. He welcomed the hot caress. Vulcan. No matter that he had spent more of his life with deck plates beneath his boots than he had treading the sandy soil of his homeworld—when he was back on Vulcan, he knew he was *home*.

The mountain villa was a low, redstone building with solar panels set into its flat roofs. Its design was deceptively simple and austere; from outside it appeared smaller and more rustic than it actually was. The surrounding foothills and the paths leading up to the mountain crests were as familiar to Spock as the corridors of his starship.

Just as he reached the *kala-thorn* hedge that enclosed the garden, a door opened onto the rearmost of the roofs and Sarek emerged. At his father's signal, Spock halted and waited for him. Sarek took the side ramp down to the ground, then skirted the edge of Amanda's garden until he stood before his son.

The Vulcan officer held up his hand in the salute of his people. "Greetings, Father," he said in their native tongue. "I trust you are well?"

Sarek nodded. "Greetings, my son. Yes, I am well. It is good to have you here."

Despite his father's reassurance, Spock was concerned about the ambassador's health. The lines in Sarek's face had deepened, and his hair was grayer than it had been a month before. His shoulders seemed smaller, and the flesh of his hand, as he returned his son's salute, was tightly drawn over the bones of his fingers.

"How is Mother?" Spock asked.

"Sleeping," his father replied. "The monitoring devices will indicate when she awakes. The Healer has stressed her need for rest." The ambassador glanced around. "We should go in."

Spock nodded. "Nevasa is . . . formidable today. One forgets, after years away."

Together they went into the villa, then sat down in the living room Amanda had decorated with handwoven wall hangings. Spock sipped appreciatively at a cup of *relen* tea, covertly watching Sarek as his father paced restlessly around the room, gazing at the bone-white walls and the desert-hued hangings as though he'd never seen them before. Finally, Sarek turned to face his son. "Your mother . . ." he began, then he fell silent.

"She . . . is dying?" Spock asked, feeling his throat contract over the words.

"Yes," Sarek said, seeming relieved that his son had spared him having to say it aloud. "The Healer holds out little hope of recovery, even though she is being treated for Reyerson's disease. The illness, in one of her age, is too debilitating."

Spock nodded silent understanding.

Father and son occupied their time while waiting for Amanda to awaken by sharing a simple lunch. It had been years since he and his father had been alone together long enough to share a meal, Spock realized, and he found himself enjoying Sarek's company. They spoke of the Klingons and the Khitomer Conference, of the current political situation in the Federation, and a host of other diplomatic concerns.

Spock rose from his seat and wandered over to examine the water sculpture in the corner of the room. Every time he came home, its design and flow were slightly altered—Amanda changed it periodically. This time, there was something different about it—the flowing lines were sharper, more angular than before. The water ran in clear perfection, instead of taking on colors from the underlying crystal and stone.

"It is different," he said to his father, indicating the sculpture.

Sarek nodded. "I programmed it this time. Your mother did not have the energy to do the work herself, but she was tired of the old design."

Studying the piece of art, Spock finally nodded. "Yes, I can see that. This design is far more . . . logical." He hesitated, trying to frame the rest of his thought in a way that would not offend.

"But not as aesthetically pleasing," Sarek finished for him. Taking in Spock's surprised glance, he nodded. "I saved the old designs, every one of them. As soon as Amanda grows tired of the current design, I will reactivate one of her programs."

Sarek hesitated for a long moment, then continued. "There is something that has been concerning me for some time now. I need your advice on a problem I am facing."

Spock's gaze sharpened with curiosity. "A problem?" he prompted. Never before had Sarek asked him—or anyone else, insofar as he knew—for advice.

"Recent events have convinced me that a serious problem is facing the Federation from an unsuspected quarter," Sarek said, steepling his fingers on the table before him. "What do you know of the Keep Earth Human League?"

Just as Spock opened his mouth to reply, the monitor in the corner beeped softly. The ambassador quickly rose to his feet. "Your mother is awake."

Soft-footed, Spock followed his father down the hall to his parents' bedroom. Even though he had thought himself prepared for his mother's illness, he was shocked by her extreme pallor and thinness, as she lay in the middle of the huge bed.

"Mother . . ." Spock said gently, leaning over her to take one of her hands in his own. The bones beneath her papery skin seemed no more substantial than those of a songbird.

"Spock . . ." she whispered, even before her eyes opened. Her familiar, loving smile shone out of her face, transforming it, making it suddenly familiar again. "Oh, Spock, it is so good to see you. . . ."

The first officer stayed with his mother for nearly an hour, talking quietly to her. When Amanda's eyes began to close, he squeezed her hand, then left.

Sarek was sitting at the table when his son reentered the dining room. Spock sank into a chair, and took a deep breath. "I did not want to believe it," he said, dully.

"I know. I experienced the same reaction," Sarek said quietly.

Father and son gazed at each other in silent accord.

Laser torch in hand, s'Kara straightened up slowly from her crouch beside the massive combination planter-harvester. Overhead, Kadura's small orange sun, Rana (Delta Eridani), was trying to break through the winter cloud cover . . . and almost succeeding. s'Kara turned her face up, enjoying the brush of warmth against her dark green Orion skin. Her short, curly black hair, liberally shot with the gold threads of age, stirred in the chill breeze that cooled the sweat on her forehead.

Looking off across the fields, rusty brown instead of summer blue-green, s'Kara let her gaze wander to her village of Melkai. There were snug little homes, painted in shades of blue, yellow, green, and mauve, their rooftops black and studded with solar collecting cells.

The Orion woman grimaced a little as she rubbed her back with one hand. Squatting beneath the combine all morning while she tried to weld its sequencer into position again was a sure guarantee of a backache to come. Still, the combine would have to be used soon for planting, for spring, despite the cold grayness of the sky, was only a few weeks away.

With a heartfelt groan, s'Kara bent her knees and prepared to squat beneath the machine again, laser torch poised.

Just as she ducked to crawl beneath the combine, a dark shadow loomed overhead. s'Kara caught it out of the corner of her eye and involuntarily looked up.

What was that? she wondered. *It almost looked like a ship going by.*

s'Kara's heart pounded as she slid back out into the open and stood up. Her eyes widened with fear.

A ship was swooping in for a landing not half a *tem* away—a Klingon ship. *Klingons! Great Mother of us all, help your children! Klingons!* Heart slamming so hard she could scarcely breathe, s'Kara fought the impulse to crawl back beneath the combine and hide.

Stories of rape, murder, and stomach-churning atrocities ran through s'Kara's mind as she began to run toward the settlement. She had to warn them!

Hearing a shout from behind her, she forced her legs to an even swifter pace, the chill air hurting her lungs. The whine of a stun ray filled her ears. Dodging frantically, she raced across the field, her feet flying so fast that she feared she'd overbalance and fall, breath sobbing in her chest.

The whine came again—

—and, without knowing quite what had happened to her, s'Kara found herself lying on her face in the field, completely helpless. Her eyelids were closed, and she couldn't open them. Frantically, she tried to pray as she lay there, wondering how long the stun beam would hold her. Her muscles screamed with pain, but she couldn't adjust her position by so much as a *sendisat*.

Time went by . . . s'Kara finally began counting her own heartbeats, and had reached 412 when she heard footsteps approaching. A voice barked an order in Klingonese, and the whine came again. Abruptly, she could move, and her entire body convulsed in agony as all her muscles went into spasms. Rough hands grabbed her, hoisted her up. Klingons . . . five of them, all armed. One of them grinned, showing a mouthful of snaggleteeth, and reached for the front of her insulated coverall, clearly intending to rip it open.

s'Kara closed her eyes tightly. She braced herself—only to have another of the Klingons reach out and strike down the hand of her would-be attacker. He snarled something that sounded like an order, and the other Klingon reluctantly stepped back.

This Klingon was wearing a more elaborate metal sash across his broad shoulders. He eyed her, then said, with a strong accent, "Do you speak Standard, woman?"

s'Kara nodded. "Yes, I do."

"Good. We talk, you translate. Help us, and you will not be harmed."

A shrill shriek rent the air, and s'Kara darted an anguished glance in the direction of the village. Another scream followed.

"We are under Federation protection, here," s'Kara told the leader. "When they find out what you are doing, it will mean war with your government."

The leader uttered a short, ugly bark of laughter. "We have no government, woman. We are our own law, our own government. I am Commander Keraz. You will address me as 'my lord.' Is that understood?"

s'Kara nodded sullenly. One of the Klingons holding her cuffed her sharply. She took a deep breath. "Yes, my lord."

"Better."

All of them glanced up as yet another Klingon bird-of-prey hurtled out of the sky. Keraz gave an order to one of his men, and the Klingon trotted off.

"We will go into the village," Keraz said to s'Kara. "We will assemble the people. You will speak to them in your own language. What you will tell them is this: We are in control, and we will stay in control. As long as they obey us, they will not be harmed. Resist, and we will kill them—or worse. Is that clear?"

s'Kara stared at him, wanting so badly to spit right into his swarthy face that her jaw muscles worked. He watched her as though she were some kind of mildly interesting insect. After long seconds, s'Kara nodded, then, as one of her guards raised his hand, said hastily, "Yes, my lord."

Another scream rose out of the village—a scream that was cut off in the middle by a whine of disruptor fire. s'Kara tensed, her throat an aching knot of despair. Keraz nodded at her guards, and they all started across the field, passing the big combine.

I will survive this, Klingon, s'Kara thought grimly. *When this is over, I will be alive, and free—and you will be sorry. By the Mother Goddess, I swear it . . .*

As the little party entered the village, s'Kara forced herself to note every horror they passed, so she could tell the authorities when they came. They *would* come, she told herself. The Federation took care of its own. They *would* come. . . .

But would anyone still be alive to be rescued?

"What is this threat to the Federation, Father?" Spock asked, later that same day, as he and Sarek walked in the gardens behind the villa. Sarek's young aide, Soran, was watching the monitors that would signal when Amanda awoke again. "You aroused my curiosity with your reference to the Keep Earth Human League."

Overhead, Nevasa was past its zenith, declining toward the horizon, but sunset was still more than an hour away. Sarek glanced about him at the stark beauty of his wife's garden. Then he quietly spoke of the Freelans, summarizing his discovery that they were actually Romulans in disguise, and speaking of his discoveries aboard the Freelan space station.

"I have been collecting data for over a year," he finished. "I would appreciate it if you would review it for yourself tonight."

Spock nodded. "If it were anyone else telling me of this, I would dismiss his words as illogical paranoia," the Starfleet officer said slowly. "That you have seen proof of your theory convinces me, but . . . how did you know? What made you suspect the Freelans?"

Sarek had known that Spock would ask. The ambassador drew a deep breath, steeling himself. "It is a long story," he began. "One that I did not think I would ever speak of to another."

His son raised an eyebrow inquiringly. "Obviously you have access to information the rest of the Federation does not. How did you obtain it? The Freelans are the most secretive of beings. . . . No one has ever seen a Freelan without his or her mask. . . ."

Slowly, deliberately, Sarek shook his head from side to side. "Not true," he said, heavily. "*I* have seen the face of a Freelan. When the incident first occurred, I remained silent about it for nearly seventy Standard years, because I could not be sure of what I saw that day. But now . . . now the puzzle is complete, and I must inform the authorities of what I have discovered."

"Seventy years?" Spock was clearly taken aback. "Please elucidate."

Pacing over to the bench that faced T'Rukh, Sarek sank down, arranging his robes meticulously while he searched for words. "It began when I was a diplomatic attaché at the Vulcan Embassy on Earth . . . some seven years before I met your mother. I had been bonded to T'Rea, the priestess"—the ambassador used the archaic Vulcan word *reldai,* which in the old days, when Vulcan was ruled by the theocracy, meant both "female religious leader" and "female ruler or princess"—"as was traditional, when we were both seven years of age. I had not seen T'Rea since we were children; she was a stranger to me."

Sarek paused, remembering his first wife as she'd looked the last time he'd seen her . . . her intense black eyes, her arrogant beauty, her proud, stern features. Mostly he remembered her hair, a rippling obsidian curtain that had hung down past her hips. It had felt as silken as her diaphanous wedding robe.

"As the newest of the diplomatic attachés on Earth, many of the routine or less-desirable tasks fell to me," Sarek continued after a moment. "One of those was being appointed the diplomatic liaison to Freelan. I was fifty-nine Standard years old, and had not yet experienced my first Time. I knew that most males undergo their first Time in their thirties or early forties, so this delay was somewhat unusual. . . ." He shrugged slightly. "But I also knew that residence off-world could affect one's cycle, and I had lived much of the past fifteen years on Tellar, Earth, and several other worlds. Many factors, as you know only too well, Spock, can affect the onset and frequency of our Times."

Spock nodded gravely.

"It was raining that day in San Francisco when the ambassador summoned me to his office," Sarek continued, his voice deepening as the memories took hold, transporting him back to the past. "I was still new enough to Earth to find such an abundance of precipitation fascinating . . . even mesmerizing.

"I had been the liaison to Freelan for three years at that time. Freelan had only come to the attention of the Federation shortly before I was appointed, so, as it happened, I was the first person to travel to that distant world to discuss trade policies."

"How many trips had you made?"

"Over the course of three years . . . seven in all," Sarek said, after a moment's thought. "Naturally, of course, I was not permitted to set foot on Freelan soil. I stayed on board their space station."

"Had you ever met a Freelan personally?"

The ambassador shook his head. "No. At that time, no one had. They did not leave their world until decades later. All contact was by comm link. Despite all this, my contact on Freelan, a diplomatic attaché named Darov, was someone I had come to know and respect over the years. Darov and I had fallen into the habit, following a day's negotiation, of playing chess after our respective evening repasts. Darov was a challenging player," the older Vulcan continued after a moment. "Many of our contests ended in a draw, and, more than once, I lost."

His son raised an eyebrow in surprise. "That is indeed . . . impressive," he murmured. It had been many years since father and son had sat down to a game, but the last time they had played, Sarek had still been able to win more than half the time.

"As we played, we talked . . . about many things. Darov was careful not to reveal much in the way of information about his people, or himself, but, over the years, I learned some things about the Freelans that outsiders did not know. For example, I knew that Darov was young, about my own age, that he was married, and had a family that he was quite . . . devoted . . . to. A son and two daughters, I believe."

"Did you gain any knowledge of Freelan society and culture?"

"Yes, though Darov was extremely cautious and secretive. I gathered that his political leanings tended toward the moderate. Darov favored increased contact with other worlds . . . while the Freelan government's official position was that outsiders constituted a potential threat to the Freelan way of life."

"Darov wanted to change the way his world interacted with others?"

"I gained that impression over the years," Sarek said, "though he never said so specifically."

"Fascinating," Spock murmured. "You did indeed learn more than is generally known even now about Freelan and its people. I had no idea the Freelans had political parties, or that not all Freelans favored their isolationist policies."

"There are many things you do not know about the Freelans," Sarek said gravely. "That day in San Francisco, Ambassador Selden assigned me to travel to Freelan to conduct trade negotiations concerning ore that had recently been discovered on a moon in the Freelan system. This ore, crysium, was a vital element in the construction and use of a new diagnostic and treatment machine recently developed by the Healers at the Vulcan Science Academy."

Sarek's mouth quirked ironically. "At the time the ambassador spoke with me, I was experiencing some minor physical symptoms of illness . . . I had not been sleeping or eating well. I considered asking him to send another in my place. But I told myself that my symptoms were simply those of mild fatigue due to overwork, and that a chance to rest aboard ship would be beneficial. . . ."

As Sarek talked, the memory of that fateful voyage and its aftermath grew in his mind, eclipsing for the moment his surroundings. Amanda's garden faded into the neutral-colored walls of his tiny cabin aboard the freighter *Zephyr.* . . .

Soft skin beneath his hands, long, silken hair spilling over his body, the brush of a mind that inflamed him past all ability to resist . . . Sarek groaned aloud as he reached for T'Rea. She wore only the diaphanous overtunic of her wedding garb, and he could clearly see her body beneath the silken fabric.

The sight of her made him gasp and tremble; his mind and body were aflame, hot as the sands of Gol, burning like the volcanoes that tormented T'Rukh, searing him beyond all ability to resist. Sarek reached for his bride, his hands catching in her garment, ripping it, and then he was touching her flesh. . . .

With a gasp and a muffled cry, he sat upright on his narrow bunk aboard the *Zephyr,* realizing that he had been dreaming. He was shaking violently, so aroused that it was several minutes before he could discipline his mind to overcome the fever racking his body.

So this is what it is like, Sarek thought finally, when he could once more think rationally. Pon farr . . . *and I am parsecs away from Vulcan, and T'Rea . . .*

Through their bond, he could sense her, knew that her body was experiencing that drawing, even as his was. For a moment he wondered what it would be like to be married to her for the rest of his life, but the rest of his life seemed like an insubstantial, faraway thing in comparison to the heat of his desire.

The drawing was physical pain, his need to mate was torture. How long before he succumbed to the madness, the *plak tow?* Grimly, Sarek set about using biocontrol techniques to subdue the *pon farr* so he could reason logically.

Minutes later, he rose from his bunk, outwardly composed, inwardly more at peace. It was early, yet. He had several days . . . perhaps a standard week . . . before the blood-fever would consume him utterly.

Vulcan was five days away. Should he request that the captain take him to Vulcan instead of docking at Freelan's space station in an hour?

Sarek shrank from the idea that anyone—any outworlder, any *human*—might see him in his extremity. And yet . . . surely he could hold out for a day, maintain control long enough to meet with Darov and formalize the ore-trade agreement. Much of the negotiation had already been accomplished via subspace messages back and forth.

Surely Sarek could handle one day's work before sealing himself into his cabin and preparing to wait out the agony before he could reach Vulcan and his wedding.

T'Rea . . . He had met her only a few times, and not ever in the past twenty years. T'Rea had become an Acolyte of Gol, and her mental skills were formidable. People spoke of her with respect, and a little awe. Rumor had it that she was a candidate to ascend to the rank of High Master.

Was she now High Master? What would it be like to be wed to the High Master of Gol, someone whose telepathic skills greatly exceeded his own modest ones? What would it be like to be wed to someone who had achieved *kolinahr*—a person who had succeeded in purging all emotion from her being? Someone who lived by Perfect Logic?

For a moment something in Sarek rebelled at the realization that there could be no personal sharing between himself and such a woman, no intimacy, no . . . companionship. No warmth. No . . . kindness, no gentleness.

After a moment he pushed the thought away, rejecting it as illogical. His work was in the diplomatic corps . . . he lived on his homeworld only a few days each year. He and T'Rea would live apart, that was the only logical solution. They would meet during their Times, and that would be all.

And children? a voice whispered inside him. *What if there are children?*

It was unlikely that the High Master of Gol would have either the time or the inclination to raise children, Sarek decided. If a child should be born as a result of this Time . . . his blood heated at the thought of the act necessary to engender a child . . . then he would take that child to raise. His work was difficult, requiring much traveling, but a child, especially an older child, would gain much from such exposure to the universe and its varied cultures.

A soft chime came from the intercom; then the steward's voice informed the Vulcan that the *Zephyr* would be docking with the Freelan station in thirty Standard minutes.

Sarek spent half of those minutes in deep meditation, checking his biocontrol, verifying that the mental barriers he had set up against the heat in his blood were holding, would hold long enough for him to accomplish his duty. The moment the negotiations with Darov were concluded, he would return to *Zephyr* and order her captain to take him to Vulcan at the freighter's maximum warp.

Then he would lock himself in his cabin for the duration of the trip, and fight to keep control over the madness that would be nibbling at the fringes of his mind.

Minutes later, dressed and outwardly as cool and composed as usual, Sarek walked through the short tunnel linking the *Zephyr*'s airlock with the Freelan station.

The station was empty at the moment, save for him . . . there were no other outworlders staying here as they met with the Freelans on the planet below via comm link. Sarek was relieved that he would be spared the necessity of engaging in small talk with other beings. He did not even enter his sleeping quarters—a neutral, pastel chamber as bland as any hotel room—but bypassed them to go directly into the adjoining office with its comm link.

Within moments, Darov's figure materialized before him. Sarek was used to facing the cowled, swathed figure, completely muffled in shimmering garments as colorless as a Taka moth's wing. Darov's mechanical voice echoed in his ears. "Greetings, Liaison Sarek! I was not expecting you until this afternoon."

"My ship made good time," Sarek said neutrally. "Greetings to you, Liaison Darov, I trust you are well?"

"Entirely, thank you," Darov said, and Sarek imagined that he could hear a touch of genuine warmth tingeing the artificial voice. "And you? Perhaps you will honor me with a game of chess after we conclude our meeting?"

Sarek bowed slightly. "I regret that I must respectfully decline, Darov. I am . . . fatigued, and am looking forward to reaching my homeworld, so I may rest."

Darov's cowl jerked slightly forward, as if the Freelan had moved his head suddenly to peer at Sarek's face. But the liaison said only, "How unfortunate that you are not feeling up to playing. I will miss our game . . . it has become one of the few pleasures I still allow myself, with my busy schedule." He straightened slightly, briskly. "If you are not well, let us by all means conclude these few points quickly, so that you may rest. Shall we begin?"

"Certainly," Sarek replied, activating half of the screen to show the data he had brought concerning the crysium ore. "Now, concerning these subsidiary mining rights . . ."

Hours later, they were nearly finished, when Darov suddenly turned his head, then announced, "Excuse me, Sarek. I am being summoned on a priority channel. Would you wait for a moment?"

"Certainly, Darov," Sarek said. The Freelan's image vanished, and he busied himself going over the points they had negotiated. He experienced a brief flare of satisfaction at his own performance. He'd protected Vulcan's interests in all major areas, while giving in on minor points that would no doubt allow Darov satisfaction regarding his own negotiation strategies.

Halfway through the list, the Vulcan attaché gasped suddenly as pain lanced through his mind and body like a phaser blast. T'Rea! Her desire called to him, reached out for him, threatened to engulf him. *Wait*, he attempted to transmit along the bond, *I am coming to you. . . .*

"Sarek? *Sarek?* Sarek, are you—" Dimly, Darov's voice reached the Vulcan. He swayed, opening his eyes, found himself still in his seat, clutching the comm board as though it were a lifeline.

"I . . . am fine," the Vulcan managed after a moment. "Perhaps a brief rest . . ."

"I did not know that Vulcans could lie . . . until now," Darov said flatly. The shrouded figure of the alien nearly filled the comm screen, as though he were leaning forward, peering intently at the Vulcan attaché. "Our station has a fully equipped automated med center. Perhaps you should—"

Agony lanced through Sarek again, rolled over him in waves so crushing that they left nothing in their wake except blackness . . . a dark so deep that it had no end, a dark that should have been cool, but was instead an inferno of black flame, and he was burning, burning, burning . . .

Hands on his shoulders, a voice in his ears, calling his name. T'Rea? He lunged blindly at the hands, at the body he sensed hovering over his, pulling at him, dragging him.

T'Rea! It had to be she, for the hands on his shoulders were not cool, as human hands were, but the same temperature as his own fevered flesh. It must be T'Rea!

Sarek called her name, reaching out, then opened his eyes to see a dark form bending over him. Moments later he was lifted in arms as strong as his own, lifted and carried. "T'Rea . . ." he gasped, only to hear a male voice say, "No, she is not here. Come, I will help you."

Not T'Rea? A male? A *rival?*

He was being challenged! T'Rea had chosen the *kal-if-fee*—how dare she? Enraged, Sarek thrashed, striking out, then found himself falling. He crashed to the deck of the space station with stunning force.

(Space station? Wasn't he on Vulcan?)

But he had no time to ponder his location, for his rival was bending over him, grappling with him. With a bellow, Sarek struck out, grabbing madly at the other male's dimly seen figure, his hands seeking the challenger's throat.

Cloth met his fingers, impeded them from their goal. Snarling, Sarek ripped savagely, felt the cloth give and come away in his hand.

(But he was on the Freelan space station, wasn't he? Wasn't this Darov, who was trying to save him? This couldn't be a rival Vulcan!)

But it was. As the shrouding cloth parted, Sarek saw features swim before his eyes—features that nearly mirrored his own! He was right! A Vulcan male was trying to take T'Rea from him! He must kill him, kill him . . . *kill* him . . .

(A voice crying out, a voice he recognized, despite its lack of mechanical quality. Darov's voice, calling his name . . . and those were Darov's features? Slanting black brows, proud black eyes, high cheekbones chiseled like his own, black hair, rumpled now from their struggle, and, amid the black locks, ears that were . . . that were—)

"I regret this, my friend," the dimly seen figure said, as Sarek froze in shocked confusion. The arm drew back; then Sarek saw the shoulder roll forward with sudden movement. Something struck him hard on the chin, and he knew no more. . . .

"What happened then?" a voice said, pulling Sarek out of the haze of memory into which he had sunk. The sun was setting behind him, and, before him, T'Rukh loomed at full phase, T'Rukhemai disappearing behind it. Spock was gazing at him intently.

"Obviously you survived to reach Vulcan. How did you manage it, if you were deep in *plak tow?*"

"When I regained consciousness," the ambassador said, "I was in the med center aboard the Freelan space station, and I was alone. The automated machinery had evidently diagnosed my condition, then administered sedatives and hormones that allowed me to function with some semblance of normalcy. It also helped that T'Rea, unknown to me, had contacted the consulate on Earth, discovered that I was several days' journey away from home, and was shielding her mind, blocking me from reading her . . . desire . . . through our bond.

"Under the influence of the medication, I reboarded my ship, which reached Vulcan before the end of the fifth day. My marriage ceremony took place less than one hour after the *Zephyr* achieved orbit around Vulcan."

"And that was when Sybok was conceived?"

Sarek slanted a surprised glance at Spock. It wasn't like his son to ask such personal questions . . . but perhaps that was because he'd never given him an opening before. "Yes," the ambassador replied simply. "T'Rea hid his birth from me, though. I did not know he existed until her death, years later. When she ascended to be High Master of Gol, two years after our wedding, she divorced me. This was legal, under the ancient laws, because the High Master is expected to sever all ties to the outside world in order to more fully embrace *kolinahr* and the teaching of that discipline to the Acolytes."

"Did you regret her action?" Spock asked. Two highly personal questions!

The ambassador took a deep breath. "No, I did not. I was immersed in my work, and had just been appointed under-ambassador. Besides," he added, with a glance at the villa, "if T'Rea had not divorced me, I would not have been free when I met your mother. My relationship with Amanda is eminently more . . . satisfying . . . than anything I shared with T'Rea during our single, brief encounter. She was . . ." Sarek paused, remembering. " . . . a typical *kolinahru.*"

"What really happened that day with Darov?" Spock asked. *"Pon farr* can . . . distort . . . one's sense of reality."

"Precisely. For that reason, I dismissed what had happened as a *plak tow*–induced hallucination," Sarek replied. "I concluded that I must have blundered around the station, at one point running into a mirror and deciding that my own reflection was a challenger in the *kal-if-fee* . . . then, by sheer happenstance, wandered into the med center, where the automated equipment took over and saved my life."

"Under the circumstances, that would be the most logical deduction," Spock agreed. "But now you know that is not true."

"Yes. My first suspicion of that was when your ship, the *Enterprise*, discovered twenty-seven Standard years ago that the Romulans, whose faces no one had ever seen, were plainly of Vulcan stock."

"Indeed," Spock said, obviously recalling the incident. One corner of his mouth twitched. "I recall the first moment when our viewscreen gave us a glimpse of the Romulan commander. It is odd that you mention that Darov bore a resemblance to you . . . because this Romulan did, also. I was rather startled when I first saw his image on-screen."

"Perhaps he and Darov were related in some way," Sarek speculated. "At any rate, from that time on, I could not dismiss the notion that the Freelans were not what they seemed. Two years ago, when the Romulans began to emerge as a serious military threat to the security of the Federation, I began researching Freelan exhaustively. As I did so, a pattern emerged."

"What kind of pattern?" Spock asked.

"I believe that the Romulans are behind the sudden popularity and high-profile activities of the Keep Earth Human League," the ambassador replied.

Spock blinked. "Please explain that allegation. How could the Freelans have anything to do with the KEHL? The KEHL is against all extraterrestrials . . . including Romulans."

Sarek rose from the bench and began pacing back and forth as he spoke. "Consider, Spock. Every time the KEHL has experienced an upsurge in growth, at least one Freelan has been attending a diplomatic, trade, or scientific conference within the same city."

Spock raised an eyebrow. *"Every* time?"

His father nodded.

"What are you postulating, Father? Some form of mass coercion? Drugs? Hypnotism?" The younger Vulcan could not disguise his skepticism.

Pausing in midstride, Sarek turned to regard his son levelly. "Mental influence." His words were clipped, terse. Quickly, he summarized his encounter with Induna, and what he'd discovered from the KEHL leader's mind.

"But Romulans do not have the ability to meld or mind-touch," Spock protested. "It could not have been a Freelan who influenced the KEHL president."

"I know that Romulans do not share the Vulcan telepathic ability," Sarek said, somewhat sharply. "I am not suggesting that they are influencing KEHL members personally. During the past three years, Freelans have begun using Vulcan secretaries and aides in increasing numbers. Have you noticed this?"

He watched his son in T'Rukh's lurid illumination as Spock mentally reviewed the data stored in his mind. "I have only recently begun attending diplomatic conferences, but you are correct. Every time I have seen a Freelan envoy, he or she *has* been accompanied by a Vulcan secretary or aide. The Khitomer Conference is a case in point."

"Yes," Sarek said. "Soran was rather taken with the Freelan aide he met there."

"Father, the practice of hiring Vulcans as administrative aides is hardly unusual."

"True," Sarek agreed. "Many young Vulcans take employment on other worlds as a way of traveling after completing the first stage of their education. However . . ." He fixed his son with an intent gaze, his voice dropping to a near-whisper. "None of those Freelan secretaries or aides were born on Vulcan."

"Indeed?" Spock blinked, then his eyes narrowed. "Fascinating . . ." he murmured, suddenly comprehending what the other was saying. "None of them?"

The elder Vulcan shook his head. "None. Including the young woman named Savel. I have traced every young Vulcan traveling off-world for the past five years . . . and no records show that any of them have been hired by Freelans."

"Yet I saw the Freelan envoy with her at his side myself," Spock said. "I recall them clearly."

"As do I," Sarek agreed. "But whoever that young Vulcan woman was, she was not born on this world."

"Then where did those young Vulcans who are influencing the KEHL leaders come from?" Spock asked.

"They came from Freelan." Sarek's voice was harsh and flat, and he swallowed to ease the dryness in his throat. "Spock, the Romulans have been systematically hijacking ships with Vulcan passengers for decades. I have studied the shipping reports, the passenger lists, for every nearby sector, and there is an eighty-six-point-seven-percent correlation between the disappearance of a ship and the presence of one or more Vulcans on board."

"Continue," Spock said, his expression grim.

"It is my belief that those abducted Vulcans were taken to Freelan and forced to produce offspring. Their resulting children grew up under Romulan influence and training—and they serve the Romulans. These children learned to use their telepathy in ways Vulcans raised on this world are taught to abhor."

Spock was quick to follow the ambassador's logic. "So now we have Freelan envoys, merchants, and scientists traveling to Earth and the Terran colonies on a regular basis, most of whom are accompanied by a Vulcan secretary, or aide. And those young Vulcans, trained in Vulcan mental disciplines, but lacking our ethical prohibitions, are using their telepathy as they mingle among the populace. They influence humans with a buried streak of xenophobia, inflaming them into becoming prime material for the KEHL."

"Exactly," Sarek said. "I must admit that at first I doubted that Vulcan telepathy, which is traditionally accomplished by touch, could be used for such a purpose." He paused for a second, then continued in a lower tone, "However, recent events have convinced me otherwise."

Spock nodded, a shadow in his eyes mirroring the sadness in his father's. "Sybok," he said. "I saw him influence minds from a considerable distance. His mental powers were . . . unusual, however. But the ability to influence minds more subtly . . . I possess that capacity myself."

This time it was the ambassador's turn to raise an eyebrow. "Really? I did not know that."

"I have done so several times," Spock admitted. "Though never to effect any lasting mental impression or change in the subject's mind. But I did it on Eminiar Seven, and again on Omega Four." He paused. "And I am only half-Vulcan. Thus I find the possibility of Vulcan offspring who possess the mental abilities, without the ethical constraints we are taught, entirely plausible. And . . . disquieting."

Spock was silent for a moment; then he asked, "Did you ever discuss with Darov what happened that day you went into *pon farr?* You said that you were friends. . . ."

"I might have," the ambassador said. "Except for the fact that I never saw Darov again. I never discovered what had become of him. I suspect he was executed for helping me that day. Darov was replaced by Taryn. My impression of him is that he is considerably younger than Darov . . . though I cannot be certain, of course, since I never knew Darov's age. He is a far different individual. Much colder . . . and possessing, I believe, a formidable intellect. We have never discussed politics, but I am certain that Taryn is far from the moderate Darov was." Sarek paused, thinking. "I have gained the impression, over the decades, that the liaison is . . . patriotic. Possibly a zealot."

Spock raised an eyebrow as he considered the ambassador's words. "If he is indeed a wing commander, that would not be surprising. Many high-ranking Romulan officers favor all-out war with the Federation."

The Starfleet officer rose from the bench to pace beside his father along the garden paths. "My final question is, *why?* Obviously, all of this . . . the Freelan base, the captured Vulcans, the KEHL—this entire plan took years . . . *decades* . . . to set into motion. What do the Romulans hope to gain?"

Sarek did not answer directly. Instead he asked, "What are the goals of the KEHL?"

"As I understand them . . . to remove all nonterrestrials from Earth itself. Especially Vulcans."

"Not just from Earth," Sarek said. "From the Federation itself. I have researched the KEHL, also. The organization is adamantly opposed to the continued presence of Vulcan as a member of the Federation."

Spock nodded slowly. "That does not surprise me." His features tightened. "If the Romulans are successful in driving a wedge between Earth and Vulcan, to the point where Vulcan either secedes or is expelled from the Federation, then Earth will have lost its most powerful ally."

"Yes," Sarek said. "A Federation without Vulcan would be weakened in many ways. Also consider: What is the current situation with the Klingons?"

"Extremely unstable. When I left the *Enterprise,* we were orbiting a planet whose colony had been devastated by a Klingon attack. Chancellor Azetbur assured us that the raiders were renegades, and that she was attempting to capture them and bring them to justice. I believe her, but many others will not. The entire Federation/Klingon situation is unstable. James Kirk referred to it last week as 'a powder keg waiting for a spark.'"

"An essentially correct, if somewhat dramatic way of putting it," Sarek said, dryly.

"Instability in the Federation could well provide such a spark," Sarek continued. "Azetbur's government is struggling to stay in power. She has popular support, but many of the older, high-ranking families object to having a woman as chancellor. A number of high-ranking officers have turned renegade, deserting the fleet and using their vessels to commit acts of piracy."

"Actions which only fuel the xenophobia the KEHL is fostering."

"Precisely." Bathed in T'Rukh's garish light, Spock's features were drawn so tightly they appeared fleshless, skull-like. "It is also possible that the Freelans are using their trained Vulcans to influence high-ranking Klingons . . . formenting dissent, inciting the Empire into civil upheaval, and then war with the Federation. The humans have an ancient phrase for such strategy: 'Divide and conquer.'"

"Indeed," Sarek agreed. He sighed wearily, feeling himself relax for the first time in . . . how long? He could not tell. . . .

"My son, it is a . . . relief . . . to speak of this all, after holding silent so long," the ambassador said, sinking down onto another bench. "I have discussed my conspiracy theory with only two people before you—Soran, just recently, and your mother. It is difficult to know who to trust. Any high-ranking official could now be under Freelan influence."

Spock shook his head slightly as he considered that. "A situation that might justifiably induce paranoia," he concurred.

"Last year, when I first began to suspect that the Freelans were using telepathy to influence people, I advised all members of Vulcan's diplomatic corps to work on strengthening their mental disciplines, so they could not only detect, but shield against, any attempt at mental influence. I traveled to Gol nearly every day for months, training with one of the high-ranking Acolytes."

"I learned similar techniques while I was at Gol," Spock was quick to assure his father. "My shielding is better than average."

"Good." Sarek gazed around him at the garden in T'Rukh's waning light. "All indications are that the Romulan plan is reaching fruition. I hypothesize that we may have only months . . . perhaps less . . . to act to stop them."

"What is your recommendation?"

"First, we must gain concrete proof of the Freelans' true identity and purpose in order to expose them. Your skills with computers equal my own. It is my hope that, working together, we can break into the Freelan system more successfully than I was able to that first time. Then we can download their memory banks."

"That would constitute indisputable proof," Spock agreed. "We must present that proof in open session of the Federation Security Council."

"I agree."

"We do have time," Spock said. "The KEHL is still a long way from influencing Earth to expel Vulcan from the Federation."

"Do not be too sure. Elections will be held in two months, and the KEHL is sponsoring many candidates . . . some openly, others with secret affiliations. Some of these candidates are vying for offices at very high levels in Earth's government."

Sarek rubbed his forehead as fatigue washed over him so strongly it seemed to gnaw at his bones; he felt every one of his 128 years. "Something else to consider, Spock: If the KEHL keeps growing, Vulcan will not struggle to remain a member of the Federation. Our people do not react well to being . . . insulted."

Spock nodded grimly. "I suggest that we discuss the matter with James Kirk and ask his help in gaining positive proof, and in bringing all of this before the Federation Security Council and the president."

"I agree," Sarek said.

It was full night now, and the temperature was dropping rapidly. The younger Vulcan glanced around him at the eerily lit garden and repressed a shiver. "It is late. We should go in."

"Yes. Your mother will be waking soon."

"So, you're Jim Kirk's nephew!" Commander Gordon Twelvetrees exclaimed, holding out his hand.

Standing stiffly at attention, Peter accepted the warm handshake from the tall, stately Lakota Indian who was Admiral Idota's aide. The admiral was one of Uncle Jim's friends, and while Peter hadn't really expected to find anyone in at such a late hour, he'd hoped to leave a message for Idota with the desk clerk. He was pleasantly surprised to find the admiral's aide still at work.

"Oh, at ease, son," the commander said, waving him to the couch in his office. He poured a cup of fresh, fragrant coffee into the fine Starfleet china that every admiral's office had, and handed it to the cadet.

Peter nodded his thanks, and took a sip. It wasn't anything like the brew at the cadet's commissary. This was a hearty, robust blend—Jamaican, probably. He relished the taste.

"You got lucky finding me here tonight," the commander said. "Usually I keep the same bankers' hours as the admiral."

The young Kirk smiled thankfully at his superior. "I'm glad you could see me. Why the late hours?"

"I was here waiting for a communiqué from the Neutral Zone. Something the admiral's been expecting. When they told me Jim Kirk's nephew had a problem . . ."

For once Peter didn't flinch at the reference to his relative. At times like this, being Uncle Jim's nephew came in handy.

"Thank you, sir. I'm most grateful for your time." He tugged his cadet's uniform into place, glad he'd taken the time to change and freshen up. He hesitated, trying to find the right place to begin, then finally started from the top, telling Twelvetrees about trying to meet Sarek for lunch, the demonstration, the riot and his involvement, and how he found himself at the local KEHL headquarters.

The story didn't take very long, and Twelvetrees never interrupted, listening to every word with complete attention. As he neared the end of his tale, Peter withdrew the three tapes with the pilfered information and showed them to the commander.

"I know it was probably a foolish thing for me to do, sir, to pretend to be a member of KEHL, but I felt it was a unique opportunity I couldn't pass up, in spite of the risks. And I think it's paid off. These tapes hold the entire files of their membership rolls, their agenda, and the stolen information they obtained from the Vulcan consulate. I think they're enough to discredit this organization for once and all. They're really getting dangerous, sir, and they're no longer willing to work within the law. Their violation of Vulcan communications alone is proof of that."

Commander Twelvetrees took the computer tapes almost reverently, staring at the innocuous bits of flat plastic as he turned them around in his big hands. "You certainly are a Kirk, son. That's the same thing Jim would've done in that very circumstance. He must be proud of you."

Peter was about to say that his Uncle Jim didn't know anything about this, when a troubling realization began gnawing at his gut. Despite the commander's words, he realized that the aide wasn't taking him seriously. Not at all.

Twelvetrees sat back against the couch, and pocketed the cassettes. "I want to thank you for the effort you took to obtain this information, Peter. Most people— working to complete their finals, cramming day and night—would only have their own personal problems in mind, and would've turned their back on this. You've got the kind of heart, the kind of backbone Starfleet needs to bring us successfully into the future. I won't forget what you've tried to do here. However . . ."

Peter felt as if ice crystals were forming in his stomach.

" . . . I have to tell you that Starfleet has had the KEHL under surveillance for quite some time. We've even had several people infiltrate the ranks. I can understand your alarm, but the truth is the KEHL is just a fringe-element, disorganized group. They've been gaining popularity due to the media exposure, and, unfortunately, we were understaffed at the consulate the day of the demonstration. But the KEHL is no threat to anyone, Peter."

"But . . . those tapes . . ." Kirk protested.

"Oh, don't worry, Peter . . . I'll take a look at these before I hand them over to Starfleet Security—just in case there's something in there we can use. They'll probably decide to warn the Vulcans about the breach in their security. But don't forget, none of the KEHL's plans have ever come to anything. And we both know there's no such thing as a Vulcan conspiracy." He stood, indicating the interview was at an end. "You have your navigational final tomorrow morning, don't you?"

"Yes, sir," Peter responded desultorily, as the commander walked him to the office door.

"You focus on that, son. I barely made it through that one myself. Don't you worry about these tapes, the KEHL, or anything but your exam. I'll make sure this information gets the attention it deserves, and if we find anything of any importance, I'll let you know." The commander extended his hand again as his doors whooshed open, practically demanding Peter's exit.

The young Kirk took the hand offered him. "Thank you, sir. And believe me, if you really look at that information, I think you'll be surprised . . . and concerned."

"Don't you worry, Peter," the commander assured him, his deep voice calming and sincere. "Starfleet Security has the situation well in hand. Thanks again for your concern."

Peter watched the doors slide closed behind him and slumped against the wall, despondently. He hadn't been born yesterday; he knew a kiss-off when he saw one. Despite the commander's promise, Peter couldn't shake the feeling that the officer was probably going to toss his tapes in the nearest recycler.

The cadet shrugged.

He could still get in a few good hours of studying if he hurried. The commander was right about one thing. If he was going to ace the navigational final, he'd need to be sharp, focused. Peter straightened up and squared his shoulders.

He'd get focused, all right. As soon as he tended to one more thing.

Minutes later, young Kirk strode briskly up to the communications center that sat in the center of the massive Starfleet Security headquarters.

"Can I help you, sir?" the young man manning the desk asked.

"Yes. I want to send a message to a Federation starship." Peter realized that he had no idea where his uncle was right now.

"And what ship is that, sir?" the operator asked casually.

"The *Enterprise*. I want to send a message to Captain James T. Kirk."

The communications clerk glanced up, faintly surprised. "Well . . . that ship is currently on assignment. A message could take a long time to . . ."

"Send it Priority One. I am Captain Kirk's nephew. It's regarding a family emergency."

"Of course, sir," the operator agreed, all business. He handed Peter a message pad and stylus. "If you'll encode your message here it will be sent on the private-messages channel, Priority One."

Peter picked up the pad, and, stylus poised, stood pondering just exactly what to say.

Spock stood waiting outside the door of his parents' room, forcing himself to remain still, hands clasped behind his back, his expression controlled, remote. Inwardly, however, the Vulcan wanted nothing more than to pace restlessly. Movement would have aided him in dispelling some of his disquiet.

This morning, the *Enterprise* had entered the Vulcan spacedock, and, in response to Spock's request that he evaluate Amanda's condition, Leonard McCoy had beamed down to the villa.

The doctor was currently in Amanda's room, examining his mother.

Spock's sensitive hearing picked up the swish of the pressure curtain moving aside, so he was prepared when the door opened, framing McCoy. The doctor's expression was somber as he walked out into the corridor.

In silence, the two officers went into Sarek's office. When the ambassador saw them, he rose from his desk and the three walked out to the living room. McCoy sank down on the couch and glanced around. "You have a lovely home, Ambassador Sarek."

The elder Vulcan inclined his head. "My wife's doing, for the most part," he said.

"The view outside is magnificent, too. I never saw anything like the Forge on any world I've visited."

"It is a relatively unique configuration," Sarek agreed.

Spock, who was sitting beside the medical officer on the couch, shifted impatiently. "Doctor . . . what did your examination indicate?"

McCoy shook his head. "I'm sorry, Spock. The Healers are correct. The Reyerson's is, for the moment, in remission. But I'm afraid that when I speak to Dr. T'Mal, I'm going to recommend that she halt your mother's treatments."

The first officer glanced quickly at his father, then back at the human. "Why, Doctor?"

"Because they're causing a tremendous strain on your mother's already frail system. While I was examining her, she suffered a small stroke—and my findings indicate that wasn't the first one."

"A stroke?" Spock half-rose from the couch.

"It was a good thing I was there. I was able to arrest it, and prevent any significant damage. My sensor readings indicate that she's had at least two others within the past week or so. Minor ones, but they take their toll."

"What is your prognosis, Dr. McCoy?" Sarek spoke for the first time in minutes.

"Well, I can't really say definitively. These things differ with individuals . . ." the human began, evasively.

Sarek stared levelly at the Starfleet medical officer. "With all due respect, I must remind you that you are not speaking to a human family, Doctor. Please do not dissemble."

McCoy took a deep breath. "All right." He stared levelly at the ambassador. "The Healer was, if anything, optimistic. I would say it's a matter of a few weeks . . . possibly only days."

Spock drew in a soft breath as the doctor's words struck him like a blow. It wasn't until that moment that the Vulcan realized, bitterly, that he'd hoped his old friend would be able to work some kind of miracle. *Illogical,* the Vulcan part of his mind whispered. *Illogical, if not irrational . . . hope is a human emotion.*

All at once he was acutely conscious of the automatic time sense marking off the hours, minutes, and seconds in his brain. Usually, the Vulcan never thought about it, unless he needed to, but suddenly, it was as pervasive as the ticking of some huge, old-fashioned Terran clock.

Time . . .

Amanda's time was running out.

Without a word to the others, he rose from his seat and headed for his room. Fingers numb, he pulled on rough, outdoor clothing and desert boots. He was not thinking, he was simply obeying a strong, almost instinctive need to move, to be outside, to walk the rough soil and climb the jagged stone of his homeworld.

The heat struck him as he headed into the hills, but Spock ignored it. He was too conscious of the seconds ticking away inexorably in his head. . . .

*   *   *

"Ambassador?" Sarek looked up at the sound of Soran's voice. The ambassador was sitting by Amanda's bedside, her hand in his, so he would be there when she awakened. On McCoy's advice, he had engaged a Healer's aide to monitor his wife's condition, but he and Spock had been taking turns remaining with her during most of their waking hours, ever since Dr. McCoy's revelation two days ago.

Now, seeing the concern in his young aide's eyes, the Vulcan hastily left the bedroom and stepped into the hallway. "What is it, Soran?"

"Ambassador, a priority call just came in for you from President Ra-ghoratrei," he said. "The president wishes to speak with you. He says it is urgent."

Sarek nodded a quick acknowledgment as he headed for his office. Moments later, he was seated before his comm link. A presidential aide recognized him, nodded briefly; then the image wavered and was replaced with that of the Deltan Federation president. Ra-ghoratrei nodded a somber greeting to the Vulcan.

"Ambassador Sarek. Your aide told me of your wife's illness. I regret having to call upon you at such a time, but I have no choice."

"What is it, Mr. President?"

"A band of Klingon renegades has captured an Orion colony—the planet Kadura—and they are holding several thousand colonists hostage. The Klingon leader is threatening to kill the hostages unless the Federation agrees to negotiate a release and monetary settlement with him." The president took a deep breath. "Ambassador . . . a great many lives hang in the balance. For this mission we need our best negotiator—and that is you. The meeting will take place on Deneb Four."

Sarek briefly reviewed what he knew of the conference center on Deneb IV. It was at least three days' journey at maximum warp. A week to go there and return, as well as whatever time the negotiations would require . . . he would probably be away from home for at least two weeks, possibly three . . .

The ambassador knew without consulting T'Mal or McCoy that, given her present condition, Amanda would probably not survive long enough for him to travel to the neutral site, handle the negotiations, and return. If he left his wife now, it was unlikely that he would ever see her alive again.

Nevertheless, there was only one logical course of action. The Vulcan took a deep breath. *It is my duty. I cannot risk so many lives. The needs of the many . . .* "I will go, Mr. President," he said, steadily.

Ra-ghoratrei breathed a sigh of relief. "The Federation thanks you, Ambassador. The hostages will now have the best chance to keep their lives and regain their freedom."

"I will need a complete report on the Klingon Commander," Sarek said. "I will depart this afternoon, provided my pilot can ready my transport. Send the information about this Klingon via subspace message, if you will."

"I will direct Admiral Burton, the head of Starfleet Security, to do so," the president promised.

"Very well. Sarek out."

"Thank you again, Ambassador. Out."

Rising from his seat, Sarek quickly gave Soran instructions to prepare for the journey. Then, knowing it was for the last time, he went to bid farewell to his wife.

"Amanda." The voice reached her in the darkness, pulling her back to light and awareness. The voice was familiar, known, beloved. An authoritative, precise voice with a faint resonance. Pleasantly deep, extremely cultured. The voice of her husband.

Amanda opened her eyes. Strong fingers grasped her hand gently but firmly. Sarek's fingers.

"Sarek," she murmured, gazing up into the face she had known and loved for so many years. "Have I been asleep long?"

"Several hours. My wife, I regret having to wake you, but I must speak with you . . . before I take my leave."

Amanda's eyes opened wider. "Leave?" she asked faintly, too weak to conceal the dismay his words caused her. "Why? Where are you going?"

"There is an emergency on the planet Kadura," Sarek said. "I just finished speaking to President Ra-ghoratrei. He asked me to negotiate the release of a Federation colony that has been seized by Klingon renegades. There are thousands of colonists whose lives are in jeopardy. I must go, Amanda. It is my duty."

Her heart contracted at his words. "How . . . how long will it take?" she asked, her words scarcely audible above the faint hum of the medical monitors. "Must you go?"

"Yes. I must take ship for Deneb Four within the hour. It is difficult to say how long I will be gone. Ten days, at the minimum. If the negotiations proceed slowly . . ." He trailed off and his fingers tightened slightly on hers.

"I see," Amanda whispered. "Very well, Sarek. I understand."

Her husband regarded her, his dark eyes shadowed with grief. Gently, he reached out and touched her hair, her cheek. "Amanda . . . if I could, I would stay here with you. You know that, do you not?"

Silently, she nodded, fighting to hold back tears. His dear, familiar face began to swim in her vision. *No!* she thought, blinking fiercely. *I will not cry. I will not let tears steal my last sight of you. I will not let weeping mar our last farewell.*

"Sarek . . ." she whispered, turning her fingers so her hand grasped his, returning the pressure. "I will miss you, my husband. I wish you did not have to go."

"I will return as soon as possible, Amanda," he promised, his eyes never leaving hers. "The instant Kadura is free, I will come home."

But you will almost certainly be too late, and we both know it. Amanda thought, her eyes never leaving his face for a moment. She hated even to blink. In a few minutes her husband would be gone, and she would never see him again . . . at least, not in this life.

"I want you to remember something," she said, struggling to keep her voice even.

"What, Amanda?"

"Never forget that I love you, my husband. Always." She gazed at him intently, holding his eyes with her own. "You will need to remember that, Sarek, very soon now. Promise me you won't forget."

"My memory is typical for a Vulcan," he said, quietly. "I forget very little, my wife."

"I know. But remembering my words in your head, and remembering them here," freeing her hand, she gently laid it on his side, where his heart lay, "are two different things. Promise me."

"You have my word, Amanda," he said, his dark eyes filled with profound sorrow.

I know that you love me, she thought, gazing up at him. *But I will not embarrass you by telling you so. . . .*

"Spock will be here with you," Sarek said. "Do not forget that, my wife."

"His presence will be a great comfort," she said, softly. Her gaze moved over his face, tracing the angular lines. Putting her hand up, she touched his cheek, his eyes, his lips, thinking of the many times she had kissed him there. "Sarek, hold me. I want to feel your arms around me. Hold me."

Gently, he reached forward, scooped her up, and cradled her against him. Amanda slid her arms around him and laid her head on his chest with a long sigh. Briefly, she abandoned herself to the moment . . . her soul was content. Finally she raised her head. "Sarek, I want you to promise me one more thing."

He had difficulty meeting her eyes . . . Amanda could tell through their bond that he was profoundly moved. "What is it, Amanda?"

"I want you to read my journals . . . afterward. Take the first one with you now, my husband. Promise me you'll read all of them. Please?"

Sarek nodded; then, with infinite gentleness, he helped settle her back onto the bed. Going into her sitting room, he returned with a slim, red-covered volume. On the spine was affixed the number 1. "This one?" he asked, holding it up.

"Yes, that one," Amanda said, regarding him steadily as she lay propped up on her pillows. "Read it. And when you've finished that one, go on and read the next . . . until you've read them all."

"I will do so, Amanda."

"I know you will," she said, and holding out her hand, two fingers extended, she smiled at him. Somewhere deep inside herself, she was crying, but she refused to let him see. *Let him remember me smiling,* she thought.

Her husband held out his hand, brushed two fingers against hers, and they remained that way for many seconds. Then, with a last, grave nod, Sarek walked away, pushing through the pressure curtain without looking back.

Spock saw the pressure curtain move; then his father appeared. The ambassador's eyes widened slightly as he realized that his son must have been listening to him as he bade farewell to his wife; then they narrowed with anger. Before his father could speak, the first officer signaled curtly for silence and beckoned the ambassador out into the hall.

Only when the *tekla* wood door was firmly closed did Spock turn to regard his father.

"Eavesdropping is discourteous, my son," Sarek said, and Spock could tell he was irritated, though his voice was carefully neutral.

Spock ignored the mild rebuke. He held his father's eyes with his own, and his own voice was cold. "Soran told me that the president called, and why. He also told me that you have ordered your transport prepared. You intend to go to Deneb Four?"

"Yes," Sarek said, eyeing his son with a touch of wariness. "I have just taken my leave of your mother."

"So I heard." Spock's voice cut like a shard of obsidian. "I must admit that I found it difficult to believe. You actually intend to *leave* her? In her present condition?"

"I must," Sarek said, quietly. "The needs of the many outweigh the needs—"

"To quote an appropriate human phrase, 'To hell with that,'" Spock broke in, his voice rough with anger and grief. "You cannot leave her like this."

"I recall a time," Sarek said, "when you chose to remain at your post, when only you could save *my* life."

Spock paused. "Yes," he said, after a moment, "but *I* have grown since then. It is a pity that you have not."

Sarek's eyebrow rose at his son's words and the unconcealed emotion. "Spock, we all have our duties to consider. The situation at Kadura is critical."

"So is my mother," the first officer said flatly. "She will not survive long enough for you to return, and you know it. Your leaving in itself will very likely hasten her end." He regarded his father unwaveringly.

The ambassador paused, and Spock knew that the thought of his leaving actually harming Amanda had not occurred to him until now. "You will be here with her," he said, finally. "She will not be alone."

"She needs her *family* with her," Spock said obdurately. "You are her bond-mate—her husband. Your loyalty should be to her. There are other diplomats on Vulcan. Senkar has handled situations of this nature before. Let him negotiate for Kadura's release."

"The president requested that I handle the negotiations personally," Sarek said.

"He cannot order you." Spock's gaze never wavered as he held his father's eyes. "Refuse . . . under the circumstances, no one will question your actions."

Sarek straightened his shoulders. "Spock, I have no more time to discuss this. I must leave now."

"You mean that you *wish* to leave," Spock said, his voice cold and flat. "You do not have the courage to stay and see her through this."

Answering anger sparked in Sarek's eyes. "I will not remain to hear such acrimonious—and illogical—outpourings, Spock. I suggest that you meditate and attempt to regain your control." He drew a deep breath, and added, in a tone that was intended to be conciliatory, "Remember, my son, you are Vulcan."

"At the moment, if you are any example, being Vulcan is hardly a condition to be desired," Spock snapped. Without another word, he brushed past his father and headed down the corridor. Behind him he could hear the ambassador's footsteps receding.

When Spock regained control, he gently opened the door to his mother's room, and entered, parting the pressure curtain with both hands.

Amanda was awake. Spock noted the unmistakable signs that she had been crying, but there were no tears present when she smiled at him wanly and held out her hand. "I was just about to eat my lunch," she said, nodding at a tray placed across her lap by the Healer's aide. "Would you like to join me, Spock?"

The Vulcan nodded and drew a chair up beside her bed. Amanda was making a valiant effort, he could tell, but she had to force herself to swallow several small mouthfuls. She smiled at him. "Do you know what I dreamt of last night?" she asked. "It was so strange . . . after all these years on Vulcan, being a vegetarian . . ."

"What, Mother?"

"I dreamt that I was eating an old-fashioned hamburger. It tasted wonderful—nice and rare, with cheese and lettuce and tomato. . . ." She smiled, shaking her head.

"If you would like one," her son said, "I will contact my ship and ask them to beam one down immediately."

"Oh, no, don't," Amanda said. "I'm sure that eating meat after all these years would make me quite ill. And the real thing could never match how good it tasted in my dream. . . ." She chuckled slightly. "But it was odd to dream about that after what . . . sixty years?"

"Indeed," Spock said, cautiously. He sensed that his mother was chattering on as a way of working herself up to what was really on her mind. Sarek, he thought, was probably aboard his transport and leaving orbit by now.

"Spock," Amanda said, softly, putting down her spoon and gazing at him directly, "what is death like?"

Spock stared at her for a long moment. How many times had he been asked this same question in the past three and a half years? Never before had he attempted an answer, but this time . . . he cleared his throat. "Mother, I cannot tell you what death is like. In a way, since my *katra* departed to reside in Dr. McCoy when my physical body expired, I was not truly dead, as humans understand the term."

"Oh," she murmured, disappointed. "I'm sorry if that question was . . . disquieting. My curiosity got the better of me . . . under the circumstances."

Spock forbore to comment on her reference to her "circumstances." Instead he said, gently, "I cannot tell you what death is . . . but I remember dying. I know what it is to die."

Amanda sat up a little straighter against her pillows, pushing her tray aside. Her blue eyes never left his. "Really? Tell me if you can, Spock."

"It was painful," Spock admitted, and if he had been human, he would have shuddered. "I had been exposed to enough radiation to literally burn me. In addition, my mind, while clear in some ways, was affected, and thus I could not control the pain. I suffered, but I knew before I even entered the chamber that I would not survive, so I also knew that I would not have to endure for long. . . ."

Amanda's eyes filled with tears. Spock knew that imagining her son burned, poisoned, and dying of massive radiation exposure was upsetting her. He hesitated, watching her. "Mother . . . if this is too painful for you, I will . . ."

"No," she said, fiercely. "It's a relief to talk about death, Spock. I couldn't, not with your father. It would have . . . distressed him too much. But you . . . you, of all people, you can understand."

"I do," he said, quietly. His hand slid across the coverlet and grasped hers, holding it tightly, reassuringly. "As my body shut down, the pain stopped, and I experienced relief when that happened. All the while I knew that I was dying, but as soon as the pain ceased, I realized with some surprise that I was not frightened, or distressed. It was more as if what was occurring was simply a further, entirely natural step in the order of things. I found myself at peace . . . such peace as I have never felt."

"Peace," Amanda whispered. "No fear?"

"Fear," Spock reminded her, "is a human emotion. No, Mother, there was neither fear nor pain. Do not forget that I had established a link between myself and McCoy, so I knew that my *katra* would . . . continue."

"No fear, no pain . . ." she mused, plainly attempting to envision such a state. "What was there, then?"

"For a moment, I had a sense that knowledge was waiting for me, infinite knowledge. It was a heady sensation, and lasted only for a moment—then my consciousness blanked out, and I did not return to awareness until I awakened on that pallet with T'Lar standing over me."

"Did you have a sense of an afterlife?"

"No, there was none of that. However, my *katra* was residing within Dr. McCoy, so I cannot categorically state that there is no afterlife."

"Do you believe in an afterlife?" his mother asked slowly.

"I do not know. I have no objective data to allow me to draw a conclusion."

Amanda smiled dryly. "Spoken like a true Vulcan, Spock."

Attempting to lighten the moment, the first officer bowed slightly. "Mother . . . you honor me."

"Oh, stop it," she said, chuckling despite everything. "You and your father . . . when you do that, I want to throw something at you!" She grasped one of the pillows, but her strength was not sufficient for her to make good on the implied threat . . . instead she sank back against her pillows, gasping.

Amanda's mention of his father caused all of Spock's anger to return full force. His mother did not miss the change in his expression, slight as it was. "Spock," she said, putting out a hand toward him, "try not to be angry with your father. Sarek is simply doing what he has to do, being who and what he is." Pride surfaced for a moment on her features. "And he *is* the best, Spock. Never forget that. Those people on Kadura could not have a better champion than your father."

"Senkar is also an experienced diplomat who has handled situations of this kind before. My father could have allowed him to negotiate with this Klingon renegade."

"You're really angry with him, aren't you?" Amanda's eyes were huge and full of distress. "Oh, Spock . . . long ago I begged Sarek to try and understand you, instead of simply judging you and finding you wanting. Now I ask you the same thing . . . try to understand your father! Forgive him . . . I know I do."

"Mother, I cannot," Spock said flatly. "You are his wife. His place is by your side."

Visibly upset, his mother closed her eyes, shaking her head as she lay limply against her pillows. "Oh, Spock . . . don't be so hard on him. We all make mistakes."

The Vulcan regarded her with concern, realizing that she was fighting back tears. He'd never meant to distress her. . . .

Spock put out a hand, closed it comfortingly over his mother's. "Very well, Mother. I will attempt to be more . . . understanding."

Amanda nodded weakly, her eyelids drooping. "Thank you, Spock. . . ."

The Healer's aide suddenly appeared from out of the shadows in the sitting room, where the monitor screens were placed. Motioning to Spock to go, she whispered, "She will sleep now, Captain Spock. I suggest you leave and return later."

The Vulcan nodded quietly, and left the chill room and the slight, silent form of his mother.

Peter Kirk unfastened the front of his uniform jacket even before the door to his apartment opened. His garments seemed to have absorbed some of the sticky fatigue that he felt must be seeping out of every pore. Stepping inside, he yanked the collar of his shirt open, feeling as if he were about to strangle.

He was so tired he wasn't even sure how well he did on his navigation exam. Oh, he was sure he'd passed, but this was one test he might not have aced. To know he might've dropped a grade because of the time he'd spent with the KEHL made him feel like a fool.

He tossed the tired uniform into the recycler. And as he did so, his comm link sounded, signaling an incoming call. Fearing it might be Lisa, Peter braced himself and accepted the call. He blinked in surprise when he found himself staring at his uncle. He'd only sent Jim that message early this morning, and the elder Kirk was the last person he'd expected to hear from. Uncle Jim couldn't possibly have gotten his message yet . . . could he?

"Hello, Peter," Kirk's image said, though he didn't smile.

"Uncle Jim!" the younger man exclaimed. "This is a surprise! I thought you were out near the Neutral Zone someplace!"

"I'm here in San Francisco," his uncle said, his words sounding clipped, as though he were rushed, or angry. He was wearing full uniform, but Peter couldn't tell where he was calling from . . . his uncle's image filled nearly the entire screen.

"You are? Well, that's great!"

"I'm at my apartment," Kirk said, solemnly. "I need to see you, Peter. Can you come over?"

The younger Kirk felt his spirits rise. If anyone would know how to deal with the KEHL, how to get around the skepticism of Commander Twelvetrees, it would be James T. Kirk.

"I need to see you, Peter," Jim repeated. "Can you come over here immediately?"

"Well . . . sure," Peter said, glancing at the chrono with an inward groan. He desperately needed about six hours' sleep. But if Jim needed him . . . "I'll be there as soon as I can. About half an hour."

"Good," Kirk said, and the comm link went dark.

Peter stared at the screen for a moment, puzzled. Something about the call seemed odd, but Peter decided his brief association with the KEHL was making him paranoid. Oh, well. He'd find out what was going on when he got there.

After a brisk sonic shower, he wearily dragged on the first clothes that came to hand—a pair of loose exercise pants and a baggy white shirt. Glancing at his chrono as he hastily ran a comb through his hair, he saw that it was a few minutes after midnight; Peter groaned inwardly. Another night's sleep ruined—and tomorrow he was supposed to work with Lisa again, bright and early. Not to mention that there were only a few days left before his *Kobayashi Maru* test!

I've got to slow down, or I'll drop in my tracks, he thought, as he left his apartment and hurried down the corridor toward the elevator.

He decided to walk; his uncle's apartment was only ten minutes away, and the brisk fall air would wake him up. It was a weekday, so there were few people out this late. The cool breeze nipped at him, and Peter wished belatedly that he'd thought to put on a jacket.

As he strode quickly down the sidewalk, not allowing his steps to lag, something moved in an alley to his left. In the glow of the streetlight, he caught a flash of silver. Peter checked, peering into the darkness, and a voice reached his ears. "Peter?"

The voice, though choked and breathless-sounding, was familiar. The cadet frowned and started toward the alley. "Lisa?" he called softly. "Is that you?"

A moment later, as his eyes adjusted to the darkness away from the streetlight, he saw her. She was walking toward him, obviously distressed. "Peter!"

"What is it, Lisa?" he asked, concerned. Much as he detested her bigoted views, he had grown attached to Lisa the woman. "Is something wrong?"

"Yes," she whispered, moving toward him. "It's . . . it's Induna. He needs us, Peter, he needs us terribly. I need you to come with me!"

"Well, I—"

The cadet caught a flash of movement out of the corner of his eye, felt a rush of air on his cheek, and, in accordance with all of Starfleet's training, ducked. As he moved to the side, a blow caught him across his upper arm with numbing force. Lisa gasped and frantically scuttled back, toward the mouth of the alley.

"Get help!" Peter yelled at her, as his assailants closed in. Two men, one tall, the other short, both burly, both obviously experienced street fighters. Peter lashed out with a side kick toward the shorter one's chest, but the man was too fast, and he hadn't struck hard enough. Accustomed to pulling blows in class, he did not connect with enough force to disable his opponent. Before he could follow up with a front punch, the taller man's fist smashed against his cheekbone with head-spinning force.

Training stood him in good stead as he reacted without thought, grabbing the man's shirtfront and turning his fall into a back roll. As he went down with the man atop him, Peter brought his knee up into the other's stomach, hearing the breath whoosh from his attacker's lungs.

Letting his opponent sail on over his head, Peter regained his feet in time to meet a rush from the shorter man. He struck at the man's neck, but again this one was too quick to allow the blow to land full-on.

Peter leaped at him, his body twisting in midair, his foot coming up in a tornado kick. *This* time he had the satisfaction of feeling his instep connect solidly with the side of the man's head. Shorty went down, and stayed down.

Whirling, hands and feet at the ready, Peter was just in time to block a blow from the tall man, but seconds later he took a smashing kick to his rib cage. Gasping for air, he aimed a back punch at the man's chest, and followed it up with a quick foot sweep.

Two down. Panting from the stabbing pain in his ribs, Peter spun, half-staggering, half-running as he headed for the mouth of the alley. He glimpsed Lisa's silver coat just ahead of him. "Run, Lisa!" he tried to shout, but his breath was too short for much sound to emerge.

As young Kirk raced toward the mouth of the alley and the comparative safety of the well-lit street, Lisa stepped out to bar his path. The cadet had only one shocked instant to realize that the faintly shining object she held in her hand, pointed straight at him, was a phaser.

No! he thought, frantically. *She set me up! It was a trap!*

"Stop right there, Peter," she commanded, in a voice he'd never heard her use before.

Peter had been trained how to deal with an armed opponent. *Hit her, hit her,* his brain screamed, but for a critical instant he hesitated.

Damn! he thought bleakly. *What would Uncle Jim do?*

But he had no time to ponder the question, for, without further ado, Lisa Tennant gave him a brilliant smile, aimed carefully, and triggered the phaser.

Peter heard the whine, glimpsed a flash of energy, and then there was only blackness. . . .

Four

Sarek sat at a comm link located in his private suite in the conference center on Deneb IV. Before him, on the screen, Chancellor Azetbur's three-dimensional image gazed out at him. "Ambassador Sarek . . ." she said, inclining her head slightly, one equal to another.

"Madame Chancellor," the Vulcan returned the greeting. "I gather that you have been briefed regarding the situation on Kadura?"

"I have," she said. "I regret what has happened, Ambassador Sarek."

"I understand, Madame Chancellor," Sarek said. "I discussed the matter with President Ra-ghoratrei upon my arrival last evening, and he informed me that you had spoken together regarding this crisis."

Azetbur's exotic features were tight with tension, and the mantle of leadership was clearly taking its toll on her. Sarek was vividly reminded that she had lost both husband and father barely a month ago. "This entire incident is unfortunate," she said. "Commander Keraz . . . I must admit that when I heard that he had initiated this raid, I was surprised. I have known the commander for years, and, while he can be . . . headstrong . . . he has always been loyal. Keraz is—was—a warrior who served the Empire with distinction, in the most honorable manner."

"I see . . ." Sarek said. "I have yet to meet the commander. Our first session begins in a few minutes. May I ask why you called, Madame Chancellor?"

"I want the renegades extradited, Ambassador Sarek. Have the Federation take Keraz and his men, and hand them over to me, so that I may make an example of them . . . an example that will speak vividly to any others who may be contemplating such treason against my government."

Sarek took a deep breath. Azetbur was many things, but "soft" or "merciful" was not one of them. "I regret, Madame Chancellor, that I cannot do that. I have no authorization from the president to do so . . . and my priority in this unfortunate situation must be the safety of the citizens of Kadura. I must decline your request."

"I see." Azetbur stared at him, her jaw muscles tight. Sarek had been prepared for her demand—Ra-ghoratrei had warned him last night of what the Empire wanted. "Do you propose, then, to simply let them go free?"

"If that is the agreement I negotiate, then that is what I must do," Sarek said. "However . . ." He paused for a moment in feigned deliberation. ". . . what happens to Keraz *after* he leaves the planet is not my affair."

"We will catch him, Ambassador. Of that you can be sure. The honor of my people depends on these traitors being captured and dealt with."

Sarek nodded.

Azetbur's expression thawed still more, and she actually chuckled aloud. "Ambassador Sarek," she said, "I understand for the first time the strength of your people. You excel at making others decide that what you want is what they, also, desire most."

The Vulcan inclined his head. "You are most gracious, Madame Chancellor."

After both parties signed off, Sarek stood at the window, gazing out at the lush wilderness that lay beyond.

Sarek approved of Deneb IV, also called Kidta, precisely because of its extreme isolation. The strictest security was being maintained: only a skeleton staff was allowed at the conference center, and Sarek, Soran, and the Vulcan ambassador to Orion, Stavel, were the only Vulcans. If Sarek had to negotiate with Klingons, he wanted to make sure he was dealing with Klingons acting on their own, under no duress from an outside influence. As nearly as he had been able to discover (and he had run extensive checks), there wasn't a single Freelan in this sector, much less on this world, or at the conference center.

Which was the way Sarek wanted it.

Any moment now, his aide would call him to the table to begin negotiations with Commander Keraz and his captains. Sarek had already braced himself to endure the presence of Klingons. Their emotions were primal and close to the surface, worse even than human emotions, and most Vulcans could sense them without being in physical contact. Sarek had no reason to suppose that Keraz would be different.

He was still puzzling over the Klingon renegade's request for negotiation as a solution to this crisis. It was out of character for Klingons to sit down and *talk* their way out of a problem, rather than just blasting everything around.

"Ambassador," someone said quietly, from behind him. Sarek turned to see Soran. "Are we ready to begin?" he asked, and the young Vulcan nodded.

Sarek straightened his formal robe, making sure the heavy, bejeweled folds hung properly, then followed Soran down the hall, into the conference room. It was a medium-sized room, with neutral-colored walls, two of which could be made transparent to show a view of the forest. A long table occupied the center of the room, and chairs suitable for humanoids surrounded it. There were two doors, one at each end of the room. From the door on Sarek's left, Admiral Smillie and an aide emerged, and from the other, four Klingons. One of the Klingons held a green-skinned Orion woman by the arm, marching her along peremptorily, but without any intentional cruelty.

Sarek raised his hand in the Vulcan salute to the Klingon in the lead. "Commander Keraz, I presume?"

The short, rather stocky Klingon nodded sharply. "Ambassador," he said. His voice was much more mellow than most Klingons'. His skin was very dark, the color of antique leather.

The representatives seated themselves around the big middle table. Sarek eyed the Orion woman and was relieved to see that, aside from stress and fatigue, she did not seem to have been harmed. She stared back at him levelly out of eyes the color of onyx. When the round of introductions reached her, she said quietly, "s'Kara. I represent the people of Kadura."

Sarek nodded, then looked over at Keraz. The Klingon seemed nervous, fingering his sash, picking at his belt as though he could not believe there were no weapons hanging there. Feeling Sarek's glance, the leader looked up, then burst out, "We desire an honorable settlement to this situation, Ambassador. My ships and crews have not damaged the planet or its inhabitants"—at this, s'Kara's eyes flashed indignantly, but she did not interrupt—"and, frankly, I have no interest in occupying a colony world composed mostly of . . . farmers." His mouth twisted with distaste. "We are warriors, not colonists. We have no wish to become planetbound—Kadura is no fit place for warriors."

Sarek inclined his head, noting that, beneath Keraz's deliberately gruff exterior, the Klingon seemed genuinely eager to negotiate. "That is promising to hear," Sarek said solemnly. "What are your terms, Commander?"

"We are prepared to withdraw . . . for the right price," Keraz said. "We must be allowed to take our payment and leave Kadura unmolested by any Starfleet vessel."

Sarek stared at the Klingon. Only a lifetime of habitual Vulcan control kept him from revealing his surprise. For Keraz to offer to withdraw at the beginning of the negotiations was the last thing he'd expected. Smoothly, giving no hint of his inner thoughts, Sarek said, "I am sure that, under the circumstances, something can be arranged."

For a moment Sarek thought about his discussion with Azetbur. If Keraz thought he could successfully leave Federation space and find refuge across the Neutral Zone, he was sadly mistaken.

Studying Keraz's face, as the Klingon began outlining his position, Sarek wondered with part of his mind what had induced the commander to turn renegade. Was it disagreement with his government's new, peaceful overtures to the Federation? Was it greed? Had Keraz snapped under pressure, and suffered some temporary madness? Or . . . was it something else?

With stern resolve, Sarek concentrated all his logic, all his experience, on bringing the Kadura situation to a peaceful, swift, and satisfactory resolution. Amanda was still alive. Perhaps he could fulfill his duty and still return home in time. Perhaps . . .

Considering the circumstances, Peter Kirk decided, it would be better if he just didn't wake up.

His most recent attempts to swim toward consciousness had been so unpleasant, he'd come to the conclusion that it simply wasn't worth it. He'd much rather stay in this dark, muzzy netherworld, not asleep, but not awake, where he could keep his various aches and pains at bay and insist to himself that they weren't real. That none of this was real. He'd just lie here, thank you, and think about the *Kobayashi Maru*. Pondering that dreaded event was infinitely preferable to opening his eyes and facing what had happened to him. Peter had a feeling that no simulation, no matter how real-seeming, could possibly equal the mess he'd somehow gotten himself into.

He groaned. Here he was. Peter Kirk, nephew of the Federation hero James T. Kirk—a Starfleet cadet so clever, so bold, that he'd allowed himself to be duped and kidnapped by a bunch of reactionary bigots too disorganized to run a successful demonstration. No. It was worse than that. He'd allowed his confused feelings for a woman he barely knew to cause him a critical moment of hesitation.

Why didn't you just surrender, *mister, and save everyone the trouble?* Would Uncle Jim have hesitated to slug a woman if the fate of the *Enterprise* was at stake? *Hell, no.*

Peter couldn't deny reality anymore; his conscience wouldn't let him. He was indisputably awake. Groaning aloud, he opened his eyes. His head throbbed as he struggled to focus on his surroundings. Squinting at the ceiling, he thought it seemed too high, and the wrong color. *Wrong color for what?* he wondered foggily, but couldn't remember.

Peter moved slowly, as painful awareness of his battle in the alley grew sharper, more persistent with every passing second. His arm and head hurt. His right side throbbed with every breath.

Cautiously, he turned his head, his gaze traveling across the small, narrow enclosure with its dingy, gray bulkheads. Reality. He swallowed, as fear finally set in. *Where the hell am I?*

Biting his lip, Peter gingerly pushed himself up until he was sitting on the edge of the standard bunk, his head in his hands. *And what is that smell?*

Sighing, he turned his attention to the plain room. It was small, barely four meters by three, and, except for the bunk, which folded out of the wall, nearly featureless.

There were a few indentations that might indicate servo panels concealed in the walls, but no windows. Peter shuddered, swallowing a sudden surge of claustrophobia. He felt light-headed and nauseated from the stun shot, and his knees were weak. Sitting silently on the bunk, he paused, just listening.

There was no sound, no sound at all.

. . . Or was there?

After a moment's intense concentration, Peter began to sense something. Was it a faint noise? A vibration? Or just a sixth sense that told him he was no longer in normal space-time? Suddenly, he *knew.*

His engineering instructor had said you could sense the spacewarp, even if you couldn't see it.

He was aboard a spaceship, traveling at warp speed, destination unknown. This wasn't a room, it was a cabin.

Peter's mouth went so dry that he couldn't even swallow. Wanting to give himself something constructive to do besides panicking, Kirk rose and systematically began to explore the cabin's flat, drab walls.

The whole place had a well-worn, grimy patina that testified to extensive use, and the panels that made up the walls were uniform and interchangeable, allowing the dimensions of the cabin to be altered according to need. The only door was heavy, with no viewing ports. While he could see where the mechanism for manual overrides probably lay, there was no way he could get through it—even if he could figure out the system—to force the doors to open. He searched for a surveillance system and couldn't find one—but that didn't mean there wasn't one trained on him at all times.

Methodically, the cadet pressed one of the innocuous indentations on the wall, and a tiny water dispenser revealed itself. He stared, mesmerized by clear, fresh-smelling fluid, but in spite of his parched mouth, passed it by. The water, he suspected, would probably be drugged. It would be the most logical way to keep a prisoner under control. He went about examining the other wall indentations and discovered an odd hole in the floor. By its smell, he decided, it could only be a head—but the style was unfamiliar to him.

When was the last time this thing was cleaned? he wondered, realizing that this was the source of some of the smell.

Water and a toilet, he mused. *But no food.* His eyes strayed back toward the water fountain. *So, how long do you think you can last without water?* The memory of the cool-looking fluid was working on him already.

Just then a soft machinery sound hummed, breaking into his thoughts. He whirled, crouching, his instincts on override, but it was just a serving panel extruding from a niche in the wall. There was a tray on the panel, as colorless as the panel itself. Whoever had designed this starship had been really fond of monochromatic schemes. Peter approached the tray.

Piled in a small, equally colorless bowl were dry ration pellets. They didn't resemble the rations he was used to, but they had that same processed-food-for-space-travel look about them—a soft gray green in color, tubular, about two centimeters in length, and maybe half a centimeter in width. He sniffed. The mealy-looking pellets had a pungent, fishy smell. They were entirely too reminiscent of the prepared food Grandma Winona used to feed her parrot.

Except this stuff is probably full of drugs, he suspected. He could see the pack-

aging now—AUNT SYLVIA'S KIDNAPPER CHOW. REDUCES STRESS. INCREASES COOPERA-
TION. Yes, there'd be something in there to keep him quiet, calm . . . cooperative. He
frowned at the food. It wouldn't be long before even its unappealing scent would
make his mouth water. While he could last without food a lot longer than he could
without water, that didn't mean that he could afford to *waste* these.

He spilled the pellets onto the tray and started lining them up in rows until he'd
spelled out, in English words, "Who are you?" Then he carefully pushed the tray
back into the wall. Of course, the "leftovers" might be jettisoned directly into the recycler, but somehow, he didn't think so. They'd want to weigh how much he'd eaten,
know how much drug he might absorb . . . to determine just how much trouble he
was going to be when they arrived.

Arrived where? he wondered, frustrated. It could be anywhere. He didn't even
know how long they'd been traveling. If they'd stunned him repeatedly (and his
headache argued that they probably had), he might have been unconscious for *days*.

Peter walked back to the bunk and sat down. Why in the world would the KEHL
kidnap him, then ship him *off-world?* That was the part that really had his head spinning. Or was that the safest way they could think of to deal with him, once they'd
figured out who he really was?

Had he been sold to the highest bidder? There were still slave traders in the
galaxy, though Starfleet had mostly shut them down. But would the KEHL have
handed him over to *aliens?* That thought was the hardest to swallow, but there was
little about this room that suggested a human-designed ship. Aliens would explain
the smell, too. It was an *alien* odor, the smell of body chemistries that were not
human in origin. Every species had its own distinct smell, Peter knew, some more
pleasant than others. While the soiled head's contribution was significant, the underlying scent was simply that of a different species—one he'd never encountered
before. Not Tellarite, or Orion, or Andorian or Horta or Vulcan . . . unfamiliar.
Alien.

Peter could understand the KEHL wanting to get rid of him. But why not simply
kill him? Why hand him over to aliens? Why go to all this trouble to get him off-world?

It had to be more than just the KEHL involved. Somebody had paid Lisa Tennant
and her goons to set him up and hand him over . . . but why?

Why in the name of the Seven Tellarite Hells would anyone want to kidnap him?
He was only a cadet . . . he had no access to restricted data. He had no rank, and he
wasn't rich. Uncle Jim made a respectable living, he supposed. But enough to make
the risk of abducting his nephew profitable? Highly unlikely.

It didn't make sense. No rank, no riches, no enemies . . .

Wait a minute. Peter straightened suddenly. *He* didn't have any enemies, as far as
he knew . . . but he knew someone who did. Someone who'd led an adventurous life,
taken plenty of risks, trodden on numerous toes. Someone who had certainly made
enemies over the years . . . more enemies than you could shake a stick at . . .

James T. Kirk.

Somebody intended to use him to get to Uncle Jim.

As for Peter, he expected to take his oath and become a Starfleet officer in a
month. Did whoever was behind all this honestly think he would just sit here and
allow his uncle's enemies to use him like that?

A prisoner's first responsibility was to escape. Right now, it didn't seem as if he
had many options while trapped in this cabin. That meant he'd have to play a prepared

hand when this ship finally stopped moving and those doors eventually opened. He'd have to overwhelm whoever was coming for him, steal this ship, and pilot it back home. He was a fair pilot, and a good navigator. That part wouldn't be difficult —it was the first part that could be trouble. How many would there be? And what species? There were numerous aliens that Peter knew he could easily fight his way through, but there were also many others whose strength was far greater than the average human's.

And that's you, mister—average. Maybe, in strength. But, he'd been studying self-defense and martial arts since he was in his teens. By the time he'd gotten to the Academy, he was already pretty good, and Starfleet put on the final polish. He could hold his own—when he was *thinking* clearly. Unbidden, the image of him falling prey to Lisa Tennant's stun gun burned in his mind.

Peter wished he could exercise, keep up his skills, his physical strength, but that wouldn't be possible. He must be under surveillance, so that meant he'd have to portray himself as passive, maybe even sickly. He'd have to sleep a lot, or pretend to, and act slow and weak. If he did that, the less on their guard they might be when they came for him. And that might be his only advantage. He really *would* be weak from lack of food, and reduced water, so he'd have to rely on surprise, if he was to have any hope at all.

Yes, his kidnappers would do what they could to keep him cooperative, compliant. But Peter had already decided just how much trouble he would be. *As much as humanly possible, mister.*

He was a Kirk, after all. And he would not be surprised again. Not if they threw the most beautiful, most interesting, most desirable females of every species in the galaxy at him.

He would get out of here, or die in the attempt. *And if I don't make it,* he thought, smiling to himself, *at least I won't have to take the* Kobayashi Maru.

Sarek sat at the negotiation table, listening as the Orion representative bickered with Admiral Smillie about Federation restitution for the attack on Kadura. To his right, the Orion woman, s'Kara, stared expressionlessly at the Orion male, but Sarek sensed her distrust, her revulsion . . . perfectly logical, under the circumstances.

Finally, he raised a hand, and as soon as Smillie and Buta, the Orion, noticed him, they fell silent. "These matters can be resolved later," Sarek said. "For the moment, I request that we finalize the agreement with Commander Keraz concerning their terms for withdrawing from Kadura. As you will recall, the commander said that he . . ."

Sarek continued, going over all the points agreed upon so far. They had come a long way in just a few days . . . but not quickly enough for him. The speedy Vulcan courier ship was standing by, ready to take him home at warp eight, but Sarek doubted he could ever get home in time to comfort his wife.

Wearily, Sarek finished outlining Keraz's demands, received a confirming nod from the Klingon. Smillie made a counteroffer to one part of Keraz's plan, wherein the renegades would be provided with dilithium as a ransom for the safe release of Kadura. Keraz countered, lowering his demand fractionally. Sarek listened with part of his mind as they came closer and closer to an agreement. If they could reach agreement, then perhaps he could be finished today. . . .

The wrangling continued for the next two hours, with Sarek mediating between them, attempting to find compromises that would work.

Finally, he realized a refreshment break was long overdue, so he dismissed the factions. The room emptied rapidly as the occupants left in search of food, lavatories, or comm links. Finally, only Sarek, Soran, Keraz, and his second-in-command, Wurrl, were left.

The Vulcan wished once again that he could arrange to speak to Keraz alone. The commander's demeanor at the negotiation table during the past days was not what one would logically expect of a Klingon renegade. Keraz was entirely too eager to negotiate, to give ground. It was almost as though he regretted having taken Kadura, and would like nothing better than to wash his hands of the whole business. . . .

Barely noticing his surroundings, occupied with his thoughts, Sarek walked slowly toward the door. Soran and Keraz were ahead of him. The Vulcan looked up, wondering where the Klingon's aide was. Movement—there was movement behind him—

—a bloodcurdling battle yell filled the air as the Klingon officer, Wurrl, leaped at the Vulcan ambassador. Sarek flung up an arm, glimpsed a flash of metal, even as something sharp sank deeply into his left bicep. He grappled with the Klingon, managing to hold him off despite his injured arm, grateful for superior Vulcan strength.

The ambassador groped for a neck pinch, but his fingers could not penetrate the heavy leather and metal of the Klingon's armor. He changed tactics, struck Wurrl sharply on the bridge of the nose, and saw the assailant's eyes cloud over. Contact with the would-be assassin's bare flesh told him that he was dealing with another case like Induna's.

Tal-shaya? Sarek wondered whether he would have to kill the Klingon outright in self-preservation. Would it work on a Klingon?

Locked together in a grisly parody of an embrace, the ambassador and the Klingon careered across the room, slamming into the conference table, scattering chairs. Suddenly Keraz was there, bellowing Klingon obscenities and threats at his aide, as he slammed a knife-hand blow into Wurrl's throat. The treacherous aide staggered, his grip on the ambassador loosening. Wurrl's breath rattled in his throat, even as steely hands grasped him and lifted, hoisting him clean off his feet. Soran swung the Klingon in an arc, then sent him crashing against the wall. Wurrl slid down it, and lay there, unconscious.

"Ambassador! Ambassador, you are wounded!" Keraz sounded thoroughly shaken. Sarek grasped his bicep, applying external pressure, even as he sought within himself for his training in biocontrol. A moment later, he felt the bleeding slow to a trickle, then stop. Automatically, he controlled the pain.

"I am not seriously injured," Sarek said. "Where did he get that dagger?" All participants in the conference were screened automatically each time they walked through the door.

Keraz went over to the downed Wurrl, and, bending over and using the tip of his metal-reinforced gauntlet, he picked up the green-smeared dagger. "Assembled," he growled, holding it out. "See? Pieces of trim from his uniform, altered so they would slide together and form a weapon. He must have put it together under the table while we met today."

Sarek raised his voice. "Security, please report to the conference chamber," he said.

His verbal request was not necessary. Barely a second later, the doors burst open, admitting four guards and Admiral Smillie. Quick questions and answers followed.

Smillie, Sarek saw, was all for taking Keraz into custody along with the seriously injured Wurrl. The Vulcan raised his hand, forestalling the Starfleet admiral. "Commander Keraz was not responsible for this incident," he said. "I am certain of that."

As Sarek spoke, he caught a quick glance from Keraz, saw the flash of gratitude in the Klingon's eyes. "Commander," Sarek said, gesturing to the open door, "let us leave security to its job. I would like to speak with you privately."

Soran stepped forward to protest, and so did Smillie, but both gave way before the ambassador's determination. Keraz nodded, and together the two left the wrecked conference chamber.

As they walked down the corridor, Sarek said, blandly, "Commander . . . I know that you are not responsible for that attack just now. I have some idea, at least generally, who is, though. Could you answer a few questions, please?"

"What kind of questions?" Keraz growled.

"In the first place, after days of discussion, I still do not have a clear idea of what you hoped to gain by your occupation of Kadura. Perhaps you might enlighten me as to your reasons?"

When Keraz only stared stonily, the ambassador added, "The greater my understanding of what you hoped to gain, the more smoothly I will be able to conclude matters. I understand the Federation mind-set on this matter . . . but I am still uncertain as to yours."

The Klingon commander hesitated; then he walked out into a courtyard and sat down by a tinkling fountain. Sarek, understanding that he thus hoped to foil any listening devices, sat down with his knees almost touching the Klingon's. "What did I hope to gain?" Keraz's effort to keep his tones low only accentuated the mellowness of his baritone. "Ambassador, at one time my actions seemed as clear as a Darlavian crystal to me, but . . . no more."

"What do you mean?"

"I cannot explain!" Keraz said, his voice lowering to a growl. "I have thrown away my warrior's honor, and my life will likely be forfeit, along with the lives of my crew. . . ." He glared at Sarek. "Do not by any chance think, Vulcan, that I am unaware that my government stands ready to capture me and punish me as a traitor without honor. If I have any hope in conducting these negotiations, it is that all of the responsibility for my actions will be focused on *me*, not on my crew."

"You are speaking as though you regret your actions since you . . . broke with your Empire," the Vulcan observed, his heart quickening. He'd never heard a Klingon speak like this before.

"I do regret them," Keraz said simply. "I did not agree with the Empire's new, craven policies toward the Federation, and I told anyone who cared to listen that. But turn renegade? Traitor? Pah!" He spat on the flagstones at his feet.

"But your actions recently have gone against orders," Sarek pointed out.

"I know!" Keraz's voice was a muted howl of frustration. "My loyalty to the Empire was complete, until . . . until one day I realized that I was being a fool, that there were riches waiting for me, and glory . . . and I realized that I could wage war on the Federation whether or not my government had the courage and the honor."

The Klingon scowled, his corrugated brow even more wrinkled than usual. "My path seemed clear, until, two days after Kadura was mine . . . I awoke one morning, realizing exactly what I had done. How my government would regard me. I knew that I would soon be surrounded by half the Federation's starships." He gave a short, bitter growl of laughter. "And you ask me *why*, Vulcan? That is your answer—that I have no answer! I do not know why!"

"But I do," Sarek said. "Or, at least, I believe that I know, Commander. Recently, I have encountered two individuals who became violent as a result of outside mental influence . . . telepathic influence. One was a human, on Terra. The other was . . . your aide, Wurrl. Just now."

"Wurrl?" Keraz stared at the ambassador incredulously. "What are you saying, Vulcan? That *I* have also been influenced? That some telepath *made* me take Kadura?"

"I do not believe they can control actions," Sarek clarified. "But they can influence, provide mental catalysts, as it were. Yes, I do believe that, Commander."

The Klingon had paled as they spoke. Not surprisingly, he found the idea of not being his own master repugnant, revolting. "How can you tell?" he whispered hoarsely. "How did you know about Wurrl?"

"I touched him," Sarek said.

"Could you tell with me?"

Sarek nodded silently. Keraz took a deep breath, then, sitting stiffly, rigidly, nodded. "Do it," he commanded.

Slowly, the ambassador raised his hand and brushed it across the Klingon's high, bony forehead. He found what he had expected to find, and Keraz read the truth without Sarek having to say it aloud. The commander threw back his head and voiced a wordless bellow of rage and frustration, then cursed vividly in at least six different languages.

Finally, Keraz subsided, panting, and sat glowering in silence for several moments. "Kamarag," he said. "This is his doing. That cursed, dishonorable slime devil has stolen my honor. For this I will rip out his gizzard and feed it to my *targ!*"

"What do you mean, he stole your honor?"

"He was trying to persuade us all to turn renegade, and ever since that meeting most of the warriors there have committed honorless raids on noncombatants—just as I did."

"What meeting?" Sarek asked.

With a savage glare that the Vulcan knew wasn't directed at him, Keraz explained about Kamarag's clandestine conclave. "Fascinating," the ambassador murmured, trying to picture Kamarag in that setting.

"Kamarag has no honor, Vulcan," Keraz said bitterly. "But you . . . you are different. You have courage, as well as honor. A coward would not have been willing to be alone with me after Wurrl's attack."

"You possess a warrior's honor," Sarek said, honestly. "I knew you would not attack me."

Keraz gave him a sideways glance. "I heard that your woman is . . . gravely ill," he said, gruffly. "You have also shown honor in remaining here in performance of your duty. I respect such honor, Ambassador."

"Is that why you agreed to speak frankly with me?" Sarek asked.

"Yes," Keraz said. "Such a demonstration of honor is admirable, no matter what species displays it."

The Vulcan inclined his head in recognition of Keraz's words. "Perhaps we may conclude the negotiations quickly," he said.

"I will keep that in mind," the Klingon replied. With a curt nod, he rose and left Sarek alone beside the fountain.

Spock sat alone in the small courtyard of the med center. This area was designed to be a peaceful refuge where friends and relatives of patients could meditate and wait in peace. The walls were pale yellow, the floor was red-ocher tiles. Benches stood ranged around the central water sculpture, facing the shining spray within its protective field. Spock gazed at the water sculpture without really seeing it.

The Vulcan was attempting to make his mind a blank, preparatory to meditating, but every time he thought he'd succeeded, thoughts, like thieves in the night, tiptoed into his consciousness.

His mother was much worse. Last night she'd had another stroke, a major one. T'Mal had ordered her beamed directly to a hospital room in the med center.

Hearing footsteps, the Vulcan glanced up to see Leonard McCoy enter the solarium. As he took in the expression on the doctor's face, the Vulcan rose slowly to his feet.

"How is she?" Spock demanded, hearing his voice ring hollowly in the silence.

Silently, the doctor shook his head. "Not good. She's still alive . . . but she can't last for long, Spock. Vital systems are just . . . closing down."

Spock stared at his friend, speechlessly. He'd thought he was braced against any eventuality, but now shock held him silent.

McCoy sat down on a bench opposite his. The doctor's face was drawn and haggard with mingled fatigue and sorrow. "We've managed to stabilize her again, but her body is just worn out. The strokes have caused metabolic imbalances and neural damage, despite everything the Healers and I could do to prevent that. Now her kidneys are shutting down . . . and her heart is compromised. I'm afraid it's just a matter of time."

"How long?" Spock asked, forcing the words past the tightness in his throat.

"Not long. Days . . . possibly only hours."

Spock rose to his feet, paced back and forth, his boot heels echoing on the tiles. McCoy's blue eyes followed his movements.

"Spock," the doctor said after a moment. "If there's anything I can do . . . if you want someone to talk to, I'm here. Jim should be beaming down any minute."

"I must make a call," Spock said, turning abruptly. "Wait here for me. I will not be long."

Minutes later he sat at the nearest public comm link, facing Sarek's aide, Soran. "Greetings," he said, curtly, in his native language. "I would speak with Sarek. It is urgent."

The young Vulcan's forehead creased, ever so slightly. "That will be difficult. The ambassador is in the midst of the afternoon's negotiations. May I relay a message?"

"No," Spock said flatly. "I must speak with my father personally. Be so kind as to summon him at once."

Soran hesitated for a long moment, then, after studying Spock's face, nodded. "I will inform him immediately, Captain Spock. Please wait."

Several more minutes passed, while Spock sat rigidly, words running through his mind. Finally a figure moved before the screen in a flash of formal ambassadorial robes, and then he was looking at Sarek. "Greetings, my son. You required a conversation with me?"

Spock nodded stiffly. "Yes, sir. Mother has suffered another stroke. Dr. McCoy says that her time is very short."

"It will not be possible for me to leave," Sarek said, his voice betraying no emotion whatsoever. Had Spock seen something flicker behind his eyes? There was no way to be sure.

"You said the negotiations were proceeding smoothly. Cannot Ambassador Stavel take over?"

"That is not an option," Sarek said firmly. "I must handle this personally. There is more at stake here than I realized."

Spock drew a deep breath. "I ask that you reconsider," he said, tightly. "My presence does not comfort her. She is calling for you."

Sarek's eyes closed, and this time the pain on his features was not masked to someone who knew him well. "Spock . . . I cannot." His face smoothed out, became impassive once more. "Farewell, Spock. I must return to the negotiation table now."

The connection was abruptly broken. Numbly, Spock rose from his seat and returned to the solarium. There he found Kirk and McCoy waiting for him. McCoy checked the tricorder he was holding. "The monitors say she's sleeping, Spock," he said. "I'll know the instant she wakes up. Sit down for a minute. You look done in."

As the Vulcan obeyed, Kirk glanced at McCoy. "How is she?"

Quickly, the doctor summarized Amanda's condition.

"Is Sarek coming home?" Kirk asked Spock.

The Vulcan's eyes narrowed. "No. The negotiations take precedence."

Kirk's hazel gaze widened slightly as the captain evidently realized he'd touched on a sensitive subject.

McCoy shook his head grimly. "Lousy timing. That Klingon commander was out of his mind to pull a stunt like this. He couldn't possibly have thought he'd get away with it!"

"Having seen Klingon 'justice' close up, I'm surprised that any amount of greed could induce a commander to commit treason against the Empire," Kirk agreed.

Spock stared at his captain for a long moment. "Interesting that you should employ that particular word, Jim. Perhaps that is indeed the case . . . that Keraz was induced to invade Kadura."

Kirk's hazel eyes were bright with curiosity. "What do you mean, Spock?"

The Vulcan hesitated, then said, "I had hoped to broach this subject when Sarek was here, so he could relate events firsthand, but . . . there is no way of knowing when my father will return to Vulcan." His voice was hard and flat in his own ears, and Spock saw Kirk and McCoy exchange quick glances.

"What do you mean? What's going on?" the captain asked.

Spock reached out and took McCoy's medical tricorder, propped it where they could all see Amanda's monitors displayed. "If she wakes, I will have to stop," he warned the others. "Sarek told me the entire story only a few days ago. . . ." The Vulcan continued, summarizing Sarek's findings about the Freelans and the KEHL.

When the first officer finished, the captain and chief surgeon exchanged glances; then both officers shook their heads dazedly. "I swear, Spock, if this were anyone but you tellin' me this," McCoy said, "I'd say he wasn't firin' on all thrusters. Romulans walking around the Federation without a by-your-leave? It sounds like the worst kind of paranoid delusion!"

"If it were anyone but a Vulcan saying this, I'd agree, Bones," Kirk said. "But Sarek is definitely sane . . . and if he's right about all this, he's right that this poses a serious threat to Federation security."

McCoy, catching sight of a change in the monitor, pointed wordlessly. Amanda was awake.

Quietly, the three officers entered the sick woman's room. Spock sat by Amanda's bedside, and his friends sat in the back of the room, their silent presence offering quiet support.

Even though Amanda was conscious, she seemed unaware of their presence. Occasionally she would call "Sarek?" in a questioning tone, then pause, plainly listening for a reply. Spock's murmured "I am here, Mother, it is Spock" made no difference. Amanda remained unresponsive to the voice of her son.

After a half-hour had passed, the Vulcan rose and motioned his friends to join him in the corridor so he could speak freely.

"I will stay with her," he said. "I appreciate your presence, but I know you have duties aboard ship."

McCoy nodded, understanding the Vulcan's unspoken plea for privacy.

Kirk cleared his throat. "If you would like some company, Spock . . ."

The Vulcan nodded. "Your offer is appreciated, Jim, but at the moment . . . I would prefer to be alone with her."

"I understand completely. If you change your mind . . ."

Spock was wearing civilian clothing, a Vulcan robe, but he reached into the pocket and removed his communicator and held it up.

"Okay," Kirk said.

McCoy put a hand on Spock's arm. "The same goes for me, Spock. She could go on like this for some time. Don't forget to eat something today, okay?"

The Vulcan nodded. "Is she in pain?"

"No, I don't believe so," McCoy said. "And, Spock?" He cleared his throat awkwardly. "It's common for stroke victims to fixate on one person or one thing. Sometimes the person can be sitting right there, but the patient won't recognize them, so . . . there's not much you can do about it. Even if your father were here, she might not realize it."

"I understand, Doctor."

Spock gazed at his two friends, knowing there was nothing more to say. Both Kirk and McCoy hesitated, then nodded, and silently turned away.

Sarek paced slowly down the corridor toward yet another negotiating session. It was morning on Kidta, but the new day brought no lightening of his spirits. The Vulcan wondered whether he should attempt to contact Spock and inquire about his wife's condition. Sarek knew, only too well, how angry Spock was over his failure to return home. He knew that, under most circumstances, his son was as logical as any Vulcan . . . but he also knew how deeply Spock cared for his mother. As he himself had once said to T'Lar, when it came to questions about the welfare of a family member, one's logic became . . . uncertain.

As the ambassador hesitated in the corridor of the conference center, wanting to contact Spock, he was strangely reluctant. Sarek found himself concentrating on Amanda, trying to feel her presence, sense her mind through their bond. He closed his eyes, concentrating . . . concentrating . . .

A thread, so faint . . . he traced it, followed it, opening his mind, sensing it. Amanda . . . she was there, in his mind, but her mental thread was weak . . . was weakening, even as he touched it. Sarek's breath caught in his throat as he realized that he was too late . . . too late. As he stood here in this hallway, his wife was dying.

Amanda! It was a mental cry of anguish that resonated within his mind. Grief struck him like a blow, grief and regret so agonizing that he swayed as he stood.

Quickly, realizing he needed solitude, Sarek turned to a small, empty conference chamber and entered it, not activating the lights. In the darkness, with nothing to distract him, perhaps he could find her, could reach her mind, even across space. It had been done before, by stronger telepaths than he . . . although he'd never been able to accomplish it.

But he had to try. . . .

Spock sat by his mother's bedside, holding her small, cold, wasted hand in both his own, as though he could somehow transfer some of his own strength to her by so doing. Amanda's blue eyes were open at the moment; she had been semiconscious all afternoon.

The room was bathed in sunlight, and the monitoring devices were subdued, nonintrusive.

As Spock watched her, wondering whether she would take a sip of water if he offered it to her, Amanda's lips parted, and she spoke. Barely more than a breath escaped—a breath that was a name.

"Sarek . . ."

She had been calling him for hours, and the sound of it wrenched her son's heart as nothing in his life ever had. Spock leaned over and said, softly but distinctly, "I am here, Mother, I am here. Spock . . . I'm here with you, Mother."

She opened her eyes again, stared vacantly at him. Fretfully, she tugged her hand away from his. "Sarek?" she murmured, turning her head on the pillow, seeking someone who wasn't there.

"Mother?" Spock called softly. Amanda turned her head to gaze at him, and for a moment he thought he saw a flash of warmth and recognition in her eyes; then it faded. Her eyes moved again, and she stirred restlessly.

"Sarek?"

Spock sighed. A few minutes later he coaxed her to take a sip of water from a straw; then she seemed to slip off into a doze.

An hour later Amanda's right hand moved restlessly, plucking at the coverlet. The Vulcan reached over to hold it. This seemed to calm her for a few minutes, and she dropped off again.

Spock fell into a doze himself; he'd scarcely slept since this had begun, and even his Vulcan constitution was wearing down. He jerked awake an hour and thirty-two point nine minutes later, hearing his mother call, "Sarek?" Her voice held such sadness, such utter desolation that his throat tightened.

Glancing up at the monitors, he saw that the levels were dropping . . . she was fading, fading away. Healer T'Mal came in, checked her patient, and when Spock, with a glance, whispered, "How long?," the physician simply shook her head.

"Sarek?" Amanda's voice cracked on the word. Spock attempted to give her some water, but she turned her head away, fretfully.

"Mother, it is Spock. I am here," he said aloud, seeing that her eyes were wide open, and she was staring straight at him.

"Sarek?" she called.

This is unbearable. Spock got to his feet and paced restlessly around the room. *There is almost no possibility that Sarek will arrive in time. But . . . unless he is here, she will have no peace. I must find a way to help her achieve tranquility, serenity . . . but how?*

Suddenly, an idea occurred to him. But was Amanda strong enough to withstand what he had in mind?

*   *   *

Sarek sat alone in the dark, his head bowed in his hands, struggling to reach his wife. With all his being he wanted to be with her at the end, wanted to give her a sense of his presence along the tenuous pathway of their bond. Sarek pressed his hands to his eyes, shutting out all light, and proceeded to systematically blank out everything except the sense of Amanda's presence in his mind. *Amanda, I am here. My wife, I am with you. Amanda . . . I am with you . . . hear me, know it is I. Amanda, my wife, I am with you. . . .*

Over and over he repeated his message, casting his mind along that fragile link, not knowing whether he was succeeding. His sense of her presence grew, eclipsing everything else; his entire existence was centered on the mental link he shared with her. Memories flashed through his mind, memories of times past—their wedding night, Spock's birth, his Times with her, the heat of the passion between them seeming to fill the whole world—and for a moment he thought he sensed that she was sharing those memories with him. But he could not be certain . . . could not even be sure that she was aware of him. If she was unconscious, he might be touching some last dream, instead of her thinking, conscious mind.

Amanda . . . my wife, I am with you. You have made my life better in so many ways, and I thank you . . . Amanda, feel my presence. I am with you. . . .

Spock glanced reflexively at the monitors, and what he saw there made him cross the room in one long stride. *Am I too late?* Spock's fingers went to her head, brushing aside Amanda's hair, seeking the proper contact points.

The Vulcan sent his mind out, searching, seeking his mother's consciousness. She was almost gone. . . . Dimly he sensed her personality, the last sparks of life and consciousness, and sent his mind surging toward hers, seeking for contact. Desperately, he tried to locate and link with that last, faint spark of life. He was determined to give her peace, give her what she wanted so badly—her husband's presence. He would call up a memory of Sarek so vividly that she would believe his father was actually present.

As he struggled to establish contact, time seemed to stretch, as though some uncanny relativistic space-time pocket had taken over the room—even though Spock's inner chrono told him that less than a minute had passed. He was failing . . . the spark that was her life, her consciousness, was falling away in the dark, fading like a burnt-out cinder. Spock tried, but he could not touch her mind, could not capture that dying spark. Beneath his fingers, Amanda twitched, then gasped reflexively, once, twice—

Spock summoned all his mental strength for one last attempt, sending his mind hurtling after that fading life-spark. . . . *My mind to yours . . . our minds are one . . .*

But it was no good. She eluded him, fading out, falling away, going too deep for him to catch and still live. *Mother!* Spock whispered silently, and knew she did not hear him . . . was not aware of him . . .

Amanda was aware, faintly, of the presence trying to touch her mind, but she had gone too far to turn back. . . .

From where?

She had no idea where she was, where she was going. All around her was darkness, shot with strange colors, hues that even Vulcans had no names for. . . . She regarded the colors with passing interest, but continued to move. Was she walking? Floating? She did not know. All she knew was that she *was* moving.

Spock... she realized, recognizing the presence that was questing after the tiny spark that remained of Amanda Grayson. She felt a rush of love and warmth for her son, but she could not halt and let him catch up to her ... she knew only that she must keep moving, that she had no choice.

For a moment she wondered where she was going, but rational thought did not seem important to her anymore. Only the need to quest, to seek ... to move ...

Seek? she wondered, vaguely. Yes, she was seeking something ... or was it someone. And that someone was ...

Sarek. She wanted Sarek. He was here, somewhere, he had to be. Her husband had been part of her mind, part of her universe for so long ... he must be here, somewhere.

Was she moving toward Sarek?

She must be, Amanda thought. Spock's presence was far behind her now, and she did not let him distract her any more. She could not turn back, she knew that instinctively.

Sarek? she thought.

Amanda had a vague impression that she was moving faster. For a fleeting moment, it occurred to her to wonder just *where* she was going, but that did not seem important, either. Only one thing still linked her to her Self, the essence of Amanda Grayson ... and that was Sarek. He had to be here, somewhere. ...

Sarek?

Something was near her. What? She had no fear of it, whatever it was. It loomed closer, closer ...

Suddenly, as she sped along, another presence was with her, enveloping her with its essence. Joyfully, Amanda recognized it.

Sarek!

He was with her, beside her, around her, within her ... he surrounded and pervaded her with the sense of his presence. *Sarek*... she thought, happy that they were together. *My husband* ...

But she was still moving ... Sarek was not the destination. He could accompany her only partway, for a short while. With a faint pang of regret, Amanda felt him drop behind her. She was moving too fast for him. ...

Moving ... rushing, now. Hurtling. Where did not matter. There was no fear, no pain, no weariness. There was ... peace. Peace and movement ...

Peace ... and nothingness ...

The last spark of individual identity that had been Amanda Grayson Sarek surrendered to the peace, losing herself, expanding beyond Self, beyond ... everything. ...

"Sarek?"

Spock's eyes snapped open in amazement at his mother's whisper. She sounded suddenly younger, almost girlish. As he watched, her cracked lips parted in a loving smile, as though she saw something he could not. "My husband ..." The words were barely discernible ... a final, soft exhalation. Amanda gasped sharply ... then her chest did not rise again.

I failed, Spock thought desolately, as his eyes automatically went to the monitors; there he read what he already knew. It was difficult to believe that his mother was dead. He let his fingers slide down her temples to her throat ... nothing. No pulse.

Spock stood there for a long moment, trying to assimilate what had happened. It seemed inconceivable that Amanda would never open her eyes again, never smile, or speak. Never . . . the word had an awful sound. Something struggled inside him to break loose, to achieve expression, but he repressed it sternly. He was a Vulcan.

Gently, Spock placed her limp hands on her breast atop the coverlet. His mother's eyes were half-open, and, automatically, he reached out and closed them. His hand lingered for a moment on Amanda's cheek; then, resolutely, he stood up. Healer T'Mal, he thought, would be here any moment, having seen Amanda's readings from the monitoring station in the med center.

The Vulcan debated whether he should draw the sheet up over his mother's face, but decided not to . . . she appeared very peaceful the way she was. Her face even bore traces of that last, faint smile.

Spock turned and walked to the door, hesitated, glanced back. There seemed no reason to stay any longer, but he could not decide what he should do. Healers, aides, and patients passed him in the corridor, and it seemed incredible and somehow unconscionable that everyone and everything should go on so normally, when there had been such a loss. . . .

Spock realized with one part of his mind that he was not reacting logically, but, for once, that did not seem important.

T'Mal came toward him, halted. She was a small, graying Vulcan, who wore a blue-green medical tunic and trousers. "Captain Spock," she said, in the most ancient and formal of Vulcan dialects, "I grieve with thee on the death of thy mother."

Spock nodded, wondering whether his expression betrayed any of his inner turmoil, but apparently it did not, for T'Mal's face did not alter as she gazed at him. The Vulcan nodded, then said, matching her formality, "We grieve together, Healer T'Mal. I thank thee for thy care of my mother these many days."

T'Mal gazed up at him, and some of her formality vanished. "Go home, Captain Spock. Rest. We will place her in stasis, until your father returns, so he may see her if he wishes. Tomorrow will be soon enough to arrange for the memorial service."

Spock nodded. "Thank you, T'Mal. I will contact you . . . later." Turning away, he headed for the med center's transporter unit.

Alone in the small room on Deneb IV, Sarek of Vulcan struggled, sending his mind out, striving to reach his wife, never knowing whether he had succeeded. And then . . . he felt Amanda die.

One moment her presence was there, a warm spark in the back of his mind, a tenuous link stretching between them—and then the link snapped . . . the warmth was gone, leaving an aching void.

Sarek leaned his head in his hands, feeling grief engulf him past any ability of his to control it. *Amanda . . . Amanda . . .* he thought, as though her name were some kind of litany or spell that could call her back. But no . . . she was gone, truly gone, and he would be forever poorer for her loss. *Amanda . . .*

Alone, in the dark, Sarek of Vulcan silently mourned. His world seemed to have tilted out of alignment, losing its focus and color. Amanda, dead? For the first time, the Vulcan realized how much of his strength, his legendary calm and wisdom had come from his wife's presence in his mind. And now . . . gone . . .

Forever.

The word was too large, too all-encompassing for even a Vulcan mind to grasp. Sarek rejected the idea. Logic might dictate that his time with Amanda was ended, but . . . one's logic was uncertain at times, when family was concerned. Someday, somehow, he would touch the essence of his wife again. Sarek knew it.

But . . . what was he to do until then?

The answer to his question returned him swiftly. He would do his job . . . his duty. He would gain freedom for the people of Kadura. He would complete these negotiations. And then, he would do what he must about the Freelan threat. He would do his duty, as he had always done. Amanda would expect that of him, as he expected it of himself.

Rising from the table, the ambassador straightened his formal robes, and his shoulders. Then, his expression calm, remote, he walked slowly back to join the others around the conference table.

Spock materialized inside the mountain villa. He could have gone to the house in ShiKahr, which was within walking distance of the med center, but there he would have had to take calls, talk to people, accept expressions of condolence and inquiries about the time of the memorial service. Here, his solitude, should he wish it, could be complete.

Spock wandered through the empty house, noting that someone had made his parents' bed. The Healer's aide, probably. The Vulcan's fingers trailed across one of Amanda's woven hangings, and he pictured her weaving it, as he'd seen her at her loom as a child.

Remembering something, he took out his communicator. "Spock to *Enterprise* sickbay," he said.

"Sickbay," replied Leonard McCoy's voice. "McCoy here."

"Doctor . . . she is gone," the Vulcan said steadily.

"Spock, I'm sorry," McCoy's voice came back.

"Please inform the captain of my mother's . . ." He searched for a human euphemism. " . . . passing, and tell him that I will speak with him soon. There will be a brief memorial service when . . . when my father returns. I will inform you as soon as a time is determined."

McCoy hesitated, then said, "I understand, Spock. Do you want me or Jim to beam down?"

"No, Doctor. At the moment, I would prefer to be alone."

"I understand," McCoy said. "Spock . . . I grieve with thee."

McCoy's High Vulcan was very weak, but Spock appreciated the gesture. "Thank you, Doctor," the Vulcan replied. "Spock out."

Some random impulse drove him out of the house. It was the middle of the night here, on this side of the planet, and Amanda's garden was quiet and serene. Spock sat on the bench, facing The Watcher, gazing around him at the beauty Amanda had created. The well-ordered paths, the graceful desert trees and shrubs from a dozen worlds, all complemented the natural stone formations that had been there when the villa had first been built. She had done this, much of it with her own hands. . . .

Spock remembered working in this garden with her as a small child, carrying colored rocks that she would arrange in swirling designs, remembered helping her rake sand into graceful patterns. . . .

Something inside the Vulcan loosened, relaxed, and this time he allowed it to surface for a brief moment. Spock leaned forward on the bench, arms crossed over his belly, as the pain of her passing filled him, engulfed him. Hot tears welled in his eyes as he sat there, but only one broke free . . . and fell, to splash the soil in his mother's garden.

Five

Journal in hand, Sarek seated himself at the desk in his cabin aboard the transport vessel. The negotiations had been completed yesterday; Kadura was, at last, free, and he was headed home for Vulcan.

Alone in his cabin, he placed the journal on the desk and, opening it, located the place where he had left off the night before. His wife's handwriting, symmetrical, flowing, and refined—a schoolteacher's elegant cursive—traveled over the white pages, bringing back memories, almost as though she were here, speaking directly to him. Yesterday he'd read her account of their first meeting and their courtship, up until the point where they had left Earth together. Now, seeing the date at the top of the next page, the ambassador braced himself for another onslaught of bittersweet memory.

September 16, 2229

Within the hour we will be in orbit around Vulcan—my new home. It hardly seems possible that so much has happened in such a short time!

I am alone in my cabin, as I have been throughout the trip . . . even though I am a married woman, by every law on Earth. But my husband follows traditional Vulcan ways, and insists that we wait until after the Vulcan ceremony before consummating our marriage. In the four months since that first walk on the beach, the first time he kissed me, Sarek has allowed me to see deeper into his mind and heart than I could ever have imagined. Not that he has been exactly . . . forthcoming. But I have learned to read even the tiniest change of expression on his face, learned to recognize every faint alteration of tone and inflection . . . learned to interpret meaning from what he doesn't say as much as from what he actually says.

And today, in anticipation of the Vulcan ceremony this evening, there was the Bonding.

How can mere human words describe what no one on my homeworld has ever experienced? Physically, it was simple, undramatic. Sarek gravely invited me into his cabin (for the first time in our week-long journey), and solemnly poured a glass of some dark, heady-smelling brew into a cup carved from a single crimson stone veined with dull gold. He added several pinches of herbs, then gestured me to a seat, all without speaking a single word. . . .

Sarek watched his betrothed sit down on the low couch in his cabin, arranging her long, pale turquoise skirts carefully. When they had taken ship for Vulcan, Amanda had adopted the traditional garb of his homeworld for the first time, commenting that they would take some getting used to after the short skirts and trousers she was accustomed to.

With a grave, formal gesture, the diplomat passed her the cup. "Here, Amanda. Drink."

Gazing up at him over the ornate rim, she took a hesitant sip. "Oh . . ." she breathed, staring mystified at the contents. "That feels like liquid fire . . . but it's not liquor, is it?"

"No, it is not ethanol," Sarek said. "The drink does have a relaxing effect, but not an intoxicating one." He paused, watching her sip again, then continued. "Amanda, you know that, on my world, husbands and wives are bound by more than law and custom."

"Yes, Sarek," she replied. "They are linked telepathically."

"We call it 'bonding,'" Sarek said. "No marriage would be complete without it. This evening my world, my people, will witness the ceremony that will make us, as your people express it, 'one flesh.' By tonight we shall be married, under the laws and customs of both our worlds. But first . . . first there must come the bonding. That is something done in private, between the betrothed pair—either when they are children, or before the marriage ceremony."

Amanda hesitated in her turn, then said, "Is it difficult? Can we do it now?"

Sarek gazed at her, intent, profoundly serious. "It is not difficult for Vulcans," he said finally. "But it has never been attempted with a human."

"I am not telepathic," she reminded him. "You know that."

"I know. But I do not believe that is necessary. Our bond will not be the same as that shared by a Vulcan couple, but I believe it will be as lasting, as deep, in its own way." The Vulcan raised his hand slowly, ceremoniously. "Will you let me try, my wife-to-be?"

"Yes," Amanda said, evenly, though he could see her pulse jump in her throat. She took a deep, final draft of the cup, then set it aside.

Sarek gave her the faint smile that he reserved for her alone, pleased by her courage. "It will seem strange to you," he warned. "My mind will merge with yours, in a very deep meld. It may feel . . . invasive. But I would never harm you, Amanda, remember that."

"I will," she said, her voice still calm—but she licked her lips, as though her mouth had gone dry.

Holding out two fingers, Sarek extended his hand toward his wife-to-be. Slowly, steadily, she raised her hand to meet his.

Sarek sent his consciousness questing outward, and felt his mind brush Amanda's. He shared her awareness of him, of the first stages of the meld; the heat of his touch against her hand . . . the seeking tendrils of his mind touching the outer fringes of her thoughts.

He went deeper, cautiously, carefully, anxious lest he cause her pain. Her love and trust surrounded him. She opened to him, like some alien flower spreading its petals to the sun. Slowly . . . very slowly . . . he eased deeper, strengthening the meld.

Raising his other hand, he spread it against the contact points on her face, feeling her cool flesh against the warmth of his. Deeper . . . deeper . . .

Amanda was now aware of him stirring in her mind, coming to life, the fibers of his being joining to hers, linking, bonding, melding: her mind was becoming sealed to his in a joining so profound that it could only be broken by a High Master—or death.

Sarek could feel her instinctive need to pull back, away—and could feel her fighting it, forcing calmness and acceptance. He send a wordless reassurance that she would not lose her individuality by this bonding, then felt her relax. He felt a wave of pride; she was brave, this woman he had chosen. Such a deep meld was enough to make even a Vulcan resist . . . but she strove for wholehearted joining.

Surrounded now by her mind, Sarek experienced Amanda's goodness, her intelligence—and her heartfelt love for him. The awareness moved him as nothing ever had. The bond he had shared with T'Rea had been a pale shadow compared to this, a travesty of intimacy.

Now he was completely within her, and the sharing they experienced was more intimate than anything either of them had ever known. He felt the last of her fear melt away, experienced her joy in their union. Amanda had longed to be one with him—and now, after so many months, she was. Her happiness suffused him, bathing him in unaccustomed emotion—but Sarek did not retreat from that emotion, here in the privacy of their joined minds. It was appropriate for a bonded couple to share such closeness. . . .

Their mental sharing was so complete, so total, that by the time Sarek withdrew his mind, his fingers encountered moisture. Tears streaked Amanda's face, and she grasped his hand tightly when he moved it away. "Oh, Sarek . . ." she whispered. "That was . . . wonderful. Will it be this way from now on?"

He nodded. "It will," he promised. "We will always be conscious of one another. We will be together as long as we both live."

Raising his hand to her lips, she kissed him gently. "Thank you," she said, softly. "I wanted to be part of you . . . and now I am. . . ."

She shook her head, put her hands up to her temples. "So many images," she murmured. "Things I never saw before are now in my mind. Those are your memories, aren't they?"

"Yes. The infusion may be . . . chaotic . . . at first, but it will sort itself out, given time."

"Faces . . . conversations . . . so much to absorb . . ." she whispered softly; then her expression tightened. "Wait a minute." She sat up straight. "There's an image . . . Sarek, *who is she?*" she demanded, in a tone that brooked no opposition.

The Vulcan had an uncomfortable notion that he knew what she was talking about, but he said only, "To whom are you referring, Amanda?"

"This woman. The one in your mind. Lovely, delicate features, masses of black hair. You . . . desired . . . her. It's in your mind. You . . . you . . ." She groped for a word. "You were *intimate* with her." Amanda's eyes flashed cobalt.

Sarek sighed. "T'Rea," he said. "My first wife."

"You were *married?* And you didn't *tell* me?" She sat bolt upright, furious. "How could you?"

Sarek regretted his lapse. Amanda's temper was not one to be trifled with. "Yes, I was married to T'Rea. Briefly. But she divorced me."

"Why didn't you tell me?"

"Because, to explain how she became my wife, I would have to reveal something so private to Vulcans that it is never spoken of to outworlders. But you are my wife-to-be, so I must tell you. I had intended to wait until after the marriage ceremony, however . . ." He spread his hands upward.

"Explain, then," Amanda said, waiting.

Sarek launched into a fairly composed, concise explanation of the Vulcan mating drive, and how a Vulcan couple in the throes of *pon farr* could mate, and yet have little interaction in each other's lives. He concluded, hesitantly, "Amanda, there is one final thing you must know. I never . . . shared . . . with her, what I experience with you. Understand that. My marriage to T'Rea was not a marriage in terms of what you and I will experience as a married couple. We have agreed to share our lives together, which is far different than the brief encounter I experienced with T'Rea when my Time came."

"I see," she said, finally, thoughtfully. "And will you experience this . . . *pon farr* again? When?"

"I cannot tell," Sarek said, honestly. "But I believe that I will, and that it will be soon. My Time with T'Rea was almost seven years ago, now."

"What a honeymoon," she murmured, shaking her head. "Oh, Sarek, I wish you had told me all this before!"

"I explained—I could not speak of it to anyone except my wife. No outworlder must know."

"I understand," she said, finally.

Just then, the ship's intercom chimed, informing them that they were about to enter Vulcan orbit. Amanda jumped up from the couch, clearly flustered. "Oh, dear. I have barely an hour to make myself presentable for the wedding!"

"You should assume the traditional garb," Sarek said. "But your appearance is . . . everything that could be desired, Amanda."

Meeting his eyes, she flushed. "What a lovely compliment," she said. "Now I know why you're such a successful diplomat. But my hair . . ." She peered at the mirror in his cabin. "I must run," she said. "I will see you in an hour."

"In an hour," he promised. . . .

Remembering his wedding, Sarek turned the page to see what Amanda had written about it.

September 16, LATER

I am so tired, and yet before I allow myself to close my eyes, I must note down my thoughts, my feelings, lest they slip away by morning's light.

I am sitting here at a small table in the corner of the bedchamber. Vulcan beds are hard, barely yielding, but I suppose I will become accustomed to that with time. I am writing by the light of my pen, clad only in my lightest nightgown—because, despite Sarek's having air-conditioning installed specially for me, it is hot. By midnight, Sarek assures me, the temperature will have dropped, as it does in desert climates.

My husband is asleep. I can hear him breathing, lightly, slowly. I wonder if any Vulcans snore? Thank all the gods that ever were, Sarek does not!

The ceremony went well, all things considered. It was held in a stone-pillared and rock-walled sort of natural amphitheater that Sarek told me was the traditional marriage site for his people for many, many generations. It reminded me of Stonehenge. 40 Eridani hovered just above the horizon as we spoke our vows, staining the red stone even redder. I managed to follow Sarek's cues without any horrible gaffes, and though the few words of Vulcan I managed to speak probably sounded like nothing ever heard before on the planet, no one reacted.

The marriage rite was presided over by two Vulcan women—T'Kar, the oldest female in the family, a wizened old creature who seemed to be half-asleep during the entire ceremony, and the person who actually officiated, named T'Pau.

I don't quite understand T'Pau's exact relationship to Sarek—Vulcan kinships are complicated, and somewhat differently structured than human families—she is something on the order of his eldest great-aunt, I believe.

T'Pau is some kind of matriarch, either by right of blood, or natural authority. Her word is, apparently, law. I suspect she's not exactly thrilled at having a human join her family . . . but she could teach Emily Post a thing or two about tradition and cutting-edge etiquette!

Fortunately, the ceremony only took about fifteen minutes — if it had been any longer, I'd have dropped from the heat, I'm sure. We then boarded ground transport and returned to the ancient family enclave, where the reception was held.

(I gather that many receptions are held outside, in the gardens, but this one, in deference to my human constitution, was held in the central hall. The temperature controls had been adjusted downward a few degrees. All the Vulcans were wearing jackets and shawls, while I could hardly wait to shed my outer robe, light and gauzy as it was!)

Earth's ambassador, Eleanor Jordan, was the only other human present. She offered a typical human toast to the wedded pair, which all the Vulcans courteously drank.

As soon as was decently possible, Sarek touched my arm, and we slipped out. He led me through stone corridors opening onto chambers filled with ancient furnishings, down a winding staircase to a transporter pad installed in the basement of the building—it looked so anachronistic set into that millennia-old red stone floor!

Sarek's house is located in ShiKahr, and is quite nice. Sparsely but impeccably furnished. It was long past sunset when we beamed here, so I received only a hazy impression of the outside. Sarek says there are gardens, which pleases me immensely. I brought some desert plant seedlings with me, in the hopes I can coax them to grow and thus have some touches of Earth here on my new home.

Even while he is asleep, I can sense Sarek's mind brushing mine.

Today, before the ceremony, Sarek enlightened me about Vulcan sexual drives. Very different from a human's libido! It seems that Vulcans undergo something he called pon farr *. . . much like the heat cycles experienced by some Terran creatures. Vulcans are capable of mating and conceiving at other times, but, during* pon farr *they must mate—if they don't, they can die!*

Sarek, my husband . . . I can scarcely believe it, even after tonight. It seems too wonderful to be true, that we can now share the same bed, and that I will wake up next to him tomorrow, and tomorrow, and for all the tomorrows we will have together. . . .

Sarek closed the journal with a sigh, unable to read any more. Resting his head in his hands, he strove to meditate, but images of Amanda intruded, filling his mind. *Amanda,* he thought, feeling grief fill him anew. *Amanda . . . that was the happiest night of my life, too.*

Valdyr watched Karg salute her uncle, then exit, leaving them alone on the cloaked warbird's small bridge. The last thing Karg did before the doors slid shut behind him was give her a long, promising leer.

I can wait for our wedding night, his expression said, *for my wait will not be long.*

Valdyr glowered at him, touching the hilt of her dagger, and her gesture was just as suggestive. His very presence sent her blood boiling with passion—but not the passion he wanted. *You will wait, Karg,* she thought with murderous hatred, *until Qo'noS's polar caps melt.* Unfortunately, with the destruction of Praxis and the subsequent environmental problems the Klingon homeworld was facing, that might not be very long indeed.

If she could only talk her uncle out of this disastrous plan of his! She turned to face the ambassador, who was absorbed, watching the surveillance screens.

"Uncle," she said with a firmness she did not feel, "we must talk."

He glanced at her, then went back to watching the image on the screen. A lone human male lay curled in an embryonic position on the narrow, shelflike bunk. "Niece, come see your charge."

Valdyr moved closer to him, staring at the silent, unmoving human. She could detect no movement, not even breathing. Was the prisoner still alive?

"He will be your responsibility," Kamarag reminded her. "The warbird's crew tells me that young Kirk has eaten nothing in the five days since his capture. He only uses his food to ask questions, and spell out his name, rank, and some meaningless number. Worse than that, he has drunk only a small amount of water. For the last day, they said, he has not moved at all."

How grotesque, Valdyr thought, *to just curl up and surrender.* This is what her uncle thought was an honorable prisoner?

"Typical," Kamarag remarked, studying the prisoner and shaking his head. "Most humans, it has been my experience, are a weak, spineless lot. I regret that this one will probably not afford you much amusement, niece."

In Klingon society, guarding prisoners of war was traditionally women's work. And, for the most hated prisoners (and humans certainly qualified for that category), the female jailers took delight in administering the *be'joy'*—the ritualized "torture-by-women."

In a world controlled by Klingon warriors, a woman could release much of the frustration engendered by the male-dominated society on a strong, healthy prisoner.

"It is critically important that this man live and be healthy, do you understand, my niece?" Kamarag's order intruded on her thoughts.

Valdyr scowled. She would have to *nurse* this feeble weakling? Klingon prisoners were not usually coddled. A touch of hope glimmered in her breast. Was her uncle finally realizing the magnitude of his actions? Was this his way of softening the offense? Yes, that had to be it. He would strengthen the dying human so as to have a healthy hostage to return in exchange for Captain Kirk. It could, perhaps, salvage some honor in the end.

"He must be strong, so that when Kirk comes to claim him," Kamarag explained in his most rational, ambassadorial voice, "this sniveling weakling can endure a good, lengthy *be'joy'*—while his uncle is forced to watch!"

Valdyr's color deepened and her eyes widened against her will. Where was the honor in that? There was no craft in this plan, no politics, just duplicity and cruelty. The shame of it made her glower at the deckplates.

"Don't worry, my dear niece," Kamarag said comfortingly, giving her a congenial hug, "*that* task will be yours as well. A reward for the distasteful work ahead of you—guarding this stinking alien, this blood kin of *va* Kirk! His torture will be my wedding gift to you—something to whet your appetites and insure a passionate night with your new husband!"

Valdyr had to bite the inside of her check to keep from erupting into gales of hysterical laughter. Had all she learned at her father's side of honor, battle, and glory been lies? Was this *really* the way Klingons conducted themselves—by betraying their leaders, lying, cheating, and abusing the helpless? Her father would have killed this man for what he was about to do.

"Now, what is it you wished to speak to me about?"

The young woman blinked, having nearly forgotten. She swallowed, knowing already how futile this would be. "I . . . I wish to speak once more . . . of my plans. The plans I made for my life, while my father was still alive."

Kamarag drew away from her, his face taking on his more "official" look.

"My father, as you must know, encouraged my learning," she reminded him. "He trained me himself, along with my four brothers, in all the warriors' arts."

Kamarag nodded. "You were your father's favorite, of that, I'm well aware. Training you was his way of proving your worth, since he made the healers work so hard to save you in infancy."

She nodded, lowering her eyes. In many families, a weak, small, sickly baby as she had been would have been allowed to die. But her father would not permit it and demanded the healers save her. Perhaps it was because she was his only daughter. Her mother liked to tell her that he'd bellowed at the doctors that Valdyr's will to live was proof that she carried a man's share of noble warrior's blood. And he'd trained her as stringently as her stronger brothers. She'd loved him for that.

"My father," she reminded Kamarag, "felt my mind was as strong as my skills, as strong as my will to live. He wanted me to continue my schooling. He knew I was not strong enough to serve as a warrior . . . but hoped I might have other skills almost as valuable to offer the Empire. He hoped—and I shared his dream—that I might follow *you*, Uncle, into diplomacy."

Kamarag raised his head in surprise. It was a compliment, and she could see he was taking it as such.

She continued quickly, before he could stop her. "At the time, it was a dream, a fantasy, but now . . . with Azetbur holding such an important political role, it would not be thought so unusual if I . . ."

The ambassador glowered. "Azetbur! The role she has usurped is a travesty! If she were a decent female she would have married again! Then, she could hand her seat over to her husband, as it should be!"

Valdyr yearned to remind her uncle that Azetbur's husband had been killed in the same attack that had killed the chancellor's father—but that it had been Azetbur herself that Gorkon had wanted to succeed him.

"And it is this depraved female you would model yourself after?"

"Oh, no, Uncle, it is *you* I would . . ."

"Do not flatter me, niece! I have been a politician since long before you were born!" He was furious now, and Valdyr had no idea how to placate him.

"But . . . my father—"

"Your father is *dead!*" he reminded her brutally. "*I* am the head of this family, and you will follow the life I prepare for you! You will marry Karg, and be a faithful wife, and bear him as many male children as your body can grow. Your glory will be in the success of your husband and male children. You will *not* live a life of perversion and depravity as that damnable Azetbur has. Do you understand me?"

Valdyr was stunned by her uncle's reaction. Stunned and heartsick. But she showed not a trace of it on her face. She would not shame her father's memory by displaying weakness. "Yes, my uncle. I understand clearly."

"Then, let us be family," he said quietly, "and never speak of this again." He turned back to regard the surveillance screens.

Valdyr struggled to control her disappointment. She'd hoped that her uncle would listen to reason . . . but he would not.

While she and her uncle had had their brief discussion, she'd been peripherally aware of the screens that displayed Karg's progress through the warbird. His lieutenant, Treegor, accompanied him. The two officers had picked up Peter Kirk from a rendezvous point on the edge of explored space, from the tramp freighter/contraband runner that had smuggled him off Earth.

Now, after landing on Qo'noS, at TengchaH Jav, the spaceport closest to Du'Hurgh, Kamarag's huge estate, it was time, at last, to remove the prisoner from his cell. As Karg stalked through the corridors, he carried in his gauntleted hand an electronic key that was the only means of opening the door to the security cell.

Through all of this, the figure on the bunk had never stirred, never twitched. *Yes, Karg,* Valdyr thought bitterly, *bring my uncle his dead prize.*

Finally, Karg and his lieutenant reached the prisoner's cabin. Karg inserted the key and left it in, so that the doors would remain open. Both men were relaxed, talking and laughing with each other, confident that the human, even in health, could be no match for them.

Karg leaned over the prisoner and shook the man's shoulder. There was no response; the captive's arm swung limply, then hung, flaccid.

"He . . . cannot be *dead?*" her uncle muttered, as if contemplating that possibility for the first time. "If he is dead . . ."

You have nothing, Valdyr thought, *nothing but shame.*

"No, he lives!" Kamarag muttered as Karg and his assistant lifted the limp form by the arms, slapping him lightly. The man seemed almost boneless, his head lolling back and forth, his eyes shut, his mouth sagging open.

He had to be alive, or his body would have stiffened with the death rictus. Karg slapped the human's face again, harder, but there was no response.

Suddenly, the prisoner groaned piteously and sagged even more. Karg and his lieutenant bowed over his form to prevent him from collapsing to the deck, and for a moment the human was lost to view, blocked by the warriors' broad backs.

Then, in the next instant, the two Klingons lurched toward each other, their heads meeting with a resounding crack. They fell backward, staggering. The human had suddenly awakened, grabbed the warriors and forced them together.

The human was upright now, his entire demeanor changed dramatically. Spinning on one foot, he lashed out with his other, catching Treegor on the chin. The warrior crashed to the deck, unconscious. Karg was up now, and in a murderous rage, blood trickling from a head-plate cut. With a roar, he charged the human, who moved low and struck the warrior with his fists hard, once, twice, three times just below the breastplate, in a warrior's most vulnerable place. The air rushed out of Karg's lungs, and all he could do was swing wildly. He managed to strike the human on the shoulder, but the man took the blow well, and punched Karg twice, in his right eye.

This human knows us, Valdyr realized. He'd wasted no energy attacking the places where warriors would feel little pain. Her gaze sharpened with interest. She had not realized that humans could fight so well—or be so clever!

Karg lunged after the human, meaning to snatch him up and throw him into the nearest wall, but the smaller male held his place until the last second, then dodged the attack. Grabbing Karg by his armor, he shoved the big warrior hard, and Karg's forward momentum ran him right into the bulkhead. His head struck with stunning force, and he slid down the wall, dazed.

Without a wasted moment, young Kirk raced out of his cell, grabbing the electronic key on his way out. Karg struggled to his feet to pursue his escaping quarry, but the doors slid shut in front of him, locking him inside. Valdyr stifled her laughter as she took in Karg's stupefied expression.

"Hu'tegh!" Kamarag cursed, slapping his palm on the alarm button. The raucous sound of the blaring klaxon instantly filled the air.

They watched the human on the surveillance screens as he raced down the corridors. Kamarag's hands flew over the control panel, and on another screen the two warriors Karg had gotten the key from suddenly appeared. They were in the mess hall, eating. They looked up in response to the alarm.

"Hurry!" Kamarag yelled through the intercom. "The human is loose in the ship!" As the warriors abandoned their meals and ran out, the ambassador secured all airlocks.

Valdyr headed for the bridge doors.

"And where are you going?" Kamarag demanded as the doors slid open before her.

"I'm going to recapture my prisoner," she informed him matter-of-factly. He seemed about to protest, but Karg's shouting as he hammered against his prison door quickly distracted him. She was in the hall before he had another second to think about it.

The human will head for the bridge, she decided. It would be the only way he could effect a genuine escape. Leaving the ship would merely strand him on a planet where he would be the only one of his kind, and entirely too easy to find. No, he'd need to get to the bridge, commandeer it. No doubt he'd figure out where it was in a matter of minutes. He was clever, this human.

Those of us that are not as strong must develop our minds all the more, she thought, grinning with the excitement of the pursuit. She was eager to go against this man. *This warrior*, she thought, shocking herself. And what else should he be called? Starved, dehydrated, and inactive for days, this human had managed to have both the strength *and* the cunning to overcome two of Kamarag's best warriors.

Valdyr raced down the corridor, heading toward the prisoner's cabin. She realized then that she had no weapon but her knife, and her fighting skills. She could not stun the man; she would have to fight him barehanded. She frowned. Would he fight her? Or would he give her that *look*, that patronizing expression warriors always gave her? *It would be shameful for a warrior to fight a* woman, she was always told.

And she always responded, *No, it is only shameful to fight her . . . and* lose. Gritting her teeth, she slid to a halt behind a juncture of corridors. This was the path to the bridge. To reach it, he would have to come through her.

Valdyr heard the thudding of feet on deckplates, then a Klingon warrior's guttural shout. She peered around the corner, her body hidden by the angled wall. The human, who'd been headed her way, spun around to face a Klingon racing toward him from the rear. Young Kirk waited until the warrior was nearly on top of him, then with an earsplitting yell of his own, leaped high in the air, smashing both feet into the warrior's face. The Klingon hit the deckplates so hard they shuddered. Kirk landed badly himself, pulling himself up with an effort. Panting for breath, he moved steadily toward her.

The Klingon woman stepped into his path from behind the curve and he stopped short. Chest heaving, he gulped for air. It had cost him, this fight, and she could see he was near the end of his strength.

"It is over," she said clearly in English. "You have fought well. Be proud. Now yield, and come with me."

Kirk was clearly surprised to hear her use his language. His shoulders sagged, as if in defeat, but she didn't trust him and went into a defensive stance. His gaze moved over her, taking in her posture, and his expression hardened with determination. "In a pig's eye!" Kirk answered.

She blinked, unable to translate the idiom. "You will yield!" she ordered, and launched herself at him.

Valdyr felt ashamed of her advantage. She doubted he would use the same force on her as he'd been willing to use on the Klingon males. His unwillingness to do that would allow her to conquer him, but she wouldn't enjoy it. She was still thinking that when his fist hit her cheek with stunning force.

Her head snapped back harshly, and she growled as blood poured from the corner of her lip. Drawing back, she landed a powerful right to his jaw, and he staggered. She moved to follow it through with a left, but he blocked the blow. Kirk brought his hand down in a hard chop at her neck, but she dodged and it landed ineffectively on her leather shoulder pad. Bringing the heel of her hand up under his chin, she snapped his head back with the force of the blow. Kirk grunted and went down.

Before he'd even finished landing, however, he'd scissored his legs between hers and knocked her to the deck. He landed on her roughly, struggling to get a grip on her hair and slam her head against the deckplates. Swinging her legs up, she flipped both of them end over end, then straddled him. "Yield, human!" she bellowed, and struck him hard in the face. His head cracked against the floor, he gave a sigh, and his eyes rolled up.

Valdyr eased off her prisoner carefully, fully aware that he might be feigning unconsciousness. Klingon boots thundered down the hall, and when she looked up, Karg, Treegor, the two crewmen, and her uncle were there, their eyes moving between the unconscious human on the floor and her. She was panting and sweating over him, the blood from her lip dripping puce droplets onto her armor.

Raging, Karg snarled, "Let me kill this *Ha'DIbah* now!" and lunged for the helpless body.

"You will not!" Valdyr heard herself shout as she thrust herself between them, shoving the warrior back roughly.

He moved on her, but by then her dagger was out of its sheath and in front of his face. He paused. Valdyr's warrior blood was coursing through her now. "Is this how a Klingon warrior kills his enemy?" she taunted her betrothed. "Waits until he's helpless and kills him in his sleep? Is that your path to honor, Karg?"

No one in the corridor moved. Karg's face flamed with shame. Valdyr was surprised when her uncle said nothing, merely stared at her reflectively.

Treegor grumbled at her, "This *human* is not worthy to be our enemy. He is a *parasite,* brought down by a *woman.* He deserves no honorable consideration."

"Be careful, Treegor," she warned. "This human brought *you* down with one blow, and outfought and outwitted the rest of you. He did that after a long fast and in a weakened state. He has earned the respect due a warrior."

Without another word, she sheathed her dagger. Then, reaching down, she grabbed the unconscious human by the wrists, hauled him up, and slung him over her shoulder. Valdyr struggled not to stagger; Kirk was heavier than he looked, but she could not afford to show weakness in front of this group now.

"Valdyr," said Kamarag quietly, "where are you taking him?"

"To the prison cell you have prepared for him," she said, managing to speak clearly in spite of her burden. "I will take him in the aircar we brought. He is my prisoner, is he not? He needs medical attention, and possibly force-feeding. Your orders on the matter of his care were very clear."

"Do . . . you not wish help?" Kamarag asked.

"Do you think I need it?" she challenged, meeting his eyes.

He raised his head as if insulted, but when Karg attempted to speak, he held up his hand to silence the warrior. Karg looked outraged. "No," Kamarag said quietly. "I do not think you need help." And with a gesture that was almost a salute, he permitted her to leave.

As Valdyr stumped toward the airlock with her heavy burden, she heard Karg say angrily to her uncle, "I will not tolerate such insolence when we are wed! I will beat that smugness out of her the first night!"

To her pleasure she heard Kamarag reply, "I do not believe a warrior's heart is so easily conquered, Karg. You may have to rethink your approach."

See, Peter told himself, *you were right the first time. You should've never woken up!* He lay perfectly still on the unyielding surface where he'd been tossed. The truth was, he was afraid to move. Every single part of him *hurt*—not just a little, but with a bone-jarring, muscle-deep, migraine-type pain the likes of which he'd never known.

Well, what did you expect, mister? You took on the whole damned Klingon army.

Klingons! He'd been kidnapped by Klingons. Well, everything he'd ever read about them was true. They could fight like mountain gorillas, and they seemed about as strong. His aching body testified to that.

But why would Klingons want to kidnap him in the first place? Ever since Jim Kirk and his crew had saved Chancellor Azetbur, his uncle had become a favored person among the Klingon populace.

But not every Klingon, he knew, supported Azetbur's rule.

He tried to recall the two soldiers who'd come for him. Their garb had been military—black and dark gray leather studded with metal, spiked boots and gloves—but the official insignia of the Klingon Empire was not pinned on their left sleeves. Instead, there'd been another insignia stitched on the leather, intertwined with what must have been the sigil of a high-ranking house.

He tried to gauge the gravity of this place by the weight of his body as it lay still. It was hard to say without moving. He was heavier than he was on Earth, just a fraction, perhaps, but there was a difference. Of course, some of that could be due to swollen muscle tissue! He wondered if he was on one of the Klingon worlds, or on Qo'noS itself. And he wondered if he'd ever find a way out of this mess. Despair washed over him like a bucket of ice water.

Klingons rarely kept prisoners, but when they did . . . there was plenty of speculation about what happened to those unfortunates. Would they kill him? Torture him?

Tales of the infamous Klingon mind-sifter ran through his memory. Determinedly, Peter took deep breaths, in through his nose, out through his mouth, until he felt calmer.

"I know you are awake, human," a highly accented feminine voice growled at him.

He knew that voice. He'd heard it at least once before. Yes. Before its owner whipped the tar out of him. He allowed one eyelid to creep open.

There she was, all right, the woman of his nightmares. She loomed over him, but carefully remained out of reach. As if he had enough energy even to lift his head, never mind take her on again. What a *punch* she had!

"You are dehydrated, human," she told him. "You need water and food. I am prepared to force-feed you if you will not cooperate with me. The choice is yours."

Her English was amazingly good, if oddly accented, Peter realized. He opened the other eye.

She was small, barely tall enough to reach Peter's shoulder, and slenderly built. Her long dark hair, braided into a rope as thick as Peter's wrist, hung over her shoulder and fell to her thighs. The Klingon woman's skin was the color of warm honey, her features delicate and feminine. Even the ridges on her forehead were elegant— sharply defined, but not as massive as those of the male Klingons. The effect was almost charming. *Like the lovely head of the cobra,* Peter thought wryly.

She wore the same military-like garb that the males had, with the same insignia on it. As Peter's eyes met hers, she lifted her chin and stared back at him levelly.

"You will sit up, or I will pull you into a sitting position," she ordered him.

The last thing he wanted was for this Amazon to handle him again. He rolled onto his side and struggled to sit up without groaning. Easing his legs over the ledge of whatever he was lying on, he settled into the ordered position, only to sag back against a wall.

"I know you now, human," the female Klingon informed him, "so do not attempt to deceive me. I defeated you once and will happily do so again."

Holding up his hands, Peter tried futilely to moisten his mouth and speak. He craved water as he'd never craved anything before; he didn't even care if it was drugged. In fact, he wished it was. It might alleviate some of this pain.

"Here, drink this," she ordered him, holding a squeeze bottle out to him.

He clutched at it, his hands covering hers, as the fluid streamed into his mouth. It was clear, clean, pure water, and tasted more wonderful than anything he'd ever consumed. Cruelly, she pulled the bottle away before he'd had more than a few swallows.

"Slowly!" she snapped. "You have been weakened by your battle. Too much fluid too soon will only make you ill. Here, swallow these, and you may have more water to wash them down."

He stared uncomprehendingly at some tiny pills in her palm.

"They are human medication. They are for pain. Take them . . . or no more water."

He took them willingly and again clutched her hands as she allowed him more water from the squeeze bottle. Her skin was so *warm.*

This time, when she took the bottle away, her face seemed to soften a little. He released his grip on her reluctantly, wondering when she'd offer the water again.

"There is warm broth in this bottle," she told him, showing it to him. "It is Klingon, but it is specially made for injured warriors. It is food and medicine all in one. I have consulted with the information we have on human physiology and I assure you it will bring you no harm. You will drink it . . . or I will feed it to you like an infant."

Peter nodded at her. He'd drink it . . . the water had awakened an echo of hunger. He moistened his lips again and asked, "Why do you care?" His voice was little more than a croak.

She frowned, confused.

"Why should you care if I eat or not? Whether I drink too much water and get sick? Why do you care?"

"My uncle has assigned me to see to your welfare," she explained, her tone curt, but no longer fierce. She handed him the bottle of broth. "I am to restore your health."

He nodded. Her job. That explained everything, and nothing. He sipped the warm brew gingerly, no longer interested in the politics of hunger-striking. Surprisingly, the liquid was savory and satisfying. As its warmth traveled through him, he found his spirits improving. Peter wondered how long it would be before the pills took effect. He was tired of pain following every faint movement.

Taking another sip of the broth, he looked around his new environment. All his great battle had done was earn him more scars and a new cell. This one was not much larger than his prison aboard the ship, but he knew very well that he was no longer in space.

The windowless walls were closely fitted blocks of stone that had been cemented over, not altogether successfully, because patches of the ancient brownish gray stonework showed through. He was perched on a sleeping platform consisting of a slab of stone with some kind of woven blanket thrown atop it.

On his left was a hole in the ground, what he now recognized as the Klingon version of a no-frills head. This one didn't appear to have been used within the last century. The door was ancient wood reinforced with metal, but the locks holding it closed were modern—incongruous against the old wood. Beside the door was a clear observation panel with a speaker set beneath it. A four-legged stool was placed near it.

The walls around him seemed as tough as neutronium. He thought of a book his uncle had brought him once—*The Count of Monte Cristo*.

Sure, he thought. *Give me a spoon, and I'll be out of here in a mere fourteen years. . . .*

This was definitely not the Klingon Hilton.

Peter took a deep breath, trying to take stock of his situation. *What would Jim Kirk do?* he wondered; then, glancing at the young Klingon woman's slender but attractive figure, he repressed a grim smile. *Yeah, right. I know just what Uncle Jim would do! Even with a Klingon, if she was as nicely built as this one . . . too bad I don't have his luck.*

Taking a few more healthy swallows of the broth, he savored the taste. It was spicy, burning his tongue, but he'd always won the chili cook-offs in school. He loved hot food. He looked at the bottle, surprised to be feeling some of his aches easing up already. "This is very good broth."

She cocked her head at him suspiciously. "I had always heard that humans were too weak to tolerate our food."

He shrugged cautiously. "I'll make you chili some day and we can discuss it. I like this well enough. And I'm feeling better. Thank you."

She seemed wary, then uncomfortable, but finally said, "I, too, thank *you*."

He stared at her, at a loss. "What for?"

"For fighting me. For treating me as an honorable opponent. It was a good battle! I believe . . . that if you were well . . . you might have won!"

Peter sat up straighter, forcing his brain into alertness. Klingons put a lot of store in honor—it was everything to them. But women didn't get much benefit from the heavily patriarchal system. He started to introduce himself. "My name is—"

She cut him off abruptly. "I know who you are."

He raised an eyebrow. Of course she knew who he was. She'd helped kidnap him, hadn't she? "And . . . my honorable opponent is . . . ?" he prodded. The ploy was deliberate. It would become harder to think of him as her victim if he started becoming a *person* to her.

She hesitated, and he wondered if she knew that. Finally, she said quietly, "I am Valdyr."

He nodded. Interesting name. He wondered if it meant anything. *Yeah. She-who-mops-the-floor-with-Starfleet-cadets!* "Valdyr, have I earned the right to know why I'm here?" He was pushing it, he knew, but what could she do, besides refuse? *And beat the hell out of you again?*

She seemed suddenly troubled, and glanced around the cell. He didn't speak, just took a few more sips of broth and waited patiently. Finally, she spoke. *"My* uncle has declared a blood feud against *your* uncle. The government no longer wants vengeance against James Kirk, since he saved the life of Chancellor Azetbur. So, to regain his honor, my uncle must act on his own. James Kirk will be sent a message to come alone to a certain place in space. There my uncle's guards will take him, and bring him here. Once he is here," she paused, staring at him for a long moment, then finally continued, "you will be released."

She's lying, Peter thought, but decided not to pursue it. He didn't have the strength to face his possible future as a Klingon prisoner. "What will happen to my uncle once Kamarag has him?" Peter asked, even though he already knew.

Valdyr refused to meet his eyes. "My uncle has a debt of honor to settle with him. If you know what that is, you know what will happen."

Torture and, eventually, execution, Peter thought grimly. "Why the blood feud, Valdyr? I know my uncle has fought your people throughout his career, but our peoples are working toward peace, now."

"Your uncle left a Klingon to perish on an exploding world," Valdyr said quietly. "That warrior was my uncle's closest friend and protégé."

"Kruge? I mean, Captain Kruge?" Peter was nonplussed. "But . . . that was over three years ago!"

" 'Revenge, like a *targ,* rouses hungry after a sleep,' " she said, obviously quoting an old proverb.

"Wait a minute. Captain Kruge ordered my cousin David's death," Peter argued. "Kruge's men murdered him in cold blood. If anyone has an old score to settle, it's *us,* not you."

Valdyr frowned. "What is this, 'cold blood'?"

"Uhhh . . . that means that Kruge thought about David's murder, then ordered it and was obeyed. He didn't kill him during a fight, or kill him by striking out blindly during an argument."

"That is not true!" Valdyr defended hotly. "David Marcus was a prisoner of war, who was executed while attacking a guard."

Peter glared at her. "That's not the way I heard it."

"My uncle told me," she said, matching his intensity.

They glowered at each other for a moment; then Peter relaxed. This was crazy, he decided. They were acting like the Hatfields and the McCoys. "Neither one of us was there, so we'll never know for sure. It's been my experience that the truth usually lies somewhere in the middle."

Valdyr gave him a surprised glance, then nodded slowly. "That has been my experience, too, Peter Kirk." The way she said his name made it sound like "Pityr."

She moved toward the heavy wooden door, but never turned her back. She wasn't going to be as easy to outwit as the goons they'd sent into his last cell, he realized. "I have brought you clean clothes." She nodded, indicating a pile of fabric that sat perched on the end of the stone bunk. "There are cloths in there . . . you would say for washing, for drying. There is soap. I will be bringing a basin for washing when you are no longer so thirsty and are ready to bathe. Your odor is too strong! If you do not willingly bathe, I will be forced to wash you myself!"

He couldn't help it. The mental image of this lovely but alien woman forcibly stripping him and lathering his naked body forced a smile onto Peter's bruised mouth. He winced even as he did it.

Her face darkened, and she advanced on him threateningly. "What is funny?"

He held up his hands placatingly. "Come on, Valdyr! Think about it. Don't Klingons have a sense of humor? Have you ever given a grown man a forced bath out of a basin before? What a . . . fascinating . . . image that idea presents!"

She scowled, but slowly her expression thawed, as if against her will. "Do not imagine that having me strip you and bathe you would be a pleasurable experience, Kirk, just because I am *female!*"

Peter widened his eyes innocently. "Why, Valdyr, such a thought never crossed *my* mind. But apparently . . . it crossed yours."

Her eyes narrowed as she digested this, then her skin visibly darkened. *She's blushing!*

"Of course . . . it is a potentially *appealing* scenario!" he continued, giving her a sidelong glance. "I don't believe humans and Klingons have ever had such . . . an intimate interaction. Truly an interstellar first!"

Valdyr's mouth dropped open, just slightly; then she whirled, opened the door, and slammed it shut almost before he realized what she was doing. Peter heard the locks on the other side activating in rhythmic succession. His jailer appeared on the other side of the observation port, glaring at him balefully.

Keep pushing your luck, mister. With a little more provocation, she just might beat you to death! He leaned forward and said quietly, "No disrespect intended to my most honorable opponent." He prayed his voice would carry through the port.

She seemed to relax at that, and her fierce expression lightened. Then, suddenly, a male Klingon appeared at her side, surprising both of them.

Oh, no, Peter thought, stunned as the man came into view. *This* was her uncle? Could it really be? He recognized Kamarag instantly—the Klingon who had declared so publicly that there would be no peace while James T. Kirk lived. Peter swallowed. Things were becoming entirely too clear.

Kamarag was big, his long dark hair and thick beard shot with gray, with heavy, jowly features that appeared never to have smiled. He glared at the young Kirk, and Peter could feel his hatred, as palpable as a clenched fist. The ambassador was *not* in uniform, but wore a longish oyster-white tunic over dark gray trousers, with a dark cape slung over one shoulder. An intricately carved leather strap held it in place. The strap bore the same insignia as the other Klingons wore—the insignia, no doubt, of the house of Kamarag.

The cadet stared at the ambassador. *Ambassador?* he thought. *What a joke. Sarek was an ambassador, a diplomat, a man of peace . . . this jerk was nothing but a warmonger, a kidnapper, a pompous ass, a . . .*

Peter ran out of silent epithets—his rage was suddenly too all-encompassing to be vented with mere insults. He had been drugged, kidnapped, beaten—and it was this man's fault. Trembling with fury, he glared at Kamarag, feeling a tirade on the verge of erupting.

Slowly, the impulse faded. What good would cursing and insulting Kamarag do? He needed to keep his wits about him, Peter realized. Jim Kirk might lose his temper at an enemy, but Sarek never would. And right now, he, Peter Kirk, needed to be *diplomatic.*

"Ambassador Kamarag," he said, and nodded politely to the older male.

But the Klingon ignored his greeting as he leaned forward and stared at the human. Slowly, his thick lips parted, and a terrible smile transformed his features. Peter felt every hair on his body rise. Then the Klingon turned to his niece. In Klingonese, he said, clearly, "He ate and drank?"

She nodded.

"Good," he continued, still in his native tongue. "I am depending on you, niece. Do not fail me. Make your prisoner strong and healthy. Treat him well." He patted the woman fondly on the shoulder. "He must be able to withstand your . . ."

Peter couldn't translate the last word, and searched his mind for its meaning, but came up blank. He'd caught the word for women, or female, in there, but as for the rest . . . he'd be willing to bet it wasn't a trip to the local equivalent of an amusement park that Kamarag was referring to. *Ordeal? Trial?* He had no way of knowing.

Kamarag was still conferring with Valdyr, smiling solicitously. When the older man turned back to stare at his prisoner once more, Peter found that the look the ambassador gave him chilled his blood. Then the elder Klingon stalked away. Peter turned back to Valdyr to ask her about what that term, *be'joy',* meant, and found, to his surprise, that her rich amber color had paled into a sickly yellow. Her eyes were wide as she watched her uncle stride away.

"Valdyr?" Peter asked softly, trying to get her attention. "What does *be'joy'* mean? I couldn't translate it. Hey, Valdyr!"

Her head snapped around and she stared at him wild-eyed. "Do *not* speak to me, human!" she commanded. "Remember your place. You are my *enemy.* My *prisoner.* And I am a Klingon!"

He was stunned to see her eyes filled with frustration and genuine grief; then she turned and stormed away, leaving him alone in his stone cell.

Sarek materialized on the windswept plateau high in the steppes above ShiKahr only minutes before sunset. Before him lay the steps leading to the top of Mount Seleya, where the ancient temple and amphitheater were located. The ambassador's robes flowed around him as he strode forward and began climbing. The stairs were steep and long; the Vulcan's heart was pounding by the time he reached the top, but he did not pause to catch his breath. Instead he detoured around the ancient, cylinder-shaped temple, heading for the small amphitheater.

The Vulcan was surprised by the number of people on the steps and ranged around the old temple. Glancing ahead, he could see that the amphitheater, reached by a narrow stone walkway that hung precariously over a thousand-meter gulf, was even more crowded.

Many people, it seemed, wished to pay last respects to the memory of his wife.

The ambassador had arrived on his homeworld only thirty minutes ago. First he had gone to the med center, where, after spending a few minutes with the physical shell that had housed his wife's spirit, Sarek authorized the cremation. Now he was at the temple, barely in time for the memorial service. The ceremony would be brief . . . his son had asked T'Lar, the High Master of Gol, to preside, and she had agreed.

As Sarek moved toward the small, shallow amphitheater, the crowd parted before him. The ambassador's gaze touched many familiar faces from his homeworld . . . diplomatic personnel and their families, as well as high-ranking government officials whom Sarek and Amanda had entertained during official functions. Members of his family whom he had not seen in years were there, heads respectfully bowed as they murmured the traditional words, "I grieve with thee."

Amanda would be gratified that so many of those who initially disapproved of our marriage have come to honor her memory, the ambassador thought, as he moved through the crowd.

As he crossed the narrow bridge, he saw that the highest-ranking officials and closest family members were awaiting him in the amphitheater—and there was his son, wearing a formal dark robe with ancient symbols embroidered in silver on the breast. Spock was standing with his crewmates from the *Enterprise*. As Sarek walked toward him, Spock glanced up, recognized his father, then, deliberately, looked away.

Sarek had not spoken to his son except for the brief, stilted words they had exchanged when Spock had called to inform his father of Amanda's passing. By the time Spock called him, the ambassador had known for nearly six hours that his wife was dead. When Sarek had attempted to speak about her, Spock had cut him off, then curtly informed his father that the final repairs to his ship would be completed within forty-eight Standard hours, and that he would be leaving Vulcan with his vessel.

As Sarek walked to the forefront of the gathering, Spock, still avoiding his father's gaze, silently took his place beside the ambassador. Together, they walked up to stand before the two huge, smooth pillars on the raised platform. From the side of one of the pillars, there was movement; then T'Lar, accompanied by two Acolytes, stepped forth. The High Master wore a dark brown robe with a pale gold overtunic.

As Sarek and Spock stood there, T'Lar began to speak: "Today we honor the memory of Amanda Grayson Sarek," she began, speaking Standard English in deference to the humans present. "She was a human who honored us with her presence on our world.

"From Amanda Grayson Sarek, we learned that our people and humans could live together in peace . . . that they could be allies, friends, and bondmates. Amanda Grayson Sarek possessed great strength, fortitude, and courage: the strength to survive a world that poses great hardships for outworlders; the fortitude to endure the suspicion and distrust in which humans were frequently held; and the courage to forever alter the way Vulcans view the people of Terra. She changed us, not through strident protest, but by quietly prevailing, becoming over the years a living testament.

"Today we honor her . . . we honor the wife, we honor the mother, we honor the teacher, we honor the person of Amanda Grayson Sarek. Her life is one to be held in highest regard and esteem."

T'Lar delivered her words in measured tones, raising her voice only to be heard above the wind, for the large crowd stood in complete, respectful silence.

After the High Master had finished, by tradition the spouse was supposed to speak. Sarek hesitated for a long moment after the last echo of T'Lar's voice had faded into silence, then said: "As a diplomat, I use words as a builder would use tools. But words will not serve me today. Grieve with me, for, with Amanda's passing, we have all lost someone very . . . rare. I can say no more."

Spock glanced at his father in surprise; then his expression hardened and he deliberately looked the other way. Sarek waited a moment to see whether his son wished to say anything, then he raised a hand in salute to the waiting crowd. "My family, my friends . . . I wish you peace and long life."

"Live long and prosper," T'Lar said aloud, speaking for the crowd. Many of the watchers held up their hands in the Vulcan salute, heads respectfully bowed.

The ceremony was over.

Unlike human funerals, etiquette following a Vulcan memorial service demanded that the family of the deceased be left in private. Sarek watched as James Kirk came up to his son and said something quietly to him; then the group of Starfleet officers silently took their leave.

"What did Kirk say?" Sarek asked, when he and Spock were alone, standing amid the stark peaks surrounding Mount Seleya.

"He asked if we could both meet with him tomorrow at nine hundred hours aboard the *Enterprise* to discuss the Freelan situation. I gave the captain a brief overview while you were gone." Spock still did not look at his father as he spoke. Instead his eyes remained fastened on the mountain peaks, scarlet from the reflection of Nevasa's sunset.

"Good," Sarek said. "I was going to request such a meeting with Kirk upon my return. I have new information to add to what I have already told you." The Vulcan hesitated. "Spock," he said finally, "about your mother . . . I would have returned home if it had been possible. I—"

"She called for you," Spock interrupted, staring straight ahead. His features seemed carved from the same rock that surrounded them. "Whenever she was conscious, she called for you. Her decline was rapid, after you left."

"The situation with Kadura was grave," Sarek said. "Lives were in jeopardy. . . . Amanda told me that she understood."

"She understood very well." Spock's voice held a bitter edge. "But the fact that she understood and forgave you does not make your actions correct. Any competent diplomat could have negotiated a settlement for Kadura's freedom. But only *you* could have eased my mother's passing."

Spock took a deep breath. "The entire time I sat there beside her . . . two *days* . . . there was only one thing in the world that she wanted—you. And you were not there. Without your presence, there was no solace for her . . . no tranquility. She called for you, and would not be comforted."

"Her ending was not . . . peaceful?" the ambassador asked, his voice a hollow whisper. Pain that was nearly physical in its intensity struck him like a blow.

Spock hesitated. "Even her sleep was restless," he said finally. A muscle twitched in his jawline. "She was not aware of my presence at all."

Sarek closed his eyes, struggling for control. He experienced a brief impulse to tell Spock how he had attempted to reach Amanda, but that was a private thing . . . not to be spoken of. Grief washed over him anew. *So . . . I did not reach her, there at the end. I thought I might have . . . I thought perhaps she could detect my presence . . . but it was not so, evidently. . . .*

"You were not there to ease her passing," Spock went on, inexorably. "Despite my presence, she died alone."

Slowly the elder Vulcan drew himself up, gazing impassively at Spock, his face a cold mask. "These highly emotional recriminations are both illogical and distasteful, Spock. Your logic has failed you, my son . . . which is regrettable, but understandable, under the circumstances. You are, after all, Amanda's child as well as mine. You are half-human . . . and it is your human half I am facing, now."

At last Spock turned his head and met his father's eyes. Their gazes locked. The younger Vulcan's mouth tightened . . . his gaze was as scorching as the desert that lay around them. But his voice, when he finally spoke, was icy. "In that case, I will take my distasteful human half and depart . . . *sir.* I bid you farewell."

Spock swung around and walked away, his pace light, even. His control was perfect; his movements betrayed nothing of the anger Sarek had sensed. The elder Vulcan hesitated, wanting to call him back, but he had been perfectly logical—and right. One did not apologize for being logical or correct. . . .

As the ambassador watched, his son crossed the narrow bridge, then strode away into the gathering darkness, leaving his father alone.

James T. Kirk sat in his conference room at 0855 hours, awaiting Sarek and his first officer. Spock had returned to his cabin aboard the *Enterprise* to spend the night, instead of remaining with his father. In Kirk's estimation, that did not bode well . . . he'd seen his friend's reaction when he spoke of Sarek's leaving when Amanda was dying. Kirk had known Spock for many years, but had never seen him like this. If he had to label it, he would call it anger.

Spock's brief revelation three days ago concerning Romulan moles masquerading as Freelans—a whole damned *planet* of them, apparently, was extremely worrisome. James T. Kirk had had many run-ins with both Romulans and Klingons in his career, and, while it could not be denied that Klingons were fierce warriors and made awesome enemies, Kirk had decided long ago that he would rather confront Klingons in a knock-down, drag-out rather than Romulans.

There was something about Romulans . . . a subtlety, a canniness . . . It was the idea of Vulcan intellect without Vulcan ethics that Kirk found frightening.

And now . . . the Romulans were planning something big, if Sarek was right. That did not bode well for the Federation. Kirk recalled the moments after he had saved President Ra-ghoratrei at Camp Khitomer. The delegates and envoys had milled around, congratulating the Starfleet officers, everyone exclaiming over the fact that the supposed Klingon assassin had actually proved to be Colonel West, a human.

While Kirk was standing there, being congratulated and thanked by President Ra-ghoratrei and Chancellor Azetbur, he'd noticed the Freelan envoy, shrouded in his or her muffling robes, facing Ambassador Nanclus, the Romulan who had plotted with General Chang and Admiral Cartwright to bring about war between the Federation and the Klingon Empire. Beside the Freelan had stood a young Vulcan woman, lovely and serene, her short black hair cropped to reveal her elegant ears.

Kirk shook his head, slowly, his mind churning with questions and speculations.

If someone had ripped the Freelan's robes away, what would they all have seen? If Sarek was correct in his reasoning . . . and Vulcans were, after all, noted for their reasoning abilities . . . then they would have all seen a Romulan face beneath that muffling cowl and mask.

If that was true, then what did the Romulans want out of all this? Was Sarek correct in his deductions? *Was* the Freelan goal to cause war between the Federation and the Klingon Empire?

The door slid open and Ambassador Sarek entered. He was wearing his formal robes of state, but even their bejeweled elegance could not disguise the Vulcan's fatigue, the deeply shadowed eyes, the hair that had turned nearly white. Sarek's expression was positively grim as he nodded to Kirk. "Captain."

Kirk, who had stood respectfully when the senior diplomat entered, nodded back. "Ambassador . . . thank you for coming. And . . ." He struggled to form the Vulcan words this ship's computer had told him were proper. "I grieve with thee . . ." He took a deep breath, returned to Standard English. "Mrs. Sarek was a wonderful woman, sir. We all respected and admired her deeply."

"Thank you, Captain," Sarek said, and for a moment the grimness relaxed fractionally, allowing just a bare glimpse of sadness to slip through.

The door slid open again, and Spock, back in uniform, entered, followed by Dr. McCoy. The Vulcan ignored his father as he nodded a quick greeting to Kirk.

Uh-oh, the captain thought. *Will they be able to work together at all?*

McCoy and Sarek exchanged greetings and the doctor expressed his condolences to the ambassador. When the formalities were finished, Kirk waved them all to seats. "Ambassador Sarek," he began, "Spock has given us a brief summary of your concerns about the Freelans. But I would like to hear the whole story from your own lips, if you don't mind. And I'd like to see the data you've compiled."

"I have already transferred it to the ship's computer, Captain," Spock said, keying in a code word on the comm link. A file menu appeared on the screen.

Sarek began to speak, his beautifully modulated tones and measured, precise delivery lending credence to what would otherwise have sounded like wild nonsense and rampant speculation, coming from anyone but a Vulcan of his reputation. Kirk listened intently, interrupting every so often to ask a question or request that the ambassador amplify a point.

Grimly, he and McCoy studied the charts and data the ambassador had accumulated over years of study and research, and with every moment that passed, Kirk's certainty that Sarek was correct in his reasoning grew. The very idea of Freelan being a Romulan world had been outrageous at first . . . now, the more Kirk thought about it, the more the whole scheme seemed like very typical Romulan reasoning . . . clever, devious, audacious . . . and, unfortunately, it seemed that it might actually work.

When Sarek finally finished his account, the captain of the *Enterprise* shook his head grimly. "This stuff about the KEHL . . . you're right about how it's growing. Two days ago I got a priority message from my nephew, Peter, telling me that he managed to gain access to the KEHL's computer systems, but that Starfleet Security hadn't paid any attention to the data he managed to get. He was asking my help in getting a full investigation of the group started."

"What kind of data did Peter have?" Spock asked.

"Membership rolls, propaganda films . . . things like that. I also gather that the KEHL has breached security at the consulate, Ambassador, and copied Vulcan data that they claimed would prove their case that your world has a master plan to take over Earth."

"Take over Earth? The *Vulcans?*" Leonard McCoy looked thunderstruck, and then he laughed out loud. "What a load of . . . uh . . ." He glanced at Sarek, and altered what he'd been about to say to "That's absurd!"

"Something happened during my negotiations with Commander Keraz that lends more credence to my theory," Sarek said.

"What was that, Ambassador?" Kirk asked.

"One of Keraz's aides, Wurrl, attempted to assassinate me. Both he and Keraz, I discovered, had been subjected to telepathic influence."

Hearing that his father had been attacked, Spock stole a quick look at the elder Vulcan, as if checking him for injury.

"Maybe what we ought to do is just grab some Freelan at a conference and rip his mask off," McCoy suggested. "Serve them right."

"In the first place, such tactics abrogate diplomatic immunity as well as civil law," Sarek pointed out evenly. "And if we engaged in such . . . peremptory . . . behavior, we would lose the goodwill of many delegates, no matter how exemplary our motives for doing so."

"Yeah, well," McCoy grumbled, "who knows what damage they've been causing, poking around in other people's minds? I'll bet the Freelans had a hand in Chang's conspiracy, too."

"I suspect you would win that wager, Doctor," Sarek said, steepling his hands before him on the table. *So that's where Spock learned that . . .* Jim thought. "During the recent crisis, President Ra-ghoratrei summoned me, Ambassador Kamarag, and Ambassador Nanclus to discuss the Klingon demand for your extradition after the assassination of Chancellor Gorkon. Just after Kamarag left, Admiral Smillie, Admiral Cartwright, and Colonel West entered the office. The Starfleet officers had prepared a military plan of action designed to rescue you and Dr. McCoy."

"I never knew that, Jim!" the doctor exclaimed, eyes widening with surprise. "I thought Starfleet just decided to throw us to the wolves."

"Admiral Smillie told me about it at Khitomer," Kirk admitted. "But he said Ra-ghoratrei wouldn't go along with it."

"That is true," Sarek affirmed. "But what is significant to us now is that, during this discussion, Ambassador Nanclus pointed out to the president that the Klingons were vulnerable . . . and that there would never be a better time to begin a full-scale military action against them. He was quite . . . emphatic."

"Nanclus was openly advocating war between the Federation and the Klingon Empire?" Even in the light of subsequent events, Kirk was surprised that the Romulan would be so overt.

"I heard him myself," Sarek said simply.

"But Nanclus was working with General Chang and Admiral Cartwright to start a war. He wasn't giving the official Romulan position. . . ." Kirk's voice faded out.

Sarek waited a beat, then lifted one elegant eyebrow. "Wasn't he?" he asked softly. "How do you know? Subsequent events made it seem that Nanclus was working in concert with Chang and Cartwright . . . but who really started the plot?"

The captain drew a deep breath. "During his court-martial, Cartwright claimed under oath that Nanclus came to *him,* and that both of them then presented the idea to Chang—who was only too happy to take over. But if the whole thing was really Nanclus's idea . . ."

"Precisely," Sarek said.

"Was the Klingon assassin's attack on you a result of telepathic influence, Ambassador?" Spock asked, his tone cool and formal. Kirk realized it was the first time he'd addressed the elder Vulcan.

"Yes, I believe so. I only gained a brief impression of Wurrl's mind during the struggle," Sarek replied. "The Klingon suffered a fractured skull during the fight, and lapsed into a coma. I have no idea whether he is still alive. Starfleet took him into custody." Sarek was looking at Spock, but, Kirk noticed, the Vulcan's return gaze was remote.

"And Commander Keraz had also been subjected to undue mental influence?" Spock pursued the topic, still in that cool, toneless fashion. "In what way?"

"When I asked the Klingon commander why he had chosen to take such an action in seizing a Federation colony, he informed me that he really did not know *why* he had done it. It was strictly an impulsive decision, one that puzzled him in its aftermath. When I told him what I had discovered about Wurrl, he asked me to determine whether he, too, had been affected. I touched him . . . and knew that he had."

"Oho," McCoy said. "You think some Freelan and his trained Vulcan pup compelled Wurrl to try and murder you, and Keraz to turn renegade and invade Kadura?"

"I would say that 'compelled' is too strong a term," Sarek said. " 'Influenced' is more apt, I believe. But as to the Freelans being involved . . . of that, I have no doubt."

"Ambassador," Kirk said, as an idea occurred to him, "is it possible that Kadura was a setup to lure you off Vulcan, so that you could be gotten out of the way? Is there any possibility that the Freelans know that you suspect them?"

Sarek blinked. Obviously, Kirk's idea was a new one to him. "Possible, I suppose," he murmured. "Taryn did seem suspicious the last time I visited their station."

"Is there any possibility that your *valit* program did not completely cover your entrance into the Romulan data banks?" Spock asked. "Could they have discovered some evidence after you left Freelan orbit?"

The elder Vulcan raised an eyebrow. "My *valit* was well designed," he said, with a touch of surprise that Spock would question his expertise with computers. "In the event any tampering *was* detected—which I consider unlikely—there would have been no way to trace the intrusion back to me."

"But circumstantial evidence might be enough to arouse Taryn to take action against you," Spock said.

"Possible," Sarek conceded.

"I think we should go to the president immediately with all of this," Kirk said. "And to Starfleet Security, Vice-Admiral Burton."

The captain looked at Sarek, was surprised to see the Vulcan shake his head in negation. "No, Kirk," he said. "Not yet. Not until I have incontrovertible proof."

"Just the fact that you're suspicious will be enough!" McCoy burst out. "A man of your reputation, Ambassador—of course the president will pay attention."

"I must speak to the president about this only in person," Sarek said. "Otherwise, I cannot be certain that his mind has not been influenced. The same applies to your Vice-Admiral Burton. Also, we must guard against any of these speculations becoming public knowledge. The consequences, should that happen, would be grave."

"What consequences?" McCoy asked, taken aback.

"The fragile peace with the Klingon Empire, for one," Spock said, before the ambassador could reply. "It might appear to Azetbur that the Federation is attempting to stir up trouble between the Romulans and the Klingon Empire . . . by accusing the Romulans of influencing the Klingons to turn renegade. Also, do not forget the KEHL. Most of the followers are undoubtedly hapless dupes . . . innocent of everything except being easily led. Charges that they are Romulan pawns could lead to witch-hunts."

"What kind of proof do you propose to get, Ambassador Sarek? If the Romulans suspect that you know, they will undoubtedly recall all their Freelan personnel, and escalate their efforts to cause war between the Federation and the Klingon Empire."

"Indeed. We must be cautious, and not move until we are ready," Sarek agreed. "I would still like to access the Freelan data banks and copy their contents. If it is done properly, we could gain proof, without alerting the Romulans that we know of their plans."

"Can you do it again? And get away with copies, this time?"

"I believe that I can," Sarek said, glancing at his son. "If Spock will assist me."

Spock sat in silence for a moment, then nodded. "I will do my best," he said. "I will need to study the *valits* you used before, to attempt to refine them so they will work more smoothly."

For a moment Kirk sensed a flash of indignation from the ambassador, even though the Vulcan's calm expression never varied. "Very well," he said. "I will provide them to you."

Kirk looked from father to son, thinking that if anyone could break past Romulan security, it would be these two. Still, he was hesitant about not going straight to Starfleet Security with news of this plot. But if delaying a few days would provide proof positive . . .

"How close would you have to be to Freelan to tap into the data banks?" Kirk asked.

"Given the resources of a starship's computer system, anywhere within the boundaries of the system should suffice," Sarek said. "I was dependent, remember, on a small tricorder. Kirk, how long would it take to reach Freelan aboard this vessel?"

"Two days, at warp six."

"Excellent," Sarek said. "That should be sufficient time for me to acquaint Spock with my plan for accessing the Freelan system." The ambassador nodded approvingly at Kirk. "I thank you for your cooperation, Captain."

"It's my duty to investigate a threat to Federation security," Kirk said simply. "When can you be ready to leave Vulcan?"

"I anticipated that I would be leaving with your ship, Kirk. I came prepared to do so."

"Scotty said the final paint job would be completed—" Kirk, who was already reaching for the intercom, broke off as it beeped. Impatiently, he opened the channel. "Kirk here. I thought I gave orders that I was not to be dis—"

"Captain," Commander Uhura's voice interrupted, "I have a Priority One personal message for you, sir, from the commandant of Starfleet Academy."

"The commandant?" Kirk was nonplussed. What could Commandant Anderson be wanting with him? "Relay it, Commander."

"Yes, sir. . . ." She paused for a moment. "Captain . . . Commandant Anderson reports that your nephew Peter has disappeared. Their investigation leads them to believe he did *not* leave of his own free will. Sir . . . the commandant reports that he suspects foul play."

Kirk swallowed. Peter was the only close relative he had. If anything had happened to him . . .

"Commander," he said tightly, "inform the bridge crew to begin preparations to depart drydock on my command." He clicked to a different channel. "Set course for Sector 53.16 . . . the Freelan system. Mr. Scott?"

"Scott here, sir," replied the familiar burr promptly.

"How soon can we cast off moorings and get out of here?"

"We'll be ready in another twenty minutes, Captain."

"You've got ten," Kirk snapped.

"Aye, sir," came the engineer's casual reply. "We'll be ready."

"Good, Scotty. Ten minutes. Kirk out."

Snapping off the intercom, the captain looked at the others grimly. "It never rains but it pours," he said. "Murphy's Law."

The ambassador raised an eyebrow. "Murphy's Law?"

"A human aphorism that states, 'Whatever can go wrong, will,'" Spock explained.

"Yeah, and at the worst possible time," McCoy added. "Jim . . . what could have happened to Peter?"

"I don't know, Bones," Kirk said. "The temptation is to think that, because he was investigating the KEHL, they're responsible for this. But that might not be true." Opening a channel to the bridge, he said, "Commander Uhura, please contact Commandant Anderson for me."

"Yes, Captain. I'll put through a call immediately, sir."

Kirk hesitated, thinking furiously. Should he turn command of the *Enterprise* over to Spock, and take a transport for Earth? He couldn't abandon Peter! And yet . . . duty came before personal concerns. "Ambassador," he said, "assuming you have your proof in a few days, what are you going to suggest that the Federation do about this situation with the Romulans?"

"Some elements in Starfleet would advise a preemptive strike," Spock said. "I can visualize Admiral Smillie approving such a tactic, given sufficient provocation."

"War? All-out war?" McCoy was aghast. "There must be some way to prevent that!" He glanced at Kirk. "Isn't there, Jim?"

"I don't know," Kirk said, forcing himself to put Peter out of his mind and concentrate on the subject at hand. "It could be that the Romulans would back off if they knew they'd lost the element of surprise, and that they couldn't push the Federation and the Klingons into hostilities."

"It is possible," Sarek pointed out, "that they might evacuate the Freelan colony and deny everything. Taryn, I believe, is ruthless enough for such an action."

"In that event, what would happen to the second-generation Vulcans?" Spock wondered. "Technically, they are hostages. We are under a moral imperative to free them."

"If these Vulcan kids have grown up brainwashed by the Romulans, they may think of themselves as Romulans, rather than as Vulcans," McCoy pointed out. "They may not want to be rescued." He turned to Sarek. "Do you have any idea how many there are?"

The Vulcan shook his head. "From the numbers of Vulcans who were abducted,

I can speculate that there may be as many as one hundred . . . perhaps two hundred. No fewer than fifty, certainly."

Kirk's hazel eyes were bleak as he held the Vulcans' gazes. "Knowing the Romulans, they're perfectly capable of simply eradicating the hostages, rather than taking any chances of them being used as an excuse for a military rescue by Federation forces."

Father and son nodded silently, grimly.

"I think we should—" Kirk began, only to be interrupted by the intercom. "Kirk here," he said.

"Sir," Uhura said, "Commandant Anderson is standing by."

"Put him through," Jim ordered.

A moment later, Kyle Anderson's features coalesced on the small screen. He was a distinguished looking black man, balding, with a heavy, iron-gray beard. "Captain Kirk," he said. "You received my message?"

"Just a few minutes ago," Kirk said. "What's happened to Peter?"

"He's vanished without a trace, Captain. Our security people have determined that he disappeared shortly after midnight on Wednesday evening of last week. But we're having finals here, so nobody realized he was missing until the day before yesterday. It took us a day to track down your ship . . . I'm sorry for the delay."

Kirk drew a deep breath. "But . . . he's been gone for days! And you still don't know where he went?"

"No. He's disappeared so thoroughly that we now suspect he was taken off-world. We're in the process of tracing all ships that departed from Earth or Earth orbit that night," Anderson said. "But, as you can imagine, that's a tall order."

Kirk nodded wordless agreement. "What makes you suspect foul play?" he asked.

"We managed to retrieve the last message that came in for him at his apartment. It had been automatically scrambled after playing . . . but they unscrambled it just this morning." He pressed a button. "Here it is."

Kirk watched with growing horror as his own features replaced Anderson's on-screen. He listened to himself demanding that Peter come over immediately. Then the screen flickered, and Anderson's dark features were back. "I never sent that message," Kirk said bleakly. "But it's no wonder he fell for it . . . he was expecting to hear from me . . ."

"We know that, Captain. We have a record of Peter encoding a Priority One message for you. May we have your permission to decode it? It might give us a clue to his whereabouts."

Kirk hesitated. They'd agreed to keep their suspicions of the KEHL being linked with the Romulans secret. "We'll investigate on our end," he said, finally. "I'll let you see the message as soon as I clear it with Starfleet Security. Can you please transmit everything you've got on that message to my communications chief, Commander Uhura? There's nobody better at tracing transmissions."

"Certainly, Captain," Anderson said. "We'll do that."

"I'll get back to you as soon as I get that clearance," Kirk said, crossing his fingers underneath the table.

"My people suspect they were waiting for him on the street," Anderson said. "And that they grabbed him there."

"So you're thinking kidnapping, rather than . . ." Kirk swallowed. " . . . murder?"

"We just don't know, Captain. But if somebody simply wanted your nephew dead, why the elaborate hoax with the faked message?"

"Logical," murmured Spock and Sarek at the same moment.

"Abduction . . . possibly kidnapping?" Kirk's mind was racing. "Has there been any kind of message? Any demands for ransom?"

"Not so far."

"If any message comes through," Kirk said, "I'll let you know. Maybe we can trace its source, and learn something from that."

"Good idea. If I hear anything, I'll contact you immediately, Captain," Anderson promised in his turn.

"Thank you, Commandant."

"Rest assured, we're doing everything we can," the man said, before cutting the connection.

Kirk turned to the others sitting around the table. "If Scotty is as good as his word, we should be casting off moorings by now. Ambassador . . . you and Spock should begin working on those *valits* you mentioned. I'll have Uhura get to work on tracing that message. I've got a hunch this is all going to wind up connected, somehow."

Minutes later, Kirk was on the bridge, ensconced in his command seat. With a glint in his eye, he surveyed the cavernous interior of the Vulcan drydock through the viewscreen. "Status, s'Bysh?" he asked his helmsman.

"All moorings cleared, Captain. Docking bay doors will open in two minutes, thirty-five point six seconds," she reported, crisply.

"Lay in a course for Freelan, Lieutenant." Kirk settled back in his seat, his eyes level, jaw set. He watched s'Bysh's green fingers fly. "Ready, Lieutenant?" he asked, scarcely more than a minute later. "Course laid in?"

"Aye, sir."

Counting seconds down in his head, Kirk reached thirty-four. "Ahead one-half impulse power, Lieutenant," he ordered, and thought he heard Chekov mutter, "Not again!"

"One-half impulse, aye, sir."

Enterprise sprang forward like a cheetah sighting prey. The ship closed on the parting bay doors with a terrifying rush of speed, blasted through them with only a few hundred meters to spare on either side, and then they were out, into free space. Chekov's sigh of relief was audible all over the bridge, and Commander Uhura chuckled softly when she heard it.

"Ahead warp six," Kirk ordered grimly.

"Warp six, aye, Captain."

Kirk settled back in his seat. No matter what speed Mr. Scott managed to coax out of the warp engines, it was going to be a long trip. . . .

After a long day spent refining *valit* programs, Sarek was weary, but sleep eluded him. Remembering his promise, he extracted Amanda's journal, and opened it, noting the date at the top of the page.

November 12, 2231

    It is the middle of the night, and quiet. I am tired . . . but I am also too excited to sleep. I cannot neglect my journal tonight of all nights!

    I have a son.

Sarek and I have a son. He was born in the early hours of this morning. Never having been through labor before, I worried that it might prove too much for me to bear (no pun intended) without shaming myself before the Healers, but I believe I did well. . . .

And our son is perfect. Even though the Healers reassured me that all their tests showed that the baby was normal, still I worried. After all, I had to be treated before I could conceive, then monitored carefully throughout the pregnancy to allow me to carry to term—nearly a full month more than the human norm!

Carrying a child for almost ten Earth months is not fun, and that is the understatement of the century. I was so big yesterday that I felt as though my sides would split open. I spent hours staring in wonderment at my belly, unable to believe the size of it. I could barely waddle to the bathroom unassisted! When I felt that dull ache in my back sharpen into an actual contraction, I could have jumped for joy. What a relief it is to return to something like my normal size!

For a while the Healers were afraid I would not be able to deliver normally . . . my son is very large for a human infant, though not particularly so for a Vulcan baby. If it had not been for the Healer-midwife's coaching, I might have given up in despair. But she was amazingly supportive for someone who must have been wincing inwardly every time I betrayed what I was feeling.

My labor was intense, and seemed to take forever. I was surprised that I was able to handle the pain as well as I did. It hurt, yes . . . by all the gods that ever were, it felt as though some diabolical presence were trying to hammer a spike into the base of my spine, while simultaneously squeezing my belly in a vise. But, unlike hangnails, stubbed toes, barked shins, and sprained ankles, this was pain with a purpose. As long as I could focus on that purpose, the pain did not . . . could not overwhelm me. I vaguely remember the midwife encouraging me, reminding that my suffering was for a purpose, and that helped me to focus on the results, not the pain.

Sarek was there for most of the time, holding my hand and thus sharing what I felt. In a way, that seemed to lessen the agony. Perhaps he used a meld to mind-block some of the worst of the pangs . . . or perhaps it was simply the quiet strength he projects that gave me courage.

I wish I could have my child with me tonight, but they have taken him to the Science Academy, to run tests and keep him under close observation.

As I held him in my arms after his first feeding, I beheld a tiny face that was so Vulcan that I wondered if there was anything of me in him. But just as I thought there was nothing human in him at all, my son opened his mouth and began to wail—sounding just like a human baby. I saw something—could it have been disappointment?—flicker across my husband's face as he heard those infant squalls.

Vulcan babies cry only for a reason—hunger or discomfort. And our son was dry and fed . . . and thus had little or no reason to wail.

Which proves that he is partly mine, after all.

Was Sarek disappointed? I suppose I will never know. I love our son too much to ask—and risk "yes" for an answer. . . .

*   *   *

The newborn infant squirmed in his tiny, heated cocoon as his father watched every movement, enthralled by the new life that he had helped create. *My son . . .* he thought, noting the tiny veins that pulsed greenish blue just beneath the thin, delicate skin. *My son . . . what will we name you? Your Name Day will not arrive for nearly a month, so we have some time to choose a suitable appellation. Your mother will not even be able to pronounce your "first" name. . . .*

Vulcan first names were always a combination of syllables in Old Vulcan that denoted lineage and birth order. But Sarek's son would be called by his last name, even as his father was. Traditionally, in honor of Surak, the name would begin with an *S*.

The infant moved restlessly again, then opened his mouth, uttering a faint squeak. His eyes opened, moved aimlessly for a moment, then fastened on his father's face. The birthing puffiness had lessened; the child's eyes were now far less slitted, and Sarek could easily discern their color. Dark, like his own, not blue, as his mother's were. Not surprising. All the Healers' tests during Amanda's pregnancy had indicated that Vulcan genes would prove dominant in a human/Vulcan pairing.

The nursery attendant, noting that the child had roused from the readings on her monitors, approached Sarek and his son. "He is awake," he announced unnecessarily.

"He is," she agreed. "Soon he will be hungry. I will give him his supplement now. Do you wish to take him to your wife for his feeding, Ambassador?"

Sarek hesitated. His son was very small . . . his own hands could nearly span that tiny body lengthwise. He had never held an infant before. . . .

"If you would prefer," the nurse said, "I will do it."

Sarek watched as she quickly, efficiently, lifted the baby and administered the oral supplement that would provide him with the nutrients that Amanda's human milk did not contain. But before she could turn away, he held out his arms. "I will take him," he said, firmly.

Obediently, the nurse placed the small, warm bundle into his arms. The Vulcan stood rigid, his arms stiff, as she settled the baby into place, making sure his head was properly supported.

The ambassador was faintly, illogically surprised to discover that his newborn son, who appeared so fragile, so helpless, actually had substance. The baby occupied space, and had mass . . . he was a warm, squirming, living, breathing entity. Sarek stared down at him, fascinated. Dark eyes regarded him, locked with his own in an unblinking regard.

As he stared into the child's eyes, all at once the infant became *real* to Sarek, in a way he never had before. For all these months he had watched his wife's belly grow, touched her delicately to feel the movement beneath her skin, observed the child's heartbeat on the monitors . . . but part of him had never truly comprehended that an actual child was forming within Amanda, and that that child was half his.

Reality had not begun to manifest itself until he had grasped Amanda's hand during labor, had directly experienced the agonizing pain that his wife was enduring. He had been amazed that a human could endure such pain without blacking out—Amanda's fierce concentration, her comparative silence except during the worst of the birthing contractions had impressed him. His wife had always seemed frail to him, delicate, with her human constitution. His own strength had always been so much greater—and yet, today, he'd found himself admiring her stoicism as she'd endured such intense pain. Amanda was stronger than he'd ever realized. Even the Healer had expressed approval of her fortitude during labor and birthing.

Now the ambassador gazed down at the tiny face with its fuzz of black hair, noting the faint traces of the slanted eyebrows, the delicately pointed ears, the slightly squashed nose.

Looking at his son, Sarek of Vulcan experienced a moment of insight so intense it was nearly painful. Past and future, then and now and tomorrow seemed to swirl around him, blending and coming together in the small body so warm and breathing in his arms. This child was a link to the long-ago, and he would be the future. Someday he would stand up and walk the sands of his homeland, would gaze at The Watcher with wonder, would go to school and learn the logic of his forebears. He would grow to adulthood, tall and strong and handsome, and someday he might hold a son of his own in his arms. . . .

"Our preliminary tests are complete," the nurse said, breaking into Sarek's reverie. "They indicate that his intelligence potential is above average, Ambassador. Considerably above average."

Sarek was not surprised, having gazed into the infant's eyes for these long seconds, but he felt a surge of pride that he did not trouble to repress.

The rigidity had somehow gone out of his arms. He held the child against his chest, instinctively cradling him close. "I will take him to his mother now," he said.

The nurse nodded, and Sarek, moving carefully so as not to jostle his son, walked away. . . .

Closing the journal, the Vulcan sighed as he recalled his encounter with his son yesterday at Amanda's memorial service. If his wife knew the things they had said to each other, she would have been terribly distressed. Remembering how she'd begged him to try and understand his son, instead of being judgmental and always finding fault, the ambassador shook his head.

And yet . . . what could he have done differently? He had only done his duty. Amanda had understood . . . why couldn't his son?

James T. Kirk sat in the captain's chair, waiting.

"Captain," Uhura said, an odd note in her voice, "I'm picking up a subspace transmission, sir. It's on the frequency reserved for personal communiqués and mail. . . ."

Kirk glanced over at her, sitting up straight. "A message?"

"Yes, sir." She looked over at him, her dark eyes compassionate. She knew, of course, that Peter was missing.

"What does it say?"

"It says, 'To Captain Kirk. Visit Sector 53.16, at coordinates 39 mark 122, before thirteen hundred hours stardate 9544.6. A certain redhead is waiting, will die if you don't show. Come alone. Tell no one.'"

Kirk drew a deep breath. "Uhura, trace that message back to its point of origin. I don't care how many substations they routed it through, follow it back all the way. Understood?"

"Aye, Captain," she said, her lovely features set in lines of determination that matched his own.

"And message Commandant Anderson that we've just received the ransom note."

Six

Wing Commander Taryn was dreaming. . . .

He did not dream often, but when he did, it was always the same dream . . . or, at least, if he dreamed other dreams, he did not remember them. The Dream (as he had come to think of it) was the only thing in the universe that he consciously feared. Each time he awakened from it, he hoped that it would be the last . . . but, though months and years of peaceful slumber passed, somehow, when he was least expecting it, the dream would come back. . . .

In The Dream he was small . . . too short to reach the viewport in normal gravity without being lifted up. He was running, running down a neutral-colored corridor, a corridor that seemed to loom inward on him as he scuttled along. His short legs pumped harder, trying to hurl him forward faster, but he was afraid—*afraid! he should not be afraid, he should be calm . . . he should be brave, he should not run away . . . but he was afraid, he was!*—and his feet kept slipping out from under him. Try as he might, he could not reach the end of the corridor . . . it seemed to expand before him almost infinitely.

He would never reach it . . . never, he would always be here, trapped, knowing that horror and absolute devastation lay behind him. And he, Taryn, deserved no better. He was a coward, a fearful, sobbing, cringing coward. . . .

Gasping, he stretched out both hands, making his short legs churn faster as he ran . . . ran . . . toward a goal that would never grow any closer. . . .

And then, with the suddenness of dreams, he was there, at the end of the corridor, standing on tiptoe, yanking frantically at the emergency release on the airlock door. The life-support pod lay in an alcove beyond that door. He knew how to open it, how to activate it, and the button to push that would launch it. Taryn knew all this, just as he knew that it was time to abandon ship, just as he'd learned in the drills.

He punched in the code, slowly, not wanting to make a mistake, his ears straining for noises from behind him. Would they come after him? What would he do if they did?

He gnawed at his lower lip, waiting, until the airlock door indicated acceptance of his code. Finally it was time to grasp the opening bar in both hands and pull it downward.

Even as he touched it, it began to move in his hands. Horrified, he leaped back, and then the door began to slide open.

Choking in terror, he fled back down the corridor, running from this new, greater fear. He reached the end of the corridor, and there was the door from whence he had come, bolting in terror and anguish, knowing himself to be a coward. The control-room door. Placing a hand on it, Taryn began to pull it open.

No! No, don't! His elder self screamed silently at his younger self, for all the good it did. Taryn pushed the door open, slowly, slowly, and saw—

—nothing except darkness as he jerked upright in bed, gasping. Slowly, reality began to trickle in. He was back on Freelan, in his own home. His wife Jolana was not here beside him, because she had gone to Romulus to visit their two grown children.

Taryn shivered, feeling cold despite the sweat on his bare chest and arms. That had been a bad one. He couldn't remember much about the dream . . . which wasn't unusual. He had a vague impression that in it, he was a frightened child, but the details were always lost. Frankly, he didn't *want* to remember that dream . . . ever.

Stress, he thought. *I've been working too hard again. But the invasion is so close . . . nothing must go wrong! The Praetor made it clear that he has complete confidence in me. He has given me more authority than I have ever had . . . and I must be worthy. Nothing must go wrong . . . we must be victorious.*

Taryn forced himself to take deep, relaxing breaths. He glanced out the window, seeing the stars, as hard and cold and sharp in the blackness as spearpoints. He knew better than to look for Vulcan's sun from here . . . it was too distant.

Vulcan's primary sun, Nevasa—or 40 Eridani, as the Federation charts recorded it. Taryn wondered, not for the first time, what it would be like to walk across the deserts of Vulcan—a world that was as hot, by all reputation, as Freelan was cold. A world where logic was revered, even over power. Sarek's world . . .

Taryn had known for days that Wurrl had failed to kill the ambassador—the Klingon hadn't been fast enough, it seemed. He'd been disappointed to learn about the Klingon's failure—but also, in a way, the officer was pleased that that particular plan had failed. It would be so much more satisfying to overcome Sarek personally; after all the times the ambassador had defeated him at chess, victory at long last would be sweet indeed.

The wing commander sighed as he slumped back against the hard bolster. *How much does Sarek know?* he wondered, for the hundredth time. Sarek, he was sure, was the only one who could alert the Federation to their plans, the only one who suspected the true nature of Freelan and its inhabitants.

He suspects, but he has no proof, he reassured himself. And things were moving so fast now, that within a few weeks—perhaps sooner, if the fleet was ready ahead of schedule, as the praetor had promised yesterday it would be—the war would begin. At that point, keeping the identity of the Freelans secret would no longer be necessary.

Taryn's mouth curved upward slightly as he thought of what it would be like to be present when Sarek realized his defeat. The Vulcan had beaten him again during their last chess game. He usually won because he baited Taryn into recklessness . . . but soon, Sarek's days of winning would be over. Soon . . .

Pleasant anticipation relaxed him; the officer lay down again, reminding himself that the dream had never come twice in one night. But it was still a long, long time before he slept. . . .

Sarek also was dreaming. Full-blooded Vulcans did not dream often, but it did happen from time to time.

The Vulcan dreamed that he was on the surface of Freelan. All around him were glaciers, jagged buttresses of ice, sharp-fanged and glittering in the sunlight. He was walking toward a house . . . Taryn's house, he knew—though the Freelan had never described anything about his home, of course. Still, this house fit in with what little was known about Freelan architectural styles. It was a black, dome-shaped dwelling, everything about it designed to maximize the capture and retention of heat, as well as keeping snowfall from crushing the building.

Sarek walked, experiencing the icy wind off the glaciers, yet not chilled by it.

Beneath his feet the snow crunched and he continued his journey.

As he neared the front of the house, the door opened and a Freelan stepped out, his muffling robes stirring in the icy breeze. "Sarek," the Freelan said, and the Vulcan recognized Taryn's voice. "Why are you here?"

"I was searching for you, Taryn," Sarek said. "My wife is dead."

"What is that to me?" the Freelan asked haughtily.

"If it were not for you, I could have been at her deathbed," Sarek said, knowing he spoke truth. "My son would not now despise me."

"What is any of this to me?" Taryn was almost sneering. "Your domestic problems are your own concern, Vulcan."

"And your deceitful world is mine!" Sarek raised his voice, and, darting forward, he savagely ripped the concealing mask from the Freelan's head and stared in shock as he saw—

Amanda's face beneath the muffling cowl and mask.

"Amanda!" Sarek said, stepping forward to touch her, to embrace her, but even as he did so, his treacherous, logical mind insisted, *Amanda is dead. . . .*

And he awoke.

He was lying in his bunk in the VIP cabin aboard the *Enterprise . . .* Freelan's icy surface and Amanda's face had been a dream, he realized. Sarek experienced once again the desolation of knowing his wife was dead. Her absence in his mind was an aching void, one that he could not imagine ever being filled.

Knowing he would not be able to sleep again, he arose from the bed, then padded barefoot across the sleeping compartment to the small lounge, a slim red-covered volume in his hand. Seating himself on the low divan, the ambassador opened the book and began to read. . . .

December 7, 2237—the Twentieth Day of Tasmeen

I have paced until I am exhausted—my legs are trembling so that I must sit . . . but I cannot rest. I see that this entry is nearly illegible, and that is because my hands are also shaking.

Spock is missing. He apparently left soon after sunset, and we have no idea where he has gone. He is only seven years old!

Sarek is in his office. I glanced at him as I went past, and he appears to be working! How can he?

If I were to ask him how he can work while our son is missing, he would gaze at me with infuriating Vulcan calm and say, "Amanda, I have reported Spock's disappearance to the authorities. They are far more fitted than I to search for him. Pacing back and forth and indulging in emotional outbursts will accomplish nothing. Simply because I am working does not mean I am not concerned about our son."

I must try to calm myself. Getting furious at my husband will not help bring my son back, and I suppose that he is right—but it is maddening when he remains so calm when I am upset.

Spock is missing—my child is out there in the desert, with all its dangers. And my husband is working!

If only he had been more understanding of Spock, made some effort to see things from a child's viewpoint—but no, the son of Sarek must be perfect, must be better than all the other children—I overheard him tell Spock that himself today. He told him that if he does not pass his kahs-wan ordeal next month, the first time he attempts it, that he, Sarek, will be disgraced. He didn't use that exact word, but the implication was clear.

This admonishment followed on the heels of Spock's fight with those schoolboys, the ones who torment him every day with taunts of "Earther!" and "Half-blood!" and "Emotional Terran—can't control himself!"

There have been times that I've had to dig my nails into my palms to stop myself from rushing out there and giving them all a slap. But of course that would only make things worse. This has been going on ever since Spock started school, at age four. . . .

It is torture to watch him try and fit in with the others. My son, so tall, so slender, with his black hair and this thin, somber little face . . . it breaks my heart to see him so abused. I've begged Sarek to talk to their parents, but he refuses. He's pointed out (logically and correctly, I'm afraid) that such intervention on his part would only make the other boys torment our son more. . . .

I cry when I see him trying to endure it, knowing how such teasing hurts. Why can't Vulcan children be as civilized as their parents?

The boys tormented him once again today, and his father was totally unsupportive, let alone sympathetic. So he has run away. Where?

After several minutes' reflection, I think I know. I believe he has set off into the wilderness in order to deliberately expose himself to danger. Spock is setting himself up for his own private survival ordeal, because he would rather die out there in the desert than disgrace his father next month.

If our son dies out there—I will blame Sarek. I know it is not just, but I also know that I will do it anyway. I will blame my husband, and I will be unable to bear the sight of him.

At least I-Chaya appears to have gone with his young master. The old sehlat wouldn't be much use as defense, I suppose, but at least the big furry creature will keep Spock warm. Nights in the desert are chilly, even by human standards.

Someone else may also have accompanied Spock, but I am less sanguine about Sarek's young cousin, Selek. Although the young man was perfectly poised and polite, I gained an impression of duplicity from him. His eyes never quite met mine when he introduced himself and explained who he was. And later . . . I caught him gazing at me when he didn't realize that I saw him doing so. There is something about Cousin Selek . . . something false. I am certain that he was lying about the purpose of his impromptu visit here. Perhaps he was lying about being related to my husband.

No, that cannot be it. There was a definite family resemblance between them. But still, there was something . . . something I cannot put my finger on. . . .

I have never heard of any Vulcan adult abusing a child. Surely Selek only went after Spock because he saw the child running away and realized Spock could be in danger! Surely Selek intends my son no harm. . . .

He seemed like a very nice young man, despite everything. There was a warmth in his eyes when he gazed at me that I found touching, despite my reservations when I realized he was not being fully truthful with us. . . .

I long to take the aircar myself and go looking for Spock. Writing in my journal usually helps to calm me when I'm upset, but not this time. I cannot sit still an instant longer—perhaps Sarek and I should take the aircar and go looking for Spock ourselves in the Llangon Mountains. It will soon be dawn. . . .

Sarek glanced up from the pages of the journal and sighed, remembering. . . .

"I cannot stand this for one more instant," Amanda burst out, pausing in her jerky pacing to glare at him. Sarek, reluctantly, had abandoned his work to join her in the living room of their residence in ShiKahr. "I don't care what you think—I'm taking the aircar and going to the Llangon Mountains to look for him myself." Turning on her heel, she headed for the door. Her husband stepped in front of her, barring her way.

"Amanda, there is no reason to—"

"Don't you *dare* use that infuriating calm voice on me!" she cried. At the moment, Amanda Grayson was a portrait in fury. "This is your fault, Sarek!" she flared, cheeks red, blue eyes blazing. "If you had tried to understand Spock, rather than demand perfection from him, just because he's your son, then this never would have happened! Now either come with me, or stay here! I don't care which!"

"Amanda." Sarek heard the steel underlying the calm tones of his own voice, did not trouble to repress it. "I will not allow you to take the aircar into the Llangon Mountains. The air currents there are treacherous, especially just after sunrise, and you are too upset to concentrate on piloting. We will wait here for the report from the authorities."

Her small hands curled into fists, and for an instant Sarek wondered if she would strike him, but she whirled and strode away. The doorway he barred was the only exit from the room, so, after a few paces she halted with a jerk, then stood stiffly, her back to him. After a moment, Sarek said, in a milder tone, "I have trained Spock in anticipation of his *kahs-wan*. He is familiar with the Vulcan plant life and the survival methods of our ancestors. Logic dictates that he will come back to us relatively unharmed, Amanda."

She stared at him wildly, then laughed, a harsh, bitter sound that had nothing of humor about it. "And I'm supposed to be comforted by that, Sarek? By logic?"

"Logic is not meant to comfort, Amanda. It simply exists. It is a way of viewing the universe that offers reason and order, instead of chaos."

"Human chaos, you mean," she snapped. "Why not just say it?" Her mouth tightened. "But you *do* say it . . . only not in words. But it's there, in your face, whenever Spock smiles or forgets himself in the slightest degree! Disapproval radiates from you—I see it, and so does Spock. The poor child will never be good enough for you, and he knows it—no wonder he's willing to risk dying out there!"

Sarek was taken aback by the accusation. Surely his wife was wrong, was simply giving vent to her illogical human emotions. . . .

"Oh, I know you won't believe me," she said, more calmly. "You excel at not seeing what's right in front of your nose, Sarek. But *I* see it. It's obvious. Spock is trying to please you, but you've set him an impossible task—perfection! Even Vulcans aren't perfect—as you ought to know!"

Her husband stared at her, wordlessly. Amanda's eyes filled with angry tears. "I won't let you ruin his life, Sarek—even if it means going home to Earth and taking him with me. Maybe he'd be better off there, among people who have some compassion, some tolerance!"

"Leave?" Sarek's breath caught in his throat. "Surely you cannot be serious, Amanda. The situation has upset you, understandably—however, there is no need to consider such drastic action."

She faced him, her hot anger dying away to something cold and, the ambassador sensed, far more formidable. "Don't underestimate me, Sarek. I love you, nothing can ever change that, but you are an adult, perfectly capable of defending and caring for yourself. Spock is my child, and I will care for and protect him in the face of every threat to his being—even if that threat is his own father."

Facing her, the Vulcan felt as though he were confronting some eternal archetypal force—the personification of maternal protectiveness. A *le-matya* with cubs could not have been more deadly in defense of her young, he realized, experiencing a mixture of shock and unwilling admiration. "I see," he said, after a moment, "I do not want you to leave, Amanda," he said, slowly and carefully.

She took a deep breath, but her expression remained hard and closed. Yet her voice betrayed just the faintest quaver. "I do not wish to leave either, my husband," she replied formally. "Yet I will do so, if I decide that action is the best thing for our son."

"I will—"

Sarek turned suddenly as his Vulcan hearing picked up a familiar sound. "An aircar," he said, starting for the door.

"Spock?" she cried, catching up with him in a long stride, then bursting through the front door ahead of him. An aircar was just settling down onto the landing pad in the large courtyard.

The aircar's side door opened, and two figures emerged, one large, one small. "Spock!" Amanda called, holding out both hands.

It was indeed their son, followed by Cousin Selek. Both turned and raised a hand in grave salute as the aircar took off, swooping back toward the center of ShiKahr.

"Spock . . ." Sarek said. He stood in the courtyard and basked in the realization that his son was safely home. . . .

On that day, Sarek recalled, his son had informed his father gravely that he had chosen Vulcan. Amanda had never again threatened to leave him . . . though the strife between them during their son's childhood had been far from over.

Following the successful completion of Spock's *kahs-wan* ordeal, Sarek had turned to the next major milestone in a seven-year-old's life—that of his bonding. Amanda had protested the whole notion—and especially Sarek's choice for his son's betrothed.

Sarek recalled his conversation with Spock. How *had* his wife known that T'Pring was dishonest and faithless? There was no logical way to explain her knowledge. . . . Sarek recalled the conversation they'd had when he'd announced his choice of Spock's bondmate to be his wife. . . .

"T'Pring? You've chosen *her?* Sarek . . . no!"* They were sitting in her garden in ShiKahr, watching Nevasa set, when he'd mentioned that he'd chosen Spock's bondmate. Amanda leaped to her feet and regarded him with dismay.

The ambassador stared at his wife in mild surprise. "Amanda, why such disapproval? The girl's lineage is impeccable. Her family is as highly placed in Vulcan society as my own. She will have property of her own, to match what our son will inherit. Why do you not approve?"

"Because," Amanda said, flatly, fixing him with a level stare, "I don't like her. That child is . . . I don't know. She's too polite, too . . . calculating. There's something . . . cold . . . about her. I don't approve of this whole business of betrothing children—it's barbaric."

"Amanda, you are not being logical. T'Pring will prove an excellent consort for our son. She is intelligent and she will have all the advantages that a well-placed family can give her . . . she will—"

"Make Spock's life miserable, Sarek," Amanda broke in, her eyes darkening with emotion. "I can tell that she's not the right girl for Spock. T'Pring reminds me of one of those beautiful little snakes we have back on Earth—the ones with the lovely, jewel-like colors, that are so delicate, so beautiful . . . and so deadly that if they bite you, you live for less than a minute."

"Such prejudice on your part is specious, Amanda," Sarek said, experiencing a moment of impatience with his wife. "You have no reason for any of these allegations."

She paused for nearly a minute before replying. "I know," she said, finally. "I know that what I'm saying isn't fair. But all my instincts tell me that T'Pring is totally wrong for Spock. Sarek . . ." She swung back to face her husband. "I want you to cancel the bonding. Or at least postpone it, until they're . . . out of school, say."

Sarek shook his head. "No, Amanda. This is my world, and we agreed long ago that Spock would be brought up according to Vulcan custom and tradition. You heard him choose Vulcan himself, after that time when he ran away to the Llangon Mountains. I have made my choice, and T'Pring is the consort I choose."

Amanda drew a deep breath, and shook her head sadly, in turn. "You're making a mistake," she said. "But you're right. I did agree, and you are following Vulcan tradition."

The slender shoulders beneath her soft green gown sagged, suddenly, and she sighed deeply. The ambassador knew that she was giving in, but his victory did not please him. "Very well, my husband," she said, tonelessly. "But I am not sanguine about this decision."

"Logic dictates that the two will be well suited to one another, Amanda."

She flashed him a contemptuous glance. "Logic? You can't use logic to predict marital harmony, Sarek. I'm sure your father was being eminently logical when he betrothed you to T'Rea . . . but we both know how well that worked out. Don't we?"

Before Sarek could arrive at a rejoinder, she turned and walked away, back into the house.

Peter Kirk laid the ornate Klingon cards down with a disgusted air. "I fold. You beat me again!"

Sitting on a stool outside the observation panel, Valdyr looked smug as she made a notation on a pad with a stylus. "You now owe me . . . five thousand, six hundred and seventy-three kilos of prime-grade dilithium crystals," she said in Klingonese.

In the two days since Peter had come to Qo'noS, Valdyr's twice-daily visits had become the high points of his days. She had treated him respectfully, and even, at times, with a rough kindness. She'd located several old Klingon books for him to read—including *The Complete Works of William Shakespeare* in, as Valdyr put it, "the original Klingon"—and had struggled to teach him an arcane Klingon card game that he was having some difficulty mastering. He insisted they speak Klingonese, so that he could become even more articulate in the difficult language.

He'd discovered that Klingons did possess a sense of humor . . . even if Valdyr's was somewhat restrained. Just getting her to relax enough to *almost* smile was a challenge.

He didn't try to kid himself—Stockholm Syndrome was setting in badly, at least on his side. He wasn't sure about Valdyr.

Between the Klingon books and his conversations with Valdyr, he ended up not needing her help in translating the odd term he'd heard her uncle speak. He'd found it easily enough in Shakespeare. *The Merchant of Venice.* Shylock used it. *Joy'* meant torture, and, as Peter already knew, *Be'* meant woman, or female. Torture by females was the rough translation.

Be'joy' referred to a specific, ritualistic torture performed on prisoners of war . . . by Klingon women.

Another subject they might never be able to discuss. *So, tell me, Valdyr, when you perform the be'joy', what do you think you'll use first? The hot irons, the electronic stunner, or will you begin by flaying my flesh? Anyone taking any bets on how long I'll last?* And to think he'd once been worried about the *Kobayashi Maru!*

He folded his hand in defeat and slipped it through the food slot. "Are you sure you've taught me *all* the rules of this game?" Peter grinned ruefully as her serious expression assured him that anything less would be dishonorable. "Well, in that case, you'll have to send me to Rura Penthe to dig those crystals."

Valdyr's dark eyes sparkled indignantly. "Never! That is a place where only the worst criminals go."

"Like my Uncle Jim and Dr. McCoy?" he asked dryly. "They're really desperate characters, both of them." He was sorry the minute he'd said it. They had a truce going, and now he'd thrown out a volley.

The Klingon woman's eyes dropped. "I know they were innocent of assassinating Chancellor Gorkon," she said, carefully shuffling the deck, then dealing cards through the food slot beneath the observation panel. "But that does not mean that your uncle never murdered a Klingon."

"He *killed* Kruge, yes, but he didn't *murder* him," the cadet insisted. "Kruge beamed down to kill Kirk because he wanted revenge for his lost crew. They were fighting on the edge of a precipice, as the Genesis planet was breaking up beneath their feet. A big chunk of rock gave way beneath Kruge, and he went over the cliff. Jim caught his hand to save him, but Kruge tried to yank him over, too. My uncle got mad and let him drop."

"Let him?" Valdyr said, skeptically.

Peter grimaced. "It was self-defense! Kruge would have killed both of them, otherwise!"

"Kamarag says that Kirk lured Kruge down to that world just as it was breaking up, then abandoned him to die," Valdyr said.

Young Kirk shook his head. "James T. Kirk doesn't operate that way. If you knew him, you'd believe me." They continued the game in silence for a few moments before Peter spoke again. "There's one thing I still don't understand, Valdyr."

"What is that?"

"It's been three years since Kruge died. Why did your uncle wait so long? Why decide to take revenge *now?*"

The young woman stared at her cards, but Peter knew well enough that she'd already planned out her moves. Finally, she said, "At first he thought the government would support him in his quest for vengeance. But when Praxis exploded, moderate voices in the councils realized that we would need the help of the Federation to survive." Valdyr examined her hand. "After that, he did not speak of Kirk for a long time. My uncle . . . has always been loyal to his government. But suddenly, a few weeks ago . . ." She sighed and moved a card. " . . . he changed. One day, revenge was all Kamarag could think of, speak of . . . plan for. Vengeance, and Kirk's death. He said that if the government would not support him, he would act on his own."

"Which is why I'm here," Peter said, and she nodded. "What caused him to change so suddenly?" he wondered aloud.

"I do not know," Valdyr said. "I only know that he is my uncle, the head of my family, and I must be loyal to him." She looked up at him. "Are you going to place a bet, Pityr?"

They placed their bets, then upped the ante several times. Peter studied Valdyr, then finally said, "Your loyalty to your uncle includes torturing me, doesn't it?" That was more than a volley, he realized. He'd just dropped a matter/antimatter bomb into their conversation.

Her eyes met his unflinchingly. "If the choice were mine . . . none of this would be happening. I am sorry, Pityr."

They said nothing for a few minutes, then continued the game, but his heart wasn't in it. He was not surprised when she beat him again. "I quit!" the human groused, struggling to keep the bitterness out of his voice. He tossed his cards back into the slot. "Life isn't fair. I've been kidnapped, held prisoner, and now my jailer turns out to be a beautiful woman who's a *card shark* to boot." He'd used the current English idiom, as he knew of no Klingon one that was appropriate.

Valdyr glanced up at him, obviously startled. "You called me . . . what did you call me?"

"Beautiful and a card shark," Peter said levelly. "Which term didn't you understand?"

"What is this . . . card shark?"

"A shark is an Earth animal, a huge fish . . . you know, fish?" He racked his brain for the Klingon word. "An animal that swims in the sea, a dangerous predator, you know?"

"Oh!" she cried. "You mean, *norgh?*"

"Yeah, *norgh.* You're like that when you play cards. Understand?"

She thought it over, then gave a soft snort of derisive laughter. "What you mean is that, since I am a woman and I beat you always, I must be ruthless. I thought Earth males treated their females equally!"

"We do," Peter protested. Valdyr just looked at him, her expression clearly distrustful. "Really, we do," he insisted, holding up his hand as if under oath. "Aren't Klingon women treated equally?" He felt guilty for asking, since he already knew the truth.

"No," Valdyr admitted. "The men have always held the . . . outward power. If women want power, they must find a man to work through, advise him, push him, make him the . . . the . . ." She groped, at a loss for a suitable term.

"A figurehead?" suggested Peter in English.

Valdyr quickly accessed the English word on her portable comm link, then nodded. "Exactly," she said.

"Well, what about Chancellor Azetbur? She's a woman."

Valdyr's eyes sparkled. "She is special. Her father made the other members of the High Council promise to uphold her as his successor, and they have done so. The people support her . . . but the warriors' code is difficult to change."

Peter fixed her with an intent stare. "What about *you*, Valdyr? What would you like to do with your life?"

She dropped her eyes. "I . . . have dreams."

"Of what?"

"When I was small," she said, "I wanted to be a warrior. It is hard for women to do . . . but possible. But I was sickly. When I realized I had attained my full size, I . . . knew I could never be strong enough to be a warrior, no matter how I studied."

"Even so, you learned to fight."

She nodded. "And I am good with a knife," she said, with a touch of pride. "But, I am too small to truly defend myself against another Klingon with nothing more than my hands."

She'd said that offhandedly, so he wouldn't feel insulted. "So you can't be a warrior. What's next?"

She glanced around, as if suddenly concerned that they might be overheard. "I hoped to become a diplomat, like my uncle."

"Are women allowed to be diplomats?"

"There is no law against it."

Peter got up off his stool, paced the cell a few times. He still ached, but he was feeling much better. "That's funny that you should say that," he admitted. "I thought about shifting to a career in the Federation diplomatic corps myself."

She cocked her head, her long braid swinging. He found himself suddenly wondering what that massive mane might look like all undone. "You did?" she asked.

He nodded. "That's why I studied Klingonese and Romulan even before the Academy."

"Then why did you change?"

"I'm not sure anymore," he said, halting and staring at her, his brow furrowed. "I guess Command was what everyone expected me to do."

"Everyone expects *me* to marry Karg and spend my time running a household," Valdyr said dryly.

Peter made a face at that, and Valdyr almost smiled. "I think," she said, "we should try very hard to do what it is we want to do, not what we are expected to do!"

"I agree!" Peter said, flashing her a smile. Then, remembering who he was, and where, and what would soon be happening to him, he sobered abruptly. They did not speak of the coming torture, but it sat there between them.

Valdyr chewed on her lower lip, her sharp, slightly crooked teeth scoring the soft flesh. "Pityr," she said softly, "please believe me. This is not something I wish to do. I . . . have no more control over this than you have."

Peter sank back onto his stool, his shoulders slumping. "Your uncle is using me to capture and kill my uncle, Valdyr. What kind of *honor* can Kamarag gain out of this?"

She drew a quavering breath, shaking her head. In the smallest voice she admitted, "There is nothing about honor in any of this. There will be nothing for our family when it is over but shame."

Peter came over to the observation panel, reached through the slot as far as he could, and just managed to brush the flesh of her arm with the tip of his forefinger. She leapt back, her knife instantly in her hand. "What—?"

"I'm *alive*, Valdyr, just like you," Peter said. "Remember when you first gave me water? You saved my life with that water. Why did you do that, when you knew what was facing me? When you knew what *you* would soon be doing to me?"

She tightened her jaw and remained silent, staring at his fingers as though they were some bizarre life-form.

"You gave me water . . . and I held your hands. Remember? They were so *warm*, your hands, so much warmer than mine. I was pretty shocky, all my blood going to my injuries . . . but I'm warm now, Valdyr, just like you. I'm alive. Feel. Feel how warm I am. Go on. . . ."

Hesitantly, she approached the panel as if mesmerized, then put out her hand, brushed his fingertips with hers. His skin tingled where she touched him. Her body temperature was slightly higher than his, although nowhere near as high as a Vulcan's. "See?" Peter said, softly. "Warm. Alive. Just like you. And I want to *stay* alive!"

She was staring down at his hand, wide-eyed, as though she'd never seen it before.

"Can you really do it, Valdyr?" he whispered, as he closed his fingers around her long, elegant ones. "Can you do this thing that has no honor in it, just because your uncle wants you to? Can you really do this . . . to me?"

She shuddered and closed her eyes. With a surprising surge of strength she clasped his hand so powerfully, her nails scored his palm, drawing blood. Then she murmured, "Yes."

What an idiot you are, mister! he thought bitterly.

Valdyr's face was flushed, her eyes bright with . . . regret? Was it really?

Yes, Peter decided. *It really is. . . .*

"I don't want to die," he said, gazing at her through the panel. "Valdyr, I especially don't want to die at your hands." He gripped her just as tightly as she gripped him. "I don't want my uncle to die either. And more than that . . . I don't want the peace our people are only now working out to crumble. . . . You know that's what will happen when all this comes to light."

She nodded grimly, raising her eyes to his.

"And I don't want to see you give up your dreams. Don't lose all the honor you've worked so hard to gain. I couldn't bear to know that my death would take that from you." He prayed she would not think his speech that of a self-serving coward willing to say anything to save his life. He was saying nothing but the plain truth.

"Valdyr," he whispered, "I've come to really care about you. As a person of honor . . . of dignity . . . and of great strength."

She looked down, staring at their joined hands, saw their commingled blood dripping onto the slot. With a choked, inarticulate sound, she yanked her hand away, then turned abruptly and bolted down the corridor, racing as though a demon was on her heels.

Peter reined in his own emotions as he pulled his abandoned hand back inside his cell. He stared at the crescent-shaped wounds on his palm, still oozing blood. He must've cut her as well, as puce-colored liquid mingled with red in his palm. He made a fist, holding their blood inside, and fought back the demons of his own fear.

As Wing Commander Taryn studied the chessboard before him, one slanting eyebrow went up in pleased surprise. "You are improving," he remarked, considering his options and finding they were limited.

His opponent was a slender young woman with delicate, almost elfin features that were emphasized by her cropped black hair and elegantly pointed ears. Her name was Savel, and she was twenty-two Standard years old. Her Vulcan parents had been killed while trying to escape when Savel was a baby; she did not remember them at all. The young woman had lived in a government-operated creche until Taryn had taken her into his household at the age of five. The commander regarded her as an adopted daughter, and had raised her with the same advantages that he had bestowed upon his two sons.

"A very interesting gambit," Taryn conceded. "Not one I ever taught you. Where did you learn it?"

Savel's black eyes sparkled with pleasure. "While I was with you at Khitomer, Ambassador Sarek's aide challenged me to a game. Soran won, using this very tactic."

Taryn stiffened in his chair. "You played chess with Ambassador Sarek's aide?"

Now it was Savel's turn to tense. "Yes," she admitted. "You did not forbid that, *Vadi.*" The word meant "uncle" in Romulan, which Savel spoke as fluently as she did Vulcan. "What harm could that do?"

"A great deal," Taryn said, sternly. The commander leaned forward in his seat, his dark eyes holding hers. "What if I had been forced to come searching for you, and encountered Sarek? I told you, he suspects us. If we had met face-to-face . . . there is no telling what he might have done. He has already unmasked one of us, and for that reason I was at great pains during Khitomer to stay out of the ambassador's way. You knew that, Savel."

The young woman hung her head. "Yes, I knew. But Soran was . . . very pleasant to me. I found our conversation enjoyable. I do not often get the chance to speak with someone near my own age, *Vadi.*"

Taryn sighed. "I know," he said. "But, Savel . . . you took an unnecessary risk. We are close to the completion of our plan, within grasp of our goal. . . ."

Now it was the woman's turn to whisper, "I know." She gazed at him with a touch of remorse plain to read in her dark eyes. As she had been raised by Romulans, her control was not as great as a native-born Vulcan's. "Forgive me, *Vadi.*"

"Very well. As long as you will promise not to take such a chance again."

"I promise," Savel said. *"Vadi . . . it is still your move."*

"So it is." Taryn studied the chessboard, then made one of the two moves possible to him. Savel's mouth twitched as she moved a piece of her own, so quickly that Taryn knew he had fallen into her trap . . . for a trap it was. The commander sighed, frowning, but inwardly he felt a wash of pleasure at her growing skill as he said, "I see it now . . . mate in two." With a near-bow of respect, he ceremoniously knocked over his king as a sign of defeat. Though losing to Sarek always rankled him, losing to Savel, whom he had taught himself, was almost pleasurable.

Taryn sat back in the overstuffed armchair in his comfortable study, with its shelves of data spindles, its ancient bas-reliefs and weapons hanging on the walls, and the glow from the fire-box chasing the last vestige of chill from the air. It was winter on Freelan, and even here, in the northern equatorial region, frost and snow were common during these long, dark months.

Taryn thought with longing of times he had lived on Romulus, in a small house on an ancient, winding street. The wind there was warm, even during the brief rainy season . . . a far contrast to the bitter gales that raged at night around his dome-shaped house on Freelan.

"Have you heard any news of Kamarag?" Savel asked. "Will we need to encounter him again?"

"I do not know," Taryn said. "The reports I have received tell me that he has had Captain Kirk's nephew kidnapped, and that he has demanded that Kirk exchange himself for the young man. Kamarag has good reason to hate Kirk, and he has sworn a blood oath to avenge his young protégé, Kruge. So it is possible that he will require no further prodding."

Savel nodded. "There was a strong core of hate in him before I ever touched his mind," she said. "Who is monitoring him now?"

"No one, at the moment," Taryn replied. "Darus was, for a time, but he has now been detailed to Earth. There is a major trade conference there, and he and Stavin were needed to attend."

She nodded. "It is possible we may have to visit Kamarag again. The ambassador may balk at actually executing Kirk, knowing that if he does that, he will surely be declared a traitor, once his actions are known to Azetbur and her councillors."

"Getting close to him may be too risky, now," Taryn said. "Even if the ambassador merely captures Kirk, that will probably be enough to touch off hostilities—especially since the raids along the Neutral Zone are increasing."

"Who is working there, *Vadi?*" Savel asked, cocking her head at him.

Taryn smiled thinly. "That is the beauty of it . . . no one. We prodded Keraz, we prodded Chang, we prodded Kruge and Wurrl and Makesh and Kardis. Now insubordination and mutiny are creeping through the Klingon forces like a spy in the night. Every week there are new reports of terrorism . . . and we are responsible for only half of them! Azetbur is holding on by her elegant fingernails—but soon, her grip on her people will be lost. And then . . ." He nodded.

"War," Savel said, with an expression Taryn could not read. It seemed to be compounded of equal parts eagerness and revulsion.

"Vadia-lya," he said, referring to her as his "little niece" for the first time in years, "what troubles you?"

"Nothing," she mumbled, gazing down at the thick-woven carpet beneath their feet. "It is only that—"

"Yes?"

"At Khitomer . . ." She bit her lip, her control visibly slipping now.

"Yes?"

"When the Federation president spoke, he sounded so . . . earnest." She looked up, met Taryn's gaze, and flushed visibly, but continued, "When he spoke of peace between the worlds, I could almost . . . visualize a galaxy where peace reigns. And that vision was attractive to me."

"Ah, but Savel, there *will* be peace," Taryn reminded her. "Soon, the purpose to which I have dedicated my life will be achieved. Soon, there *will* be peace. Of course a little strife must precede it, that is unavoidable. The war between the Federation and the Klingons will not last long, and the conflict between what remains of the

Federation and our forces will be even briefer. But soon . . . within a year or two, we will have a lasting peace . . . and survival as well as victory for the Romulan Empire. Otherwise, what will happen to us?"

"The Federation will try to destroy us," she replied without much conviction.

Taryn gazed at her thoughtfully, but finally nodded. "Another game?" he asked, waving at the chessboard.

Savel's grave features brightened, though her control was back in place, and she did not smile. "Oh, yes, *Vadi*," she said, eagerly, and moved to set up the pieces.

Stepping off the turbolift, Sarek walked down the narrow corridor, halting outside Kirk's quarters. He signaled the door. "Come," the captain's voice responded.

Kirk was just fastening the belt of his uniform jacket. He halted abruptly as he saw who his early-"morning" visitor was. "Ambassador!" he exclaimed, "Good morning."

The Vulcan did not waste time on pleasantries. "Kirk, we must speak for a moment," he said. "I have been giving a great deal of thought to your nephew's abduction, and logic indicates that it is connected to our problem with the Freelans."

"I was wondering the same thing myself," Kirk said. "I called it instinct instead of logic, but it sounds like we've reached the same conclusion. What's your reasoning?"

"While I was negotiating on Kidta, Commander Keraz told me that Ambassador Kamarag called a meeting of Klingon officers, and attempted to induce them to turn against Azetbur and her government. If Keraz and Wurrl were influenced by Freelan telepaths, why not the ambassador? With the history of events between you, Kamarag would prove an excellent candidate for mental influence."

"You think *Kamarag* kidnapped Peter?"

"Not personally, no. But that he was behind it . . . yes, I do."

Kirk looked thoughtful. "That's an interesting idea," he said. "I know he hates me . . . I've been told many times how he's denounced me publicly at every opportunity . . . but is his hatred strong enough to lead him to betray his government?"

"Perhaps not on his own, but with sufficient telepathic prodding . . ." Sarek countered. "Logic seems to favor Kamarag as a likely suspect in Peter's abduction."

"But how does that connect with Peter investigating the KEHL?"

"If the same person or persons are influencing both groups . . . it would be simple to induce the KEHL to turn Peter over to someone who would then take him to Kamarag."

"You think there's a third party involved?"

"I would suspect so. That way, the KEHL would not have to deal with an alien ship."

"Makes sense. Uhura is trying to track down the ships that departed Earth during the time in question. But that's a tall order. She's been working on it since yesterday, so maybe she'll have something soon."

"Have you heard any reports about the KEHL and its activities?" Sarek asked. "I have not yet scanned today's communiqués."

"The leader, Induna, was finally released on bail," Kirk said. "Last I heard, he was calling for—" The captain broke off as the intercom signaled. He activated it. "Kirk here."

"Captain?" It was Commander Uhura's voice. "Sir, I've managed to locate the points of origin of both the message sent to Peter in his apartment, and the subspace one that reached us."

"Good work. What did you find out?"

"The first transmission, the one patched together with clips from old transmissions of yours, was sent from a vessel in Earth orbit . . . the *Bobino*."

"What kind of ship? What registry?"

"*Bobino* is a freighter, registered to an Otto Whitten, who owns her but is not her pilot."

"Did you check him out?"

"Yes, Captain. This Whitten is a man with a past. A con artist . . . but clever. Arrested many times, but the charges were always dropped. The vessel is registered as a 'freighter,' but 'smuggler' is probably a more accurate description."

Kirk glanced at Sarek. "Sounds about right," he said. "Who is the pilot?"

"*Bobino*'s pilot is a woman named Erika Caymor. Same thing as Whitten. She's been arrested a number of times, but she always gets off. Extortion, credit fraud, theft, smuggling . . . the list of charges against her goes on. But the authorities could never make anything stick. They're a nasty—but clever—pair."

"They sound like scum," Kirk said, bitterly. Smugglers who had smuggled not contraband, but Peter Kirk, offworld. "What about the other transmission? The subspace one?"

"That message originated on Qo'noS, Captain. I can't pin it down any further than that."

"Damn!" Kirk muttered, looking over at Sarek and nodding ruefully. "Good work. Thank you, Commander."

"I was glad to be of help, sir," she said. "I put in a call to Vice-Admiral Burton's office, asking them for any information they have on *Bobino*'s registered course. I'll let you know when I hear from them."

Kirk clicked off the intercom and turned back to the Vulcan. "Looks like logic and instinct are both paying off," he said.

"What will you do now, Kirk?" Sarek asked. "Will you stay on course for Freelan? What about the ransom demand that you exchange yourself for your nephew?"

"At the moment, our course is taking us toward both destinations," Kirk said. "I plan to get to the closest possible approach to the stated coordinates, then hand over the *Enterprise* to Spock and order him to take you to Freelan. I can hire a small ship at the nearest starbase and make that rendezvous myself."

"Why not use the *Enterprise*?"

Kirk shook his head. "I can't justify using the starship for a personal mission like this."

"But . . . Kirk. Going to keep that rendezvous alone will be extremely . . . hazardous," Sarek said, raising an eyebrow.

"Oh, I don't plan to just waltz in with my eyes shut, Ambassador. The *Enterprise*'s speed has given me nearly a two-day lead that the kidnappers don't expect. If they keep that rendezvous, I plan to be there well ahead of time, so I can find out where they come from."

"Logic suggests that they will come across the Neutral Zone from Qo'noS," Sarek said. "Kamarag told me once that his ancestral estate is located there."

The captain programmed the food dispenser in his cabin for a cup of coffee, then, when it arrived, took a grateful sip. "It's frightening," he said, "to think that the Romulans could plan something like this for so long. Planting a colony on Freelan, disguising their appearance, all that security for decades . . . and the gradual acquisition of Vulcan children to raise so they could control their telepathic abilities. All of this beginning in the days before we even knew what the Romulans looked like! By my calculation, they've been working on this plan for seventy-five years!"

"Possibly longer," Sarek said, sitting down on the edge of the bunk. "We have no idea when Freelan was first colonized. However, do not forget, Captain, that, like Vulcans, Romulans have a considerably greater life span than humans."

The ambassador spoke without thinking, but, suddenly hearing his own words, he experienced a vivid memory of Amanda. They had been sitting together in her garden, watching T'Rukh, when she'd said, suddenly, "Sarek . . . I want you to know that I expect you to remarry after I am gone."

Her husband had regarded her with mild surprise. "Amanda . . . is this statement a result of your having turned forty yesterday? I understand that this particular anniversary of birth is frequently stressful for humans. . . ."

She'd smiled at him. "No, my husband. My remark was entirely logical. We've never spoken of it before, but it's obvious that, barring some kind of accident, you will outlive me by at least sixty years. You should not deprive yourself of companionship, out of some misguided sense of loyalty. To do so would not be logical."

"But—"

She'd smiled again and stopped his words with a shake of her head. "I know this is premature. But someday you'll remember this conversation. Someday you'll be relieved to know that you have my blessing in choosing another consort. Let's leave it at that."

And they had.

He looked up, to find Kirk regarding him intently from across the small room. "My apologies, Captain," the ambassador said. "My thoughts turned . . . elsewhere. You were saying?"

The human shook his head slightly, his hazel eyes softening. "I want you to know, Ambassador, that I admire you and Spock for continuing with this mission . . . despite everything that's happened."

"Work is an anodyne to grief, Kirk," Sarek said. "Or, at least . . . it presents a distraction."

"Yes, I know," the captain replied simply. "Ambassador . . ." He hesitated.

"Yes?" Sarek said, raising an eyebrow.

"I may be overstepping, here, but I just wanted you to know that . . . that Spock . . ." Kirk was struggling to find words. Sarek nodded encouragingly. The captain tried again. "He's taking his mother's death very hard," he said in a rush. "With some people, it's a relief to transmute grief into anger. If you don't mind a word of advice . . . be patient. Let him work through this on his own. He'll . . . come around."

The Vulcan regarded the human steadily. "I will keep your words in mind, Kirk," he said quietly. "Patience is a virtue on Earth . . . on Vulcan, we are taught that it is an essential component of life."

Kirk sipped his coffee in silence for several moments. "Kamarag," he said, finally. "Ambassador, if he does have Peter, I'll have to go to Qo'noS . . . and stage a rescue."

Sarek shook his head. "Captain . . . alone? That would be . . . most illogical."

"Rescuing Peter isn't an official mission," Kirk pointed out. "But . . . maybe I don't have to go to Qo'noS alone. Chancellor Azetbur was rather grateful that I saved her life . . . possibly she'd be interested in knowing about what's going on."

"I would not tell her directly, Kirk," Sarek cautioned.

"Why not?"

"There is no way for us to know who may be under the Freelan influence now," Sarek reminded him. "Azetbur herself might even be suborned."

"They'd never get close enough to her," Kirk said, but the captain was clearly taken aback at the idea.

"Possibly you are correct. But what about her aides? If they discover what you know, and that you have shared your knowledge with the chancellor, that would make her, in turn, a prime candidate for assassination."

"You're right. . . ." Kirk set his coffee cup down so hard it sloshed into the saucer. "Damn! This entire situation breeds paranoia. You can't trust anyone!"

"I will speak with Azetbur. I may be able to discern from her expressions and speech patterns whether she has been influenced. I will attempt to warn her . . . subtly, as well as discover whether she knows anything about Peter."

"Thank you, Ambassador. I'd appreciate that."

Minutes later, Sarek sat before the comm link in his cabin, waiting patiently as the screen flickered. Finally it cleared, and familiar features coalesced before him. Sarek inclined his head respectfully. "Madame Chancellor."

Azetbur inclined her head in turn. "Ambassador Sarek. I trust you are well?"

"I am, Madame. And you?"

"Entirely," she said. "Allow me to offer condolences on your recent bereavement."

"Thank you, Madame Chancellor."

The Klingon woman gazed at him, and, for the first time since he'd known her, seemed at a loss. "I heard about the attempt on your life, Ambassador. It was a relief to know that Wurrl had failed. I take oath on my father's honor, Ambassador, that neither Keraz nor Wurrl was acting under my direction."

"I know that, Madame Chancellor," Sarek assured her. "I sensed Wurrl's mind telepathically during the struggle. He was definitely not allied with your government."

The chancellor visibly relaxed. "What is the purpose of your call, Ambassador?"

Sarek hesitated for a second, carefully phrasing his inquiry in the most subtle and least revealing terms he could manage. "Madame Chancellor . . . there was an . . . illegality, a violent act, perpetrated against a Federation citizen on Earth eight Terran Standard days ago. I am . . . disquieted . . . to inform you that this . . . incident, at least on the surface, appears linked to Qo'noS. Evidence indicates that this . . . link may be highly placed in your government."

Azetbur blinked, and Sarek was quick to note the faint flicker of surprise cross her face. She was learning fast . . . her expression barely altered before her features were, once more, an impassive mask. But the ambassador knew that, whoever had been responsible for young Peter Kirk's abduction, it had not been done with the chancellor's knowledge or sanction. "Qo'noS?" she repeated. "I assure you, Ambassador, I have no knowledge of any such crime. Unless, of course, you are referring to the renegades who captured Kadura?"

"No, Madame Chancellor, this concerns a different matter altogether," Sarek said. "Incidentally, may I inquire as to whether Commander Keraz has been captured?"

"Not to my knowledge," Azetbur said. "He is still at large." She gave the Vulcan an impatient glance. "Ambassador, if there has been violence done on Earth by Klingons—especially by any who are government officials, then I must demand that you be more specific."

"Madame Chancellor, your zeal does you credit—but you have misunderstood. I am neither accusing nor identifying any Klingon official as having committed crimes."

"Then what *are* you saying, Ambassador?" she snapped. "I do not care for verbal swordplay; I am a Klingon."

Sarek nodded. "I assure you that I would be more specific if I could, Madame Chancellor, but I regret that I am not at liberty to explain at this time."

"When you are free to explain, will you, Ambassador? I must confess that my . . . curiosity . . . is aroused." Her dark eyes sparkled dangerously.

"You have my word," Sarek promised. "Madame Chancellor . . . I am not at liberty to do more than make a suggestion, for I have no way to substantiate my suspicions, but . . ." He paused while she listened intently. "If . . . individuals within your government appear to behave in a manner that is suspicious, or uncharacteristic . . ." He hesitated again, choosing his words with infinite care. "It is possible that . . . an external agency is exerting undue influence upon them. I believe that these external agencies were responsible for Commander Keraz's actions at Kadura."

Now it was Azetbur's turn to raise an eyebrow. "Really, Ambassador? What an extraordinary statement."

"I make it only as one living being to another, Madame . . . not in any official or diplomatic capacity. Guard yourself, Madame Chancellor. I have reason to believe the intent is to subvert the peace process your government and the Federation have recently embarked upon."

"What kind of undue influence?" she demanded. "Bribery? Torture of family members? Drugs, or other chemical forms of coercion?"

Sarek shook his head. "No, Madame. None of those methods. I regret that I cannot be more specific; however, I have overstepped my authority in divulging even this much to you."

She gave him a long, thoughtful look, but forbore to ask, evidently realizing he could not be persuaded to say any more. Sarek took a deep breath. One final test, now. "Incidentally, Madame Chancellor . . ."

"Yes?"

"Captain Kirk requested that I express his wishes for your continuing good health and success in your administration."

The Klingon woman's expression brightened . . . for a moment she nearly smiled. "Please express my thanks to Kirk, and tell him I wish him success, too. We were . . . gratified . . . to learn that he and the *Enterprise* will continue to serve the Federation."

Sarek nodded. "I have enjoyed our talk, Madame Chancellor; however, I know your schedule is a busy one. I shall say farewell."

"Thank you for your . . . warning, Ambassador. Be assured I shall be watchful."

Sarek nodded, then held up his hand in the formal salute. "Peace and long life, Madame Chancellor."

Again the faintest of smiles touched the Klingon woman's mouth. *"Qapla'!,* Ambassador Sarek," she said, wishing him success.

"Captain?" Uhura turned to regard her superior officer. "I have an incoming call for you. It's Vice-Admiral Burton, sir."

"I'll take it in my quarters, Commander," Kirk said, and then he added, in an undertone too soft for anyone but her to catch, "Put this on a shielded frequency, Uhura."

She nodded as he left the bridge.

In his quarters, Kirk turned on his screen and Vice-Admiral Burton, Starfleet's chief of security, appeared. After the captain had outlined the problem of Peter's disappearance, concluding with Uhura's finding that the ransom message had originated on Qo'noS, the admiral, a beefy man with a shock of thick white hair, frowned. "More terrorism," he concluded. "This is obviously not your ordinary kidnapping for profit."

"I agree," Kirk said. "How do you want me to handle this, sir?"

"Investigate your nephew's disappearance without any public fanfare," Burton said. "And if there's any possibility that this is reprisal against you personally, by the Klingons, you'd better abandon this notion of going in alone. I'm officially authorizing you to use the *Enterprise* for this mission. If the Klingons are involved, then it becomes a matter of Federation security—and that makes it official. But . . . Kirk. I meant it about keeping this quiet. The KEHL is gaining converts every day. Something like this would add fuel to the fire."

"I understand, Admiral. Did your office come up with any information on that smuggler's destination?" the captain asked.

"We've got a copy of *Bobino*'s official flight plan, Captain. They were scheduled to take a load of gourmet foodstuffs to Alpha Centauri A . . . but they're overdue. Way overdue."

"Any idea where they went instead?"

Burton nodded grimly. "They picked up a cargo of high-grade dilithium ore in Sector 51.34 two days ago."

Sector 51.34 was only a parsec or so from the Klingon Neutral Zone. Kirk nodded, unsurprised.

"Captain, this clinches it. I want you to get to the bottom of this . . . and soon."

"I will, sir," Kirk replied.

"Mr. President," Sarek said, to the image on his comm link. "Greetings." Gravely, he saluted the chief executive.

"Ambassador Sarek," Ra-ghoratrei said. "Allow me to offer my most sincere condolences on your bereavement. I very much . . . regret . . . having called you to duty at such a time."

"I discussed my mission to Kidta before leaving, Mr. President," Sarek said, uncomfortable at having to speak of this now. "My wife understood its importance. But I did not call you to discuss Kidta, Mr. President."

"What is it, Ambassador?"

"Sir . . . I believe that I have discovered a threat to Federation security. I have discovered evidence—evidence that I will soon be able to share with you—that the Keep Earth Human League may be funded and supported by off-world interests."

Ra-ghoratrei's pale eyes widened. "What? The KEHL? But they are . . ." He hesitated. "They are more than they seem, apparently. . . ."

"Yes, Mr. President. I suggest that you authorize a full-scale investigation into the group. I believe that such an investigation may turn up surprising information."

"Can you be more specific, Ambassador?"

"No, Mr. President," he said, "I cannot, at this time. But I will be contacting you within a few days with, I hope, conclusive proof. In the meantime, I ask that you authorize a full investigation—although I do not believe that it should be a public inquiry. I will explain my reasoning later."

"Ambassador," Ra-ghoratrei said thoughtfully, "your service to the Federation is legendary. I will do as you ask . . . but I do insist upon the explanation you promised."

"You will receive one, Mr. President. Two days—three at the most—should prove sufficient."

"Very well," the president said. "Until we speak again, then, Ambassador Sarek."

"Live long and prosper, Mr. President." Sarek raised his hand in salute.

After cutting the connection, the Vulcan sat for several minutes composing a detailed message to Ra-ghoratrei, with additional copies to the head of Starfleet Security, Vice-Admiral Burton, and the chairman of the Security Council, Thoris of Andor. The message gave a complete summary of his suspicions and findings, plus the data he had collected so far.

Then the Vulcan placed each message under a time lock. If the *Enterprise* did not return from this mission, Ra-ghoratrei would receive the message in five days, with the others receiving theirs in six.

When he finally got off duty that evening, Kirk was weary to the bone. They were now en route for the Klingon Neutral Zone. A few hours ago, he'd received official orders from Starfleet affirming Vice-Admiral Burton's verbal orders. He was to attempt to locate and rescue Peter Kirk; then he was directed to place himself and his vessel at the disposal of Ambassador Sarek, who was currently on a special fact-finding mission for the Federation president.

Unsealing his maroon uniform jacket, Kirk slumped into a chair. The captain had a hunch that the entire mess was only beginning—that it was only going to get worse before it got better. *Assuming it does get better, which is a big assumption,* he reminded himself.

And besides, he thought, *you've got it easy, compared to Peter.* What might the Klingons be doing to the young man, while he sat here, safe aboard his orbiting fortress? Thoughts of Klingon torture, mind-sifters and beatings, raced through his mind, and the captain shuddered.

At least Qo'noS isn't Rura Penthe, he thought, trying to find comfort in the fact—but he was tormented by images of Peter being brutalized by Klingons like Old One-Eye. Klingon jailers weren't noted for their kindness and compassion, to put it mildly.

He and Peter had grown close, over the years; Kirk knew his nephew better than the cadet suspected. He was aware of Peter's feeling that he had to live up to his illustrious uncle's example, and regretted inadvertently placing his nephew under that kind of pressure. But Peter was a Kirk, and he was bound to pressure himself to achieve, no matter what anyone said to him.

An image of the young man's features drifted before his eyes, and Kirk shook his head wearily. Would he ever see him again . . . alive? Where was Peter? Was he even now being tortured?

With a muffled groan, Jim Kirk leaned his head in his hands. *Hang on, Peter,* he thought. *Just hang on a little longer. . . .*

Seven

Savel stared at herself in the mirror as she brushed her thick, shining hair. Today she was wearing a long blue dress instead of her usual silvery padded tunic and snug trousers, and she felt more feminine than she had in a long time.

For a moment, she indulged herself by imagining what Soran might think if he could see her in this garb. He had been so courteous, so quietly attentive . . . it had been very flattering. Savel knew that most Vulcans were bonded by the time they were adults . . . was Ambassador Sarek's young aide betrothed?

Surely not; if he'd been promised to another, he wouldn't have stared at her quite so intensely. His eyes had been very dark, very earnest. . . .

Savel suddenly wondered what would happen to Soran if her adopted uncle's most cherished dream was realized, and war erupted between the Federation and the Klingons—followed swiftly by a full-scale Romulan invasion. Everyone knew that Vulcans were pacifists . . . but that word was not at all synonymous with "cowards." If pushed to defend their homeworld, Savel was quite sure that the Vulcans would fight, and fight well.

And what if Soran was hurt . . . even killed?

Savel's throat tightened, and she told herself she was being ridiculous. She'd only met the young Vulcan for a few hours; thinking about him now was senseless . . . illogical!

She stared at her reflection, wondering where Soran was, what he was doing at the moment. Would she ever see him again? Would she ever find someone on Freelan that she found as attractive? The odds against that happening were great—and not simply because she was so drawn to Soran. The young Vulcans residing on Freelan were technically free to intermarry with the Romulans . . . but few did.

To put it bluntly, the majority of the transplanted Vulcans on Freelan were regarded with suspicion and disapproval . . . though there were exceptions. Savel knew of several Vulcans-by-blood who had risen to high-ranking positions in the Romulan military—some had intermarried. One or two had even received vital political appointments.

But generally the transplanted Vulcans tended to seek each other's society, rather than looking to the Romulans for mates or companionship. Was this because they had all grown up with the knowledge that they were a captive people? Or did their telepathic abilities set them apart?

Some Romulans were willing to accept and welcome the new additions into their society . . . but many more were like Taryn's wife Jolana. Why? Was Jolana cold and withdrawn because she suspected Savel's loyalty? Since many Vulcans-by-blood served in the military, and served well, that attitude was illogical. Or was their distrust and aversion due to jealousy or fear of the Vulcan telepathic abilities? There was no way to be sure without a deep mind-meld, and Savel had no desire for such intimacy with her adopted "aunt" . . . so she would never know.

With a sigh, she smoothed down the skirt of the blue dress, and headed for the door of her room. Tonight she and Taryn would be leaving aboard his ship. The commander would take command of the invasionary force that was being assembled and supplied near Remus. Savel held no military rank, but her telepathic skills made her invaluable in espionage efforts.

As she stepped through the door, Savel thought for a moment more about Soran, but she forced the image of the handsome young aide's face from her mind. She would never see him again . . . thinking about him was illogical.

Squaring her slender shoulders, head high, Savel resolutely went to find her uncle, so they could plan what their strategy would be during the upcoming war.

Peter Kirk paced restlessly, turning again and again to stare through the observation port at the front of his cell. It had been three days since Valdyr had fled from him. Three days.

He was still fed regularly, his meals brought now by different Klingon guards, but she had not returned. The guards had come and gone as quickly as possible, sparing him barely a glance.

The cadet discovered that, for the first time since this whole thing had started, he was afraid—gut-wrenchingly, genuinely afraid—but not for himself.

Could Kamarag have observed Valdyr's behavior toward her prisoner and considered it disloyal or treacherous? Could she have been punished for their conversations, for . . . touching him? He ran his thumb over the healing wounds on his palms, as if trying to reassure himself that that passionate handclasp had actually happened, that he hadn't imagined the entire thing. No, it had happened. He glanced at his hand. Oh yes, it had happened.

But where was Valdyr? What if she never returned?

At the thought of never seeing the young Klingon woman again, Peter swallowed painfully. *Valdyr* . . .

Peter opened his fist and stared down at the marks of her nails. What had happened between them?

Or, at least . . . what had happened to *him?* He scowled, fighting the reality, struggling against the truth. . . . Peter groaned inwardly and struck the wall of his cell with his fist so hard that he winced from the pain. But even that couldn't distract him. The truth was still there, immutable, unmistakable. . . .

How long was he going to go on lying to himself?

All right, dammit! Peter finally admitted. *I love her. I'm a fool!*

It was inconceivable that he should love her—a Klingon! When had it happened? How could it have happened? Were Klingons and humans even biologically compatible? Who even knew? And yet . . . trying to deny how he felt would be like denying that he had two hands, or two eyes . . . or one heart.

Very little was known about the complexities of Klingon society, though there was plenty of speculation. Some of the things he'd heard about the sexual capacity of Klingon women would've made an Orion slaver blush. It was probably nothing but sleazy speculation, he knew—the same kinds of things had been said about other groups at other times. Peter had paid such gossip little mind . . . until now. But now thinking of those things brought images to his mind . . . images. . . .

Did Klingons love like humans? Were they even capable of similar emotions? More importantly, was there any hope at all that Valdyr might ever have the same feelings for him, or would she just find the whole thing one more dishonorable complication in a situation that was causing her considerable soul-searching and anguish?

There had been women in Peter's life, and some of them he'd loved—or, at least, he'd thought so at the time. Yet the most intimate moments with them had not moved him the way that touching Valdyr's hand had. Peter tried telling himself this was just a greater manifestation of Stockholm Syndrome, but neither his emotions nor his hormones were listening.

Love? Yeah, let's get really kinky, here, Peter. You'll probably never see her again until they haul you out to that platform, where she'll be waiting to perform the be'joy' on you, with Uncle Jim as a witness. You'll really enjoy that, won't you? You'll love that, right?

Suppose . . . suppose . . . she'd refused to perform the *be'joy'*. Maybe that was why she hadn't returned. Suppose one of the guards who'd been delivering his meals got the job because she'd refused and her uncle was furious. What if he died without ever seeing her again, at the hands of a stranger?

The cadet sank onto his bunk, cradling his head in his hands, feeling despair ready to overwhelm him.

Something made him glance back at the observation portal, and suddenly, as if his desire had conjured her up, Valdyr stood there, staring at him expressionlessly. She said nothing, standing at attention like the good Klingon warrior she yearned to be.

Slowly, he got up and walked toward the portal, trying to frame words. Valdyr's eyes widened almost imperceptibly and he stopped dead in his tracks, suddenly wary. Something was wrong. . . .

She wasn't alone. Without warning, Kamarag stepped into view. With him was another soldier, one Peter dimly remembered seeing before. Hadn't this guy been one of the goons who had come to get him out of his cell aboard the transport vessel?

Valdyr no longer met his eyes. Was it time for the *be'joy'?* Peter swallowed, but stood tall, head high. He would not shame himself. . . .

"Ah, the young Kirk," the ambassador murmured approvingly, addressing Valdyr in Klingonese. "He looks fine, niece. Strong. Healthy. You have done well." Kamarag eyed Peter through the portal as if sizing up a side of beef. "Cadet Kirk!" he said in English. "Do you know what day it is?"

"No, Ambassador," Peter replied, in the same tongue, "I do not."

"It is the day I will have my revenge!" Kamarag informed him. For a Klingon, his demeanor was positively jovial. "Even now your uncle speeds to our rendezvous, where I will take him prisoner. As soon as I have him, Karg here will bring you and Valdyr to join us." He indicated the other male. Peter stared at the warrior. So this was Karg . . . no wonder Valdyr hated him.

"Aboard my flagship, *HoHwi'*, we shall all enjoy an old Klingon ritual. Tell me . . . do you find my niece attractive, young Kirk?"

Peter refused to show fear. "Any male would," he said, honestly.

"Good, good! I like your spirit . . . it will add immeasurably to the *be'joy'*! No doubt you have longed in the past days to find yourself . . . close . . . to her, hungered for her touch? Even human males are not immune to a lovely female's charms, that is obvious. Well . . . I am happy to tell you that you will soon have your wish granted. Soon, you will be very close to Valdyr indeed—while she separates your skin into its many fragile layers inch by bloody inch! By the time she is finished with you, she will know you . . . intimately. Outside . . . and inside."

Kamarag guffawed, and Karg did, too. *Good grief*, Peter thought, refusing to feel the fear that wanted to claw its way out of him with a shriek. *Where did this guy learn English? Reading Edgar Rice Burroughs? He sounds like he comes from Barsoom. . . .*

Kamarag was still grinning. "No doubt your uncle will enjoy the spectacle; he will, after all, be the next to succumb to it!"

Peter said nothing. He would not let himself be baited . . . besides, Kamarag was, finally, saying something of real interest.

"And as soon as the *be'joy'* is finished, my fleet will speed into Federation territory—and all the riches that await us there."

Peter was stunned. He had thought that Kamarag's only interest lay in torturing him and his uncle. He'd had no idea the ambassador had a "fleet" of his own and was planning to start a war!

"Your fleet?" he dared to ask, hoping Kamarag would keep talking, keep boasting. *He must mean the renegades who were causing so much trouble. . . .*

"Yes indeed. I have a sizable force accumulated of captains who are ready to take back their honor as Klingon warriors! Together, we will reduce your Starfleet to scrap metal."

Dream on, Peter thought. The ambassador had lost his mind if he seriously thought he and his "fleet" could conquer the Federation. Starfleet would wipe them out, there was no doubt. But—Peter repressed a shiver—he also had no doubt that Kamarag and his cohorts would wreak terrible destruction on the worlds closest to the Neutral Zone before they were stopped.

The ambassador turned so that his niece would be sure to hear him. "By the time *Chancellor* Azetbur learns of our action, it will be too late. At last, we will all regain our honor!" He faced Peter again, noted how the young man was eyeing the walls of his cell. "It is a terrible thing to be held prisoner while events of such magnitude unfold around you, is it not, young Kirk?"

Peter refused to give him the satisfaction of a reply.

Valdyr's face never changed expression, yet she seemed to be struggling with emotion. "My uncle," she said softly, pitching her words for Kamarag's hearing alone, turning her back on Karg, "I ask that you reconsider what you are about to do. Attacking the Starfleet is *Hoh'egh.*"

Of course Valdyr realizes it's suicide, Peter thought, his spirits rising slightly. *Kamarag may be crazy, but she's not. . . .*

The ambassador stared down at her. "You are worried for me, niece?"

Valdyr nodded. "Not only for you, Uncle. For all of our people. Our world is *dying,* my uncle," she insisted, still speaking softly, but passion now tinged her voice. "We have neither the technology nor the means to save our people. By working with the Federation, Chancellor Azetbur hopes . . ."

"Enough of this!" Kamarag growled, losing his patience. "I will not hear another word about that depraved female and how she will save the Klingon Empire! Mention that name again, Valdyr, and you will have more to fear from Karg than your wedding night!"

Valdyr flushed deeply, and she set her jaw. She drew herself up as tall as she could, and this time she addressed both males. "Is this how you would control me, Uncle, by *threatening* me with a husband? Is this how a Klingon male earns his female's loyalty—through fear? Where is your honor? You—"

Karg's fist shot out faster than Peter's eyes could follow, smashing brutally into her jaw. She hit the ground hard, but never uttered a sound.

Valdyr's face was swelling, and her lip was split and bleeding, but he knew from personal experience she could handle that. Her hand went for her dagger automatically, but Karg anticipated it and grabbed her wrist, twisting it painfully. She endured it without flinching, as the powerful warrior leaned down close to her face.

"Your disrespect to your uncle is disturbing, Valdyr," he warned her. "Do not think I will tolerate such attitudes from my wife. Where are your loyalties? To your *family,* or to that perverted female who has usurped the rightful role of a male?"

"I am a Klingon!" Valdyr snarled. "My respect and my loyalties are to my family, Karg—of which you are not a part!"

"That will be rectified soon enough," Karg reminded her. "We will be wed as soon as James T. Kirk dies beneath your knife. Then you will be mine! And you will learn respect. . . ." Hauling her up by the front of her armor, he backhanded her hard enough to snap her head back. She blinked, dazed.

Peter slammed against the viewing port before he even realized he'd moved forward. He pounded his fists against the glass. "Karg, you coward!" he heard himself shouting, barely remembering to speak English. "You want someone to fight, come in here and take me on. I'll flatten you, you bastard, just like I did the *last* time."

His taunts had the effect he intended. Karg's face suffused with rage and he released Valdyr and moved toward the viewing port. Kamarag stopped him with a gesture.

"Enough of this," Kamarag said to Karg. "I must fetch James T. Kirk. Wait for my call, then bring Cadet Kirk to me at the head of my fleet. Once this business is done, you can enjoy your wedding night in Federation space, as we head for the nearest colony!"

Karg gave Valdyr a last, sneering glance; then the two males left.

Peter pressed against the port, straining to see down the hallway, trying to determine if Karg and Kamarag were out of earshot. He turned back to Valdyr, and was surprised to find her intense black eyes focused on his face, as if she were trying to look through him. "Valdyr!" he whispered. "Are you all right? Valdyr?"

She glanced down the hallway, then finally climbed to her feet and came over to face him. "You meant what you said to Karg, didn't you?"

"What?" He shook his head, unsure he'd fully understood her.

"Do you understand what you said to him, how he interpreted it?" she asked again.

Peter just stared. "What was not to understand? If I could've gotten my hands on him, I'd've mopped the floors up with him, I'd've . . ."

She shook her head. "You challenged him as an equal. Warrior to warrior. You refused to let him view you as a helpless human prisoner. You challenged him—over his woman."

Peter felt his barely suppressed rage bubble over. Clenching his fists, he pounded one hand hard against the viewing port. "You're *not* his woman!"

"My uncle has arranged the mating. It will be done."

"Like hell it will!" Peter raged, feeling jealousy overwhelm him. The thought of Karg "claiming" Valdyr on the much-referenced wedding night made him crazy. "He'll touch you over my dead body! He can't have you!" Hearing himself beginning to sputter incoherently, he wound down.

"I will ask you the same question you asked me so many days ago, Pityr," Valdyr said softly, in a tone he had never heard her use. "Why do you care? What does it matter to you who touches me?"

He ground his teeth. Better to say nothing than to have her laugh in his face, or give her something to taunt him with when he had to endure her knife. But something in her eyes compelled truth. "It matters to me. It matters a lot. The man . . . who touches you . . . should do so with respect. . . ."

She never took her eyes from his. "That will never happen, Pityr. My uncle is about to betray his government, a course of events that will eventually bring about either the destruction of our world, or, at the very least, of our family. And the man . . . who would touch me with . . . respect . . . will soon be dead . . . by my hand. . . ."

What . . . what does she mean by that? Peter stood plastered against the window, as close to her as he could get, afraid to interpret her words too freely . . . afraid to hope.

"Pityr . . ." Her voice was hoarser than usual. "I cannot stay long. I—"

"Where were you?" he demanded. "You've been gone for three days!"

"I was here," she said tonelessly, not looking at him. "I came down once, while you were asleep, to look at you. But I could not talk to you until I . . ." She trailed off.

"Until you what?" he asked softly.

"Until I knew my own mind," she admitted.

"What does that mean?"

"After the other day . . . I sent a message to my uncle, asking him to release me from this duty. But he . . . he refused."

"Why did you ask to be released?" Peter asked, wishing she'd look up at him.

But she kept her eyes downcast. "Qo'noS . . . is not a good place to live, since Praxis exploded. Half of the moon was blown into a very long elliptical orbit that in fifty years will finally intersect with this world . . . which will mean the end for life on this planet. So many meteors will impact that it will destroy our atmosphere, crush our homes and land. Even now, Qo'noS is encircled by a ring of debris that reminds us night and day that our time is limited.

"Meteor showers are now common. One of your human months ago, my mother was at home in HatlhHurgh with my oldest brother. A shower fell, and our home was destroyed, my mother and brother killed. My father had died three years ago, when your uncle destroyed his own vessel to trap Kruge's crew. So my three living brothers and I had no one. Kamarag took us all in. He is now the head of my family, Pityr!" Her voice was tight and brittle, and she shook her head so hard her thick braid slid across her breastplate. "Honor demands that I serve him, and do as he wishes!"

"Well, you are doing that," Peter said, feeling his throat tighten as he glimpsed her expression.

"But to serve him, I have to be prepared to betray the leader of the Empire, Chancellor Azetbur. I have to share the responsibility for the death of our homeworld. Without the Federation to help us, everyone on Qo'noS will eventually die! And . . . worst of all . . . I must personally bring about your death!" She moved closer to the window, until she was pressed against the glass, even as he was. "Pityr . . . Pityr-oy . . ." She closed her eyes, but the anguish in her voice was unmistakable.

The cadet froze as he took in what she had just said, feeling a surge of incredulous joy. The suffix "oy" was used as an endearment. "Valdyr . . ." he whispered. "Valdyr, look at me . . ."

Finally, she looked up. Carefully, Peter stuck his hand through the slot, until his fingertips brushed hers. He stroked the tips of her fingers, his heart pounding. "Valdyr-oy . . ." he whispered, his blue eyes holding her dark ones.

She gazed at him incredulously; then he felt her fingertips slide over his, and suddenly she was touching his palm gently, rubbing her fingertips against the crescent wounds there. He in turn felt the small scabs from his own nails that were sheltered in her palm. "How can this be?" she whispered, her voice a mixture of anguish and joy. "It is not possible. We are not the same people. We are alien to one another. Enemies by blood . . ."

"Not anymore," he protested softly, "not enemies. Not by blood. We have shared blood. We are part of each other."

"Impossible," she repeated, as if trying to convince herself. "Humans are weak and cowardly. They have no heart, no endurance. They cannot fight, they have no will to do it. They stink of fear. Human males have no stamina, no passion. All they can do in bed is talk. A Klingon woman would kill any human male foolish enough to bed her."

"Is that what they say?" Peter murmured, losing himself in her dark eyes. "Well, on my world they say things, too. Klingons never bathe, so they smell. They are stupid, ignorant savages who live on base emotions, allowing their passions to rule their lives. They rut like animals. Klingons cannot weep . . . because they cannot love."

She looked shocked to hear that Terrans had prejudices that equaled those on her own world. "Do they say that?" she murmured, and he nodded, silently. "But Pityr . . . I am learning that what they say is not true. I have seen you fight like the finest warrior, against odds so great, there was no way to win. You fought . . . and almost won. I had never seen such heart, such will to win . . . such stamina . . ."

He clasped her hand in his tightly. "I am learning, too. You're always clean, and your fragrance reminds me of apricots. You're so smart, you're the only one here who has the sense to see what the future holds. And I've heard anguish in your voice . . . a sorrow too noble for tears. I know you don't want to hurt me. I understand you are just doing what you must."

She shook her head. "You believe it is true, then?"

It was his turn to be confused.

"That, because we cannot weep," she explained, "we cannot love."

"No, I don't believe that."

"But you believe that I could still bring about your death? Even now?"

"I thought . . . when you explained about your uncle . . ."

"The days I stayed away . . . I did so . . . because no matter how I felt about my family loyalty, I realized . . . that I could not live with the betrayal of Azetbur, and the destruction of my planet . . . and more than that . . . I could not live with your death."

"What are you going to do, then?"

She released his hand, glanced up and down the hallway. "I do not know yet. You will have to trust me."

He shrugged, smiling. "My fate has been in your hands since I first arrived here, Valdyr."

A look of pleasure washed across her face, and then she was gone, leaving him with nothing but the memory of her touch.

Commander Taryn sat in his quarters aboard the Romulan bird-of-prey *Shardarr*, reviewing intelligence communiqués from Romulus. Savel, who sat opposite him, watched alertly as the commander's expression darkened. "What is it?" she asked, when he finally looked up.

"Matters may be moving more precipitously than we anticipated," he replied, the lines in his craggy, raptor-beaked countenance deepening. "Kamarag has gathered a squadron of renegade captains around him by offering them Federation plunder and amnesty from the new government he claims he will head. He is clearly planning some kind of coup to coincide with his raid into Federation space. His squadron is currently assembling in space, not far from Qo'noS."

Savel digested this news in silence. It *is* really going to happen, she thought. The war . . . the war that Taryn had planned for his whole life. And *she* had been the one to bring it about. Vividly, she remembered touching Kamarag's mind, inflaming his hatred for Kirk. It hadn't been difficult . . . the Klingon's hatred had already been like magma beneath a planet's crust. . . . "But this is what you wanted, what we planned for," she said, finally.

"But the speed with which this is happening is a problem for us." Taryn rose from his antique carved desk and paced restlessly across the small office, stopping for a moment to regard the extensive collection of ancient weapons hanging on the wall. Some of them were so old that they predated the Romulan exodus from Vulcan, following the Surak reformation. The commander stood for a moment, ostensibly studying a training *lirpa*—one with a hollow bludgeon and a dulled blade.

Savel had a good knowledge of the tactical situation they now faced. But she had no idea of what information Taryn had gained from those communiqués. "What problem?" she asked.

Taryn handed her the communiqués, inviting her to scan them for herself. "Kamarag is doing far more than we expected. He plans to topple Azetbur's government—not simply to lead a renegade raid. We did not anticipate this."

Savel scanned the messages quickly, then nodded agreement. "He has gone too far to simply go home after his raid. There is no way that Kamarag can keep his actions secret, now . . . not with this many people involved. The ambassador has evidently decided that the time has come to make his break with Chancellor Azetbur's government. How do you think he will proceed, *Vadi?*"

"I believe that, once Kirk is dead, the ambassador will initiate hostilities by leading his squadron across the Neutral Zone in an all-out attack on the nearest Federation world. He will use the publicity from that to declare himself a war leader, and thus sway the public to his side. Staging a military coup will then be easy."

Savel raised an eyebrow as that notion sank in. "If Kamarag does that . . . such an action would indeed precipitate all-out war between the Federation and the Klingon Empire." Silently, the young Vulcan woman considered, as she had been considering for the past several days, the ramifications of interstellar war.

Memories surfaced in her mind, from the days before she'd come to live with Taryn and his family. There had been eleven Vulcan children in the creche, many of them orphans whose parents had suicided rather than be forced to engender more children to live on Romulus, Remus, or Freelan. And in the very early days . . . there had been an old one, an ancient Vulcan who had been brought in to teach them their native language. Sakorn had been his name, and he was blind.

Savel vividly remembered the afternoons she and the other children had spent with Sakorn during those language lessons. The ancient Vulcan had also, whenever he could avoid the watchful eye of the other teachers, attempted to imbue his charges with Vulcan ethics and values.

"War is an unconscionable waste of resources, and the most illogical of tactics," she remembered him saying quietly, one summer afternoon, as they'd all sat in the school courtyard together. "There are no winners in war . . . only losers. The innocent pay, and the guilty grow ever richer and ever greedier. Violence breeds violence, and the cycle of avarice and corruption is nearly impossible to break. There is no excuse for a civilized being to resort to war . . . there are always alternatives to bloodshed."

Savel didn't know whether she completely agreed with Sakorn's pronouncements—but her memories of the old one were still vivid enough to make her breath catch in her throat as she imagined what he'd say if he knew what she'd done.

"War . . ." she repeated, hearing the doubt in her own voice. "What you have been working to achieve for all these many years . . ."

"Indeed," the commander replied, taking down an ancient Vulcan *senapa* and examining the scythelike obsidian blade, careful to touch only the handle, for the cutting edge was dipped in the traditional poison. He frowned down at the weapon, seemingly studying the flowing streaks of red amid the black stone. "This development will, in all likelihood, benefit us in the end. The more fragmented the Klingon Empire is, the easier it will be to conquer. But Kamarag is moving so much faster than I had anticipated . . . he is proceeding too swiftly. Our forces are days away from being able to take full tactical advantage. And if Kamarag kills Kirk tomorrow, and then proceeds full-scale into Federation space . . . the Federation and the Klingons could be engaged in all-out war within a handful of days. The praetor has ordered full mobilization of all forces, under my direct command . . . but I do not know whether we can be ready to invade in time."

Savel glanced at the small viewscreen that showed the vista of stars as seen from *Shardarr*'s bridge. Events, like the stars, seemed to be moving toward them too fast. "Is there anything we can do to slow the ambassador?"

"I cannot think of anything," Taryn said.

At the sound of the intercom, both turned toward the comm link. "Taryn here," the commander snapped as he activated it.

"Commander, I have that tactical analysis prepared that you requested," came the voice of Taryn's second-in-command.

"Excellent," Taryn said. "Call a meeting of all senior officers in my conference chamber. We will be there directly."

Motioning to Savel to join him, the commander strode out of his office and down the narrow, utilitarian corridor.

Once they reached the sparsely furnished conference chamber, with its huge comm link that dominated the bulkhead, the young Vulcan woman sat in her accustomed place on the commander's left. One by one, his senior officers filed into the room. They were all young, handpicked by Taryn to serve aboard his ship and intensely loyal to him.

Taryn began the meeting by having his second-in-command, Poldar, give a briefing on the current tactical situation. Savel watched as he pinpointed the location of Kamarag's renegade squadron, then pointed out the locations of their own vessels. Several would reach the area within two days, but others would not arrive for another five or six.

The fleet was massing . . . the largest fleet ever assembled in Romulan history. And *Shardarr* would spearhead the attack, if all went according to plan.

"What about Federation vessels?" Taryn asked.

"There are a number in Sector 53.16," Poldar said, "but none close enough to trouble us until we are well across the Neutral Zone. With the exception of one vessel, Commander."

Taryn raised one slanting eyebrow, inviting the centurion silently to continue. "Commander, I speak of the *Enterprise*. Kirk's ship lies directly in the course Kamarag's squadron will take across the Neutral Zone."

"*Enterprise* lies in the path of Kamarag's invasionary force?" Taryn repeated slowly, plainly taken aback.

"Yes, Commander," Poldar said. "We received a new batch of intelligence reports just as I was leaving the bridge for this meeting. We have a positive identification on the ship . . . it is definitely Kirk's."

"That is not good," Tonik, the senior helm officer, said flatly. "If Kamarag's squadron encounters the *Enterprise*, they may be decimated."

"Not even *Enterprise* can defeat half a score of ships," Taryn pointed out, the faintest touch of scorn in his voice. "And Kirk . . . Kirk is not with the ship. He is keeping a rendezvous elsewhere." Despite the commander's confident air, Savel noted the lines of strain deepen between his brows.

"Even if Kirk is not there, he will have left one of his senior officers in command of his vessel," Tonik pointed out, mildly. "And even if Kirk is not with his vessel, that by no means makes *Enterprise* easy prey."

"Yes," one of the junior officers chimed in, "and with only five or six Klingon ships remaining, Kamarag's force might not be threatening enough to bring out the Federation fleet in force. And the fewer Starfleet ships assembling to defend the Neutral Zone, the fewer captains we can induce to cross into Klingon space . . . should that tactic prove necessary to gain our ends."

"I regret to say that I have more news that may not please you, Commander," Poldar said, pausing to glance at another communiqué. "Intelligence has confirmed the presence of Ambassador Sarek aboard the *Enterprise*."

Taryn straightened abruptly, and now he *was* frowning. "Sarek . . ." he repeated, and his officers watched him silently.

After a moment's contemplation of their newest piece of news, Taryn rose from his seat and brusquely dismissed his officers. Savel stayed, knowing that the order did not apply to her. When the chamber had emptied, she stepped closer to her adopted uncle, touched his sleeve. Taryn, who had been gazing straight ahead, eyes hooded, his expression unreadable, startled slightly and looked around.

"What is it, *Vadi?*" she asked, softly.

"Why is Sarek aboard that ship?" Taryn asked, his jaw muscles tight with tension. "What is he planning? Sarek never does anything without a reason. . . ."

"I do not know, *Vadi*," Savel said. "The one time I was in his presence, at Camp Khitomer, I tried to 'read' him—and could not. His shielding is surprisingly good."

"How much does he know?" demanded Taryn, thinking aloud. "He tried to break into our data banks . . . I am certain he was somehow responsible for the malfunction that nearly shut the entire system down that night he was aboard our station."

"How do you know that?" Savel was taken aback to hear about the data banks.

Taryn made an impatient gesture. "I cannot prove it. He left no betraying trace. But I am certain that malfunction masked some espionage attempt on his part. Did he gain access? Copy data? Is it possible that he actually obtained *proof* of our plans?"

Grinding one fist into his palm, he strode restlessly around the conference chamber, frowning. "No," he said, after a moment, answering his own question. "He has no proof. He would have contacted Ra-ghoratrei if he did . . . and our contact in the president's office would have informed us."

"But he did speak to Ra-ghoratrei yesterday," Savel pointed out. "The report said so."

"Yes, but only to warn him against the KEHL. No . . . he has no proof. I am sure of that. But now . . . to make sure he does not gain proof . . . I must lure him to me . . . and kill him." Taryn said the last slowly, as though he almost regretted the necessity.

"Are you sure that he did not somehow warn Ra-ghoratrei, *Vadi?*"

He turned to regard her as though he'd forgotten her presence. "No . . . I know Sarek. He is too proud, too stubborn to go to Ra-ghoratrei with a tangle of speculations for which he has no concrete proof. He is aboard the *Enterprise* at this moment because he has come in search of that proof! Now we have a few days before the fleet assembles. During that time . . ." A muscle tightened in Taryn's jaw. "Sarek must die."

"But if he is aboard the *Enterprise* . . . As Tonik said, she will not be an easy ship to destroy."

"No . . . but if I can lure Sarek to Freelan, I could order one of the squadrons on Freelan to waylay *Enterprise* and destroy her en route."

"And if Sarek refuses to come to Freelan?"

"Then we will have to lure *Enterprise* away from her present position, possibly across our Neutral Zone."

"Why? What purpose would that serve?"

"Two things would be accomplished." Taryn's expression lightened into almost one of pleasure. "First," he held up one finger, *"Enterprise* would be out of the way of Kamarag's squadron, allowing the Klingon to enter Federation space in full force. And, two"—he held up a second finger—"the delay involved while I allowed *Enterprise* to search for *Shardarr*—"

"Without finding her until you choose, I presume."

"Correct . . . that time delay will allow at least one or two of our other ships to join us. Facing three, even four cruisers or birds-of-prey, the starship will be outgunned. During the time they waste while hunting us, we will jam their communications to keep Sarek from sending a message to Raghoratrei. Then, when we are certain of victory, *Shardarr* and the other ships will decloak . . . and we will finish them."

"A good plan, *Vadi,*" Savel said hollowly. Suppose Sarek had brought Soran with him? *He* would be killed, too. "But . . . is there no other way? Sarek . . . I have heard you speak of him so many times as almost a . . . friend. Is there no way to spare him?"

"It is regrettable," Taryn said bleakly, the expression in his dark eyes revealing his own turmoil. "However, I can think of no other way to insure that the ambassador does not warn Ra-ghoratrei of what he may have learned about us and our plans."

"He may have already told the president. Killing Sarek may not prevent the Federation from discovering what is happening."

"He has not told him. I am certain he has not. I know Sarek . . . I have studied his mind during our chess games. He is stubborn, and proud. He would insist on having incontrovertible proof . . . not mere suspicions." Taryn sighed as he stared at the battle plan still frozen on the wall screen. "I do regret the necessity. I could have wished to keep Sarek alive, so he could be of use as a negotiator."

Unable to sleep, Sarek rolled out of the narrow bunk and paced restlessly around the cramped cabin. Then, driven by an impulse he did not stop to analyze, he slipped on his robe and soft boots and, picking up Amanda's journal, headed for the observation deck.

It was the middle of the shipboard "night," so the ambassador encountered only a few crew members in the corridors or the turbolift. Halting before the door to the observation deck, Sarek touched the entry panel, then stepped into the starlit dimness.

While *Enterprise* was in warp, the stars appeared different than in subspace . . . each bore a trail of light caused by the effect of the spacewarp that allowed the vessel to exceed the speed of light. The closer the star, the more distinct the trail appeared to an observer. On the bridge, the ship's viewscreens automatically filtered out the trails, in order to clarify the image, but here they showed distinctly.

Moving as silently as a shadow, Sarek walked to one of the chairs scattered about, and seated himself. He gazed outward, attempting to clear his mind, preparatory to finding his center. It had been so long since he had gained the tranquility found only in meditation.

Down . . . seek the center . . . concentrate effortlessly. Allow all external stimuli and surroundings to slip away. . . .

Sarek felt his mind and body responding, as he sought out and touched his own center—

The sound of a step intruded into his consciousness. Sarek's eyes opened as he sensed a familiar presence, and he turned to see Spock hesitating just inside the door of the observation lounge.

"I regret the intrusion," Spock said, coolly, formally, as he turned to go.

Sarek hesitated, wanting to call him back, not wishing to have this enmity between them. But he could not quite force himself to speak.

Suddenly the ambassador was struck by an overpowering sense of what humans called déjà vu—this had happened before . . . nearly forty-five Standard years before. Sarek blinked, and the memory surged up, as fresh and real as though it were actually happening. . . .

The three of them were gathered around the table for the evening meal, and Amanda had prepared many of their favorite dishes herself, not trusting the selectors to season and spice every dish perfectly. Always sensitive to his wife's moods, because of their bond, Sarek soon realized that Amanda was both preoccupied and nervous . . . though he could not think of any reason for her to be uneasy.

Eighteen-year-old Spock sat on his right, and the youth's appetite, customarily healthy, was noticeably lacking.

Today Sarek had met with the head of the Vulcan Science Academy to discuss possible curricula for Spock's education, which would begin next term. Sekla, the ambassador recalled (experiencing a flash of pride he did not trouble to suppress), had openly expressed his eagerness to guide and foster young Spock's intellectual and logical development. His son's intelligence profiles and school records were, in Sekla's word, "impressive." For a Vulcan, that was quite a compliment.

Sekla, Sarek had noted, had been careful *not* to say, "Impressive for one of half blood." No mention had been made of his son's shared heritage.

Now Sarek glanced inquiringly from his wife to his son. "My wife, this meal is exemplary. I thank you. Yet I note that neither of you appears to be hungry. Is something wrong?"

Amanda started, then obviously forced herself to relax as she turned to face her husband. Her brown hair had recently begun to show a few streaks of silver, but her soft features were relatively unlined, and her blue eyes were as sapphire-intense as ever. "Nothing is wrong, Sarek," she said, but he could tell through their bond that she was equivocating . . . not actually telling an untruth, but coming perilously close to it. "However, I have determined to finish that translation of T'Lyra's ancient poetry cycle tonight. My editor messaged me today to inquire about when it would be completed, and I have only two poems left. So I will take my leave of you. Spock"—she turned her gaze on her son, and there was an intensity in her eyes that hadn't been there when she'd spoken to her husband—"will you help your father clear the table? That will give you a chance to talk."

"But, Mother—" Spock began, half-protesting, but Amanda merely gave him a too-bright smile as she collected her own dishes and headed for the autocleaner in the kitchen. Her son avoided his father's gaze as he snatched up his dishes and followed his mother into the kitchen.

Sarek hastily rose, gathered his own dishes, and followed him. *What is transpiring here?* he wondered, disquieted.

The elder Vulcan was just in time to hear Amanda insist, "You have to tell him, Spock. You know that." Sarek hesitated, half-shielded by the doorway, and saw his wife give his son an encouraging smile. Spock gave her a wan half-smile in return. Sarek tensed as he saw it. His son's control was virtually perfect in front of him, but, in the company of humans, it slipped occasionally. Once, on Earth, the ambassador had actually seen him grin when he'd thought he was alone, as the youth observed the antics of a pair of his grandparents' kittens.

I will insist that Spock reside at the Science Academy during his course of study, Sarek thought. *There are no humans there, and that should enable him to perfect his control.*

Then Amanda left the kitchen, and Sarek stepped in. Silently, father and son tidied the kitchen and dining area. When they were finished, the elder Vulcan caught and held his son's eyes. "What is it that you must tell me, Spock?" he asked bluntly.

His son took a deep breath. "Perhaps we might walk outside, Father? The Watcher should be just past full phase."

"Certainly," Sarek agreed.

Together, the two left the villa and walked into Amanda's garden. As father and son walked slowly, Sarek glanced at his son's face, saw that Spock's mouth was drawn tight, making him appear older than his eighteen years. "Tell me what concerns you, Spock," Sarek said, finally, seeing that the youth was not disposed to break the silence.

Spock drew a deep breath and halted, turning to face his father. His eyes were level, but for a moment a muscle jumped in the corner of his jaw . . . twitched once, twice, then was forcibly repressed. "Father, I decided some time ago that I did not wish to attend the Vulcan Science Academy," he said, carefully enunciating each word. "I applied instead to Starfleet Academy. I learned today that I have been accepted as a cadet."

Sarek heard the words, but it took a second for them to register. Ever since Spock's early childhood, Sarek had watched his eager fascination with the universe, observed and fostered the development of his logical, scientific mind. For years science had been Spock's consuming interest in life. And now he was talking about giving that up in order to wear a *uniform?*

The ambassador gazed at his son, searching for words, knowing that he must make the youth recognize the gravity of this error in judgment.

"Spock," he began, careful to keep his voice low, "it is obvious that this constitutes an unconsidered decision on your part. That is understandable . . . you are young, after all. But I cannot allow you to . . . waste your years of study. Your thinking processes and logical abilities are eminently suited for a scientific career."

"I do not intend to give up science, Father," Spock said, a spark of eagerness animating his features slightly when he realized that his father was willing to discuss his decision rationally. "Starfleet . . . serving aboard a starship . . . will provide an unparalleled opportunity for scientific exploration, observation, and study. As a science officer, I will be able to study the universe as I never could if I remained here on Vulcan."

Spock's control was slipping; his father could hear the passion tingeing his voice. Sarek stared at the youth stonily. "Spock . . . your control," he chided.

The other's eyes fell . . . all animation drained from his features. "I ask forgiveness," he said, and Sarek caught just a hint of sullenness in his tone. "At any rate, Father, I have made my decision."

"Spock, what happened just now is an excellent example of why I demand that you reconsider this decision," Sarek pointed out. "In Starfleet, you will be among mostly humans. Your control is precarious enough. In the company of humans, it may be irrevocably damaged. You could disgrace your people . . . your entire lineage if you do this."

"I will endeavor to perfect my control—" Spock began.

Sarek shook his head and continued, adamantly, "Spock, every time your control falters, you reflect poorly upon all of Vulcan."

Spock's features hardened. "My control is my own affair," he said, coldly. "I wonder how my mother would react if she knew you were warning me against being 'contaminated' by her species."

"Your mother has no part in this," Sarek said curtly, feeling his anger at his son's stubbornness threatening his own control. "She is not Vulcan, and this does not concern her."

"Mother is in favor of my decision," Spock said evenly. "She believes it will be beneficial for me to interact with many different kinds of beings. And I should point out that gaining acceptance into Starfleet Academy is far from easy, Father. Starfleet chooses only the top five percent of applicants." The youth gave him a sideways glance. "Mother is proud that I have been accepted."

Sarek heard the implied rebuke, but did not acknowledge it. "Assuming you graduate," he said, "are you aware that you will be required to take an oath stating that you will do whatever is necessary to carry out your orders? Including *kill?* Starfleet vessels carry formidable weapons, Spock! You would have to be trained in the use of them, as well as hand weapons. It is eminently possible that you would be called upon to kill another, in the performance of your duty."

Spock's expression did not alter. "There is talk of commissioning an all-Vulcan science vessel," he pointed out. "Perhaps I will be assigned to that ship . . ."

"And perhaps you will not," Sarek snapped. His own control was slipping, but, at the moment, he did not care. He paced up and down the garden path, his strides quick and jerky. "You will be a puppet, a toy for Starfleet to order about as they please. You will have no free will. Starfleet officers are respected by the masses, that is true. But no Vulcan has ever graduated from the Academy, my son! Our people are not suited for a life in the service!"

"That is something that remains to be seen, Father," Spock said, with maddening calm. "I have decided that this is a step I wish to take. Do not think you can dissuade me. My mind is made up."

"Your future is bright," Sarek said, changing tactics. "I have little doubt that you will distinguish yourself as a scientist if you attend the Vulcan Science Academy. If you pursue this other path, however, you will have disgraced your family . . . your lineage. What would T'Pau say, if she could hear you planning to bring ruin upon yourself?"

"I have determined that this path is mine," Spock said. "I cannot allow family opinion to dissuade me."

"If you do this," Sarek said, holding his son's eyes with his own, putting every bit of intensity he was experiencing into his formal words, "you will not be welcome in my lands, your name will not be known to me. If you persist in disgracing yourself and your lineage, I will not be able to excuse you, either publicly or privately. You will be *vrekasht* to me, Spock, do you understand?"

Vrekasht . . . the ancient word meant "exile," or "outcast." Sarek regretted having to say it, but it was obvious that strong measures were required to make his son see reason in this.

Spock's features hardened, and his mouth was a grim slash. *"Vrekasht?"* he repeated. "Is that not rather . . . overstating the gravity of the situation, Father? I have only chosen my life's path . . . not murdered or mind-violated another."

"If you persist in joining Starfleet, then I have no doubt that you will be called upon to do both, in the course of time," Sarek said, inexorably. "I insist that you reconsider this disastrous course."

Spock gazed at him for a long moment; then his shoulders straightened, and he raised his chin slightly. "No," he said, coldly. "My decision stands. If you wish to name me *vrekasht,* then so be it. Farewell, Father."

Without another word, the youth turned and strode away, up the garden path, toward the villa. Sarek watched him go, fighting with himself. Spock was correct: to name his son *vrekasht* was extreme . . . and unjustified. Sarek wished he had not done it. The word "Wait!" surged through him, wanting to burst from his lips . . . but the ambassador clenched his teeth and the word died in his mouth, unspoken.

Spock's tall figure was at the garden perimeter now . . . was still moving . . . it was not yet too late . . . it was—too late. Over. There was a last flicker of a Vulcan robe, and then his son vanished into the villa.

Go after him, one part of Sarek's mind insisted, but he could not. He was correct, and he would not grovel, would not recant. Logic dictated that he wait for Spock to consider his words. Surely his son would come to his senses.

Sarek stared blindly at T'Rukh, waiting for Spock to reappear. An hour passed . . . two. Three, and the ambassador still waited, barely stirring.

Finally he heard a step beside him, and turned, only to find that it was Amanda who stood there. Traces of weeping still showed around her eyes, but her features were composed. "Where is Spock?" Sarek demanded.

"He beamed out an hour ago," she replied, her expression as cold as the snows of her homeworld. "Our son is gone, Sarek."

The Vulcan heard her words, unable to believe that Spock had not reconsidered, had accepted the sentence his father had imposed on him, and had left to pursue this illogical, distasteful career choice. "Spock . . . is gone?" he asked, finally.

"That is what I said." Amanda's voice was flat. "He told me that you declared him *vrekasht*, my husband. How could you?"

"I was trying to make him come to his senses," Sarek muttered, still stunned by her pronouncement.

"That was a terrible, unjust thing to do, Sarek," Amanda said. "You have done the unforgivable. Spock is my son, and I will not support you in this." She took a deep breath. "I cannot stay with someone who could do what you have done today. I am leaving you, Sarek."

"You are . . . leaving? Amanda," he said, carefully, "I do not wish you to leave."

"You have no choice, Sarek. I cannot stay with you anymore . . . after this." For the first time, Amanda's voice faltered slightly.

Sarek, noting that, said, "But you will be back, Amanda. You will return. . . ."

She shook her head. "I don't know, Sarek. Perhaps. Or perhaps not. I only know that I can't bear the sight of you at the moment. Farewell."

Without giving him a chance to say anything more, she turned and walked away, just as her son had. Sarek stood in his wife's garden, bathed in T'Rukh's harsh light, alone.

Alone . . .

Sarek watched as the door to the observation deck slid shut behind his son. His fingers tightened on Amanda's journal. Today he would read of her days without him. She had been gone for nearly a year, and they had never spoken of that time after she'd returned. What had she done in all those days?

Today he would find out.

Those days without her had been the worst of his life . . . in some ways, worse even than now.

Why had she come back? Sarek still wasn't sure. His father, Solkar, had died, and she had appeared without warning at the memorial service. At its conclusion, Amanda had simply walked over to him, taken his arm, and gone home with him as though she had never been away.

They had never discussed the separation.

Sarek took a deep breath and opened the slim red volume. . . .

Spock walked along the corridor leading from the observation deck, almost wishing he had not left. His father had appeared so . . . alone. For a moment, Sarek had appeared actually . . . vulnerable.

But then memories of Amanda's last hours surfaced, and the Vulcan's lips tightened. Vulnerable? His father?

Reaching Kirk's cabin, the Vulcan identified himself and was admitted. Kirk was still in uniform, though the captain had been off duty for over an hour.

"We will reach the rendezvous coordinates in one hour point thirty-two minutes," Spock said, without preamble. "What are you planning to do, Captain?"

"We're almost a full two days ahead of the deadline, Spock," Kirk said. "Your father and I discussed this yesterday. He thinks, and I agree with him, that Kamarag is behind this. I believe he's holding Peter on Qo'noS."

"And?" Spock prompted, when the officer paused.

"And I'm going in to rescue him," Kirk said. "With luck, I can take a shuttlecraft in, locate him by sensor, grab him, and get back to the *Enterprise* before Kamarag even reaches the rendezvous site."

Spock nodded; he'd been expecting something like this. "I will go with you, Captain," he said. "You cannot go alone."

"I was planning to," Kirk said. "Invading the Klingon homeworld single-handed is pretty foolhardy . . . even for me." He shook his head, as if wondering at himself. "I can't expect anyone to join me on such a harebrained mission."

"You can expect your friends, Jim," said a new voice, and Spock turned to see Leonard McCoy framed in the doorway behind him. "You know better than to think Spock and I would let you go off to tackle a whole planet of Klingons by yourself!"

Kirk grinned ruefully. "I guess I do," he said finally, gazing at his friends and shaking his head. "After all, three stand a *much* better chance than just one, against a whole planet . . . right?"

"You got it," McCoy said. "Right, Spock?"

"Right, Doctor," the Vulcan said, firmly.

Kirk spread his hands in a gesture of defeat. "All right, then . . . next stop, Qo'noS. I'll meet you on the shuttlecraft deck in an hour."

Eight

"Approaching Qo'noS, Captain," Spock reported. "ETA to orbit, twelve point two minutes."

Kirk, who was piloting the shuttlecraft *Kepler*, nodded in acknowledgment of the Vulcan's words. "Anything within sensor range?"

"I detect no military craft, just freighters."

The captain checked his screens, wishing he had some idea of where on Qo'noS Kamarag's ancestral home lay. Northern or southern hemisphere? Eastern or western continent?

"Spock," he said, "what are our chances of tapping into the Klingon data banks and accessing some information?"

"I may be able to do so, Captain," the Vulcan said, turning away from his sensor array. Like Kirk and McCoy, Spock wore a black jumpsuit designed for night raids. "What information do you wish me to access?"

"Kamarag's home address," Kirk said, dryly.

"I will attempt to access its location, Captain," Spock said, turning back to his instruments.

"Y'know, Jim, this will be the first time we've actually *seen* Qo'noS," McCoy pointed out. The doctor was sitting in the passenger seat behind the captain. "Last time we were there, we were shut up like mice in a shoebox, and shuttled around in closed vehicles."

Kirk nodded. "We didn't even see the planet from orbit."

Spock regarded his console intently. "I have Qo'noS on-screen."

Intently, Kirk watched as the tiny dot grew until, with magnification on maximum, they could see their destination. "Look at that," Kirk whispered, after a moment. "I didn't realize it had a ring!"

"That ring is much of what remains of Praxis," Spock said. "There are several large chunks of the moon still orbiting Qo'noS, and corresponding gaps in the ring. This ring is . . ." He consulted his sensors. " . . . approximately two thousand kilometers across, and it orbits Qo'noS's equator at a mean distance of eleven thousand, five hundred seventy-one kilometers."

Kirk glanced at his own sensors. "There's also a lot of asteroidal material in the system," he said.

"Correct. A large number of asteroids will impact the planet in approximately fifty years."

Kirk stared at the planet that was growing in their viewscreens. "Now all we have to do is avoid detection by the Klingons while we locate Peter." He gave McCoy a lopsided grin. "Sure you don't want to change your mind about coming, Bones?"

"Too late for that, Jim," he pointed out, smiling back at his friend.

Spock cleared his throat. "Piloting the shuttlecraft across the plane of that ring will be difficult, Captain. The *Kepler*'s shielding is limited."

"Why go near the ring at all?" McCoy asked. "You can surely plot a course that will keep us away from it."

Kirk glanced at the ringed world, watching it grow steadily in their viewscreen. "If we go in directly, bold as brass, the Klingon sensors will be bound to pick us up, and we'll have unwelcome surface-to-air company in no time," he explained. "I think what Spock is planning"—he slanted an inquiring look at the Vulcan—"is to use the ring as a cover."

"Precisely," said Spock. "As I mentioned before, sensors indicate that the ring has several gaps, caused by large chunks of Praxis acting as ring shepherds. Their gravitational force clears a small gap around them. I recommend that we traverse the ring plane through one of the larger gaps. Matching orbit with the ring, we can use it as a shield while we locate Peter."

"How are you going to find him?" McCoy asked, staring mesmerized at the ringed planet. "It's a big world."

"I did manage to locate Kamarag's ancestral compound in the Klingon data banks," Spock said. "Thus we have an approximate idea of where to search. Mr. Scott and I modified the sensors to detect any human life readings. If Peter is the only human in that compound, we should be able to trace him."

"It's a good plan," Kirk said, "but crossing the plane of the ring, even through the longest gap, will require some tricky piloting."

"It is fortunate for us that the presence of the ring, and all the attendant meteor showers since the demise of Praxis, has evidently forced the Klingons to abandon whatever early-warning defense system their planet boasted," Spock said, studying his instrument readouts.

"They probably still have a lot of meteor showers," Kirk said, eyeing the ring. They were now close enough to it that, under the highest magnification, the ring was revealed to be made of millions of chunks of rock, ranging from pieces no bigger than a marble to huge boulders larger than the *Kepler*.

Minutes later, the shuttlecraft was approaching the gap in the ring. Kirk sent the little vessel skimming along its edge, matching its speed; then he boosted the *Kepler*'s velocity slightly, aiming for the break, which was now clearly visible.

Qo'noS was an awesome sight: below them the planet turned, brown and greenish blue, its continents separated by shallow azure seas speckled with atolls. The three largest landmasses were edged by volcanic mountain chains, and it was evidently a far more seismically active planet than Earth.

From this distance, signs of civilization, at least on the daylight side, appeared minimal. Only a few angular blotches on the western side of the continent below them betrayed the presence of large cities.

But even the world turning below him could not hold the captain's attention for long. As they sped along, Qo'noS's ring dominated their view, spreading out before them like a golden plain studded with nuggets of all sizes. The ring was nearly two thousand kilometers wide at this point—and yet, it was far from solid. Glimpses of the surface beyond it came and went, depending on its density. Kirk's eyes widened as he studied the vista.

"Shields at maximum, Captain," Spock said. "Ready for crossover."

"It's a good thing we'll be crossing over on the dayside of the planet," Kirk said. "Otherwise, dust vaporizing against our shields would spotlight us from the surface, if we tried this on the nightside."

"Will the shields hold?" McCoy asked tensely.

"Long enough to get us through," Kirk said, hoping he wasn't being overly optimistic. He kept his eyes glued to the last-minute course corrections flashing up at him. "Barring any major collisions, of course," he added.

"Even though the gap is relatively free of large rocks, it still contains quantities of dust and small particles. The shuttlecraft's shields were not designed for continuous bombardment, Captain," Spock warned. "They may burn out."

Moments later, the ring gap lay directly below them. Kirk's fingers skipped nimbly across the controls as he delicately jockeyed the shuttlecraft into position. With a short blast of the maneuvering thrusters, the captain began the crossover.

Even here, in this relatively "clear" portion of the ring, they were buffeted by debris. The little craft bucked as the shields absorbed the impacts of direct hits from gravel-sized rocks—one, two, three . . . a dozen—Kirk lost count. All the while his hands moved, keeping them on course, heading them down and through the sparsest portion of the gap.

He was aware, peripherally, of Spock backing him from the copilot's seat, making tiny adjustments that helped stabilize the *Kepler.*

"Shields are weakening," the Vulcan reported matter-of-factly. And then, a second later, he added, with a touch of excitement, "Captain, I am picking up Peter's readings. . . ."

"Where?" Kirk said. "Can you plot a course to bring us down near him?"

"Affirmative," Spock replied, and, only a few seconds later, the heading the Vulcan had computed appeared on Kirk's screen. Quickly, the captain laid it in.

"Shields are down by eighty percent," Spock cautioned.

"We're almost out of it," Kirk said tightly, fighting the controls of the bucketing *Kepler.* "Ten more seconds, and we're home free!"

"Shields are weakening . . . weakening . . ." Spock said. Then the Vulcan added, matter-of-factly, "Shields are burned out, Captain."

"We're okay," Kirk said, his throat raw with tension. "We're out of it. Now all we have to do is—"

There was a sharp crack of sound as something struck the *Kepler,* rocking the shuttle violently; then Kirk heard the high, thin shriek of escaping air pressure. "Bones, check the air pressure! Spock, take over!" he ordered, moving to locate the impact and exit points of the tiny rock that had struck them. Moments later, the captain saw with satisfaction that *Kepler*'s automatic sealant system was working as it was designed to, covering the tiny holes. The whine of escaping air lessened, then stopped. Jim returned to his board.

Moments later, he knew they were in trouble. The shuttlecraft's directional controls now responded sluggishly to his exploratory commands. "Damn it," Kirk said, feeling the *Kepler* yaw. "Piloting this thing down through atmosphere won't be easy."

"You goin' to be able to land this crate, Jim?" McCoy asked, his voice carefully casual.

"We're sure going to try," Kirk said. Grimly, he fought the controls, struggling to keep the shuttlecraft on course. It wouldn't help them to land safely in one of Qo'noS's oceans, and he certainly didn't want to find himself setting down thousands of kilometers from Peter.

It was a bumpy ride, nursing the crippled shuttle down through Qo'noS's turbulent upper atmosphere, fighting to keep the little craft stable and on course.

Finally, they were approaching their destination. Red sunlight from Qo'noS's setting sun splashed them as they headed down. Kirk wished for Sulu as he struggled to keep the *Kepler*'s landing skids parallel to the ground. It had been a long time since he'd landed anything in these conditions. Glancing at his course readouts, he realized that they were about six kilometers from his intended destination, and thought, *Close enough. I don't mind walking. . . .*

Glimpsing a gap in the tree cover below, the captain sent the craft down into it, and suddenly they were engulfed by huge trees with strange, feathery leaves and giant red seedpods.

"Come on," he whispered to the little ship. "You can make it . . . almost there . . ." He made a last-minute adjustment, saw the ground rushing up toward them. Too fast!

"Brace for crash landing!" Kirk managed to shout, even as *Kepler's* nose plunged downward.

The shuttlecraft hit, bounced wildly, struck again, bounced again, then, finally, stopped. Kirk pushed himself upright in his seat, looking around dazedly as he unsnapped his safety harness. "We made it," he said, disbelievingly. He turned to regard his companions, who were both sitting up, their expressions somewhat dazed.

"Captain," Spock said, "we should leave the vicinity quickly. Our erratic approach may have been sighted."

"We obviously can't escape in the *Kepler,*" Kirk said, gazing ruefully at the damaged shuttle as they prepared to abandon ship. "Can you tell if there are any spaceports nearby?"

Spock held up his tricorder, nodded. "Fifteen and a half kilometers due west," he said, "lies the port called TengchaH Jav." He slung the instrument over his shoulder. Working quickly, the Vulcan opened the weapons locker, extracted three small phasers, checked their settings and power packs, then distributed one to each of them.

"I'm going to set the shuttle to self-destruct," Kirk said, his fingers moving over the controls.

"Be sure you give us time to get out of range, Jim," McCoy admonished, scrambling hastily out of the craft.

After setting up the self-destruct sequence, Kirk, with Spock and McCoy behind him, walked away from the doomed *Kepler.* Jim gave the little craft a valedictory pat as he left, wishing there were some way to salvage the ship.

The three set off, walking quickly into the forest, picking their way over rocks and fallen logs, as the night gathered around them.

Once you step upon this path, Valdyr warned herself, *your life as a Klingon will be over.* There would be no place for her anywhere in Klingon society, not on Qo'noS, not on her colonies, not anywhere. She would be outcast, scorned and marked for death. She closed her eyes, struggling not to let the magnitude of her plan stay her hand. *This is the path before you,* she reminded herself. *For you, it is the road of honor, whether any other Klingon anywhere in the universe ever realizes that.*

For the final time, she checked her weapons. Under her sleeve, against her forearm sat her small, wicked, three-pronged dagger, where a sudden jerk of her wrist would release it. At her right hip hung the small, silent crossbow that had been her favorite weapon since childhood. While it was best used in close conditions, it did not have the hum and whine of modern weapons, and would not reveal a concealed shooter. Under her breastplate sat two hand disrupters, their battery packs fully charged. She touched the weapons one final time. Then she took the key to Peter's cell. He was still her prisoner.

Straightening her armor and tunic, she left her room and headed for her uncle's private quarters. Du'Hurgh, Kamarag's ancient family estate, was a massive, old fortress, with dozens of rooms and numerous passageways and staircases. Taking an obscure route, she came to her uncle's quarters stealthily, concerned that Karg might have guards posted, but there were none. And why should there be? After all, who would dare enter Kamarag's private quarters in the ambassador's own home? His simpleminded, weak niece? And even if she did, what could she do there?

Moving silently, Valdyr slipped into her uncle's favorite study. Once inside, she stood perfectly still, waiting, listening, but there was no one, not even a serving woman.

Valdyr was nearly overcome by memories once she stood inside the cavernous chamber. Every kind of ancient armament hung from its walls, as well as paintings and tapestries of the finest warriors of their family's lines. Her father had brought his children here every summer, and the compound and this place, in particular, called up vivid memories of him. Valdyr stared at the images of long-dead heroes and re-membered her father's thrilling tales of their exploits. How she'd longed to be like them! Her gaze fixed on the portrait of a woman, her many times great-grandmother who had fought at her husband's side in so many decisive battles hundreds of years ago. That image had always been her favorite. She gazed upon it now, knowing she would never see it once she left here.

Then, so be it.

Moving to the computer that appeared so out of place in this ancient hall, she paused for one last moment before using the private code of her dead father to acti-vate this link with the outside world. Then she sent a carefully composed message to Brigadier Kerla, consort to Chancellor Azetbur. Her father had served under Kerla many years ago, before he was promoted and sent to serve with Kruge. Her father and Kerla had been good friends, trusted allies.

Valdyr knew Azetbur trusted Kerla as well. She would have to take a chance with him. The message, at first, would seem like a normal piece of correspondence. She had to make sure that it would be sent through the relays, that no one would pay it any mind and stop it on its journey. The relays would slow it down, she knew, but she could think of no other way to insure that Brigadier Kerla would receive it. She was, after all, only the daughter of a dead hero, only the niece of an ambassador. Perhaps her father's name would take her message to Kerla's hands. If it did not, than Peter, his uncle, and Valdyr herself were all doomed.

Peter lay on the stone bench, reading and trying to keep his eyes from staring at the vacant glass portal. The waiting was becoming unbearable. Would Uncle Jim really just give himself up to Kamarag? He couldn't! He would know kidnappers never live up to their promises, especially a kidnapper as crazed as Kamarag. Peter sighed, trying not to wear himself out worrying over a situation he could do nothing about.

He heard the slightest click, and his gaze snapped to the portal, but no one was there. Another click followed, and Peter was on his feet instantly. It was happening. They were coming to take him . . . to Valdyr. Uncle Jim had actually done it, given himself up. His mind raced wildly.

His door swung open, and Valdyr entered, pointing a wicked-looking Klingon hand disrupter at him. So, she'd had to come for him herself. Boy, these people did nothing to make things easier, did they?

"Are you ready?" she demanded.

He stood up straight. "Yes. I'm ready."

With a quick flip of her wrist she tossed the disrupter at him. He snatched it clumsily, then stared at the weapon in his hand. He realized she was holding a small crossbow by her side. "What's going on?" he whispered.

"Shhhh," she warned him, then stuck her head out the door, looking both ways. "Be prepared to use that. We have a long, dangerous journey ahead of us. You must stay close to me, Pityr."

He grinned. "Try and stop me."

They moved quickly through endless, ancient stone corridors in stealthy silence, and the whole time he hadn't a clue as to their destination.

After a good fifteen minutes of climbing dark, winding staircases, and tiptoeing down long unused hallways, Valdyr finally halted. Turning to him, she pressed her mouth against his ear and whispered, "Now it becomes difficult."

Now? he thought, and stared at her.

"To leave the dungeons is easy if you take the back passageways," she explained quietly. "They are no longer used. But to enter the secret tunnels, you must go through the heart of the compound. We will have to be even more cautious. And we must be ready to fight."

"I'm ready," he assured her. "Lead the way."

She opened the antique door cautiously, indicating that he should wait behind in the stairwell. He watched her through a crack in the wood as she stepped into a spacious, well-lighted hallway. She had just begun to signal him to follow her when two burly Klingons rounded a corner. She froze, as he did.

"Valdyr!" one of them said to her congenially. "Karg has been looking for you. He wishes you to join him at the midday meal. You'd better hurry."

She stiffened and frowned. "And because Karg wishes it, Malak, I am to obey? I am no trained *targ*, and I take no backhand summons from my uncle's pet." Her tone dripped contempt.

Peter rolled his eyes, unable to believe that she was going to get into a row with these two apes now. But the guard merely laughed, apparently enjoying her display of spirit.

"I told him you would not listen to me, Valdyr," Malak agreed, "but I, too, must do as I am bid by my commander."

Suddenly the soldier with him sniffed. "Do you smell something?"

Malak tested the air and looked thoughtful.

Damn it! Peter swore silently. He hadn't had a real bath in over a week, and his sponge baths, no matter how thorough, were a poor substitute. *Besides, you're a human. You smell as different to them as they do to you.*

Before Malak could answer, Valdyr sneered, "Who could smell anything while Karg walks these halls?"

Malak laughed again. "Oh, Valdyr, you were always a terror. I miss serving with your brother. If Karg were wise, he'd seek another wife. Make things easy for yourself and hurry along. You might still get a choice cut of meat. Come, Darj, we have work to do."

The laughing soldiers moved on, but Peter could see Darj looking about the hall, as if trying to find the source of the odor he'd detected. Valdyr watched them for a few minutes, then yanked open the door.

"Hurry, there is no time! Karg will come looking for me if I do not answer his summons shortly." Clutching his sleeve, she towed him through the hallway. Finally, she stood before a huge piece of furniture. She peered around behind it, then glanced at Peter, as if assessing his size. "The passageway is behind this closet. I think you are thin enough. . . ."

"I *knew* I smelled something foul!" an angry voice said behind them.

They spun, and Peter found himself facing Darj. He was alone, holding a weapon on both of them. He glanced at Valdyr, who was still half behind the closet, half exposed. There was no way they could pretend she was just "moving the prisoner." Their attempt to escape was plain.

"Malak thinks little of his commander," Darj said, moving carefully around them. "Fortunately for Karg, I am loyal! Malak will be demoted, but if he's fortunate, he'll be allowed to live. You two, however, will not have that privilege. Valdyr, move away from that closet, now."

"Certainly, Darj," she said demurely, surrendering. She stepped away from the massive wooden piece, revealing the crossbow held firmly in her right hand. She fired at the same instant, and the quarrel buried itself deep in the soldier's throat.

Darj collapsed heavily, gurgling, then lay still. Before Peter could react, Valdyr snatched up the soldier's weapon and pocketed it, then rifled through his uniform. She shoved several small items into the pouch she wore on her belt; then she began tugging the heavy body toward the closet. "Help me!" she gasped, and Peter, who'd been standing there, stunned—he'd never seen anyone killed before—jumped to obey.

"Into the closet," she ordered, and the two of them wrestled the heavy body inside the massive wooden structure. "This way!" she snapped, and he followed her as she squeezed behind the heavy furniture.

In back of the old wooden object was a small door that opened inward. Valdyr pulled out an ornate iron key, and unlocked the secret door. It slid open easily. And then they were inside, the door shut securely behind them. Peter stood stock-still, in total darkness. If she abandoned him here . . .

A light flared and he winced at the sudden brightness. Valdyr was in front of him, holding a tiny but powerful lantern. "We will be safe for a while now. The only one who knows these passages is my uncle, and he is not here. Karg knows nothing of them . . . the fool can search the entire compound and never find us. And even if they find Darj's body and discover this passageway, by that time we will be deeply into the hidden chambers."

She started moving along the narrow tunnel, and Peter followed her. "But how long can we stay here?" he wondered.

"We only need to stay until dark," she explained. "Then, we can follow the tunnels, and leave the compound."

"You mean these passageways will actually take us *outside* this fortress?"

"That's correct. They were built hundreds of years ago, and have been used by entire armies during local conflicts and feuds. There are dozens of warrens and chambers, enough to hide an entire squadron of soldiers. We will be safe . . . until we leave. Once outside the compound we must try to reach the spaceport—but by then Darj will surely be missed, and your escape discovered. They will be searching for us."

They moved swiftly through the tunnels, saying little, as Valdyr guided them to safety. Finally, she ushered him into a small, cozy chamber, then set about lighting battery-powered lamps that hung on the wall. "This place had always been special to my oldest brother and myself. We used to play war in these tunnels, and hide from our nurses down here." She moved over to a narrow bed, her only furniture in the room, and sat down. "We spent hours down here, making up stories, planning our futures. . . ."

Peter remembered her speaking of her brother's death. "You must miss him."

She nodded. "He was a lot like my father. He treated me more like a little brother than a sister." She looked about the dimly lit chamber. "It is almost as if I can feel his spirit here. . . ."

Peter watched as her eyes moved around the room. She had just killed one of her countrymen. She was giving up everything in her life to do this for him. He didn't know what to say to her. "I . . . wish I could've known your brother. I would like to think . . . we could've found a common ground. . . ."

She turned to him. "My brother and father would approve of what I'm doing. They would know I'm fighting for Qo'noS, for the future of all Klingon people."

Peter nodded. "I'm sure they would. You've chosen a very difficult path, Valdyr—much more difficult than armed combat. You bring honor to their memory."

They sat in awkward silence for a few minutes. Finally, she said, "I have sent a message to Azetbur. Once she receives it . . ."

"When did you send it?" he asked, interested. "What did it say?"

She explained about sending the message to her father's old friend, Brigadier Kerla, and how she had addressed and phrased it cautiously, so it would go through the channels without being intercepted. "However, I know that will slow it down. I cannot say how long it will take before Azetbur will even see it."

Peter thought she was being optimistic. Realistically, it could be hours before the thing even got into the hands of this Kerla, assuming some well-meaning staff member didn't misinterpret it and delay it even further. "When the chancellor finds out what you've done, she will surely reward you."

Valdyr looked away, her expression grim. "I have betrayed my family. She may personally be grateful, but . . . family honor is very important to our people. There will be no rewards for what I've done. I expect to be outcast . . . you would say, homeless, shunned . . . when this is over. But I will have my own personal honor. No one can take that from me. Not Karg. Not Kamarag. No one."

He admired her obstinate courage. "Valdyr . . . I want to thank you for helping me. And as long as I live, you will always have a place in *my* family . . . for whatever that's worth."

She looked at him, her expression shocked. "You would accept me in your family? And how would your people feel about that, a Klingon woman coming to them? What of your uncle—he hates us. How will he feel about this?"

"My uncle is fair," Peter insisted. "The tragedy of Gorkon's death changed the way he regards your people. He is as close to me as you were to your father. I assure you, my uncle would welcome any warrior as brave as you into our family."

"Then I hope we all live long enough to meet, Pityr. I have heard much of this James Kirk. It would be interesting to face him and see if the man and legend are the same."

Peter started to smile when a mark on her neck caught his eye. He squinted. It was a terrible-looking bruise. He touched it gently. "What happened, Valdyr? How did you get this?"

She flinched and moved away, so he pulled his hand back, fearing he'd been too familiar. She looked away, and he thought he could see her color darkening in the chamber's muted light. "It is just . . ." she began hesitantly. "It is nothing. . . ."

Then he realized. "Karg did this to you." His voice was low as he tried to suppress the outrage he felt. "That's what happened, isn't it? This is from Karg."

She turned, met his gaze defiantly. "It is Karg's mark. He marked me so everyone would know to whom I belonged. I fought him, but he's . . . too strong for me. . . ."

Peter's fury flared. "I'd love to have about ten minutes alone with that guy in a locked room," he grumbled.

She watched him curiously. "This bothers you, Pityr, this mark from Karg?"

"Of course it bothers me!" he blurted. "He touched you against your will. No one should be allowed to do that."

She actually laughed then, and the lightness of that sound startled him. "Oh, Pityr, you humans are unusually funny! If I were strong enough, I could keep Karg in his place—it might be a good marriage then—but because I am small, he has all the advantage."

"It shouldn't have anything to do with strength, Valdyr," he argued. "You should only be touched when you choose to be, and by whom you choose to be."

"I see. And because Karg forced his touch on me, you are angry with me about this?" she asked.

"Of course I'm not angry with *you!* I'm furious at *Karg.*"

"Furious enough . . . to fight for me?" She asked the question so quietly, Peter instantly understood that the question meant more to her than its simplicity indicated.

He stared into her deep, dark eyes, realizing that this was the first interaction they'd been able to enjoy without having the viewing port between them since she'd first dumped him into his cell. They were together, here in this small room, with no one around, just the two of them. He swallowed, wanting to make sure he said just the right thing. "My people believe that fighting is the last resort, that there are always alternatives to violent confrontation . . . but . . . I must confess . . . that guy . . . Yes, Valdyr. If I had the chance, I would fight Karg for you."

Her eyes widened as if she could not believe he'd actually said that. She looked as if she might say something, then hesitated, and finally murmured, "Pityr. What are . . . apricots?"

He blinked, momentarily confused. Then he remembered telling her that was how she smelled to him. He smiled. "They're a delicious fruit from Earth. They're only available a short time each year, so they're highly prized. They have a wonderful perfume, and a bowl of them in the warm summer air will scent a whole room. My grandmother grew them and we couldn't wait every year until they were ready to be eaten."

"And . . . I have this same scent?"

"Yes. . . ." He leaned closer and deliberately inhaled her odor. Moving slowly, for fear of shattering the mood between them, he touched her face, turning it to him, as he allowed his lips to graze her cheek lightly.

"What . . . are you doing?" she whispered, holding perfectly still.

"Kissing you," he explained, pressing his mouth to the edge of her jaw, then the corner of her mouth. "Do Klingons kiss?"

"Yes," she murmured.

He met her gaze unflinchingly. "What do you want? Do you want me to touch you?"

"I want only one male on Qo'noS to touch me," she admitted. He started to pull back slightly, afraid he'd misinterpreted her interest. "I want Pityr Kirk . . . a *human*! . . . and a warrior . . . to touch me!" She said it as if it amazed her.

Then, as if her confession suddenly granted Peter total freedom, he took the woman in his arms, armor and all, and pressed his mouth against hers.

The kiss began tenderly, but almost immediately it ignited all the stored-up emotion of his long days of captivity. Peter pulled Valdyr fiercely against him, and was aware of her arms coming up to encircle him with a strength he found exhilarating. "*Hlja'!*" she whispered, between kisses. "*MevQo'*, Pityr . . ."

There was no way in hell he *could* stop.

Finally, when they pulled away, she laughed and bit his chin hard. He yelped and bit her back. And in the next instant they fell upon the bunk, wrestling, yanking at each other's clothing, rolling over and over in strenuous love-play that sent them crashing to the floor, laughing, biting, tussling. Finally, he landed on his back, Valdyr straddling him, pinning his shoulders to the ground.

"I like this way of kissing. You will teach me this human kissing, Pityr Kirk!" she demanded before dissolving in laughter again.

He heaved her up and tossed her off him, rolling over to pin her down this time. "I will teach you this human kissing, Valdyr-oy. And you will teach me . . . ?" He had no idea what to ask for.

She touched his cheek, her eyes glimmering. "Everything, Pityr-oy. I will teach you everything."

He leaned down and began their lessons. . . .

"Ambassador Sarek?" Commander Uhura's voice was as cool and professional as usual, but there was an underlying note of tension in it that made the Vulcan raise an eyebrow as he activated the intercom in his cabin.

"Sarek here, Commander," he replied.

"I have a message coming in for you, Ambassador," she said. "The codes accompanying it identify it as being from Freelan. . . ." The way she trailed off alerted the ambassador.

"Is it originating there?"

"All the codes are correct, and the directional frequency is right . . . but I don't believe it's actually coming from there. My guess is that the transmission is being relayed via Freelan from some other location."

Sarek nodded. "That does not surprise me, Commander Uhura. Please patch the message through to me here . . . and, if you can do so without arousing suspicion, trace the actual origination coordinates of the message."

"Understood, Ambassador," she replied. Almost immediately the comm screen in Sarek's cabin flickered, and, a moment later, he found himself facing a Freelan. Despite the fact that Freelans appeared virtually identical in their shrouding robes, the Vulcan was certain that his caller was Taryn. "Greetings," Sarek said, cautiously. "This is Ambassador Sarek. Whom do I have the honor of addressing, please?"

"This is Liaison Taryn," the image's mechanical tones responded, without preamble. "Ambassador . . . I must ask you to meet with me on a matter of some urgency."

"Where would you like to meet?" Sarek said. "As you have already discovered, I am not on Vulcan."

Taryn's shrouded figure moved slightly, and the Vulcan thought he detected tension in the dark form. "Why . . . I had hoped you could come here, as is our custom," the Freelan liaison said.

"When would you prefer to meet?"

"As soon as possible."

Sarek shook his head. "I fear that will be difficult, Liaison. The ship that is my transport has been diverted to patrol the Neutral Zone. I will be unable to meet with you until the *Enterprise* has completed its current mission. Why do you need to meet with me, Liaison?"

Taryn did not reply for a long moment. "That trade agreement we negotiated last month concerning *kivas* shipments," he said, finally. "My government has overridden some of the provisions I agreed to. I have no choice but to ask you to reconvene the negotiations."

Sarek raised an eyebrow in feigned surprise. "Overridden?" he asked. "Liaison, when we met, I trusted that I was dealing with someone with sufficient authority to negotiate in good faith. I am . . . disappointed . . . to discover that you no longer have the backing of your government."

When the liaison replied, the Vulcan could hear the anger lacing his voice, even through the mechanical tones. "I assure you, Ambassador, that this is simply a temporary setback. I have not lost the backing of my government. I do have the power to negotiate in good faith for my world."

For the first time, Sarek permitted a touch of sarcasm to tinge his own voice. "Your world? Which world is that?"

"What do you mean?" Taryn demanded angrily.

"My apologies," Sarek said, smoothly. "My mind must be . . . confused. Age catches up with all of us, as the human aphorism would have it. For just a moment I thought I was speaking with someone else . . . a diplomat from another world altogether, by the name of . . . Nanclus. You never met him, of course. He was executed for treason last month."

"When can you meet with me?" Taryn asked, and the mechanical tones could not disguise the cold fury in his voice.

"I do not know," Sarek said, honestly. "I will have to consult with the ship's officers to discover that. I will speak with you again by the end of today, Liaison."

"I may be away . . . at a government conference," Taryn said. "My aide will take your message, Ambassador."

"Very well." Sarek inclined his head and raised his hand in the Vulcan salute. "I wish you peace . . . and long life, Taryn."

Without replying, the Freelan broke the connection.

Sarek sat staring at the screen for a moment, until Uhura's face flickered into view. "Ambassador Sarek . . . I was correct, sir. That call was patched through Freelan channels, but its actual point of origin was in a sector of the Romulan Neutral Zone. The exact coordinates are a few hours' journey from our present location."

Sarek inclined his head graciously. "I thank you for your diligence,

Commander," he said. "I find that information unsurprising . . . but . . ." His mouth curved slightly as he thought about his son's reaction. " . . . fascinating."

In his office aboard *Shardarr,* Commander Taryn pulled off his muffling Freelan cowl and inhaled a deep breath of "fresh" air before turning to face Savel, who was sitting across the desk from him. "He knows." The commander's deep voice was grim. "He knows everything. Now he mocks me with his knowledge. There is no question anymore. Ambassador Sarek must die . . . and as quickly as possible."

Quickly, the commander contacted Poldar over the intercom and ordered him to plot a course that would take them within subspace jamming range of the *Enterprise.*

"Our foremost ships are still half a day's journey away from our present location, Commander," the centurion reported, when asked.

"What will you do now?" Savel inquired softly.

The commander gave her an enigmatic glance. "Delay, Savel. Make *Enterprise* notice me, then hunt me, then chase me . . . until it is my pleasure to turn the tables, and hunt *her."*

Savel gazed at him, her eyes wide and haunted, full of silent apprehension and sadness. *Where is Soran? If he dies . . . I will be the cause of it . . . of all of this . . .*

"Pityr," Valdyr whispered against the cadet's ear, "we have to leave now."

Peter Kirk groaned, not certain whether he'd actually slept, or simply lain, half-drugged with exhaustion and satisfaction. The room appeared the same as it had when they'd entered it, the lantern still illuminating the dimness, and he had no sense of time.

"Pityr," she whispered, "it is time. We must go."

"Not yet," he argued. "Just a few more minutes . . ."

She sighed, then relaxed against him. "One more minute," she said. "Perhaps two. But no more, *'Iwoy . . ."*

The human stroked her back, feeling the contours of flesh over bone that weren't quite human. He realized that he ached. *I must be covered with bruises,* he thought, remembering what had passed between them and marveling at it. *Not to mention toothmarks . . .* A faint taste lingered in his mouth, sweet and somewhat smoky. Peter ran his tongue over his raw, bruised lips. The faint saltiness of his own blood now mingled with the alien taste of hers.

He tightened his arms around her, then kissed her again. He didn't want to leave now. He didn't even want to move, though the floor they were lying on was so cold and hard that he was shivering.

Finally he raised his head, resisting the urge to kiss her again, to savor the taste and texture and *feel* of her strange mouth again . . . and again. "What time is it?"

"It is the middle of our night," she explained, as she picked up her small lantern. "The few soldiers my uncle left here with Karg should be weary from searching for us since the midday meal. Karg would've come looking for me shortly after I failed to heed his summons. I don't know how long it would be before they missed Darj. Eventually, someone would've thought to check your cell." He was surprised to see her grin.

She stood, and began pulling her clothing into place, then redonned her armor. "They will search the road to TengchaH Jav—the closest spaceport. Even if Karg were bright enough to figure out that we hid on the premises—which he's not—he will have to search very discreetly. Kamarag gave orders that nothing should arouse suspicion from any official agency of the Klingon government."

"So, what's our plan?" he asked, as he slipped on his boots.

"We will take the tunnels to the farthest exit, and come out in the woods near the south road. We can stay in the forest and follow the road to the spaceport. It will be perhaps nine of your kilometers to the port."

"Can't they scan for me while we're under here?" he asked. "After all, I *am* the only human in the nearby vicinity."

She patted a wall. "There is so much selonite in these walls that scanning rays cannot penetrate. That is why they cannot follow us here—to the scanners, this does not exist."

"And once we're out of the tunnels?"

"I have a small tracer for you. It will give off a false registration—make the scanners think you are another Klingon. Soldiers carry them so they can be found where they fall in battle, so they might receive their warrior's ritual. It will mask your readings."

"Suppose we're seen?" Peter asked. He tapped his forehead. "Don't you think someone might notice?"

"I have a hooded cloak for you," she said. "I cached one here yesterday." She opened a recessed drawer under the stone sleeping shelf and pulled it out.

"You've thought of everything," Peter said, "I think. What happens when we get to the spaceport?"

"We will have to get past the security gates, and keep a close eye out for Karg's troops. Then, I will help you find a ship." She hesitated, glancing at him sideways. "You will escape Qo'noS. . . ."

"You mean *we* will. Right?" he demanded, taking her by the shoulders. "You're coming with me, back to Earth. Aren't you?"

Valdyr gazed up at him, smiling sadly. "That is what I thought too, at first. But . . . I've reconsidered. Pityr . . . be realistic. A Klingon, on Earth? How could I live? I would be an exile, an outcast, living among a species that hates my people—even as my people hate yours. . . ."

"We don't have to stay on Earth," Peter insisted. "There are colonies where even *we* wouldn't be noticed."

"And your career in Starfleet?"

"Listen, all that time alone in that cell made me think, too, and one of the things I've realized is that I'm *not* James T. Kirk—and I never will be. I want to be *myself.* I'm not cut out to be a legend, Valdyr. I'm just not cut out for command." He regarded her worriedly. "Valdyr-oy . . . think what will happen if you stay behind! Your uncle . . . when he catches up with you . . ."

Her exotic alien beauty almost glowed as she responded assuredly, "Do not worry, Pityr-oy. He will not catch me. I will die by the *Heghba'*, with my honor intact."

It took the human a second to realize that she meant ritual suicide, and when he did, his hands tightened convulsively on her shoulders. "No!" he cried. "Don't even think it!"

"I have betrayed my family by helping you," she pointed out reasonably. "There is no other path left to regain my honor."

"Don't *talk* like that," he said fiercely, his heart pounding with fear for her.

"You're *not* doing that! I won't let you! You'll have to fight me, Valdyr . . . !" He stopped, realizing how frantic he sounded.

Her face was very close to his in the confines of the dusty, stone-walled chamber. Peter felt her breath touch his face as she said, softly, "The last time I fought you, I won. But you were exhausted, at the end of your stamina. I do not think it will be so easy for me the next time."

He pressed his cheek against hers and held her to him. If that was the best she could do for capitulation, he'd take it. But at least she knew if she attempted to stay behind at the spaceport, he wouldn't give in without a struggle.

"Now, we *must* go," she whispered and, taking his hand, led him out of the room.

She led Peter along dark, dusty corridors that twisted and turned without rhyme or reason. They traveled a surprisingly long time, saying nothing, with no light but Valdyr's small hand-held lantern.

Finally, the corridor they were in ended in a tunnel that ran straight *up,* with an ancient-looking, battered wooden ladder traveling up into the darkness. Without a word, Valdyr began climbing, and Peter followed without hesitation. Finally, she halted, and Peter could see an opening in the stone before her.

"Good," Valdyr whispered. "They have not discovered this exit. Quickly, now!" She was out of the opening in seconds, and Peter clambered out after her. And then for the first time he stood on Qo'noS's soil, conscious and aware. Despite Valdyr's urgency, he paused to glance around.

In the darkness, the forest looked like any forest at night—heavy tree trunks crowding in on one another, with tangled, shapeless underbrush at their roots. In the daylight, the colors and textures that would make this forest unique—alien—would be revealed, but for now, all that was lost.

Then Peter glanced skyward—and stood transfixed. Overhead, washed in gold by the reflected light of the sun on the planet's other side, Qo'noS's ring arched like a bridge—a broken bridge. The shadow of Qo'noS bisected the middle of the ring, leaving it in darkness.

Valdyr threw the cloak over his shoulders and fastened the tracers. "Pull your hood up," she commanded him. "We must hurry."

James T. Kirk picked his way cautiously down a narrow animal trail, squinting in the darkness. From the look of Qo'noS's ring, it was nearly midnight. His night vision was excellent, almost as good as Spock's. (Unfortunately, the same could not be said for his regular eyesight—and he'd now gone through so many pairs of spectacles for reading that Bones McCoy claimed to have exhausted the supply in all the antique shops in San Francisco.)

The rescue party had had to detour around several large, private estates, which had nearly doubled their hike through the dark forest. Now, finally, the trees were thinning ahead of them. "How far are we from Kamarag's compound?" Jim whispered ahead to Spock. "My sense of direction has been off ever since we made that last detour."

"We are almost—" The Vulcan broke off, and halted. "Correction. We are here."

Kirk pushed his way through the last screen of undergrowth, McCoy following him. Together, the little party looked down from a high ridge, seeing the huge, fortresslike house down in the hollow, surrounded by both high stone walls and modern security fields.

"There seems to be a lot of activity going on," Kirk said, noting the brilliant security lights and the presence of many armed figures racing to and fro.

Spock regarded his tricorder intently. "Peter is no longer within the compound," Spock said.

"Not there? Then where is he? Did they take him off-world?" Kirk demanded, startled. Had Kamarag decided not to meet at the rendezvous? Had the Klingon ambassador somehow discovered that Kirk had no intention of obeying his instructions, and had returned to execute his nephew in revenge?

"Peter has vanished," Spock said. "He is not in the compound at the present moment. However," the Vulcan added, fiddling with his tricorder, taking readings, "that does not necessarily mean that he is now off-world. The rock formations in this area contain traces of selonite . . . the same material that forms the basis for the cloaking device. It makes readings impossible. If some of that selonite-impregnated rock is between us and Peter, that would make it impossible to scan him."

Kirk groaned aloud. "Just what we need!"

"I believe I should continue scanning," Spock said. "I may be able to pick him up again . . . if he is in the area."

Leonard McCoy plopped himself down on the ground with a groan. "Haven't hiked this much since Yellowstone," he grumbled, digging into his belt pouch and taking out a small flask and container of ration pellets.

The three officers silently shared the skimpy provisions as Spock continued to study the screen of his tricorder. "Fascinating," the Vulcan murmured, after a few minutes. "I am picking up something . . . confusing. For a moment I thought I had detected Peter, but now the human readings are blending and merging . . . becoming intermixed with Klingon readings."

"Where? What location?" Kirk demanded, jumping up.

"Due north," Spock said, pointing. "On the other side of the compound."

"Is it possible that it might be Peter, somehow masking his readings?" McCoy asked, peering at the tricorder's tiny screen.

"I believe it may be," Spock muttered.

"Well, it's the best lead we've got," Kirk said.

"Captain . . . these readings are moving toward the spaceport," Spock said. "Slowly . . . at a walking pace." Spock glanced up at his friend. "I believe, Jim, that your nephew has not waited for rescue. He has, instead, effected his own escape."

Kirk felt a slow grin spread across his features. "Well, that was damned inconsiderate of him, wasn't it?"

"Now what?" McCoy wondered aloud.

"Guess our next stop will be the spaceport, too," Kirk said, glancing at his wrist chrono. "See that ground vehicle that just pulled up there, outside the security gate?" He pointed down into the hollow.

"Yes, Captain," Spock replied.

"Think you could hot-wire that thing?"

"I believe I can, Captain," Spock said.

"Good. Let's make our way down there . . . slowly. Keep low. Take no chances. We've got plenty of time; we're going to hijack that car in just about . . . forty-five minutes."

The three officers cautiously made their way down the little ridge, crawling commando-style where they was no ground cover. Finally, they huddled crouched in a thicket about thirty meters from the guard station. The driver and the guard were standing outside, talking desultorily. The fugitive trio waited in silence, until, finally, Kirk glanced at his chrono again. "Ready, Spock?"

"Ready, Captain."

Kirk counted seconds in his head, and then, right on schedule, came the moment he'd been waiting for. A dull boom erupted from the forest they'd left behind, and a gout of distant yellow and red flame brightened the night. Half a second later, the ground beneath their feet shuddered.

"That's it!" Kirk said, grabbing McCoy and propelling him out of their hiding place. "Go!"

Spock was already racing forward. The guard was still outside his security station, his gaze fixed on the fire in the foothills. He never saw the Vulcan's dark figure, never realized that anyone was there—until a hand clamped onto the juncture of neck and shoulder, and he sagged, limp.

The driver turned toward his fallen comrade, then launched himself at Spock's dimly seen shape with a loud war cry. Kirk darted up behind him, chopped him hard on the neck, then kicked his feet out from under him. When the Klingon, dazed but still game, tried to get up, the captain stunned him with his phaser.

The captain caught his breath, then turned toward the car. "Want me to drive?" he asked, heading for the open door.

"With all due respect . . . *no*," Spock said, firmly, heading him off. "I have analyzed the controls with my tricorder, and *I* would prefer to drive. Your efforts at chauffeuring during our sojourn on Iotia are still vivid in my memory."

Kirk chuckled as the three would-be rescuers piled into the ground vehicle. It was a matter of moments to activate the engine and turn the car. Kirk crouched beside Spock and felt adrenaline course through his body. He glanced back at McCoy, who was gripping the edge of the backseat with both hands, holding on as Spock sent their stolen transportation barreling down the road.

"Jim, how the hell did you know that would happen?" the doctor demanded, pointing in the direction of the explosion.

"That was the *Kepler*," Kirk said. "You told me to give us plenty of time to get away . . . and it came in handy as a diversion."

With a sharp cry, the doctor grabbed the seat again and held on for dear life as the car slewed around a sharp curve. "Dammit, Spock, watch it! You're a Starfleet officer, not a chauffeur!"

"Spock, how long till we reach the spaceport?"

"ETA is . . . fifteen point seven minutes, Captain," Spock said, intent on driving. He sent the vehicle skidding into another tight turn, frowning slightly in the lights of the controls. "This road, unfortunately, winds about rather than going directly through the woods. I apologize for the . . . instability . . . of the ride."

Kirk grinned, feeling the car surge forward. "Just as long as it gets us there before Peter gets off-world, Spock. That way we'll only have to steal *one* ship."

"I shall endeavor to avoid that eventuality," Spock promised gravely, and increased speed until the groundcar seemed ready to take flight.

Peter and Valdyr had alternately walked and jogged for over an hour before they reached the edge of the forest, which ran almost up against the spaceport. The two paused for a moment, staring down at TengchaH Jav's perimeter security gate—the first of several hurdles they had to surmount in their quest to get off Qo'noS.

Valdyr glanced over her shoulder, then fished in her pocket, as they approached the gate. "This gate is programmed to admit any valid identification," she told him.

He gazed at the security device that would scan the number of people approaching and only admit those with the proper ID. "That's great," Peter remarked, watching her take out a small ID disk. "I don't have one."

"Yes, you do," she said. "I took Darj's." Handing him a disk, she fed hers into the scanner. "Before I killed him, I'd wondered how I would get you past this point."

Peter followed suit, and the gate swung open. Quickly, the two headed for the nonmilitary side of the port. If they were in luck, they would find a small, private vessel that was unsupervised while its crew was on shore leave. "Maybe we can find a trader or a smuggler's ship," Peter told Valdyr, "with a Federation registry. Federation vessels have standarized controls. I know I can pilot one of those. What other checkpoints do we have to cross?" he asked in a low voice, as they hurried along, watching keenly for any sign of Karg or his troops.

"There is an inside gate that leads to the civilian landing fields, but it is not always guarded," she whispered. "If there is a guard . . ." She patted her crossbow.

Peter swallowed hard. "Valdyr, there's got to be another way. If there's a guard . . . distract him somehow—act helpless, or something."

She spun, glaring at him.

"Just for a *second!*" he argued. "While he's helping you, I'll come up behind him and knock him cold."

"Are you sure you can?" she asked pointedly. "You'll only get one chance. Perhaps *you* should act helpless!"

"Let's not argue technique, okay?"

She nodded, if reluctantly. "Once we're inside that gate, we'll have to choose a ship. Of course, they are all locked. . . ."

"I should be able to break the codes," Peter assured her. "I learned the basics for breaking computer codes back when I was in my teens, and most freighters—especially the older models—don't have the most up-to-date security systems."

"That would be—" Valdyr began; then she glanced back over her shoulder again, only to halt in her tracks. "Lights! A ground vehicle!" she whispered, shoving the human toward a stack of vacuum-proof packing crates. "Hide!"

Peter leaped for cover and Valdyr joined him. They crouched, rigidly still, scarcely daring to breathe. After a moment, he peered around the nearest container, making sure he was in shadow. He watched the vehicle as it skidded to a stop. "Someone's in a big hurry," he whispered, with a sinking feeling in his midsection.

"It is one of Kamarag's vehicles," Valdyr said, with despair in her voice. "They have tracked us, somehow."

Without discussing it, the two fugitives both took out their disrupters and prepared for battle. They watched anxiously as the vehicle's doors opened, and three black-clad shapes emerged. Two were tall and lean, the other shorter and stocky. They moved furtively, and one kept glancing at some device in his hand—probably a scanner or tricorder. Peter groaned inwardly. Valdyr took his hand, gripping it so hard she made the bones grind.

Then his eyes narrowed as he stared at the three shapes. The stockier man was obviously in charge . . . both of the others turned to report to him as they searched. There was something about the way that one moved. Something familiar. . . . They wore no traditional Klingon garb that he had ever seen. And none of these figures looked big enough to be any of Karg's men. The shapes of their heads in the shadows seemed . . .

"We must kill them with the first shot," Valdyr murmured softly in his ear, "or we will never escape."

He nodded distractedly, even as the three searching figures drew closer to their hiding place. "Wait," he whispered, "let them get closer first. We can't afford to miss."

She aimed her weapon, even as he did. But then he lowered the disrupter. He was too busy staring at the tallest of the three figures. There were too many things all wrong about this. The tall searcher suddenly moved through a beam of light, and his face was illuminated. Peter saw a flash of a familiar arching eyebrow, and the unmistakable curve of a pointed ear.

Valdyr took deadly aim at the stocky male who was now almost on top of them. Peter lurched, grabbed her firing hand, and called, "Valdyr, no!"

She turned to him, her face twisted in confusion. The three stealthy figures turned in unison toward the sound. Peter surged to his feet, distantly hearing the Klingon woman's shocked growl. She clutched at him, attempting to pull him down, but he yanked free and bolted away, trying to get clear of the crates. "Uncle Jim!" he called softly. "It's me! Peter!"

"Peter?" Kirk halted on the pavement, staring wildly around until he spotted his nephew. "Peter!"

The young Kirk launched himself at his relative, and Jim seized his nephew in a bear hug, nearly lifting the taller man off the ground. They pounded each other's backs until they wheezed, grinning wildly.

"Gentlemen, I hate to intrude." Spock's cool tones cut across their emotional give-and-take. "However, if we are to effect our escape, we must not lose any time."

"I'm with Spock on that, Jim," Leonard McCoy agreed, glancing furtively around. "We can't afford to get caught now."

"Right," Kirk said, stepping back and regarding Peter fondly. Then the cadet watched his uncle's expression change to surprise, then alarm.

Peter turned to see Valdyr cautiously emerging from behind the stacks of crates. She was still clutching the disrupter. All three men wheeled in her direction, even as Jim Kirk's hand dropped to his phaser.

"No, Jim! Wait! She's with me! That is . . ." He paused, collected his wits as all three men glanced between him and the Klingon woman. He walked over to the crates and took Valdyr by the arm. He murmured to her, "Time to holster the weapon." Then, leading her somewhat reluctantly to the small group, he introduced her. "Captain James T. Kirk, Dr. Leonard McCoy, Captain Spock . . . this is Valdyr. I wouldn't be here without her. She helped me escape. She's . . . on our side." Peter trailed off, his face growing hot. The captain stared at his nephew, as if wanting to be sure he meant what he said.

"So," Valdyr said, eyeing the senior Kirk up and down, "this is the famous legend?"

The captain looked slightly abashed. "Well . . . I *am* out of uniform. . . ."

"I presume she provided you with the Klingon robe," Spock asked, reaching over to pull an object from it, "and the tracer?"

Peter nodded.

The Vulcan examined the device. "Yes. Here is the cause of those confusing tricorder readings. It very nearly kept us from locating you."

"It kept Kamarag's men from finding us, as well," Peter explained while Valdyr glowered.

"I can well imagine," Spock agreed dryly. "It is fortunate that Federation technology is more advanced than . . ."

McCoy elbowed Spock, and the Vulcan abruptly fell silent. The doctor stepped smoothly into the breach, all his Southern courtliness in evidence. "Well, if you've been helpin' Peter out, miss, we're all mighty grateful. Aren't we, Jim?"

Kirk paused for a second, then finally said quietly, "Of course we are. Thank you for helping Peter. For . . ." He glanced quizzically at his nephew. " . . . everything. . . ."

"Not to belabor Spock's point," McCoy added, "but it's time we got ourselves out of here."

Peter gave him a sharp glance. "Valdyr's coming with us. Where's your ship?"

Before Jim could say anything, Spock cleared his throat. "We . . . are currently without one."

Peter rolled his eyes. "So we *still* have to steal a ship? That's where we were at before you showed up!"

"Miss . . . Valdyr," McCoy said, still exuding polite charm, "do you know the layout of this spaceport?"

"The commercial freighters and off-world vessels are on that side," she said, pointing southwest, "and the military vessels are in a shielded underground hangar—to protect them from meteor showers—over there." She pointed in the opposite direction.

"I was hoping to find a freighter," Peter said.

"Forget that," Kirk told him. "We're going to need something with a cloaking device if we hope to get out of here in one piece. A bird-of-prey should do the job nicely."

Peter's mouth dropped open. *Is he crazy?* But Valdyr nodded in agreement. "My uncle's men will not expect us to go for a ship that would be impossible for two people to pilot."

"Your *uncle* . . . ?" Jim Kirk said.

Peter sighed and nodded. "Her uncle is Kamarag."

None of the three Federation officers said anything for another long moment while Valdyr drew herself up stiffly. Peter wondered if any human male in history ever had such an uncomfortable family introduction.

The entire group climbed back into the crowded vehicle and turned toward the manned gate half a kilometer away that was the entrance to the military side of the spaceport. They drove toward a cluster of outbuildings until Valdyr directed them into a convenient alley. They were able to position the vehicle so that the gate was within sight, while keeping the groundcar in darkness. The group huddled inside began to confer.

"There are two guards," Valdyr told them.

"We can handle that," Kirk said, touching his pocket. "We're armed. Phasers on stun." Spock, McCoy, and Kirk drew their weapons. "Spock and I will move along the fence line. . . ."

"Jim," McCoy interrupted, "you'll be out in the open. Don't you think they'll see you?"

Kirk gazed out of the vehicle, mulling over options.

"The chances of our approaching the guards without being seen," Spock informed him, "are approximately . . ."

"Spare me," McCoy groaned.

The Vulcan raised a surprised eyebrow.

"There is a simpler way," Valdyr said suddenly, with a sigh. "If your weapon can stun, then give one to me. I can approach the guards as if I were—how do you say it?—a *helpless* woman." She glowered at Peter, who only smiled back at her. "They will not be expecting trouble from one as small as myself. When I am close to them they will be easy to stun, and there will be no chance of them sounding an alarm."

Kirk nodded and Spock handed his weapon over to the Klingon female. When she was out of the vehicle, Kirk regarded his nephew. "You *do* trust her, Peter?"

Peter nodded. "Valdyr has not only given up everything—including her *heritage*—to save my life, but, I . . . I'm in love with her!" He took a deep breath.

The sudden silence in the car was shocking. McCoy's eyebrows had climbed to his hairline, while Spock began an intense examination of the vehicle's interior. Kirk gaped at his nephew. Peter swallowed. He had wanted to find the perfect moment to discuss this with Jim; he hadn't meant to just blurt it out in front of *everyone*.

"Does she know that?" the captain finally asked quietly.

Peter shook his head. "She knows . . . I care for her. I know she cares for me. We really haven't had the time or opportunity to have the kind of meaningful discussions people like to have in a developing relationship."

There was another uncomfortable pause, and then Spock interrupted: "She is at the gate."

The four men watched the Klingon woman as she sauntered up to the two guards, twitching portions of her compact form provocatively. One of them started grinning as soon as he saw her. Peter found himself wondering how one acted *sexy* while wearing armor . . . but, in a flash of insight, he realized that the armor itself was exciting for Klingon males! Whatever Valdyr was saying to the two guards made both of them focus on her, and lose all interest in their post. This small spaceport must not see many problems, he imagined. No doubt these two men spent most of their time bored and restless.

Suddenly, Valdyr arched her back, stared up at the closest guard, and bared her teeth. He grabbed her by the hair and tried to yank her over to him, even as the other one grabbed her, pressed himself against her, and bent his head to her neck. Peter's temper flared and his hand had grabbed the handle of the car door when Spock's reasonable voice intruded. "Wait," the Vulcan cautioned. "One moment . . ."

No sooner did he say that than the two Klingon guards suddenly looked amazed, then crumpled to the ground. Valdyr grimaced, spat on the one who had clutched her, and then matter-of-factly grabbed the closest by the heels and began struggling to wrestle him into the guard station.

"That's our cue!" Jim announced, and opened the vehicle's doors.

At the gate, Spock lifted one of the unconscious Klingons effortlessly and arranged him at his station inside the small building, while the captain and McCoy struggled with the other one.

Peter grabbed Valdyr by the shoulders. "Are you all right?"

"Uuughh!" she grunted. "I had to let those *veQ-nuj* handle me. I'm sorry now I didn't just kill them!"

"Valdyr . . ." Peter said warningly. She gave him a knowing look, then handed Spock back his phaser.

Suddenly, a mechanical whine intruded, and the entire party turned to look out the windows at the source of the sound. Feeling a rumble beneath his feet, Peter glanced over at a portion of the pavement that was rising into the air, like a huge trapdoor. Distant figures surrounded a small vessel that was on the platform rising up level with the landing field.

"Looks like a miniature bird-of-prey," Kirk said.

"That is essentially what it is," Valdyr confirmed. "A small, armed shuttle, very fast and maneuverable, it usually has a crew of three to six."

"I'd say that's exactly what the doctor ordered," McCoy said, "if only we could get to it."

Peter shook his head. "Forget it. I can see at least three crew members out there, as well as four maintenance staff. We wouldn't have a prayer of swiping that ship."

Kirk sighed. "Probably not," he admitted. But the expression on his uncle's face said otherwise.

"A *helpless* woman will not get you that ship," Valdyr warned.

"No," Jim agreed. "And if we try to take out the crew *and* the maintenance staff, even with three hand phasers and two disrupters against all of them, we'd be spread awfully thin. It would be hard to get close enough to stun them. These little jobs don't have much range."

Valdyr lifted her head proudly as the captain casually included her.

Jim continued to eye the ship speculatively. "It'll be tough enough just taking off, much less avoiding pursuit and setting a course that will bypass that ring. . . ."

"What he's sayin', miss," McCoy translated for the Klingon woman, "is that we're goin' for it, soon as he finishes tellin' us how impossible it is!"

Suddenly, an alarm began to whoop. The crew near the ship looked up, and automatically the fugitives ducked so that they wouldn't be seen through the guard-house windows. Valdyr pointed excitedly through the front windows, toward the automatic gate she and Peter had entered with their coded disks.

Several vehicles had just arrived, and armed Klingons, small in the distance, were aiming heavy disrupter rifles at the gate with its blaring alarm. Suddenly, the gate blew apart, its metal structure screaming, its beams and support hardware twisting and shattering. The Klingons poured through the perimeter, over the blasted chunks of debris that had been the entrance.

"Karg's men!" the Klingon woman said. "They have finally traced us."

"Karg must've decided that they couldn't capture us undetected, so they're staging an all-out assault!" Peter agreed.

The warriors surrounding the small bird-of-prey had noticed the invasion, too, and were pointing at the running figures.

"Stay down!" Valdyr ordered everyone. "Don't let them see you!" Tossing her disrupter at Peter, she leapt out of the guardhouse, brandishing her dagger. In Klingonese, she shouted at the men guarding the small bird-of-prey. "Enemies have come to steal your vessel! Defend yourselves!" Waving her weapon at the ship, she beckoned the crew. With a roar, the ship's crew members drew their own weapons and charged forward to confront the invaders. With a mighty yell, Valdyr raced toward Karg's troops, and the soldiers from the ship followed her blindly.

"Valdyr, no!" Peter yelled, and lurched after her, but Jim grabbed him roughly by the arm.

"She's bought us the time we need!" Jim told him. "We can't go up against that firepower with three phasers! Now come on, we've got to get that ship!"

"She'll be killed!" Peter argued. "I'm not leaving her!"

"Spock," the captain ordered.

"Peter, please," the Vulcan said quietly, taking the cadet's arm in a formidable grip, "I would regret being forced to carry you to safety."

McCoy was peering out the doorway at the ensuing melee of soldiers firing at each other. Disrupters whined and crackled. "Time, gentlemen!"

The captain stuck his head out the door to confirm McCoy's diagnosis. "You've got Peter, Spock?"

"Yes, Captain."

Peter stared at the Vulcan, calculating his chances at pulling away from the taciturn science officer without leaving his arm behind. Uncle Jim, McCoy, and Spock left the guardhouse at a dead run, and Peter had to either move his feet or be dragged. Pulling back as much as possible against the Vulcan's immovable strength, he turned his head, straining to see Valdyr, but it was impossible to pick her small frame out from the mass of huge, fighting men. If he left her this way, he knew he'd never see her again. He'd never be able to live with himself, either.

"Spock!" he implored. "They'll *kill* her!"

The Vulcan's expression softened just slightly, but he didn't slow down. "Once we're aboard the ship we may be able to effect her rescue."

Peter told himself that Vulcans never lie, and prayed that the old saying was true.

He heard the disrupter fire cease, and looked back at the mob of Klingons. He was shocked to see a number of bodies sprawled on the ground, dead, and realized that the remaining soldiers, as a group, had turned and were staring, and pointing, at them.

Spock saw it, too. "That is, if we get to the ship . . ."

A loud voice Peter recognized as Karg's suddenly shouted, "HALT, HUMANS!"

"We can make it!" Kirk insisted, as they drew closer to the ship.

"Halt, now!" shouted Karg again. "Or, we will kill this female *maghwl'!*" A jolt of disrupter fire charged the air, blasting the ground a few meters in front of Peter and Spock. The next blast nearly took off McCoy's leg.

Spock stopped running, and, even so, they nearly piled into McCoy, who had skidded to an abrupt halt. "Jim!" the doctor bellowed. "Stop, dammit! They've got our range!"

The captain halted, and turned, his face grim and set.

The combined group of soldiers closed the gap between them. As they did, Peter shook his arm where Spock still gripped him. "Spock! Let me go!"

Spock stared at the cadet. "If I do, you will do nothing foolish?"

Peter hesitated.

Spock's eyebrow went up; then he sighed, loudly. "Never mind. It was a poor choice of words. You are, after all, a Kirk." He released the human's arm.

"They killed the ship's crew, her maintenance staff," McCoy murmured in a shocked tone.

Peter's heart sank. And now Karg had them all, Valdyr, himself . . . his Uncle Jim. The cadet decided he must be some kind of bad-luck hex. After all, Uncle Jim had gotten out of a million scrapes worse than this *before*. As Karg drew near them, he could see he was towing Valdyr by the hair. She was unarmed. There was magenta blood splashed on her arm, and some smeared on her face, but he didn't think any of it was hers.

"Won't Kamarag be pleased!" Karg gloated as the soldiers drew abreast of them. "No doubt he's having some trouble finding his quarry in the immensity of space. When he returns, won't he be impressed when we present him with not only James T. Kirk and his wretched kin, but also the gutless Vulcan computer and the butcher who calls himself a physician! You will all pay for your crimes against Qo'noS!"

Peter heard McCoy murmur a bitter, "Oh, brother . . . not again!"

"I have committed no crimes against Qo'noS," the captain said, coolly. "I only came here to rescue my brother's son, who is also innocent of any crime. Besides," he added, "Chancellor Azetbur invited me to visit her world anytime after I saved her life at Khitomer."

The watching troops stirred when they heard their chancellor mentioned, though Karg was undismayed by Kirk's reference. The captain glanced around at the circle of armed Klingons. "Chancellor Azetbur knows nothing of your betrayal . . . *yet*," the officer reminded them boldly. "If you abandon this scheme of Kamarag's now, you can still save . . ."

"*Chancellor* Azetbur is our *enemy!*" Karg bellowed furiously.

However, Peter noted that several of the soldiers shifted uneasily, glancing at each other surreptitiously. Others glanced around, uncomprehending, not understanding the captain because they didn't speak English.

Peter studied them, an idea growing in the back of his mind. Perhaps not all of these men were totally committed to betraying their government. There came a time when even good soldiers had to question bad orders. . . .

The cadet recognized one of them, Malak, and saw that he, particularly, seemed uncomfortable. In the harsh glow of the spotlighted landing field, he saw two gleaming weapons on Malak's belt. One of the daggers was small . . . delicate. He had Valdyr's blade.

Karg was still ranting. "That slut! Azetbur is a *pretender!* She is . . ."

"*Appointed* by her father," Peter said loudly in Klingonese, raising his voice to be heard over Karg's baritone, "and *ratified* by the Klingon High Command. She is no *pretender*, but the legal head of your Empire. A *rightfully* appointed head of state, who is working toward saving your planet!"

All eyes turned to him as, dramatically, he swung his hand overhead, pointing to the ring, the debris of Praxis that encircled Qo'noS. "It's still there, isn't it? It hasn't gone away, has it? The symbol of your world's inevitable demise. You all know that, without the help of the Federation, Qo'noS is doomed. Your military vessels are housed in *underground* shelters to keep them safe from meteors that gouge your world. How many of you have lost loved ones to the meteors? Is that the way warriors want to die? Being struck by *veQ* from the sky?"

Peter realized that his uncle, the doctor, and Spock were staring at him. Even the captain and McCoy, who were probably hearing him over the Universal Translators they carried, seemed impressed. Several of the soldiers looked uncomfortable, glancing at Karg guiltily as if wondering what they were all doing there in the first place.

"Azetbur is working with the Federation to guarantee you a *future*," Peter reminded the Klingons. "She's not dwelling on the past, like this *qoH*"—he pointed at Karg—"who thinks that he can make the past into the future, when anyone who raises his eyes can *see* that is impossible! Azetbur, like yourselves, looks up at the sky and reads what is written there—change. Change and continued life for Klingons and Qo'noS! Your chancellor wants to make sure there is a future for *all* Klingons—not just the wealthy ones who can hide in the fortresses, and not worry about what falls from the sky. Your chancellor is loyal to the people of Qo'noS—and she needs your loyalty in return. Do not betray her!"

It wasn't a bad speech, Peter realized. He suspected that he had more than one convert in the crowd.

"Listen to him!" Valdyr implored. "You heard from Treegor how he can fight! He defeated two Klingon warriors at once! Peter Kirk *is* a warrior, like yourselves. He speaks from his heart."

"Silence, you *Iam be'!*" Karg snarled, and swung a vicious blow at her face.

Before Peter could react, Valdyr blocked the blow and slammed an elbow into Karg's midsection, under his breastplate. Then she punched him hard in the face with the back of her own fist, making his nose spout blood.

Karg never released the grip on her hair. Enraged, he swore violently and, in a blur, yanked his dagger out of his belt and stabbed the woman viciously in the gut, twisting the knife and drawing it up as hard as he could before yanking it out.

Valdyr's eyes widened, but she didn't cry out. Instead, she spat directly in Karg's face. Blinded, he released her, and stepped back. Valdyr's eyes rolled up and she crumpled to the ground, her hands folded over the wound. Blood gushed through her fingers.

The Klingon soldiers seemed stunned by Karg's action, as though they could not believe that their commander could be so foolish as to kill Kamarag's own *niece*.

Peter screamed "NO!" and bolted to Valdyr's side, barely realizing that McCoy moved with him, some medical diagnostic tool already in his hand. "Valdyr! Valdyr!" the cadet shouted as McCoy swung the tool around, recalibrated it, swung it again, muttering wildly to himself.

She can't be dead! he thought frantically.

The Klingon woman's eyes fluttered feebly, finally opened. The dark light in her eyes was dim, barely focused. "Pityr . . ."

"Valdyr! Hold on! Fight like the warrior you are! Don't give in!"

"Pityr . . . ? You must flee. . . ."

"Valdyr, listen. You'll be okay, just listen. Oh God, Doctor, do something! Valdyr . . . you've got to live. You've got to! I love you, Valdyr. Do you hear me? I love you!"

A smile flickered across her face, revealing crooked teeth as McCoy fumbled in his medical kit. He found a hypo, adjusted it, then pressed it against her neck. "You love me?" she gasped. "This is true?"

"It's true, I swear it before all Qo'noS. I love you."

She nodded. "We cannot weep. But we can love, Pityr. You are my mate. With you I would take the vow. I love you, too." Then her eyes closed again, and her head rolled to the side. McCoy cursed vehemently and gave her something else.

"Bones?" the captain asked softly.

McCoy shook his head, but continued working feverishly.

Peter felt every emotion he'd suffered through and repressed well up in him and explode in a blinding rage. He touched the blood still seeping through her locked fingers, then enclosed it in his fist. Clenching his teeth in fury and bitter sorrow, he slowly rose . . . and turned toward Karg.

"Son, wait," his uncle warned quietly, but Peter ignored him.

Taking a step toward the Klingon, he thrust out his fist, still dripping with Valdyr's blood, and growled, in Klingonese, "One of you who still possesses a warrior's honor, give me a dagger, so I may deal with this traitor who has no pretense to honor left him—to attack an unarmed *female!*"

"*You* would challenge *me?*" Karg asked him incredulously, shifting the dagger that still gleamed with Valdyr's blood.

"It is his *right*," Malak said, stepping forward. "Valdyr has named him her mate." The soldier removed the woman's dagger from his belt and tossed it to Peter, who caught it by the hilt.

"It is a good day to *die*," Peter announced, smiling wolfishly as he advanced on the officer.

"Peter! No!" Jim shouted, lurching forward.

But Spock caught his captain by the arm before he could interfere, saying quietly, "Jim. This is a cultural issue."

"Dammit, Spock," Kirk growled.

"It is *Peter's* choice," Spock reminded him.

Karg charged the young man, his dagger extended. Peter deflected it, and punched the Klingon hard in the eye with the fist that held Valdyr's knife. With a second swipe, he opened a shallow cut on the Klingon's corrugated forehead. It bled freely. Karg howled, and his eye began to swell and close, even as the blood dripped down, further blinding him.

Peter spun around the warrior, the small blade licking out, caressing him as delicately as a lover, nicking his ear. Flick . . . and Valdyr's dagger scored the back of Karg's gauntleted hand. Flick . . . now his cheek was laid open.

The small cuts humiliated the warrior, enraging him past all caution. Karg lurched forward, stabbing blindly, as Peter danced out of the way, leaving a razor-thin line of blood along the Klingon's neck.

The officer recovered himself slightly, holding back, and when Peter came in again, he sliced the cadet's arm. The human ignored the wound, though it burned like fire, and, *flick*—this time the little dagger cut the small leather strap that held the right side of Karg's armor close to his body. The armor flapped annoyingly now, distracting the warrior.

Roaring with rage, he charged the rapidly moving human, but Peter stepped aside like a matador, and, as he did so, he chopped his fist down on the Klingon's bull-like neck, deadening the nerves in his arm, nearly causing Karg to drop his dagger. He aimed a powerful kick at the soldier's midsection, but Karg was ready, and blocked, numbing his foot and halfway up his leg.

Limping, Peter staggered out of range, then came back in, and landed a ringing blow to Karg's chin, making his head snap back. The Klingon's teeth clacked shut, and blood suddenly poured from his mouth. Before he could recover, Peter grabbed the healthy mass of hair that was a Klingon warrior's pride.

"We humans call this 'death by humiliation,'" he whispered in his enemy's ear. "Think of it as return payment for the way you abused Valdyr." With a swift flash of her wicked blade, he severed most of the long hair from Karg's head. Behind them, he could hear the other Klingons laugh uproariously.

Karg went wild, bellowing and swearing as he charged the human. Peter side-stepped him, and clubbed him hard where his neck and back joined. Karg's eyes rolled up, and he fell heavily, face forward, onto the pavement, then lay unmoving, unconscious. Peter, his rage still unspent, hovered over the body, sweating, heaving for air. He wanted Karg to get up, again and again, so that he could beat him to a bloody pulp—then slice him like a holiday roast.

"Kill him, young Kirk!" Malak urged. "It is your right. He will have no honor left to him, if you let him live."

No one moved as Peter shifted Valdyr's blade and stared at the back of the unconscious soldier.

Then a weak, tremulous voice cut the air. "Pityr . . ."

He blinked, looked around, saw Valdyr lying on the pavement, with McCoy still working on her. Her eyes were half-open, her bloody hand raised slightly, beckoning him.

"Dammit, man!" McCoy snapped at him. "Will you get yourself over here before she burns up the little reserves she has left tryin' to get your attention!"

Peter glanced up at Malak. "Karg doesn't deserve any honor. He's a traitor, a man who brutalizes those who are weaker than he is. Let him live with the shame of his defeat." He left the unconscious Klingon and moved to Valdyr's side.

He took her hand as she whispered in a thin voice, "You fought for me?"

"And won," he said, slipping her dagger back in its place. "With your knife."

"My warrior . . ." she whispered, and lost consciousness again.

As the Klingon woman slipped back into unconsciousness, McCoy continued to work on the hideous wound in her abdomen. He worked swiftly with the tiny electronic microcautery, but she had lost so much blood already!

Jim and Spock drew near the fallen woman. "Bones, will she make it?"

The doctor never looked up, never lost his focus. But before he could answer, a harsh, accented Klingon voice called out, *"This* is the man who killed Chancellor Gorkon!" McCoy glanced up, saw one of the soldiers pointing at him. "Now he will kill Kamarag's niece!"

"Not bloody likely," McCoy swore. "I'm not goin' to let her die."

The shame of that failure still burned within him. The fact that the chancellor's death had caused him—and his best friend—to be sent to that hellhole Rura Penthe was bad enough . . . but really, it was the death of Gorkon himself that upset McCoy. He had never before lost a patient because of his own *lack of knowledge.* Working on the chancellor for those few, futile moments had been the blackest point in his entire career. To struggle to save a dying man . . . and know so little about his most rudimentary needs . . . *First, do no harm,* the law of healers said, the law that ruled McCoy's life. After Rura Penthe, he'd sworn that would never happen to him again. Not ever. Ignoring the soldier's insult, he focused on his patient.

"In the time since the chancellor's death," Spock suddenly said, addressing the crowd, "Dr. McCoy has studied Klingon physiology extensively. He is completely qualified to assist this woman."

The warriors did not seem mollified. Then Malak stepped forward. "It is well known that Vulcans do not lie."

Does everyone still believe *that load of horse-puckey?* McCoy wondered, sealing the wound, and packing it with a sterile, inflatable foam from a small container in his kit.

The doctor noticed Spock's expression change, as if he suddenly realized what an opening he'd just been given. "Warriors, know this," the Vulcan intoned. "You serve Kamarag loyally, yet even Kamarag does not know that the plans he has made have been influenced by the mind of an alien. Kamarag's thoughts and plans are not his own—he is little more than a puppet."

The Klingons all looked at one another, then at Malak, who seemed stunned.

"Why else would Kamarag," Spock continued, pressing his advantage, "after three years of silence, suddenly concoct this plan to kidnap Peter Kirk and lure James Kirk to his death, when James Kirk himself was responsible for saving Azetbur's life? Did none of you question Kamarag's motives? Did none of you question his plans to commit treason? Did none of you question the lack of *honor* in his scheme?"

Malak answered for the group. "We did have questions, the same questions Valdyr had from the beginning. But we are loyal to Kamarag's house, as our families have been for generations. Now I look at what it has brought us, and I have no answers. We have lost some of our brothers, and have been forced to kill warriors we had no feud with." He gestured back at the dead soldiers that had been protecting their ship.

"If we can get off Qo'noS, and meet with Kamarag," Spock explained, "we hope to prove to him how he has been influenced, and sway him from his course."

Malak nodded. "Vulcans do not lie, so I believe you." He looked down at McCoy. "Do you believe you can save Valdyr?"

McCoy wiped the sweat beading on his brow. "I've got her stabilized . . . barely. If I could get her to the *Enterprise,* to our sickbay . . ."

"Take her," Malak said, startling the doctor. These fierce-looking warriors were actually going to let them *go?* Malak looked at Captain Kirk and Spock. "Take the bird-of-prey. If you can outrun those who will surely come after you, do so. Save Valdyr. And, if you can, save Kamarag. Then I will have done my duty to my lord." He turned to his men, as if waiting for a challenge, but none came.

"Can we move her?" Peter asked McCoy. The boy's face was nearly white with worry.

"Carefully," McCoy warned, worried that any sharp motion would reopen some of those bleeders.

Spock leaned down and asked, "Shall I?" Gratefully, McCoy nodded, watching protectively as the Vulcan gently lifted the unconscious woman and stood up with her cradled in his arms.

McCoy trotted alongside Spock as they all headed for the small warbird.

"Spock," Peter said, "I can override the lock, but I'll need your tricorder." At the Vulcan's nod, Peter unfastened the device from around Spock's waist, then made himself busy with the lock that would extrude the gangplank. His fingers flashed over the controls of his tricorder as he searched for the proper sequence. Suddenly there was a soft thunk; then, with a hiss of pressurized air, the ramp extended out and down. Kirk was in the lead, already heading for the ship's bridge.

"Put her here, Spock," McCoy directed the Vulcan, and the science officer lowered Valdyr onto a padded seat set back away from the tiny bridge, then went forward. McCoy crouched beside the woman, checking her wound and reading his diagnostic tool. Everything had held. The wound was secure. McCoy glanced around the tiny cabin. Wouldn't this ship have its own medikit, with Klingon-specific drugs and equipment?

"How bad is it?" Peter asked, his eyes searching the older man's face.

McCoy hesitated. Finally, he admitted, "There's a lot of internal damage, but, Peter, with her spirit . . . if anyone can make it with this much damage, I'd say she can."

Peter nodded, and tried to smile wanly. McCoy looked up to see Jim hovering over his nephew's shoulder.

"We're going to need you up front, Peter," the captain ordered.

"Aye, sir," the cadet responded and, with a final glance back at Valdyr and McCoy, moved up to the bridge.

Good, thought the doctor, *get him out of my hair so I can get some real work done.*

Peter watched his uncle Jim swing himself into the pilot's seat and begin powering up the ship. Spock, to Peter's surprise, elected to take the gunner's seat, leaving the navigation console to the cadet.

Moments later, the tiny shuttle lifted off and swooped upward. Peter could see the change come over his uncle as Kirk gloried in the small ship's skyward rush. The cadet called off a course, and Kirk fed it into the ship's computer.

Suddenly, a harsh Klingon voice came over the intercom, demanding to know the ship's flight plan, its registration number, and a half a dozen other required things ships had to have before leaving the spaceport. Peter found it ironic that even Klingons had bureaucracy.

"Any way we can bluff our way out of this?" the captain asked his crew.

"I can speak enough Klingon, Uncle Jim," Peter told him, "but I just don't have the answers to their questions."

"Nor do I, Captain," Spock told him.

"Fine," the captain said casually, and slapped the intercom into silence, cutting the speaker off in mid-tirade. "That's enough of that."

"Company coming," Peter reported tersely, as he watched his instruments. "Two cruisers."

"Where's the damned cloaking device?" Kirk grumbled, peering at controls covered by Klingon symbols. "On the *Bounty,* Scotty labeled everything in English!"

Peter craned his neck to see around his uncle. "It's on your left, that third switch, with the red telltale beside it."

"It is possible, Captain," Spock warned, "that other Klingon vessels may well have technology to identify this ship's energy signature, and thus allow them to track us, even if we activate it."

"Well, it won't hurt to try," Kirk said. He quickly flipped the appropriate switch. "There it is, Spock. . . ."

Peter felt a subtle hum course through the shuttle, and the viewscreen changed abruptly, revealing a view of the planet below that was wavy and distorted, as though seen through a haze.

The shuttle was almost out of the atmosphere, almost into space, when one of the ships nearly caught them. "Cruiser at oh-four-three mark six," Peter announced. "They've powered up their weapons and they're tracking us!"

Spock was setting up the gunner's targeting screen, all his attention fixed on their opponent. The other ship fired, and the shuttle shuddered violently.

"Direct hit!" Peter shouted. "Our amidships shield is down by eighty percent. Another hit there, and we won't have to worry about confronting Kamarag."

"What the hell's going on up there?" McCoy shouted. Quickly, he examined Valdyr. Puce swirls colored the white packing foam in her wound. *Oh no, she's sprung a bleeder!* He had no time to check the Klingon kit, and grabbed his micro-cautery. The ship suddenly veered sharply before he could engage the instrument. If that had happened while he was working in the wound, he could have caused irreparable damage! He had to have a steady working field.

"Another jolt like that and I may as well throw this patient out the airlock for all the good I'm doin' her!" he yelled.

He saw Peter turn to look at Valdyr, then heard Jim's "captain" voice order sharply, "Focus on your job, mister! Let the doctor handle his patient." The cadet's face flamed as he turned back around.

Let the doctor handle his patient! McCoy mentally mocked Kirk's order. The ship lurched again, then zagged hard right. Bones had to grab Valdyr's unconscious form to keep her secure in the chair. *Handle, indeed!* he fumed. *I'm a doctor, not a damned juggler!*

"Spock?" Jim Kirk asked, not turning his head to see his officer. "I'm coaxing every bit of speed out of this ship that I can—"

"Understood, Captain," the Vulcan said, his voice preternaturally calm. "Targeting . . . locking on . . . and firing."

The little bird-of-prey shivered with the force of the blast. Jim spared a glance for the viewscreen, in time to see the disrupter blast score a direct hit on their opponent.

"That's got them!" the captain said exultantly. "Nice shooting, Spock! No loss of life, but they'll have to break off pursuit and make a manual landing. Peter, let's up the stakes on this pursuit. Locate one of the ring shepherds and plot us a course past it. Find us a way through that ring."

Peter worked at his controls feverishly. "Course computed and laid in, sir," he reported, moments later, his voice professionally confident.

"Looks good," Jim responded, standing by to make minute course corrections. Then the ship shot toward the ring field at maximum speed.

"Cruiser approaching, dead astern! Six-four-three mark nine!" the captain heard his nephew shout. "They're going to follow us—weapons targeting!"

"Spock," Kirk said, "remember what happened to the *Kepler?*"

"I do indeed, Captain," the Vulcan said, targeting his weapons.

The shuttle hurtled into the gap. On their right side, close enough almost to touch, loomed the huge granite ring shepherd. They were beside it—they were past it—

"Now, Spock!"

"Firing aft weapons," Spock announced, and the little warbird trembled with the force of the blasts.

The powerful beams shot into the ring shepherd, blowing it apart in a shower of debris, spreading directly into the path of the oncoming cruiser.

Shards and chunks of rocks spun wildly, in eerie silence; then Peter's voice reached Kirk, suddenly exultant. "Captain, the debris has overloaded their shielding! They're breaking off!"

The Vulcan nodded. "Even Klingons can understand diminishing returns. Pursuing us at the cost of their own vessel was not worth the effort. Eminently logical."

"Have you all finished turnin' this blasted shoebox upside down?" McCoy bellowed from the rear.

The three men glanced at one another in exasperation. "Yes, Doctor," Jim assured him. Then Kirk turned to look at his nephew. "Go on back if you want to, Peter. Spock and I can handle this now."

Peter nodded his gratitude and slipped out of the seat to join McCoy. "How is she?" He still found it hard to believe they'd survived that flight through the ring gap!

"A little the worse for wear, I'm afraid," McCoy admitted grumpily. He had an odd-looking kit opened up beside him. "Fortunately, I found this ship's medical kit. But I'm havin' a little trouble with the diagnostic tool—language barrier, you know? Maybe you can help."

Peter smiled wanly. He desperately wanted to do something for Valdyr, anything. . . . McCoy waved the device over the pale, comatose woman. Peter translated what he could, giving McCoy the terms phonetically, since none of them meant much to him, but the doctor kept nodding and saying, "Uh-huh," as if *he* at least understood it. McCoy dug around in the kit, found something, and slapped it in his hypo. "This'll be a big help," he mumbled, as he pressed it to Valdyr's neck. "Though, heaven knows she's got a damned *pharmacy* in there now."

Suddenly, the woman's eyes fluttered open. "Pityr . . ." she gasped.

"He's right here, miss," McCoy told her. "Don't move now. Talk to her, son, before she starts thrashin'."

"Valdyr." The cadet took her hand, squeezed it gently. Her returning grip was weak, and that shocked him more than even her appearance.

"My warrior," she whispered, "you cannot only fight . . . you can speak . . . so well . . . like a diplomat . . . as well as Azetbur . . ."

Peter flushed with pride, knowing the high opinion Valdyr had of the female chancellor.

"I'd say he's every bit as eloquent as his uncle, young miss," McCoy agreed, checking her signs, and examining her wound for fresh blood.

Valdyr frowned, blinking drowsily. "Pityr, what am I missing?"

The cadet shook his head, not following her.

"This McCoy, he keeps saying to me, 'miss,' 'miss'—what is this I am missing? I do not want to be missing anything!"

McCoy heard her, and raised his eyebrows. Peter nodded, trying to assure the doctor it was all right. "It's okay, Valdyr. You're not missing anything. 'Miss' is an archaic title, what humans sometimes call young, unmated females. It's old-fashioned, but it's a sign of respect."

Her gaze drifted to McCoy. "Thank you for that respect, Doctor. I did not think that would be such an easy thing to get from humans."

"You *earned* that, miss," McCoy assured her. "Now, please, just lie still."

Suddenly, she turned back to the young Kirk, her eyes widening. "Pityr, do not forget to tell your uncle . . . about Kamarag. . . ."

"He knows all about Kamarag, Valdyr," the cadet tried to reassure her.

"No," she insisted, "he does not! You must tell him about Kamarag's fleet. I do not know how many ships, but he had many officers that he spoke to! Do not let Kirk fly right into his ambush. . . ."

"I'll tell him, Valdyr, I'll tell him. You've got to take it easy."

"Pityr, please, kiss me," she demanded, her voice hoarse and breathless. "If I am to die, I want to take the memory of your kiss with me, Pityr-oy."

"You're not going to die, Valdyr," Peter told her. "I'll fight death for you, just like I fought Karg. And I'll win." Gently, he touched her mouth with his.

She laughed lightly as he did. *"Hlja'!"* she whispered. *"MevQo',* Pityr. . . ." Then she slid back into unconsciousness.

Peter glanced at McCoy, alarmed, but for once the doctor seemed unconcerned. "It's okay," the older man assured him. "Her body's shutting down its less important functions, to preserve its energy. She's holding on."

The cadet sighed, relieved. "Call me if she comes to," he asked, and McCoy nodded as Peter returned to his station.

His uncle and Spock acknowledged his arrival as Peter relayed the message from Valdyr to Jim Kirk about Kamarag's forces.

"Don't worry, Peter. We can still beat him back to the rendezvous point. We'll warn *Enterprise* in time."

"And then what?" Peter demanded, bleakly.

Kirk shrugged. "Maybe there will be another ship or two around. I'll contact Scotty, and have him call for help."

"The nearest starbase is two days' journey away," Peter pointed out darkly.

"Take it easy for the moment, Peter," Kirk tried to reassure him. "We'll find a way to handle Kamarag. And, by the way, you *were* pretty damned eloquent, cadet."

"Thanks, Uncle Jim."

The elder Kirk patted the helm and changed the subject. "This is one sweet little ship, isn't she?" he said to the other two men. "So . . ." he patted the console again, "what'll we name her?"

"Actually, Klingon ships are called 'he,'" Peter said, tightly. "And he has a name. It's painted on his bow. I spotted it as we boarded him." His face was an expressionless as Spock's, belying the turmoil of emotions inside him. "He's called the *Taj.*"

Spock looked pensive. "Ironic . . ." he muttered.

"What does it mean?" Jim asked.

"Dagger," Peter said, a shadow crossing his face.

No one said anything more as *Taj* flew on, swift and alone in the blackness.

Nine

Hours later, a weary James T. Kirk piloted the *Taj* into the *Enterprise*'s docking bay. Waiting for him in the docking bay was a welcoming committee consisting of a medical team, a grim-faced Mr. Scott, Commander Uhura, and Ambassador Sarek.

Within moments a medical team spirited Valdyr away, with McCoy and Peter in tow. Kirk stood at the top of the gangplank and watched the two of them, his heart aching a little for his nephew. *Peter* in love with a *Klingon?* But it had happened, there was no denying it. It was obvious that this was no casual affair; Peter had fallen, and fallen hard. Was there any possibility of a future for the two of them together? Any hope of happiness? He didn't know. . . .

Ten minutes later, once more in uniform, the captain hurried down the corridor, fastening the flap of his maroon jacket.

When he reached the conference chamber, he found his officers, plus Sarek, already assembled. Spock, also, was back in uniform. In contrast to his own weary dishevelment, the Vulcan was, of course, impeccably groomed and seemed as fresh as if he hadn't played hide-and-seek on Qo'noS for the past fifteen hours.

Kirk lowered himself into a seat and addressed his chief engineer. "Status, Mr. Scott?"

"Well, Captain . . . I dinna know exactly what's goin' on, but something worrisome is happening. Half an hour ago, we picked up a blip for about five seconds on our sensors—and then it was gone. Three minutes later, another . . . not far away. Just . . . *blip,* then gone. Over and over, sir. Never in the same space twice . . . but stayin' just barely within the boundary of the Neutral Zone—th' *Romulan* Neutral Zone."

"What do the sensors indicate?" Kirk asked. "Could it be Kamarag's fleet?"

"Noo, sir, it's not large enough for that. We canna get a full readin', Captain, because it comes and goes so quickly. Just bits and pieces. It isna small, that's for sure. I'd say ship-sized."

"No possibility of it being a natural phenomenon?"

"Noo, Captain. My guess is that it's a ship. A cloaked ship. It decloaks just long enough to register on our sensors as a blip, then it recloaks and moves. But never very far away."

"A bird-of-prey," Kirk said, and Scott nodded. "Klingon?"

"Possibly," Spock said, studying the limited sensor data Scott displayed for their benefit. "But I think not. The ion traces are different from those we detected from cloaked Klingon vessels."

"And, Captain," Uhura spoke up, "there's something else that's suspicious about it. The instant we first picked it up, something began jamming our long-range communications. We can't send subspace messages, sir."

"Hmmmm . . ." Kirk sipped coffee, thinking hard. "Show me the blips," he said, and Scott obediently called up a three-dimensional schematic on the conference table's screen. Kirk studied the pattern as he finished his coffee. "What do you make of this, Spock?"

"I would like the opportunity to study it further," the Vulcan said, gazing intently at the screen. Sarek also stared at the screen, barely blinking. Kirk could almost hear the Vulcan wheels turning.

"What would happen," the ambassador said quietly, "if we were to move closer to it?"

"We can try," Kirk said. "Mr. Scott, Commander Uhura, please report to the bridge to oversee maneuvers. Scotty, see how much of an ion trail our visitor is leaving. Uhura, try and determine the range their jamming signal has."

"Yes, Captain."

"Aye, sir."

Minutes later, with the two senior officers standing by, Kirk instructed the helm to head for the last recorded blip at one-eighth impulse power.

"Look!" Uhura exclaimed over the intercom as another blip abruptly flashed on, then off. This one was deeper into the Neutral Zone by several hundred kilometers.

"It's like a game," Kirk said, staring hard at the screen. "They want to lure us into the Neutral Zone."

"A game," Sarek repeated softly, an undercurrent of excitement in his voice. "Yes indeed . . . a game! But not follow-the-leader . . . watch closely . . ." The Vulcan's long-fingered hands flashed swiftly over the computer controls.

As Kirk watched, the three-dimensional schematic was replaced by a three-level grid pattern—a familiar pattern. He turned to Sarek incredulously. "A chessboard, Ambassador?"

"Yes," the Vulcan said, his dark eyes shining with pleasure from solving the puzzle. "And I recognize the game. Taryn is in command of that vessel. And those moves, those coordinates—they are identical to the moves Taryn made in one of our recent games." He shook his head, adding, mostly to himself, "A *Vulcan* gambit . . . of course he would employ one. A Vulcan gambit . . . it makes perfect sense. I should have realized it before."

"But assuming that *is* Taryn, why would he come here?" Kirk said.

"Because he wants me. He knows that I have uncovered the Freelan plan. I spoke to him while you were gone, and I deliberately baited him, trying to lure him into some reckless action . . . as I have done many times during our chess games. Now he is responding to my implicit challenge. He is moving his ship in the pattern of the last game we played that he won. He employed T'Nedara's gambit, and there"—Sarek swiftly outlined a series of moves in red—"it is. The exact pattern of his moves in the game we played."

"How many moves did he make during the entire game?" Spock asked, obviously fascinated. As they had been speaking, several more blips had appeared on the schematic.

"It was a long, hard-fought game. Each of us made hundreds of moves."

"Are you *sure*, Ambassador?" Kirk asked, wonderingly. "Do you have any other evidence that this is Taryn? When he contacted you, what did he want?"

"He demanded a meeting between us in the Freelan system. I told him I would be unable to attend. As I said, I baited him. I could tell that he was angry, though of course I could not see his features. Now he does this," he gestured at the screen, "as his next move."

"But if he was on Freelan only hours ago—"

Sarek shook his head. "No. He merely *said* he was on Freelan. Commander Uhura confirmed that the message from Taryn was only routed through Freelan communications systems. The actual transmission originated inside the Romulan Neutral Zone."

On Kirk's order, *Enterprise* moved again, and again the unseen vessel responded with a series of moves. "The pattern is exact," Sarek said. Catching Kirk's still-skeptical glance, he marked a new location on the screen in purple. "The next move," he said.

As the Vulcan had predicted, when *Enterprise* moved again, the blip materialized for a second in those exact coordinates. Kirk shook his head. "Okay, let's assume you're right, for argument's sake. But why the game? What does he want?"

"The game grid for his ship's maneuvering coordinates is not the main point, Captain. Taryn would probably be surprised to realize that I have identified the pattern. He is simply amusing himself while he seeks to draw us closer to his ship . . . and away from the rendezvous point."

Kirk turned to the monitor that showed Uhura and Scotty, who were listening in from the bridge, as ordered. "Commander, have you discovered the range of their jamming capability?"

"Yes, sir," she replied promptly. "It extends for nearly a light-year in all directions. We'll definitely have to move to get any kind of message out."

"Great . . ." Kirk said, grimly. "Starbase Eight is two full days away, and that's the closest help we can expect. And now we can't even get a message out."

"Captain," Scotty put in, "what I dinna understand is why the devil the Romulans try to lure you away now, if they're the ones who forced you to come out here in the first place? It doesna make sense!"

"It does if the Romulans wish to begin a war," Sarek said, "between the Federation and the Klingon Empire. If Taryn has gone to this trouble to initiate hostilities, he undoubtedly wishes Kamarag and his fleet to cross into Federation space unimpeded."

"Good point," Kirk said. "So, really, Peter's kidnapping was almost extraneous to the rest of this situation. The Romulans inflamed Kamarag—and this is the form his revenge took. In addition to attacking the Federation, he decided he had to get back at *me*, personally."

"That would seem the logical deduction, Captain," Spock said.

Sarek was staring at the growing schematic as if mesmerized. "We cannot continue to allow them to jam *Enterprise*'s subspace communications. We must be able to send a message to Starfleet Command . . . and the president."

"Why?" Kirk demanded. "I mean . . . to request reinforcements, yes, that I know. But why the president?"

"Taryn must realize now that I know about their plans. He is trying to prevent me from revealing what I know to Ra-ghoratrei or your Starfleet Admiral Burton."

"It is fortunate," Spock observed quietly, "that you sent that time-locked message."

"At your suggestion," Sarek reminded the first officer. "However, that message may not activate in time to prevent both a Romulan and a Klingon invasion."

"So . . . what's next?" the captain asked, rubbing his forehead.

"What do you mean, Captain?" Sarek asked.

"I mean that you've convinced me that that's a Romulan ship, and that Taryn is commanding it. But as long as he doesn't cross the Neutral Zone, I have no authority to go after him. And I can't go far . . . Kamarag is on his way, remember, with that fleet. So what do I do now?"

"Our original goal remains unchanged, Kirk. We must obtain indisputable proof of the true nature of Freelan, and of the Romulan plot to instigate war . . . and to do that, I must transport over to Taryn's ship and speak with him personally."

Kirk regarded Sarek, his eyes narrowing. "Slow down, Ambassador. Why would you want to transport aboard that Romulan ship? Assuming I'd allow it . . . which I won't. Beaming aboard a cloaked vessel? Something we can't even get a reliable transporter lock on? That could be suicide. And even if you survived the beaming, don't forget your destination."

"I am willing to take the risks, Captain," Sarek said gravely. "In fact, I insist upon it."

"What could you hope to gain from dropping in on Taryn?" Kirk heard the exasperation in his own voice.

"Two things, Kirk," Sarek said. "First, if I can catch Taryn without warning, he will not have time to assume his disguise. If I beamed over and recorded our interview on some type of scanning device, that would constitute the proof we seek. And, secondly, if Taryn knows that their plot is known to the Federation, he might be willing to negotiate for the lives of the Vulcans on Freelan . . . allow us to rescue those who wish to leave that world."

"Why do you think he'd do that?" Kirk asked.

"Because of something I only now realized about the esteemed liaison . . . something I should have deduced long ago. Taryn has a vested interest in saving those Vulcans."

Kirk gave Spock a "what the hell is going on?" look. The captain sighed. "All right, I grant you your point about getting your proof. But why should the Romulans care whether the Federation knows about their plan? Won't they simply proceed with it anyway?"

Spock shook his head. "Unlikely, Captain. The entire Freelan plan was dependent on secrecy and surprise . . . and on the Klingons attacking the Federation, thus diverting troops and resources, forcing Starfleet to spread its defenses too thinly. If the fleet were warned, and war with the Klingons averted, the Romulans would stand no chance against the Federation."

"Precisely," Sarek said.

"Okay, I see what you're getting at . . . but, Ambassador, I can't allow you to beam over to that vessel, proof or no proof, kidnapped Vulcans or no kidnapped Vulcans. Starfleet would bust me down to yeoman duty for risking a person of your reputation on such a stunt."

"I am willing to take the risk, Kirk," Sarek replied. "Just as you have your duty, I have mine . . . and it is to do everything in my power to prevent a war . . . or the probable slaughter of transplanted Vulcan citizens."

Kirk's eyes met Sarek's and held for a long moment. Slowly, Jim shook his head. "No," he said. "I'm sorry, Ambassador Sarek, but the answer is no. It's too risky. We can't pinpoint the location of the ship closely enough."

"Yes, we can," Spock said, suddenly. "If the ambassador can predict its next location, then I can program the transporter to lock on to the bridge before it even appears."

Kirk stared dubiously at the Vulcan officer. "Do you think he can accomplish anything over there, Spock?"

"I do not know," Spock said, quietly. "It depends upon his plan."

"Kirk," Sarek said, earnestly, "I have known Taryn for more than sixty years. I believe I can predict his actions and reactions accurately enough to be able to choose the best technique for approaching him."

"They'll shoot you on sight, Ambassador!" Kirk replied.

"Not if I am beamed onto the bridge, where Taryn can see me. He will not summarily execute me. He may decide at some point that that is what he must do, but he will let me speak, first. And if I can speak with him . . . I can negotiate. If he will not listen, and chooses to kill me . . . I am willing to take that chance."

"The ambassador does not have to go alone, Captain," Spock said, stiffly. "I am volunteering to accompany him."

You wouldn't even know they're father and son if you saw them like this, Kirk thought, inwardly shaking his head. *Vulcans!*

"Captain," Spock said, "as soon as you beam us aboard, you must use the diversion to warp far enough away to be out of jamming range. Then you must transmit the data we will relay."

Kirk hesitated, wavering. Finally, hearing an invisible clock ticking in his head, knowing that Kamarag's fleet was on the way, he nodded curtly. "All right."

The next minutes flew by in a blur as Sarek and Spock prepared the transporter coordinates that would place them aboard the Romulan vessel. Beaming would indeed be tricky: the transporter chief would have barely a second to fine-tune the location in order to make sure they arrived on the ship—and not in an area of space beside her, or beneath her.

"This recording device will function automatically," Spock told his father in the transporter room, fastening a small instrument into place between two of the large cabochon gems on the ambassador's formal robe. "It will transmit, and the *Enterprise* will record what it sends. If Taryn is indeed aboard, and you can induce him to identify himself, while showing his true features, that should constitute the proof we need."

"All right. I pick up your transmission, warp out of here, and then message Starfleet and the president," Kirk said. "Then what? I've got to come back here and intercept Kamarag. What do you want me to do about you two? Try to lock on and beam you back?"

"As soon as the message is sent, return to the rendezvous point," Sarek said. "If my talk with Taryn has been successfully concluded, I will contact you to arrange for us to return. If not . . . there is not much chance that we will be alive to be retrieved," he added, matter-of-factly.

Kirk sighed and nodded. *I hope to hell this works. . . .*

Spock and Sarek stepped up onto the transporter pads. The captain nodded at the transporter chief. "Energize."

Sarek heard the distinctive whine, felt the *Enterprise*'s transporter chamber begin to dissolve around him . . .

And then he was materializing again. He saw, with a moment of brief, intense relief that he was again surrounded by bulkheads. At his side, Spock was re-forming. They had made it. He was aboard Taryn's ship.

As he had requested, Spock had programmed their coordinates to place them on the bridge—a logical choice, since it was one of the largest, relatively open areas.

The ambassador heard gasps of shock, startled exclamations as the Romulans recognized both of them. Then, all around them, hands drew disrupters. In less than a second after they had finished beaming, Sarek found himself facing seven drawn weapons.

If I am wrong, the ambassador thought, *and Taryn is not here—or is not the man I believe him to be—neither Spock nor I will live another minute.*

But no blast of energy tore through him. Slowly, the ambassador pivoted, studying his surroundings. The bridge of a bird-of-prey was considerably more cramped than that of a Federation starship. All around him, uniformed Romulans sat before instrument consoles, their seats swiveled to face the intruders, the disrupters in their hands leveled unwaveringly.

Uniformed *Romulans?* The Ambassador stared around him in surprise. *No . . . not Romulans. At least . . . not most of them.*

Sarek was astonished to realize that the individuals surrounding him at the various command posts were *not* Romulans—they were Vulcans. He'd been expecting to find at least one Vulcan aboard Taryn's ship—but not nine of them!

But these officers were, indisputably, Vulcans.

He could tell by the faint mental vibrations they exuded. On his own world, Sarek was used to that, and, like most of his species, had learned to ignore it, overlook it, tune it out. But to encounter it here?

"What is this?" a voice barked harshly in Romulan. Despite the millennia separating their peoples, the languages of Vulcans and Romulans still held some of the same cadence and flow, though their vocabularies and syntax had mutated greatly over the years. Swiftly, the voice changed to English. "What is going on? Who are you?"

Sarek turned to regard the speaker. "You know who I am, Commander."

The individual facing him, one of the two present who was *not* holding a drawn weapon, had to be Taryn. Sarek studied him unblinkingly. Yes, this was Taryn . . . even without the insignia on his uniform, he would have known him. Everything fit. The arrogance he'd come to know so well shone in this individual's eyes. Those eyes were dark and hooded amid his craggy, hawklike features. He wore the uniform of a high-ranking Romulan officer—a wing commander.

And from him, as from many of the other officers, Sarek sensed now unshielded mental activity. It also emanated from the young woman standing beside him, her eyes wide and startled. She, alone of the bridge crew, was unarmed. Sarek nodded at both of them. "Commander Taryn," he said. "And Savel? My aide, Soran, has spoken of how much he enjoyed playing chess with you. Allow me to present my . . . associate, Captain Spock."

The ambassador had seen something flare in the girl's eyes when he'd spoken of Soran. Recalling Soran's expressed interest in her, Sarek noted her reaction and silently filed that information away for further consideration. It could prove useful. . . .

"What are you two doing here?" Taryn demanded, his voice harsh and rasping with surprise and anger he did not trouble to conceal. "How dare you," he almost sputtered, "invade my ship in this manner?"

"I recognized your game strategy, Taryn," Sarek said, attempting to make it clear that the commander was responding to that name. He only hoped that Kirk was picking up everything from the tiny recorder. "T'Nedara's gambit. A *Vulcan* gambit. I took it for a tacit invitation to call upon you." The ambassador smiled faintly. "A Vulcan gambit, Taryn . . . how appropriate, under the circumstances."

Taryn bolted up out of his seat, and for a moment Sarek knew that his life hung in the balance. The commander's hand dropped to the grip of the hand disrupter he wore. Then he took a deep breath . . . another. Forced a faint, wry smile. "Perhaps I was *too* clever, Sarek. I did not think you would recognize the coordinates as being the same pattern as the moves in our chess game."

"How could I not recognize them, Taryn?" Sarek asked simply. "That was one of the few that you won. Naturally, I would remember." Exultation surged inside him. Taryn had responded to Sarek's use of his name, and he'd made reference to their games on Freelan—which were chronicled in Sarek's diplomatic records of his negotiations with the Freelans. At last, he had the proof he had risked his life to achieve.

Leave, Kirk, the Vulcan urged, silently. *Take your starship and transmit the message. . . .*

"Why have you come here, Sarek?" Taryn asked, almost pleasantly. "You know that I cannot permit either of you to return."

"I came to negotiate for the release of the Vulcans who reside on Freelan," the ambassador replied. "The Federation has been warned. The war you attempted to instigate will not come to pass. Starfleet will be standing ready, should your forces attempt to initiate hostilities. We both know that the Romulan Empire is not prepared to take on a battle-ready Federation . . . a strong Federation that is still allied with the Vulcans." Sarek took a deep breath and glanced slowly around the bridge, at all the faces of the officers.

"And, finally," he concluded, "there will be no war with the Klingons." He spoke decisively, not allowing any of his inner doubts to show. There *could* still be war, and he knew it—but Taryn and his officers must not.

"Why not?" Savel blurted. Taryn glared at her, and she subsided immediately, but not before Sarek glimpsed relief in her eyes.

"Because Captain Kirk managed to safely rescue his nephew," Spock said, speaking for the first time since their beam-over. "And, even if Kamarag's fleet manages to destroy the *Enterprise,* Starfleet has been warned. The renegade ambassador will not get far into Federation space before he is stopped. Azetbur has proved she will not support the renegades . . . your plan has failed."

"Enough of this!" the commander snapped, his temper obviously fraying. "Why are you here, Sarek? Surely you know your life is forfeit, should I give the word. What did you hope to gain?"

"The lives of the Vulcans on Freelan," Sarek said steadily. "As I told you before. You are the wing commander for the Freelan operation. Only the praetor can countermand your orders. If you give the word, the Vulcans will be permitted to leave—those that choose to do so. The *Enterprise* will take them away from Freelan before bloodshed can occur."

"Bloodshed?" Savel glanced at the wing commander, and this time his quelling glance only made her stiffen her spine and repeat her question. "What do you mean, Ambassador?"

"Consider, Savel . . ." Spock said. "What will the praetor do with Freelan once the Federation president and Security Council know the truth about your world?"

"If he follows precedent," Sarek pointed out, "he will, as the humans put it, 'cut his losses.' Possibly abandon the colony. And certainly destroy all evidence of the plot. And the most tangible evidence of what Romulus planned are the individuals such as yourself."

"In a way, miss," Spock added, "the Vulcans on Freelan can be considered prisoners of war. The fact that you were born and grew up on that world does not change the fact that you reside there due to acts of terrorism and piracy committed by the Romulan military. Have you studied history?"

She nodded slowly.

"Then perhaps you can tell me . . . how often are prisoners of war actually *returned* to their native soil after such a long passage of time?"

"I cannot think of a single instance," Sarek said, in answer to his son's rhetorical question. The Vulcan ambassador gazed around him at the closed, hard young faces of the bridge officers. "It is far safer—and politically sounder—to kill them or allow them to die."

Savel turned to the wing commander, her dark eyes full of distress. "Would they do that, *Vadi?*" she demanded. "Would you allow that?"

"If he does nothing, that is very likely what will happen," Spock said.

"Taryn," Sarek said, his voice deepening, "if we do not take your people off Freelan, the chances are excellent that they will be considered a failed experiment— or prisoners of war—and eliminated. Will you risk a pogrom, Taryn? Will you allow your own people to be slaughtered?"

"My own people . . ." the commander repeated tonelessly. His face was expressionless, but Sarek did not miss the tension in his jaw muscles. "I do not understand what you mean."

"Certainly you do," Sarek said, holding the commander's eyes with his own. "You are as Vulcan as I . . . and as Vulcan as they are," he said, his eyes flicking from one to another of the bridge officers. He pointed to Savel. "As Vulcan as she is."

Silence fell on the bridge. Sarek glimpsed the surprise in Spock's eyes, quickly masked. One by one, the young bridge officers turned to regard their commander. Only Savel did not betray any amazement. *She knew,* Sarek thought.

Taryn shook his head, unable to summon words. The commander was pale beneath the weathering of his features. "No," he said, forcing the word out. "No!"

"Come now," Sarek said, gently. "It is illogical to deny the truth. Will you continue to deny your heritage, knowing that you risk death for the other Vulcans on Freelan?"

The young officers were recovering from the shock of Sarek's revelation. They stirred and murmured among themselves.

"Even if what you say is true, what could possibly induce me to relinquish the Vulcans on Freelan?" Taryn demanded, his expression darkening. "If I did that, I would be committing treason!"

"If you do not, you will be committing murder," Spock said quietly. "And, in a manner of speaking, genocide. Is that what you wish for them? Imprisonment and eventual death?" He indicated the officers.

"And for her?" Sarek nodded at Savel. The ambassador was impressed at how well Spock was handling his part in this—obviously, he had underestimated his son's abilities in the field of diplomacy.

"No!" Taryn cried, in what was almost a howl of pain. He smashed a fist down on the arm of his command seat, bending it visibly. "I will *not* betray my adopted people. I am *Romulan*, NOT Vulcan. I have dedicated my life to the service of the praetor! My Vulcan blood is nothing but an accident of birth—it means nothing to me!"

"Does Savel mean nothing to you?" Sarek asked, quietly. He was thinking quickly, wondering what other inducement he could offer. There was one possibility: Taryn, he knew, would not allow himself to lose face before his crew. "We have known each other for a long time," he said. "I know you, Taryn. I am willing to offer you what you want most, in exchange for the lives of the Vulcans."

"What—what do you mean?" Taryn demanded. Whatever the commander had expected, it obviously wasn't this.

"The chance to defeat me. Does that tempt you? You have wanted to win in a contest between us for decades, Taryn."

The ambassador knew he was treading a very delicate line. "One final contest, Taryn. One last chance to beat me." Sarek fixed the commander with an intent gaze. "I will wager with you for their lives. A game, Taryn. If I win, you allow them to go free, you agree to help me in any way necessary to free the Vulcan captives. If I lose . . ." The ambassador drew a deep breath. "If I lose, you will get the battle you desire. I suspect your fleet is on the way. Time, at the moment, is my enemy . . . but it is your friend. A game will take several hours. Will you gamble that your fleet will reach here before endgame?"

"A game?" Taryn actually laughed. "A *game*, Vulcan? Are you insane? We play for far higher stakes than simply a mere game! We play for lives here. Are you willing to play the game as it should be played?"

Sarek suddenly realized what Taryn was talking about, even as Spock did. His son gave him a warning glance. But the ambassador squared his shoulders. "I am willing to do whatever is necessary to gain the lives and the freedom of your captives, Taryn. I have the courage to do what I must." He paused for a long, significant second. "Do you?"

Taryn was clearly taken aback. The officer glanced around at the faces of his officers, seeing their waiting expressions.

"Old man, you surprise me," Taryn said, and then he smiled . . . a predatory, dangerous smile. "No one has ever before dared to question my courage."

Slowly, the wing commander got to his feet. Standing, he was taller and heavier-built than Sarek—and probably at least thirty years younger. "Very well, then, Ambassador. I challenge you!" His voice rang out so loudly that Savel jumped.

"I challenge you by the ancient laws and rite of the *Toriatal. T'kevaidors a skelitus dunt'ryala aikriian paselitan . . . Toriatal*," he intoned solemnly. Sarek recognized the language as Old High Vulcan. Taryn faced him, head high. "So . . . you want their lives, Sarek—then fight for them! Win their lives, or your life—and that of your son's—are forfeit!"

Sarek recognized the words. This was a challenge so old that it was still common to both the Vulcan and Romulan cultures. The *Toriatal* dated back to the days before Surak had brought his message of logic and peace to their mutual homeworld.

In the ancient days of the *Toriatal*, two warring Vulcan nations would, in a land already devastated by conflict, choose champions to represent them in battle, and agree to victory or defeat on the basis of that single-combat-to-the-death outcome. At least now the *Enterprise* would be safe from any Romulan ship in Taryn's fleet, Sarek thought. Under the terms of the *Toriatal*, a truce remained in effect until the champions had completed their fight. No Romulan vessel would initiate hostilities once he agreed to the *Toriatal*—until the battle was concluded, and either he or Taryn lay dead.

"State the terms of the challenge," Sarek said, buying time while he thought.

Was this the only way? In any kind of physical contest, Taryn would be the undisputed favorite. He was a full-blooded Vulcan, younger, stronger than the ambassador—and a soldier, in fighting condition. The odds were not good.

"Very well. If you win, Ambassador, I agree that I will release any of the Vulcans residing on Freelan should they wish to go. I will help you in whatever way is necessary to allow you to offer them that choice. I will break off the planned attack, and not initiate hostilities with the *Enterprise*. Acceptable?"

Sarek nodded. "I understand."

"And, if *I* win, Ambassador, you agree that your life—in the unlikely event you survive the challenge itself—and the life of your son are mine to do with as I please. The ship you call *Enterprise* and its crew will be fair game for my fleet, when it arrives."

The ambassador turned to look at Spock. "I am willing to wager my own life in this challenge," he said. "But I cannot ethically stake the life of my son."

"What I am staking is far greater than what you are willing to wager, as it is, Ambassador," Taryn pointed out, truthfully. "A challenge is a challenge. Do you accept, or not?" The Romulan exuded confidence as he stood there.

Sarek drew a deep breath. *The needs of the many* . . . he thought, but he could not do it. Not with the life of his son at stake. Slowly, he shook his head, and opened his mouth—

"Do it," Spock said in an undertone, without turning his head. "Accept his terms. If you do not, our lives are forfeit in any case."

Sarek glanced at the first officer, then straightened his shoulders. "Very well, Commander. I accept your challenge. I will fight you in the *Toriatal*."

"As challenger, the choice of type of combat is mine," Taryn said, a gleam of anticipation in his eyes.

"Yes."

All around him he heard murmurs of anticipation from the young officers. Only Savel seemed distressed by what was happening. Out of the corner of his eye Sarek saw her shaking her head as she whispered, "No, *Vadi!*"

Sarek wondered what kind of duel Taryn would choose. He hoped Taryn's arrogance would lead him to choose unarmed combat. The ambassador was an expert at several Vulcan martial arts, including *tal-shaya*. In unarmed hand-to-hand, he might stand a chance. Although Sarek had trained with traditional Vulcan weapons in his youth, and had become proficient with them, he had not done any sparring with weapons for years.

Also . . . if they fought without weapons, there was a good chance that neither of them would die. Sarek did not want to die—nor did he want to kill Taryn.

"I choose weapons, Ambassador," Taryn said, and paused for a beat. "Specifically, the *senapa*." The commander sat back with a faint, cold triumphant smile.

Sarek took a deep breath. The *senapa* . . . the deadliest, most painful of weapons in the ancient Vulcan arsenal. A combatant could survive one cut, or perhaps two—if he was strong and received an immediate blood filtering and transfusion—but three was almost always a death sentence. "I will prepare myself," the ambassador said.

"You will need a second," Spock said. "I offer myself, Ambassador."

Sarek turned to look at his son, and, finally nodded. "I accept."

Turning back to face Taryn, Sarek gave him the ancient, ceremonial salute. "As soon as you are ready, Commander."

Taryn nodded. "Fifteen minutes, Ambassador. Savel will guide you to the gymnasium."

In one corner of *Shardarr*'s gymnasium, Spock quickly prepared Sarek for the coming combat. Swiftly, efficiently, he stripped off the heavy, formal robe and hung it on the wall, carefully arranging the folds so the jeweled borders faced the combat square Poldar and Tonik were marking off. When his son leaned close to unfasten the ambassador's undertunic, Sarek whispered quietly, "How long will it take Kirk to send the message and return?"

"Approximately an hour, from the time we left," Spock reported, sotto voce. Then he added, "You are not in any condition to attempt this."

"I am well aware of my limitations," Sarek agreed, bleakly. "If I can hold out long enough, perhaps Kirk will return. If I am only wounded, the estimable Dr. McCoy might be able to save me."

"The closest supply of *senapa* poison antidote is on Vulcan," Spock whispered grimly. "It is hardly standard provisioning for starships. I do not like this. A duel with *senapas* . . . Taryn will have a definite advantage. He is younger, taller, and doubtless far quicker than you."

"Do not think that knowledge has escaped me," Sarek admitted, with a flare of mordant humor. "But, as the challenger, it was his right to choose the contest and the weapon to be used."

"When was the last time you trained?"

"It has been several months," Sarek admitted. "Since before . . . before your mother's illness was diagnosed."

Sarek heard his son's indrawn breath, sensed his apprehension. It echoed his own. All the commander had to do was stay out of range, and use his greater reach and faster reflexes to cut Sarek several times . . . and it would be all over. Even one cut, the ambassador reflected, would eventually slow him down . . . and, as the minutes went by, and the poison permeated his system, Sarek would grow dizzy and drop his guard, thus becoming an easy target.

When he saw Taryn walking toward the improvised challenge square, Sarek quickly rose to his feet. As was traditional, both combatants were clad only in short, loose trousers, so that most of their bodies would be bare—and thus more vulnerable to the poisoned blades.

Accompanied by Spock, Sarek walked to meet his opponent. The centurion Taryn had addressed as Poldar—another of the transplanted Vulcans—stood impassively awaiting them in the center of the combat square. In his arms rested a carved display case, and within it, in recessed niches, the two *senapas*. When he reached the middle of the square, Taryn, with a mocking salute, indicated that the ambassador should take the first choice of weapons.

Sarek studied the two *senapas*. They appeared identical; a curved, half-moon blade, wickedly sharp, with a handgrip and a padded rest for the knuckles, so they would not touch the blade. Sarek selected the weapon nearest him, grasped it, then stepped back, waiting while Taryn took the other. He hefted the *senapa* . . . it had been a long time since he'd practiced with one. It was, of course, a slashing weapon rather than a stabbing one.

Poldar motioned the two seconds, Spock and Savel, to back away from the square. Sarek took a deep breath, trying to loosen his muscles. He rolled his weight onto the balls of his feet, and assumed a balanced stance, right foot slightly ahead of the left.

"Begin," said Poldar, and Sarek was surprised to hear the centurion say the word in Vulcan. He glanced at the young Vulcan—and that nearly proved his undoing, for Taryn, moving with the silent deadliness of a *le-matya,* sprang forward. Only his son's reflexive gasp made the Vulcan leap backward, and he avoided Taryn's blade by centimeters.

Backing away cautiously, keeping one eye out for the boundary lines of the combat square (for to step over one was to lose automatically and face execution), Sarek was careful to stay near the middle of the marked-off enclosure. A square enclosure was far more dangerous than a circular one—a combatant could be trapped in a corner, and it was a rare fighter indeed who could fight his way out of that situation and remain unscathed.

The Vulcan tried a few experimental swipes with his *senapa,* getting the feel of the weapon. At one time, Sarek had been able to flip the *senapa* in the air and catch it by the handle with either hand—but that was over a hundred years ago.

Taryn had evidently been sizing his opponent up, for he came in again, low and fast, feinting to the right, then slashing quickly left. Again Sarek managed to dodge and twist, avoiding the blade by a hairbreadth. But the effort left him short of breath . . . and Taryn, seeing that, smiled.

The ambassador continued his slow circle in the center of the enclosure, watching for an opening. "Step over the line, old one," Taryn said, mockingly. "Make it easy on yourself."

"Did no one ever teach you that insulting your opponent is the mark of a coward and a bully?" Sarek asked, keeping his voice maddeningly calm.

Taryn's face twisted with anger, and he lunged again at Sarek. The ambassador sidestepped, his foot lashing out, tripping Taryn, even as he brought his unweaponed fist down on the back of his opponent's neck. With a grunt, Taryn fell forward, but he had been well trained—the commander turned the fall into a roll, and was back on his feet before Sarek could take advantage. Taryn eyed his opponent warily, and the smug, overconfident expression in his eyes had now altered to a look of respect.

Sarek began planning his next strategy—until he saw Taryn's eyes widen, and then gleam excitedly. At the same moment, he felt a faint, stinging burn along his left side, over his ribs. Looking down, he saw the thin line of green. A tiny slash— but, over time, it would be enough. The ambassador's breath hissed between his teeth. Deliberately he began circling again, hoping that Taryn would be content not to close with him for the moment.

Centering himself, the Vulcan reached inward with his sense of his physical self. Like all Vulcans, he'd been trained in biocontrol and biofeedback. The poison . . . yes, it was spreading outward from the little wound. Just a tiny amount, but it would make him sluggish, and, eventually, disable him. Concentrating fiercely, the ambassador managed to slow down his circulation, stemming the spread of the poison. It was all he could do. . . .

Tired of waiting for Sarek to succumb to the poison, Taryn attacked again, lashing out in a hard, flat arc that would have slashed the Vulcan's throat had he not ducked under it. Sarek came in close, his elbow up and out, and it struck the commander hard, not in the throat as he'd planned, but on the side of his jaw. Taryn grunted and staggered back, but when Sarek attempted to follow his advantage, the commander kicked him hard in the left patella.

Pain seared through Sarek's leg, and it nearly buckled beneath him. Somehow, the Vulcan managed to stay on his feet, but he was gasping painfully. Fire shot through his veins, and for a moment he couldn't decide whether it was from the poison, or lack of air. Blackness hovered at the edge of his vision, but several deep, gasping breaths forced it to retreat.

"You are better than I expected, Ambassador," Taryn said. Sarek was too winded to be gratified by the sweat that shone on the commander's face and chest. "But you are in no condition for this and you know it. Step out, and I guarantee you a quick, clean death with honor. Why prolong this?"

I must end this soon, Sarek thought. Then a possible strategy occurred to him, and he began shuffling toward the commander, feigning (he did not have to playact much, actually) weakness along his entire left side.

Right-handed as usual, Sarek aimed an awkward, underhand slash at Taryn's shoulder. The commander, as he'd planned, leaped to Sarek's left, closing in for the kill. Sarek pivoted away from the other's blade, and then with every ounce of control he could muster, the ambassador flipped the *senapa* into the air—

—and caught it left-handed.

Taryn was still leaning into his swing, unaware that his entire side was now a target. With a flick of his left wrist, Sarek slashed him lightly, along the ribs, once . . . and then again.

Two slashes. Enough poison to disable even a strong opponent in a matter of minutes. Dimly, Sarek heard Savel's anguished gasp. Quickly, he disengaged, stepping back, still careful not to step into one of the corners.

Feeling the sting along his ribs, Taryn checked, then stared down at himself incredulously. Slowly, he looked back up at the weapon Sarek still held left-handed. The commander chuckled faintly, hollowly. "Better and . . . better . . . old one." He was beginning to gasp. "Very well, then . . . finish me. Go . . . ahead."

"I have no desire to kill an old friend," Sarek said. "Let us declare the challenge at an end. All I want are the Vulcan youths."

"You think . . . I wish . . . them harm?" Taryn's breath came hard, now, and it was painful to hear. "No . . . I never . . ."

"I did not think you wished them harm," Sarek was quick to say. "Let us stop this now, Taryn. With a doctor's help, it is possible we both can survive. I ask you . . . as a friend . . ."

"Please, *Vadi!*" Savel cried out, unable to restrain herself.

"No!" Taryn roared, and lunged forward, slashing wildly. Sarek parried with his own *senapa,* and the brittle blades rang against each other—and shattered. Taryn gasped, his eyes rolled up in his head, and he fell.

Sarek stood staring at him, his eyes widening in distress as he saw the small streak of green crawl across the commander's knuckle. Three slashes . . . fatal, in all likelihood.

"Where is your physician?" the ambassador demanded, dropping down beside the commander's still form. "Bring the physician immediately!"

"No . . . forbid it . . ." Taryn mumbled, his eyes closed. "Poldar . . . take command . . . do whatever you must . . . to honor the outcome . . . of the challenge . . ."

"I will, Commander," the young centurion promised, bending over his dying officer.

"He might be saved!" Sarek insisted, touching Taryn's forehead, feeling the life throbbing within his body and his mind—though it was ebbing fast. "Bring the doctor!"

Poldar steadfastly shook his head. Even when Savel added her voice to the ambassador's, the young centurion stood firm, obviously determined to honor Taryn's last orders.

In a final effort to save the commander, Sarek slid both hands around Taryn's head, instinctively finding the correct points. "Make them bring a doctor," he ordered Savel and Spock, who was crouched beside him, and then he sent his mind into the commander's, melding with him, lending him strength, keeping him alive—at the risk of his own life.

The meld deepened as Sarek poured more mental energy into the dying commander. He and Taryn shared each other's minds, each other's lives. In vivid flashes, the ambassador relived events from Taryn's past. The births of his children. His wedding. His promotions. Their chess games. Political allies, and deadly enemies . . .

But all the while the other Vulcan's mind was growing weaker, weaker, forcing the ambassador to pour more and more of his own strength into this last, desperate effort. Sarek deepened the meld, and felt himself going back, back in time, to Taryn's youth . . . then his childhood. Back all the way to his earliest memory—one that, even in his dying, weakened condition, filled the commander's mind with horror and revulsion. . . .

Taryn remembered . . . and Sarek shared that memory, for they were One.

Sarek was Taryn, only his name was different—Saren—and he was four years old, aboard his parents' small trading vessel. All the Vulcans in that sector knew that ships were disappearing . . . piracy and hijackings were assumed to be the cause. Orion slavers roamed the spaceways, and the tales of rape, pillage, murder, and enslavement were rampant—and horrifying.

So when their small freighter was suddenly seized in a tractor beam, and a huge, unknown ship loomed over them, seemingly materializing out of nowhere, Taryn's parents had made a decision that seemed right to them.

In whispers, his father and mother had decided that they would fight, to the death if necessary, rather than allow themselves to be taken captive and probably enslaved. If they were not killed in the fight, they resolved to link their minds, and use their training in biocontrol to stop each other's hearts. After long minutes of discussion, they decided that they must include Taryn in their link . . . they did not want their son to suffer, and growing up as a slave seemed to them worse than not living to grow up at all.

"Saren . . ." said Mother, holding out her hand to her child, who stood wide-eyed and trembling in the doorway to the tiny control room. "Come here. Give me your hand."

"Yes, Saren," echoed Father, reaching out for his son. "Come here. Take our hands."

Instinctively, Taryn knew that if he did as they bade, he would come to harm. Trembling, he shook his head wordlessly.

"Come now, Saren," said Father impatiently. "You are letting your emotions rule. We are Vulcans . . . fear has no part in our lives. Do you wish to be a coward?"

"No . . ." little Taryn whimpered, tears beginning to trickle down his face. He hadn't cried since he was a baby, and he was profoundly ashamed of himself. He was a Vulcan, and Vulcans didn't cry! Or let themselves be afraid. But he couldn't help it.

"Saren, my son." Father's voice was stern. "Come here—now!"

The little ship shuddered as something clamped on to their airlock. Mother cried out that they must hurry—hurry! Both Vulcans removed weapons from a locker. Old-style stunners . . . little defense against phasers or disrupters.

"Saren!" Father commanded, coming toward him. "Give me your hand!"

The child's remaining control snapped, and he shrieked aloud, "No! I'm afraid!"

Sobbing with terror, Taryn turned and bolted out of the control room. It was only after he'd reached the airlock door, and it had begun its ominous turn the moment he'd touched it, that the child's terror of the unknown had overcome his fear of his parents, and what they'd decided they must do.

As the invaders pushed their way into the ship, weapons drawn, Taryn had bolted back up the corridor. He'd flung himself inside, and was immediately struck by the stun beam. Helpless, he'd lain there, unmoving, forced to watch as the invaders in their uniforms had burned down the door, shot his father with a disrupter, vaporizing him immediately, and then turned their attentions to his mother. As they'd reached for her, she'd stiffened suddenly, her eyes glazing, then crumpled in their arms, dead.

Sarek understood so much now about the commander . . . why he'd issued the challenge, why he could not abide the charge of cowardice or fear.

The ambassador knew that the commander had locked those memories away, repressed them until they haunted him only in dreams. *You were only a child,* he told the stricken commander. *A small child. You are not responsible for what happened. You could not have changed it. Know this, and let the pain go . . . let it go . . .*

Sarek sensed Taryn's understanding, sensed that the commander was finally released from the terror and guilt of that time—but his new understanding would do him little good, because, despite his best efforts, the Freelan was slipping away. Sarek clung to the meld with stubborn, dangerous persistence, clung even when he felt the change, the dissolving sensation seize his body.

Death? he wondered, dimly. *Is this death?*

But moments later, he recognized the sensation for what it was—he was caught in a transporter beam.

James T. Kirk stood in the transporter room, watching Dr. McCoy and his medical team struggle to stabilize the dying Romulan. "Tri-ox!" the doctor shouted, and a nurse slapped a hypo into his hand.

Sarek was crouched beside the Romulan, both hands pressed to his head, clearly melding with him—but, even as Kirk watched, the ambassador, who was clad only in his undergarments, suddenly slumped over onto the pad.

"They are suffering from *senapa* poisoning, Doctor," Spock said, his voice incongruously calm in the organized melee of the medical team. "It may be possible to reproduce the antidote." Grabbing a stylus from a technician, he scribbled a chemical formula and diagram. "This is it."

McCoy quickly pushed the formula at a tech, and the man hurried out to get it replicated. "What else do you know about how to treat this?" he grunted, giving Sarek a tri-ox hypo also. "It sure as hell messes up the blood's ability to carry oxygen!"

"The ancient text mentioned treating it by blood filtration and transfusions."

"Okay," McCoy said. "Set up sickbay for filtration and transfusions. Check our supply of Vulcan Q-positive blood. That's a common type, we should have some on hand."

"But . . . he's a Romulan," Kirk said. "Or do they have the same blood types?"

"I have no idea," McCoy said. "But *this* one's a Vulcan, Jim."

Spock looked over at the captain and nodded confirmation.

"All right, Spock, you're going to have to play donor for your father again," the doctor snapped. "Get ready."

"I am prepared, Doctor," the Vulcan said, removing his jacket and rolling up the sleeve of his shirt.

"Okay, I think they're stable enough to move! Get those antigrav stretchers over here, Nurse!" the doctor ordered.

The captain turned to McCoy. "Will he make it?"

"Don't know yet, Jim," McCoy grunted, his fingers flying as he injected the Romulan with a hypo. "Maybe. These Vulcans are tough . . . as well as stubborn," he added, giving Spock a sidelong glance.

Kirk watched as they loaded both unconscious Vulcans onto the stretchers and followed them into the hall. He was halfway to sickbay when Uhura's page reached him. "Captain Kirk . . . Captain Kirk, please report to the bridge immediately."

A quick slap on the nearest intercom panel brought him into contact. "This is the captain. What's going on, Commander?"

Chekov's voice responded, sounding breathless and a little scared. "Sir, I am picking up ships on our long-range sensors. Ten of them. Coming out of the Neutral Zone, and heading straight for us."

"On my way," Kirk said, and began running for the turbolift. *It never rains but it pours,* he thought grimly. *What a time for Kamarag to show up. . . .*

Ten

"Right on time," Kirk muttered to himself as he reached the bridge and glanced at the chrono. "I suppose punctuality is a must for a diplomat. . . ."

Chekov turned to regard him questioningly. "I beg your pardon, Captain?"

Kirk shook his head as he headed for his command seat. "Nothing, Mr. Chekov. Status?"

"We have picked up ten ships coming out of the Klingon Neutral Zone."

"ETA, Commander?"

"Three point six minutes, sir."

"What type?"

"I am scanning four cruisers and six birds-of-prey, sir."

Kirk's heart sank even further. Klingon cruisers were almost a match for the *Enterprise,* unlike the smaller warbirds. The captain turned over plans in his mind . . . run for it, try to stay ahead of them until reinforcements could arrive? No . . . because as soon as they crossed the Neutral Zone, they'd probably split up, in order to do the most possible damage to the maximum number of planets.

"Commander Uhura, try to hail Kamarag's ship."

"Yes, sir."

Kirk was surprised when the Klingon's ship, the *HoHwi',* accepted the contact. Moments later, the ambassador's heavy features coalesced on the screen. The moment his eyes fixed on the captain, he scowled, and his glare would have drilled neutronium. "Kirk . . ." he growled. "How dare you contact me? We have nothing to say to each other—unless you want to beg me for your life, and that of your crew. I would enjoy that sufficiently to allow you several minutes for that. . . ." At the thought, he smiled, but it was anything but a pleasant expression.

"Ambassador," the captain said, forcing himself to use his most reasonable voice, when the very sight of the Klingon made him furious, remembering how he'd agonized over Peter's disappearance, "we need to talk. There are some things I have to tell you. Break off your attack, because you're doing this as a result of alien mind influence. Ambassador Sarek is aboard, and he has proof of what I'm telling you— proof I'd be happy to let you see for yourself. I'm sure that, under the circumstances, if I explain everything to Chancellor Azetbur, she'll—"

Kamarag interrupted with a sound that was halfway between a growl and a snarl. "Kirk, you lying, cheating murderer! I know you have kidnapped my niece and are holding her prisoner. Your thrice-cursed nephew has attacked my finest officer, Karg! For this you will die in writhing agony. When I free my niece, she will perform the *be'joy'* on both Kirks, and I and my troops will wager as to which of you shrieks the loudest and longest!"

Turning his head, he addressed one of his officers. "This is an order. Target Kirk's ship to *cripple* only—do you understand? I want him alive! He is mine!"

Kirk, watching, would have found the ambassador's blustering amusing, under different circumstances. *He sounds like one of the villains in a dime novel,* he thought, sardonically.

"Ambassador Kamarag," he began, only to have the Klingon's image abruptly disappear.

"He broke contact, Captain," Uhura said, unnecessarily.

"Just as well," Kirk muttered.

"Vell," Chekov said, dourly, "I guess that is that. Ve are the only ship between them and the Federation colonies . . . so I guess ve stay put."

"We'll give them a fight," Kirk said.

Then something occurred to the captain, and he turned to Uhura. "Commander, open a wide-beam frequency to all those ships. I'm going to see if some of those other commanders aren't a little more open to reason."

"Frequency open, Captain."

Kirk took a deep breath. "This is Captain James T. Kirk of the Federation starship *Enterprise*. I believe most of you know me—as an opponent, in the past, and as a friend to your Empire in recent days. I swear to you on my honor as a Starfleet officer that you are following a man who is under the influence of alien mind control. Kamarag is no longer thinking independently. If you will break off the attack, and not intrude into Federation space, I will personally speak to Chancellor Azetbur on your behalf. Ambassador Sarek of Vulcan is aboard this vessel and he will speak for you. It is my belief, under the circumstances, that the chancellor will agree to grant clemency for any commander who breaks off the attack. I ask you to consider what you are doing—betraying your own government, to follow a madman. Kirk out."

The ships were almost within firing range. Kirk waited tensely, but none of them broke formation—the warbirds clustered together in groups of threes, with the cruisers between them and to either side.

"Well," he said, to no one in particular, "it was worth a try . . . guess we go it alone . . ."

"Captain," Uhura said, plainly startled by what she was hearing, "we're being hailed."

"By the Klingons?"

"No, sir . . . by the Romulan vessel!"

"On-screen."

The bridge crew watched as the screen flickered; then the oncoming Klingon vessels were replaced by the features of an officer in Romulan uniform. "I am Centurion Poldar," he said.

"I am Captain Kirk."

"Yes, I know. Captain, my commander's orders were to honor his word to Ambassador Sarek. I hereby place my ship at your disposal. I am prepared to fight alongside you as long as necessary." Kirk glanced at the tactical schematic, and saw that *Shardarr* had drifted over until she was behind the Federation vessel, clearly preparing to defend her from the rear.

"I appreciate your assistance, Centurion," Kirk said. "Too bad the odds aren't more even."

Poldar drew himself up. "I stand by my orders, Captain Kirk," the young officer said expressionlessly. "You will find *Shardarr* prepared for battle." He cut the connection.

"Well," Kirk muttered, "that's one for the history books. . . ."

"Stand by phasers and photon torpedoes," Kirk said. "Target the *HoHwi'*, and fire on my order."

"Aye, Captain!"

As the Klingon vessels came closer, they slowed, and spread out until they encircled the Federation and the Romulan vessel. *HoHwi'* was still the closest. There wasn't much Kirk could do about tactics; surrounded as he was, evasive action would be limited to only a few hundred thousand square kilometers of space.

His eyes fixed on the tactical screen, Kirk watched the blips, then snapped, "Fire, Mr. Chekov!"

Two deadly phaser blasts shot out, striking the Klingon vessel's shields.

"Slight damage to their forward shield, Captain," Chekov reported.

The flagship returned fire, and the *Enterprise* shuddered violently as she was struck amidships. "Port shield down twenty percent, Captain."

Oh hell, this is it, Kirk thought.

Just what I need, with a full sickbay, Leonard McCoy thought grumpily, *another damned space battle!*

The *Enterprise* shuddered violently as she was hit. Beside the doctor, on the couch where he was lying for the transfusion to his father, Spock struggled to sit up. The Vulcan had already given more blood than was good for him—he was pale and unsteady, but still determined to gain his feet.

"And where in hell do you think *you're* going, Spock?" McCoy snapped.

"The ship is obviously engaged in battle, Doctor." Spock was halfway up now, swaying like a ship in a gale. "I must report to the bridge."

McCoy gave him an evil grin and reached in his pocket for a hypo he'd prepared specially and been saving, knowing he'd probably need it. "I told you twenty-six years ago that my patients don't walk out on me during medical procedures," he said, jamming the hypospray against the Vulcan's arm. Spock sagged back onto the couch, unconscious.

The ship shuddered again. Leonard McCoy ignored the motion. He was a doctor, and he had lots of work to do. . . .

"Target *HoHwi'* with a photon torpedo and fire, Mr. Chekov!"

"Firing, Captain!"

The *Enterprise* gave a different, more internal shudder as the weapon was launched. Kirk held his breath, then pounded his fist on the arm of his chair in disappointment. At the last possible second, the Klingon vessel managed to evade the torpedo. Chekov was crestfallen. "A clean miss, Captain."

Behind them, *Shardarr* fired, catching a warbird and shearing off half a wing. "Good going, Centurion!" Kirk whispered, just as *Enterprise* shuddered again. "Forward shield down to fifty percent, Captain!" Chekov reported.

Kirk groaned inwardly. *We're going down this time. There's no way around it.* "Lieutenant, evasive—five-oh-six mark four!"

Enterprise heeled over, but the disrupter blast caught her glancingly on the saucer. The entire bridge lurched violently.

"One of the birds-of-prey is preparing to fire, Captain!" Chekov exclaimed.

But, to everyone's utter astonishment, the Klingon vessel wheeled around like a nervous horse and loosed a blast at Kamarag's ship!

"What the *hell?"* Kirk demanded.

"Captain, we're being hailed!"

"Captain Kirk? Ambassador Sarek?" A strongly accented voice came over the ship-to-ship, audio only. "This is Commander Keraz aboard *BaHwil'*. I request that you and Ambassador Sarek speak for me and my crew . . . should we by any chance survive this. I will fight with you—and we will die as true warriors, with honor!"

"Glad you could join us," Kirk said, dryly.

With a graceful dip of her painted wings, the bird-of-prey moved out of formation and joined the other two ships in the middle of the circle.

"Commander Keraz, Commander Poldar—you stay behind us, and use our shields to augment your own," Kirk instructed. "See if you can't take out a couple of those ships for me."

Both commanders signaled their assent to Kirk's plan. Moments later, the captain was rewarded with a view of *Shardarr* and *BaHwil'* moving in a corkscrew evasive pattern, firing at the warbirds on the *Enterprise*'s port and starboard sides. *BaHwil'* got lucky—or its gunner was extremely skillful. Keraz's disrupters penetrated the renegade's shields like a phaser slicing rock, and, for a moment, space lit up with a mini-nova as the bird-of-prey exploded violently.

Kirk shook his head. *This is the craziest fight I have ever been in . . . look at this! A Federation, a Klingon, and a Romulan ship, ready to duke it out with a whole squadron of Klingon renegades? I never thought I'd be fighting battles with Klingons and Romulans, instead of against them!*

Enterprise bucked like a spurred horse under another blast from *HoHwi'*.

"Aft shield down sixty percent, Captain! We can't take another hit there!"

Kirk glanced at the schematic, saw that *HoHwi'* had drifted closer to *Shardarr*. "Ship to ship, Uhura! Tight beam to *Shardarr!*"

"Aye, Captain!"

"Centurion Poldar—I want you to fire at Kamarag's ship in exactly thirty Federation Standard seconds," Kirk said, tersely. "Target coordinates seven-six-three mark nine. I know she isn't there now—but she will be! On my mark, and counting!"

Without waiting for acknowledgment from the Romulan, he turned to Chekov. "Target the flagship on its port side and fire, Mr. Chekov. Targeting coordinates seven-six-six mark two."

"Aye, Captain! Targeting . . . and firing!"

As Kirk had hoped, *HoHwi'* evaded most of their blast, swinging to port—which brought the cruiser directly into the line of *Shardarr*'s blast. Fire flared along the Klingon ship's side, and Chekov yelled, "Captain, she's lost all maneuvering power!"

"Target weapons array and fire, Mr. Chekov!"

The phasers blasted the listing ship, wiping out her weapons with one shot. The bridge crew whooped in triumph.

Three down, seven to go, Kirk thought grimly, just as one of the warbirds fired on them.

Enterprise lurched so violently that Kirk was nearly flung from his seat. Quickly, he activated his restraint system.

"Captain, we've lost our aft shield," Chekov reported. "Another hit there, and we're dead."

"Chekov, target that vessel, and fire on my order."

"Aye, Captain!"

James T. Kirk drew a deep breath, thinking that it might be his last. He opened his mouth, said, "Fi—"

—and stopped in midword.

Suddenly, the long-range scanners showed a huge fleet of ships pouring out of the Klingon Neutral Zone! Dozens of ships . . .

"Captain? We're being hailed!" Uhura's eyes were wide with amazement.

"On-screen, Commander."

A gruff, familiar voice filled the air, even as the forward viewscreen filled with well-known features. "Kirk? This is General Korrd. The chancellor tells me our *former* ambassador is giving you some trouble." The general's fleshy, squint-eyed features were wreathed in a malicious smile. Kirk noted the emphasis on the word "former."

"Well, yes, General . . . just a little trouble."

Korrd guffawed heartily at the captain's attempt at humor, which, to be frank, did not quite come off. "Get that Vulcan of yours to man the guns, then!" the general advised, genially. "He's one *Hu'tegh* fine gunner!"

Kirk glanced at the sensor array, saw that the renegade vessels were streaking off in all directions. He realized suddenly that his uniform was sticking to him, and that his face was covered with sweat.

"Kirk?" It was General Korrd again.

"Yes, General?"

"Looks like I'll have a good hunt for the next few days. Wish me success, Kirk! Korrd out."

The captain cut the connection with a grin, shaking his head.

The bridge crew looked as though they didn't know whether to laugh or cry, cheer or curse. Chekov seemed to be doing a little of everything, mostly in Russian.

"Well, I'll be damned," Kirk said, to no one in particular. "That was . . . close."

Eleven

The first thing Sarek was conscious of upon waking was that the pain from the *senapa* wound was gone . . . vanished. He did not have to exert biocontrol to repress it. The second thing the ambassador realized, as soon as he opened his eyes, was that he was in the *Enterprise*'s sickbay.

The bed he was resting in was in a secluded alcove. Glancing around, Sarek saw that his son occupied a bed across from him. Spock's eyes were closed . . . he was breathing deeply. Asleep.

Events rushed back as the ambassador stretched cautiously. The fight with Taryn . . . beaming over to the *Enterprise*. McCoy's fight to save the wing commander. The last thing Sarek remembered was being hooked up to a blood-filtration device, at the same time as Spock was readied for a massive transfusion. Spock's blood now coursed through his veins . . . Spock's blood had helped to preserve his life.

Just as it had all those years ago . . .

Slowly, the ambassador sat up, then reached for the intercom switch beside the bed. He summoned one of McCoy's nurses, and, when the man appeared, he made a request.

Minutes later, Sarek held in his hands one of the red volumes of his wife's journal. Swiftly, the Vulcan flipped through the pages, searching for a particular entry . . . and found it. . . .

December 7, 2267
  Sarek is safe . . . Dr. McCoy operated on his heart, and he will be fine—mere words cannot convey my relief. I really thought that I was going to lose him. Oh, Sarek . . . if you weren't in my life anymore, I don't know how I would go on. I would NOT want to go on. But, thankfully, I don't have to face such desolation. Something . . . the gods, fate, fortune . . . if there is a governing force to the cosmos, today It was kind.
  And today . . . for the first time in eighteen long years . . . today we were a family again. It was wonderful. I had given up hope that those two stubborn Vulcans would ever reconcile—and, yet today they were both teasing me about logic, and the glint of humor in Spock's eyes matched the one in Sarek's.
  This evening McCoy agreed to let us all have dinner in sickbay, and we ate together as a family—with an honored guest, of course. Captain Kirk is such a charmer! (And he knows it, too . . .)
  It has indeed been an eventful day. I am tired out, yet I don't want to sleep, yet. I want to savor the knowledge that we are a family again, and that my son and husband are on good terms.
  Family . . . what a lovely word. I don't think there is a better one in the entire language. . . .
  After so many years of enmity and anger . . . family. I pray that their goodwill toward each other will continue. They are both so stiff-necked, so stubborn! Neither is ever willing to admit that he was wrong . . . especially Sarek.

But today the fates were kind, and we were spared a tragedy. I wonder if I would truly have hated my son for the rest of his life if he had allowed his father to die because he felt he could not give over command of his vessel? Or would I have forgiven him eventually?

Thank heavens I will never have to find out. . . .

The entry ended there. Slowly, thoughtfully, Sarek closed the journal, struck by his wife's words, written so long ago. Amanda could almost have been describing the present situation between Spock and himself. . . .

Amanda . . . he thought, gazing across the room at his son's sleeping face. *Amanda, what should I do now?*

As it happened, Spock was *not* asleep. He lay quietly, breathing deeply, relaxed, but he was fully aware that his father was reading one of his mother's journals. As he watched surreptitiously, he saw the elder Vulcan put the slim volume down with a sigh.

The first officer thought of the events of the previous day, recalling, with a chill, Sarek's duel with Taryn. Several times, as he'd watched from the sidelines, Spock had been convinced that the ambassador was finished . . . but always, Sarek had rallied and fought back with a skill that had surprised and impressed his offspring.

Spock had never realized that his father, the diplomat, had so mastered the ancient fighting techniques. And then, as Taryn had lain there, gasping his last, Sarek had melded with him, saving the wing commander's life. The first officer repressed a surge of envy. His father had never chosen to meld with *him* . . . but he had not hesitated to join his mind with a stranger's. . . .

Glancing around the sickbay as McCoy bustled around in the next room, checking on several patients who had been injured during the *Enterprise*'s battle with Kamarag's ship, Spock experienced a strong flash of déjà vu.

The Vulcan remembered that day his mother had come to his quarters, begging him to go to his father and give Sarek the blood transfusion that would enable McCoy to operate, and thus save Sarek's life. Amanda had come to him, had begged with tears in her eyes . . . and he, Spock, had refused to go.

Because of duty.

He had told his mother that he could not, would not go to Sarek, and the reason he had given her was that duty demanded that he remain in command of the *Enterprise*. . . .

Remembering Amanda's response to his words, the Vulcan raised a hand to his cheek. For a moment he almost reexperienced the slap she had given him . . . for a moment he could almost feel the sting. Spock recalled being surprised by the strength of the blow—he'd received many in fights that hadn't matched its impact.

Duty . . . duty . . . duty . . .

The word whispered through his mind, sounding vaguely obscene when it was repeated enough times to lose all meaning. Spock glanced over at his father, remembering the way he had condemned Sarek for doing exactly what he himself had done, twenty-six years before.

I am sorry, Mother, he thought, not quite sure what he was apologizing for . . . the events of that day twenty-six years ago, or what he'd said to his father only days ago? He thought he'd grown more than his father. But had he really?

Perhaps not . . .

"Spock . . ." Sarek's voice reached him. Instantly Spock sat up and regarded the ambassador.

"I am here . . . sir," he said.

"Are you . . . well?" the elder Vulcan asked, eyeing him measuringly.

"I am," Spock said. "And you?"

"Well," Sarek said, sounding slightly surprised. "Though thirsty. And rather weak."

Spock glanced around the sickbay, saw no attendants, and, rather than buzz for one, got up himself, poured a glass of water, and took it to his father. "Here," he said, prepared to help the elder Vulcan sit up if he needed it, but Sarek was able to do so unaided.

The ambassador sipped gratefully at the cool water. "And you, my son?" he asked, putting the glass down.

"I am well," Spock said.

"The Klingon fleet?" Sarek asked.

"The *Enterprise* engaged Kamarag's ship, backed by Poldar aboard *Shardarr*." Spock raised an eyebrow. "And it seems that your old acquaintance Keraz threw in his lot with the forces of law and order. The captain was in to visit me several hours ago, and told me that Azetbur has promised the commander a full pardon."

Sarek nodded. "What of Kamarag?"

"*Enterprise* managed to cripple his ship. I gather that Kamarag did not choose to live through his defeat."

The ambassador nodded. "Loss of life is always regrettable, but . . . perhaps . . . this is one time it is better so." The elder Vulcan glanced over at the other diagnostic couch. "Commander Taryn's readings are almost normal, now," he observed.

"Yes, McCoy says he's sleeping normally. He'll be able to return to his ship within a day." Spock gazed at Sarek. "From what little I heard of what he said to you and Poldar, his experience during the duel and the mind-meld evidently . . . changed Taryn."

"He is grateful to me for saving his life," Sarek said. "But, even more, he feels that he has regained his Vulcan heritage, apparently through our mental link. I gather that his past had haunted him all his life. When he faced, with me, what he most feared . . . it lost its power over him."

"What will happen now with the Vulcans on Freelan?"

"Taryn will escort us to Freelan and authorize any of them that choose to leave aboard the *Enterprise* as free to go," the ambassador replied.

"But after the Vulcans who wish to emigrate are released," Spock ventured, after a few minutes, "what will happen to Taryn? Do you think he will come to Vulcan with the others?"

Sarek shook his head. "No," he said, and there was more than a touch of sadness in his expression. "Taryn will go back to Romulus, to face his superiors and his praetor. He has not said so, but I know his mind, now."

"But . . . if he does that, he will be executed for treason," Spock said.

"Yes," Sarek agreed, holding his son's eyes with his own. "But he believes it is his duty . . . and, after my recent actions, who am I to tell anyone not to fulfill his duty, no matter what the cost?"

The two Vulcans shared a long, unblinking look; then Spock swallowed. His voice, when he spoke, had a rough edge, like a jagged tear in dark velvet. "Father . . ." The word emerged with difficulty after all these days. "About what I said after mother's memorial service . . ." He paused, searching for words.

Grief mixed with a touch of hope flared in the ambassador's eyes. "Yes, my son?" Before Spock could continue, he raised a hand. "I must tell you that I have thought a great deal on what you said, after the memorial service. I only hope that my actions did not hasten Amanda's end. You may have been right when you accused me of going because I lacked the courage to stay, Spock. . . ."

"And I may have been wrong, Father," Spock said, forcing the words out. "I know, now, that my mother's death was inevitable. Remember, Dr. McCoy told us that she had only days. And . . . there is something else I must tell you. . . ."

"Yes?"

"When I told you that Mother could not find peace, I . . . may not have been entirely correct."

Sarek raised an eyebrow.

"I was angry," Spock said, not allowing himself to sound defensive at the admission, "and what I said, for the most part, was the truth . . . but . . . at the very end . . ." He had to stop, take a deep breath, before he could go on. "She relaxed. She even smiled. She appeared peaceful."

Sarek nodded silently, and it was a long time before the ambassador spoke. Finally he stirred. "Thank you, my son," he said softly. "Your words have meant a great deal to me."

Valdyr watched Dr. McCoy check the regenerated tissue on her wound. She had on a bizarre, blue, two-piece outfit one of the female nurses brought for her to wear until her own clothes could be cleaned and repaired. The garments were comfortable—too comfortable, she thought—but they were so *flimsy* she wasn't entirely convinced they would survive her normal activities. McCoy had discreetly lifted the top over her abdomen and was running his hand gently over the new tissue. She grimaced, peeking at it herself.

"That doesn't hurt, does it?" McCoy asked her, as he poked around.

"Of course not," Valdyr said sternly. As if any Klingon would have admitted if it did! McCoy looked at her and she could see the amusement etched on his face. He'd been so kind to her, she couldn't help but relax around him. "Well," she admitted reluctantly, "it did at first—just a little. Now, all it does is itch."

"That won't last, miss," he assured her. "Another day or so, and you won't even know anything ever happened there."

She made a face at him, and he grinned. "How can you say that when that place is all *pale* and *soft!*"

"As your own cells replace it," McCoy said, "that'll be fixed, too. We wouldn't want you looking like a patched-up battleship!" The sickbay doors whooshed open, making both of them turn to see Peter enter the exam area. The cadet looked at them quizzically, as if wondering if he'd come at a bad time. McCoy waved him over as he covered the wound. "However, I should tell you, Valdyr, human males like a little softness in a woman." He raised an eyebrow at Peter, who gave them an embarrassed smile.

"Not that one," Valdyr said confidently—and her words made Peter's face turn crimson.

The cadet glowered at her disapprovingly. "I think *you're* feeling too well," he decided.

"She's doing great," confirmed McCoy, "thanks to her amazing constitution. I take it you're here to take my favorite patient away from me?"

"Yes, sir," Peter said. Turning to Valdyr, he told her, "We've got your quarters all prepared. It's time you gave up that bed to someone who really needs it." At that moment, the doors opened, and Jim Kirk entered.

"You've had half the ship locked away in here, Bones," the captain complained good-naturedly. Eyeing Valdyr, the captain smiled and nodded. "How are you feeling?"

She nodded back reservedly. He had come to her, himself, to tell her of her uncle's death following the *Heghba'*. It had been a sign of great respect, and she'd appreciated it. He had not flinched, either, when she'd voiced the ritual howl. Valdyr was coming to think humans weren't nearly as weak as she'd been led to believe.

"We were just about to inspect Valdyr's quarters, Uncle Jim," Peter told him. "Dr. McCoy told me this morning she could be released."

Kirk nodded and turned back to Valdyr. "I'm here on official business." He looked at Valdyr meaningfully. "A little more pleasant business than the last time, thank goodness. Miss Valdyr, Chancellor Azetbur has asked to speak with you."

"With me?" Valdyr said, incredulously. "The chancellor would speak with me?"

Kirk walked over to the wall viewscreen and tapped a sequence on the control panel. A Klingon face appeared. "Tell the chancellor that Valdyr is here, ready to speak with her."

Valdyr's heart was hammering.

Suddenly, Chancellor Azetbur's image filled the screen. She looked so stern, so powerful, so impossibly noble and honorable that Valdyr simply stared, transfixed. She reminded the young Klingon woman of the portrait in her uncle's home. "Chancellor . . ." Valdyr finally managed to whisper.

Azetbur's face warmed into a gracious smile. "Valdyr! It is an honor to speak with you. And a pleasure."

Azetbur felt *honored* to meet *her?* Valdyr's gaped. "Oh, no, Chancellor. I have no honor . . . I betrayed——"

"Nonsense!" the chancellor interrupted briskly. "None of our people has more honor. You risked *everything* to save Qo'noS and our people—and you succeeded. You received an honorable wound in battle. You helped to save the honor of your family, from Kamarag's attempt to destroy it. Qo'noS will never forget your sacrifice. While you were recovering, I have spoken to the people who know you well. They have told me of your dreams for the future."

Valdyr glanced over at Peter quickly; he was smiling as he winked at her.

"I want you to know that I, personally, wish to assure you that your future will be as bright as the one you granted your people through your courage." Azetbur leaned closer to the screen, her expression softening, becoming less formal, more earnest. "You were born to be a leader, Valdyr, and I shall make sure that is what you will become. You will be trained as diplomat, under my auspices and tutelage. Our Empire needs people like you to insure her welfare. Our people are facing a time when they can no longer solve problems the way they have in the past. We need warriors who will gain our ends with *words*, not weapons. You *are* our future, Valdyr."

"Me?" Valdyr stammered, but after a second, she managed to regain her compo-

402   A.C. Crispin

sure enough to say, "Chancellor, you honor me too greatly. I do not know what to say."

"What is there to say? It is only what you deserve. Kirk has told me that his ship is currently on a vital mission to Freelan. As soon as his mission is fulfilled, when you are completely recovered, General Korrd will be sending a crew to fly the *Taj* home. He has instructions to bring you to me, so we may discuss your education, and your future, at greater length. Grow strong, Valdyr. I will see you soon." And then, abruptly, she signed off.

Valdyr just sat there, completely taken aback. She'd been resigned to giving up her life as a Klingon, to adjusting to this new life. Now . . . She looked at the men standing around her. Azetbur must have spoken to them. She turned to Peter. "You told her . . . about me?"

"I told her the truth," Peter explained. "I told her about your dreams of getting an education, about being a diplomat. . . ." He trailed off. "Isn't that what you wanted?"

That was what she'd wanted . . . *before*. Did she still want it? "But . . . if I go back to school . . ." She turned and looked at Captain Kirk. Was this his way of pulling her and Peter apart? She didn't know what to think.

"Valdyr," the captain said softly. "You're being given a wonderful opportunity. You're very young. This could shape your whole life. Think carefully before you decide."

McCoy suddenly stood in front of her. "Come on, Jim. These kids need time to talk." Nodding farewell, the two older men left.

Peter pulled himself up to sit beside her on the bed. He had said little so far.

"If . . . I do this, Pityr," she said quietly, "then . . . we must part . . . Is that what you want me to do? You want me to leave you?"

He didn't answer for a long moment; then finally he said, "Remember that talk we had, where I told you that everyone expected me to be like my uncle Jim and take the Command track, and you said . . ."

"That I was expected to marry and bear children and spend all my time scheming for their advancement. Yes, I remember."

"Well, you made that sound like a fate worse than death, Valdyr. If you pass this opportunity up . . . that's all that will be left for you to do. If you married me, and had my children, and worked to improve our lives—someday you'd wake up and realize you ended up living the very same life everyone wanted you to have on Qo'noS. And then, I think, you'd be very unhappy."

The truth of his words hit her hard. But why did her future as a diplomat require her to leave him? "Why can't our futures somehow . . . be closer together? Why must I be on Qo'noS and you on Earth? Why can't things be better than that?"

He slipped an arm around her and pulled her close to him. "I'm not sure it can't be, Valdyr. We'll have to work at it, and we'll have to be willing to suffer separations. . . . Did you know that Mr. Spock's parents are of mixed species?"

"No, I did not."

Peter nodded. "His mother was human." Then he chuckled. "And his father is a diplomat. What I'm trying to say is, that Sarek and his wife had to spend a lot of time apart, because of their work. She was a teacher, and a mother, and that kept her at home."

"I understand about Mr. Spock's parents," Valdyr said, "but what has that to do with . . ."

"Us? Well, I just mention that because they enjoyed many years of marriage, even though they spent a lot of time apart. It was a good marriage. I've been thinking about them because, well, Mr. Spock's mother just died . . . while Sarek was on this last diplomatic mission."

Valdyr was startled by that. "That was a difficult thing to do, to serve with honor while one is grieving."

"Yes, but Sarek *is* a Vulcan. My point, Valdyr, is that other people maintain relationships even when they aren't always together. Even when they have to spend large amounts of time far apart."

"You are saying, if they can do it, that we could, too?"

Peter shrugged. "I mean, if a *mere* Vulcan can maintain a relationship with a human over time and space . . . what can a Klingon accomplish?"

She rested against him. "Now I know what it is I will be missing, Pityr. I will be missing you so terribly." She felt him swallow, and knew that was one of his ways of controlling the emotions he didn't want her to see.

"We'll find a way, Valdyr," he promised her, hugging her tight. "We'll find a way to be together. We'll just have to be patient."

Smiling, she let him help her off the bed, and lead her to her quarters.

During the next two days, the *Enterprise* warped toward Freelan, accompanied through space by *Shardarr*. When they reached the fringes of the Freelan stellar system, the ships dropped out of warp. Sarek accompanied Taryn to the transporter chamber so he could reclaim his ship from Poldar.

The wing commander, having a typically strong Vulcan constitution, was fully recovered from the effects of the *senapa* poison. He had resumed his uniform. For the first time, Sarek was able to study his features freely, without either a mask of fabric or anger to conceal them. The two Vulcans stood facing each other in the transporter chamber, while the *Enterprise*'s transporter chief discreetly busied herself with duties.

"What has been the reaction to your orders to allow the Vulcans to leave, should they choose to do so?" Sarek asked.

The officer drew himself up, his expression taking on a touch of the old arrogance. "I am still wing commander. I am being obeyed," he said. "As soon as I have beamed over, I will send Savel back . . . and then any of my officers who wish to leave. The Vulcans on Freelan have been told to gather at a central point, so they may be beamed up efficiently. They will do so."

"Of course," Sarek said, with a touch of humor. "They are Vulcans. Efficiency is in their blood."

"You gave me your word that Savel will be under your personal guidance in establishing her new life," Taryn reminded the ambassador.

Sarek raised a hand formally. "I gave you my word. She will be given every opportunity and advantage it is possible for me to offer."

The wing commander relaxed slightly. "Very well, then. I must go. If you will wait for Savel, she will not be long."

"Taryn . . ." Sarek began, and the officer, who had begun to turn away, turned back. "Come with us," the ambassador said, aware of a note of entreaty in his voice he did not entirely trouble to repress. "Your people will need leadership, you are correct in that. You could provide that leadership yourself. And . . ." The ambassador's mouth quirked upward slightly. "And we could play chess. . . ."

A slight smile touched the wing commander's grim mouth. "And have you continue to beat me? I think not. It is my duty to take *Shardarr* back to Romulus, and to face the praetor with what I have done."

"But you know what will happen."

"Of course," Taryn said. "But this is what I must do, Sarek. I am a Romulan officer. I have lived as a Romulan . . . and I will die as one."

Sarek sighed. "I was not expecting anything else," he said. "But I had to ask. . . ."

Taryn nodded curtly, then stepped up on the transporter pad. Again that faint smile touched his mouth, as he lifted his hand, and, with a slight grimace, spread his fingers into the Vulcan salute. "Peace and long life, Sarek," he said, quietly—

—just as the transporter beam took him.

Minutes later, Savel and Taryn stood together in *Shardarr*'s transporter room. The young Vulcan woman's features were composed, but her voice trembled uncontrollably. "I do not want to leave you, *Vadi!* Let me go back with you to Romulus. Perhaps I can bear witness for you, and they will understand."

Commander Taryn smiled faintly. "Understand? The praetor? Why, Savel, I never knew you to make jokes before. . . ."

"But . . ." She was trembling, thinking of what would happen to him back on Romulus. "Please, *Vadi!*"

"Savel," he said, chidingly, "remember your control. You are a Vulcan, and under Ambassador Sarek's guidance. He has promised me that he will sponsor you, until you are ready to take your place on your rightful world. You must look to the future."

"*You* are a Vulcan, too," she said, an edge in her voice that betrayed her anguish at parting from him. "Come with us. . . ."

He was already shaking his head. Taryn drew himself up proudly. "I am a Romulan," he corrected her. "And I must take *Shardarr* back to Romulus and make my final report."

A number of the young Vulcan bridge officers were already aboard the *Enterprise*, and were leaving with the Federation vessel . . . but a surprising number of the senior officers—including Centurion Poldar—had announced their decision to accompany Taryn on their last voyage home.

"Besides," the commander added, "the ambassador will need help to gain the trust of the Vulcans who have chosen to go home to their native world. They will need a leader. You have the strength to guide them, Savel."

"What will happen to the others?" she wondered. At least fifty of the Vulcans, mostly those who had married into Romulan families, had chosen to stay.

"They will have to go underground, to live as Romulans for the rest of their lives." He sighed. "The Plan has failed. I would not be surprised if the praetor decides to evacuate Freelan entirely. The repercussions of the failure of the Plan will echo through the Empire for many years . . . perhaps decades."

"What will the praetor do?" Savel asked.

"What we Romulans always do in the face of adversity . . . pull back, regroup, wait. The Empire is patient, Savel. That is why it has endured so long. The Empire will wait, and plan . . . until it is time to try again."

"If only there could be peace," she whispered.

He raised an ironic eyebrow. "If only there could be," he echoed. "But not today, I fear." He glanced up at the waiting transporter technician. "Come, it is time."

Savel straightened her shoulders and nodded, her features calm . . . though her eyes were full of anguish. With her bag of personal belongings in hand, she slowly took her place on the transporter pad. Taryn gave her a Romulan salute. "Farewell, *Vadia-lya.*"

Squaring her shoulders, Savel hesitantly lifted her hand, spreading her fingers apart as she had seen Sarek do. "Peace, *Vadi* . . . peace and—" She broke off. To say "long life" under these circumstances was ridiculous. "Farewell," she said, instead.

Just as the beam of the transporter began to whine, Savel saw him smile at her fondly. "Give my regards to Soran," he said, just before she winked out of existence.

Wing Commander Taryn took a deep breath, squared his own shoulders, and left the transporter room without a backward glance.

Peter Kirk and Valdyr stood together in the *Enterprise*'s docking bay, at the foot of *Taj*'s gangplank, to say their farewells. They did not embrace, because there were three Klingon officers in the doorway, eyeing them interestedly. Peter smiled unsteadily at the young Klingon woman. "You'll get home days ahead of me," he reminded her. "Uncle Jim finally introduced me to Ambassador Sarek and he said he would grant us access to the diplomatic commnet. I expect to find a communiqué waiting when I get back to Earth. I want to hear all about your schooling, Valdyr. I want to know everything that happens to you, until we can see each other again. Promise me."

She nodded in turn. "On my honor, I will. You must do the same."

"On my honor, I will."

She gave him a faint smile. "Then . . . I wish you safe voyage back to your world. I know you will pass your warrior's test with honor, Pityr. You have already faced far worse. . . ."

"Yes, but then I had you to help me be strong," he said, and for a moment felt his control slipping. "Farewell Valdyr-oy. Safe voyage. Until we meet again. May it be soon. . . ."

"Farewell, Pityr-oy. We will *make* it be soon," she replied fiercely, giving him a warrior's closed-fist salute.

As he watched, she turned and ran up the gangplank. The last glimpse he had of her was the gleam of her armor, and a final toss of her long braid.

Hearing over the intercom that the bay was about to depressurize, Peter hastily left, without looking back. . . .

Twelve

Sarek sat on the divan in the small VIP cabin aboard the Earth-bound *Enterprise*, Amanda's journal open in his lap. The ambassador was rereading the entry his wife had made on the day that the news of her father-in-law's death had reached her.

April 5, 2249

I just received a communiqué from T'Pau, telling me that Solkar died yesterday. He was the last surviving member of Sarek's immediate blood-kin—except, of course, for Spock . . . whom Sarek has declared vrekasht.

I find myself thinking about how lonely Sarek must be. Of course, after what he did, he deserves to be alone . . . but time, I am discovering, has a way of putting things in perspective.

This past year, as I look back on it, has, in a way, been a good one. It was a thrill to go back to teaching, and, because of my celebrity (notoriety?), I've been given the best and brightest that Earth had to offer. My students have been wonderful—watching them grow and expand their horizons has been so rewarding.

Also, living here in San Francisco while Spock attends Starfleet Academy has been a good opportunity to renew closeness with my son.

It was also good to spend time with Mom and Dad . . . Aunt Matilda passed away this year, and she was younger than Dad . . . it made me realize, for the first time, that my parents will not go on forever. Neither will I, come to think of it.

Neither will Sarek.

It's funny how death puts things in perspective. I think . . . I think it's time to go home to Vulcan. Spock will soon, as second-year cadet, be going off on training missions. He has made the admittedly difficult adjustment to living in close quarters with so many human students, and he is finally beginning to make a few friends.

He doesn't need me here anymore . . . he needs the company of people his own age, cadets who are learning the things he is learning.

And, of course, there is the thought of Sarek, alone. When I asked T'Pau, rather hesitantly, how Sarek was these days, she stared straight at me, her imperious expression unchanged—but her words, uttered in her slightly lisping, accented speech, surprised me. "Thee asks how Sarek is, Amanda? In all this year of exile from thy homeworld, thee hast never asked. Why now?"

"I ask because I know how Sarek would grieve for his father, T'Pau," I said, regarding her steadily. "I am . . . concerned about his welfare."

Her black eyes blinked at me, from out of her bony, once-beautiful features. "Thee is right, Amanda. Sarek grieves for Solkar . . . but he grieves a hundredfold more for thee."

Her bluntness startled me. "Really?" I murmured, unable to think what to say, trying to repress the stab of anguish her words brought.

T'Pau paused, then stared straight at me. "Wilt thee attend Solkar's me-

morial service, Amanda? If thee tells me thee wishes to attend, I will delay the service until thee can come home."

Home. She said "home" in referring to Vulcan. T'Pau said that, to me . . . an off-worlder. My breath caught in my throat as I remembered so much . . . the beauty, the desolation, the heat . . . Sarek's arms around me, the closeness of our bodies no more intimate than that of the bond we share . . .

For the first time in a year, I allowed myself to sense Sarek's mind through the bond. It was always there, of course, in the back of my mind—I'd have known if anything had happened to him. But I've been too angry to let myself touch his mind. And, of course, I'm not a telepath, so my ability is limited. . . .

But I sensed him. And what I sensed made tears stream down my face.

She didn't even avert her eyes from the sight of so much rampant emotionalism when I wept. When I managed to regain my control, she said, only, "Wilt thee come home, Amanda?"

I nodded at her, and she gave me the date, location, and time of the service, then cut the connection.

So now . . . I must pack, and board the transport. I have only a few hours to finish, so I can't spend any more time on this journal until I'm bound for Vulcan.

Sarek, I am coming back to you. I have learned a great deal this past year, and one of the things I have learned is that in punishing you, I was punishing myself just as much. It is no longer worth it.

If I know you—and I do—you won't ever bring up the subject of my self-imposed exile from you and Vulcan. You'll simply want to go back to the way things were—except that our son will not be part of our family anymore, as far as you're concerned.

Can I live with that? Yes, I believe I can. You see, if I can forgive you, then I have to believe that you and Spock will, someday, forgive each other.

I must hurry . . . time and that transport won't wait. . . .

Sarek closed the volume and sighed. It was painful to read those words . . . to think of the time they had spent apart, and of how he would give up nearly everything he possessed to regain that lost year. Putting that volume aside, he picked up the next, then located the spot where he'd left off the night before. Noting the date on the next entry, the ambassador steeled himself to read what she had written.

March 14, 2285

No entry for three days . . . I can scarcely see to write this . . . I am so tired that I ache all over, but every time I lie down and close my eyes, the images I see are too awful to bear. So, after dozing for the first time in days, I am awake barely an hour later, writing . . . because doing nothing is even worse.

Is there a God? If there is a Supreme Being, how could he, she, it, or they allow this to happen?

My son is dead. Spock is . . . dead. Writing those words . . . I am trembling, shaking, and my heart feels as though some giant is squeezing it in an inexorable fist. Spock, dead? It seems impossible. I keep thinking there has been some mistake, that Starfleet will call us and tell us it isn't true. How *can it be true? Spock is—oh God, was—half-Vulcan! I expected him to out-live me for decades! Why did this have to happen, why? My child, dead? How could this happen?*

Of course I know how it happened. Even in the midst of my own anguish I could find it in my heart to pity poor Jim Kirk . . . he tried so hard to break it gently. Spock was his best friend, they were so close, serving together all these years. I could tell that the captain had been crying too. . . .

Sarek did not cry, of course. I found myself, for a moment, hating him for that. As though his lack of human tears meant that he did not care for Spock . . . when I know that he did care, that our son was the most important person in the galaxy to him . . . except, possibly, for me. I stared at him, the tears welling up and coursing down my face, sobs racking me until it seemed that my body could not hold them—and I came so close to lashing out at him. For a horrible instant I wanted to slap him, scream at him, and demand that he weep for our son. . . .

I am thankful that I did not. I would never have forgiven myself. That would have made an intolerable situation even worse.

Sarek takes comfort in the fact that Spock died well, in the performance of his duty, sacrificing himself to save his shipmates. A hero, to use the human term . . . a word which does not translate into modern Vulcan.

But there is no comfort for me. Last night I clutched myself, rocking back and forth, feeling as though I might explode with sorrow. Sarek came and sat beside me, trying to comfort me with his presence. He rested his hand on mine, silently, and when he finally spoke, it was only to say the traditional words . . . "My wife, I grieve with thee. . . ."

I know he does. But I feel that a mother's love is stronger, and thus her grief is also greater. Illogical, perhaps . . . but true, I know it.

Spock, my son . . . if only you had died on Vulcan! Then you would not be lost to us forever. At least your living spirit, your katra, could have been saved, could have been placed in the Hall of Ancient Thought. If only—

Abruptly, the precise, elegant handwriting broke off. Sarek knew why. Vividly, he remembered the afternoon his wife had burst into his study, her reddened eyes wide and wild. . . .

"Sarek!" Amanda's normally cultured, lovely voice shattered like fine crystal in the stillness. "What about Spock's *katra?* It wouldn't have died with his body, if he found someone to entrust it to . . . his living spirit could still be found!"

Sarek turned from his computer terminal to see his wife standing in the doorway, clutching it with both hands, as though she might fall without the support. She was wearing a dressing gown pulled carelessly over her nightdress, and her hair was mussed, in contrast to her usual impeccable grooming.

Amanda's eyes flashed with incredulous hope as she continued, breathlessly, "From what James Kirk told us, our son *knew* his actions would kill him—so he would certainly have established the mental link necessary to entrust his *katra* when he died! Spock was a good telepath—he could have done it very quickly."

"But Kirk did not mention—" Sarek began, reasonably.

"Kirk's *human!*" Amanda burst out. "He may not even know what he holds in his mind! Most humans wouldn't—oh, Sarek, if there's even a chance—" She gazed at her husband pleadingly. "—even a small chance, we can't afford to ignore it! We're talking about our son's living spirit—what humans would call a soul, I suppose. We can't let him be lost forever!"

Sarek stared at her, his mind turning over what she had said. "Your deduction is most unlikely, Amanda," he said at last, his tones gentle. "From the scenario that Kirk described, the ship was in great peril, in imminent danger of destruction. Spock could hardly have found time to meld with Kirk before he went down to the engine room."

"It doesn't take a full meld, and you know it, Sarek," she insisted, her blue eyes flashing stubbornly. "Our son was a trained telepath, he'd melded with Kirk many times. He could have established the link that would make Kirk his Keeper in a bare instant!"

Sarek experienced a flare of hope. Amanda was quick to notice the tiny change in his expression. "You must go to Earth and see Kirk, my husband," she said formally. "You will be able to tell whether Kirk holds our son's essence in his mind. Go, Sarek. Spock *would* have found a way! I know it!"

The ambassador stood up, crossed the room to stand beside his wife. Slowly, formally, he held out two fingers, and she returned the gesture. They stood together, their mutual grief flowing between them, both gaining strength from their closeness. Through their bond, Sarek shared some of Amanda's hope that their child was not totally lost, and it slowly, gradually, became his own hope.

Finally, Sarek nodded. "I will go to Earth, Amanda," he promised. "I will speak with Kirk in person. If necessary, I will touch his mind, and discover whether he is unconsciously Keeping our son's living spirit."

Amanda smiled at him gratefully. "Thank you, Sarek," she said, softly. "Thank you, my husband. Spock would have found a way . . . I know it. My son is not completely gone . . . if he were, I think I would know. You must find him, Sarek. . . ."

"If he is to be found, I will do so," Sarek said, his tone as grave and earnest as if he took a solemn oath. "I will bring his living spirit back to Vulcan . . . so he may be at peace."

Sarek looked up from the journal and sighed, remembering what had followed. His son was alive today because of Amanda's unwavering faith that he was not truly—not *completely*—lost to them.

I must give these journals to Spock, allow him to read them when I am finished, he thought. *My son deserves to gain the insight into his mother's mind that they have given me. . . . Despite the bond we shared for so many years, there are things about Amanda that I never knew until now. . . .*

If only his wife were still alive. If only he could express aloud, for once, the emotions he had allowed only to surface in the silent privacy of their bond. It would have meant so much to her to have heard him say it out loud . . . just once.

But she was dead. Amanda was dead.

Dead . . . and nothing could change that. Amanda, unlike a Vulcan woman, had no future . . . at least, no future that was perceivable or verifiable. As a human, she had not possessed a *katra* . . . so nothing could be placed in the Hall of Ancient Thought, to linger until it was ready to go on to whatever lay next.

If Amanda had been Vulcan . . . if Kadura had not been taken hostage . . . Sarek could have been the Keeper of her *katra* . . . her living spirit could have resided within him until it was released into the energy nexus of the Hall of Ancient Thought.

If Amanda had been Vulcan, her husband and son could have gone to that ancient citadel, stood within its confines and gained a sense of her presence. By the time his wife's *katra* was ready to depart, Sarek would have been prepared, would have had ample time to bid her farewell. Had his wife been Vulcan, her death would not have meant such an abrupt and shocking end, a complete and utter severing of their bond. Even if he had been on Kadura, Spock could have been her Keeper....

But Amanda *had* been human, and the ambassador had never, until a few weeks ago, wished it otherwise. But when he'd learned that she was ill, Sarek had been forcibly reminded of something he'd determinedly managed to forget . . . that his wife was almost certain to predecease him by years . . . probably decades.

The ambassador sighed aloud, thinking that if Amanda had been Vulcan her *katra* would probably now be residing within him—or within Spock. She would, in a sense, still be alive....

But if Amanda had been Vulcan, she would not have been Amanda....

Sarek sighed, and his eyes returned to the volume on his lap. He began reading again, finished that one, and, with a sense of deep regret, picked up the last of the red-bound books. Opening this one, he paged through it, saw that it was only a third filled. He took a deep, painful breath, and determinedly began to read.

The last brief series of entries made him sit up straighter, his eyes moving quickly over the page. When he finished them, he went back and read them again, slowly. He could almost hear her voice....

September 17, 2293

Frankly, I am worried about Sarek. The days since I have been diagnosed have been a great strain, far worse for him than for me. After all, he bears the burden of not allowing me to glimpse his fear for me . . . of not letting me sense his pain. The only comfort I can offer is to let him think that I remain unaware of his inner turmoil, so that is what I do....

September 18, 2293

Sarek left today to negotiate for the release of Kadura, a planet taken by Klingon renegades. The president asked him personally to handle the negotiations, and he had to accept. It is his job, his duty to use his skills for the benefit of others, and I understand that. He is the best in the galaxy at what he does, and I know that. I am proud of him.

Which doesn't mean that I don't miss him, and wish he had stayed here with me. I miss him more with each passing hour. You would think I would be used to his absences by now, but this time . . . I am not a saint . . . I am facing something that frightens me, and I wish he were here to help me face it. But I am strong. I can manage by myself . . . I always have, whenever it was necessary.

Besides, there is still our bond. I miss his presence in the back of my mind, but there is still a small sense of him remaining. Since I am not telepathic, it is faint . . . but, in a sense, he is always with me.

Will I ever see him again?

I fear not.

Something about the way I feel . . . Spock mentioned a sensation of "shutting down," when we spoke about dying. Is that what I am feeling?

Difficult to keep my thoughts organized enough to write. Hard to concentrate . . . so tired.

LATER
Spock . . . I am worried about him. His eyes are haunted, his mouth a knife-thin slash. Beyond his worry for me, his constant concern and grief, I can sense his anger. . . .

Anger at death, perhaps. Anger at age, at the cruel fate that is turning his mother into a shriveled, feeble stranger. Normal emotions—except that my son is a Vulcan. But I have sensed more barely masked emotion from Spock since his father left today than I have since he was a small child. They say everyone has a weak point—and apparently I am Spock's.

Spock's main anger . . . is directed at his father.

How can I help him learn to understand, and accept and forgive—as I have learned to do over the past decades? How can I help Spock, when I will not be here much longer?

Tired now . . .

September 19, 2293
So glad that I made Sarek promise to read these journals. Comforting to know that he will understand, someday, what I was thinking, feeling, here at the end. Will I be here tomorrow? I sit here in my bedroom and gaze around me at my beloved things . . . and I am at peace, finally. If only Spock could share my acceptance.

If only I had the strength to explain Sarek to my son. Spock cannot forgive his father for leaving me, but it's not that he doesn't love me, not that at all. Spock is half-Vulcan, raised to be Vulcan . . . why can't he understand?

What a reversal . . . usually it is Spock who has to explain Vulcan behavior to me. Never forget that time in his quarters aboard Enterprise when Sarek was dying. I slapped him, slapped my son. The crack of that blow still rings in my ears. Only time I ever struck him in his life. Oh, Spock . . . you understood then! Why can't you understand now?

Don't hate your father.

Love him, as I do. Understand him, as I do.

Sarek . . . you are reading this. I know you are. Show Spock this entry, even if you don't choose to let him see the others. Show him. Perhaps it will help . . .

So much still to do, to say. Wish I could visit my garden again. My favorite place . . .

Sarek, remember that, afterward. My garden. I want to be in my garden, afterward.

More to write, but tired . . . so tired.

Sarek . . . I can still sense you . . . in the back of my mind. If only I could touch you, see your face . . . just once more . . .

Peter Kirk stood before the closed bridge doors and found himself clenching his fists. *Relax,* he ordered himself, but his body refused to listen. *What's the big deal? It's only your first command!* He took a deep breath, let it out slowly, and moved forward just far enough to activate the doors. They opened with a familiar whoosh.

The minute he stepped onto the bridge, the crew came to attention, but Peter barely noticed them as more than shadowy shapes, he was so keyed up. This was it. The moment of truth. He walked forward, trying to conceal his tension.

The bridge seemed dimmer than he was used to. "As you were," he ordered the crew, trying to sound normal, even cavalier as he approached the captain's chair. *The captain's chair. Your chair.* Even now he was still amazed that he was here. That he was finally in command of the *Enterprise*. He'd thought the commandant was joking when he'd told him. His first command. The *Enterprise*. He eased himself in the command seat, and touched the armrest console almost reverently.

"Present location, navigator?" he asked.

"Sector 3414, approaching the Loop Nebula, Captain," a familiar voice replied.

Peter's head snapped up. For the first time, he really *looked* at the crew. He'd known he'd be working with senior officers, of course, but . . . "Commander Chekov," he said quietly. "I didn't expect to see you here."

"Vell, sir," Chekov replied with a saucy grin, "ve vere just in the neighborhood. . . ."

Peter blinked, and looked around him. Lieutenant s'Bysh sat at the helm, by Chekov's side. A glance to his left showed Commander Uhura fussing with her communications board. She nodded at him when she noticed him watching her.

He stiffened in surprise when the seat before the Life Sciences and Support station revolved, revealing Dr. McCoy. The doctor's expression was one of sheer delight, as he reported, "Life-support operating at peak efficiency, sir, and sickbay's fully staffed and *ready for action."*

"Thank you, Doctor," Peter said blandly, in spite of the bead of sweat he suddenly felt tracking down his face. He didn't want to look over at the science station, but he had to. "First Officer, anything to report?"

"Not at this time, sir," Spock's familiar, placid baritone replied.

So, it was old home week, huh? He shook his head. Either that or it was a dream he'd wake up from . . . but that wasn't bloody likely.

Most of the cadets "fortunate" enough to make it to the *Kobayashi Maru* had to contend with a bridge crew of half cadets and half experienced officers. It wasn't unusual for a well-known visiting ship's crew to offer to man the simulator, but Peter had never heard of anyone taking the test with the entire bridge crew from a *Constellation*-class starship! Usually, there were other cadets being tested, not just the command officer, but Peter was so late taking his test, there were no longer any cadets left to be part of his crew. The experienced bridge crew's job was to "push" the captain, see if he or she had the confidence to override their experience and advice. But to have *this* crew . . . ?

Maybe he could lodge a protest with the exam board. *Yeah. After I finish the test!* There was no getting out of it. He glanced around the bridge once more. Uncle Jim was nowhere to be found—at least he could be thankful for that. He licked his lips.

Hell, it's just a test. It can't be half as bad as flying through the ring around Qo'noS, or escaping from Kamarag's prison! Then why was he so nervous? He could feel Spock's unwavering gaze searing the back of his head.

Suddenly, Uhura sat up straight. "Incoming transmission, sir. It's . . . garbled. . . ."

"Put it on speakers, Lieutenant," he ordered, swiveling his chair.

"Enterprise, can you hear me? This is the *Kobayashi Maru,"* a heavily accented Slavic voice reported. Peter strained to hear the woman, but the broadcast was dim and full of static.

"Can't you boost that, Commander?" he asked.

Uhura shook her head. "That *is* boosted, sir. That transmission is coming straight through the Loop Nebula, sir. It's a miracle we can hear it at all." She frowned, concentrating intensely, and manipulated her board.

"We have suffered a rupture in our matter-antimatter containment field," the woman on the *Kobayashi Maru* continued. "We have had severe damage to our life-support system. We've ejected our fuel to keep the ship intact, but we're down to batteries now."

"Kobayashi Maru." Uhura shouted, "what are your coordinates?"

The transmission grew even fainter, and Peter strained to hear it. "Coordinates 3417, mark 6. We are five hundred thousand kilometers away from the Cygnus Loop Nebula, and drifting. Battery power can maintain life-support for one hour . . . repeat . . . one hour. If we don't get help soon, three hundred sixty-two lives will be lost. *Enterprise,* can you hear me? We have one hour or less . . ." The voice broke up into garbled static.

"Mr. Chekov, can you bring up schematics on the location of *Kobayashi Maru?"* Peter asked.

"Aye, sir," Chekov replied, and within seconds a graphic image appeared on the big viewscreen.

The viewscreen before him showed *Enterprise* currently moving toward a huge nebula, a massive cloud of gas and dust, in colors of hazy blue, white, and pink. On the other side of the nebula, if the coordinates they had given were correct, the dying freighter, *Kobayashi Maru,* was drifting.

Peter frowned. So far, the rumors had been correct. This *was* a new scenario. With the exception of the familiar, damaged vessel, most of what was happening had been changed. For example, he now had to rescue the people on the ship, not simply the ship itself. Once they were aboard—assuming he got that far, which was highly unlikely—*then* he'd worry about how to put a tractor beam on the vessel herself. Could he tow her?

Peter forced himself to consider the big picture. "Mr. Chekov," Peter said crisply, "where are we in relation to the Klingon Neutral Zone?"

Chekov's hands moved over his board, and the viewscreen presented an image of the Neutral Zone in relation to the injured ship. "Three parsecs," Chekov reported, "sir."

If they didn't have to go *into* the Neutral Zone, then what . . . ? Never mind, the *Maru* didn't have much time. "Mr. Chekov, plot us fastest optimal course, skirting the nebula as closely as we can without encountering interference. ETA to intercept?"

Chekov acknowledged the order, did some quick calculations, then finally reported. "We can circle the nebula around its smallest side, and arrive at *Kobayashi Maru* in fifteen minutes, sir. Optimal speed this close to the nebula . . . warp two."

"If I might suggest, Captain," Spock interjected, "we could reduce that time by ten point eighteen minutes by going *through* the nebula at warp one."

Peter looked back at the colorful schematic. That was true, but why did that make him uneasy?

"We are the only ship in this quadrant, sir," Spock continued. "And, as you yourself confirmed, we are a safe distance from the Klingon Neutral Zone. Going through the nebula would seem to be the most efficient course of action."

Peter set his jaw. "All of that is true, Mr. Spock, but going through the nebula leaves us blind, deaf, dumb, and helpless. We can't even engage our shields in there. When we come out the other side there would be several seconds before we became reoriented." He smiled at the Vulcan. "For some reason, that makes me uneasy," he added, dryly.

"Lieutenant s'Bysh." He swung his chair back around. "Take us around the nebula using Mr. Chekov's suggested course. Warp two."

He turned to address his first officer. "Mr. Spock, I want you to send a buoy with a long-range sensor scan in it *through* the nebula, that can send us back information on the conditions on the other side of the nebula, before we arrive there. It'll stay ahead of us and help us pinpoint the *Maru*, or warn us of any *other* possible problems before we stumble into them."

Spock reported the firing of the sensor buoy. Then, Peter slapped the console. "Engineering!"

"Aye, sir!" a thick Scottish burr responded.

Why am I not surprised to hear you? "Scotty, we're going to need to beam over more than three hundred people in less than thirty minutes. . . ."

"It isna possible, Captain! If we used every transporter in the bloody ship it wouldn't . . ."

"The cargo transporters, Mr. Scott. Can't they be adjusted to transport people?"

"Aye, sir, but—" Scott began hesitantly.

"Use all the cargo bays, and get everyone you've got on this. We need to be able to get those people on board fast, and from long range. There's a cranky matter-antimatter pod floating somewhere around this area, so we're not going to be able to get too close. We'll be on site in ten minutes."

"Ten minutes!" the Scotsman protested. "But, Captain . . . !"

"You're running out of time, Mr. Scott!"

"Halfway around the rim of the nebula, sir," Chekov reported dutifully.

"Anything new from the *Maru*, Uhura?" Peter asked.

"I can't raise them, sir," she informed him.

"Long-range scanning, Mr. Chekov. Any signs of enemy ships out there?" Peter found himself twitching in the chair.

Chekov shrugged, totally unconcerned. "Nothing, sir. But there have been no reports of hostile activity in this region."

"Is that right?" he murmured. This was wrong, all wrong. Where were the damned Klingons? Where was the enemy? This was too *easy*. He realized his mouth was dry. "Mr. Spock, are we getting any reports from that buoy?"

"Yes, sir, data coming in now."

"Put it on the screen." A new image came up, one that did not have the nebula. The nebula would be behind the buoy, so it would be offscreen. Before the buoy hung nothing but the blackness of space, and the twinkling of far distant stars. And in the foreground, but still at a distance, the crew could see a damaged ship, drifting aimlessly. Dangerously close to it remained the matter-antimatter pod. He'd have to make Scotty transport those people from the farthest reach of transporter range. *Oh, damn, damn, damn . . . this is too easy.*

He blinked, staring at the viewscreen so hard his eyes burned.

"Approaching the other side of the nebula, sir," Chekov said quietly.

"Course and speed, Captain?" s'Bysh asked.

Peter's head jerked up, and he stared at the innocent-looking viewscreen. "Lieutenant Uhura, any word from the *Kobayashi Maru*?"

"Nothing, sir," she reported. "I keep hailing, but . . ."

"We're past the nebula, they should be able to respond," Peter said to himself.

"Unless their accident has destroyed their communications abilities," Spock suggested. "Shall we increase speed, Captain? We are still only traveling at warp two. . . ."

Peter cut him off with a quick chop of his hand. "Helm, full stop."

s'Bysh hesitated, and Peter shot her a look.

"Full stop, aye," she repeated, and obeyed.

"Captain!" McCoy snapped. "We're runnin' out of time! Those people are breathin' away the last of their air!"

"Those people," Peter informed his crew tightly, "are sitting in the middle of a trap. Mr. Chekov, what is our position relative to the Romulan Neutral Zone?"

"Ve are just outside it, sir."

Oho! They almost got me there. If I'd gone straight in, I'd have been over the Neutral Zone before I knew it. Nudging Chekov over, Peter tapped in a sequence on his board. A scrolling line of data ran down the side of the viewscreen for the crew to see. "Check out those readings. There are five anomalies surrounding the *Maru*, and each of those anomalies possesses a specific energy signature—a sure sign of cloaked vessels."

The cadet took a deep breath. "The *Kobayashi Maru* is being used as the bait in an elaborate trap. Yellow alert, everyone." He turned to Spock. The Vulcan was clearly surprised by Peter's announcement and was double-checking the readings. "They're there, aren't they, Mr. Spock?"

Amazingly, Spock hesitated. "Data does seem to show certain anomalies. . . ." He trailed off, and continued to check his viewscreen.

McCoy came barreling out of his chair. "Well, what are we gonna do about those people? You can't just leave 'em there, Captain!"

"I have no intention of abandoning those people, Dr. McCoy," Peter assured him, even as he began to unbutton his uniform jacket.

"Captain, what is it that makes you think these anomalies are the readings of cloaked *Romulan* vessels?" Spock asked.

Peter finished removing his jacket and draped it over the command chair. "Well, since we're on the edge of the Romulan Neutral Zone, and we're currently waging *peace* with the Klingons, my guess is those cloaked vessels are Romulan cruisers . . . from the size of them. Call it a 'gut feeling,' Spock, but we're about to test it out." He pressed the intercom. "Mr. Scott, have one of your staff program the synthesizer to manufacture *two* Vulcan *lirpas*." He turned to McCoy. "Doctor, please bring those *lirpas* back to me as soon as they are ready."

"*Lirpas?*" McCoy drew himself up. "Me? What are you talking about, *lirpas?*"

At the same moment, Scotty was saying, "*Lirpas?* Sir?"

Peter's voice took on an edge. "That was an order, Doctor! That was an order, Engineer!"

McCoy cleared his throat, grunted, and left the bridge without further comment.

"*Lirpas?*" Spock said, incredulously.

"Mr. Scott!" Peter called, slapping the console hurriedly. "What's happening with those transporters?"

"We're almost ready, sir," Scott reported.

"Power it up, Mr. Scott. Two minutes. On my signal." He slapped off the con before Scott could protest again.

"Excuse me, Captain," said Mr. Spock in his driest tone. "If you believe we are confronting Romulan vessels, shouldn't we engage our shields?"

"No," Peter countermanded, shaking his head. "We're not in firing range, and we're not going to be for three minutes. However, Mr. Spock, if any of those 'anomalies' move within the next several minutes, indicating that one or more of those vessels is approaching, you are to raise shields immediately. Understood?"

"Aye, sir," Spock agreed.

"Enterprise," a gasping voice called over the intercom, "batteries have ruptured and are draining. We have less than ten minutes' air. . . ." The garbled message was drowned out in static.

"Lieutenant Uhura," Peter instructed, removing his vest, "beam a message to the *Maru.* Remind them of standard Federation evacuation drills. They should already have all personnel in spacesuits or encased in protective fields in accordance with abandon-ship procedures. We can't afford to rush in there."

Peter turned at the sound of the bridge doors and saw Dr. McCoy entering, dragging two heavy *lirpas* behind him. With a baffled expression, the doctor handed them over to the young captain.

"Commander Uhura," Peter continued, "open a hailing frequency in the direction of those cloaked coordinates. Prepare to transmit a message on wide beam."

He smiled at the bridge crew, knowing they must think he'd gone crazy. Maybe he *was* crazy, because he was starting to enjoy himself. This whole situation was a real challenge, and he already knew he'd kept his ship from being blown to smithereens far longer than most candidates made it. Of course, it was all for nothing if he couldn't pull off the rescue of at least the personnel aboard *Kobayashi Maru.*

He looked over at Communications inquiringly.

"Sir, hailing frequencies are open." She looked over at Spock and shrugged.

"This is Captain Peter Kirk hailing the commander of the fleet surrounding the injured ship *Kobayashi Maru.* We are aware of the trap you have set and, frankly, Commander, I find your clumsy ploy *insulting.* In response to this slight, I now have something to say to you: *T'kevaidors a skelitus dunt'ryala aikriian paselitan . . . Toriatal."* He heard Spock take a sharp breath that was almost a gasp. "Commander"—Peter dropped back into Standard English—"I issue this challenge under the ancient law of *Toriatal.* By rights, you must respond to my declaration."

Silence. Total, dead silence.

Peter waited, sweating. It no longer mattered that it was just a simulation. He was as charged up as if he really were facing an invisible enemy. Clutching the two *lirpas,* he listened to the blood rushing in his ears.

The simulation program, he thought as he waited. *It's trying to figure out how to respond to my challenge.*

Suddenly, Uhura's mouth dropped open. "Captain," she said breathlessly, "we're being hailed . . . by the Romulan commander!"

"On-screen, Lieutenant," he said, as he lifted one of the *lirpas* and held it in a defensive position. The screen shifted, changing, showing the interior of a Romulan cruiser, and an image of a Romulan commander standing there.

"Who are you to issue the ancient challenge?" the holo-commander demanded. "You are merely *human.* I am not obligated to respond to an *outworlder* who dares to issue the *Toriatal."*

"You *are* obligated," Peter insisted, trying to remain cool. His shirt was sticking to him as he held the heavy *lirpa* at the ready, with the other leaning against the command chair beside him. "The law is clear. 'Whoever issues the *Toriatal* challenge has the right to be answered. No leader may ignore a properly given challenge.' I have issued it in the tradition of your oldest laws. What do you say? Do you accept the challenge? Or are you afraid to fight a human?"

Again the long pause. Finally, the holo-commander said, hollowly, "I accept the challenge."

"The choice of weapons is mine," Peter announced, "and I have chosen *lirpas.*"

"Captain," Spock said clearly, "several of the Romulan vessels are bringing their weapons on-line."

"Will you disobey your own law, Romulan, and allow your ships to fire upon us, even after I have issued the challenge?" Peter demanded. "If you do, you dishonor your own heritage! The *Toriatal* mandates a state of truce while it is in effect!"

The holo-commander was still for nearly a minute; then the image turned its head and spoke to someone not in visual range.

Peter saw Spock's eyebrow climb. "Weapons . . . are being taken off-line, sir."

"Mr. Spock, I order you to beam me over to those coordinates," Peter instructed his science officer. "While I am engaging the Romulan commander, you and Mr. Scott will beam over every survivor from the *Kobayashi Maru.* As soon as you have them all, order full astern speed, and retreat back into the nebula. The Romulans will not be willing to follow you in there. From there, you can make your escape."

Before Spock could offer his own protest, McCoy blurted, "Are you crazy? He's gonna slice you into ribbons with that thing, and while he's doin' it, his other ships are gonna play target practice with us!"

"No, they won't," Peter told McCoy. "While the commander and I are in combat, his troops must, by law, hold their fire, *as must we.* But there's nothing in the law that says you can't quietly transport those people off the *Maru* and get the hell out of here."

"Captain, I cannot allow you to do this," Spock said, quietly. "Even if you were to defeat the Romulan commander, it is unlikely they will return you to us. This is suicide."

Peter paused. "It's a no-win situation, Mr. Spock, I'll give you that. But only for me. The *Enterprise* and the *Kobayashi Maru* will be safe. And as the captain, my job is to insure the safety of the ship." He picked up the second *lirpa* and keyed the intercom. "Mr. Scott, stand by with those cargo transporters. Transporter Chief?"

A mechanical-sounding voice said, "Transporter room, aye."

"Beam me directly from the bridge to the bridge of the Romulan vessel," Peter said, and, checking Chekov's readouts, gave the coordinates. "Energize!" *What's going to happen now?* he wondered. Would they actually beam him someplace? Would he really have to fight someone?

Suddenly, a voice outside the bridge doors called out, "Wait a minute, wait a minute! Open these doors! Lights on!" The bridge doors slid open and Commandant Kyle Anderson stormed in. "What the hell is going on here? Cadet, where did you come up with these 'anomalies' and energy readings you're talking about? This is totally irregular."

Peter had to blink to reorient himself out of the simulation and back to real life. His blood pressure was up, and he was really ready for a good fight. "Here, sir," Peter said, putting down his *lirpa* and walking over to Chekov's console. "The anomalies are hard to spot, but the energy signature gives you something to look for. . . ."

"That's impossible!" the commandant protested, not even looking at the readout. "No one can spot a cloaked vessel!"

Spock suddenly cleared his throat. "With all due respect, Commandant, I am afraid that Cadet Kirk is correct. While he was aboard the *Enterprise*, I acquainted him with some research that Mr. Scott and I have been conducting. Our discoveries are still in the developmental stage, but, during our escape from Qo'noS, Cadet Kirk had occasion to monitor electromagnetic signatures on Klingon vessels."

"I see," the commandant said, as Spock showed him the anomalies. "All right. I can see where that gave you an advantage in this scenario, but what's all this nonsense about ancient Romulan challenges? Those ships would've blown you out of space while you were waving that thing"—he pointed to the *lirpa*—"in their faces."

Again, Spock came to his rescue. "With all due respect, sir, that's not the case. That challenge dates from Pre-Reformation times on Vulcan, and is respected by the Romulans. Cadet Kirk issued it correctly, Commandant. Even his pronunciation in Old High Vulcan was nearly perfect."

"Hmmm," the commandant said, "and they'd have to cease hostilities while he fought the commander?"

Spock nodded.

Anderson's features suddenly broke out in a wide grin. "Well . . . damn! Looks like you've spent too much time in space, Cadet Kirk. This test is designed for *inexperienced* trainees!" He shook his head. "Believe me, we'll fix those readings for the next poor fool who has to face this scenario! But for now . . . it looks like you're the second Kirk to beat the no-win scenario. And you didn't have to reprogram the computer to do it!" He extended his hand to the cadet, who took it, shaking it heartily.

"But sir," Chekov protested, "the Romulans would have surely killed him!"

"But he would've saved his ship and the people from the *Kobayashi Maru*, and all without firing a shot!" another voice added from the bridge doors.

Peter looked up to see his uncle standing there, smiling at him.

"A captain must be willing to sacrifice himself for his ship," Kirk reminded everyone. "That's his job. Congratulations, Peter. That was one hell of a test."

Peter nodded at everyone as they filed out. It was several minutes before Peter and his uncle had privacy. The captain held out his hand and, when his nephew took it, clapped him on the shoulder, grinning proudly. "I knew you could do it," he exclaimed.

"I was inspired by recent events," Peter said, dryly.

"Obviously—but that doesn't take away from the fact that you kept your head, and figured it all out. You're going to make a great captain someday."

The younger man shook his head. "With all due respect, Uncle Jim . . . I'm quitting Command track today. I'm requesting reassignment to the Starfleet diplomatic corps. Ambassador Sarek is giving me a recommendation. Recent events have made me realize that that's what I *really* want to do with my life."

Kirk regarded his nephew intently for nearly a minute, then nodded. "It's your choice, Peter, and I respect you for making a difficult decision." Humor glinted in the hazel eyes. "You weren't influenced in your decision by the notion of attending long diplomatic conferences with the Klingons, were you?"

Peter grinned. "Let's just say that I'll be taking a lot more classes in Klingon language and culture," he admitted.

The two fell into step and went out into the corridor, through the gleaming lobby of the Starfleet Academy. "You're writing to her?" the captain asked.

"Yes . . . and I got a reply last week. She's in school already and likes it. *She's* taking a course in advanced Standard English!"

"By the time you two meet again, any language barrier should be a thing of the past," Kirk said, as they crossed the broad plaza that lay at the foot of Starfleet's gleaming towers.

"By the time we meet again, let's hope a lot of barriers will be a thing of the past," Peter said. "We'll both be working toward that, Uncle Jim."

James Tiberius Kirk smiled at his brother's son. "It isn't often that personal interest and duty coincide."

Peter nodded. "But when it does . . . it's great."

"I wish both of you the best of luck, Peter, I mean that."

The younger Kirk smiled. "I know you do. And that means a lot to me, Uncle Jim."

"And I want you to know something else," Jim admitted. "I also think you would've been a hell of a starship captain."

Peter beamed. He knew that, in his uncle's eyes, this was the finest compliment he could give anyone. "Thanks, Uncle Jim. But I'd never hold a candle to you."

The senior Kirk grinned and slapped his nephew on the back. The captain of the *Enterprise* quickened his pace. "Come on . . . everyone's waiting for us." Then, suddenly, the hazel eyes twinkled. *"Ambassador* Kirk, do you think? Someday?"

Peter shrugged. "You never know . . ."

"Ambassador Kirk . . ." the captain muttered, trying it on for size. "The more I say it, the better it sounds. . . ."

Spock stood in the huge, skylighted conference chamber on the world called Khitomer. The new peace conference boasted dozens of beings from many worlds . . . but not one Freelan. The absence of the cloaked and masked delegates had been noted and commented upon, but only the member worlds of the Federation Security Council knew the truth.

In the weeks since the *Enterprise* had brought the captive Vulcans out of the Neutral Zone, the tensions in the galaxy had eased considerably. The ringleaders of the KEHL, including Lisa Tennant, had been arrested and charged with breaking into the computer system at the Vulcan consulate, and for assaulting and abducting Peter Kirk. With its most dedicated members out of action, the group was gradually returning to its status as a harmless fringe organization.

Azetbur's dramatic rescue operation against the Klingon renegades had restored the Federation's faith in the new chancellor, and this new peace conference was a result. Scientists from many worlds had been asked to join with governmental delegates to advise the Federation on how best to help the Klingon homeworld solve its many problems. Today's sessions had been devoted to discussion of how the effects of Praxis's explosion on Qo'noS might be overcome. Tomorrow the agenda included the possibility of economic aid.

The Vulcan was attending the conference as one of Starfleet's representatives. He'd enjoyed the day's session; searching for scientific solutions to the problems facing Qo'noS was a stimulating challenge. Now, as the delegates milled around, talking in groups after the formal meetings had broken up, Spock searched the room for his father. He had not seen Sarek since his arrival yesterday.

"A good session today, don't you think, Captain Spock?" came a voice from behind him. Turning, Spock saw the new Romulan delegate, Pardek, standing beside him. The Vulcan had been somewhat surprised when the Empire had sent a delegate to replace Nanclus, in light of recent events with Freelan, but, then, the Romulans had always excelled at talking peace while plotting war.

"I agree," he said. Pardek was a little older than the Vulcan, with rather heavy features and thick brow ridges. He was stocky and compactly built, with the air of one who has known military service. Not unusual in a Romulan.

"It is an honor to meet you, Captain," Pardek said. "Your name has been . . . prominent . . . in the Empire for a long time, now."

Spock raised an eyebrow, amused at the word choice. "Indeed?" he asked dryly.

"You and your father both are well known to my government," Pardek said, and the Vulcan knew he hadn't missed the irony. "Especially in the light of recent events."

Spock had to conceal surprise that the Romulan was being even this direct. "Recent events," Spock repeated, "have certainly been . . . stimulating."

"Undeniably," Pardek agreed. "By the way . . . what has become of that radical organization that was causing Earth so much trouble in the recent past? That group of xenophobes. I have scanned nothing about it in the media reports for days."

Spock slanted the Romulan an ironic glance, but Pardek remained unruffled. "The Keep Earth Human League has been singularly quiet lately," the Starfleet officer replied. "The membership seems to be . . . dissolving. Odd, isn't it?"

"Isn't it?" Pardek agreed, blandly. "I was thinking, Captain Spock. A discussion of . . . recent events might prove interesting between us. An . . . *unofficial* discussion, you understand."

"The human phrase for what you mean is 'off the record,' Delegate Pardek."

"I like that term." Pardek smiled faintly, reminiscently. "English is such a colorful language . . . so descriptive. I enjoyed learning it."

"You were saying there were matters you wished to discuss . . . off the record?"

Pardek hesitated, then said, "Your name and your father's—but especially the name of Sarek—have been on everyone's lips lately. Including the praetor's."

"For some reason," Spock said, "that does not surprise me. My father has a . . . friend . . . who was setting off on a journey to see the praetor. Perhaps you know of him?"

Pardek's fleshy features were carefully neutral. "Possibly," he admitted. "Are we speaking of someone in the military?"

"Yes. He is rather highly ranked."

Pardek looked away. " 'Was' is a more appropriate term, I fear."

"Ah," Spock said. "I am . . . grieved . . . to hear you say that."

Pardek raised an eyebrow. "But hardly surprised."

"No."

"It is regrettable," Pardek said, after a moment. "He was my friend, too."

"Indeed?"

"Yes, I knew him for many years. And I cannot find it in myself to condemn his actions in effecting the release of a number of captives. Far better," Pardek said thoughtfully, "to allow those who wished to leave to do so."

"But not all of those in question chose to leave," Spock pointed out. "Which concerns me. There was a possibility of . . . bloodshed. Reprisal, on those who stayed."

"I am pleased to tell you that no such tragedy has occurred," Pardek said earnestly. "The individuals who did not choose to leave have gone underground, merging into the general population. No active search for them has been mounted, under the circumstances. Most of the ones who stayed did so because they had married into Romulan families. The praetor understands this. He values public opinion, like any head of state."

"Understandably. These individuals we are speaking of—" Spock began.

"Off the record, of course. Not in any official capacity . . ." Pardek reminded him.

"Of course. These individuals . . . they have successfully managed to infiltrate, to mingle and become lost amid the rest of your society?"

"Quite successfully. It was remarkable how quickly they simply . . . melted away. I suspect most of them have changed their names, and will simply keep a low profile as a part of their Romulan families. They will raise their children, grow old . . . live ordinary lives as respectable citizens of the Empire. In time, they will be virtually indistinguishable from native-born Romulans."

"The praetor is not searching for them?"

"Not at all. As long as none of them surface to cause trouble, I expect that policy to continue."

"Fascinating," Spock murmured. "Who knows how this . . . mingling will affect your people, in years to come . . ."

"I have been wondering the same thing, Captain," the Romulan said.

"Perhaps this is not so surprising after all," Spock murmured thoughtfully. "In days past, we were, after all, one people."

"Millennia past," Pardek pointed out. "Still, as recent events have shown, there are still . . . cultural links."

"Indeed," Spock agreed, thinking of the challenge and the *senapa* duel. Watching it had brought home to him, as nothing else ever had, that Vulcans and Romulans had once been one people. They were still far more similar than they were different, at least physically . . .

"Perhaps we might discuss our idea further. During the conference . . . and afterward."

"I would like that, Spock," the delegate said, and the Vulcan realized they were speaking almost as if they both took some kind of vow to explore this concept together. "After I return to Romulus . . . perhaps we might stay in contact? Correspond?"

"I would be honored," Spock said.

"Spock?" A third voice reached them, and the Vulcan turned to see Sarek approaching through the thinning crowd of diplomats.

After quickly introducing his father to the Romulan delegate, Spock excused himself to leave the chamber with his father. Together, they walked out of the conference center and down the massive steps.

As Sarek and his son walked down the steps leading from the conference chamber, he reminded himself not to push: the rapprochement between them was still very fragile. It was extremely . . . satisfactory . . . to simply walk beside his son again, shoulder to shoulder.

"For a first day, the negotiations went well," the ambassador observed as they strolled across a manicured lawn beneath a vivid blue sky. In the east, the sun was setting in a magnificent splash of coral and fuchsia.

"I agree," Spock replied. "It seems possible that Qo'noS the planet may indeed be salvageable. Destruction of the ring would be a colossal task . . . but, given the time frame, it is feasible."

Sarek nodded; then the curiosity he had been holding back overcame him. He searched for an appropriate opening. "I was not expecting the Romulans to send a delegate," he began.

"I must admit I was surprised myself," Spock said.

Then Spock hesitated, and his father gained the impression that he was about to say something, but changed his mind. "It has been nearly three weeks since the *Enterprise* brought the captured Vulcans back to their native world," he observed. "Tell me, Father, how are they doing? Are the efforts at reeducating them regarding the ethics of mental contact succeeding?"

"Their teachers are optimistic," Sarek said. "Particularly since Savel seems to have emerged as a leader for them, and she is committed to using her telepathic abilities ethically, to help others. She told me the last time I saw her that she intends to train to become a Healer, and work as a telepathic therapist. I am encouraged that the newcomers will be able to adjust and prosper in our society."

"I believe they can," Spock said. "I spent considerable time talking with Savel on the voyage back to Vulcan. She seems like a young person with a great deal of potential. I was impressed by her."

"Not as impressed as young Soran is," Sarek said dryly.

Spock raised an eyebrow. "Indeed? And does she return his interest?"

"My impression is that she does."

"Soran is unbonded, is he not?"

"Yes. His parents did not hold with the tradition of bonding as children. That trend appears to be growing," Sarek said, thoughtfully.

"Then Soran is free."

"For the moment," Sarek said, with a glint of humor in his dark eyes. "I do not expect that state of affairs to continue for long, however."

His son cocked an eyebrow at him, and there was an answering glint in his own dark eyes.

Reaching the edge of the parklike grounds, father and son halted to watch the sunset for a few minutes in silence. "On the whole," Spock said finally, "I am impressed with Pardek. He strikes me as an intelligent individual, one who is something of a visionary."

Sarek glanced up at his son, realizing that Spock was deliberately granting him an opening. "Indeed? What makes you say that?"

"Our discussion at the end of today's session."

Sarek raised an eyebrow. "Yes? And what were you two discussing, if I may ask? You seemed very intent."

"We were," Spock admitted. "We began by speaking about the KEHL," he said, with a faint glimmer of humor. "And then we moved on to speaking, off the record, about the young Vulcans who elected not to go with the *Enterprise* . . ." Spock went on to summarize that portion of the conversation with Pardek.

"Knowing that the praetor has decided to ignore their existence is good news," Sarek said, when his son had finished. "Did Pardek give any hint as to Taryn's fate?"

Spock nodded, his expression darkening. "Taryn is dead, Father," he said. "I regret that I must be the one to tell you."

Sarek closed his eyes briefly. "I have been expecting to discover that," he said, heavily. "It is hardly a surprise, under the circumstances."

Finally, Sarek took a deep breath and broke the resulting silence. "Was it Taryn's fate that you and Pardek were speaking of so intently, as I approached?"

His son slanted a sidelong glance at him. "Curious, Father?"

"I must admit that I am."

Spock took a deep breath, and began walking again, in the general direction of the delegates' living quarters. "Very well. Pardek was saying that it was surprising how easily the young Vulcans were able to adapt to Romulan society. I observed that, after all, we were one people long ago." The officer hesitated, then continued, "I wonder if we might ever hope to be one people again."

Sarek stopped in midstride and stared at the other, barely troubling to conceal his consternation. "My son, surely you are not serious."

"Why not?" Spock's expression held a glint of stubborn resolve that his father well remembered. "We are working toward peace with the Klingons. Why not peace—and eventual cooperation—with the Romulans?"

Sarek struggled to repress his dismay. "You are speaking of . . . a fusion of the two cultures?"

"Yes, I was . . . although I concede that it would be . . . difficult."

The ambassador sighed, shaking his head. "Spock . . . my son, do you have any idea how unrealistically idealistic you sound? You are speaking of *Romulans*, remember? They have grown so far apart from our ideals that there is no longer any common meeting ground, I assure you. Witness their actions on Freelan—witness Nanclus's treachery and meddling!"

"Witness Taryn," Spock pointed out, quietly. "Witness his response to your challenge. A challenge so old that both our peoples share it."

"Taryn," Sarek reminded him curtly, "was a *Vulcan.*"

"He died a Romulan," Spock countered, with an edge in his voice, "upholding his concept of Romulan honor and duty."

Sarek sighed. "Spock . . . Spock . . . your dedication to the cause of peace does you credit, my son. But the entire notion is . . . ridiculous."

"I do not believe so. I intend to explore the concept with Pardek, but I do not choose to discuss the topic further. Your mind is closed, Father."

Sarek's eyes flashed, but his features never changed. "As you wish," he said, coldly. But then, thinking of how Amanda would react if she could hear them at the moment, the ambassador modulated his tones, attempting to conciliate, using his best diplomatic manner. "Perhaps you are right, Spock . . . perhaps there is nothing to be gained from discussing a subject on which we will never agree. But there are other topics we might discuss . . . say, over dinner?"

His son turned to regard him, his features cold and composed, but then, in response to what he saw in his father's eyes, they softened fractionally, and he nodded. "You are right. There are other topics." Spock's expression lightened. "Very well, Father. At dinner, then," he agreed.

Father and son walked on, together, as the shadows of evening lengthened around them.

Epilogue

Sunrise on Vulcan . . .

Sarek stood alone in Amanda's garden, waiting for the first light of dawn. As sunrise approached, the darkness of the sky was untouched, stars strewn everywhere—except behind the giant shape of Vulcan's sister world. The Watcher was lit only by light reflected from Vulcan, and so was nearly invisible, a dark ashen color in its newness. Here in the mountains near Gol, dawn came 1.6 hours late, delayed by the intervention of The Watcher.

As the ambassador watched, a glow appeared on the upper limb of The Watcher, subtle at first, but growing brighter. The Vulcan had seen many sunrises from orbit, and was always struck by the similarity to the way Vulcan's sun rose over T'Rukh. The sister planet's tenuous atmosphere, carrying enormous amounts of dust and SO_2 from its myriad volcanoes, caught Nevasa's ruddy light in a thin layer like high cirrus clouds.

Sarek turned and picked up a small container that had been resting on the bench behind him. It was an ancient jar carved from white stone.

His eyes fixed on the sky, Sarek ran his fingernail around the jar's seal, opening it. Carefully, he worked the stopper loose. Above him, the arc of red spread outward; then, suddenly, the star itself appeared. The hot glow grew brighter, visibly swelling. Vulcan's sky brightened, hiding T'Rukh behind rosy curtains of light. Slowly, as Nevasa came out of eclipse, a delicate down-curving crescent of light became visible, growing toward the horizon. The stars faded, grew dim, disappeared.

But they will return, Sarek thought. *Tonight they will shine again. The stars . . . outlive us all.*

Dawn. It was time.

Taking a deep breath, the Vulcan tilted the jar slightly, allowing some of the gray powder within it to fall. The morning breeze caught part of it, wafting it away, but much fell, to land in the soil below.

Sarek moved on a few steps, to a new location. This time he tilted the jar into his hand, letting the ashy powder fill his palm. *This is the last time I will touch her,* he thought, clenching his fist around the ash, grasping it as he would have her hand. By this time Nevasa had risen farther, separating from the enormous arc that was T'Rukh, brightening the Vulcan sky to its normal, searing color.

Day had begun.

A time to gain, a time to lose . . . Sarek thought, remembering one of Amanda's favorite quotations. Slowly, one by one, he forced his fingers to open, letting the ash sift down, between them. Letting go.

As the dawn breezes began to die, Sarek upended the jar, shaking it, so the last trace of the ash within could sift out, to drift and finally settle over the stones, the soil, the living plants from so many worlds.

Farewell, Amanda . . . The Vulcan's lips moved, but no sound emerged.

Carefully, the ambassador replaced the stopper in the now-empty jar. Then, his steps slow but steady, he turned and left the silent garden behind.